PRAISE FOR
MARY

D0091484

A SECRET AFFAIR

"This neatly choreographed romance . . . will fascinate readers as Balogh gradually peels away the layers of [the] complex, secrets-laden story with tantalizing skill and sympathetic care. . . . Poignant, thought-provoking, deliciously sensual, and completely entralling, this polished gem is the last in the Huxtable quintet and one that Balogh's fans have been anxiously awaiting."
—*Library Journal*

"Balogh has saved the best for last; Constantine—dark, wicked, and cryptic—has a perfect foil in Hannah, and their encounters are steamy, their romance believable. Though series fans will be disappointed to see it come to a close, they couldn't ask for a better way to go out."
—*Publishers Weekly*

"Mary Balogh has masterfully woven a romantic tale of the importance of family, of compassion, and of love and forgiveness in this fifth book in her series about the Huxtable family. A *Secret Affair* will not disappoint, and you'll be pleasantly surprised by the 'secrets.' "
—Fresh Fiction

SEDUCING AN ANGEL

"With her inimitable, brilliantly nuanced sense of characterization, elegantly sensual style, and droll wit, best-seller Balogh continues to set the standard to which all other Regency historical writers aspire while delivering another addictively readable addition to her Huxtable family series." —*Booklist*

"One of [Balogh's] best books to date."
—A Romance Review

AT LAST COMES LOVE

"Sparkling with sharp wit, lively repartee, and delicious sensuality, the emotionally rewarding *At Last Comes Love* metes out both justice and compassion; totally satisfying." —*Library Journal*

"*At Last Comes Love* is the epitome of what any great romance should be.... This novel will leave you crying, laughing, cheering, and ready to fight for two characters that any reader will most definitely fall in love with!"
—Coffee Time Romance

THEN COMES SEDUCTION

"Exquisite sexual chemistry permeates this charmingly complex story." —*Library Journal*

"Balogh delivers another smartly fashioned love story that will dazzle readers with its captivating combination of nuanced characters, exquisitely sensual romance, and elegant wit." —*Booklist*

"Mary Balogh succeeds shockingly well."
—Rock Hill *Herald*

FIRST COMES MARRIAGE

"Intriguing and romantic . . . Readers are rewarded with passages they'll be tempted to dog-ear so they can read them over and over." —McAllen *Monitor*

"Wonderful characterization [and a] riveting plot . . .
I highly recommend you read *First Comes Marriage*."
—Romance Reviews Today

"Peppered with brilliant banter, laced with laughter . . . and tingling with sexual tension, this story of two seemingly mismatched people struggling to make their marriage work tugs at a few heartstrings and skillfully paves the way for the stories to come."
—*Library Journal*

"The incomparable Balogh delivers a masterful first in a new trilogy. . . . Always fresh, intelligent, emotional and sensual, Balogh's stories reach out to readers, touching heart and mind with their warmth and wit. Prepare for a joyous read." —*Romantic Times*

SIMPLY PERFECT

"A warm-hearted and feel-good story... Readers will want to add this wonderful story to their collection. *Simply Perfect* is another must-read from this talented author, and a Perfect Ten." —Romance Reviews Today

"With her signature exquisite sense of characterization and subtle wit, Balogh brings her sweetly sensual, thoroughly romantic Simply quartet to a truly triumphant conclusion." —*Booklist*

SIMPLY MAGIC

"Absorbing and appealing. This is an unusually subtle approach in a romance, and it works to great effect."
—*Publishers Weekly*

"Balogh has once again crafted a sensuous tale of two very real people finding love and making each other's lives whole and beautiful. Readers will be delighted."
—*Booklist*

SIMPLY UNFORGETTABLE

"When an author has created a series as beloved to readers as Balogh's Bedwyn saga, it is hard to believe that she can surpass the delights with the first installment in a new quartet. But Balogh has done just that." —*Booklist*

"A memorable cast... refresh[es] a classic Regency plot with humor, wit, and the sizzling romantic chemistry that one expects from Balogh. Well-written and emotionally complex." —*Library Journal*

SIMPLY LOVE

"One of the things that make Ms. Balogh's books so memorable is the emotion she pours into her stories. The writing is superb, with realistic dialogue, sexual tension, and a wonderful heart-wrenching story. *Simply Love* is a book to savor, and to read again. It is a Perfect Ten. Romance doesn't get any better than this."
—Romance Reviews Today

"With more than her usual panache, Balogh returns to Regency England for a satisfying adult love story."
—*Publishers Weekly*

SLIGHTLY DANGEROUS

"*Slightly Dangerous* is the culmination of Balogh's wonderfully entertaining Bedwyn series.... Balogh, famous for her believable characters and finely crafted Regency-era settings, forges a relationship that leaps off the page and into the hearts of her readers." —*Booklist*

"With this series, Balogh has created a wonderfully romantic world of Regency culture and society. Readers will miss the honorable Bedwyns and their mates; ending the series with Wulfric's story is icing on the cake. Highly recommended." —*Library Journal*

SLIGHTLY SINFUL

"Smart, playful, and deliciously satisfying... Balogh once again delivers a clean, sprightly tale rich in both plot and character.... With its irrepressible characters and deft plotting, this polished romance is an ideal summer read." —*Publishers Weekly* (starred review)

SLIGHTLY TEMPTED

"Once again, Balogh has penned an entrancing, unconventional yarn that should expand her following."
—*Publishers Weekly*

"Balogh is a gifted writer.... *Slightly Tempted* invites reflection, a fine quality in romance, and Morgan and Gervase are memorable characters."
—*Contra Costa Times*

SLIGHTLY SCANDALOUS

"With its impeccable plotting and memorable characters, Balogh's book raises the bar for Regency romances." —*Publishers Weekly* (starred review)

"The sexual tension fairly crackles between this pair of beautifully matched protagonists.... This delightful and exceptionally well-done title nicely demonstrates [Balogh's] matchless style." —*Library Journal*

"This third book in the Bedwyn series is... highly enjoyable as part of the series or on its own merits."
—*Old Book Barn Gazette*

SLIGHTLY WICKED

"Sympathetic characters and scalding sexual tension make the second installment [in the Slightly series] a truly engrossing read.... Balogh's sure-footed story possesses an abundance of character and class."
—*Publishers Weekly*

SLIGHTLY MARRIED

"*Slightly Married* is a masterpiece! Mary Balogh has an unparalleled gift for creating complex, compelling characters who come alive on the pages.... A Perfect Ten." —Romance Reviews Today

A SUMMER TO REMEMBER

"Balogh outdoes herself with this romantic romp, crafting a truly seamless plot and peopling it with well-rounded, winning characters." —*Publishers Weekly*

"The most sensuous romance of the year." —*Booklist*

"This one will rise to the top." —*Library Journal*

"Filled with vivid descriptions, sharp dialogue, and fantastic characters, this passionate, adventurous tale will remain memorable for readers who love an entertaining read." —*Rendezvous*

WEB OF LOVE

"A beautiful tale of how grief and guilt can lead to love."
—*Library Journal*

By Mary Balogh

The Mistress Series
More than a Mistress
No Man's Mistress
The Secret Mistress

The Huxtable Series
First Comes Marriage
Then Comes Seduction
At Last Comes Love
Seducing an Angel
A Secret Affair

The Simply Series
Simply Unforgettable
Simply Love
Simply Magic
Simply Perfect

The Slightly Series
Slightly Married
Slightly Wicked
Slightly Scandalous
Slightly Tempted
Slightly Sinful
Slightly Dangerous

Beloved Classic Novels
A Summer to Remember
One Night for Love
The Ideal Wife
The Secret Pearl
A Precious Jewel
The Gilded Web
Web of Love
The Devil's Web
A Christmas Promise
Dark Angel/Lord Carew's Bride

More than a Mistress

No Man's Mistress

MARY BALOGH

DELL
NEW YORK

Sale of this book without a front cover may be unauthorized. If this book is coverless, it may have been reported to the publisher as "unsold or destroyed" and neither the author nor the publisher may have received payment for it.

More than a Mistress and *No Man's Mistress* are works of fiction. Names, characters, places, and incidents are the products of the author's imagination or are used fictitiously. Any resemblance to actual persons, living or dead, events, or locales is entirely coincidental.

2011 Dell Mass Market Omnibus Edition

More than a Mistress copyright © 2000 by Mary Balogh
No Man's Mistress copyright © 2001 by Mary Balogh
Excerpt from *The Secret Mistress* by Mary Balogh copyright © 2011 by Mary Balogh

All rights reserved.

Published in the United States by Dell, an imprint of The Random House Publishing Group, a division of Random House, Inc., New York.

DELL is a registered trademarks of Random House, Inc., and the colophon is a trademark of Random House, Inc.

More than a Mistress originally published in hardcover in the United States by Delacorte Press, an imprint of The Random House Publishing Group, a division of Random House, Inc., in 2000. *No Man's Mistress* originally published in hardcover in the United States by Delacorte Press, an imprint of The Random House Publishing Group, a division of Random House, Inc., in 2001.

This book contains an excerpt from the forthcoming novel *The Secret Mistress* by Mary Balogh. The excerpt has been set for this edition only and may not reflect final content of the forthcoming edition.

ISBN 978-0-345-52904-6
eBook ISBN 978-0-345-53164-3

Cover design: Lynn Andreozzi
Cover photograph: Herman Estevez

Printed in the United States of America

www.bantamdell.com

2 4 6 8 9 7 5 3

Dell mass market edition: June 2011

More than a Mistress

1

THE TWO GENTLEMEN WHO WERE IN THEIR SHIRT sleeves despite the brisk chill of a spring morning were about to blow each other's brains out. Or attempt to do so, at least. They were standing on a secluded stretch of dew-wet lawn in London's Hyde Park, facing in different directions, each ignoring the other's existence until the moment should come to take aim at each other and shoot to kill.

They were not alone, however, this being a duel of honor in which due process had been followed. A gauntlet had been thrown down, even if not literally, and challenger and challenged had progressed toward this morning's meeting through the medium of their seconds. Both seconds were now present, as were a surgeon and a gathering of interested spectators, all male, who had risen early from their beds—or had not yet gone to them after the revels of the night before—for the sheer exhilaration of watching two of their peers attempt to put a period to each other's existence.

One of the duelists, the challenger, the shorter and stockier of the two, was stamping his booted feet, flexing his fingers, and licking his dry lips with a drier tongue. He was almost as pale as his shirt.

"Yes, you may ask him," he told his second through teeth that he tried in vain to keep from chattering. "Not that he will do it, mind, but one must be decent about such matters."

His second strode off smartly to confer with his counterpart, who in his turn approached the other duelist. That tall, elegant gentleman showed to advantage without his coat. His white shirt did nothing to hide the powerful muscles of his arms, shoulders, and chest, as his breeches and top boots only accentuated those of his long legs. He was nonchalantly engaged in smoothing the lace of his cuffs over the backs of his long-fingered, well-manicured hands and holding a desultory conversation with his friends.

"Oliver is shaking like a leaf in a strong breeze," Baron Pottier observed, his quizzing glass to his eye. "He could not hit the broad side of a cathedral from thirty paces, Tresham."

"His teeth are clacking like trotting hooves too," Viscount Kimble added.

"Are you intending to kill him, Tresham?" young Mr. Maddox asked, drawing to himself a cool, arrogant stare from the duelist.

"It is the nature of duels, is it not?" he answered.

"Breakfast at White's afterward, Tresh?" Viscount Kimble suggested. "And Tattersall's after that? I have my eye on a new matched pair of grays for my curricle."

"As soon as this little matter has been taken care of." But the duelist was distracted both from straightening his cuffs and from his conversation by the approach of his second. "Well, Conan?" he asked, a touch of impatience in his voice. "Is there good reason for this delay? I must confess myself eager for my breakfast."

Sir Conan Brougham was accustomed to the man's cool nerve. He had served as his second during three previous duels, after all of which his friend had consumed a hearty breakfast, unharmed and perfectly composed, as if he had been engaged for the morning in nothing more lethal than a brisk ride in the park.

"Lord Oliver is prepared to accept a properly worded apology," he said.

There were jeering noises from their acquaintances.

Eyes of such a dark brown that many people mistook their color for black looked back into Sir Conan's without blinking. The narrow, arrogant, handsome face to which they belonged was expressionless except for one slightly elevated eyebrow.

"He has challenged me for cuckolding him but is willing to settle for a simple apology?" he said. "Do I need to spell out my answer, Conan? Did you need to consult me?"

"It might be worth considering," his friend advised. "I would not be doing my job conscientiously if I did not thus advise you, Tresham. Oliver is a pretty decent shot."

"Then let him prove it by killing me," the duelist said carelessly. "And let that be within minutes rather than hours, my dear fellow. The spectators are displaying distinct signs of boredom."

Sir Conan shook his head, shrugged, and strode away to inform Viscount Russell, Lord Oliver's second, that his grace, the Duke of Tresham, did not acknowledge the necessity of any apology to Lord Oliver.

There was nothing for it then but to proceed to business. Viscount Russell in particular was anxious to have the meeting over with. Hyde Park, even this secluded corner of it, was a rashly public place in which to hold a duel, illegal as such meetings were. Wimbledon Common, the more usual venue for affairs of honor, would have been safer. But his friend had insisted on the park.

The pistols had been loaded and carefully inspected by both seconds. While an expectant hush fell over the spectators, the protagonists each picked up a weapon without looking at the other. They took up their positions back to back and at the agreed-upon signal paced out the regulation number of steps before turning. They took careful aim, each standing sideways in order to offer as narrow a target as possible to the other. They waited for Viscount Russell to drop the white handkerchief he held aloft, the signal to fire.

The hush became an almost tangible thing.

And then two things happened simultaneously.

The handkerchief was released.

And someone shrieked.

"Stop!" the voice cried. *"Stop!"*

It was a female voice, and it came from the direction of a grove of trees some distance away. An indignant buzz arose from the spectators, who had held themselves properly silent and motionless so that the protagonists would have no distraction.

The Duke of Tresham, startled and furious, lowered his right arm and turned in order to glare in the direction of the person who had dared interrupt such a meeting at such a moment.

Lord Oliver, who had also wavered for a moment, recovered fast, corrected his aim, and fired his pistol.

The female screamed.

His grace did not go down. Indeed at first it did not appear that he had even been hit. But a bright red spot appeared on his calf, an inch or two above the top of one perfectly polished leather boot, just as if suddenly painted there by an invisible hand with a long-handled brush.

"Shame!" Baron Pottier called from the sidelines. "For shame, Oliver!"

His voice was joined by others, all censuring the man who had taken unfair advantage of his opponent's distraction.

Sir Conan began to stride toward the duke while the crimson spot increased in diameter and the surgeon bent over his bag. But his grace held up his left hand in a firm staying gesture before raising his right arm again and taking aim with his pistol. It did not waver. Neither did his face show any expression except intense, narrow-eyed concentration on his target, who had no choice now but to stand and await his death.

Lord Oliver, to his credit, stood very still, though the hand that held his pistol to his side was trembling noticeably.

The spectators were silent again. So was the unidentified woman. There was an air of almost unbearable tension.

And then the Duke of Tresham, as he had done at every previous duel in which he had been engaged, bent his arm at the elbow and shot into the air.

The red spot on his breeches spread outward in rapidly expanding concentric circles.

IT HAD TAKEN IRON willpower to remain standing when it felt as if a thousand needles had exploded in his leg. But even though incensed with Lord Oliver for firing his pistol when any true gentleman would have waited for the duel to be reorganized, Jocelyn Dudley, Duke of Tresham, had never had any intention of killing or even wounding him. Only of making him sweat awhile, of giving him time to watch his life flash before his eyes and wonder if this would be the one occasion when the duke, famed as a deadly shot but also known as a man who contemptuously wasted his bullet on the air during duels, would act untrue to form.

The needle points had taken over his whole person by the time he had finished and tossed the pistol onto the wet grass. He felt like agony personified and remained upright only because he would be damned before giving Oliver the satisfaction of being able to claim that he had been felled.

He was also still angry. An understatement. He was in a white-hot fury that might have been directed against Oliver had there not been a more obvious target.

He turned his head and looked with narrowed gaze to the spot at the edge of the trees where she had been standing a few moments ago, shrieking like a banshee. A serving girl, running an early-morning errand, no doubt, and forgetting one of the primary rules of service—that one minded one's own business and left one's betters to mind theirs. A girl who needed to be taught a lesson she would never forget.

She was still there, staring as if transfixed, both hands pressed to her mouth, though she had stopped her caterwauling. It was a pity she was a woman. It would have given him intense satisfaction to set a horsewhip whistling about her hide before being carted away to have his leg attended to. Deuce take it, but he was engulfed in pain.

Only a few moments had passed since he had fired his pistol and tossed it down. Both Brougham and the surgeon were hurrying toward him. The spectators were buzzing with excitement. He heard one voice distinctly.

"Well done, by Jove, Tresh," Viscount Kimble called. "You would have contaminated your bullet by shooting it into the bastard."

Jocelyn held up his left hand again without looking away from the woman by the trees. With his right hand he beckoned imperiously to her.

If she had been wise, she would have turned and run. He was hardly in a position to go chasing after her, and he doubted that anyone else present would be interested in running to earth on his behalf an unappealing, gray-clad slip of a servant girl.

She was not wise. She took a few tentative steps toward him and then hurried the rest of the way until she was standing almost toe-to-toe with him.

"You fool!" she cried with angry disregard for her place on the social scale and the consequences of talking thus to a peer of the realm. "What an utterly idiotic thing to do. Have you no more respect for your life than to become embroiled in a stupid *duel*? And now you have been hurt. I would have to say it serves you right."

His eyes narrowed further as he determinedly ignored the pulsing pain in his leg and the near impossibility of standing any longer on it.

"Silence, wench!" he commanded coldly. "If I had died here this morning, you would as like as not have hanged for murder. Have you no more respect for *your* life than to interfere in what is no concern of yours?"

Her cheeks had been flushed with anger. They paled at his words, and she stared at him wide-eyed, her lips compressed in a hard line.

"Tresham," Sir Conan said from close by, "we had better get that leg attended to, old chap. You are losing blood. Let me carry you with Kimble here over to the blanket the surgeon has spread out."

"*Carry?*" Jocelyn laughed derisively. He had not taken his eyes off the serving girl. "You, girl. Give me your shoulder."

"Tresham—" Sir Conan sounded exasperated.

"I am on my way to work," the girl said. "I will be late if I do not hurry."

But Jocelyn had already availed himself of her shoulder. He leaned heavily on it, more heavily than he had intended. Moving at last, shifting the weight off his injured leg, he found that the wave of agony made a mockery of the pain hitherto.

"You are the cause of this, my girl," he said grimly, taking one tentative step toward the surgeon, who suddenly seemed an impossible distance away. "You will, by God, lend me your assistance and keep your impertinent tongue safely housed behind your teeth."

Lord Oliver was pulling his waistcoat and coat back on while Viscount Russell packed away his pistol and came striding past Jocelyn to retrieve the other one.

"You would do better," the girl said, "to swallow your pride and allow your friends to carry you."

Her shoulder did not bow beneath his weight. She was rather tall and slender, but she was no weakling. She was doubtless accustomed to hard manual labor. She was probably equally accustomed to cuffings and beatings for impudence. He had never heard the like from a servant girl.

He was well-nigh swooning by the time he reached

the blanket the surgeon had spread on the grass beneath an oak tree.

"Lie down, your grace," he instructed, "and I will see what damage has been done. I do not like the look of the positioning of that wound, I must confess. Or all the blood. I daresay the leg will need to come off."

He spoke as if he were a barber who had discovered a tuft of hair that did not blend well with the rest of the head. He was a retired army sawbones, supplied by Lord Oliver. Bloodletting and amputation were probably his answer to every physical ailment.

Jocelyn swore eloquently.

"You cannot possibly know that from a single glance," the serving girl had the temerity to observe, addressing the surgeon, "or make such a dire prediction."

"Conan," Jocelyn said, his teeth clamping tightly now in a vain attempt to control the pain, "fetch my horse." It was tethered not far away.

There was a chorus of protests from his friends who had gathered around him.

"Fetch his horse? He is as mad as ever."

"I have my carriage here, Tresham. Ride in that. I'll go and have it brought up."

"Stay where you are, Brougham. He is out of his mind."

"That's the fellow, Tresham. You show them what you are made of, old sport."

"Fetch my damned horse!" Jocelyn spoke from between his teeth. He had a death grip on the girl's shoulder.

"I am going to be very late," she scolded. "I will lose my employment for sure."

"And serve you right too," Jocelyn said, throwing her own words back at her, his voice devoid of all sympathy as his friend strode away to bring his horse and the surgeon launched into a protest.

"Silence, sir!" Jocelyn instructed him. "I will have my own physician summoned to Dudley House. He will have more regard for his future than to suggest sawing off my leg. Help me to my horse, girl."

But Lord Oliver appeared in front of him before he could turn away.

"I am not satisfied, I would have you know, Tresham," he said, his voice breathless and trembling as if he were the one who had suffered injury. "You will doubtless use the distraction with the girl to throw dishonor on my name. And everyone will laugh *at me* when it is known that you contemptuously shot into the air."

"You would rather be dead, then?" Death was seeming to be a rather desirable state to Jocelyn at that particular moment. He was going to black out if he did not concentrate hard.

"You will stay away from my wife in the future if you know what is good for you," Lord Oliver said. "Next time I may not accord you the dignity of a challenge. I may shoot you down like the dog you are."

He strode away without waiting for an answer, while another chorus of "Shame!" came from the gallery, some of whose members were doubtless disappointed that they were not about to witness the sawbones plying his trade on the grass of Hyde Park.

"My horse, girl." Jocelyn tightened his hold on her shoulder again and moved the few steps to Cavalier, whose head Conan was holding.

Mounting was a daunting task, and would have been quite impossible if his pride had not been at stake—and if he had not had the assistance of his silent but disapproving friend. It amazed Jocelyn that one small wound could cause such agony. And there was worse to look forward to. The bullet was lodged in his calf. And despite his words to the surgeon, he was not quite confident that the leg could be saved. He gritted his teeth and took the horse's reins from Conan's hands.

"I'll ride with you, Tresham," his friend said curtly. "You bloody idiot!"

"I'll ride on your other side," Viscount Kimble offered cheerfully. "And then you will have someone to catch you whichever side you choose to slide off. Well done, Tresh, old chap. You gave that old sawbones a right set-down."

The serving girl stood looking up at Jocelyn.

"I must be at least half an hour late by now," she said. "All because of you and your foolish quarreling and more than foolish dueling."

Jocelyn reached for one of the pockets of his coat, only to be reminded that he was still wearing just his shirt and breeches and top boots.

"Conan," he said testily, "oblige me by finding a sovereign in my coat pocket and tossing it to this wench, will you? It will more than compensate her for the loss of half an hour's wages."

But she had turned on her heel and was striding away over the grass, her back bristling with indignation.

"It is a good thing," Baron Pottier said, looking after her, his quizzing glass to his eye, "that shopgirls do not challenge dukes to duels, Tresham. You would be out here tomorrow morning again for sure." He chuckled. "And I would not wager against her."

Jocelyn did not spare her another thought. Every thought, every sense, every instinct became focused inward on himself—on his pain and on the necessity of riding home to Grosvenor Square and Dudley House before he disgraced himself and fell off his horse in a dead faint.

FOR TWO WEEKS JANE Ingleby had searched for employment. As soon as she had accepted the fact that there was no one in London to whom to turn for help and no going back where she had come from, and as soon as she had realized that the little money she had brought to town with her would not keep her for longer than one month even if she were very careful, she had started searching, going from one shop to another, one agency to another.

Finally, when depleted resources had been adding anxiety to the almost paralyzing fear she had already been feeling for other reasons, she had found employment as a milliner's assistant. It involved long hours of dreary work for a fussy, bad-tempered employer who did business as Madame de Laurent complete with French accent and expressive hands, but whose accent became pure cockney when she was in the workroom at the back of her shop with her girls. The pay was abysmal.

But at least it was a job. At least there would be wages enough each week to hold body and soul together and pay the rent of the small room Jane had found in a shabby neighborhood.

She had had the job for two days. This was her third. And she was late. She dreaded to think what that would mean even though she had a good enough excuse. She was not sure Madame de Laurent would be sympathetic to excuses.

She was not. Five minutes after arriving at the shop, Jane was hurrying away from it again.

"Two gents fighting a duel," Madame had said, hands planted on hips, after Jane had told her story. "I was not born yesterday, dearie. Gents don't fight duels in Hyde Park no longer. They go to Wimbledon Common."

Jane had been unable to supply the full names of the two gentlemen. All she knew was that the one who had been wounded—the dark, arrogant, bad-tempered one—had been called Tresham. And that he lived at Dudley House.

"On Grosvenor Square? Oh, *Tresham*!" Madame had exclaimed, throwing her hands in the air. "Well, that explains everything. A more reckless, more dangerous gent than Tresham it would be impossible to find. He is the very devil himself."

For one moment Jane had breathed a sigh of relief. She was going to be believed after all. But Madame had tipped back her head suddenly and laughed scornfully. And then she had looked around the workshop at the other girls, and *they*, sycophants that they were, had all laughed scornfully too.

"And you would have me believe that the Duke of Tresham needed the help of a milliner's assistant after taking a bullet through the leg?" Madame had asked. The question was clearly rhetorical. She had not paused for a reply. "You cannot take me for a fool, dearie. You saw some excitement and stayed around to have a gawk, did you? Did they take his breeches down to tend to his leg? I can hardly blame you for stopping to gawk at that sight. There is no padding in *them* breeches, I would have you know."

The other girls had tittered again while Jane had felt herself blush—partly with embarrassment, partly with anger.

"Are you calling me a liar, then?" she had asked incautiously.

Madame de Laurent had looked at her, transfixed. "Yes, Miss Hoity Toity," she had said at last. "That I am. And I have no further need of your services. Not unless—" She had paused to look about at the girls again, smirking. "Not unless you can bring me a note signed by the Duke of Tresham himself to bear out your story."

The girls had dissolved in convulsions of giggles as Jane had turned and left the workshop. As she strode away, she remembered she had not even asked for the two days' wages she had earned.

And what now? Return to the agency that had found her this job? After working for only two days? Part of the problem before had been that she had no references, no previous experience at anything. Surely worse than no references and no experience would be two days of work ended with dismissal for tardiness and lying.

She had spent the last of her money three days ago on enough food to last her until payday and on the cheap, serviceable dress she was wearing.

Jane stopped on the pavement suddenly, her legs weak with panic. What could she do? Where could she go? She had no money left even if she did decide belatedly that she wanted to go in search of Charles. She had no money even with which to send a letter. And perhaps even now she was being hunted. She had been in London for longer than two weeks, after all, and she had done nothing to mask her trail here. Someone might well have followed her, especially if…

But she blanched as her mind shied away from that particular possibility.

At any moment she might see a familiar face and see the truth in that face—that she was indeed being pursued. Yet she was now being denied the chance to disappear into the relatively anonymous world of the working class.

Should she find another agency and neglect to mention the experience of the past few days? Were there any agencies she had not already visited at least half a dozen times?

And then a portly, hurrying gentleman collided painfully with her and cursed her before moving on. Jane rubbed one sore shoulder and felt anger rising again—a familiar feeling today. She had been angry with the bad-tempered duelist—apparently the Duke of Tresham. He had treated her like a thing, whose only function in life was to serve him. And then she had been angry with Madame, who had called her a liar and made her an object of sport.

Were women of the lower classes so utterly powerless, so totally without any right to respect?

That man needed to be told that he had been the means of her losing her employment. He needed to know what a job meant to her—survival! And Madame needed to know that she could not call her a liar without any proof whatsoever. What had she said just a few minutes ago? That Jane could keep her job if she brought a note signed by the duke attesting to the truth of her story?

Well then, she would have her note.

And he would sign it.

Jane knew where he lived. On Grosvenor Square. She knew where that was too. During her first days in London, before she had understood how frighteningly alone she was, before fear had caught her in its grip and sent her scurrying for cover like the fugitive she now was, she had walked all over Mayfair. He lived at Dudley House on Grosvenor Square.

Jane went striding off along the pavement.

2

THE EARL OF DURBURY HAD TAKEN ROOMS AT the Pulteney Hotel. He rarely came to London and owned no town house. He would have preferred a far less expensive hotel, but there were certain appearances to be kept up. He hoped he would not have to stay long but could soon be on his way back to Candleford in Cornwall.

The man standing in his private sitting room, hat in hand, his manner deferential but not subservient, would have something to do with the duration of the earl's stay. He was a small, dapper individual with oiled hair. He was not at all his lordship's idea of what a Bow Street Runner should look like, but that was what he was.

"I expect every man on the force to be out searching for her," the earl said. "She should not be difficult to find. She is just a green country girl, after all, and has no acquaintances here apart from Lady Webb, who is out of town."

"Begging your pardon, sir," the Runner replied, "but there are other cases we are working on. I will have the assistance of one or two other men. Perfectly able men, I assure you."

"I would think so too," the earl grumbled, "considering what I am paying you."

The Runner merely inclined his head politely. "Now,

if you could give me a description of the young lady," he suggested.

"Tall and thin," his lordship said. "Blond. Too pretty for her own good."

"Her age, sir?"

"Twenty."

"She is simply a runaway, then?" The Runner planted his feet more firmly on the carpet. "I was under the impression that there was more to it than that, sir."

"There certainly is." The earl frowned. "The woman is a criminal of the most dangerous kind. She is a murderess. She has killed my son—or as good as killed him. He is in a coma and not expected to live. And she is a thief. She ran off with a fortune in money and jewels. She must be found."

"And brought to justice," the Runner agreed. "Now, sir, if I may, I will question you more closely about the young woman—any peculiarities of appearance, mannerisms, preferences, favorite places and activities. Things like that. Anything that might help us to a hasty conclusion of our search."

"I suppose," his lordship said grudgingly, "you had better sit down. What is your name?"

"Boden, sir," the Runner replied. "Mick Boden."

JOCELYN WAS FEELING QUITE satisfyingly foxed. Satisfying except that he was horizontal on his bed when he preferred the upright position while inebriated—the room had less of a tendency to swing and dip and weave around him.

"'Nuff!" He held up a hand—or at least he thought he did—when Sir Conan offered him another glass of brandy. "'f I drink more, th'old sawbones will have m'leg off b'fore I can protest." His lips and tongue felt as if they did not quite belong to him. So did his brain.

"I have already given you my word that I will not amputate without your concurrence, your grace," Dr. Timothy Raikes said stiffly, no doubt aggrieved at being referred to as a sawbones. "But it looks as if the bullet is deep. If it is lodged in the bone . . ."

"Gerr irr—" Jocelyn concentrated harder. He despised drunks who slurred their words. "Get it out of there, then." The pain had been pleasantly numbed, but even his befuddled mind comprehended the fact that the alcohol he had consumed would not mask the pain of what was about to happen. There was no point in further delay. "Ged on—get on with the job, man."

"If my daughter would just come," the doctor said uneasily. "She is a good, steady-handed assistant in such cases. I sent for her as soon as I was summoned here, but she must have left Hookham's Library before the messenger arrived."

"Blast your daughter!" Jocelyn said rudely. "Get—"

But Conan interrupted.

"Here she is." There was marked relief in his voice.

"No, sir," Dr. Raikes replied. "This is merely a housemaid. But she will have to do. Come here, girl. Are you squeamish? Do you faint at the sight of blood as his grace's valet does?"

"No to both questions," the housemaid said. "But there must have been some mis—"

"Come here," the doctor said more impatiently. "I have to dig a bullet out of his grace's leg. You must hand me the instruments I ask for and swab the blood so that I can see what I am doing. Come closer. Stand here."

Jocelyn braced himself by grasping the outer edges of the mattress with both hands. He caught a brief glimpse of the housemaid before she disappeared beyond Raikes. Coherent thought vanished a moment later as everything in his body, his mind, his world exploded into searing agony. There was nowhere, no corner of his being, in which to hide as the physician cut and probed and dug deeper and deeper in search of the bullet. Conan was pressing down with both hands on his thigh to hold his leg immobile. Jocelyn held the rest of himself still by dint of sheer willpower and a death grip on the mattress and tightly clenched eyes and teeth. With dogged determination he concentrated on keeping himself from screaming.

Time lost all meaning. It seemed forever before he heard the physician announce with damnable calm that the bullet was out.

"It's out, Tresham," Conan repeated, sounding as if he had just run ten miles uphill. "The worst is over."

"Damn it to hell!" Jocelyn commented after using a few other more blistering epithets. "Can't you perform the simple task of removing a bullet, Raikes, without taking all morning over it?"

"I worked as fast as I could, your grace," his physician replied. "It was embedded in muscles and tendons. It is difficult to assess the damage that has been done. But haste on my part would almost certainly have crippled you and rendered amputation unavoidable."

Jocelyn swore again. And then felt the indescribable comfort of a cool, damp cloth being pressed first to his forehead and then to each of his cheeks. He had not realized how hot he was. He opened his eyes.

He recognized her instantly. Her golden hair was

dressed with ruthless severity. Her mouth was in a thin line as it had been the last time he saw her—in Hyde Park. She had shed the gray cloak and bonnet she had been wearing then, but what was beneath them was no improvement. She wore a cheap, tasteless gray dress, primly high at the neckline. Despite his inebriation, which his pain had largely put to flight, Jocelyn seemed to recall that he was lying on his own bed in his own bedchamber in his own London home. She had been in Hyde Park on her way to work.

"What the devil are *you* doing here?" he demanded.

"Helping to mop up blood and now sponging away sweat," she replied, turning to dip her cloth in a bowl and squeeze it out before pressing it to his forehead again. Saucy wench.

"Oh, I say!" Conan had obviously just recognized her too.

"Who let you in?" Jocelyn winced and swore as Dr. Raikes spread something over his wound.

"Your butler, I suppose," she said. "I told him I had come to speak with you, and he whisked me up here. He said I was expected. You may wish to advise him to greater caution about the people he admits. I might have been anyone."

"You *are* anyone!" Jocelyn barked, tightening his grip on the mattress as his leg was moved and a universe of pain crashed through him. The doctor was beginning to bandage his wound. "What the devil do you want?"

"Whoever you are," the doctor began, sounding nervous, "you are upsetting my patient. Perhaps you—"

"What I *demand,*" she said firmly, ignoring him, "is a signed note to the effect that you detained me against my will this morning and thus caused me to be late for work."

He must be drunker than he had realized, Jocelyn thought.

"Go to the devil," he told the impertinent serving girl.

"I might well have to," she said, "if I lose my employment." She was dabbing at his chin and neck with her cool cloth.

"Perhaps—" Dr. Raikes began again.

"Why should I care," Jocelyn asked her, "if you lose your job and are tossed out onto the street to starve? If it were not for you, I would not be lying here as helpless as a beached whale."

"I was not the one aiming a pistol at you," she pointed out. "I was not the one who pulled the trigger. I called to both of you to stop, if you will remember."

Was he actually, Jocelyn wondered suddenly, scrapping with a mere laboring girl? In his own home? In his own bedchamber? He pushed her arm away.

"Conan," he said curtly, "give this girl the sovereign she ran away from earlier, if you will be so good, and throw her out if she refuses to go on her own feet."

But his friend had time for only one step forward.

"She certainly *does* refuse to go," the girl said, straightening up and glaring down at him, two spots of color reddening her cheeks. She was having the unmitigated gall to be angry and to show it to his face. "She will not budge until she has her signed note."

"Tresham," Conan said, sounding almost amused, "it would take you only a moment, old chap. I can send down for paper, pen, and ink. I can even write the note myself, and all you will need do is sign it. It is her livelihood."

"The devil!" Jocelyn exclaimed. "I will not even dignify that suggestion with a reply. She may grow roots where she stands until a burly footman comes to toss her out on her ear. Are you finished, Raikes?"

The doctor had straightened from his task and turned to his bag.

"I am, your grace," Dr. Raikes said. "There is much damage, I feel it my duty to warn you. It is my hope that it will not be permanent. But it most certainly will be if you do not stay off the leg and keep it elevated for at least the next three weeks."

Jocelyn stared at him, appalled. Three weeks of total inaction? He could not think of a worse fate.

"If you will not write the note," the girl said, "then *you* must offer me employment to replace my lost job. I simply refuse to starve."

Jocelyn turned his head to look at her—the cause of all his woes. This was his fourth duel. Before today he had not suffered as much as a scratch. Oliver would have missed by a yard if this girl's screeching had not given him a broader target at which to aim and the luxury of aiming at an opponent who was not also aiming at him.

"You have it," he snapped. "You have employment, girl. For three weeks. As my nurse. Believe me, before the time is up you will be wondering if starvation would not have been a better fate."

She looked steadily at him. "What are my wages to be?" she asked.

JANE AWOKE DISORIENTED EARLY the following morning. There were none of the noises of drunken men bellowing and women shrieking and children crying and quarreling, none of the smells of stale cabbage and gin and worse to which she had grown almost accustomed. Only silence and warm blankets and the sweet smell of cleanliness.

She was at Dudley House on Grosvenor Square, she remembered almost immediately, and threw back the bedcovers to step out onto the luxury of a carpeted floor. After she had gone yesterday to give notice to her landlord and fetch her meager belongings, she had reported to the servants' entrance of Dudley House, expecting to be put into an attic room with the housemaids. But the housekeeper had informed her that the house had its full complement of servants and there was not a bed available. His grace's nurse would have to be placed in a guest room.

It was a small room, it was true, at the back of the house overlooking the garden, but it seemed luxurious to Jane after her recent experiences. At least it offered her some privacy. And comfort too.

She had not seen her new employer since yesterday morning, when she had so boldly—and so despairingly—demanded that he provide her with employment if he would not help her keep the job she already had. He had apparently taken a dose of laudanum after she and the physician had left, which the housekeeper had sneaked into a hot drink without his knowledge, and it had reacted with the enormous amount of alcohol in his system to make him violently sick before it plunged him into a deep sleep.

Jane guessed that the size of his headache this morning would be astronomical. Not to mention the pain in his leg. It was only through the skill of a superior physician, she knew, that he still had two legs today.

She washed in cold water, dressed quickly, and brushed out her hair before plaiting it with expert fingers and coiling it tightly at the back of her head. She pulled on one of the two white caps she had bought yesterday out of the wages she had earned at the milliner's. She had gone back there officially to give her notice and explain that she would be working for the Duke of Tresham. Madame de Laurent had paid up, too surprised to do otherwise, Jane guessed.

She left her room and made her way down to the kitchen, where she hoped to have some breakfast before she was summoned to begin her work as nurse.

He would make her prefer starvation to her current employment, he had predicted yesterday. She had no doubt he would try his best to make her life uncomfortable. A more arrogant, bad-tempered, ill-mannered man it would be difficult to find. Of course, there had been extenuating circumstances yesterday. He had been in considerable pain, all of which he had borne stoically enough, except with his tongue. *That* had been allowed to run roughshod over everyone within earshot of it.

She wondered what her duties would be. Well, at least, she thought, entering the kitchen and discovering to her chagrin that she must be the last servant up, her working life was unlikely to be as monotonous as it had been at Madame Laurent's. And she was earning twice the wages with board and room in addition.

Of course, it was to last for only three weeks.

HIS LEG WAS THROBBING like a mammoth toothache, Jocelyn discovered when he woke up. From the quality of the light in the room, he judged that it was either early morning or late dusk; he guessed the former. He had slept the evening and night away and yet had lived a lifetime of bizarre dreams in the process. He did not feel in any way refreshed. Quite the contrary.

It behooved him to concentrate on the mammoth toothache in his leg. He did not want even to think about the condition of his head, which felt at least a dozen times its usual size, every square inch of it throbbing as if some unseen hand were using it as a drum—from the inside. His stomach was best ignored altogether. His mouth felt as if it might be stuffed with foul-tasting cotton wool.

Perhaps the only positive note in an overwhelmingly negative situation was that if first impressions were anything to judge by, at least he was not feverish. It was the fever that killed after surgery more often than the effects of the wound itself.

Jocelyn jerked impatiently on the bell rope beside his bed and then vented his irritability on his valet, who had not brought his shaving water up.

"I thought you would wish to rest this morning, your grace," he said.

"You thought! Do I pay you to think, Barnard?"

"No, your grace," his man replied with long-suffering meekness.

"Then fetch my damned shaving water," Jocelyn said. "I have bristles enough on my face to grate cheese."

"Yes, your grace," Barnard said. "Mr. Quincy wishes to know when he may wait upon you."

"Quincy?" Jocelyn frowned. His secretary wished to wait upon him? "Here? In my bedchamber, do you mean? Why the devil would he expect me to receive him here?"

Barnard looked at his master with considerable unease. "You *were* advised to stay off your leg for three weeks, your grace," he said.

Jocelyn was speechless. His household actually expected him to remain in bed for three weeks? Had they taken collective leave of their senses? He informed his hapless valet with colorful eloquence what he thought of the advice and interference of physicians, valets, secretaries, and servants in general. He threw back the bedcovers and swung his legs over the side of the bed—and grimaced.

Then he remembered something else.

"Where is that damned woman?" he asked. "That interfering baggage whom I seem to remember employing as my nurse. Sleeping in the lap of luxury, I suppose? Expecting breakfast in bed, I suppose?"

"She is in the kitchen, your grace," Barnard told him, "awaiting your orders."

"To attend me here?" Jocelyn gave a short bark of laughter. "She thinks to be admitted here to ply my brow with her cool cloths and titillate my nerves with her sharp tongue, does she?"

His valet was wise enough to hold his tongue.

"Send her to the library," Jocelyn said, "after I have retired there from the breakfast room. Now fetch my shaving water and wipe that disapproving frown from your face."

Over the next half hour he washed and shaved, donned a shirt, and sat while Barnard arranged his neckcloth the way he liked it, neat and crisp without any of the silly artistry affected by the dandy set. But he was forced to concede that the wearing of breeches or pantaloons was going to be out of the question. If current fashion had not dictated that both those garments be worn skintight, perhaps matters might have been different. But one could not fight fashion altogether. He did not possess breeches that did not mold his legs like a second skin. He donned an ankle-length dressing gown of wine-colored brocaded silk instead, and slippers.

He submitted to being half carried downstairs by a hefty young footman, who did his best to look so impassive that he might almost have been inanimate. But Jocelyn felt all the humiliation of his helplessness. After he had sat through breakfast and read the papers, he had to be half carried again into the library, where he sat in a winged leather chair beside the fire rather than at his desk, as he usually did for an hour or so in the mornings.

"One thing," he said curtly to his secretary when that young man presented himself. "Not one word, Michael, about where I should be and what I should be doing there. Not even half a word if you value your position."

He liked Michael Quincy, a gentleman two years his junior who had been in his employ for four years. Quiet, respectful, and efficient, the man was nevertheless not obsequious. He actually dared to smile now.

"The morning post is on your desk, your grace," he said. "I'll hand it to you."

Jocelyn narrowed his gaze on him. "That woman," he said. "Barnard was supposed to have sent her in by now. It is time she began to earn her keep. Have her come in, Michael. I am feeling just irritated enough to enjoy her company."

His secretary was actually grinning as he left the room.

His head now felt about fifteen times larger than normal, Jocelyn thought.

When she came into the room, it was clear that she had decided to be the meek lamb of an employee this morning. Doubtless word had spread belowstairs that he was in one of his more prickly moods. She stood inside the library door, her hands folded in front of her, awaiting instructions. Jocelyn immediately felt even more irritated than he had already been feeling. He ignored her for a couple of minutes while he tried to decipher a lengthy, crossed letter written in his sister's atrocious handwriting. She lived scarcely a ten-minute walk away, but she had written in the greatest agitation on hearing about the duel. It seemed she had suffered palpitations and vapors and other indecipherable maladies so serious that Heyward, her husband, had had to be fetched from the House of Lords.

Heyward would not have been amused.

Jocelyn looked up. She looked hideous. She wore yesterday's gray dress, which covered her from neck to wrists to ankles. There was no ornament to make the cheap garment prettier. Today she wore a white bonnet cap. She stood straight and tall. It was altogether possible, he thought, mentally stripping her with experienced eyes, that she looked quite womanly beneath the garments, but one had to be dedicated to observe the signs. He seemed to recall through yesterday's nightmare of pain that her hair was golden. It was invisible now.

Her stance was meek. But her eyes were not directed decently at the floor. She was gazing steadily at him.

"Come!" He beckoned impatiently.

She came with firm strides until she was three feet

from his chair. She was still looking directly at him with eyes that were startlingly blue. Indeed, he realized in some surprise, she had a face that was classical in its beauty. There was not a fault to find there, except that he remembered yesterday's thinned lips. In repose today they looked soft and exquisitely shaped.

"Well?" he said sharply. "What do you have to say for yourself? Are you ready to apologize to me?"

She took her time about answering.

"No," she said at last. "Are you ready to apologize to me?"

He sat back in his chair and tried to ignore the rampaging pain in his leg. "Let us get one thing straight," he said in the quiet, almost pleasant voice that he knew had every last member of his staff instantly quaking in his or her boots. "There is not even the smallest semblance of equality between us—" He paused and frowned. "What the devil is your name?"

"Jane Ingleby."

"There is not the smallest semblance of equality between us, Jane," he continued. "I am the master and you are the servant. The very *lowly* servant. You are not required to cap everything I say with some witty impertinence. You will address me with the proper respect. You will tack 'your grace' onto everything you do say. Do I make myself clear?"

"Yes," she said. "And I believe, your grace, you should watch your language in my hearing. I do not approve of having the devil's name and the Lord's name bandied about as if they were in everyone's nursery vocabulary."

Good Lord! Jocelyn's hands curved about the arms of the chair.

"Indeed?" He used his iciest voice. "And do you have any other instructions for me, Jane?"

"Yes, two things," she said. "I would prefer to be called Miss Ingleby."

His right hand found the handle of his quizzing glass. He half raised it to his eye. "And the other thing?"

"Why are you not in bed?"

3

JANE WATCHED THE DUKE OF TRESHAM RAISE HIS glass all the way to his eye, grotesquely magnifying it, while his other hand came to rest on top of the pile of letters in his lap. He was being enormously toplofty, of course, trying to frighten her. And half succeeding. But it would be certain suicide to show it.

His servants, she had gathered at breakfast, were all terrified of him, especially when he was in one of his black moods, as he was this morning, according to his valet. And he looked rather formidable, even clad as he was now in dressing gown and slippers over a crisp white shirt and expertly tied neckcloth.

He was a powerful-looking, dark-haired man with black eyes, prominent nose, and thin lips in a narrow face, whose habitual expression appeared to be both harsh and cynical. And arrogant.

Of course, Jane conceded, this must not be one of his better days.

She had approached the room with Mr. Quincy, the duke's pleasant, gentle-mannered secretary, and had decided to be what she was supposed to be—a quiet, meek nurse who was fortunate to have this position even if only for three weeks.

But it was difficult not to be herself—as she had discovered at great cost almost a month ago. Her stomach lurched and she withdrew her mind firmly from those particular memories.

"I beg your pardon?" he said now, lowering his glass to his chest again.

A rhetorical question. He did not, she guessed, suffer from defective hearing.

"You were told to stay in bed for at least three weeks and keep your leg elevated," she reminded him. "Yet here you sit with your foot on the floor and obviously in pain. I can tell from the tension in your face."

"The tension in my face," he told her with an ominous narrowing of his eyes, "is the result of a giant headache and of your colossal impudence."

Jane ignored him. "Is it not foolish to take risks," she asked, "merely because it would be tedious to lie abed?"

Men really were foolish. She had known several just like him in her twenty years—men whose determination to be men made them reckless of their health and safety.

He leaned back in his chair and regarded her in silence while despite herself she felt prickles of apprehension crawl up her spine. She would probably find herself out on the pavement with her pathetic bundle of belongings in ten minutes' time, she thought. Perhaps without her bundle.

"*Miss Ingleby.*" He made her name sound like the foulest curse. "I am six and twenty years old. I have held my title and all the duties and responsibilities that go with it for nine years, since the death of my father. It is a long time since anyone spoke to me as if I were a naughty schoolboy in need of a scolding. It will be a long time before I will tolerate being spoken to thus again."

There was no answer to that. Jane ventured none. She folded her hands before her and looked steadily at him. He was not handsome, she decided. Not at all. But there was a raw masculinity about him that must make him impossibly attractive to any woman who liked to be bullied, dominated, or verbally abused. And there were many such women, she believed.

She had had quite enough of such men. Her stomach churned uncomfortably again.

"But you are quite right in one thing, you will be pleased to know," he admitted. "I am in pain, and not just from this infernal headache. Keeping my foot on the floor is clearly not the best thing to be doing. But I'll be damned before I will lie prone on my bed for three weeks merely because my attention was distracted long enough during a duel for someone to put a hole in my leg. And I will be double damned before I will allow myself to be drugged into incoherence again merely so that the pain might be dulled. In the music room next door you will find a footstool beside the hearth. Fetch it."

She wondered again as she turned to leave the room what exactly her duties would be for the coming three weeks. He did not appear to be feverish. And he clearly had no intention of playing the part of languishing invalid. Nursing him and running and fetching for him would not be nearly a full-time job. Probably the housekeeper would be instructed to find other tasks for her. She would not mind as long as her work never brought her in sight of any visitors to the house. It had been incautious to come into Mayfair again, to knock on the door of a grand mansion on Grosvenor Square, to demand work here. To put herself on display.

But it was such a pleasure, she had to admit to herself

as she opened the door next to the library and discovered the music room, to be in clean, elegant, spacious, civilized surroundings again.

There was no sign of a footstool anywhere near the hearth.

JOCELYN WATCHED HER GO and noticed that she held herself very straight and moved gracefully. He must have been quite befuddled yesterday, he thought, to have assumed that she was a serving girl, even though as it had turned out she really was just a milliner's assistant. She dressed the part, of course. Her dress was cheap and shoddily made. It was also at least one size too large.

But she was no serving girl, for all that. Nor brought up to spend her days in a milliner's workshop, if he was any judge. She spoke with the cultured accents of a lady.

A lady who had fallen upon hard times?

She took her time about returning. When she did so, she was carrying the footstool in one hand and a large cushion in the other.

"Did you have to go to the other side of London for the stool?" he asked sharply. "And then have to wait while it was being made?"

"No," she replied quite calmly. "But it was not where you said it would be. Indeed, it was not anywhere in plain sight. I brought a cushion too as the stool looks rather low."

She set it down, placed the cushion on top of it, and went down on one knee in order to lift his leg. He dreaded having it touched. But her hands were both gentle and strong. He felt scarcely any additional pain.

Perhaps, he thought, he should have her cradle his head in those hands. He pursed his lips to stop himself from chuckling.

His dressing gown had fallen open to reveal the bandage cutting into the reddened flesh of his calf. He frowned.

"You see?" Jane Ingleby said. "Your leg has swollen and must be twice as painful as it need be. You really must keep it up as you were told, however fretful and inconvenient it may be to do so. I suppose you consider it unmanly to give in to an indisposition. Men can be so silly that way."

"Indeed?" he said frostily, viewing the top of her hideous and very new cap with extreme distaste. Why he had not dismissed her with a figurative boot in the rear end ten minutes ago he did not know. Why he had hired her in the first place he could not fathom since he blamed her entirely for his misfortune. She was a shrew and would worry him to death like a cat with a mouse long before the three weeks were over.

But the alternative was to have Barnard fussing over him and blanching as pale as any sheet every time he so much as caught sight of his master's bandage.

Besides, he was going to need something to stimulate his mind while he was incarcerated inside his town house, Jocelyn decided. He could not expect his friends and family to camp out in his drawing room and give him their constant company.

"Yes, indeed." She stood up and looked down at him. Not only were her eyes clear blue, he noticed, but they were rimmed by thick long lashes several shades darker than her almost invisible hair. They were the sort of eyes in which a man might well drown himself if the rest of her person and character were only a match for them. But there was that mouth not far below them, and it was still talking.

"This bandage needs changing," she said. "It is the one Dr. Raikes put on yesterday morning. He is not returning until tomorrow, I believe he said. That is too long a time for one bandage even apart from the swelling. I will dress the wound afresh."

He did not want anyone within one yard of the bandage or the wound beneath it. But that was a craven attitude, he knew. Besides, the bandage really did feel too tight. And besides again, he had employed her as a nurse. Let her earn her keep, then.

"What are you waiting for?" he asked irritably. "Permission? Is it possible that you deem it necessary to have my *permission* to supersede one of London's most eminent physicians and to maul my person, Miss Ingleby?" It annoyed him that he had not insisted upon calling her Jane. A nice meek name. A total misnomer for the blue-eyed dragon who looked calmly back at him.

"I do not intend to maul you, your grace," she said, "but to make you more comfortable. I will not hurt you. I promise."

He set his head back against the headrest of his chair and closed his eyes. And opened them hastily again. Headaches, of course—at least the caliber of headache that he had been carrying around with him since he regained consciousness a couple of hours before—were not eased when experienced from behind lowered eyelids.

She closed the door quietly behind her, he noticed, as she had done when she had gone in search of the footstool. Thank God for small mercies. Now if only she would keep her mouth shut. . . .

FOR THE FIRST TIME in a long while Jane felt as if she were in familiar territory. She unwound the bandage with slow care and eased it free of the wound, which had bled a little and caused the bandage to stick. She looked up as she freed it.

He had not winced even though he must have felt pain. He was reclined in his chair, one elbow resting on the arm, his head propped on his hand while he regarded her with half-closed eyes.

"I am sorry," she said. "The blood had dried."

He half nodded and she set about the task of cleansing the wound with warm water before applying the balsam powder she had found among the housekeeper's supplies.

She had nursed her father through a lingering illness until the moment of his death a year and a half ago. Poor Papa. Never a robust man, he had lost all his will to live after Mama's passing, as if he had allowed disease to ravage him without a fight. By the end she had been doing everything for him. He had grown so very thin. This man's leg was strong and well muscled.

"You are new to London?" he asked suddenly.

She glanced up. She hoped he was not going to start amusing himself by prying into her past. It was a hope that was immediately dashed.

"Where did you come from?" he asked.

What should she say? She hated lying, but the truth was out of the question. "From a long way away."

He winced as she applied the powder. But it was necessary to prevent the infection that might yet cost him his leg. The swelling worried her.

"You are a lady," he said—a statement, not a question.

She had tried a cockney accent, with ludicrous results. She had tried something a little vaguer, something that would make her sound like a woman of the lower classes. But though she could hear accents quite clearly, she found it impossible to reproduce them. She had given up trying.

"Not really," she said. "Just well brought up."

"Where?"

It was a lie she had already told. She would stick with it since it immediately killed most other questions.

"In an orphanage," she said. "A good one. I suppose I must have been fathered by someone who could not acknowledge me but who could afford to have me decently raised."

Oh, Papa, she thought. And Mama too. Who had lavished all their love and attention on her, their only child, and given her a wondrously happy family life for sixteen years. Who would have done their utmost to see her settled in a life as happily domesticated as their own if death had not claimed them first.

"Hmm" was all the Duke of Tresham said.

She hoped it was all he would ever say on the subject. She wrapped the clean bandage securely but loosely enough to allow for the swelling.

"This stool is not high enough even with the cushion." She frowned and looked around, then spied a chaise longue adorning one corner of the library. "I suppose you would rain down fire and brimstone on my head if I were to suggest that you recline on that," she said, pointing. "You could retain all your masculine pride by remaining in your library, but you could stretch your leg out along it and elevate it on the cushion."

"You would banish me to the corner, Miss Ingleby?" he asked. "With my back to the room perhaps?"

"I suppose," she said, "the chaise longue is not bolted to the floor. I suppose it could be moved to a place more satisfactory to you. Close to the fire, perhaps?"

"The fire be damned," he said. "Have it moved close to the window. By someone considerably more hefty than you. I will not be responsible for your suffering a dislocated spine even if there would be some poetic justice in it. There is a bell rope beside the mantel. Pull on it."

A footman moved the chaise longue into the light of the window. But it was on Jane's shoulder that the duke leaned as he hopped from his chair to take up his new position. He had flatly refused, of course, to allow himself to be carried.

"Be damned to you," he had told her when she had suggested it. "I shall be carried to my grave, Miss Ingleby. Until then, I shall convey myself from place to place even if I must avail myself of some assistance."

"Have you always been so stubborn?" Jane asked while the footman gawked at her with dropped jaw as if he expected her to be felled by a thunderbolt in the very next moment.

"I am a Dudley," the Duke of Tresham said by way of explanation. "We are a stubborn lot from the moment of conception. Dudley babes are reputed to kick their mothers with unusual ferocity in the womb and to give them considerable grief while proceeding into the world. And that is just the beginning."

He was trying to shock her, Jane realized. He was looking at her intently with his black eyes, which she had discovered from close up were really just a very dark brown. Foolish man. She had assisted in the birthing of numerous babies from the time she was fourteen. Her mother had raised her to believe that service was an integral part of a life of privilege.

He looked more comfortable once he was settled and had his foot resting on the cushion. Jane stood back, expecting to be dismissed or at least to be directed to present herself to the housekeeper for further orders. The footman had already been sent on his way. But the duke looked at her consideringly.

"Well, Miss Ingleby," he said, "how are you planning to amuse me for the next three weeks?"

Jane felt a lurching of alarm. The man was incapacitated, and besides, there had been no suggestive note in his voice. But she had good reason to be distrustful of gentlemen in their boredom.

She was saved from answering by the opening of the library door. It did not open quietly, as one might have expected, to admit either the butler or Mr. Quincy. Indeed, its opening was not even preceded by a respectful knock. The door was thrown back so that it cracked against the bookcase behind it. A lady strode inside.

Jane felt considerable alarm. She was a young and remarkably fashionable lady even if she would never earn full marks for good taste in dress. Jane did not recognize her, but even so in that moment she realized clearly the folly of being here. If the visitor had been announced, she herself could have slipped away unseen. As it was, she could only stand where she was or at best take a couple of steps back and sideways and hope to melt into the shadows to the left of the window curtains.

The young lady swept into the room rather like a tidal wave.

"I believe my instructions were that I was not to be disturbed this morning," the duke murmured.

But his visitor came on, undaunted.

"Tresham!" she exclaimed. "You are alive. I would not believe it until I had seen it with my own eyes. If you just knew what I have suffered in the past day, you would never have done it. Heyward has gone off to the House this morning, which is bothersome of him when my nerves are shattered. I declare I did not get one wink of sleep last night. It was most unsporting of Lord Oliver actually to shoot at you, I must say. If Lady Oliver was indiscreet enough to let him discover that she is your latest amour, and if he is foolish enough to proclaim his goat's horns to all the world with such a public challenge—and in Hyde Park of all places—then *he* is the one who should get shot at. But they say that you shot gallantly into the air, which shows you for the polished gentleman that you are. It would have been no more than he deserved if you had killed him. But of course then they would have hanged you, or would have if you had not been a duke. You would have had to flee to France, and Heyward was provoking enough to tell me that he would not have taken me to Paris to visit you there. Even though all the world knows it is the most fashionable place to be. Sometimes I wonder why I married him."

The Duke of Tresham was holding his head with one hand. He held up his free hand while the young lady paused to draw breath.

"You married him, Angeline," he said, "because you fancied him and he was an earl and almost as wealthy as I am. Mostly because you fancied him."

"Yes." She smiled and revealed herself to be an extremely pretty young lady despite her resemblance to the duke. "I did, did I not? How *are* you, Tresham?"

"Apart from a throbbing leg and a head ten sizes or so too large for my neck," he said, "remarkably well, I thank you, Angeline. Do have a seat."

The last words were spoken with considerable irony. She had already sat down on a chair close to the chaise longue.

"I will leave instructions on my way out," she said, "that no one but family is to be allowed in to see you. You certainly do not need any visitor who might be inclined to talk your head off, poor thing."

"Hmm," he said, and Jane watched as he raised his quizzing glass to his eye and looked suddenly even more pained than before. "That is a repulsive bonnet," he said. "Mustard yellow? With that particular shade of pink? If you were intending to wear it to Lady Lovatt's Venetian breakfast next week, I am vastly relieved to inform you that I will be unable to escort you."

"Heyward said," the young lady continued, leaning forward and ignoring his opinion of her taste in bonnets, "that Lord Oliver is telling everyone he is not satisfied because you did not try to kill him. Can you imagine anything so idiotic? Lady Oliver's brothers are not satisfied either, and you know what *they* are like. They are saying, though not one of them was present, I understand, that you moved like a coward and prevented Lord Oliver from killing you. But if they challenge you, you simply must not accept. Consider my nerves."

"At the precise moment, Angeline," he assured her, "I am preoccupied by my own."

"Well, you may have the satisfaction of knowing that you are the talk of the town anyway," she said. "How splendid of you to *ride* home, Tresham, when you had been shot through the leg. I wish I had been there to observe it. At least you have diverted talk from that tiresome Hailsham affair and that business in Cornwall. Is it true that a beggar girl screamed and distracted your attention?"

"Not a beggar exactly," he said. "She is standing there by the curtain. Meet Miss Jane Ingleby."

Lady Heyward swiveled on her chair and looked at Jane in considerable astonishment. It was quite clear that she had not noticed there was anyone else in the room except her and her brother. Not that the curtain offered any great degree of shelter, but Jane was dressed as a servant. It was a somewhat reassuring realization that that fact made her virtually invisible.

"You, girl?" Lady Heyward said with an hauteur that gave her an even more marked resemblance to the duke. She could be no more than a year or two older than herself, Jane estimated. "Why are you standing there?"

"She is my nurse," the duke said. "And she prefers to be called Miss Ingleby rather than *girl*." There was a deceptive meekness in his voice.

"Indeed?" The astonishment in the young lady's face increased. "How peculiar. But I have to run along. I was to meet Martha Griddles at the library twenty minutes ago. But I had to come here first to offer what comfort I could."

"What are sisters for?" his grace murmured.

"Precisely." She bent over him and aimed a kiss at the air in the vicinity of his left cheek. "Ferdie will probably be calling on you later. He was incensed by the dishonor

Lady Oliver's brothers were trying to throw upon you yesterday. He was all for calling them out himself—every one of them. But Heyward said he was merely making an ass of himself—his very words, I swear, Tresham. He does not understand about the Dudley temper." She sighed and left the room as abruptly as she had entered it, leaving the door wide open behind her.

Jane stood where she was. She felt cold and alone and frightened.

What was the drawing-room gossip to which the Duke of Tresham's sister had so fleetingly referred? *At least you have diverted talk from . . . that business in Cornwall.*

What business in Cornwall?

"I believe," the duke said, "the brandy decanter is called for, Miss Ingleby. And inform me at your peril that imbibing more alcohol will merely intensify my headache. Go and fetch it."

"Yes, your grace." Jane was quite uninclined to argue.

4

LORD FERDINAND DUDLEY CAME LESS THAN AN hour after Lady Heyward had left. He crashed the door back against the bookcase just as she had done and strode into the library unannounced.

Jocelyn winced and wished he had not sent the brandy decanter away as soon as he had set eyes upon it. He had just finished drinking a cup of chocolate, which Jane Ingleby had told him might settle his stomach and soothe his head. It had not achieved either desirable effect yet.

She melted back against the curtains again, he noticed.

"Devil take it!" his younger brother said by way of greeting. "Old Gruff-and-Grim tried to stop me from coming in here, Tresham. Can you imagine? Where do servants get such cork-brained notions?"

"Usually from their employers," Jocelyn said.

"Good Lord!" His brother stopped in his tracks. "You really are playing the invalid. Mama used to languish on that chaise longue whenever she had been dancing and gaming for three nights or so in a row and fancied herself at death's door. There's no truth to the rumor, is there?"

"There usually is not," Jocelyn replied languidly. "To which particular rumor do you refer?"

"That you will never walk again," his brother said, throwing himself down onto the chair on which Angeline had sat. "That you had to wrestle old Raikes down onto the floor to prevent his hacking off the leg. Honestly, Tresham, physicians these days would just as soon pull a saw out of their bags as take the time to dig around for a bullet."

"You may rest assured," Jocelyn told him, "that I was in no mood for wrestling anyone to the ground yesterday except perhaps that nincompoop of a surgeon Oliver took out to Hyde Park. Raikes did his job admirably well and I will certainly walk again."

"Just what I said," Ferdinand said, beaming at him. "It is in the betting book at White's. I have fifty pounds on it that you will be waltzing at Almack's within a month."

"You will lose." Jocelyn raised his quizzing glass to his eye. "I never waltz. And I never show my face at Almack's. All the mamas would instantly assume I was in the marriage mart. When are you going to dismiss that sad apology for a valet of yours, Ferdinand, and employ someone who can refrain from cutting your throat every time he shaves you?"

His brother fingered a small nick under his chin. "Oh, that," he said. "My fault, Tresham. I turned my head without warning him. The Forbes brothers are after your blood. There are three of them in town."

Yes, they would be. Lady Oliver's brothers had almost as bad a reputation as hell-raisers as he and his siblings did, Jocelyn thought. And since the lady was the only sister among five brothers, they were more than usually protective of her even now, three years after her marriage to Lord Oliver.

"They will have to come and take it, then," Jocelyn said. "It should not be at all difficult since it seems my butler will admit anyone to my house who deigns to step up and rap on the knocker."

"Oh, I say!" Ferdinand sounded aggrieved. "I am not just anyone, Tresham. And I must protest your not asking me to be your second or even informing me that there was to be a duel. Is it true, by the way, that it was a servant girl who caused all the fracas? Brougham says she came storming into the house after you and got all the way to your bedchamber and gave you a tongue-lashing because she had lost her job." He chuckled. "I daresay that it is a very tall story, but it is a damned good one nevertheless."

"She is standing over there by the curtain," Jocelyn said, nodding in the direction of his nurse, who had stood like a statue ever since his brother's arrival.

"Oh, I say!" Ferdinand leaped to his feet and gazed at her with the keenest curiosity. "What the devil is she doing here? It is really not the thing, you know, girl, to interfere in a matter of honor. That is gentlemen's business. You might have caused Tresham's death, and then you would have swung for sure."

She was looking at Ferdinand the way she usually looked at him, Jocelyn saw. He recognized the signs—the further straightening of already straight shoulders, the thinning of the lips, the very direct stare. He waited with a certain relish for her to speak.

"If he had been killed," she said, "it would have been by the bullet of the man with whom he was dueling. And how foolish to call such a meeting a matter of *honor*. You are right to call it men's business, though. Women have a deal more sense."

Lord Ferdinand Dudley looked almost comically

nonplussed as he took a scolding from a hideously clad servant.

"She comes equipped with a mind, you see, Ferdinand," Jocelyn explained with studied boredom, "with a double- edged tongue attached."

"I say!" His brother turned his head and looked at him, aghast. "What in thunder is she doing here?"

"Conan did not complete the story?" Jocelyn asked. "I have employed her as my nurse. I do not see why the rest of my servants should be at the receiving end of my temper for the coming three weeks while I am incarcerated in my own home."

"Devil take it," his brother said. "I thought he was funning!"

"No, no." Jocelyn waved one careless hand. "Meet Jane Ingleby, Ferdinand. But do have a care if it ever becomes necessary to address her again. She insists upon being called *Miss Ingleby* rather than *Jane* or *girl*. Which point I have conceded since she has stopped calling me nothing at all and has begun occasionally addressing me as *your grace*. My younger brother, Lord Ferdinand Dudley, Miss Ingleby."

He half expected her to curtsy. He half expected his brother to explode. This must surely be the first time he had been presented to a servant.

Jane Ingleby inclined her head graciously, and Ferdinand flushed and made her an awkward little bow and looked downright embarrassed.

"I say, Tresham," he said, "has the injury turned you daft in the head?"

"I believe," Jocelyn said, setting one hand to the aforementioned head, "you were about to take your leave, Ferdinand? Some advice, my dear fellow, though why I waste my breath giving it I do not know since Dudleys are not renowned for taking advice. Leave the Forbeses to me. Their quarrel is with me, not with you."

"Damned rogues and gangsters!" His brother bristled. "They would be better employed giving their sister a good smacking. How you could have got involved with plowing that particular piece of skirt, I do not know. I—"

"Enough!" Jocelyn said coldly. "There is—" He was about to say there was a lady present, but he caught himself in time. "I am not answerable to you for my affairs. Take yourself off now, there's a good fellow, and send Hawkins in to me. I intend to attempt to make clear to him that his future employment in this house depends upon his letting no one else beyond the doorstep for the rest of the day. If my head does not explode before nightfall and cause my brains to rain down on the books, I shall be very surprised."

Lord Ferdinand left and the butler stepped into the library a minute or two later, looking apprehensive.

"I do apologize, your grace—" he began, but Jocelyn held up one hand.

"I will concede," he said, "that it would probably take a whole regiment of seasoned soldiers and a battery of artillery to keep Lord Ferdinand and Lady Heyward out when they are determined to come in. But no one else today, Hawkins. Not even the Prince Regent himself should he deign to come calling. I trust I have made myself clear?"

"Yes, your grace." His butler bowed deferentially and withdrew, closing the door behind him with merciful quietness.

Jocelyn sighed aloud. "Now, Miss Ingleby," he said, "come and sit here and tell me how you plan to amuse me for the next three weeks. You have had plenty of time to think of an answer."

"YES, I PLAY ALL the most common card games," Jane said in answer to a question, "but I will not play for money." It had been one of her parents' rules—no gambling in their home for higher stakes than pennies. And no playing at all after half a crown—two shillings and sixpence—had been lost. "Besides," she added, "I have no money with which to play. I daresay you would derive no pleasure from a game in which the stakes were not high."

"I am delighted you presume to know me so well," he said. "Do you play chess?"

"No." She shook her head. Her father had used to play, but he had had strange notions about women. Chess was a man's game, he had always said with fond indulgence whenever she had asked him to teach her. His refusal had always made her want even more to be able to play it. "I have never learned."

He looked at her broodingly. "I do not suppose you read," he said.

"Of course I *read*." Did he think her a total ignoramus? She remembered too late who she was supposed to be.

"Ah, of course," he repeated softly, his gaze narrowing. "And write a neat hand too, I daresay. What sort of an orphanage was it, Miss Ingleby?"

"I told you," she said. "A superior one."

He looked hard at her but did not pursue the matter.

"And what other accomplishments do you have," he asked, "with which to entertain me?"

"Is entertaining you a nurse's job, then?" she asked.

"My nurse's job is exactly what I say it is." His eyes were looking her over as if he could see beneath all her garments. She found that gaze more than a little disconcerting. "It is not going to take you twenty-four hours of every day to change my bandage and lift my foot on and off cushions after all, is it?"

"No, your grace," she admitted.

"Yet you are eating and living at my expense," he said. "And I believe I am paying you a rather handsome salary. Do you begrudge me a little entertainment?"

"I believe," she told him, "you will soon be heartily bored with what I have to offer."

He half smiled, but rather than softening his face, the expression succeeded only in making him look rather wolfish. He had his quizzing glass in his hand, she noticed, though he did not raise it to his eye.

"We will see," he said. "Remove that cap, Miss Ingleby. It offends me. It is remarkably hideous and ages you by at least a decade. How old are you?"

"I do not believe, your grace," she said, "that my age is any of your business. And I would prefer to wear a cap when on duty."

"Would you?" He looked suddenly haughty and not a little frightening with his eyebrows raised. His voice was softer when he spoke again. "Take it off."

Defiance seemed futile. After all, she had never worn a cap before yesterday. It had just seemed like a good sort of disguise, like something beneath which she could at least half hide. She was not unaware of the fact that her hair was her most distinctive feature. She reluctantly untied the bow beneath her chin and pulled off the cap. She held it with both hands in her lap while his eyes were directed at her hair.

"One might say," he said, "that it is your crowning glory, Miss Ingleby. Especially, I daresay, when it is not so ruthlessly braided and twisted. Which poses the question of why you were so determined to hide it. Are you afraid of me and my reputation?"

"I do not know your reputation," she said. Though it would not tax the imagination overmuch to guess.

"I was challenged to a duel yesterday," he said, "for having, ah, *relations* with a married lady. It was not the first duel I have engaged in. I am known as an unprincipled, dangerous man."

"Spoken with pride?" She raised her eyebrows.

His lips twitched, but whether with amusement or anger it was impossible to tell.

"I do have some principles," he said. "I have never ravished a servant. Or assaulted any woman beneath my own roof. Or bedded any who were unwilling. Does that reassure you?"

"Absolutely," she said. "Since I believe I qualify for sanctuary on all three counts."

"But I would give a monkey," he said softly, sounding as dangerous as he had just described himself, "to see you with your hair down."

THE LILLIPUTIANS WERE SWARMING all over the Man Mountain, securing him with the greatest ingenuity—even his long hair—to the ground.

She was reading *Gulliver's Travels* to him, a book to which he could hardly object since he had left the choice of reading material up to her. She had wandered about the library shelves for a half hour, looking and fingering and occasionally drawing out a book and opening it.

She handled books with reverence, as if she loved them. She had turned to him finally and held up the volume from which she was now reading.

"This one?" she had asked. "*Gulliver's Travels*? It is one of those books I have always promised myself I would read."

"As you wish." He had shrugged. He was perfectly capable of reading silently to himself, but he did not want to be alone. He had never particularly enjoyed his own company for any length of time—no, that was not true. But for the past ten years or so it had been.

He had been feeling considerable irritation as the true nature of his plight had become clearer to him during the course of the day. He was a restless, energetic man, who engaged in a dozen or more activities every day, most of them involving physical exercise like riding and boxing and fencing and—yes—even dancing, though never the waltz and never at that most insipid of all institutions, Almack's. Making love was a favorite activity too, of course, and that could be the most energetic exercise of all.

Now for three weeks, if he could bear the torture that long, he was to be inactive, with only visiting friends and relatives for company. And the prim, shrewish Jane Ingleby, of course. And pain.

He had distracted himself by dismissing his nurse and spending the afternoon with Michael Quincy. The monthly reports from Acton Park, his country estate, had arrived that morning. He had always been conscientious about them, but he had never before pored over them with quite such determined attention to detail.

But the evening threatened to be endless. The nights were the time when he did most of his living and socializing, first at the theater or opera or whatever fashionable ball or soiree was likely to draw the greatest crowd, and then at one of his clubs or in bed if the sport offered there seemed worth the sacrifice of a night with his male friends.

"Do you wish me to continue?" Jane Ingleby had paused and looked up from the book.

"Yes, yes." He waved one hand in her direction, and she looked down and resumed her reading.

Her spine, he noticed, did not touch the back of her chair. And yet she looked both comfortable and graceful. She read well, neither too fast nor too slowly, neither in a monotone nor with theatrically exaggerated expression. She had a lovely soft, cultured speaking voice. Her long lashes fanned her cheeks as she looked down at the book she held with both hands close to her lap. Her neck was long and swanlike in its elegance.

Her hair was pure spun gold. She had done an admirable job of making it look severe and insignificant, but the only way she could hope for success in that endeavor was to shave her head. He had noticed the beauty of her face and the loveliness of her eyes during the morning. It was only when she had removed her cap that he had discovered how far reality surpassed his growing suspicion that she was an extraordinarily handsome woman.

He watched her read as he rubbed the heel of his right hand hard over his thigh as if to ease the pain in his calf. She was a servant, a dependent beneath his roof, and without any doubt a virtuous woman. As she had observed in her usual pert manner during the morning, she was thrice protected from him. But he would dearly like to see that hair with all the pins and coils and braids removed.

He would not be totally averse, either, to seeing her person without the dreary, cheap, ill-fitting dress and anything else she might be wearing beneath it.

He sighed, and she stopped reading again and looked up.

"Would you like to go to bed now?" she asked him.

She could always be relied upon to return her own particular brand of sanity to a situation, he thought. Her expression was without the slightest hint of suggestiveness despite her choice of words.

He glanced at the clock on the mantel. Good Lord, it was not even ten o'clock. The evening had scarcely begun.

"Since neither you nor Gulliver is a particularly scintillating companion, Miss Ingleby," he said brutally, "I suppose that is my best option. I wonder if you appreciate how low I have been brought."

A NIGHT OF SLEEP without either liquor or laudanum to induce slumber had not improved the Duke of Tresham's temper, Jane discovered early the next morning. The physician had arrived and she was summoned from her breakfast in the kitchen to the duke's bedchamber.

"You have taken your time," he said by way of greeting when she entered the room after tapping on his door less than a minute after the summons. "I suppose you were busy eating me out of house and home."

"I had finished my breakfast, thank you, your grace," she said. "Good morning, Dr. Raikes."

"Good morning, ma'am." The physician inclined his head politely to her.

"Take that monstrosity off!" the duke commanded, pointing at Jane's cap. "If I set eyes on it again, I shall personally carve it into very thin ribbons."

Jane removed her cap, folded it neatly, and put it into the pocket of her dress.

Her employer had turned his attention to the doctor.

"It was Miss Ingleby who changed the bandage," he said, apparently in answer to a question that had been asked before her arrival, "and cleansed the wound."

"You did an admirable job, ma'am," the doctor said. "There is no sign of infection or putrefaction. You have had some experience in tending the ailing, have you?"

"Yes, a little, sir," Jane admitted.

"She spooned purges into all the damned orphans when they overate, I daresay," the duke muttered irritably. "And I am not *ailing*. I have a hole in my leg. I believe exercise would do it more good than coddling. I intend to exercise it."

Dr. Raikes looked horrified. "With all due respect, your grace," he said, "I must advise strongly against it. There are damaged muscles and tendons to heal before they are put to even the gentlest use."

The duke swore at him.

"I believe you owe Dr. Raikes an apology," Jane told him. "He is merely giving you his professional opinion, for which you summoned him and are paying him. There was no call for such rudeness."

Both men looked at her in sheer astonishment as she folded her hands at her waist. And then she jumped in alarm as his grace threw his head back on the pillow and roared with laughter.

"I do believe, Raikes," he said, "that a splinter from the bullet in my leg must have flown up and lodged in my brain. Can you believe that I have suffered this for a whole day without putting an end to it?"

Dr. Raikes clearly did not. "I am sure, ma'am," he said hastily, "that his grace owes me no apology. One understands that his injury has severely frustrated him."

She could not for the life of her leave it alone. "That is no excuse for speaking abusively," she said. "Especially to subordinates."

"Raikes," the duke said testily, "if I could go down on bended knee in humble sorrow at my words, I would perhaps do so. But I may not so exert myself, may I?"

"No indeed, your grace." The doctor, who had finished rebandaging the duke's leg, looked considerably flustered.

It was all her fault, of course, Jane thought. It came of having grown up in an enlightened home, in which servants had invariably been treated as if they were people and in which courtesy to others had been an ingrained virtue. She really must learn to curb her tongue if she was to have this chance of earning three weeks' salary to take with her into the unknown beyond it.

The Duke of Tresham submitted to being carried downstairs, though not before he had dismissed Jane and instructed her to stay out of his sight until he summoned her. The summons came half an hour later. He was in the drawing room on the first floor today, reclining on a sofa.

"My head appears to have returned to its normal size this morning," he told her. "You will be pleased to learn that you will not be much called upon to use any of your considerable resources in entertaining me. I have given

Hawkins leave to admit any visitors who may call, within reason, of course. He has express instructions to exclude any milliners' assistants and their ilk who rap on the door."

Jane's stomach lurched at the very thought of visitors.

"I will excuse myself, your grace," she said, "whenever someone calls."

"Will you indeed?" His eyes narrowed. "Why?"

"I assume," she said, "it will be mostly gentlemen who will call. My presence can only inhibit the conversation."

He startled her by grinning at her suddenly, completely transforming himself into a gentleman who looked both mischievous and far younger than usual. And almost handsome.

"Miss Ingleby," he said, "I do believe you are a prude."

"Yes, your grace," she admitted. "I am."

"Go and fetch that cushion from the library," he instructed her. "And set it under my leg."

"You might say please once in a while, you know," she told him as she turned toward the door.

"I might," he retorted. "But then again, I might not. I am in the position to give the commands. Why should I pretend that they are merely requests?"

"Perhaps for the sake of your self-respect," she said, looking back at him. "Perhaps out of deference to the feelings of others. Most people respond more readily to a request than to a command."

"And yet," he said softly, "it appears that you are in the process of obeying my command, Miss Ingleby."

"But with a mutinous heart," she said, leaving the room before he could have the last word.

She returned with the cushion a couple of minutes later, crossed the room without a word, and, without looking at him, positioned it carefully beneath his leg. She had noticed in his bedchamber earlier that yesterday's swelling had gone down. But she had noticed too his habit of rubbing his thigh and baring his teeth occasionally, sure signs that he was in considerable pain. Being a proud man, of course, he could not be expected to admit to feeling any at all.

"Apart from the thin line of your lips," the duke said, "I would not know you were severely out of charity with me, Miss Ingleby. I expected at the very least that you would jerk up my leg and slam it down onto the cushion. I was all ready to deal with such a show of temper. Now you have deprived me of the opportunity to deliver my carefully rehearsed setdown."

"You are employing me as a nurse, your grace," she reminded him. "I am to comfort you, not harm you for my own amusement. Besides, if I feel indignation on any subject, I have the vocabulary with which to express it. I do not need to resort to violence."

Which was as massive a lie as any she had ever told, she thought even as the words were issuing from her lips. For a moment she felt cold and nauseated, her stomach muscles clenching in the now-familiar feeling of panic.

"Miss Ingleby," the Duke of Tresham said meekly, "thank you for fetching the cushion."

Well. That silenced her.

"I do believe," he said, "that almost elicited a smile from you. Do you ever smile?"

"When I am amused or happy, your grace," she told him.

"And you have been neither yet in my company," he said. "I must be losing my touch. I am reputed to be rather superior, you know, in my ability to amuse and delight women."

Her awareness of his masculinity had been a largely academic thing until he spoke those words and looked at her with the characteristic narrowing of his dark eyes. But suddenly it was no longer academic. She felt a totally unfamiliar rush of pure physical desire that did alarming things to her breasts and her lower abdomen and inner thighs.

"I do not doubt it," she said tartly. "But I daresay you have already used up this month's supply of seductive arts on Lady Oliver."

"Jane, Jane," he said gently. "That sounded remarkably like spite. Go and find Quincy and fetch the morning's post. *Please,*" he added as she moved toward the door.

She turned her head to smile at him.

"Ah," he said.

5

ANGELINE CAME AGAIN IN THE LATE MORNING, escorted this time by Heyward, who had accompanied her in order to inquire civilly after his brother-in-law's health. Ferdinand came before they left, but more with the purpose of talking about himself than out of any great concern for his brother's recovery. He had become embroiled in a challenge to race his curricle to Brighton against Lord Berriwether, whose skill with the ribbons was rivaled by no one except Jocelyn himself.

"You will lose, Ferdinand," Heyward said bluntly.

"You will break your neck, Ferdie," Angeline said, "and my nerves will never recover so soon after this business with Tresham. But how dashing you will look tearing along the road as fast as the wind. Are you going to order a new coat for the occasion?"

"The secret is to give your horses their heads whenever you have a straight stretch of road," Jocelyn said, "but not to get too excited in a pinch and not to take unnecessary risks on sharp bends as if you were some circus performer. For both of which vices you are famous, Ferdinand. You had better win, though, now you are committed. Never make a boast or a challenge you are incapable of backing up with action. Not especially if you are a Dudley. I daresay you *were* boasting."

"I thought perhaps I might borrow your new curricle, Tresham," his brother said carelessly.

"No," Jocelyn said. "Absolutely not. I am surprised you would waste breath even asking unless you think a hole in my leg has made me soft in the brain."

"You are my brother," Ferdinand pointed out.

"A brother with a working brain and a fair share of common sense," Jocelyn told him. "The wheels on your own curricle were round enough when last I saw them. It is the driver rather than the vehicle that wins or loses a race, Ferdinand. When is it to be?"

"Two weeks," his brother said.

Damn! He would not be able to watch any part of it, then, Jocelyn thought. Not if he was obedient to the commands of that damned quack, Raikes, anyway. But in two weeks' time, if he was still confined to a sofa, his sanity might well be at stake.

Jane Ingleby, standing quietly some distance away, had read his mind, Jocelyn would swear. A single glance at her showed her with her lips compressed in a thin line. What did she plan to do? Tie him down until every last day of the three weeks had passed?

He had refused her request to be excused when his family members arrived. He refused it again later when more visitors were announced while she was taking his letters one at a time from his hand as he perused them and dividing them into three piles according to his instructions—invitations to be refused, invitations to be accepted, and letters whose replies would necessitate some dictation to his secretary. Most of the invitations, except for those to events some time in the future, of course, had to be refused.

"I will leave you, your grace," she said, getting to her feet after Hawkins, who seemed far more in control of his own domain in the front hall today, had come to announce the arrival of several of his friends.

"You will not," he said, raising his eyebrows. "You will remain here."

"Please, your grace," she said. "I can serve no function here while you have company."

She looked, he thought, almost frightened. Did she expect that he and his friends were going to indulge in a collective orgy with her? He would probably have dismissed her himself, he supposed, if she had not announced that she would leave. Now, out of sheer stubbornness, he could not let her go.

"Perhaps," he said, "all the excitement will bring on a fit of the vapors and I will need the ministrations of my nurse, Miss Ingleby."

She would doubtless have argued further if the door had not opened to admit his visitors. As it was, she scurried for the farthest corner of the room, where she was still standing when it occurred to him to look a few minutes later. She was doing an admirable job of blending into the furniture. Her cap was adorning her head again and covering every last strand of her hair.

They had come in a collective body, all his closest friends—Conan Brougham, Pottier, Kimble, Thomas Garrick, Boris Tuttleford—bringing hearty good cheer with them. There was a great deal of noise as they greeted him, asked rhetorically after his health, jeered over his dressing gown and slippers, admired his bandage, and found themselves seats.

"Where is your claret, Tresham?" Garrick asked, looking about him.

"Miss Ingleby will fetch it," Jocelyn said. That was when he looked and noticed her in the far corner. "My nurse, gentlemen, who runs and fetches for me since I am unable to reach the bell rope from where I recline. And who scolds and worries me into and out of the dismals. Miss Ingleby, ask Hawkins for the claret and the brandy, and have a footman bring a tray of glasses. Please."

"*Please*, Tresh?" Kimble chuckled. "A new word in your vocabulary?"

"She makes me say it," Jocelyn said meekly, watching Jane walk out of the room, her face averted. "She scolds me when I forget."

There was a raucous guffaw from his gathered friends.

"Oh, I say," Tuttleford said when his mirth had subsided a little, "isn't she the one who squawked out, Tresham, just when you were unnerving Oliver with your pistol trained at the bridge of his nose?"

"He has employed her as his nurse," Conan replied, grinning. "And has threatened to make her sorry she was born or something like that. *Is* she sorry, Tresham? Or are you?"

Jocelyn played with the handle of his quizzing glass and pursed his lips. "You see," he said, "she has a damnably annoying habit of answering back, and I have a damnable need for mental stimulation, penned and cribbed and incarcerated as I am and as I am likely to be for a couple of weeks or so longer."

"Mental stimulation, ho!" Pottier slapped his thigh and roared with merriment, and everyone else followed his example. "Since when have you needed a female for mental stimulation, Tresham?"

"By Jove!" Kimble swung his quizzing glass on its ribbon. "One cannot quite picture it, can one? How else does she stimulate you, Tresh? That is the question. Come, come, it is confession time."

"He has one immobilized leg." Tuttleford laughed again. "But I'll wager that does not slow you down one whit, does it, Tresham? Not in the *stimulation* business. Does she come astride? And do all the bucking so that you can lie still?"

The laughter this time was decidedly bawdy. They were all in fine fettle—and getting finer by the minute. Jocelyn raised his quizzing glass all the way to his eye.

"One might casually mention," he said quietly, "that the female in question is in my employ and beneath my own roof, Tuttleford. Even I have some standards."

"My guess is, fellows," Conan Brougham said, more perceptive than the others, "that the notorious duke is not amused."

Which was a mistake on his part, Jocelyn thought a moment later as the door opened and Jane came back into the room, carrying two decanters on a tray. A footman came behind her with the glasses. She was, of course, the instant focus of everyone's curious attention, a fact that should have amused him as it would surely disconcert her. But he felt only annoyance that any of his friends would for one moment think him capable of the execrable taste of dallying with his own servant.

She might have tried to escape with the footman, but she did not do so. She retired to her corner with lowered eyes. Her cap was pulled lower than ever over her brow.

Viscount Kimble whistled softly. "A beauty in hiding, Tresh?" he murmured, too low for her to overhear.

Trust Kimble's eyes to penetrate her disguise. Kimble,

with his blond god's good looks, was very much a ladies' man, of course. A connoisseur to equal Jocelyn himself.

"But a servant," Jocelyn replied, "under the protection of my own roof, Kimble."

His friend understood him. He grinned and winked. But he would not make any improper advances to Jane Ingleby. Jocelyn did wonder fleetingly why he cared.

The conversation quickly moved off into other topics since they could hardly discuss Jane in her presence. But no one seemed to consider it improper to discuss in her hearing Lady Oliver's apparent enjoyment of her notoriety as she had played court to a host of admirers at the theater last evening; the presence of three of her brothers with her and Oliver in their box; the avowed determination of the brothers to call the Duke of Tresham to account for debauching their sister as soon as he was on his feet again; the ridiculous lengths to which Hailsham was going to prove that his eldest son, now nine years old and reputed to be mentally deficient, was a bastard so that he could promote the claims of his second and favorite son; the latest sensational details of the Cornish scandal.

"It is being said now that Jardine is dead," Brougham said on that last topic. "That he never did recover consciousness after the attack."

"It must have been one devil of a bash on the head," Kimble added. "The more sensational accounts insist that his brains were fully visible through hair and blood. London drawing rooms are filled with swooning females these days. Which makes life interesting for those of us who can be close enough to some of them when it happens. Too bad you are incapacitated, Tresh." He chuckled.

"As I remember it," Pottier said, "Jardine did not *have* a great deal of hair. Not too many brains either."

"He never regained consciousness." Jocelyn, attempting to shift his position to rid himself of a few cramps, inadvertently knocked the cushion to the floor. "Come and replace this, Miss Ingleby, will you? He never regained consciousness and yet—according to some accounts—he was able to give a perfectly lucid account of the attack and his own spirited and heroic defense. He was able to identify his attacker and explain her motive for breaking his skull. A strange sort of unconsciousness."

Jane bent over him and placed the cushion in just the right spot, lifted his leg onto it as gently as she always did, and adjusted the top of the bandage, which had curled under. But she was, he noticed when he glanced at her, white to the very lips.

He was almost sorry then that he had insisted upon her remaining in the room. Clearly she was uncomfortable in the company of all men. And no doubt with their talk. As stoic as she had been over his injury, perhaps the talk of hair and blood and brains had been too much for her.

"News of his death may be just as exaggerated," Garrick said cynically, getting to his feet and helping himself to another drink. "It could well be that he is simply ashamed to show his face after admitting to having been overpowered by a mere slip of a girl engaged in a robbery."

"Was she not clutching a pistol in both hands?" Jocelyn asked. "According, that is, to the man who never regained consciousness from the time she struck him with one of them until the moment of his demise? But enough of that nonsense. What sort of a cork-brained scheme is this that Ferdinand has got himself into? A curricle race against Berriwether of all people! Who made the challenge?"

"Your brother," Conan said, "when Berriwether was boasting that you will be eating humble pie at all your old sports now that you will have one lame leg to drag about. He was claiming that the Dudley name would never again be one to be uttered with awe and admiration."

"In Ferdinand's hearing?" Jocelyn shook his head. "Definitely not wise."

"No, not exactly in his hearing," his friend explained. "But Ferdinand got wind of it, of course, and came striding into White's with flames roaring from his nostrils. I thought for one moment he was going to slap a glove in Berriwether's face, but all he did was ask as polite as you please what Berriwether thought your finest accomplishment was apart from your skill with weapons. It was your skill with the ribbons, of course. Then came the challenge."

"And how much has Ferdinand wagered on the outcome?" Jocelyn asked.

Garrick provided the answer. "One thousand guineas," he said.

"Hmm." Jocelyn nodded slowly. "The family honor worth one thousand guineas. Well, well."

Jane Ingleby was no longer standing in her corner, he saw idly. She was sitting there very straight-backed on a low stool, her back to the room.

She did not move until his friends took their leave more than an hour later.

* * *

"GIVE ME THE DAMNED thing!" The Duke of Tresham was holding out one imperious hand.

Jane, standing beside the sofa, where he had summoned her the moment after the drawing room door had closed behind his visitors, unfastened the ribbons beneath her chin and removed the offending cap. But she held it in her own hands.

"What are you intending to do with it?" she asked.

"What I am intending to do," he said irritably, "is send you to fetch the sharpest pair of scissors my housekeeper can provide you with. And then I am going to have you watch while I cut that atrocity into shreds. No, correct that. I am going to have *you* cut it into shreds."

"It is mine," she told him. "I paid for it. You have no right whatsoever to destroy my property."

"Poppycock!" he retorted.

And then to her horror Jane knew why he had suddenly blurred before her eyes. An inelegant sob escaped her at the same moment as she realized that her eyes had filled with tears.

"Good God!" he exclaimed, sounding appalled. "Does the wretched thing mean that much to you?"

"It is mine!" she said vehemently but with a lamentably unsteady voice. "I bought it and one other just two days ago. They cost everything I had. I *will* not allow you to cut them up for your own amusement. You are an unfeeling bully."

Despite the anger and bravado of her words, she was crying and sobbing and hiccuping quite despicably. She swiped at her wet cheeks with the cap and glared at him.

He regarded her in silence for a few moments. "This is

not about the cap at all, is it?" he said at last. "It is because I forced you to remain in the room with a horde of male visitors. I have hurt your sensibilities, Jane. I daresay in the orphanage the sexes were segregated, were they?"

"Yes," she said.

"I am weary," he said abruptly. "I believe I shall try to sleep. I do not require your presence here to listen to me snore. Go to your room and remain there until dinnertime. Come to me again this evening."

"Yes, your grace," she said, turning from him. She could not say thank you even though she knew that in his way he was showing her a kindness. She did not believe he wished to sleep. He had merely recognized her need to be alone.

"Miss Ingleby," he said when she reached the door. She did not look back. "Do not provoke me again. In my service you will wear no cap."

She let herself out quietly and then raced upstairs to her room, where she shut the door gratefully on the world and cast herself across the bed. She was still clutching the cap tightly in one hand.

He was dead.

Sidney Jardine had died and there was no way anyone on this earth was going to believe that she had not murdered him.

She clutched a fistful of the bedspread in her free hand and pressed her face into the mattress.

He was dead.

He had been despicable and she had hated him more than she had thought it possible to hate anyone. But she had not wanted him dead. Or even hurt. It had been a pure reflex action to grab that heavy book and the pure, mindless instinct of self-defense to whack him over the head with it. Except that she had swung the tome rather than lifting it and bringing it down flat, because it had been so heavy. The sharp corner had caught him on the temple.

He had not fallen but had touched the wound, looked down at his bloodied fingers, laughed, called her a vixen, and advanced on her. But she had sidestepped. He had lost his balance as he lunged and had fallen forward onto the marble hearth, cracking his forehead loudly as he went down. Then he had lain still.

There had been several witnesses to the whole sordid scene, none of whom could be expected to tell the truth about what had happened. All of whom doubtless would be eager to perjure themselves by testifying that she had been apprehended while stealing. The gold, jewel-studded bracelet that would seem to prove them right was still at the bottom of her bag. All those people had been Sidney's friends. None of them had been hers. Charles—Sir Charles Fortescue, her neighbor, friend, and beau—had been away from home. Not that he would have been invited to that particular party anyway.

Sidney had not been dead after the fall even though everyone else in the room had thought he was. She had been the one to approach him on unsteady legs, sick to her stomach. His pulse had been beating steadily. She had even summoned a few servants and had him carried up to his room, where she had tended him herself and bathed his wounds until the doctor arrived, summoned at her command.

But he had been unconscious the whole while. And

looking so pale that a number of times she had checked his pulse again with cold, shaking fingers.

"Murderers hang, you know," someone had said from the doorway of the bedchamber, sounding faintly amused.

"By the neck until they are dead," another voice had added with ghoulish relish.

She had fled during the night, taking with her only enough possessions to get her to London on the stagecoach—and the bracelet, of course, and the money she had taken from the earl's desk. She had fled not because she believed that Sidney would die and she would be accused of his murder. She had fled because—oh, there were a number of reasons.

She had felt so very alone. The earl, her father's cousin and successor, and the countess had been away at a weekend house party. They had little love for her anyway. There was no one at Candleford to whom to turn in her distress. And Charles was not home. He had gone on an extended visit to his elder sister in Somersetshire.

Jane had fled to London. At first there had been no thought of concealment, only of reaching someone who would be sympathetic toward her. She had been going to Lady Webb's home on Portland Place. Lady Webb had been her mother's dearest friend since they made their come-out together as girls. She had often come to visit at Candleford. She was Jane's godmother. Jane called her Aunt Harriet. But Lady Webb had been away from home and was not expected back any time soon.

For more than three weeks now Jane had been well-nigh paralyzed with terror, afraid that Sidney had died, afraid that she would be accused of his murder, afraid that she would be called a thief, afraid that the law would come looking for her. They would know, of course, that she had come to London. She had done nothing to hide her tracks.

Worst of all during the past weeks had been knowing nothing. It was almost a relief to know at last.

That Sidney was dead.

That the story was that she had killed him as he had been apprehending her in the process of robbing the house.

That she was considered a murderess.

No, of course it was not a relief.

Jane sat up sharply on the bed and rubbed her hands over her face. Her worst nightmares had come true. Her best hope had been to disappear among the anonymous masses of ordinary Londoners. But that plan had been dashed when she had so foolishly interfered in that duel in Hyde Park. What had it mattered to her that two gentlemen who had no better use for their lives were about to blow each other's brains out?

Here she was in Mayfair, in one of the grand mansions on Grosvenor Square, as a sort of nurse/companion to a man who derived some kind of satisfaction out of displaying her to all his friends. None of them knew her, of course. She had lived a secluded life in Cornwall. The chances were that no visitors to Dudley House over the coming weeks would know her. But she was not quite convinced.

Surely it was only a matter of time. . . .

She got to her feet and crossed the room on shaking legs to the washstand. Mercifully there was water in the pitcher. She poured a little into the bowl and scooped some up in her cupped palms, into which she lowered her face.

What she ought to do—what she ought to have done at the start—was simply turn herself over to the authorities and trust to truth and justice. But who were the authorities? Where would she go to do it? Besides, she had made herself look guilty by running away and by staying out of sight for longer than three weeks.

He would know what she ought to do and where she should go with her story. The Duke of Tresham, that was. She could tell him everything and let him take the next step. But the thought of his hard, ruthless face and his disregard for her feelings made her shudder.

Would she hang? *Could* she hang for murder? Or even for theft? She really had no idea. But she had to grip the edge of the washstand suddenly to stop herself from swaying.

How could she trust in the truth when all the evidence and all the witnesses would be against her?

One of the gentlemen downstairs had said that perhaps Sidney was not dead after all. Jane knew very well how gossip could twist and change the truth. It was being said, for example, that she had been holding a pistol in each hand! Perhaps word of Sidney's death had spread simply because such an outcome titillated the senses of those who always liked to believe the worst.

Perhaps he was still only unconscious.

Perhaps he was recovering quite nicely.

Perhaps he was fully recovered.

And perhaps he was dead.

Jane dried her still-hot cheeks with a towel and sat down on the hard chair beside the washstand. She would wait, she decided, looking down at her hands in her lap—they were still shaking—until she had discovered the truth more definitely. Then she would decide what was best to do.

Was there a search on for her? she wondered. She pressed her fingers against her mouth and closed her eyes. She must stay out of sight of future visitors just in case. She must remain indoors as much as possible.

If only she could continue to wear her caps. . . .

She had never been a coward. She had never been one to hide from her problems or cower in a corner. Quite the contrary. But she had suddenly turned craven.

Of course, she had never been accused of murder before.

6

Mick Boden of the Bow Street Runners was standing in the Earl of Durbury's private sitting room at the Pulteney Hotel again, one week after his first appearance there. He had no real news to impart except that he had discovered no recent trace of Lady Sara Illingsworth.

His failure did not please him. He hated assignments like this one. Had he been summoned to Cornwall to investigate the murder attempt on Sidney Jardine, he could have used all his skills of detection to discover the identity of the would-be murderer and to apprehend the villain. But there was no mystery about this crime. The lady had been in the process of robbing the absent earl when Jardine had come upon her. She had hit him over the head with some hard object, doubtless taking him by surprise because he knew her and did not fully realize what she was up to, and then she had made off with the spoils of the robbery. Jardine's valet had witnessed the whole scene—a singularly cowardly individual in Mick's estimation since the thief had been a mere girl with nothing more lethal than a hard object to swing at him.

"If she is in London, we will find her, sir," he said now.

"If she is in London? *If*?" The earl fumed. "Of course she is in London, man. Where else would she be?"

Mick could have listed a score of places without even

taxing his brain, but he merely pulled on his earlobe. "Probably nowhere," he admitted. "And if she did not leave here a week or more ago, she will find it harder now, sir. We have questioned every coaching innkeeper and coachman in town. None remember a woman of her description except the one who brought her here. And now we are keeping a careful watch."

"All of which is laudable," his lordship said with heavy irony. "But what are you doing to find her within London? A week should have been time enough and to spare even if you put your feet up and slept for the first five or six days."

"She has not returned to Lady Webb's, sir," Mick told the earl. "We have checked. We have found the hotel where she stayed for two nights after her arrival, but no one knows where she went from there. According to your account, sir, she knows no one else in town. If she has a fortune on her, though, I would have expected her to take another hotel room or lodgings in a respectable district. We have found no trace of either yet."

"It has not occurred to you, I suppose," the earl said, going to stand in front of the window and drumming his fingernails on the sill, "that she may not wish to draw attention to herself by spending lavishly?"

It would strike Mick Boden as decidedly odd to steal a fortune and then neglect to spend any of it. Why would the young lady even have stolen it, if she was living at Candleford in the lap of luxury as the daughter of the former earl and relative to this present one? And if she was twenty years old and as lovely as the earl had described her, would she not be looking forward to making an advantageous match with a wealthy young nob?

There was more to this whole business than met the eye, Mick thought, not for the first time.

"Do you mean she might have taken employment?" he asked.

"It has crossed my mind." His lordship continued the finger-drumming while he frowned out through the window.

How much money had been taken? Mick wondered. Surely it must have been a great deal if the girl had been willing to kill for it. But of course there had been jewels too, and it was time he explored that possible means of tracing the girl.

"I and my assistants will start asking at the employment agencies, then," he said. "That will be a start. And at all the pawnbrokers and jewelers who might have bought the jewelry from her. I will need a description of each piece, sir."

"Do not waste your time," the earl said coldly. "She would not pawn any of it. Try the agencies. Try all likely employers. *Find* her."

"We certainly would not want a dangerous criminal let loose on any unsuspecting employer, sir," Mick agreed. "What name might she be using?"

The earl turned to face the Bow Street Runner. "What name?"

"She used her real name at Lady Webb's," Mick explained, "and at the hotel those first two nights. After that she disappeared. It has struck me, sir, that she has realized the wisdom of concealing her identity. What name might she use apart from her own? Does she have any middle names? Do you know her mother's maiden name? Her maid's name? Her old nurse's? Any that I might try at the agencies, sir, if there is no record of a Sara Illingsworth."

"Her parents always called her Jane." The earl scratched his head and frowned. "Let me think. Her mother was a Donningsford. Her maid . . ."

Mick jotted down the names he was given.

"We will find her, sir," he assured the Earl of Durbury again as he took his leave a few minutes later.

Though it was a strange business. A man's only son was in a coma, one foot in the grave, the other on an icy patch. He might even be dead at this very moment. And yet his father had left him in order to search for the woman who had tried to kill him. But the man never left his hotel suite, as far as Mick knew. The would-be murderess had stolen a fortune, yet the earl suspected she might be seeking employment. She had stolen jewels, but his lordship was unwilling to describe them or to have them hunted for in the pawnshops.

A very strange business indeed.

AFTER ONE WEEK OF moving between his bed upstairs, the sofa in the drawing room, and the chaise longue in the library, Jocelyn was colossally bored. Which was probably the understatement of the decade. His friends called frequently—every day, in fact—and brought him all the latest news and gossip. His brother called and talked about little else except the curricle race that Jocelyn would have given a fortune to be running himself. His sister called and talked incessantly on such scintillating topics as bonnets and her nerves. His brother-in-law made a few courtesy calls and discussed politics.

The days were long, the evenings longer, the nights endless.

Jane Ingleby became his almost constant companion. The realization could both amuse and irritate him. He began to feel like an old lady with a paid companion to run and fetch and hold the emptiness at bay.

She changed his bandage once a day. He had her massage his thigh once, an experiment he did not repeat despite the fact that her touch was magically soothing. It was also alarmingly arousing, and so he rebuked her for being so prudish as to blush and told her to sit down. She ran errands for him. She sorted his mail as he read it and returned it to Quincy with his instructions. She read to him and played cards with him.

He had Quincy in to play chess with him one evening and instructed her to sit and watch. Playing chess with Michael was about as exciting as playing cricket with a three-year-old. Though his secretary was a competent player, it never took great ingenuity to defeat him. Winning, of course, was always gratifying, but it was not particularly exhilarating when one could see the victory coming at least ten moves in advance.

After that Jocelyn played chess with Jane. She was so abysmally awful the first time that it was a measure of his boredom that he made her try it again the next day. She was almost ready that time to have given Michael a marginally competitive game, though certainly not him. The fifth time they played, she won.

She laughed and clapped her hands. "That is what comes, you see," she told him, "of being bored and toplofty and looking down your nose at me as if I were a speck on your boot and yawning behind your hand. You were not concentrating."

All of which was true. "You will concede, then," he asked, "that I would have won if I had been concentrating, Jane?"

"Oh, assuredly," she admitted. "But you were not and so you lost. Quite ignominiously, I might add."

He concentrated after that.

Sometimes they merely talked. It was strange to him to *talk* to a woman. He was adept at chitchatting socially with ladies. He was skilled at wordplay with courtesans. But he could not recall simply talking with any woman.

One evening she was reading to him and he was amusing himself with the observation that with her hair ruthlessly scraped back from her face, her eyes were slanted upward at the corners. It was her little rebellion, of course, to make her head as unattractive as possible even without the aid of the cap, and he hoped uncharitably that it gave her a headache.

"Miss Ingleby," he said with a sigh, interrupting her in the middle of a sentence, "I can listen no longer." Not that he had been doing much listening anyway. "In my opinion, with which you may feel free to disagree, Gulliver is an ass."

As he had expected, her lips tightened into a thin line. One of his few amusements during the past week had been provoking her. She closed the book.

"I suppose," she said, "you believe he should have trodden those little people into the ground because he was bigger and stronger than they."

"You are such a restful companion, Miss Ingleby," he said. "You put words into my mouth and thereby release me from the necessity of having to think and speak for myself."

"Shall I choose another book?" she asked.

"You would probably select a collection of sermons," he retorted. "No, we will talk instead."

"What about?" she asked after a short silence.

"Tell me about the orphanage," he said. "What sort of life did you have there?"

She shrugged. "There is not a great deal to tell."

It must certainly have been a superior sort of orphanage. But even so, an orphanage was an orphanage.

"Were you lonely there?" he asked. "*Are* you lonely?"

"No." She was not going to be very forthcoming with her personal history, he could see. She was not like many women—and men too, to be fair—who needed only the smallest encouragement to talk with great enthusiasm and at greater length about themselves.

"Why not?" he asked, narrowing his gaze on her. "You grew up without mother or father, brother or sister. You have come to London at the age of twenty or so, if my guess is correct, doubtless with the dream of making your fortune, but knowing no one. How can you not be lonely?"

She set the book down on the small table beside her and clasped her hands in her lap. "Aloneness is not always the same thing as loneliness," she said. "Not if one learns to like oneself and one's own company. It is possible, I suppose, to feel lonely even with mother and father and brothers and sisters if one basically does not like oneself. If one has been given the impression that one is not worthy of love."

"How right you are!" he snapped, instantly irritated.

He was being regarded from very steady, very blue eyes, he noticed suddenly.

"Is that what happened to you?" she asked.

When he realized just what it was she was asking, the

intimately personal nature of the question, he felt such fury that it was on the tip of his tongue to dismiss her for the night. Her impertinence knew no bounds. But a conversation, of course, was a two-way thing, and he was the one who had tried to get a conversation going.

He never had conversations, even with his male friends. Not on personal matters. He never talked about himself.

Was that what had happened to him?

"I was always rather fond of Angeline and Ferdinand," he said with a shrug. "We fought constantly, as I suppose most brothers and sisters do, though the fact that we were Dudleys doubtless made us a little more boisterous and quarrelsome than most. We also played and got into mischief together. Ferdinand and I were even gallant enough on occasion to take the thrashing for what Angeline had done, though I suppose we punished her for it in our own way."

"Why does being a Dudley mean that you must be more unruly, more vicious, more dangerous than anyone else?" she asked.

He thought about it, about his family, about the vision of themselves and their place in the scheme of things that had been bred into them from birth onward, and even perhaps before then.

"If you had known my father and my grandfather," he replied, "you would not even ask the question."

"And you feel you must live up to their reputations?" she asked. "Is it from personal choice that you do so? Or did you become trapped in your role as eldest son and heir and eventually the Duke of Tresham yourself?"

He chuckled softly. "If you knew my full reputation, Miss Ingleby," he said, "you would not need to ask that question either. I have not rested on the laurels of my forebears, I assure you. I have sufficient of my own."

"I know," she said, "that you are considered more proficient than any other gentleman with a wide range of weapons. I know that you have fought more than one duel. I suppose they were all over women?"

He inclined his head.

"I know," she said, "that you consort with married ladies without any regard to the sanctity of marriage or the feelings of the spouse you wrong."

"You presume to know a great deal about me," he said mockingly.

"I would have to be both blind and deaf not to," she said. "I know that you look upon everyone who is beneath you socially—and that is almost everyone—as scions to run and fetch for you and to obey your every command without question."

"And without even a please or thank you," he added.

"You engage in the most foolhardy wagers, I daresay," she said. "You have shown no concern this week over Lord Ferdinand's impending curricle race to Brighton. He could break his neck."

"Not Ferdinand," he said. "Like me, he has a neck made of steel."

"All that matters to you," she said, "is that he win the race. Indeed, I do believe that you wish you could take his place so that you could break yours instead."

"There is little point in entering a race," he explained, "unless one means to win it, Miss Ingleby, though one also must know how to behave like a gentleman when one loses, of course. Are you scolding me, by any chance? Is this a gentle tirade against my manners and morals?"

"They are not my concern, your grace," she said. "I am merely commenting upon what I have observed."

"You have a low opinion of me," he said.

"But I daresay," she retorted, "my opinion means no more to you than the snap of your fingers."

He chuckled softly. "I was different once upon a time, you know," he said. "My father rescued me. He made sure I took the final step in my education to become a gentleman after his own heart. Perhaps you are fortunate, Miss Ingleby, never to have known your father or mother."

"They must have loved you," she said.

"Love." He laughed. "I suppose you have an idealized conception of the emotion because you have never known a great deal of it yourself, or of what sometimes passes for it. If love is a disinterested devotion to the beloved, Jane, then indeed there is no such thing. There is only selfishness, a dedication to one's own comfort, which the beloved is used to enhance. Dependency is not love. Domination is not love. Lust is certainly not it, though it can be a happy enough substitute on occasion."

"You poor man," she said.

He found the handle of his quizzing glass and lifted it to his eye. She sat looking back at him, seemingly quite composed. Most women in his experience either preened or squirmed under the scrutiny of his glass. On this occasion its use was an affectation anyway. His eyesight was not so poor that he could not see her perfectly well without it. He let the glass fall to his chest.

"My mother and father were a perfectly happy couple," he said. "I never heard them exchange a cross word or saw them frown at each other. They produced three children, a sure sign of their devotion to each other."

"Well, then," Jane said, "you have just disproved your own theory."

"Perhaps," he said, "it was because they saw each other for only a few minutes three or four times a year. As my father came home to Acton Park, my mother would be leaving for London. As she came home, he would be leaving. A civil and amicable arrangement, you see." One he had thought quite normal at the time. It was strange how children who had known no different could adapt to almost any situation.

Jane said nothing. She sat very still.

"They were wonderfully discreet too," he said, "as any perfect couple must be if the harmony of the marriage is to be maintained. No word of my mother's legion of lovers ever came to Acton. I knew nothing of them until I came to London myself at the age of sixteen. Fortunately I resemble my father in physical features. So do Angeline and Ferdinand. It would be lowering to suspect that one might be a bastard, would it not?"

He had not spoken those words to hurt. He remembered too late that Jane Ingleby did not know her own parents. He wondered who had given her her last name. Why not Smith or Jones? Perhaps it was a policy of a superior orphanage to distinguish its orphans from the common run by giving them more idiosyncratic surnames.

"Yes," she said. "I am sorry. No child should have to feel so betrayed even when he is old enough, according to the world's beliefs, to cope with the knowledge. It must have been a heavy blow to you. But I daresay she loved you."

"If the number and splendor of the gifts she brought with her from London are any indication," he said, "she doted on us. My father did not depend upon his months in London for pleasure. There is a picturesque cottage in a remote corner of Acton Park, Jane. A river flows at the foot of its back garden, wooded hills grow up around it. It is an idyllic setting indeed. It was home during several of my growing years to an indigent relative, a woman of considerable charm and beauty. I was sixteen years old before I understood just who she was."

He had always intended to give the order to have that cottage pulled down. He still had not done so. But it was uninhabited now, and he had given his steward specific orders to spend not a single farthing on its upkeep. In time it would fall down from sheer neglect.

"I am sorry," she said again as if she were personally responsible for his father's lack of taste in housing his mistress—or one of them anyway—on his own estate with his children in residence there. But Jane did not know the half of it, and he was not about to enlighten her.

"I have much to live up to, you see," he said. "But I believe I am doing my part in perpetuating the family reputation."

"You are not bound by the past," she told him. "No one is. Influenced by it, yes, perhaps almost overwhelmingly drawn to live up to it. But not compelled. Everyone has free will, you more than most. You have the rank, the wealth, the influence to live your own life your own way."

"Which, my little moralist," he said softly, narrowing his eyes on her, "is exactly what I am doing. Except now, of course. Such inaction as this is anathema to me. But perhaps it is a fitting punishment, would you not agree, for having taken my pleasure in the bed of a married woman?"

She flushed and looked down.

"Does it reach your waist?" he asked her. "Or even below?"

"My hair?" She looked back up at him, startled. "It is only hair. Below my waist."

"Only hair," he murmured. "Only spun gold. Only the sort of magic web in which any man would gladly become hopelessly caught and enmeshed, Jane."

"I have not given you permission for such familiarity, your grace," she said primly.

He chuckled. "Why do I put up with your impudence?" he asked her. "You are my servant."

"But not your indentured slave," she said. "I can get up and walk out through that door any time I please and not come back. The few pounds you are paying me for three weeks of service do not give you ownership of me. Or excuse your impertinence in speaking with lascivious intent about my hair. And you may not deny that there was suggestiveness in what you said about it and the way you looked at it."

"Certainly I will not deny it," he agreed. "I try always to speak the truth, Miss Ingleby. Go and fetch the chess board from the library. We will see if you can give me a decent game tonight. And have Hawkins fetch the brandy while you are about it. I am as dry as a damned desert. And as prickly as a cactus plant."

"Yes, your grace." She got to her feet readily enough.

"And I would advise you," he said, "not to call me impertinent again, Miss Ingleby. I can be pushed only so far without retaliating."

"But you are confined to the sofa," she said, "and I can walk out through the door at any time. I believe that gives me a certain advantage."

One of these times, he thought as she vanished through the door—at least *one* time during the remaining two weeks of her employment—he was going to have the last word with Miss Jane Ingleby. He could not remember *not* having the last word with anyone, male or female, any time during the past ten years.

But he was relieved that their conversation had returned to its normal level before she left. He did not know quite how she had turned the tables on him before that. He had tried to worm out of her something about herself and had ended up telling her things about his childhood and boyhood that he did not care even to think about, let alone share with another person.

He had come very close to baring his heart.

He preferred to believe that he had none.

7

COME HERE," THE DUKE OF TRESHAM SAID TO JANE after a game of chess a few days later, in which he had prevailed but only after he had been forced to ponder his moves and accuse her of trying to distract him with her chatter. She had spoken scarcely a word during the whole game. Jane had moved away to return the chess board to its cupboard.

She did not trust the tone of his voice. She did not trust *him* when she thought about the matter. There had been a tension between them during the past few days that even in her inexperience she had had no difficulty in identifying. He saw her as a woman, and she, God help her, was very much aware of him as a man. She breathed a prayer of gratitude as she approached the sofa for the fact that he was still confined to it, though she would no longer be employed if he were not, of course.

The thought of leaving her employment—and Dudley House—in another week and a half was becoming more and more oppressive to her. In their careless conversation, his friends had several times referred to the fact that her father's cousin, the Earl of Durbury, was in London and that he had the dreaded Bow Street Runners looking for her. The friends and the duke himself appeared to be on her side. They jeered over the fact that she had overpowered Sidney, a man who was apparently not universally liked. But their attitude would change in a moment if they discovered that Lady Sara Illingsworth and Jane Ingleby were one and the same person.

"Show me your hands," the duke said now. It was, of course, a command, not a request.

"Why?" she asked, but he merely raised his eyebrows in that arrogant way he had and stared back at her.

She held them out toward him hesitantly, palms down. But he took them in his own and turned them over.

It was one of the most uncomfortable moments of Jane's life. His hands dwarfed her own, cupping hers loosely. She could easily have pulled away, and every instinct urged her to do so. But then she would reveal her discomfort and its only possible source. She felt the pull of his masculinity like a physical force. She found it difficult to breathe.

"No calluses," he said. "You have not done much menial work, then, Jane?"

She wished he would not sometimes lapse into calling her by the name only her parents had ever used. "Not a great deal, your grace," she said.

"They are beautiful hands," he said, "as one might expect. They match the rest of your person. They change bandages gently without causing undue pain. One wonders what other magic they could create with their touch. Jane, you could be the most sought-after courtesan in all of England if you so chose."

She pulled her hands back then, but his own tightened about them a little faster than she moved.

"I did add 'if you chose,' " he pointed out, a wicked gleam in his eyes. "What other magic can they create? I wonder. Are they musical hands? Do you play an instrument? The pianoforte?"

"A little," she admitted. Unlike her mother, she had never been any more than a proficient pianist.

His hands were still tight on hers. His dark eyes burned upward into her own. Her claim to be able to escape him at any time by simply walking out through the door was ridiculous now. By just a slight jerking on her hands he could have her down across him in a moment.

She glared at him, determined not to show fear or any other discomfort.

"Show me." He released her hands and indicated the pianoforte on the far side of the drawing room. It was a lovely instrument, she had noticed before, though not as magnificent as the one in the music room.

"I am out of practice," she said.

"For God's sake, Miss Ingleby," he retorted, "do not be coy. I always withdraw in haste to the card room whenever the young misses of the *ton* are about to demonstrate their party pieces at any fashionable entertainment. But I have degenerated to the point at which I am almost eager to listen to someone who openly admits that she plays only a little and is out of practice. Now go and play before my mind turns to other sport while you are still within grabbing distance."

She went.

She played one of the pieces she had committed to memory long ago, a Bach fugue. By happy chance she made only two errors, both in the first few bars and neither glaring.

"Come here," the duke said again when she had finished.

She crossed the room, sat in the chair she usually occupied, and looked directly at him. She had discovered that doing so protected her from being bullied. It appeared to suggest to him that she was capable of giving as good as she got.

"You were right," he said abruptly. "You play a little. A very little. You play without flair. You play each note as if it were a separate entity that had no connection with what came before or after. You depress each key as if it were simply an inanimate strip of ivory, as if you believed it impossible to coax *music* out of it. You must have had an inferior teacher."

The criticism of herself she could take quite philosophically. She had never had any illusions about her skills. But she bristled when he cast such aspersions on her mother.

"I did not!" she retorted. "How dare you presume to judge my teacher by my performance. She had more talent in her little finger than I have in my whole body. She could make it seem as if the music came from *her* rather than from a mere instrument. Or as if it came *through* her from some—oh, from some heavenly source." She glared indignantly at him, aware of the inadequacy of words.

He gazed at her in silence for a moment, a strange, unfamiliar glow in his eyes.

"Ah," he said at last, "you do understand, then, do you? It is not that you are unmusical, just that you are without superior talent of your own. But why would such a paragon come to an orphanage to teach?"

"Because she was an angel," Jane said, and swiped at the tears that threatened to spill onto her cheeks. What was the matter with her? She had never been a watering pot until recently.

"Poor Jane," he said softly. "Did she become a mother figure to you?"

She almost told him to go to hell, language that had never passed her lips before. She had almost sunk to his level.

"Never mind," she said weakly. "You do not own my memories, your grace. Or me either."

"Prickly," he said. "Have I touched a nerve? Go away now and do whatever it is you do during your hour off in the afternoons. Send Quincy to me. I have letters to dictate to him."

She walked in the garden as she did most afternoons except when it rained. Spring flowers were in glorious bloom, and the air smelled sweet. She was missing the air and exercise that had been so much part of her life in Cornwall. But fear was something that was closing about her more and more. She was afraid to go beyond the front doors of Dudley House.

She was afraid of being caught. Of not being believed. Of being punished as a murderess.

Sometimes she found herself on the verge of blurting the whole truth to the Duke of Tresham. Part of her believed he would stand as her friend. But it would be foolishness itself to trust a man renowned for ruthlessness.

AFTER TWO WEEKS JOCELYN decided that if he had to spend another week as he had spent the last two he would surely go mad. Raikes had been quite correct, of course, damn his eyes. The leg was not yet ready to bear his weight. But there was a middle ground between striding about on both legs and lying with one elevated.

He was going to acquire crutches.

His determination to delay no longer strengthened after two particular afternoon visits. Ferdinand came first, bursting with the latest details of the curricle race, set for three days hence. It seemed that betting at White's was brisk, almost all of it against Ferdinand and for Lord Berriwether. But his brother was undaunted. And he did introduce one other topic.

"The Forbes brothers are becoming increasingly offensive," he said. "They are hinting that you are hiding out here, Tresham, pretending to be wounded because the thought of them waiting for you has you shaking in your boots. If they ever so much as whisper as much in my hearing, they will all have gloves slapped in their faces hard enough to raise welts."

"Keep out of my concerns," Jocelyn told him curtly. "If they have anything to say about me, they may say it to my face. They will not have long to wait."

"Your concerns *are* mine, Tresham," his brother complained. "An insult to one of us is an insult to all. I just hope Lady Oliver was worth it. Though I daresay she was. I have never known a woman with such a slender waist and such large—" But he broke off suddenly and glanced uneasily over his shoulder at Jane Ingleby, who was sitting quietly some distance away, as usual.

Ferdinand, like Angeline and Jocelyn's friends, seemed uncertain how to treat the Duke of Tresham's nurse.

Trouble was brewing, Jocelyn thought restlessly after his brother had left. Just as it usually was over something or other. Except that normally he was out there to confront it. He had always reveled in it. He could not remember thinking, as he sometimes caught himself doing these days, that there was something remarkably silly and meaningless in his whole style of life.

The sooner he got out and back about his usual activities, the better it would be for his sanity. Tomorrow he would want to know the reason why if Barnard had not acquired the crutches he had asked for.

And then came the second visitor. Hawkins, come to announce the caller, looked disapproving. Jane Ingleby gathered up the book from which she had been reading and retreated to the corner where she always hid out while he entertained.

"Lady Oliver, your grace," Hawkins said, "wishing for a private word with you. I informed her ladyship that I was not sure you were well enough to receive visitors."

"Bloody hell!" Jocelyn roared. "You know better than to allow her over the doorstep, Hawkins. Get the woman out of here."

It was not the first time she had come to Dudley House. The woman knew no better, it seemed, than to call upon a gentleman in his bachelor home. And she had come at a time when half the fashionable world was out and about and might happen by and see her or evidence of her presence.

"I suppose," he asked rhetorically, "she came in Lord Oliver's town coach and that it is waiting for her outside?"

"Yes, your grace." Hawkins bowed.

But before Jocelyn could renew his command that the woman be removed from the premises immediately if not sooner, the lady herself appeared in the doorway. Hawkins, Jocelyn thought grimly, would be fortunate indeed if he did not find himself demoted to the position of assistant boot boy before the day was over.

"Tresham," she said in her sweet, breathy voice. She raised a lace-edged handkerchief to her lips as visual evidence of the distress of a woman of sentiment.

She was, of course, a vision of delicate loveliness in varying shades of coordinating greens to complement her red hair. She was small and slender and dainty, though she did also, of course, have the bosom that Ferdinand had referred to earlier.

He scowled at her as she wafted into the room, her hazel eyes clouded with concern for him. "You ought not to be here."

"But how could I stay away?" She continued wafting until she reached the chaise longue. She sank to her knees beside him and possessed herself of one of his hands with both her own. She raised it to her lips.

Hawkins, the arrant knave, had withdrawn and closed the door behind him.

"Tresham," she said again. "Oh, my poor, poor dear. You shot gallantly into the air, it is said, when you might easily have killed Edward. Everyone knows your prowess with a pistol. And then you bravely allowed him to shoot you in the leg."

"It was the other way around," he told her curtly. "And there was nothing brave about it. I was not paying attention at the time."

"A woman screamed," she said, kissing his hand again and holding it against one cool, powdered cheek. "I am sure I do not blame her, though I would have swooned quite away if I had been there. My poor, brave darling. Did he nearly kill you?"

"The leg is far from the heart," he said, firmly repossessing himself of his hand. "Do stand up. I will not offer you a seat or refreshments. You are leaving. Now. Miss Ingleby will show you out."

"Miss Ingleby?" Two spots of color appeared in her cheeks suddenly, and her eyes flashed.

He indicated Jane with one hand. "Miss Ingleby, meet Lady Oliver. Who is leaving—*now*!"

But Lady Oliver's look of jealous annoyance turned to indifference mingled with disdain when her eyes lit on Jane. What she saw, obviously, was a maidservant.

"You are cruel, Tresham," she said. "I have been worried half to death about you. I have been languishing for a sight of you."

"Which you have now had," he said briskly. "Good day to you."

"Tell me you have been pining for me too," she said. "Ah, cruel that you make me beg for one kind word."

He looked at her with something like loathing. "Frankly," he said, "I have scarce spared you a thought since I last saw you—at the Georges', was it? Or on Bond Street? I do not remember. And I daresay I will not spare you another thought once you have gone."

She was holding her handkerchief to her mouth again and looking at him reproachfully over the top of it.

"You are angry with me," she told him.

"My feelings, I assure you, ma'am," he said, "do not go beyond irritation."

"If you would let me explain—" she began.

"I beg you will spare me."

"I came here to warn you," she said. "They are going to kill you, you know. My brothers, that is, Anthony and Wesley and Joseph. In defense of my honor, which they do not believe Edward did convincingly enough. Or if they do not kill you, they will find another way to hurt you. They are like that."

Behaving with a ruthless disregard to honor must be a family trait, then, Jocelyn thought.

"Miss Ingleby," he said, "would you please conduct

Lady Oliver to the door and see her on her way? And instruct Hawkins that I will have a word with him."

Lady Oliver was weeping in earnest. "You are hard-hearted, Tresham, as everyone warned me," she said through her sobs. "I thought I knew better. I thought you loved me. And I do not need a maid to show me out. I can see myself out, thank you."

Which she proceeded to do in a tragic performance that surely would have brought whistles from the pit of any theater had she been on stage, and a demand for an encore.

"Well, Miss Ingleby," Jocelyn said after an unseen hand had closed the library door, "what do you think of my paramour? Can you blame me for climbing into the lady's bed, married or not?"

"She is very lovely," she admitted.

"And your answer to my second question?" He glared at her as if she were somehow to blame for Lady Oliver's continued indiscretions. He would have expected the woman to avoid him above all others for the next lifetime or two.

"I am not your judge, your grace," Jane Ingleby said gravely.

"You condone adultery, then?" he asked, looking at her with narrowed gaze.

"No, of course not," she said. "It must always be wrong. Nevertheless, you were cruel to her just now. You spoke to her as if you loathed her."

"I do," he said. "Why pretend that I do not?"

"And yet," she said, "you lay with her and made her love you. But now you have spurned her when she braved propriety in order to come and see you and warn you."

He smiled. "Is it possible," he asked, "to be so incredibly naïve? I made Lady Oliver love me, Jane? The only person Lady Oliver loves is Lady Oliver. And she has braved propriety so that the *beau monde* will believe that she and I are flouting convention and danger by continuing our liaison. The woman is an exhibitionist. It pleases her to be notorious, especially with someone like me. It delights her to have it said that she has tamed the heart of a Dudley—of the Duke of Tresham himself. She would love nothing better than for me to be compelled to shoot into the air three more times while her brothers use me for target practice. Five times if the other two brothers should descend upon town."

"You trivialize the lady's sensibilities," Jane said.

"I thought," he said softly, "you were not my judge."

"You would tempt a saint," she told him tartly.

"I hope so." He grinned. "But tell me, what has you so convinced that I have lain with Lady Oliver?"

She stared at him blankly for a few moments. "Everyone knows it," she said at last. "It is why the duel was fought. *You* told me."

"Did I?" he asked. "Or did I just allow you to make the assumption?"

"I suppose," she said, sounding indignant, "you are going to deny it now."

He pursed his lips and took his time about answering. "No, I think not," he said. "To deny it would be to give the impression that your good opinion matters to me, you see, Jane. I could not have you believing that, could I?"

She came closer and sat down on her chair again. She arranged the book open on her lap without any apparent care that she turned to the right page. She set her hands flat on the pages. She was frowning.

"If it is untrue," she asked, "why did you not deny it? Why did you fight a duel and risk death?"

"Jane, Jane," he said, "is a gentleman publicly to contradict a lady?"

"But you loathe her."

"I am still a gentleman," he said, "and she is still a lady."

"That is ridiculous!" Her brows snapped together. "You would allow her husband to believe the worst of you and her without telling him the truth? You would allow all of fashionable society to believe the worst of you?"

"Ah," he said, "but they love me for it, Jane. I am the bad, dangerous Duke of Tresham. How I would disappoint the *ton* if I were to insist that on this occasion I am as innocent as a newborn lamb. Not quite, of course. I did flirt with the lady on a few occasions. I often flirt with married ladies. It is expected of me."

"What nonsense you speak!" she said crossly. "And I do not believe you. You are telling me all this only so that you may laugh at me later and tell me what a simpleton I am to believe in your innocence."

"Ah, but, Miss Ingleby," he said, "I have already told you that your opinion matters not one whit to me."

"You are despicable," she said. "I do not know why I remain in your employ."

"Perhaps, Jane," he said, "because you need a roof over your head and food in your stomach. Or perhaps because you enjoy scolding me and chastising me with your barbed tongue. Perhaps because you are growing just a little fond of me?" He deliberately made his voice into a caress.

Her lips were set in a thin line. She stared grimly at him.

"Just remember one thing," he said. "I do not tell lies, Jane. I may acquiesce in other people's lies, but I do not tell lies of my own. You may believe me or not as you wish. Now put down that book and go and fetch me some coffee. And my mail from Michael Quincy. And the chess board."

"You will *not* call me Jane," she said, getting to her feet. "One day I will beat you at chess again even when you are concentrating. And wipe the complacency from your face."

He grinned at her. "Go and do what you have been told to do," he said. "*Please,* Miss Ingleby?"

"Yes, your grace," she said vindictively.

Why, Jocelyn wondered as she left the room, had it seemed so important to him, despite his denial, that she know the truth about Lady Oliver? He did not care tuppence what anyone thought. Indeed, he had always reveled in his rakish reputation even on the rare occasion like this when it was unearned.

Lady Oliver had boasted to her husband, probably during a quarrel, that the Duke of Tresham was her lover. And said husband, in high dudgeon, had issued his challenge. Who was Jocelyn to contradict the lady?

Why had he wanted Jane Ingleby to know that he had never bedded Lady Oliver? Or any other married lady, for that matter?

If Barnard did not have those crutches by tomorrow, Jocelyn thought suddenly, he would beat the man about the head with them as soon as they were in his possession.

8

"WHAT DO YOU THINK YOU ARE DOING?" JANE asked, startled, when she walked into the library the following morning to discover the Duke of Tresham standing facing the window, propped on crutches.

"I *think* I am standing at the window of the library," he said, looking back over his shoulder at her, his eyebrows raised haughtily. "In my own home. Deigning to answer an impertinent question from an impertinent servant. Fetch your cloak and bonnet. You may accompany me outside into the garden."

"You were told to keep your leg still and elevated," she said, hurrying toward him. She had not remembered that he was quite so tall.

"Miss Ingleby," he said, without changing his expression, "go and fetch your cloak and bonnet."

He was a little awkward with the crutches at first, she noticed later, but that fact did not deter him from strolling outside with her for half an hour before they sat side by side on a wrought-iron seat beneath a cherry tree. Her shoulder was almost touching his arm. She sat very still while he breathed in slowly and audibly.

"One takes many things for granted," he said, more to himself than to her, it seemed. "Fresh air and the perfumes of nature, for example. One's health. One's ability to move about freely."

"Deprivation and suffering can certainly act like wake-up calls," she agreed. "They can remind us to stop squandering our lives in unawareness and in attention to mere trivialities." If she were ever free again...

Her mother had died after a shockingly brief illness when Jane was barely seventeen, and her father had taken to his bed and died a little over a year later. She had been left with memories of happiness and security, which she had been young and innocent enough to expect to last forever. She had been left with Papa's cousin inheriting his title and taking over Candleford. And resenting her and courting her favor all at the same time and devising plans for her future that suited his vision but not her own. If she could have back just one of those days of her innocence...

"I suppose," the duke said, turning his head to look down at her, "I should turn over a new leaf now, shouldn't I, Miss Ingleby? Become that rarest of all social phenomena, a reformed rake? Defy my heritage? Marry a saint and retire to my country estate to become a model landlord? Sire a brood of model children and raise them to be model citizens? Live happily ever after in a monogamous relationship?"

He had made himself sound so abjectly meek that she laughed.

"It would be a fine thing to behold, I am sure," she said. "Have you proved your point for this morning? Your leg is hurting, is it not? You are rubbing your thigh again. Come indoors and I shall make you comfortable."

"Why is it," he asked her, "that when you say such things, Jane, I forget any idea of turning over a new leaf and feel very unsaintly indeed?"

He had leaned slightly sideways. His arm was against

her shoulder and there was no space on her other side to shuffle across to. She stood up.

That feeling of almost unbearable tension was happening altogether too often. With him, of course, it was deliberate. She believed he delighted in making suggestive remarks to her and looking at her with his eyes half closed. He was amusing himself by teasing her, knowing very well that she was affected. And she *was* affected. She could not deny that the sight of him—even the very *thought* of him—could quicken her blood. That the careless touch of his hand could make her ache for more.

"Take me back inside, then," he said, getting up and onto his crutches without her assistance, "and perform whatever nursing duties you deem necessary. I will come meekly, you see, since you are not in the mood for dalliance."

"And never will be, your grace," she assured him firmly.

But it was a statement and a resolve that were to be tested later that very night.

JOCELYN COULD NOT SLEEP. He had been suffering from insomnia for a week or more. It was understandable, of course, when there was nothing to do after eleven o'clock at night—sometimes even ten—but go to bed and picture in his mind all the balls and routs then in progress and to imagine his friends moving on afterward to one of the clubs until dawn sent them homeward.

Tonight his sleeplessness was combined with a terrible restlessness. He could feel temptation grab almost irresistibly at him—the sort of temptation that had often got him into trouble when he was a boy until he had learned to curb his urges, especially when his father was at Acton. Finally he had suppressed them completely—except when occasionally they burst through all his defenses and would not leave him alone.

On such occasions he usually went to a woman and stayed with her until there was no energy left for anything but sleep and a return to his normal way of life.

He thought with brief wistfulness of Jane Ingleby, but he turned his mind quickly away from her. He enjoyed teasing her, flirting with her, annoying her. And of course she was powerfully beautiful and attractive. But she was off-limits. She was a servant beneath his own roof.

Finally, at something past midnight, he could resist no longer. He threw back the bedcovers, hoisted himself upward with his crutches, and hobbled through to his dressing room, where he donned shirt and pantaloons and slippers but did not bother with either waistcoat or coat. He did not light a candle as he did not have a third hand with which to carry it. He would light some downstairs.

He made his way slowly and awkwardly down to the ground floor.

JANE COULD NOT SLEEP.

The Duke of Tresham no longer needed a bandage. The wound had healed. He was getting about with crutches. He was restless and bad-tempered and would soon be going out. He would not need her.

He never had really needed her.

She would probably be dismissed even before the

three weeks were at an end. But even if not, there was only one week left.

The world beyond the doors of Dudley House had become a frightening place that she dreaded having to step into. Every day one visitor or other referred to what was known as the Cornish incident. Today the duke and his friends had chatted merrily on the subject.

"I wonder," the blond and very handsome Viscount Kimble had said, "why Durbury stays shut up in the Pulteney almost all the time instead of enlisting the aid of the *ton* in apprehending his niece or cousin or whatever the devil relationship the woman has to him. Why come to town to search for her and then hide away and let the Runners do all the work?"

"Perhaps he is grieving," the brown-haired, pleasant-faced Sir Conan Brougham had suggested. "Though he does not wear mourning. Could it be that Jardine is not dead after all but is merely skulking in Cornwall with a broken head?"

"That would be in character," the duke had said dryly.

"If you were to ask me," Viscount Kimble had observed, "the woman should be awarded a medal rather than a noose if he *is* dead. The world will be a better place without the presence of Jardine in it."

"But you had better watch your back with the rest of us once you leave the sanctuary of this house, Tresham," Sir Conan had added with a chuckle. "Look out for a fierce wench wielding a pair of pistols or a hefty ax. Accounts vary on which she used to do the dastardly deed."

"What does she look like, pray?" the duke had asked. "So that I may duck out of sight when I see her coming."

"A black-eyed, black-haired witch as ugly as sin," Sir

Conan had said. "Or a blond Siren as beautiful as an angel. Take your pick. I have heard both descriptions and several others between the two extremes. No one has ever seen her, it seems, except Durbury, who is keeping mum. Have you heard about Ferdinand's new team? I daresay you have, though, and from the horse's mouth itself, so to speak. Will they decide to travel north when he gives them the signal to proceed south, do you suppose?"

"Not if he is a true brother of mine," the duke had said. "I suppose he bought a frisky pair that will take a year to tame?"

The conversation had proceeded on that topic.

Now Jane could not sleep. Or even lie still. She kept seeing Sidney's parchment-pale face and the blood on his temple. She kept thinking of the earl's coming to London to search for her. And of the Bow Street Runners combing its streets and questioning its inhabitants to discover her whereabouts. She kept imagining herself taking her fate in her own hands and leaving Dudley House to confront the earl at the Pulteney Hotel.

It would be such a relief to come out of hiding, to have everything out in the open.

To be thrown into jail. To be publicly tried. To be hanged. *Could* an earl's daughter be sentenced to hang? An earl could not. But could his daughter? She did not know.

Why was her father's cousin not wearing mourning? Was it possible that Sidney was not dead after all? But it would be foolish to hope.

She threw back the bedcovers eventually and stopped even pretending to be settled for the night. She lit her candle, threw her cloak about her shoulders, and left her room, not even bothering to dress or to put on shoes. Perhaps she could find a book in the library into which to escape until her brain quieted down.

But she became gradually aware of something as she descended the stairs. Some sound. By the time she reached the bottom it was quite obvious what it was.

Music. Pianoforte music.

Coming from the music room.

But who could be producing it? It was far too late for visitors. It must be well past midnight. Besides, there was no light in the hall. The servants had all retired to bed. There was a thin thread of light beneath the music room door.

Jane approached it gingerly and rested her hand on the knob for several moments before turning it and opening the door.

It was the Duke of Tresham.

He was seated on the pianoforte bench, his crutches on the floor beside him. He was hunched over the keys, playing without sheet music, his eyes closed, a look almost of pain on his face. He was playing something hauntingly beautiful, something Jane had never heard before.

She stood transfixed, listening. And experiencing again, with a constriction of the heart, the feeling that the music came not from the instrument or even from the man but through them from some divine source. She had not believed there could be another musician with a talent to match her mother's.

But now she was in his presence.

Five minutes or more must have passed before the music ended. He sat, his hands lifted an inch above the keyboard, his head bowed, his eyes still closed. It was only in that moment that Jane realized she was a trespasser.

But it was too late. Even as she thought of withdrawing and closing the door quietly behind her, he turned his head and opened his eyes. For a moment they looked blankly into hers. And then they blazed.

"What the devil are you doing here?" he thundered.

For the first time she was truly afraid of him. His anger appeared somehow different from any she had seen in him before. She half expected him to get up and come stalking toward her.

"I am so sorry," she said. "I came down for a book and I heard the music. Where did you learn to play like that?"

"Like what?" he asked, his eyes narrowing. He was recovering from his shock, she could see, and was looking more himself. "I dabble, Miss Ingleby. I was amusing myself, unaware that I had an audience."

He had retreated, she realized suddenly, behind a familiar mask. She had never thought of him before as a man who needed defenses. It had never occurred to her that perhaps there were depths to his character that he had never shown her, or any of his visitors either.

"Oh, no," she said, aware even as she spoke that perhaps it would be wiser to remain silent. She stepped right into the room and closed the door. "You are no dabbler, your grace. You have been gifted with a wondrous and rare talent. And you were not amusing yourself. You were embracing your talent with your whole soul."

"Poppycock!" he said curtly after a brief silence. "I have never even had a lesson, Jane, and I do not read music. There goes your theory."

But she was staring at him with wide eyes. "You have never had a lesson? What were you playing, then? How did you learn it?"

She realized the truth even as she asked the questions. He did not answer her but merely pursed his lips.

"You do not wear it loose even to bed?" he said.

Her hair. He was talking about her hair, which was in a thick braid down her back. But she was not to be distracted.

"It was your own composition," she said. "It *was*, was it not?"

He shrugged. "As I said," he told her, "I dabble."

"Why does your talent embarrass you?" she asked. "Why are you eager to belittle and even deny it?"

He smiled then, slowly. "You really do not know my family," he told her.

"I suppose," she said, "that playing the pianoforte, composing music, loving it, is something quite unworthy of a Dudley male."

"Bordering on the effeminate," he agreed.

"Bach was a man," she said, walking toward him and setting her candle down on the pianoforte beside the candelabrum that had been giving him light. "Were all the famous composers effeminate?"

"They would have been if they had been Dudleys." He grinned rather wolfishly at her. "Bare feet, Jane? Such shocking dishabille!"

"According to whom?" She would not allow him to change the subject. "You? Or your father and grandfather?"

"We are all one," he said. "Like the trinity, Jane."

"That is blasphemous," she told him firmly. "Your father must have been aware of your talent. Something like that cannot be hidden indefinitely. It will burst forth, as it has tonight. He did not encourage you to develop it?"

"I soon learned never to play when he was at home," he said. "Not after he caught me at it twice. I never did particularly enjoy having to sleep on my front all night because my rear was too sore."

Jane was too angry to say anything. She merely stared at him with compressed lips—at the hard, cynical, dangerous rake who had had all traces of his more sensitive, artistic nature thrashed out of him by a father who had been ignorant enough and weak enough to fear all things feminine. Why was it that men of that type did not realize that the mature, balanced person, regardless of gender, was a fine mix of masculine and feminine qualities? And here was this foolish man trying to live up to the ideal set him by ignorant men—and doing rather a good job of it most of the time.

He turned his attention back to the keyboard and began to play softly. This time it was a familiar tune.

"Do you know it?" he asked without looking up.

"Yes," she said. "It is 'Barbara Allen.' " One of the lovelier and sadder folk songs.

"Do you sing?" he asked her.

"Yes," she admitted softly.

"And do you know the words?"

"Yes."

"Sing them, then." He stopped playing and looked at her. "Sit on the bench here beside me and sing. Since you have come, you might as well make yourself useful. I shall try to play as if my fingers were not all thumbs."

She did as she was bidden and watched his hands as he played some introductory bars. She had noticed before that he had long fingers. Because he was the Duke of Tresham, it had not occurred to her then that they were artistic hands. It was obvious now. They caressed the keys as if he made love to the music rather than merely produced it.

She sang the song through from beginning to end, long as it was. After an initial self-consciousness, she forgot everything but the music and the sad story of Barbara Allen. Singing had always been one of her greatest joys.

There was silence when the song came to an end. Jane sat straight-backed on the pianoforte bench, her hands clasped in her lap. The duke sat with his hands poised over the keys. It was, Jane thought, without quite understanding the meaning of the thought, one of life's most blessed moments.

"My God!" he murmured into the silence. It did not sound like one of his all-too-common blasphemies. "Contralto. I expected you to have a soprano voice."

The moment passed and Jane was very aware that she was sitting beside the Duke of Tresham in the music room, clad only in her nightgown and outdoor cloak, her braid loose down her back. With bare feet. He was wearing very tight pantaloons and a white shirt open at the neck.

She could think of no way to stand up and remove herself from the room without making a grand production out of it.

"I have never in my life," he said, "heard such a lovely voice. Or one that adapted itself so perfectly to the music and the sentiment of the song."

She was pleased despite her discomfort.

"Why did you not tell me," he asked her, "when I had

you play for me and gave you an honest assessment of your talent? Why did you not tell me that you sing?"

"You did not ask," she told him.

"Damn you, Jane," he said. "How dare you keep yourself so much to yourself? A talent like yours is to be shared, not hidden away from the world."

"Touché," she said quietly.

They sat side by side in silence for a while. And then he took her hand in his and held it on the bench between them. Suddenly half the air seemed to have been sucked from the room.

"You ought not to have come down," he said. "Or you ought to have crept into the library and chosen your book and ignored your curiosity. You have caught me at a bad time."

She understood his meaning. It was a bad time for her too. They were firmly caught in a situation that was unfamiliar to them. In a mellow, somewhat melancholy mood. Alone together—as they often were, of course. But entirely alone this time, with no servants moving about beyond the door. Late at night.

"Yes" was all she could think of to say. She stood up then, drawing her hand free of his. Yet everything except her common sense yearned to stay.

"Don't go," he said, his voice unusually husky, and he swiveled around on the bench until he sat with his back to the pianoforte. "Don't leave me yet."

It was a moment—and only a moment—of decision. She could listen to common sense, say a firm good night, and walk from the room. He could not—and would not—stop her. Or she could stay in a situation that was charged with tension and against which her defenses had been lowered. There was no time to debate the matter with herself. She took the couple of steps that brought her directly in front of him.

She lifted both hands and set them on his head as if in benediction. His hair was silky and warm beneath her fingers. His hands came to rest on either side of her waist and drew her toward him. He sighed and leaned forward to bury his face between her breasts.

Fool, she told herself as she closed her eyes and reveled in the physical sensations of his touch and his body heat and the smell of his cologne. *Fool!* But the thought was without conviction.

When he finally lifted his head and looked up at her, his dark eyes fathomless, she went down onto her knees on the floor between his spread thighs. She did not know why she did so, whether at the guidance of his hands or from some instinct that did not require thought. She set her arms along the tight fabric over his thighs, feeling their firm, muscled strength, and lifted her head.

He was leaning over her, and his fingers touching her face were feather-light and tipped with a heat that scorched its way into the depths of her femininity. He cupped her face with his hands before kissing her.

She had been kissed before. Charles had been her beau for four years as well as her dearest friend forever. On a few occasions she had been alone with him and had permitted him to kiss her. She had liked his kiss.

Now she realized she had never been kissed before. Not really. Not like this.

Ah, never like this.

He scarcely touched his lips to hers. His eyes were open, as were hers. It was impossible to lose herself in sheer physical sensation even though every part of her body sizzled with awareness and ached with desire. It was impossible not to know fully what was happening and with whom. It would be impossible afterward to tell herself that she had been swept away by mindless passion.

This was not mindless.

He feathered kisses over her cheeks, her eyes, her temples, her nose, her chin. And returned to her mouth, which he touched softly, teasingly, with his lips, coaxing her to kiss him back in the same way.

A kiss was not necessarily just lips pressed to lips, she discovered in growing wonder. There was the warm, moist flesh behind her lips, which he touched and stroked with his tongue. There was her own tongue moving lightly across his top lip and back over the bottom one. He touched its tip, sliding over the top of it deep into the cavity of her mouth. There were sucking and stroking and soft, wordless moans in her voice, in his.

And then his arms closed about her as he leaned farther over her, half lifting her against the taut strength of his chest, and they shared a deep, hard, openmouthed embrace that had her clinging and pressing and yearning for more.

At last she was down on her knees again, his hands spread over her own on his thighs, his dark, heavy-lidded eyes gazing down into hers.

"We will have to punish each other for this in the morning, Jane," he said. "It will be amazing how different it will all seem then. Forbidden. Impossible. Even sordid."

She shook her head.

"Oh, yes," he insisted. "I am just a rake, my dear, with nothing on my mind except covering you on the floor here and taking my wicked pleasure deep inside your virgin body. And you are the wide-eyed, innocent dove. My servant. My dependent. It is quite impossible. And definitely sordid. You think that what has happened is beautiful. I can see it in your eyes. It is not, Jane. That is merely what an experienced rake can make a woman think. In reality it is the simple lustful, raw desire for sex. For the quick, vigorous mating of bodies. Go to bed now. Alone."

Both his face and his voice were harsh. She got to her feet and stood away from him. But she did not immediately turn to leave. She searched his eyes with her own, looking into the mask that he had settled firmly in place. The impenetrable mask. He was gazing back at her with a mocking half smile on his lips.

He was right. What had happened had been entirely physical. And very raw.

But he was wrong too. Her mind could not yet grapple with what exactly was wrong with what he had said. It just was. He was wrong.

But yes, it was quite impossible. And without a doubt this would all appear very different in the morning. She would not be able to look calmly at him tomorrow as she was doing now.

"Good night, your grace," she said.

"Good night, Jane."

He had turned back to the pianoforte by the time she had picked up her candle, left the room, and closed the door behind her. He was playing something quiet and melancholy.

She was halfway up the stairs before she remembered that she had come down for a book. She did not turn back.

9

"YES, A STOOL WILL DO NICELY," JOCELYN SAID with a careless wave of his hand to the servant who had asked.

It would do more than nicely. He had come to White's Club in his town carriage rather than riding, but he really ought to have used his crutches after descending instead of just a stout cane. His boot was pressing uncomfortably against his still-tender right calf. If he was not careful he was going to be compelled to have the boot cut off again when he returned home. He had already lost his favorite pair that way the day of the duel.

"And fetch me the morning papers too," he instructed the servant, lifting his leg onto the stool without any outer appearance of effort but with a grateful inward sigh.

He had left the house early so that he would not have to encounter *her* before leaving, and she was herself an early riser. He picked up the *Morning Post* and scanned the front page, scowling as he did so. What the devil was he about, escaping early from his own home so that he could postpone coming face-to-face with a servant?

He was not sure which of two facts he was most ashamed of—if shame was the right word. Embarrassment might be more accurate. But neither was an emotion with which he had much recent acquaintance.

She had caught him playing the pianoforte. Playing

one of his own compositions. And he had kissed her. Damnation, but he had been alone and inactive for too long and had broken one of his cardinal rules and had sunk to a new low in his own esteem. If his leg had not been aching enough to distract him, he probably would have laid her on the floor and availed himself of the treasure that had lain beneath the flimsy barrier of her nightgown. She would not have stopped him, the silly innocent.

"Tresham? By God, it is! How are you, old chap?"

Jocelyn was happy to lower his newspaper, which he had not been reading anyway, in order to greet acquaintances, who were beginning to arrive for their morning gossip and perusal of the papers.

"Hale, hearty, and hopping along at roughly my usual speed," he replied.

The next several minutes were taken up with cheerful greetings and jocular witticisms about the Duke of Tresham's leg and the elegant stool on which it reclined and the stout cane propped beside his chair.

"We were beginning to think you were enjoying playing court at Dudley House, Tresh," Viscount Kimble said, "and were going to settle to it for life."

"With the delectable Miss Ingleby to minister to your needs," Baron Pottier added. "You are wearing your boots again, Tresham?"

"Would I come to White's in my dancing slippers?" Jocelyn raised his eyebrows.

But Sir Isaac Wallman had picked up on an interesting detail. "The delectable Miss Ingleby?" he said. "The nurse? The one who screamed during the duel? Ho, Tresham, you rogue. Now how exactly has she been ministering to your needs?"

Jocelyn raised his quizzing glass and regarded the little dandy through it, looking him over slowly from head to toe.

"Tell me, Wallman," he said in his most bored accents, "at what ungodly hour of the night did you have to rise to give your valet time to create that artistry with your neckcloth?" It would have been overelaborate even for the grandest of grand balls. Though maybe not for a soiree with the Regent, that prince of dandies.

"It took him a full hour," Sir Isaac replied with some pride, instantly distracted. "And he ruined eight neckcloths before he got it right with this one."

Jocelyn lowered his glass while Viscount Kimble snorted derisively.

The pleasantries over with, the conversation moved to the London-to-Brighton curricle race set for two days hence and to the somewhat reclusive presence in London of the Earl of Durbury, who had come to search for his son's murderess. It was a major disappointment to several of the gentlemen present that the earl was not appearing everywhere in order to regale a bored *ton* with the macabre details.

Sidney Jardine, who had been elevated to the position of heir to an earldom on the accession of his father to the title a year or so before, had never been popular with his peers. Jocelyn's only dealings with him had come during a *ton* ball a couple of years before when Jardine, in his grace's hearing, had made a coarse remark fully intended for the ears of a young lady and her mama, who had both declined his invitation to the former to dance. Jocelyn had invited the man to stroll with him on the terrace beyond the ballroom.

There he had instructed Jardine pleasantly enough to

take himself off home without further ado or to hell if he preferred unless he chose to stay and have his mouth washed with soap. And when a furiously bristling Jardine had tried to issue a challenge, Jocelyn had raised his quizzing glass to his eye and informed his would-be adversary that it was an immutable rule with him to duel only with gentlemen.

"I am of the school of thought," he said now, "that Lady Sara Illingsworth should be congratulated rather than censured. If she is wise, though, she will have removed herself far from London by now."

"She did not go by stage, though, Tresh," Viscount Kimble said. "I have heard that the Runners have done a thorough investigation. No one of her description has been traveling on any one of them."

"She has learned wisdom since her arrival here, then," Jocelyn said. "Good for her. I daresay she was provoked. Why else would any young lady bash a gentleman over the head?"

"You should know, Tresham," Sir Isaac said with a titter, and won for himself another steady perusal through the ducal quizzing glass.

"Where is Ferdinand stabling his new horses?" Jocelyn asked of the group at large, though he was still looking at an enlarged and visibly uncomfortable Sir Isaac. "And where does he exercise them? I daresay he is busy preparing them for the race. I had better get over there and see if he is like to murder himself on Friday. He was never the world's most skilled judge of horseflesh."

"I'll come with you, Tresh," Viscount Kimble offered as Jocelyn lowered his foot from the stool and turned to grasp his cane. "Do you need any assistance?"

"Come within three feet of me at your peril!" Jocelyn

growled while he hoisted himself upright as gracefully as he was able and gritted his teeth at the needle-sharp pain that shot up his right leg. "And I don't need your escort, Kimble. I came in the carriage."

It was an admission that aroused a fresh burst of amusement and witticisms from his acquaintances, of course.

Jane would give him a royal scolding for this when he got home, Jocelyn thought, and was instantly annoyed at himself for even thinking of home.

He found his brother exactly where he expected to find him, exercising and training his new horses. At least Ferdinand had a good eye for his matched pair, Jocelyn discovered with some relief. They were not just a pretty pair, but superb goers too. The trouble was, of course, that Ferdinand had not had the handling of them for nearly long enough to race them, besides which point he was a restless and impulsive and reckless young man—a typical Dudley, in fact—with impatient hands and a tendency to make colorful use of all the most profane words in his vocabulary when he was frustrated.

"You have to let your hands talk firmly yet seductively," Jocelyn said with a sigh after one particularly hair-raising tirade occasioned by the horses' refusal to act as a team. "And you have to give your voice a rest, Ferdinand, or by the time you reach Brighton there will be none of it left with which to cheer your own victory."

"Damned cattle," his brother grumbled. "I have bought a couple of prima donnas."

"What you have bought," Jocelyn told him, "is an excellent pair that was cheap at the price. What you have to do, preferably before Friday, is teach them who is master."

He was not entirely without hope of winning his substantial bet at White's. Ferdinand was a notable whip though a somewhat erratic one, who appeared to believe that superiority consisted in taking unnecessary risks.

"Now, with *your* curricle, Tresham," Ferdinand said with studied nonchalance, "I would leave Berriwether five miles behind my dust. It is lighter and better sprung than my own."

"You will have to be content to leave him only two miles behind your dust, then," Jocelyn said dryly.

"I'll be giving Wesley Forbes a thrashing one of these days," Ferdinand said later when the brothers were relaxing in his bachelor rooms, Jocelyn with his right foot up on a low table. "He was making offensive remarks at Wattier's last night about people who stagger about on crutches to convince the world of their weakness but forget which leg they are supposed to have injured. Sometimes they lurch along with the right leg raised, he said, and sometimes with the left. He thinks he is the world's sharpest wit."

Jocelyn sipped on his glass of claret. "He could not have been referring to me, then, could he?" he remarked. "Don't be drawn, Ferdinand. You do not need a brawl this side of the race. And never on my behalf. The very idea!"

"I would have planted him a facer right there in the card room," Ferdinand said, "if Max Ritterbaum had not grabbed my arm and dragged me off to Brookes's. The thing is, Tresh, that not a one of them will have the bottom to say anything like it to your face. And you can be damned sure that none of them will be decent enough to slap a glove across your cheek. They are too craven."

"Leave them to me," Jocelyn said. "Concentrate on the race."

"Let me refill your glass," Ferdinand said. "Have you seen Angeline's latest monstrosity?"

"A bonnet?" Jocelyn asked. "The mustard one? Atrocious."

"Blue," his brother said, "with violet stripes. She wanted me to take her walking in the park with it perched on her head. I told her that either it or I would go strolling with her, but not both together. I would be the laughingstock, Tresham. Our sister was born with a ghastly affliction: no taste. Why Heyward encourages her by paying the bills is beyond me."

"Besotted with her," Jocelyn said. "As she is with him. No one would ever guess it to see them together, or *not* together, which is more often the case. They are as discreet about it as if they were clandestine lovers."

Ferdinand barked with laughter. "Lord," he said, "imagine anyone besotted with Angie!"

"Or with Heyward," his brother agreed, idly swinging his quizzing glass from its ribbon.

It was an enormous relief, he reflected some time later as he made his way home, to be getting his life back to normal.

IF JANE HAD THOUGHT for one moment that what had happened the night before had meant something to the Duke of Tresham, it did not take her long to learn the truth. Not that she *had* thought it, but sometimes one's emotions defied reason.

He did not return home until late in the afternoon. And even then he did not summon Jane, but closeted himself in the library with Mr. Quincy. It was almost dinnertime before he sent for her.

He was still in the library. He was seated on the chaise longue, his right leg elevated on the cushion. He was fully dressed minus his right boot. He was also scowling.

"Not one word," he said before she had even thought of opening her mouth. "Not a single word, Miss Ingleby. Of course it is sore and of course Barnard had the devil of a time pulling off my boot. But it is time it was exercised, and it is time I took myself off out of here during the daytime. Else I will descend to rape and debauchery."

She had not expected him to refer to last night after being absent all day. Last night seemed rather like a dream. Not perhaps their embrace, which was something so far beyond her experience or expectations that she could not possibly have imagined it, but the sight and sound of the Duke of Tresham playing the pianoforte and coaxing magic from its keys.

"I suppose," he said, turning his black eyes and his blacker scowl on her for the first time, "you thought it was love, Jane? Or affection? Or some fine emotion at least?"

"No, your grace," she said. "I am not as naïve as you seem to think me. I recognized it as physical desire on both our parts. Why should I believe that a self-acknowledged rake would have any fine feelings for his servant? And why would you fear that a woman like me would fall for your dangerous and legendary charm when I have been subjected to your ill temper and profane tongue for more than two weeks?"

"Why would I *fear*?" His eyes narrowed. "I might have guessed that you would have the last word on the subject, Jane. How foolish of me to imagine that I seriously discomposed you last night."

"Yes," she agreed. "I daresay your leg is somewhat swollen. You will need to bathe it in cold water. Keep it submerged for a while."

"And freeze my toes?"

"I imagine," she told him, "that that discomfort is better than watching them turn black over the coming weeks."

He pursed his lips and there seemed for a moment to be a smile lurking in his eyes. But he did not give in to it.

"If you are planning to go out again tomorrow," she said, "I beg leave to be given the morning free, your grace."

"Why?" His frown returned.

Her clasped hands turned cold and clammy at the very thought of her reason, but she could no longer give in to the paralysis of terror. She must sooner or later venture beyond the sheltering doors of Dudley House.

"It is time I looked for other employment," she said. "I have less than one week left here. Indeed, I am not really needed now. I never have been. You never needed a nurse."

He stared at her. "You would leave me, would you then, Jane?"

She had been firmly repressing the pain she felt at the thought of doing just that. The pain just did not have either a rational or worthy cause. Though, of course, she had seen a startlingly different side to him in the music room last night.

"My employment here will soon be at an end, your grace," she reminded him.

"Who says so?" He was staring at her broodingly. "What poppycock you speak when you have nothing else to which to go."

Hope stirred. She had half thought of asking him—or of asking the housekeeper, who hired the servants—if she could stay on as a housemaid or scullery maid. But she did not believe she would do so. She would not be able to bear living on at Dudley House in a more menial capacity than the one she had held so far. Not that she could allow pride to dictate her actions, of course.

"It was agreed," she said, "that I remain to nurse you while your injury forced you to remain inactive. For three weeks."

"There is still almost a week left, then," he said. "I will not hear of your searching for something else, Jane, until your time here has been served. I do not pay you to spend your mornings flitting all over London looking for an employer who will pay you more than I do. How much *do* I pay you?"

"More than I earn," she said. "Money is not the issue, your grace."

But he was being stubborn. "I will hear no more about it for at least another week, then," he said. "But I have a job for you on Thursday evening, Jane. Tomorrow. And I will pay you well for it too. I will pay you what you deserve."

She looked warily at him.

"Don't stand by the damned door as if poised for flight," he said irritably. "If I wished to pounce on you, I would do so no matter what the distance. Come closer. Sit down here."

He pointed to the chair where she usually sat.

There was no point in arguing that at least. She did as she was told even though doing so brought her uncomfortably within the aura of his masculinity. She could smell his cologne and remembered how it had been very much a part of last night's sensual experience.

"I am hosting a grand entertainment here tomorrow evening," he said. "Quincy is just now writing out the invitations and having them delivered. There will be only a day's notice for the invited guests, of course, but they will almost all come. Invitations to Dudley House are rare enough to be coveted, you see, despite my reputation. Perhaps because of it."

She would remain for every moment of the evening behind the closed door of her room, Jane thought, clasping her hands very tightly in her lap.

"Tell me," the duke said, "do you possess any garment more becoming than that atrocity you are wearing and the other one you alternate with it, Miss Ingleby?"

No. Oh, no. Definitely not. Absolutely, without question not.

"I will not need it," she said firmly. "I am not going to be one of your guests. It would be unfitting."

His eyebrows arched arrogantly upward.

"For once, Miss Ingleby," he said, "we are in perfect accord. But you have not answered my question. Do take that mulish look off your face. It makes you look like a petulant child."

"I have one muslin frock," she admitted. "But I will not wear it, your grace. It is unsuited to my employment."

"You will wear it tomorrow evening," he informed her. "And you will do something prettier with your hair. I will find out from Barnard which of the maids is most adept at dressing hair. If there is none, I will hire one for the occasion."

Jane was feeling somewhat sick to her stomach.

"But you have said," she reminded him, "that I cannot be one of your guests. I will not need a muslin dress and an elaborate coiffure to sit in my room."

"Do not be dense, Jane," he said. "There will be dinner and cards and conversation and music—provided by a number of the ladies I am inviting. All ladies are accomplished, you know. It is a common fallacy among mothers, it seems, that the ability to tinkle away at a pianoforte keyboard while looking suitably decorative is the surest way to a man's heart and fortune."

"I wonder," she said, "what has made you so cynical."

"Do you?" He smiled in that wolfish way of his. "It comes of growing up with an earl's title and the rank of a marquess, Jane. And of becoming a duke at the tender age of seventeen. Time and again I have proved myself to be the blackest-hearted villain in all England. But every mama with a marriageable daughter still fawns over me as if I were the Angel Gabriel, and every papa courts my acquaintance. Not to mention the simpering young maidens themselves."

"One of these days," she said tartly, "you are going to fall in love with one of those maidens only to discover that she will laugh your courtship to scorn. You have little respect for female intelligence, your grace. You believe yourself to be the greatest matrimonial prize in Christendom and therefore despise all those whom you believe to be angling after you. There are *some* sensible ladies in this world, I would have you know."

He pursed his lips again, a gleam of definite amusement in his eyes now. "For my pride's sake, Jane," he said, "might we extend that to include the Islamic world as well as just Christendom?"

He was quickly learning, Jane thought, how to burst her bubble.

"But we digress." He looked at her more soberly, and Jane felt fingers of apprehension creep up her spine. "You, Miss Ingleby, are going to be the main attraction of the evening. You are going to sing for my guests."

"No!" She stood up abruptly.

"Ah yes," he said softly. "I will even accompany you. I believe I must have admitted to the *ton* from time to time that I dabble. I do not fear that my manhood will be in jeopardy if I merely accompany a vocalist. Do you believe I should?"

"No," she said. "No to the whole thing, I mean. I will not do it. I am not a public performer and have no wish to be. You cannot make me and do not think you can. I will not be bullied."

"I will pay you five hundred pounds, Jane," he said softly.

She drew breath to continue and snapped her mouth shut again. She frowned.

"Five hundred pounds?" she said incredulously. "How ridiculously absurd."

"Not to me," he said. "I want you to sing in public, Jane. I want the *beau monde* to discover what I discovered last night. You have a rare talent."

"Do not think to flatter me into agreeing," she said. But her mind had already whirled into motion. Five hundred pounds. She would not need to work for a long time. She could disappear into a more secure hiding place than this house. She could even move away to somewhere the earl and the Bow Street Runners would not think of looking.

"Five hundred pounds would free you from the necessity of searching out instant employment, would it not?" he said, obviously reading her thoughts, or at least some of them.

But first she would have to face a houseful of guests. Was there anyone in London, she wondered, apart from the Earl of Durbury, who knew her real identity, who had ever set eyes on her as Lady Sara Illingsworth? She did not believe so. But what if there *were* someone?

"I will even say please, Jane," the Duke of Tresham said, his voice falsely humble.

She looked reproachfully at him. Was there even the remotest chance that the earl would be among the guests? There was one way of finding out, of course. She could ask Mr. Quincy if she could look at the guest list.

"I will think about it," she told him while her stomach performed an uncomfortable flip-flop.

"I suppose," he said, "that is the best I can expect from you for now, is it, Jane? You cannot capitulate too soon or it will seem that you have allowed yourself to be overpowered. Very well. But your answer must be yes. My mind is set upon it. We will do some rehearsing tomorrow afternoon."

"You are rubbing your leg again," she said. "I suppose you will not admit that you were foolish to go out today and more foolish to stay out so long. Let me call someone to help you up to your room, and let me have some cold water sent up to you."

"I have been attempting to teach my brother to distinguish the front end of a horse from the rear," he said. "I have wagered a hefty amount on him at White's, Miss Ingleby, and am quite determined that he will win the race."

"How terribly foolish men are," she said. "Their minds are totally bent on trivialities, their energies spent on matters of insignificance. If Lord Ferdinand is hurt on Friday, you will perhaps realize that he is of far more importance to you than the mere winning of a bet."

"If you have finished your scolding," he told her, "you may do what you yourself suggested, Miss Ingleby, and summon the heftiest footman you can find."

She left the room without another word.

What if her description was circulating London? she thought suddenly. What if she stepped into the music room on Thursday evening and the assembled guests arose en masse to point accusing fingers at her?

She could not help the foolish feeling that in some way it would be a relief.

10

JOCELYN DID NOT OFTEN ENTERTAIN, BUT WHEN he did, he did it in lavish style. His chef grumbled belowstairs at having been given no notice at all of the monumental task of preparing a grand dinner to begin the evening and a tasty supper to sustain it at midnight. But he set about the task with a flurry of creative energy instead of resigning on the spot as he threatened to do whenever he stopped work long enough to draw breath.

The housekeeper did not complain, but marshaled her troops with grim determination to banish every speck of dust from the rooms that would be used for the entertainment and to have every surface polished and gleaming. She arranged the lavish mounds of flowers that Michael Quincy had ordered.

As Jocelyn had predicted, almost everyone accepted his invitation even though doing so doubtless involved the breaking of other commitments at the last moment. The chance to attend a dinner and soiree at Dudley House did not come often.

Jocelyn instructed his housekeeper to select or to hire a maid accomplished at dressing a lady's hair. He did toy with the idea of also taking Jane Ingleby to a fashionable modiste and commanding that an evening gown be made up with all haste—he had considerable influence with two or three of London's most exclusive dressmakers—but he did not do so. She would without doubt make a fuss and end up refusing to sing. Besides, he must not make her look too much the lady, he decided, or his guests would be wondering about the propriety of her having spent almost three weeks beneath his roof as his nurse.

He spent some time during the afternoon in the music room with her, rehearsing two contrasting songs to show off her voice as well as an encore, the possibility of which she protested was nonsense, but which he insisted was not.

He found, as he dressed for the evening, that he was feeling nervous. A fact that thoroughly alarmed him and made him despise himself heartily.

WHEN SHE HAD BEEN younger, when her parents had both been alive and healthy, there had been frequent picnics, dinners, and dances at Candleford Abbey. They had loved entertaining. But Jane did not believe they had ever invited anywhere near fifty guests at one time. And even those parties she remembered had been a long time ago. She had been just a girl.

She sat in her room for several hours before getting ready to go downstairs, listening to the distant sounds of voices and laughter, imagining what was happening, what was yet to happen before she was summoned to sing. But it was impossible to predict the exact time of the summons. *Ton* parties, Jane was aware, were quite unlike their counterparts in the country, which almost never continued past eleven o'clock or midnight at the very latest. Here in town no one seemed to consider it strange to be up all night—and then, of course, to sleep all the following day.

She might not be called down before midnight. She would collapse in a heap of the jitters if she had to wait that long.

But finally she could see from the clock on the mantel that Adele, the French maid who had been hired for the evening just to dress her hair, would be knocking on her door in ten minutes' time. It was time to get dressed.

It was far too late to regret agreeing to this madness. There was no one among the guests—she had perused the guest list with great care—who might know her identity. But the Earl of Durbury was in town. What if everyone at tonight's gathering had been furnished with her description? Her stomach lurched. But it was too late.

She determinedly pulled off her maid's frock and drew over her head the carefully ironed sprigged muslin dress she had set out on her bed earlier. It was a dress perfectly suited to afternoon tea in the country. It was not at all appropriate for an evening party even there, of course, but that did not matter. She was not a guest at tonight's entertainment, after all.

She shivered with mingled cold, excitement, and fear.

She had never meant to hide when she fled to London. What she should have done after making the ghastly discovery that Lady Webb was not at home, Jane thought belatedly, was to stay at the hotel where she had taken a room and apply to the earl's man of business in town for funds. She should have boldly proclaimed to all the world that she had been abused and assaulted by a drunken rogue during the earl and countess's absence from Candleford and had quite justifiably defended herself by hitting him with a book and removing herself far from proximity to him.

But she had not done it, and it was too late now.

She was in hiding. And about to show herself to fifty members of the crème de la crème of British society.

What *utter* madness.

A female voice laughed shrilly in the distance.

Someone tapped on Jane's door, making her jump foolishly. Adele had arrived to dress her hair.

AT ELEVEN O'CLOCK LADY Heyward, Jocelyn's hostess for the evening, announced the end of the card games that were in progress, while Jocelyn himself directed a few footmen in the moving of the drawing room pianoforte to the center of the room and the arrangement of chairs about the room's perimeter. The musical part of the evening was about to begin.

Several of the younger ladies volunteered or were persuaded to play the pianoforte or to sing. One gentleman—Lord Riding—was brave enough to sing a duet with his betrothed. All the recitals were competent. The guests listened more or less attentively and applauded politely. This was, after all, a familiar form of evening entertainment to them all. Only a few of the acknowledged patrons of the arts ever hired professional artists, but on those occasions the evening was heralded as a private concert.

Finally Jocelyn got to his feet with the aid of his cane.

"Do feel free to stand up and move about for a few minutes," he said when he had everyone's attention. "I have engaged a special guest for your entertainment before supper. I shall go and bring her down."

His sister looked at him in surprise. "Whoever can she be, Tresham?" she asked. "Is she waiting in the kitchen? Where on earth did you find her when you have been almost shut up here for the past three weeks?"

But he merely inclined his head and left the room. Fool that he was, he had scarce been able to think of anything else all evening but this moment. He just hoped she had not changed her mind. Five hundred pounds was a considerable inducement, of course, but he was of the opinion that if Jane Ingleby had decided she did not want to sing, even five thousand pounds would not convince her.

He had been pacing the hall, leaning heavily on his cane, for two minutes after sending Hawkins up for her before she appeared on the staircase. She stopped on the third stair up and turned into a decent imitation of a statue—a pale, grim statue with its lips set in a thin, hard line, who nevertheless looked like an angel. The light, simply styled muslin dress did wonders for her form, accentuating her tall, slender grace. Her hair—well, he simply could not remove his eyes from it for a long moment. It was not elaborately styled. It was not a mass of curls and ringlets, as he had half expected. It was dressed up, but all the usual severity was gone. It looked soft and healthy and shiny and elegant. And pure gold.

"Well, well," he said, "the butterfly has fluttered free of its cocoon."

"It would be much better if we did not do this," she said.

But he moved to the bottom of the staircase and reached up a hand for hers, holding her eyes with his own.

"You will not turn craven on me now, Jane," he said. "My guests await my special guest."

"They will be disappointed," she warned him.

It was entirely unlike her to cower. Not that she was doing that exactly. She was standing straight with her chin lifted proudly. She also looked as if she might have sent roots down into the third stair.

"Come," he said, using his eyes shamelessly to compel her.

She came down to the second stair, and when he turned his hand palm down, she set her own hand on his and allowed him to lead her toward the drawing room. She had the bearing of a duchess, he thought with what might have been amusement under different circumstances. And in the same moment he felt as if scales had fallen from his eyes. An orphan? Raised in an orphanage? Turned out on the world to make her own way in life now that she had grown up? He did not think so. He was a fool ever to have been taken in by that story.

Which made Jane Ingleby a liar.

"'Barbara Allen' first," he said. "Something that is familiar to my fingers while they limber up."

"Yes. Very well," she agreed. "Are *all* your guests still here?"

"Hoping that forty-eight or forty-nine of them have retired to their homes for their beauty sleep, are you?" he asked her. "Not one has left, Jane."

He felt her draw deep, steadying breaths as a liveried footman leaped forward to open the drawing room doors. She lifted her chin a little higher.

She looked like a fresh garden flower amid hothouse plants, he thought as he led her inside and between two lines of chairs, on which his guests were seating themselves again and from which they looked with curiosity at his guest.

"Oh, I say." It was Conan Brougham's voice. "It is Miss Ingleby."

There was a buzz as those who knew who Miss Ingleby was explained to those who did not. They all, of course, knew about the milliner's assistant who had distracted the Duke of Tresham's attention during his duel with Lord Oliver and had then become his nurse.

Jocelyn led her into the open space occupied by the pianoforte at the center of the room. He released her hand.

"Ladies, gentlemen," he said, "I have persuaded Miss Ingleby to share with you what is surely the most glorious singing voice it has ever been my privilege to hear. Unfortunately she does not have an accompanist who can do her justice, only me. I dabble along, you see, with five thumbs on each hand. But I daresay no one will notice once she begins to sing."

He arranged the tails of his coat behind him as he seated himself on the bench, set his cane on the floor beside him, and curved his fingers over the keys. Jane was standing exactly where he had left her, but in truth he was not paying her much mind. He was terrified. He who had faced the wrong end of a pistol in four separate duels without flinching shied away from playing the pianoforte for an audience who would not even be listening to him, but to Jane. He felt exposed, almost naked.

He concentrated his mind on the task at hand and began playing the opening bars of "Barbara Allen."

Her voice was breathless and slightly shaking for the first two lines of the first verse. But then she settled down, as did he. Indeed, he soon forgot his own task and played more from instinct than deliberate intent. She sang the song better, more feelingly, than he had yet heard it, if that were possible. She was the sort of singer, he realized, who responded instinctively to an audience. And his guests were a very attentive audience indeed. He was sure no one moved in any way at all until the last syllable of the ballad had faded away. And even then there was a pause, a moment of absolute silence.

And then applause. Not the muted applause of a gathering of the *beau monde* being polite to one of its own, but the enthusiastic appreciation of an audience who had for a number of minutes been transported into another dimension by a truly talented artist.

Jane looked surprised and somewhat embarrassed. But quite composed. She inclined her head and waited for the applause to die away and be replaced by an expectant hush.

She sang Handel's "Art Thou Troubled?" It was surely one of the loveliest pieces of music ever composed for a contralto voice. Jocelyn had always thought so. But this evening it seemed that it must have been written especially for her. He forgot about the difficulty he had had in improvising an authentic-sounding accompaniment for the words. He simply played and listened to her rich, disciplined, but emotionally charged voice and found his throat aching, as if with tears.

"'Art thou troubled?'" she sang. "'Music will calm thee. Art thou weary? Rest shall be thine; rest shall be thine.'"

He must have been troubled and weary for a long, long time, Jocelyn found himself thinking. He had always known the seductive power of music to soothe.

But it had always been a forbidden balm, a denied rest. Something that was soft, effeminate, not for him, a Dudley, a Duke of Tresham.

"'Music.'" She drew breath, and her rich voice soared. "'Music calleth, with voice divine.'"

Ah, yes, with voice divine. But a Dudley only ever spoke with a firm, manly, very human voice and rarely ever listened at all. Not at least to anything that was outside the realm of his active daily life, in which he had established dominance and power. Certainly not to music, or to the whole realm of the spirit that music could tap into, taking its listener beyond the mere self and the finite world of the senses to something that could only be felt, not expressed in words.

The pain in his throat had not eased by the time the song came to its conclusion. He closed his eyes briefly while applause broke the silence again. When he opened them, it was to see that his guests were rising one by one to their feet, still clapping, while Jane looked deeply embarrassed.

He got up from the bench, ignoring his cane, took her right hand in his, and raised it aloft between them. She smiled at last and curtsied.

She sang the light and pretty but intricate "Robin Adair" for an encore. He would doubtless inform her tomorrow that he had told her so, Jocelyn thought, but he knew that tonight he would be unable to tease her.

She would have fled from the room after that. She took a couple of hurried steps toward the opening between the lines of chairs that led to the doors. But his guests had broken ranks and had other ideas. The entertainment was over. It was suppertime. And Ferdinand had stepped into her path.

"I say, Miss Ingleby," he said with unaffected enthusiasm. "Jolly good show. You sing quite splendidly. Do come to the supper room for refreshments."

He was bowing and smiling and offering his arm and using all the considerable charm of which he was capable when he turned his mind from horses and hunting and boxing mills and the latest bizarre bets at the clubs.

Jocelyn felt unaccountably murderous.

Jane tried to escape. She offered several excuses, but within seconds Ferdinand was not the only one she had to convince. She was surrounded by guests of both genders eager to speak with her. But though her position at Dudley House as his nurse and the circumstances of her hiring were doubtless intriguing to people who throve on gossip and scandal, Jocelyn did not believe it was those facts alone that drew so much attention her way. It was her voice.

How could he have listened to it two nights ago, he wondered now, without realizing that it was not just an extraordinarily lovely voice? It was also a well-trained voice. And good voice training was surely not something anyone came by at an orphanage, even a superior one.

She was borne off toward the dining room on Ferdinand's arm, with Heyward walking at her other side, engaging her in an earnest discussion of Handel's *Messiah*. Jocelyn turned his attention to his other guests.

HER VOICE TEACHER, WHOM her father had brought to Cornwall at considerable expense, had given it as his opinion that she could sing professionally if she chose, that she could hold her own in Milan, in Vienna, at

Covent Garden—anywhere she liked. That she could be an international star.

Her father had pointed out gently but firmly that a career, even such an illustrious one, was out of the question for the daughter of an earl. Jane had not minded. She had never felt the need to win public acclaim or fame. She sang because she loved to sing and because she liked to entertain friends and relatives.

But this evening's success at Dudley House was seductive, she had to admit. The house itself had been transformed into a splendid wonderland with every candle in every chandelier and candleholder lit and vases of lavish and expertly arranged flowers everywhere. Everyone was flatteringly kind. Almost all the guests approached her in the dining room, some just to smile and tell her how much they had enjoyed her performance, many to talk with her at greater length.

She had never been to London before. She had never moved in exalted circles. But there was a wonderful feeling of *rightness* about being with this company. These were her people. This was the world to which she belonged. If her mother had lived longer, if her father had retained his health, she would as a matter of course have come to London for a Season. She would have been brought to the great marriage mart for the serious business of selecting a suitable husband. She felt at home with the Duke of Tresham's guests.

She had to make a deliberate effort to remind herself that she was not really one of them. Not any longer. There was a huge obstacle between herself and them, put there when Sidney, drunk and offensive, had decided to try to seduce her as an inducement to persuade her to marry him. He had been going to ravish her—

with the full connivance of his equally drunken friends. But she had never been one to endure bullying meekly. She had swung a book at his head.

And so had begun the string of events that had made a fugitive of her. But some fugitive! Here she was in the very midst of a select gathering of the *ton*, behaving as if she had not a care in the world.

"You must excuse me," she murmured, smiling and getting to her feet.

"Excuse you?" Lady Heyward regarded her with gracious surprise. "Absolutely not, Miss Ingleby. Can you not see that you have become the guest of honor? Heyward will persuade you to stay, will you not, my love?"

But Lord Heyward was deep in earnest conversation with a dowager in purple topped by a matching plumed turban.

"Allow me," Viscount Kimble said, taking Jane by the elbow and gesturing to the chair she had just vacated. "You are the mystery of the hour, Miss Ingleby. One moment hurrying to work across Hyde Park, the next nursing Tresh like a gray shadow, and now singing like a trained nightingale. Permit me to interrogate you." He smiled with practiced charm, softening the effect of his words.

Lady Heyward, still on her feet, was clapping her hands to draw all attention her way.

"I absolutely refuse to allow everyone to drift away after supper," she said, "when it is scarce past midnight. I refuse to allow Tresham to be the laughingstock tomorrow. We are going to have dancing in the drawing room. Mrs. Marsh will play for us, will you not, ma'am? Shall I give the order for the carpet to be rolled back, Tresham, or will you?"

"Dear me," his grace said, his fingers curling about the handle of his quizzing glass. "How extraordinarily kind of you to be so solicitous of my reputation, Angeline. I shall give the order." He left the room.

"You really must excuse me," Jane said firmly a few minutes later, after giving vague answers to the questions Lord Kimble had asked her. "Good night, my lord."

"I shall have a new reason for calling upon Tresham during the next few days," he told her, bowing over her hand, which he raised to his lips. His eyes looked appreciatively into her own.

Another dangerous gentleman, Jane thought as she hurried from the room, bidding several people good night as she went. And one who must surely know how devastatingly attractive pale blue and silver evening clothes looked with his blond hair.

But slipping off to the privacy of her room was not to be easy at all tonight, she saw as she approached the drawing room. The Duke of Tresham was coming out, leaning on his cane. Several of his guests were already back there, she could see through the open door. More were coming from the supper room.

"Going to bed, Jane?" he asked her. "When it is not even an hour past midnight?"

"Yes, your grace," she said. "Good night."

"Poppycock!" he told her. "You heard Angeline. In her estimation you have become the guest of honor. And despite her appalling taste in dress—shocking pink, you will have observed, does not become her, especially when accompanied by frills and flounces and those unfortunate blue plumes she has in her hair—despite all that, Jane, there is no higher stickler than my sister. You will come into the drawing room."

"No," she said.

He raised his eyebrows. "Insubordination? You will dance, Jane. With me."

She laughed. "And your cane too?"

"Now, that, Jane," he said, lifting it and pointing it at her, "is a low blow. I shall dance without my cane. A waltz, in fact. You will waltz with me."

He had moved to stand between her and the route to the staircase. She could tell from a glance at his face that he was in one of those moods that would not brook denial. Not that she would not put up a good fight on that account. He could not force her to dance, after all.

"You never waltz," she told him.

"Now who told you that?" he asked her.

"You did," she reminded him. "In my hearing. When someone mentioned Almack's one day."

"I will make an exception tonight," he said. "Do you waltz, Jane? Do you know the steps?"

It was her way out. All she needed to do was say no. And indeed she had never performed the steps at any public assembly, only with Charles and a few of their friends at private gatherings. But she was suddenly assailed by a deep longing to waltz here at Dudley House among her peers before she disappeared somewhere she would never be found. To waltz with the Duke of Tresham. Suddenly the temptation was overwhelming.

"She hesitates," the duke murmured. He leaned closer. "You must not deny it now, Jane. Your silence has betrayed you." He offered his arm. "Come."

She hesitated only a moment longer before laying her arm along his and turning into the drawing room.

To dance.

To waltz with the Duke of Tresham.

* * *

ONE THING WAS VERY clear to Jocelyn as he sat conversing with a few of his more elderly guests while the younger ones danced an energetic country dance. Jane Ingleby was going to have to go soon. Away from Dudley House. Away from him.

She had indeed become the focus of attention. She was not dancing, but she was surrounded by a veritable court of admirers, among them Kimble and Ferdinand, both of whom should have been dancing. She looked somewhat incongruous in her sprigged muslin dress and simple coiffure when every other lady present was decked out in silks and satins and jewels with elaborate plumes and turbans. But she made every one of them look fussy and overdressed.

She was simplicity itself. Like a single rose. No, a rose was too elaborate. Like a lily. Or a daisy.

There would indeed be questions if he kept her here any longer. Surely it must be apparent to all his guests, as it should have been to him for the past three weeks, that she was a lady from the top of her head down to her toenails. The impoverished orphan of an impoverished gentleman, at a guess. But a lady nonetheless. An extraordinarily lovely one.

He was going to have to find her employment elsewhere—a thoroughly depressing thought, which he would put out of his head for tonight. The country dance had ended. He got to his feet, leaving his cane propped against the chair. Putting his full weight on his right leg did not cause undue pain, he was relieved to find. He made his way toward Mrs. Marsh at the pianoforte.

"Take your partners, gentlemen," he announced after consulting her, "for a waltz." He moved in the direction of Jane and had the misfortune to meet the eyes of both Kimble and Brougham as he did so. Both were looking at him rather as if he had sprouted another head. He knew why. It was common knowledge that the Duke of Tresham never waltzed. He extended his right hand. "Miss Ingleby?"

"You will suffer for this," she warned him as they took their places on the polished floor, from which the carpet had been rolled back. "You will probably be forced to spend the next two weeks with your leg up on a cushion."

"Then you may have the satisfaction of saying you told me so," he said, setting his right hand behind her waist and taking her right hand in his left.

He never waltzed, for the simple reason that it was far too intimate a dance for a man who had become adept at avoiding matrimonial traps. But he had always thought that if the occasion and the woman were ever right, he would find the waltz truly enchanting.

The time was right and so was the woman.

Her spine arched pleasingly beneath his hand. The curve of her other arm and her hand resting on his shoulder brought her tantalizingly close to him though their bodies did not once touch as they twirled about the room, their eyes on each other, the other dancers and the spectators forgotten, as if they did not exist. He could feel her body heat and smell the faint aroma of roses that seemed to cling about her.

She danced divinely, as if her feet did not quite touch the floor, as if she were a part of himself, as if they were both a part of the music or it a part of them. He found himself smiling at her. Although her face remained in repose, it seemed to him that an answering warmth beamed through her blue eyes.

It was only as the music drew to an end that he realized two things—that he had inadvertently let go of his customary haughty aloofness, and that his leg was aching like a thousand devils.

"I am going to bed," she said breathlessly.

"Ah, Jane," he said softly, "I cannot come with you. I have a houseful of guests."

She withdrew herself from his arms as everyone changed partners or returned to the sidelines.

"But I will escort you to your room," he told her. "No, you may not look significantly down at my leg. I am not a cripple, Jane, and will not behave like one. Take my arm."

He did not care who saw them leave together. He would not be gone long. And she would not be here at Dudley House much longer to fuel any gossip. That was clearer than ever to him.

The hall and staircase seemed very quiet in contrast to the buzz of conversation they had left behind in the drawing room and could still hear. Jocelyn did not attempt conversation as they ascended slowly—he had not brought his cane with him. He did not speak at all until they were walking along the dimly lit corridor to Jane's room.

"You were as much of a success as I knew you would be," he said then. "More so, indeed."

"Thank you," she said.

He paused outside her room, standing between her and the door.

"Your parents," he said, "must have been very proud of you."

"Y—" She caught herself in time. She looked keenly at him, as if to see whether his words had been a mere slip of memory. "The people who knew me were," she said carefully. "But a talent is not something to be unduly proud of, your grace. My voice is something for which I can take no credit. It was given me, just as was your ability to play the pianoforte as you do."

"Jane," he said softly before dipping his head and setting his lips to hers.

He did not touch her anywhere else. She did not touch him. But their lips clung softly, warmly, yearningly for many moments before one of them drew back—he was not sure who.

Her eyes were dreamy with latent passion, her cheeks flushed with desire. Her lips were parted and moist with invitation. And his own heartbeat was drumming in his ears and threatening to deafen him to reality. Ah, Jane, if only…

He searched her eyes with his own before turning and opening her door. "It is as well that I have guests below, Jane. This will just not do, will it? Not for much longer. Good night."

JANE FLED INTO HER room without a backward glance. She heard the door close behind her before spreading her hands over her hot cheeks.

She could still feel his hand at her waist as they waltzed. She could still feel his heat, still smell his cologne, still feel the sense of perfect rhythm with which they had moved to the music. She could still feel the waltz as an intimate, sensual thing, not the sheer fun it had been when danced with Charles.

Yes, it was as well there were guests downstairs.

She could still feel his kiss, not fierce, not lascivious. Much worse. A soft, longing kiss. No, it would not do. Not for much longer. Not for *any* longer, in fact. A great yawning emptiness opened up somewhere deep inside her.

11

THE BRIGHTON RACE WAS TO BEGIN AT HYDE Park Corner at half-past eight the following morning. Fortunately it was shaping up to be a clear, windless day, Jocelyn discovered when he stepped outside, leaning on his cane.

He climbed up unaided to the high seat of his curricle, and waved away his groom, who would have jumped up behind. He was only going to the park and back, after all. He was going to give Ferdinand some last words of encouragement—not advice. Dudleys did not take well to advice, especially from one another.

He was very early, but he wanted to spend a few minutes with his brother before the crowds arrived to cheer the racers on their way to Brighton. There were a number of gentlemen who would ride their horses behind the curricles, of course, so that they could witness the end of the race and celebrate with the winner in Brighton. Ordinarily Jocelyn would have been one of them—no, ordinarily he would have been one of the *racers*—but not this time. His leg was considerably better than perhaps it should feel when he had waltzed on it last evening, but it would be foolish to subject it to a long, bruising ride.

Ferdinand was flushed and restless and eager as he checked his new team and chatted with Lord Heyward, who had arrived even before Jocelyn.

"I am to be sure to tell you from Angeline," Heyward was saying with an ironic lift of one eyebrow, "that you are to win at all costs, Ferdinand, that you are to take no risks that will break your neck, that the honor of the Dudley name is in your hands, that you are not to worry about anything but your own safety—and a great deal more in the same contradictory vein, with which I will not assail your ears."

Ferdinand grinned at him and turned to bid Jocelyn a good morning.

"They are as eager as I to be on the way," he said, nodding in the direction of his horses.

Jocelyn raised his quizzing glass to his eye and looked over the curricle, which his brother had bought impulsively a few months before entirely on the grounds that it looked both smart and sporty. He had complained about it ever since, and indeed there was something clumsy about it that one detected only in the handling of it. Jocelyn had driven it once himself and had never felt any burning desire to repeat the experience.

The odds were against Ferdinand in this race, though Jocelyn did not despair of his wager. Youth and eagerness were on his brother's side as well as a certain family determination never to come in second at any manly sport. And those chestnuts were certainly a pair that Jocelyn coveted himself. The curricle was the weakness.

Lord Berriwether, Ferdinand's opponent, was driving up amid a veritable cavalcade of horsemen come to cheer him on. All of them would have wagered on him, of course. A few of them called good-naturedly to Ferdinand.

"A prime pair, Dudley," Mr. Wagdean cried cheerfully. "A pity they have three lame legs apiece."

"Even more of a pity when they win," Ferdinand retorted, grinning, "and show up Berriwether's pair, which has no such excuse."

Berriwether was showing his unconcern with the opposition by flicking at an invisible speck of dust on his gleaming top boots with his whip. The man looked more suitably dressed for a stroll on Bond Street than a race to Brighton. But he would be all business, of course, once the race was under way.

"Ferdinand," Jocelyn said impulsively, "we had better switch curricles."

His brother looked at him with undisguised hope. "You mean it, Tresham?"

"I have a better regard for my wager than to send you off to Brighton in that bandbox," Jocelyn replied, nodding at the red and yellow curricle.

Ferdinand was not about to argue the point further. In a matter of minutes—and with only five minutes to spare before the scheduled start of the race—his groom had unhitched his curricle from the chestnuts and switched it with the duke's.

"Just remember," Jocelyn said, unable after all to resist the urge to give advice, "it is somewhat lighter than yours, Ferdinand, and more instantly responsive to your maneuvering. *Slow down* on the bends."

Ferdinand climbed up to the high seat and took the ribbons from his groom's hand. He was serious now, concentrating on the task ahead.

"And bring it back in one piece," Jocelyn added before stepping back with the rest of the spectators, "or I'll skin you alive."

One minute later the Marquess of Yarborough, Berriwether's brother-in-law, raised the starting pistol skyward, there was an expectant hush, the pistol cracked, and the race began amid a roar of cheers and a cloud of dust and a thundering of hooves.

It looked, Jocelyn thought, gazing rather wistfully after the curricles and the throng of riders, rather like a cavalry charge. He turned toward Ferdinand's curricle and exchanged a few pleasantries with some other spectators.

He wished then that he had brought his groom after all. He would have to go home in order to have his horses stabled and the curricle put away in the carriage house before proceeding to White's. But he need not go inside the house. He had no reason to do so and every reason *not* to.

He had kissed her again last evening. And had admitted that they could not go on as they were. The matter had to be dealt with. She had to go.

The trouble was, he did not want her to go.

He should have driven around to the mews, he remembered as he drove into Grosvenor Square and approached the front doors of Dudley House. He was not concentrating. He would drive around the square and back out of it.

But just as he gave his horses the signal to proceed, a series of incidents, which happened so fast that even afterward he was not sure of the sequence, changed all his plans. There was a loud snapping sound, a sudden lurching of the curricle to the left, a snorting and rearing of the horses, a shout in a male voice, a scream in a female's. And a painful collision of his body with something hard enough to knock the breath out of him.

He was lying facedown on the roadway outside his own doors when rational thought returned. With the sound of frightened horses being soothed behind him, with the feeling that every bone in his body must have been jarred into a new position, and with someone stroking his hair—what the devil had happened to his hat?—and assuring him in a marvelous exercise of utter female stupidity that he would be all right, that everything would be all right.

"Bloody hell!" he exclaimed ferociously, turning his head to one side and viewing from ground level the ruin of his brother's curricle, which was listing sharply to one side on its snapped axle.

Every house on the square, it seemed, was disgorging hordes of interested and concerned spectators—had they all been lined up at the windows to witness his humiliation?

"Just catch your breath," Jane Ingleby said, her hand still in his hair. "A couple of the servants will carry you inside in a moment. Don't try to move."

That was all he would need to cap the mortification of one of the most wretched months of his life.

"If you cannot talk sense," he said, shaking his head irritably to rid himself of her hand, "I suggest that you not talk at all."

He planted his hands on the ground—there was a ragged hole in the palm of one of his expensive leather gloves, he noticed, with raw flesh within—and hoisted himself upward, ignoring the silent screaming of muscles that had just been severely abused.

"Oh, how foolish you are!" Jane Ingleby scolded, and to his shame he was forced to set a heavy hand on her shoulder—again.

But he was gazing narrow-eyed at Ferdinand's curricle.

"It would have snapped when he was out in the country driving at breakneck speed," he said.

She frowned up at him.

"It is Ferdinand's curricle," he explained. "The axle has broken. He would have been killed. *Marsh!*" he bellowed at his head groom, who was still soothing the horses while someone from another house was unhitching them from the vehicle. "Examine that curricle with a fine-tooth comb as soon as you have a chance. I want a report within the half hour."

"Yes, your grace," his groom called.

"Help me inside," Jocelyn commanded Jane. "And stop your fussing. I'll have bruises and scrapes for you to tend to your heart's content once we have reached the library, I do not doubt. I have not broken any bones, and I did not land on my right leg. At least, I do not think I did. Someone did this. Deliberately."

"To kill Lord Ferdinand?" she asked as they went inside. "So that he would lose the race? How absurd. No one could want to win a bet or a race that badly. It was an accident. They do happen, you know."

"I have enemies," he said curtly. "And Ferdinand is my brother."

He hoped fervently that the curricle was all that had been tampered with. This had the signature of the Forbes brothers all over it. Underhanded, sneaky bastards.

JANE HAD RISEN WITH a firm determination to take her leave of Dudley House that very day. Her usefulness here, what little there had been, was at an end. The three weeks were over. And what she had agreed to and done last evening for the entertainment of the duke's guests had been the ultimate madness. Fifty members of the *beau monde* had seen her—really *seen* her—when she was dressed, if not quite in the splendor of evening garments that would have set her on a level with them, at least in a manner that set her noticeably above the level of a maid.

It was surely only a matter of time before the search for her led to the circulation among the *ton* of a description of her appearance. Indeed she was puzzled that it had not already happened. But when it did, a number of last evening's guests were going to remember Jane Ingleby.

She had to leave Dudley House. She had to disappear. She would take the five hundred pounds—another madness, but she had every intention of holding the Duke of Tresham to his end of their bargain—and go into hiding. Not in London. She would go somewhere else. She would walk clear of town before trying to board any public conveyance.

Jane was determined to leave. Even apart from every other reason, there was last night's lingering kiss, which had come alarmingly close to exploding into uncontrolled passion. It was no longer possible for her to remain at Dudley House. And she would not allow herself to indulge in any personal longing. For the moment at least she could not allow herself to have any personal feelings.

She fetched warm water and ointments and bandages as soon as she had settled him in the library. She was sitting on a stool before the fireside chair, rubbing ointment into his badly scraped palms, when his groom was admitted.

"Well?" his grace demanded. "What did you find, Marsh?"

"The axle had definitely been tampered with, your grace," his groom told him. "It was not natural wear and tear that made it go like that."

"I knew it," the duke said grimly. "Send someone reliable over to my brother's stable, Marsh. No, better yet, go yourself. I want to know exactly who has had access to that curricle during the past few days. Especially yesterday and last night. Deuce take it, but surely both he and his groom were careful enough to inspect the vehicle when it was to be used in a lengthy race."

"I know you and I both would if it had been you, your grace," the groom assured him.

He went on his way, and Jane found herself being scowled at.

"If you are planning to use those bandages," he said, "forget it. I am not walking around with two mittened paws for the next week or so."

"Those cuts will be painful, your grace," she warned him.

He smiled grimly at her, and Jane sat back on the stool. She knew that his mind was distracted with the morning's events and with anxiety for his brother's safety. But the time had come. She could wait no longer.

"I am going to leave," she said abruptly.

His smile became more crooked. "The room, Jane?" he said. "To put the bandages away again? I wish you would."

She did not answer but merely stared at him. He had not for a moment misunderstood her, she knew.

"You would leave me, then?" he said at last.

"I must," she said. "You know I must. You said so yourself last night."

"But not today." He frowned and flexed the fingers of his left hand, which was less badly scraped than the other. "I cannot cope with another crisis today, Jane."

"This is not a crisis," she told him. "I have had temporary employment here and now it is time for me to leave—after I have been paid."

"Perhaps," he said, "I cannot afford to pay you today, Jane. Did I not agree to give you the colossal sum of five hundred pounds for last evening's performance? I doubt Quincy keeps that much petty cash on hand."

Jane blinked her eyes, but she could not quite clear them of the despicable tears that rushed to them.

"Do not make a joke of it," she said. "Please. I must leave. Today."

"To go where?" he asked her.

But she merely shook her head.

"Don't leave me, Jane," he said. "I cannot let you go. Can you not see that I need a nurse?" He held up his hands, palms out. "For at least another month?"

She shook her head again and he sat back in his chair and regarded her, narrow-eyed.

"Why are you so eager to leave me? Have I been such a tyrant to you, Jane? Have I treated you so badly? Spoken to you so irritably?"

"That you have, your grace," she told him.

"It is because I have been pampered and fawned over since my youth," he said. "I did not mean anything by it, you know. And you have never let me browbeat you, Jane. *You* have been the one to browbeat *me*."

She smiled, but in truth she felt like bawling. Not just because of the frightening unknown into which she would be going but because of what she would be leaving behind, though she had tried determinedly not to think of it all morning.

"You must leave here," he said abruptly. "On that we are agreed, Jane. After last night it is even more imperative that you leave."

She nodded and looked down at her hands in her lap. If she had hoped he would try harder to persuade her to stay on the slim excuse of his scraped hands, she was to be disappointed.

"But you could live somewhere else," he said, "where we could see each other daily away from the prying eyes and gossiping tongues of the *beau monde*. Would you like that?"

She raised her eyes slowly to his. She could not possibly misunderstand his meaning. What she could not believe was her own reaction, or lack of it. Her lack of outrage. Her yearning. The temptation.

He was looking steadily back at her, his eyes very dark.

"I would look after you, Jane," he said. "You could live in style. A home and servants and a carriage of your own. Clothes and jewels. A decent salary. A certain freedom. Far more freedom than a married woman enjoys, anyway."

"In exchange for lying with you," she said quietly. It was not a question. The answer was too obvious.

"I have a certain expertise," he told her. "It would be my delight to use it for your pleasure, Jane. It would be a very fair exchange, you see. You cannot tell me in all honesty, can you, that you have never thought of sharing a bed with me? That you have never wanted it? That you are in any way repelled by me? Come, be honest. I will know if you lie."

"I do not have to lie," she said. "I do not have to answer at all. I will have five hundred pounds plus my three weeks' salary. I can go wherever I want and do whatever I want. That is a fortune for a frugal person, your grace. I am not compelled to accept *carte blanche* from you."

He laughed softly. "I do not believe, Jane," he said, "that I would ever be fool enough to try to compel you to do anything. I am not seducing you. I am not tempting you. I am offering you a proposition, a business one, if you wish. You need a home and a source of income beyond what you already have. You need some security and someone to take your mind off your lone state, I daresay. You are a woman with sexual needs, after all, and you are sexually drawn to me. And I need a mistress. I have been womanless for an alarmingly long time. I have even taken to cornering nurses outside their rooms when I escort them there and stealing kisses. I need someone I can visit at my leisure, someone who can satisfy my own sexual needs. You can, Jane. I desire you. And of course I have the means with which to enable you to live in style."

And in hiding.

Jane looked at her hands, but her mind was considering his offer. She could not quite believe that she was doing so, but she deliberately stopped herself from reacting with simple horror and outrage.

Even assuming she was never caught, she could never go back to being Lady Sara Illingsworth. She could never come into the inheritance due her on her twenty-fifth birthday. She had to think practically of her future. She had to live somewhere. She had to work. Five hundred pounds would not last forever no matter how frugally she lived. She was perfectly capable of taking employment fitted for a gentlewoman—as a teacher or governess or lady's companion. But to do so she would have to make application, she would have to have references, she would have to risk discovery.

The alternative was to grub out an existence at menial tasks. Or to become the Duke of Tresham's mistress.

"Well, Jane?" he asked into the lengthy silence that had followed his last words. "What do you say?"

She drew a deep breath and looked up at him.

She would not have to leave him.

She would lie with him. Outside wedlock. She would be a mistress, a paid woman.

"What sort of a house?" she asked. "And how many servants? How much salary? And how are my interests to be protected? How am I to know you will not dismiss me out of hand as soon as you have tired of me?"

He smiled slowly at her. "That's my girl," he said softly. "Feisty."

"There is to be a contract," she told him. "We will discuss and agree to its terms together. It is to be drawn up and duly checked and signed by both of us before I become your mistress. In the meanwhile I cannot stay here. Is there already a house? Are you one of those gentlemen who keeps a house especially for your mistresses? If so, then I will move to it. If we cannot come to an agreement on a contract, then I will, of course, move out again."

"Of course I have such a house," he said. "Empty of all but two servants at present, I hasten to add. I will take you there later, Jane, after Marsh has returned with news from my brother's stable. I have to do something to fill in the time before word comes from Brighton. We will discuss terms tomorrow."

"Very well." She got to her feet and picked up the bowl and the bandages. "I will have my bag packed and will be ready to leave whenever you summon me, your grace."

"I have the feeling," he said with deceptive meekness as she reached the door and turned the handle, "that you are going to drive a very hard bargain, Jane. I have never before had a mistress who insisted upon a contract."

"The more fool they," she said. "And I am not your mistress yet."

He was chuckling softly when she closed the door.

She leaned back against it, thankful that there were no servants in sight. All her bravado went from her, and with it all the strength in her legs.

What on earth had she just done?

What had she agreed to—or *almost* agreed to?

She tried to feel a suitable degree of horror. But all she could really feel was enormous relief that she would not be leaving him today, never to see him again.

12

IT WAS A HOUSE HE HAD OWNED FOR FIVE YEARS. It was on a decent street in a respectable neighborhood. He had had it decorated and furnished at great expense. He had hired decent, reliable servants, two of whom had been there for all five years, staying to maintain the house even when it had no occupant.

It was a house of which Jocelyn was fond, representing as it did a world of private and sensual delights. And yet as soon as he stepped across the threshold with Jane Ingleby, he felt uncomfortable.

It was not just the house. It was the whole idea of her becoming his mistress. He wanted her, yes. In bed. In all the usual ways. Yet somehow the idea of Jane Ingleby as his mistress did not seem quite to fit.

"Jacobs," he said to the butler, who bowed deferentially, "this is Miss Ingleby. She will be living here for a while. You and Mrs. Jacobs will take your orders from her."

If Jacobs was surprised to find his master choosing a mistress from among the working classes—she was, of course, wearing the cheap gray cloak and bonnet she had worn in Hyde Park—he was far too well trained to show it.

"We will do our best to see to your comfort, ma'am," he said, bowing to her.

"Thank you, Mr. Jacobs," she said, inclining her head

regally before he withdrew discreetly to the nether regions of the house.

"They will hire more servants, of course," Jocelyn said, taking Jane's elbow and beginning a tour of the house with her. "Shall I give the orders, or would you prefer to be in charge of it yourself?"

"Neither yet," she said coolly, looking around the sitting room with its lavender carpet and furnishings, its pink draperies and frilled cushions. "I may not be staying longer than a few days. We have no agreement yet."

"But we will." He guided her toward the dining room. "I shall come in the morning for our discussion, Jane. But first I will take you to a modiste I know on Bond Street. She will measure you for the clothes you will need."

"I will wear my own clothes, thank you," he was not surprised to hear, "until I am your mistress. If we come to an agreement on that point, then you may summon a dressmaker here if you wish. I am not going to set foot on Bond Street."

"Because it will be known that you are my mistress?" he asked, watching her run her fingertips over the polished surface of the round dining table—it could be considerably enlarged to seat guests, but when dining alone with his mistress he preferred to be within touching distance. "You think that a matter for shame? I assure you it is not. Courtesans of the highest class, Jane, are almost on a par with ladies. Above them in some ways. They often have considerably more influence. You will be highly respected as my mistress."

"If I become your mistress, your grace," she said, "I will be neither ashamed nor proud. I will be taking the purely practical step of securing employment that will be both lucrative and congenial to me."

He laughed. "Congenial, Jane?" he said. "You bowl me over with your enthusiasm. Shall we go upstairs?"

He wondered if she felt as passionless as she looked. But he remembered the two embraces they had shared and drew his own conclusions, especially from the one in the music room. She had been anything but passionless on that occasion. And even outside her room, after she had sung for his guests, there had been a yearning that he might have kindled had he chosen.

He was still in the doorway of the bedchamber when she, a few steps ahead of him, turned toward him.

"One thing must be made perfectly clear even today," she said, her hands clasped at her waist, her chin lifted as if for battle, a martial gleam in her eyes. "If I decide to stay, everything in this house has to be changed."

"Indeed?" He raised his eyebrows and his quizzing glass and took his time looking about the room. The wide, canopied, mahogany bed with its intricately carved posts was covered in brocaded silk, with the same silk pleated in a rosebud design on the canopy. The bed curtains were of heavy, costly velvet, as were the window draperies. The carpet was soft and thick underfoot.

All were a rich scarlet.

"Indeed!" she replied firmly, pure scorn in her voice. "This house is disgusting. It is a caricature of a love nest. I will not sleep in this room even alone. I will certainly not lie here with you. I would feel like a whore."

Sometimes one had to take a stand with Jane Ingleby. The trouble was he was unaccustomed to taking stands since nobody had ever made it necessary before now.

"Jane," he said, planting his booted feet apart, clasping his hands at his back, schooling his features into their most forbidding aspect, "I believe it is necessary to remind you that I am not the one being offered employment. I have made you an offer, which you are free to accept or reject. There are plenty who would rush to take your place here given half a chance."

She stared at him.

"My mistake, your grace," she said after a few silent moments, during which he had to concentrate hard not to shift uncomfortably from foot to foot. "I thought we had agreed to discuss terms. But I see you have reverted to that ridiculous posturing as autocratic aristocrat, whose will no sane person would even dream of crossing. You had better go and give someone else half a chance. I am leaving."

She took one purposeful step toward him. Only one. He stood his ground in the doorway. She could try going through him if she wished.

"What is so objectionable about the house?" he was weak enough to ask her. "I have never before had a single complaint about it."

But she was quite right, damn it. He had felt it as soon as he had stepped inside the house with her. It was is if he had been entering a strange dwelling and seeing it for the first time. This house was just not Jane.

"I can think of two words to describe it," she said. "I could probably think of a whole dictionary full if I had more time. But those that leap to mind are *sleaze* and *fluff*. Neither of which is tolerable to me."

He pursed his lips. Those two words perfectly described the house. He had had the sitting room designed for a feminine taste, of course, not his own. Or what he had imagined was feminine taste. Effie had always appeared perfectly at home there. So had Lisa and Marie and Bridget. And this room? Well, in candlelight it could always heighten his sexual desire. The predominant reds did marvelous things to the color of naked female flesh.

"It is one of my first conditions," she said. "This room and the sitting room. They are to be redone to my instructions. This point is not negotiable. Take it or leave it."

"*One of?*" He raised his eyebrows. "Tell me, Jane, am I to be allowed to write some conditions of my own into this contract of ours? Or am I to be your slave? I would like to know. Actually the prospect of being a slave has a certain appeal. Does it come with chains and whips?" He grinned at her.

She did not smile.

"A contract is a two-way agreement," she said. "Of course there will be certain things that you will insist upon. Like unlimited access to my—"

"Favors?" he suggested when she floundered.

"Yes." She nodded briskly.

"Unlimited access." He gazed steadily at her and was gratified to see that the rosiness in her cheeks owed nothing to the redness of her surroundings. "Even when you are unwilling, Jane? Even when you have a headache or some other malady? You would agree in writing to act the martyr even if my appetites prove insatiable?"

She thought for a moment. "I imagine it would be a reasonable demand for you to make, your grace," she said. "That is what mistresses are for, after all."

"Poppycock!" He narrowed his gaze on her. "If that is the attitude with which you approach the liaison, Jane, I want none of you. I do not want a body to plow whenever my sexual urges are out of control. There are innumerable brothels I might use for such a purpose. I want someone with whom to relax. Someone with whom to take the ultimate pleasure. Someone to pleasure in return."

The color deepened in her cheeks, but she kept her spine straight and her chin raised.

"What if you came here ten days in a row and I said no each time?" she asked him.

"Then I would consider myself a damnable failure," he said. "I would probably go home and blow my brains out."

She laughed suddenly and looked so vividly beautiful and golden amid the scarlet that he felt his breath catch in his throat.

"How absurd!" she said.

"If for ten straight days a man cannot entice his mistress into bed," he said meekly, "he might as well be dead, Jane. What is there for him to live for if his sexual appeal is gone?"

She tipped her head to one side and regarded him thoughtfully. "You are joking," she said. "But you are half serious too. Being a *man* is very important to you, is it not?"

"And being a *woman* is not important to you?"

She considered her answer. It was characteristic of her, he had noticed before, not always to rush into saying the first thing that came into her head.

"Being *me* is important to me," she said. "And since I am a woman, then I suppose being a woman is important too. But I do not have a mental image of what a perfect woman is, of what other people look for in me because I am a woman. I do not slavishly pattern my appearance or my behavior on any image. I need to be true to myself."

Jocelyn felt a sudden wave of amusement.

"I have never stood in this doorway before," he said, "halfway across the room from a woman, discussing the nature of gender and sexuality. We should by now, you know, have consummated our intent to contract a certain relationship. We should be lying exhausted and naked and mutually satisfied on that bed."

This time there was no other way to describe her face than to say she blushed.

"I suppose," she said, "you expected that once you had got me here I would succumb to your devastating charm and the allure of this room?"

It was exactly what he had expected—or hoped for anyway.

"And I suppose," he said with a sigh, "you will not allow me to lay one lascivious finger on you until this room looks like a monk's cell. Go ahead, then, Jane. Give your orders to Jacobs. Do whatever you wish with my house. I will do my part and pay the bills. Shall we go back downstairs? I daresay Mrs. Jacobs has a tea tray ready and is bursting with curiosity to catch a glimpse of you."

"She can bring it to the dining room," Jane said, sweeping past him when at last he stepped to one side of the doorway.

"Where will you sleep tonight?" he asked, following her down. "On the dining room table?"

"I will find somewhere," she assured him. "You need not concern yourself about it, your grace."

He walked away from the house an hour later, cane and painfully scraped palm and all, having dismissed his town carriage earlier. He was eager to hear Marsh's report from Ferdinand's stable. It might be impossible to prove that any of the Forbeses had had access to the curricle. But all he needed was the possibility that the broken axle had come courtesy of one of them.

Then they would have the Duke of Tresham to deal with.

He wondered if word had yet arrived about the result of the race. Unusually for him, all he was really concerned about was that Ferdinand had got to Brighton safely.

He should never have suggested that Jane Ingleby become his mistress, he thought. There was something all wrong about it.

And yet his loins ached for her.

Why had the damned woman not simply tiptoed on past that morning in Hyde Park when she had seen that there was a duel pending, as any decent woman would have done?

If he had never set eyes upon her, he would not now be walking around with the curious sensation that either he or his world was standing on its head.

SHE SLEPT ON THE sitting room sofa. The color scheme and all the frills and knickknacks were in atrociously bad taste, but at least it was not as vulgar a room as the bedchamber.

While they had talked in that room during the afternoon, she had had lurid, uncomfortable images of lying tangled with him on the bed amid all that scarlet silk. She did not know what full sexual arousal felt like, but it must be something very like what she had felt then.

What she had agreed to—or was about to agree to—had become appallingly real to her.

How could she be his mistress? she had asked herself, sitting upright on the sofa before lying down to sleep. She simply could not do it unless she felt something for him as a person. Did she? She did not *love* him, of course—that would be patently rash. But did she like him? Feel some affection for him? Some respect?

She thought of their endless verbal scraps—and smiled unexpectedly. He was a haughty, tyrannical, thoroughly irritating man. But she had the distinct impression that he enjoyed the way she stood up to him. And he *did* respect her opinions, even if he never admitted as much. The fact that she was alone tonight, their liaison unconsummated, was proof enough of that. And there was his strangely admirable sense of honor. He had faced Lord Oliver in a duel rather than call Lady Oliver a liar.

Jane sighed. Ah, yes, she liked him well enough. And, of course, there was the artistic, more sensitive side to his nature, which she had glimpsed that night in the music room. And his intelligence. And his sense of humor. All the many fascinating facets of his character that he kept carefully hidden away from the world.

And there was their mutual desire for each other. Jane felt no doubt that it *was* mutual. If she had been just any woman, any prospective mistress to him, he would have sent her on her way as soon as she raised the question of a contract. But she must remember—always, for as long as their liaison lasted—that it was only passion he felt. Sexual passion. She must never mistake the feelings of the Duke of Tresham for love.

It was not going to be easy to be his mistress.

Jane slept on the sofa and dreamed of Charles. Her closest friend. Her beau. Like someone from another lifetime. He was sitting in the rose arbor at Candleford with her, telling her about his sister's new baby and telling her too how they would set up their own nursery as soon as they were able after her twenty-fifth birthday freed her to marry whomever she chose.

She awoke with wet cheeks. She had deliberately not thought of Charles after her flight from home. She had succeeded all too well. Why had she not thought of going to him now that she had the money with which to travel? Was he still at his sister's in Somersetshire? Or had he returned to Cornwall? She could have found a way to reach him without being caught. He would surely know what to do, how to protect her, how to hide her if necessary. Most important of all, he would believe her story. He knew how desperately eager the new Earl of Durbury was that she marry his son. He knew how despicable Sidney could be, especially when he was in his cups.

She could still do it, of course. She had been paid yesterday before leaving Dudley House. She had not yet become the Duke of Tresham's mistress. She could leave before he came back and avoid the necessity of giving up her virtue.

The very idea of such a fate would surely have brought on a fit of the vapors just a few weeks ago. Now, with surprising belatedness, she had thought of a decent alternative.

But the trouble was that she did not love Charles. Not as a woman should love her husband. Not as Mama had loved Papa. She had always known it, of course. But she had always *wanted* to love Charles because she liked him and because he loved her.

If she went to him now, if he somehow extricated her from the tangle she was in, she would be bound to him for life. She would not have minded just a few weeks before. Friendship and affection would have been enough.

No longer.

Was being the duke's mistress preferable to honorable marriage with Charles, then?

It was a question Jane could not answer to her own satisfaction before his grace's arrival in the middle of the morning. It was a question whose answer she recognized with some reluctance after she had heard his knock and had opened the sitting room door to see him step into the hall and hand his hat and gloves and cane to Mr. Jacobs. He brought all his energy and restlessness and sheer maleness with him—and Jane realized she had missed him.

"Jane." He strode toward her, and they retreated into the sitting room together. "He won. By scarcely the length of his horses' noses. He was behind a full length coming into the final bend, but he accelerated into it and took Berriwether by surprise. They thundered into Brighton almost neck and neck. But Ferdinand won, and three-quarters of the members of White's have gone into mourning."

"He came to no harm, then?" she said. "I am glad." She might have commented again on how foolish such races were, but he looked so very pleased with himself. And she really was glad. Lord Ferdinand Dudley was a pleasant, charming young man.

"No. No harm." He frowned suddenly. "He does not choose his servants wisely, though. He has a valet who does not allow for the fact that a man sometimes turns his head without warning while being shaved. And he has a groom who allows half the world into his stable and carriage house the day before a race in order to admire the tools of his master's trade. There is no proving who arranged for Ferdinand's death during that race."

"But you suspect Sir Anthony Forbes or one of his brothers?" she asked him. She seated herself on the sofa, and he sat beside her.

"More than suspect." He looked about the room as he spoke. "It is the way they work. I did something to their sister; they do something to my brother. They will be sorry, of course. I will deal with them. What have you done to this room?"

She was relieved at the change of subject.

"I have just removed a few things," she told him. "All the cushions and a few of the ornaments. I have ideas for extensive changes to both this room and the bedchamber. I would not be needlessly extravagant, but even so the cost would be considerable."

"Quincy will take care of the bills," he said with a careless wave of one hand. "But how long is all this going to take, Jane? I have the feeling you are not going to allow me to bed you until everything is to your liking, are you?"

"No," she said with what she hoped was suitable firmness. "A week should be sufficient once the order is given. I have spoken to Mr. Jacobs, and he says the suppliers will fall all over themselves to be prompt as soon as he mentions your name."

The duke did not answer her. Obviously the truth of that statement was no surprise to him.

"Let us discuss this contract, then," he said. "Apart

from *carte blanche* to tear down my house and rebuild it, what are your demands, Jane? I will pay you a monthly salary five times higher than what I paid you as a nurse. You will have your own carriage and as many servants as you deem necessary. You may clothe yourself in as much finery as you wish with all the accessories and direct the bills to me. I will be generous with jewels, though I would prefer to buy those myself. I will take on full responsibility for the support and future placement of any children of our liaison. Have I missed anything?"

Jane had turned suddenly cold. Her own naïveté quite mortified her.

"How many children do you presently have?" Foolishly she had not thought of becoming with child.

His eyebrows rose. "You can always be relied upon to ask unaskable questions, Jane," he said. "I have none. Most women who make their living by such arrangements as this know how to prevent conception. I assume you do not. You *are* a virgin, are you not?"

It took a great deal of fortitude to keep her eyes from sliding away from his very direct gaze. She wished blushes were as much within her control.

"Yes." She kept her chin up. "There is one expense you do not need to burden yourself with. I do not need a carriage."

"Why not?" He rested one elbow on the back of the sofa and set his closed fist against his mouth. His dark eyes did not look away from hers. "You will need to shop, Jane, and get out to see the sights. It would be unwise to rely upon me to take you about. Shopping bores me. When I come here, I will be far more eager to take you to bed than out for a drive."

"The servants can shop for food," she said. "And if

you object to the clothes I wear, you can send dressmakers here. I have no wish to go out."

"Is what you are about to do so shameful to you, then?" he asked her. "You really feel you cannot show your face to the world ever again?"

She had answered that the day before. But it would be as well, she thought, if he believed it. Strangely, it was not true. Life had become a practical business, which she must direct and control as best she was able.

He did not speak again for some time. The silence stretched between them while he stared broodingly at her and she gazed back, uncomfortable but unwilling to look away.

"There is an alternative," he said at last. "One that would bring you fame and fortune and great esteem, Jane. One that would save you from the degradation of bedding with a rake."

"I do not consider it degrading," she told him.

"No?" He lifted his free hand and cupped her chin. He ran his thumb lightly across her lips. "I am not intimate with the inner circles of high culture, Jane, but I daresay my word carries some weight almost everywhere. I could introduce you to Lord Heath or the Earl of Raymore, two of the more prominent patrons of the arts. I have every confidence that if either one of them heard your voice, he would set your feet on the road to fame. You are that good, you know. You would not need me."

She gazed at him in some surprise. He wanted her—she did not doubt that. But he was prepared to let her go? Even to help her be independent of him? Quite unconsciously she parted her lips and touched her tongue to the pad of his thumb.

His eyes met and held hers. And she felt raw desire

knife down inside her. She had not intended to provoke such a moment. Neither had he, she suspected.

"I do not want a career as a singer," she said.

It was the truth even apart from the fact that she could not flirt with danger by going before the public gaze again. She did not want to use her voice to earn a living. She wanted to use it for the pleasure of people who were close to her. She had no yearning for fame.

He leaned forward and set his mouth where his thumb had been. He kissed her hard.

"But you do want one as my mistress?" he said. "On your terms? What are they, then? What do you want that I have not already offered?"

"Security," she said. "I want your agreement to pay my salary until my twenty-fifth birthday even if you should dismiss me before then. Provided I am not the one to break our agreement, of course. I am twenty now, by the way."

"For five years," he said. "And how will you support yourself after that, Jane?"

She did not know. She was supposed to come into her inheritance then—all of her father's fortune that had not been entailed on his heir. But of course she might never be able to claim it. She would not suddenly stop being a fugitive simply because she had reached the magic age of freedom.

She shook her head.

"Perhaps," he said, "I will never tire of you, Jane."

"Nonsense!" she told him. "Of course you will. And long before four and a half years have passed. That is why I must protect my future."

He smiled at her. He did not smile nearly often enough. And altogether too often for her peace of mind.

She wondered if he knew what devastating charm his smile hinted at.

"Very well, then," he said. "It will be written into the contract. Salary until dismissal or your twenty-fifth birthday, whichever comes later. Anything else?"

She shook her head. "What about your conditions?" she asked him. "We have come to an agreement on what you will do for me. What must I do for you?"

He shrugged. "Be here for me," he said. "Have sexual relations with me whenever I can persuade you that you want them as much as I do. That is all, Jane. A relationship between a man and his mistress cannot be legislated, you know. I will not even try to insist upon obedience and subjection, you see. You would not be able to keep such a promise even if you could be persuaded to make it. And damn me for a fool for saying this aloud, but I believe it is your very impudence that attracts me. Shall I have Quincy draw up the contract and bring it here for your perusal? I imagine he will be vastly diverted by such a task. I will not bring it myself, Jane. I will not come again until you send for me. I will assume when I do hear from you that the bedchamber abovestairs is ready for use."

"Very well, your grace," she said as he got to his feet. She stood up too. A week was going to seem like an eternity.

He framed her face with his hands. "That will have to change too, Jane," he said. "I cannot have you *your gracing* me when we are in bed together. My name is Jocelyn."

She had not known his name. No one had ever used it in her hearing. "Jocelyn," she said softly.

His very dark eyes were normally hard and quite opaque. It was impossible to see more of the man than he was willing to reveal—and that was usually not very much, she suspected. But for a moment after she spoke his name, Jane had the distinct feeling that something opened up behind his eyes and that she was falling into them.

For only a moment.

He dropped his hands and turned toward the door.

"One week," he said. "If the renovations are not complete by then, Jane, a few heads are going to roll. You will warn all the workmen involved?"

"Yes, your grace," she said. "Jocelyn."

He looked over his shoulder at her and opened his mouth to speak. But he changed his mind and strode from the room without saying another word.

13

MANY OF MICK BODEN'S ACQUAINTANCES ENvied him his job. There was a certain glamour about being one of the famed Bow Street Runners. The common fallacy was that he spent his working days literally running to earth all of London's and half of England's most desperate criminals and hauling them off to the nearest magistrate and the just reward for their dastardly deeds. They saw his life as one of endless adventure and danger and action—and success.

Most of the time his job was routine and rather dull. Sometimes he wondered why he was not a dockyard worker or a crossing sweeper. This was one of those times. Lady Sara Illingsworth, a lady of a mere twenty years who had grown up in the country and presumably had no town bronze, was proving to be unexpectedly elusive. In almost a month of searching he had discovered no trace of her beyond those first few days.

The Earl of Durbury still stubbornly insisted she was in London. There was nowhere else she could have gone, he claimed, since she had no friends or relatives elsewhere apart from an old neighbor now living with her husband in Somersetshire. But she was not there.

Something told Mick that the earl was right. She was here somewhere. But she had not returned to Lady Webb's, even though the baroness was now back in town. She had not contacted either her late father's man of business or the present earl's. If she had been spending lavishly, she had not been doing it in any of the more fashionable shops. If she had been trying to sell or pawn any of the stolen jewels, she had not done it at any of the places Mick knew about—and he prided himself on knowing them all. If she had tried to secure respectable lodgings in a decent neighborhood, she had not done so at any of the houses on whose doors he and his assistants had tirelessly knocked. She had not sought employment in any of the houses at which he inquired—and he had asked at all the likely possibilities except the grandest mansions in Mayfair. She would not have been foolhardy enough to apply at one of those, he had concluded. None of the agencies had been applied to by anyone bearing any of the names Mick thought she might be using. None remembered a tall, slim, blond beauty.

And so he found himself yet again with nothing to report to the Earl of Durbury. It was lowering. It was enough to make a man think seriously about changing his line of work. It was also enough to arouse all a man's stubborn determination not to be thwarted by a mere slip of a girl.

"She has not gone into service, sir," he said with conviction to an exasperated, red-faced earl, who was doubtless thinking of the hefty bill he had run up at the Pulteney in a month. "She would not have sought employment as a governess or lady's companion—too public. For the same reason she would not have taken work as a shop clerk. She would have to work somewhere she would not be seen. Some workshop. A dressmaker's or a milliner's, perhaps."

If she was working at all. The earl had never told him

exactly how much money the girl had stolen. Mick was beginning to suspect it could not have been much. Not enough to enable her to live in style, anyway. Surely such a young, inexperienced woman would have made mistakes by now if she had had a vast fortune to tempt her into the open.

"What are you waiting for, then?" his lordship asked coldly. "Why are you not out searching every workshop in London? Are the illustrious Bow Street Runners to be outsmarted by a mere girl?" His voice was heavy with sarcasm.

"Am I searching for a murderess?" Mick Boden asked. "How is your son, sir?"

"My son," the earl said irritably, "is at death's door. You are searching for a murderess. I suggest you find her before she repeats her crime."

And so Mick began his search anew. London, of course, had more than its fair share of workshops. He just wished he knew for sure what name the girl was using. And he wished that she had not somehow managed to hide her blond hair, apparently her most distinctive feature.

IT WAS A LONG week. Jocelyn spent far too much of it drinking and gaming by night and trying to whip himself into shape during the day by spending long hours honing his fencing skills and building his stamina in the boxing ring at Gentleman Jackson's. His leg was responding well to exercise.

Ferdinand was incensed when he learned what had happened to his curricle and was determined to ferret out the Forbes brothers, who had dropped out of sight the day after the duel, and slap a glove in all their separate faces. At first he would not agree that it was his brother's quarrel. It was his life, after all, that had been threatened. But Jocelyn was insistent.

Angeline had had a fit of the vapors at the news of the broken axle, had summoned Heyward from the House, and then, to divert her shaken nerves, had bought a new bonnet.

"I wonder that there is any fruit left on any of the stalls at Covent Garden, Angeline," Jocelyn observed, viewing it with a pained expression through his quizzing glass as he rode through Hyde Park at the fashionable hour one day and came across her sporting it as she drove in an open barouche with her mother-in-law. "I daresay it is all decorating that monstrosity on your head."

"It is all the crack," she replied, preening, "no matter what you say, Tresham. You simply must promise not to drive a curricle again. You or Ferdie. You will kill yourselves and I will never recover my nerves. But Heyward said it was no accident. I daresay it was one of the Forbeses. If you do not discover which one and call him to account, I shall be ashamed to call myself a Dudley."

"You do not now," he reminded her dryly before tipping his hat to the Dowager Lady Heyward and riding on. "You took your husband's name when you married him, Angeline."

He was not as impatient as his brother and sister to find the Forbeses and punish them. The time would come. They must know it as surely as he did. In the meantime, let them remain in their hiding place, imagining what would happen when they finally came face-to-face with him. Let them sweat it out.

Several people asked about Jane Ingleby. She had created even more of a stir with her singing than he had expected. He was asked who she was, if she was still employed at Dudley House, if she was to sing anywhere else, who her voice teacher had been. Viscount Kimble even asked him outright one evening at White's if she was his mistress—a question that won for himself a cool stare through the ducal quizzing glass.

Strange, that. Jocelyn had never before been secretive about his mistresses. Indeed, he had often used the house for dinners and parties when he wished them to be a little less formal than such occasions at Dudley House inevitably were. His mistresses had always also been his hostesses—a role that would fit Jane admirably.

But he did not want his friends to know she was in his keeping. It seemed somehow unfair to her, though he would not have been able to explain if he had tried. He told them she had had temporary employment with him and was now gone, he knew not where.

"A devilish shame, Tresham," Conan Brougham said. "That voice ought to be brought to the attention of Raymore. She could earn a more than decent living with it."

"I would have offered her employment myself, Tresh," Kimble said, "on her back, that is, not with her voice. But I feared I might be trespassing on your preserves. If you hear where she is, you might drop a word in my ear."

Jocelyn, feeling unaccustomedly hostile to one of his closest friends, changed the subject.

He walked home alone later that same night despite the danger of attack by footpads. He had never feared them. He carried a stout cane and he was handy with his fives. He would rather enjoy a scuffle with two or three ruffians, he had often thought. Perhaps any ruffians who had ever spotted him had been intelligent enough to estimate correctly their chances against him. He had never been attacked.

The mention of Jane Ingleby had made him unbearably restless. It had been five days, and it had seemed more like five weeks. Quincy had personally taken over that silly contract on the second day. To Jocelyn's surprise she had signed it. He had expected her to haggle over a few small details out of sheer perverseness.

She was officially his mistress.

His virgin, unbedded mistress. How everyone who knew him would jeer if they knew he had engaged a mistress who had banished him from his own house, insisted upon a written contract, and kept the relationship unconsummated a full week after he had made her the proposition.

He laughed aloud suddenly, stopping in the middle of an empty, silent street. Ornery Jane. Even during the consummation she would doubtless not play the part of timid, shrinking virgin being deflowered.

Innocent, naïve Jane, who did not realize how clever she was being. He had desired her a week ago. He had yearned for her five days ago. By now he was on fire for her. He was finding it difficult to think of anything else. Jane with her golden hair, into whose web he could hardly wait to be ensnared.

He was forced to wait two more days before a note finally arrived. It was characteristically brief and to the point.

"The work on the house is complete," she wrote. "You may call at your convenience."

Cool, unloverlike words that set him ablaze.

* * *

JANE WAS PACING. SHE had sent the note to Dudley House immediately after breakfast, but she knew that often he left home early and did not return until late at night. He might not read the note until tomorrow. He might not come for another day or two.

But she was pacing. And trying in vain not to look through the front-facing windows more often than once every ten minutes.

She was wearing a new dress of delicate spring-green muslin. High-waisted, with a modest neckline and short, puffed sleeves, it was of simple design. But it was expertly styled to mold and flatter her figure above its high waistline and to fall in soft folds to her ankles. It had been very costly. Accustomed to the prices of a country dressmaker, Jane had been shocked. But she had not sent the Bond Street modiste and her two assistants away. The duke had selected them and sent them with specific instructions on the number and nature of garments she was to have.

She had selected the fabrics and designs herself, favoring light colors over vivid ones and simplicity of design over the ornate, but she had not argued over the number or the expense, except flatly to insist upon only one walking dress and only one carriage dress. She had no intention of walking or driving out any time soon.

He would not have given her *carte blanche* over the house renovations if he had not intended coming back, she thought as she leaned close to the window yet again early in the afternoon. He would not have sent the modiste or the contract. Indeed, he had sent the latter twice, first two copies for her to peruse and sign and return, and then just one copy to keep, with his own signature—*Tresham*—scrawled large and bold beneath her own. Mr. Jacobs had witnessed her signature, Mr. Quincy his.

But she could not shake the conviction that he would not come back. The week had been endless. Surely by now he must have forgotten her. Surely by now there was someone else.

She could not understand—and did not care to explore—her own anxiety.

But all anxiety fled suddenly to be replaced by a bursting of joy when she saw a familiar figure striding along the street in the direction of the house. He was walking without a limp, she noticed before turning and hurrying to open the sitting room door. She stopped herself from rushing to open the front door too. She stood where she was, waiting eagerly for his knock, waiting for Mr. Jacobs to answer it.

She had forgotten how broad-shouldered he was, how dark, how forbidding in aspect, how restless with pent-up energy, how—male. He was frowning as usual when he handed his hat and gloves to the butler. He did not look at her until he had done so. Then he strode toward the sitting room and fixed his eyes on her at last.

Eyes that looked not only at her dress and face and hair, she thought, but on everything that was her. Eyes that burned into her with a strange, intense light she had not seen there before.

The eyes of a man come to claim his mistress?

"Well, Jane," he said, "you have finished playing house at last?"

Had she expected a kiss on the hand? On the lips? Soft lover's words?

"There was much to do," she replied coolly, "to convert this house into a dwelling rather than a brothel."

"And you have done it?" He strode into the sitting room and looked around, his booted feet apart, his hands at his back. He seemed to fill the room.

"Hmm," he said. "You did not tear down the walls, then?"

"No," she said. "I kept a great deal. I have not been unnecessarily extravagant."

"One would hate to have seen Quincy's face if you had been," he retorted. "He has been somewhat green about the gills for the past few days as it is. I understand that bills have been flooding in."

"That is at least partly your fault," she told him. "I did not need so many clothes and accessories. But the dressmaker you sent said you were adamant and she dared not allow your orders to be contradicted."

"Some women, you see," he said, "know their place, Jane. They know how to be submissive and obedient."

"And how to make a great deal of money in the process," she added. "I kept the lavender color in here, as you can see, though I would not have chosen it had I been planning the room from scratch. Combined with gray and silver instead of pink, and without all the frills and silly knickknacks, it looks rather delicate and elegant. I like it. I can live here comfortably."

"Can you, Jane?" He turned his head and looked at her—again with those burning eyes. "And have you done as well with the bedchamber? Or am I going to find two hard, narrow cots in there and a hair shirt laid out on each?"

"If you find scarlet a necessary titillation," she said, trying to ignore the thumping of her heart and hoping it did not betray itself in her voice, "then I daresay you will not like what I have done to the room. But I like it, and that is what counts. I am the one who has to sleep there every night."

"I am being forbidden to do so, then?" He raised his eyebrows.

That foolish blush again. The one sign of emotion it was impossible to disguise. She could feel it hot on her cheeks.

"No," she said. "I have agreed—in writing—that you are to be free to come and go as you please. But I daresay you do not intend to *live* here as I do. Only to come when you . . . Well, when you . . ." She had lost her command of the English language.

"Want sex with you?" he suggested.

"Yes." She nodded. "Then."

"And I am not allowed to come when I do not?" He pursed his lips and regarded her in silence for a few uncomfortable moments. "Is that in the contract? That I can come here only for sex, Jane? Not for tea? Or conversation? Or perhaps just to sleep?"

It would be like a real relationship. It was too seductive a thought.

"Would you like to see the bedchamber?" she asked.

He regarded her for a few moments longer before the smile came—that slight smile that lit his eyes and lifted the corners of his mouth and turned Jane's knees weak.

"To see the new furnishings?" he asked her. "Or to have sex, Jane?"

She found his raw choice of words disconcerting. But any more euphemistic way of phrasing it would mean the same thing.

"I am your mistress," she said.

"Yes, so you are." He strolled closer to her, his hands still at his back. He dipped his head closer and gazed into her eyes. "No sign of steely martyrdom. You are ready for the consummation, then?"

"Yes." She also thought she was ready to collapse in an ignominious heap at his feet, but that fact had nothing to do with a weak resolve, only with weak knees.

He straightened up and offered his arm.

"Let us go, then," he said.

THE FURNISHINGS HAD NOT changed, only the color scheme. But he would scarcely have known he was in the same room if someone had blindfolded him, picked him up bodily, and deposited him here. It was all sage green and cream and gold. It was elegance itself.

If there was one thing Jane Ingleby had an abundance of, it was good taste, plus an eye for color and design. Another skill learned at the orphanage? Or at the rectory or country manor or wherever the devil it was she had grown up?

But he had not come to inspect the room's furnishings.

"Well?" Her eyes were bright, her cheeks flushed. "What do you think?"

"What I think, Jane," he said, narrowing his gaze on her, "is that I will see your hair down now at last. Take out the pins."

It was not dressed with its customary severity. It was waved and coiled in a manner that complemented the pretty, elegant dress she wore. But he wanted to see it flowing free.

She removed the pins deftly and shook her head.

Ah. It reached to below her waist, as she had said it did. A river of pure, shining, rippling gold. She had appeared beautiful before. Even in the hideous maid's dress and the atrocious cap she had been beautiful. But now...

There simply were not words. He clasped his hands behind him. He had waited too long to rush now.

"Jocelyn." She tipped her head to one side and looked directly at him with her very blue eyes. "I am on unfamiliar ground here. You will have to lead the way."

He nodded, wondering at the great wave of—oh, not desire exactly that washed over him. Longing? That sort of gut-deep, soul-deep yearning that very occasionally caught him unawares and was shaken firmly off again. He associated it with music and painting. But now it was his name that had aroused it.

"Jocelyn is a name that has been in my family for generations," he said. "I acquired it when I was still in the womb. I cannot think of a single soul until now who has spoken it aloud to me."

Her eyes widened. "Your mother?" she said. "Your father? Your brother and sister? Surely—"

"No." He shrugged out of his tight-fitting coat and opened the buttons of his waistcoat. "I was born heir to my present title. I was born with an earl's title, Jane. My family all used it until I became Tresham at the age of seventeen. You really are the first to call me by my given name."

He had suggested it. He had never done so with his other mistresses. They had called him by his title, just like everyone else. He remembered now being shaken to hear his name on Jane's lips a week ago. He had not expected it to bring such a feeling of—of intimacy. He had not realized how he had longed for such intimacy. Just that. Someone calling him by name.

He tossed his waistcoat aside and untied the knot of his neckcloth. She was watching him, her hands clasped at her waist, cloaked in gold.

"Jocelyn," she said softly. "Everyone should know what it is like to be called by name. By the name of the unique person one is at heart. Do you want me to undress too?"

"Not yet." He pulled his shirt off over his head and pulled off his Hessian boots. He kept his pantaloons on for the time being.

"You are very beautiful," she surprised him by saying, her eyes on his naked torso. Trust Jane to make such a remark! "I suppose I have offended you by using that particular word. It is not masculine enough, I daresay. But you are not handsome. Not in any conventional sense. Your features are too harsh and angular, your coloring too dark. You are only beautiful."

An experienced courtesan could not have aroused him so deftly even with the most cunningly erotic words.

"Now what have you left me to say about you?" he asked, stepping forward and touching her at last. He framed her face with his hands, sliding his fingers into the warm silk of her hair. "You are not pretty, Jane. You must know that. Prettiness is ephemeral. It passes in a season. You will be beautiful when you are thirty, when you are fifty, when you are eighty. At twenty you are dazzling, breathtaking. And you are mine." He dipped his head and touched his parted lips to hers, tasting her with his tongue before withdrawing a couple of inches.

"Yes, Jocelyn." Her teeth bit into her soft, moist lower lip. "For now I am yours. According to our contract."

"That damned thing." He chuckled softly. "I want you to want me, Jane. Tell me it is not just the money or this house or the obligation that wretched piece of paper has put you under. Tell me you want me. *Me*—Jocelyn. Or tell me truthfully that you do not and I will leave you to the enjoyment of your home and salary for the next five years. I will not bed you unless you want me."

He had never particularly cared before. All conceit aside, he knew he was not the sort of man who repelled women who earned their living in bed. And it had always been a matter of pride with him to give pleasure where he took it. But he had never cared whether a woman wanted *him* or just the wealthy, rakish aristocrat with the dangerous reputation. In fact, if he had thought about it, he probably would have decided that he did not want any woman close enough to desire *him*.

He had never before been Jocelyn to anyone. Not to anyone in his family. Not to any woman. Not even to his closest friends. He would rather turn and leave now and never return than let Jane lie on her back on that bed simply because she felt obliged to. It was a somewhat alarming realization.

"I want you, Jocelyn," she whispered.

There was no doubt she meant it. Her blue eyes were focused fully on his. She was speaking the simple truth.

And then she leaned forward, letting every part of her body rest lightly against him. She set her lips to the hollow at the base of his throat. It was a gesture of sweet surrender.

All the sweeter because it seemed uncharacteristic of

Jane. He knew her well enough to realize it was something she would never do merely because surrender was expected of her.

He felt strangely gifted.

He felt curiously wanted. In a way he had never felt in his life before.

"Jane," he said, his face in the silk of her hair. "Jane, I need to be inside your body. Inside *you*. Let me in."

"Yes." She tipped back her head and gazed into his eyes. "Yes, I will, Jocelyn. But you must show me how. I am not sure I know."

Ah. Jane to the end. She spoke in her cool, practical voice—which he suddenly realized was a mask for nervousness.

"It will be my pleasure," he told her, his mouth against hers as his fingers tackled the buttons down the back of her dress.

14

SHE WAS NOT NERVOUS.

Oh, yes, she was.

She was nervous in the sense that she did not know quite what to do and was afraid of being gauche.

But she was not afraid. Or in any way horrified at what she was doing. Or ashamed. And she had spoken no lie. She wanted him. She desperately desired him. And he *was* beautiful—all solid, hard muscle with broad shoulders and chest, narrow waist and hips, long legs. He was warm and smelled of some musky cologne.

He was Jocelyn, and only she had ever spoken the intimacy of his name. She knew all about the importance of names. Only her parents had ever called her by her middle name, her *real* name, the one that seemed somehow to encompass her true identity. Her parents and now Jocelyn. She had tried to stop him from calling her Jane, but he had done so regardless.

And so in some inexpressible way they knew each other intimately even before the physical knowing, which was just beginning. He was unclothing her. Her nakedness did not embarrass her. She saw herself through the look in his dark eyes and knew that she was beautiful and desirable.

She gave him back the look.

"Jane." He set his hands lightly at her waist and drew her against him. She inhaled slowly at the feel of his bare chest brushing her nipples. "We are ready for bed. Come and lie down."

For a moment the coldness of the sheet against her back took her breath. She had changed the colors of the room but not the materials. Satin, she had guessed, was an erotic accompaniment to what would happen in this bed.

She watched him finish undressing. He did not turn his back and she did not look away. She was to become as familiar with the look and feel of his body as she was with her own. Why begin with shyness or coyness?

She knew pretty well what happened. She had lived all her life in the country, after all. But even so she was shocked. There surely could not be room.

He was smiling that half-inward smile of his when he climbed onto the bed beside her and propped himself on one elbow to look down at her.

"You will become accustomed to both the sight and feel of it, Jane," he said. "I have never had a virgin. I suppose there will be pain and blood this first time, but I promise you pleasure too. And I will not put this terror inside you until your body is ready for it. It is my task to see that it is made ready. Do you know anything of foreplay?"

She shook her head. "I have never even heard the word."

"It means what it says." His eyes still laughed gently at her. "We will play, Jane, for as long as we need before I mount your body and ride us both to satiety. I daresay you do not know much if anything about the ride either, do you? The pain will be over before it begins. You will enjoy it, believe me."

She did not doubt it. There was already an ache of

something that was not quite pain along her inner thighs and up into her belly. Her breasts had tightened to a strange, tingling soreness.

"You are doing it already, are you not?" she said. "Playing? With words?"

"We could sit at opposite ends of a room and arouse each other to fever pitch with only words," he said, grinning suddenly. "And maybe we will do it one of these days. But not today. Today is for touch, Jane. For exploring each other with hands and mouths. For stripping away the otherness that holds us from merging into the oneness we crave. We *do* crave it, do we not? Both of us?"

"Yes." She lifted a hand and cupped one of his cheeks. "Yes, Jocelyn. I want to be a part of your name, a part of the person who bears that name, a part of the soul inside that person. I want to be one with you."

"You, me, we, us." He lowered his head and spoke against her mouth. "Let us invent a new pronoun, Jane. The unity of I and the plurality of we melded into a new numberless word for Jane and Jocelyn."

She opened her mouth beneath his, suddenly ravenous and shaken by the words they had spoken—and those they had not. This was not the way she had expected it to be. This was not man and mistress. This was lover and beloved.

It had not been a part of the bargain. Either for her or—surely—for him.

But it was what was happening.

She realized too late, as his tongue plundered her mouth and his hands gave her an intimation of the magic and sensual delights ahead, what this was all about. She understood, far too late, why she had taken this option rather than any of the other more proper and rational ones. She understood why she had accepted his proposition without either outrage or horror.

This was love. Oh, perhaps not *love* exactly. But this was being in love. This was wanting to give and give to the beloved until everything that was oneself had been gifted away. And wanting to receive and receive until the emptiness had been filled again with a mingling of what was herself and him.

He was right. There was no word. No pronoun. There never was a word for the deepest realities.

"Jane."

His hands, his skilled fingers, his mouth were everywhere. He knew unerringly where and how to touch her, where to brush with feather-light fingertips, where to tickle, where to pulse his fingers, where to massage, where to pinch and scratch. He knew where to kiss, where to lick, to suck, to nip with his teeth.

She had no idea how long it went on. And she had no idea how she knew where to touch him, how to caress him, when to change the nature of each caress. But she did know, as if she had always known, as if there were a deep well of femininity on which to draw for the beloved without the necessity of any lesson.

Perhaps it was that hers was not just any woman's body and his not just any man's. Some instinct told her that this was usually done in darkness and with eyes tightly shut, that usually all the pleasure was hugged tightly to oneself, the pleasure-giver shut out. Even in her inexperience she sensed that lovers did not always love with eyes open and focused on each other's whenever it was feasible to do so.

"Jane."

He spoke her name over and over, as she did his. She was his beloved, as he was hers.

The ache, the yearning, the need became more persistent and more localized. She needed him *there*.

Here.

Now.

His hand, between her thighs, worked light, deft magic in her most secret place and built a frenzy of desire.

"Jocelyn." She set her hand over his wrist. "Jocelyn." She did not know what she needed to say. But he understood.

"Slick and warm and ready," he said, his mouth coming to hers again. "I am going to mount, Jane. Lie still and stay relaxed. When I am deep, we will begin the final pleasure."

"Come," she said to him. "Oh, please come."

His whole weight bore her down into the mattress, holding her immobile while his thighs came between hers and pressed them wide and his hands slid beneath her. By sheer instinct she twined her legs about his. And then he raised his head and looked down into her face, his eyes heavy-lidded with passion. But not blind passion. He looked deep into her own eyes.

And then she felt him hard against the pulsing ache of her entrance. And pressing through it, pushing slowly but firmly, filling her, stretching her, alarming her. There was the sudden premonition of pain, the certainty that he could come no farther. He was too big.

"Jane." There was something like contrition in his eyes. "If I could only take the pain for you. But it always falls to the woman to do the suffering." He pushed hard, frowning as he gazed into her eyes.

There was an involuntary tensing, a fear of pain, and—and an awareness that the moment had passed, that he was deep. That he was inside her body. And inside her heart. Inside herself. She smiled at him.

"I am still alive."

He grinned and rubbed his nose across hers.

"That's my girl," he said. "I could not expect tears and vapors from Jane Ingleby, could I?"

She clenched her muscles about the unfamiliar thick hardness inside her and closed her eyes to revel in the wonder of it. But he had promised more. And now that the dreaded moment of her lost virginity was over, all the longing, all the aching came flooding back.

"What is the ride?" she asked, opening her eyes again. "Show me, Jocelyn."

"Lie still if you wish," he told her. "Ride with me if you wish. There are no rules here in our bed, Jane, and nothing in that foolish contract either that applies to this. Just you and me and what is mutually pleasurable."

He lowered his head then to rest in her hair on the pillow. He withdrew slowly to the brink of her—and pressed inward again.

There was no pain this time. Only wetness and heat and soon the rhythmic thrust and withdrawal of a riding motion to which her own body soon adjusted and matched. A carnal, energetic, blissful mating of bodies that was focused *there,* where her woman's body had opened to him and his man's body had penetrated deep. And yet the sensation went beyond that localized physical point. This was the mating of man and woman, of Jocelyn and Jane. It was a ride to union, to that wordless moment at which the I and the you of the two of them would lose focus and meaning. The moment in which the plurality of we would become singular.

Desire, yearning, need—all became pain and reaching, reaching...

"Now, Jane." He lifted his head again. His lips touched hers. His eyes looked into her own. "*Now.* Come. Come with me. Now, Jane."

Yes, now. All the way. Now. All the way to nothingness, to everything. To oblivion, to the ultimate knowing. To oneness.

Yes, now.

"Jocelyn!"

Someone cried his name. Someone murmured hers.

She felt a final, blissful gush of heat and knew that the mating was complete.

There was murmuring after that, and lightness and coolness as he moved off her, and more murmuring, and the comfort of his damp chest against hers as he drew her onto her side against him, his arm about her, and the coziness of bedcovers over her shoulders.

"Jane." She heard her name once more. "I am not sure you are still capable of saying you are alive."

She smiled sleepily. "Mmm," she said with a sigh. "Is this heaven, then?"

She was too tired to hear his chuckle. She slid into a delicious slumber.

JOCELYN DID NOT SLEEP. He was thoroughly sated but also uneasy. What the devil had he been babbling? He hoped she had not been listening.

Of course she had been listening.

What they had just done had been done together.

They had not been separate entities giving and taking a purely physical pleasure. They had been—damnation, he could not stop thinking the way he had been speaking. He had become her, and she had become him. Not that that was it either. They had both, together, become a new entity that was both of them and neither of them.

He was going to end up in Bedlam if he was not careful.

It had been something quite beyond his experience. And certainly beyond his intentions. He had wanted a mistress again. Someone to bed at will. Something really quite basic and simple. He had desired Jane. She had needed a home and employment.

It had all made perfect sense.

Until she had let her hair down. No, that had only fueled his desire.

Until she had called him by name. And said something else. What the devil was it she had said? He rubbed his cheek over the warm silk of her hair and hugged her a little closer.

Everyone should know what it is like to be called by name. By the name of the unique person one is at heart.

Yes, that was what had done it. Those few foolish words.

From birth he had been an earl with the rank of a marquess, heir to a dukedom. All his education, formal and informal, had been designed to train him to take over his father's title and his father's character when the time came. He had learned his lessons well. He had taken over both at the age of seventeen.

. . . the unique person one is at heart.

He had no heart. Dudleys generally did not.

And he had no unique character. He was what his father and everyone else had always expected him to be. For years now he had hugged about himself like a cloak his reputation as a dark, ruthless, dangerous man.

Jane's hair was fragrant with the smell of roses that always clung about her. It made him think of country gardens in the early summer. And filled him with a strange yearning. Strange, because he hated the country. He had been to Acton Park, his own estate, only twice since leaving there after a bitter quarrel with his father when he was sixteen—once for his father's funeral less than a year later, and once for his mother's four years after that.

He had intended never to go back until he was carried there one day for his own burial. But he could close his eyes now as he held Jane tightly and remember the rolling, wooded hills to the east of the house, where he and Ferdinand and Angeline had played robbers and highwaymen and Robin Hood and explorers. And where sometimes, when alone, he had played poet and mystic, breathing in the smells of elemental nature, sensing the vastness and the mystery of this nebulous thing called life, trying to formulate his thoughts and feelings and intuitions into words, trying to write them down as poetry. And occasionally liking what he had written.

He had torn up every word in a passion of anger and disgust before he left home.

He had not thought of home in a long age. Not of *home* at least, even though he kept a careful eye on the running of the estate. He had even forgotten that Acton Park ever had been home. But it had. Once upon a time. There had been a nurse who had given them discipline and affection in generous measures. She had been with them until he was eight or nine. He could even remember why she had been dismissed. He had had a toothache and she had been holding him on her lap in the nursery, cradling his sore face with her large, plump hand and crooning to him. His father had come into the nursery unannounced—a rare event.

She had been dismissed on the spot.

He, Jocelyn, had been sent down to his father's study to await the thrashing that had preceded the pulling of his tooth.

The Duke of Tresham, his father had reminded him with every painful swish of the cane across his backside, did not raise his sons to be girls. Especially not his heir.

"Jocelyn." Jane was awake again. She tipped back her head to look at him. Her beautiful face was flushed and heavy-lidded, her lips rosy and swollen from his kisses. She seemed cloaked and hooded in fragrant, shining gold. "Was I dreadfully gauche?"

She was one of the rare women, he thought, for whom passion and sexuality were instinctive. She had given both unstintingly this afternoon as if she did not know what it was to be hurt. Or belittled. Or rejected.

But before he could answer, she set one fingertip lightly to the bridge of his nose to cover the frown line there.

"What is it?" she asked. "What is the matter? I *was* gauche, was I not? How foolish to have imagined that because it was earth-shattering for me, it must have been so for you too."

Foolish Jane so to expose herself to ridicule and pain. He took hold of her wrist and lowered her hand.

"You are a woman, Jane," he told her. "An extraordinarily lovely woman. With everything in the right place. I was well pleasured."

Something happened to her eyes. Something closed up behind them. He recognized his sudden irritation for what it was. It was shame that his throat and chest were aching with unshed tears. And anger that she had brought him so low.

He should never have told her to call him by name.

"You are angry," she said.

"Because you talk of earth-shattering experiences and make me feel that I must have misled you," he said curtly. "You are employed as my mistress. I have just been putting you to work. I always take pains to make work congenial to my mistresses, but work is what it is. You have just been earning your living."

He wondered if she felt the lash of his words as stingingly as he. He hated himself, which was nothing new except that the passion of his self-hatred had long ago become muted to a disdain for the world in general.

"And giving good value for money," she said coolly. "I would remind you, your grace, that you employ me for the use of my body. You are not paying for my mind or my emotions. If I choose to find part of my employment earth-shattering, I am free to do so provided at the same time I open my body for your use."

For one moment he was in a towering rage. If she had dissolved into tears, as any normal woman would have done, he could have lashed himself harder by treating her with scorn. But typically of Jane, she was scolding him with cool dignity despite the fact that she was lying naked in bed with him.

He chuckled. "Our first quarrel, Jane," he said. "But not our last, I suspect. I must warn you, though, that I would not have your emotions engaged in this liaison. I would not have you hurt at its inevitable ending. What happens in this room is sex. Nothing else. And you were not gauche. It was as good a session of sexual intercourse as I have ever experienced. Better, in fact. There, are you reassured?"

"Yes," she said, her voice still cool. "Thank you."

He was aroused again—by his anger, by her cool refusal to be chastised, by her golden beauty, by the faint smell of roses. He did what he had to do to reassert his control over the afternoon's business. He turned her onto her back and mated with her again, but this time he concentrated all his powers on keeping the act carnal, even clinical. Man and mistress. Nothing more.

And then he slept, lulled by the sound of rain against the window.

"I THOUGHT PERHAPS YOU would wish to stay for dinner," she said.

"No."

They were dressed again and back downstairs in the sitting room. But he had not seated himself as she had. He had gone first to stand in front of the fireplace to stare down into the unlit coals. Then he had paced to the window to stare out at the rain.

He filled the sitting room with his presence and energy. Looking at his immaculate elegance, his proud, erect posture, his powerful shoulders and thighs, Jane found it hard to believe that just half an hour ago he had been lying naked with her in the bed upstairs. It was already hard to believe any of it had happened despite the physical evidence of soreness and tender breasts and unsteady legs.

"I have a dinner engagement," he said. "And there is an infernal ball to be attended tonight. No, I did not come to stay, Jane. Merely to consummate our liaison."

It was not going to be easy, being his mistress. She had never expected it to be. He was an arrogant man of uncertain temper. He was accustomed to having his own way, especially with women. But it was going to be especially hard to cope with his strange, sudden mood swings.

She would have felt hurt by his words, belittled by them, as she had when he had spoken in a similar manner in bed earlier. But she realized that the words were not spoken carelessly but quite deliberately. She was not sure why. To remind her that she was his mistress, not his lover?

Or to convince himself that she meant nothing to him beyond a female body to be used for his pleasure?

Despite all her ignorance and inexperience, she would swear that the first time he had entered her he had not been using her. She had not been a mere woman's body. It had not been just carnal pleasure.

He had made love to her. *With* her.

He was ashamed now of having shown such weakness.

"That is a relief, then," she said coolly. "There are several rearrangements to some of the other rooms that I hoped to start today, but I have already lost most of the afternoon."

He looked over his shoulder at her without turning and regarded her steadily.

"You will not be put in your place, Jane, will you?"

"If you mean," she replied, "that I will not allow you to make me feel like a whore, your grace, the answer is no, I will not. I will be here whenever you need me. It is our agreement. But my life will not revolve around your visits. I will not spend my days gazing wistfully from the window and my evenings listening expectantly for the door knocker."

She remembered guiltily how she had paced back and forth to the windows all morning. She would not do it again.

"Perhaps, Jane," he said softly, his eyes narrowing dangerously, "I should send a message in advance whenever I wish to bed you to ask if you can fit me into your busy schedule."

"You were not listening," she told him. "I signed a contract, and I mean to keep it and to see that you do too."

"What *do* you do with your time?" He turned from the window and looked about the empty room. "Do you go out?"

"Into the garden at the back," she said. "It is rather pretty, though it needs work. I have ideas and have started to implement them."

"Do you read?" He frowned. "Are there any books here?"

"No." He should know very well there were not.

"I will take you to Hookham's Library tomorrow morning," he said abruptly, "and buy you a subscription."

"No!" she said sharply. She relaxed again. "No, thank you, Jocelyn. I have plenty to do. It takes a great deal of time and energy to convert a brothel into a home, you know."

"That was unprovoked impudence, Jane, and unworthy of you." He looked very large and menacing, standing before her chair, his booted feet apart, his frown still in place. "I suppose if I told you I would come to take you walking in Hyde Park, you would be too busy for that too?"

"Yes." She nodded. "You do not need to put yourself out on my account."

He stared at her for a long time, his expression so unreadable that she could see nothing in him of the man who had loved her with unmistakable passion such a short time ago. He looked hard and humorless and untouchable.

Then he bowed to her abruptly, turned, and strode from the room.

She gazed in surprise at the door he had closed behind him and listened to the sounds of the front door being opened and then shut again. He was gone. Without a word of farewell or any hint of when he might come again.

This time she felt hurt.

Desolate.

15

THE ROOM NEXT TO THE SITTING ROOM HAD been furnished with a daybed, a plusher than plush carpet, an inordinately large number of mirrors, which multiplied one's reflection at least ten times, depending on where one stood, sat, or lay, and the inevitable cushions and knickknacks.

In Jane's estimation it had been used either as a private retreat by the duke's ex-mistresses who enjoyed their own company more than anyone else's, or as an alternative to the bedchamber. She suspected the latter.

It was a room she had ignored while the two main rooms were being refurbished. But now, at her leisure, she was making it into her own domain. The lavender sitting room was now elegant, but it was not *her*.

The mirrors and the daybed were banished—she did not care what happened to them. She sent Mr. Jacobs out on a special commission to purchase an escritoire and chair and paper, pens, and ink. Mrs. Jacobs in the meantime was sent to buy fine linen and an embroidery frame and an assortment of colored silken threads and accessories.

The den, as Jane thought of the room, would become her private writing and sewing room. She would indulge there her passion for embroidery.

She sat stitching in her den, a fire crackling cozily in the hearth, during the evening following the consummation of her liaison. She pictured Jocelyn at a grand dinner party and then moving on to a great squeeze of a ball, and tried not to feel envious. She had never had her come-out Season. There had been the year of mourning for her mother. Then her father had been too ill though he had urged her to accept Lady Webb's offer to sponsor her. But she had insisted on staying to nurse him. And then there had been his death and her year of mourning. And then the circumstances that had brought her under the new earl's guardianship.

Would Jocelyn dance tonight? she wondered. Would he waltz?

But she would not indulge in depressing thoughts.

For a moment her heart lifted when she heard a tap on the den door. Had he come back? But then she saw the butler peering around the door, his expression wary.

"I beg your pardon, ma'am," Mr. Jacobs said, "but there are two great boxes just now arrived. What would you like done with them?"

"Boxes?" Jane raised her eyebrows and set her embroidery aside.

"From his grace," the butler explained. "Almost too heavy to lift."

"I am not expecting anything." She got to her feet. "I had better come and see for myself. You are sure his grace sent them?"

"Oh, yes, ma'am," he assured her. "His own servants brought them and explained they were for you."

Jane was intrigued, especially when she saw two large crates in the middle of the kitchen floor.

"Please open one of them," she said, and Mrs. Jacobs fetched a knife and the butler cut the string that held one of the boxes closed.

Jane pushed back the lid, and all the servants—the butler, the housekeeper, the cook, the housemaid, and the footman—leaned forward with her to peer inside.

"Books!" The housemaid sounded vastly disappointed.

"Books!" Mrs. Jacobs sounded surprised. "Well. He never sent books here before. I wonder why he sent them now? Do you read, ma'am?"

"Of course she does," Mr. Jacobs said sharply. "Why else would she want a desk and paper and ink, I ask you?"

"Books!" Jane said almost in a reverential whisper, her hands clasped to her bosom.

She could see from the ones on top that they were from his own library. There were a Daniel Defoe, a Walter Scott, a Henry Fielding, and an Alexander Pope visible before she touched a single volume.

"It seems a funny sort of gift to me," the housemaid said, "begging your pardon, ma'am. P'raps there's something better in the other box."

Jane was biting hard on her upper lip. "It is a priceless gift," she said. "Mr. Jacobs, are the boxes too heavy for you and Phillip to carry into the den?"

"I can carry them on my own, ma'am," the young footman said eagerly. "Shall I unpack them for you too?"

"No." Jane smiled at him. "I shall do that myself, thank you. I want to see all the books one at a time. I want to see what he has chosen for me."

By happy chance there was a bookcase in the den though it had been covered with tasteless ornaments before Jane had cleared it off.

She spent two hours kneeling beside the boxes, drawing out one book at a time, arranging them pleasingly on the shelves, pondering over which she would read first.

And occasionally blinking her eyes fast and even swiping at them with her handkerchief when she thought of him going home this afternoon and hand-picking all these books for her. She knew he had not simply directed Mr. Quincy to do the choosing for him. The books included ones she had mentioned as her particular favorites.

If he had sent her some costly piece of jewelry, she would not have been one fraction as well pleased. Such a gift would not even dent his purse. But his books! His own books, not ones he had purchased for her. He had taken them from his own shelves, and among them were his personal favorites too.

Some of the loneliness had gone from the evening. And some of the bewilderment at his leaving so abruptly during the afternoon, without a word of farewell. He must have gone straight home and spent time in his library. Just for her sake.

She must not, Jane told herself firmly, allow herself to fall any deeper in love with him. And she must not—she absolutely *must not*—let herself *love* him.

He was a man humoring a new mistress. Nothing more.

But she read happily until midnight.

THE NEXT MORNING THE Duke of Tresham rode in Hyde Park at an hour when he often met some of his friends there on Rotten Row. The rain had stopped sometime during the night and the sun shone, making diamonds of the moisture on the grass. Fortunately for his need for distraction, he ran into Sir Conan Brougham and Viscount Kimble almost immediately.

"Tresh," the viscount said by way of greeting as Jocelyn joined the group, "we were expecting you at White's for dinner."

"I dined at home," Jocelyn told him. And he had. He had been unable to dine with Jane as his feelings had been rubbed raw and he had not wanted her to know it. And although he had dressed to go out, he had not done so. He was not quite sure why.

"Alone?" Brougham asked. "Without even the delectable Miss Ingleby for company?"

"She never did dine with me," Jocelyn said. "She was a servant, if you will remember."

"She could be my servant any time," Kimble said with a theatrical sigh.

"And you were not at Lady Halliday's," Brougham observed.

"I stayed home," Jocelyn said.

He was aware of his friends exchanging glances before they broke into merry laughter.

"Ho, Tresham," Brougham said, "who is she? Anyone we know?"

"A fellow cannot claim to have spent an evening at home alone without incurring suspicion?" Jocelyn spurred his horse into a canter. But his friends, who adjusted the speed of their mounts to match that of his, were not to be deterred. They rode one on either side of him.

"Someone new if she kept him from dinner at White's and the card room at Lady Halliday's, Cone," Kimble said.

"And someone who kept him awake all night if this

morning's ill temper is anything to judge by, Kimble," Brougham observed.

They were talking across Jocelyn, both grinning, just as if he were not there.

"Go to the devil," he told them.

But they both greeted his uncharitable invitation with renewed mirth.

It was a relief to see Angeline approaching on foot beyond the fence with Mrs. Stebbins, one of her particular friends. They were out for a morning stroll.

"Provoking man!" Angeline exclaimed as soon as Jocelyn rode within earshot. "Why are you always out when I call, Tresham? I made a particular point of going to Dudley House yesterday afternoon as Heyward informed me you had left White's before luncheon. I was quite sure you must have gone home."

Jocelyn fingered the ribbon of his quizzing glass. "Were you?" he said. "It would be redundant to inform you that you were wrong. To what, may I ask, did I owe the show of sisterly affection? Good morning, Mrs. Stebbins." He touched the brim of his hat with his whip and inclined his head.

"Everyone is talking about it," Angeline said while her friend made his grace a deep curtsy. "I have heard it three times in the past two days, not to mention Ferdie's speaking of it when I saw him yesterday. So I daresay you have heard it too. But I must have your assurance that you will do nothing foolish, Tresham, or my nerves will be shattered. And I must have your promise that you will defend the family honor at whatever cost to yourself."

"I trust," Jocelyn said, "you intend sooner or later to enlighten me on the topic of this fascinating conversation, Angeline. Might I suggest sooner as Cavalier is still frisky?"

"It *was* being said," she explained, "that the Forbes brothers fled town in fear of retaliation from you for what they tried to do to Ferdie."

"As well they might," he commented. "They have some modicum of wisdom among the three of them if that was indeed the reason for their disappearance."

"But now," she said, "it is known for absolute certain—is it not, Maria?" She turned to Mrs. Stebbins for confirmation. "Mr. Hammond mentioned it at Mrs. Bury-Haugh's two days ago and everyone knows that his wife is second cousin to Mrs. Wesley Forbes. So it must be true."

"Incontrovertibly, I would say," Jocelyn agreed dryly, using his quizzing glass to peruse the other walkers beyond the fence and the other riders within.

"They are not satisfied," Angeline announced. "Can you imagine the gall of them, Tresham? When Ferdie might have been killed? They are not satisfied because you took the curricle and came to no worse harm than to ruin a pair of leather gloves. *They* are still vowing vengeance on *you*! When everyone knows that *you* are now the one with the grievance. They have gone for reinforcements and are expected back at any moment."

Jocelyn turned about with a flourish to look at the grassy expanse behind him. "But not quite yet, Angeline," he said. "The reinforcements to which you refer are presumably the Reverend Josiah Forbes and Captain Samuel Forbes?"

"It will be five against one," she declared dramatically. "Or five against two if one counts Ferdie as he insists one must. It would be five against three if Heyward would not insist in his odious manner that he will not involve himself in childish capers. I will wheedle a gun out of him and start practicing my marksmanship again. I am a Dudley, after all."

"I beg you to desist," Jocelyn said firmly. "None of us would know which side was in more danger from you if you were to prove as adept at shooting now as you were as a girl." He raised his glass again and looked her over from head to ankles. "That is a surprisingly elegant bonnet you are wearing," he said. "But the poppy red flowers are a lamentably poor match for the pink of your walking dress."

"Lord Pym met us ten minutes ago," she said with a toss of her head, "and observed, foolish man, that I look like a particularly delectable meadow in which he could only wish he were strolling alone. Did he not, Maria?"

"Indeed?" Jocelyn's manner became instantly frosty. "I trust, Angeline, you reminded Lord Pym that you are the sister of the Duke of Tresham?"

"I sighed soulfully and then laughed at him," she said. "It was harmless gallantry, Tresham. Do you believe I would allow any man to take liberties with me? I shall tell Heyward about it and he will toss his glance at the ceiling and then tell me . . . well." She blushed and laughed again, nodded to Kimble and Brougham, took Maria Stebbins's arm, and resumed her promenade.

"London needs some new scandal," Jocelyn observed as he rode onward with his friends. "It seems that no one has anything else to talk about these days except those cowardly scoundrels who claim kinship with Lady Oliver."

"They are doubtless shaking in their boots, by Jove," Viscount Kimble said, "since Joseph Forbes was rash enough to claim responsibility on behalf of all of them for your scraped palms. But they are probably hatching more mischief too—nothing as direct as a challenge, of course."

"They may not have a choice—except loss of face and the last vestiges of their honor," Jocelyn said. "But enough on the subject. I am sick to death of it. Let us enjoy the fresh air and sunshine."

"To blow away the cobwebs?" Brougham asked. He looked beyond Jocelyn to address their other friend again. "Did you notice, Kimble, that according to Lady Heyward, Tresham was from home yesterday afternoon? Was he with you?"

"He was not with me, Cone," the viscount replied, all seriousness. "Was he with you?"

"I did not set eyes on him between yesterday morning and this," Brougham said. "She must be *very* new and *very* frisky."

"The devil!" Kimble drew his horse to such an abrupt halt and threw back his head to laugh with such loud merriment that he was almost unseated and had to exercise considerable skill to bring his mount under control again. "Right under our noses, Cone," he said when he was able. "The answer, I mean."

Conan Brougham's and Jocelyn's horses were prancing a little distance away.

"The delectable Miss Ingleby!" Kimble announced. "You rogue, Tresh. You lied. You do have her in your keeping. And she kept you from your friends and your obligations and your bed—your own bed, that is—most of yesterday and all night. She must have lived up to all the considerable promise she showed."

"It has been staring us in the face, has it not?"

Brougham agreed with a grin. "You actually danced—*waltzed*—with her, Tresham. And could not take your eyes off her. But why the secrecy, old chap?"

"I do believe," Kimble said with an exaggerated sigh, "I am going to go into mourning. I have been considering hiring a Bow Street Runner to search for her."

"You two," Jocelyn said with his customary hauteur, "may go to the devil with my blessing. Now if you will excuse me, breakfast awaits at Dudley House."

At first silence and then their laughter followed him as he rode off unhastily in the direction of home.

It was not like that, he kept thinking foolishly. It was not *like* that.

But if it was not like that—a man with a new mistress enjoying the novelty of a new female body with which to pleasure himself—then what *was* it like?

He hated the thought of even his closest friends snickering over Jane.

SHE MUST HAVE HEARD him coming. She was standing in the doorway of the sitting room again, wearing primrose yellow today—another new dress of classically simple design. She had perfect taste in clothing, it seemed, once she had been forced out of the cheap gray monstrosities.

He handed his hat and gloves to the butler and moved toward her. She smiled at him with dazzling warmth and held out both hands, completely throwing him off stride. He had been feeling out of charity with the world and even with her and had been irritated with himself for being unable *not* to come to her again this afternoon.

"Thank you," she said, and squeezed his hands when

he gave them to her. "How can I ever thank you sufficiently?"

"For the books?" He frowned. He had forgotten about the books. He had intended to take her straight up to bed today, to have his brisk pleasure of her before leaving to get on with the rest of his day, undistracted by thoughts of her. He had intended to get this relationship properly on track. At the same time he had hated the thought of Kimble's or Brougham's ribald remarks, which he was sure to hear this evening, and his own knowledge that there was truth in them.

"A mere nothing," he said curtly. He freed his hands and motioned for her to precede him into the sitting room.

"To you, perhaps," she said. "But to me, everything. You cannot know how I have missed reading since I came here."

"Then why the devil," he asked her irritably, closing the door and looking about the room, "did you not let me take you to the library?"

And why the deuce was she so ashamed to be seen? His other mistresses had never been more happy than when he escorted them somewhere where they would be seen in his company.

She was probably the daughter of a damned clergyman. But he would be double damned before he would start feeling guilt at having had her virtue.

She would not answer his question, of course. She smiled again, tipping her head to one side.

"You are in a black mood this afternoon," she observed. "But I am not to be cowed by it. Has something happened that you would like to talk about?"

He almost laughed.

"The Forbes brothers have slunk off out of town to bring on reinforcements," he said. "They are afraid to confront me with the odds of three against one. They are planning to increase them to five against one. They will discover that the odds are still in my favor. I derive a certain relish out of dealing with bullies and cowards."

She sighed. "Men and their pride," she said. "I suppose you will still be brawling when you are eighty, if you should live so long. Will you sit down? Shall I order tea? Or do you wish to go straight upstairs?"

Suddenly, strangely, alarmingly, he did not want her. Not in bed. Not now. It just seemed too—too what? Sordid? He almost laughed again.

"Where are the books?" he asked. "In the bedchamber? The attic?"

"In the next room," she said. "I have converted it for my own use when you are not here. I think of it as my den."

He hated the sitting room. Even though it was now elegant and tasteful, it still reminded him of a waiting room, an impersonal space in which certain civilities were observed before the inevitable adjournment to the bedchamber. And there were no personal touches here that made it Jane's sitting room.

"Take me there," he commanded.

He might have guessed that Jane would not simply turn and meekly lead the way.

"It is my room," she said. "This is where I entertain you—and occasionally, perhaps, in the dining room. The bedchamber is where I grant you your contractual rights. The rest of the house I consider my personal domain."

Jocelyn pursed his lips, undecided whether to bark at her for the satisfaction of seeing her jump with alarm or to throw back his head and laugh.

Contractual rights, by thunder!

"Miss Ingleby." He made her his most elegant bow. "Would you grant me the privilege of seeing your den?"

She hesitated, bit her lower lip, and then inclined her head.

"Very well," she said, and turned to leave the room ahead of him.

The room was Jane. He felt that as soon as he stepped through the door. He felt as if for the first time he was entering her world. A world that was elegant and genteel on one hand, industrious and cozy on the other.

The fawn-colored carpet and draperies had always made the room look dreary, and all the attempts of her predecessors to brighten the room with cushions and shawls and garish gewgaws had only emphasized the gloom. The mirrors, added by Effie, had merely multiplied the gloom. He had made it a habit never to set foot in here.

Now the fawn colors, which Jane had made no attempt to mask, made the room seem restful. The daybed was gone. So, not surprisingly, were all the mirrors. Some graceful chairs had been added as had a desk and chair, the former strewn sufficiently with papers to indicate that it was not for display purposes only. The bookcase was filled with his books though one lay open on the small table next to a fireside chair. In front of the chair at the other side of the hearth was an embroidery frame over which was stretched a piece of linen. About it were strewn silken threads and scissors and needles.

"May I sit down?" he asked.

She indicated the chair by the book.

"If you wish," she said, "you may deduct the cost of the desk and chair from my salary since they were purchased for my private use."

"I seem to recall," he said, "that I gave you *carte blanche* for the house renovations, Jane. Do stop saying ridiculous things and sit down. I am too much the gentleman, you see, to seat myself before you do."

She felt uncomfortable, he could see. She perched on the edge of a chair some distance away.

"Jane," he said impatiently, "sit at your embroidery frame. Let me see you work. I suppose it is another skill you learned at the orphanage?"

"Yes," she said, moving her place and picking up her needle.

He watched her in silence for a while. She was the picture of beauty and grace. A lady born and bred. Fallen indeed on hard times—forced to come to London to search for employment, forced to take work as a milliner's assistant, forced to become his nurse, forced to become a mistress. No, not forced. He would not take that guilt on himself. He had offered her a magnificent alternative. Raymore would have made her a star.

"This has always been my vision of domestic bliss," he said after a while, surprising himself with the words, which had been spoken without forethought.

She looked up briefly from her work.

"A woman beside the fire stitching," he said. "A man at the other side. Peace and calm about them and all well with the world."

She lowered her head to her work again. "It was something you never knew in your boyhood home?" she asked.

He laughed shortly. "I daresay my mother did not know one end of a needle from the other," he said, "and no one ever told either her or my father that it is possible occasionally to sit around the hearth with one's family."

No one had told him those things either. Where were these ideas coming from?

"Poor little boy," she said quietly.

He got abruptly to his feet and crossed to the bookcase.

"Have you read *Mansfield Park*?" he asked her a minute or so later.

"No." She looked up briefly again. "But I have read *Sense and Sensibility* by the same author and enjoyed it immensely."

He drew the volume from the shelf and resumed his seat.

"I shall read to you while you work," he said.

He could never remember reading aloud, except at his lessons as a boy. He could not remember being read to either until Jane had done it when he was incapacitated. He had found the experience unexpectedly soothing though he had never listened attentively. He opened the book and began reading.

" 'About thirty years ago, Miss Maria Ward, of Huntingdon, with only seven thousand pounds, had the good luck to captivate Sir Thomas Bertram, of Mansfield Park. . . .' "

He read two chapters before stopping and lowering the book to his lap. They sat in silence for a while after that. In a silence that seemed to him thoroughly comfortable. He was sprawled in his chair, he realized. He could nod off to sleep with the greatest ease. He felt . . . How *did* he feel? Contented? Certainly. Happy? Happiness was something he had little or no acquaintance with and set no store by.

He felt shut off from the world. Shut off from his usual self. With Jane. Who was certainly shut off from her world and usual self, whatever they might be. Could this be perpetuated? he wondered. Indefinitely? Forever?

Or could it at least become an occasional retreat, this room that was so much Jane and in which he felt comfortable, restful, contented—all alien to his normal way of life?

He should put an end to these foolish, unrealistic, and uncharacteristic dreams without further ado, he thought. He should take his leave—or take her to bed.

"What is it you are working on?" he asked her instead.

She smiled without looking up. "A tablecloth," she said. "For the dining room table. I had to find *something* to make. Embroidery has always been a passion with me."

He watched her for a while longer from beneath lazy eyelids. The frame was tilted away from him so that he could not see the pattern. But the silks were autumnal colors, all tastefully complementary.

"Will your hackles rise," he asked, "if I come and look?"

"No indeed." She looked surprised. "But you are under no obligation to be polite, you know. You can have no interest in embroidery."

He did not deign to answer. He hauled himself out of the deep, comfortable chair, setting his closed book on top of her open one as he did so.

She was working a scene of autumn woods across one corner of the cloth.

"Where is the pattern from which you work?" he asked her. He wanted to be able to see the whole picture.

"In my head," she told him.

"Ah." He understood then why it was a passion with her. It was not just that she was skilled with her needle. "It is an art with you, then, Jane. You have a fine eye for color and design."

"Strangely," she said, "I have never been able to capture my visions on paper or canvas. But through my needle pictures flow easily from my mind to the fabric."

"I was never any good at portraying scenes," he said. "I always felt that nature did so much better than I could possibly do. Human faces are a different matter. There is so much life and character to capture."

He could have bitten his tongue as soon as the words were out. He straightened up in some embarrassment.

"You paint portraits?" She looked up at him, bright interest in her eyes. "I have always thought that must be the most difficult form of art."

"I dabble," he said stiffly, wandering to the window and gazing out at the small garden, which was looking remarkably well tended, he noticed. Had those roses always been there? "Past tense. I dabbled."

"I suppose," she said quietly, "it was not a manly pursuit."

His father's language had been far more graphically scathing.

"I would like to paint you," he heard himself saying. "There is a great deal in your face even apart from exquisite beauty. It would be an enormous challenge."

There was silence behind him.

"Upstairs we will satisfy our sexual passions," he said. "In here we could indulge all the others, Jane, if you wished it. Away from the prying eyes and sneering lips of the world. This is what you have created in this room, is it not? A den, as you call it, a haven, where you can be yourself, where all the other facts of your life, including being my mistress, can be set aside and you can be—simply Jane."

He turned his head. She was looking steadily at him, her needle suspended above her work.

"Yes," she said.

"And I am the last person with whom you would wish to share the room." He smiled ruefully at her. "I will not insist. In future you will entertain me in the sitting room whenever we are not in the bedchamber."

"No." She let a few moments pass before elaborating. "No, I will no longer think of this room as mine but as ours. A place in which our contract and our relative stations in life have no application. A place where you may paint and read, where I may embroider and write, a place where there can be a woman at one side of the hearth and a man at the other. A place of quiet and peace, where all is well with the world. You are invited to make yourself at home here whenever you wish, Jocelyn."

He gazed at her over his shoulder for a long time without saying anything. What the devil was happening? There could be only one reason, one passion to bring him to this house. He did not want any other reason. He might become dependent upon it—upon her. And yet his heart ached and yearned with hope.

For what?

"Would you like tea?" She was threading her needle

into the linen and getting to her feet. "Shall I ring for the tray?"

"Yes." He clasped his hands at his back. "Yes, please."

He watched her do so.

"There is plenty of spare room in here," he said. "I am going to have a pianoforte brought here. May I?" He could scarcely believe he was actually asking permission.

"Of course." She looked gravely at him. "It is *our* room, Jocelyn. Yours as well as mine."

He thought for one moment that it might be happiness that rushed to engulf him. But he soon recognized it as an equally unfamiliar emotion.

Terror.

16

JANE WENT TO BED EARLY, BUT SHE COULD NOT sleep. She stopped trying after half an hour. She got out of bed, lit a candle, pulled a warm dressing gown over her linen nightgown, slipped her feet into her slippers, and went back downstairs to her den. Their den. Their haven, he had called it.

Mr. Jacobs was still up. She asked him to build up the fire again. The young footman brought the coals and asked if there was anything else he could fetch for her.

"No, thank you, Phillip," she said. "That will be all. I can find my own way to bed when I am tired."

"Yes, ma'am," he said. "Don't forget to put the guard about the fire, then, when you leave, ma'am."

"I won't." She smiled. "Thank you for reminding me. Good night."

"Good night, ma'am," he replied.

She would read until she was too tired to keep her eyes open, she decided. She seated herself beside the fire, in the chair Jocelyn had occupied during the afternoon, and picked up a book. Not the one from which he had read. She left that where it was. Perhaps he would wish to continue with chapter three next time he came. She opened her book to the page at which she had left off reading the night before and set it on her lap.

She gazed into the fire.

She should not have allowed him in here. She knew

that she would no longer think of this room as hers. It was theirs. She could *feel* his presence here. She could see him as he had been earlier, sprawled comfortably but not inelegantly in this chair. She could hear his voice reading from *Mansfield Park* as if he were as lost in the story as she had been. And she could see him standing at the window. . . .

It was unfair. She could have coped with her new life if their relationship had proceeded, as she had expected, along purely sexual lines. She knew enough to realize that sex was not love, especially sex between a rakish duke and his mistress. She did not know what *this* was.

He had spent longer than two hours in this room with her this afternoon—with his mistress—without once touching her. He had not taken her to bed. After tea, during which they had discussed the war and political reform—she was a pacifist, he was not; she was unreservedly in favor of reform, he was far more cautiously so—he had got to his feet quite abruptly, made her a bow, bade her a good afternoon, and gone on his way.

He had left her feeling empty inside. Though that could not be strictly true or she would not also have felt all churned up—her body, her mind, her emotions.

For almost the whole time they had been here together in the den, he had not been the Duke of Tresham. He had been Jocelyn. But Jocelyn with far fewer reservations than she was accustomed to. Jocelyn without any mask. A person in need of being himself as he had never been before. A man in need of friendship and acceptance and—ah, yes.

Jane sighed aloud.

A man in need of love.

But she doubted he would ever accept that ultimate gift even if he acknowledged the need to himself.

She doubted even more that he was capable of returning the gift.

And who was she to offer? A fugitive. A murderess—no, not that. She was even beginning to believe it herself. She did not think the blow she had given Sidney would have killed him in itself.

She shuddered at the memories.

And then she set her head back against the chair and listened to the sounds of Mr. Jacobs or Phillip at the front door, locking up for the night. A moment later there was a tap on her door.

"Come in," she called. It must be midnight or later. The servants should be in bed.

He looked powerful and satanic, covered from neck to ankles in a long black opera cloak. He stood in the doorway, one hand still on the knob, while her stomach performed a complete somersault and she knew that indeed the afternoon had been disastrous to her.

"Still up?" he asked. "I saw light beneath the door."

"Do you have your own key?" she asked him.

"Of course," he replied. "This is my house."

She got to her feet and moved toward him. She had simply not expected him.

And then a strange thing happened. He took his hand from the doorknob as she approached and spread his arms to the sides, revealing the white silk lining of the cloak and the elegant black and white evening clothes he wore beneath. But Jane did not really notice the splendor of his appearance. She kept walking and was soon enveloped in the folds of his cloak while she lifted her face and he lowered his own both at the same time.

It was a long and deep and fierce embrace. But the strange thing was that it was not sexual—not entirely so anyway. Jane had little experience with embraces, but she knew instinctively that he was not just a man kissing his mistress prior to taking her to bed. He was Jocelyn. And he was kissing her, Jane.

By the time the embrace ended he was the Duke of Tresham again.

"I will be putting you to work tonight, Jane," he said.

"Of course." She stood back and smiled.

And then gasped with alarm when he caught her hard by the wrist and gazed down at her with hard, cold eyes.

"No!" he said fiercely. "You will not smile at me in that way, Jane, like a jaded coquette hiding her weary cynicism behind a cool smile of invitation. There is no *of course* about it. If you do not want me, then tell me to go to hell and I will go."

She jerked her wrist out of his grasp. "What do you expect when you speak of putting me to work?" she asked angrily. "Does a woman go to *work* for a man in bed when she wants him? When you call it work you make a whore of me."

"You are the one," he reminded her, his eyes as cold as steel, "who speaks of contractual obligations and rights. What does that make of me? It makes me someone who has purchased access to your body. Someone who has bought the services of a whore. It makes of you a woman who is working when she lies on her back for me. Don't use righteous anger on me, Jane, and expect me meekly to bow my head. You may go to the devil for all I care."

"And you may…" But she forced herself to stop and

to draw a steadying breath. Her heart was pounding like a hammer. "We are quarreling again. Was it my fault this time? I am sorry if it was."

"It is that infernal contract that is to blame," he grumbled.

"Which is my fault." She smiled briefly at him. "I really am pleased to see you, Jocelyn."

The anger and the coldness faded from his face. "Are you, Jane?"

She nodded. "And I really do want you."

"Do you?" He gazed broodingly at her, his eyes very black.

Could this be the Duke of Tresham? Unsure of himself? Uncertain of his welcome?

"I am saying it inside the room where we agreed our contract would bear no sway," she said, "so it has to be the truth. Come to bed with me."

"I have come from the theater," he explained. "I was invited back to Kimble's for supper with his party and said I would walk there rather than crowd a carriage. But I found my legs carrying me here instead. How do you interpret that, Jane?"

"I daresay," she said, "you were in need of a sharp quarrel with someone who would not back down from you."

"But you were the first to apologize," he reminded her.

"Because I was wrong," she told him. "I do not insist upon winning an argument at any cost, you see. Not like some I know."

He grinned wolfishly at her. "Which means, I suppose," he said, "that as usual you have had the last word,

Jane. Come, then. Since it is what I came for and since you have invited me, let us go to bed."

Physical desire made her breathless again as she stepped past him and preceded him up the stairs. He did not come immediately after her, she noticed. He had paused to set the guard in front of the dying fire.

Which was probably, she guessed with an inward smile, one of the most domesticated things he had ever done.

KIMBLE WOULD TEASE HIM mercilessly in the morning. Jocelyn did not care. When had he ever cared what anyone—even his closest friends—thought or said about him? And the teasing would at least be good-natured.

The truth was he had had to come back tonight. He had been more disturbed by the strange events of the afternoon than he cared to admit. He had had to come back just to get some normalcy back into his relationship with his mistress. To put her to work.

It had been a mistake to use those exact words to her, of course. But he was not accustomed to tiptoeing his way about other people's sensibilities.

He undressed, doused the candles, and climbed into bed with her. He had instructed her to keep on her prim and pretty nightgown. There was something surprisingly erotic about grasping its hem and lifting it up her legs and over her hips to her waist. He did not want foreplay tonight. He wanted to do what he had come to do before somehow the whole scene became unfamiliar again. He slid his hand between her thighs and felt her. She was ready enough. He turned onto her with his full weight, spread her legs wide with his knees, slid his hands beneath her, and entered.

She was soft, warm, relaxed heat. He began to work her with firm, vigorous strokes. He tried to think of her simply as a woman. He tried to think of his need as simply sexual.

He failed miserably on both counts.

He rarely kissed in bed. It was unnecessary, and it was too personal for his taste. He kissed her.

"Jane," he murmured into her mouth, "tell me you wanted me to come back, that you have thought of nothing but me since this afternoon."

"Why?" she whispered. "So that you can warn me again not to become dependent upon you? I am not sorry you came. I am glad. This feels good."

"Damn you," he said. "Damn you."

She was silent while he worked. But just as he felt the climax approach and was about to deepen and quicken his rhythm, he felt her arms close about his waist and her feet slide up the bed and her thighs hug his hips while she tilted her pelvis to allow him deeper access.

"Jocelyn," she whispered, "don't be afraid. Please don't be afraid."

He was driving toward release and did not hear the words consciously. But after he had finished, when he lay exhausted beside her, he heard their echo in his mind and thought he must have imagined them.

"Come here," he said, reaching out a hand to touch her.

She curled up against him, and he lowered her nightgown, drew up the bedclothes, wrapped his arms about her, pillowed his cheek against the top of her head, and fell asleep.

He had frequently spent nights at the house and staggered home at dawn to sleep. He had never *slept* a night at the house. When he had come this time, he had intended a few hours of vigorous sport just to remind both Jane and himself of the basic nature of their liaison.

He awoke when daylight was pouring into the room. Jane, tousled and flushed and delicious, was still asleep in his arms.

He drew free of her and swung himself out of bed, waking her in the process. She smiled sleepily at him.

"My apologies," he said stiffly as he pulled on his evening clothes. "I daresay according to that infernal contract I have no right intruding on your privacy when I am not actually asserting my rights. I will be gone in a moment."

"Jocelyn," she said with soft reproach, and then she had the unmitigated gall to laugh.

With glee.

At him.

"I amuse you?" He scowled at her.

"I do believe," she said, "you are *embarrassed* that you slept instead of spending the night demonstrating your renowned prowess as a lover. You seem always to have to prove your superior manhood."

The fact that she was perfectly right did not improve his mood.

"I am delighted to have amused you at least," he said, throwing his cloak about him with a vicious swing of his arm and buttoning it at his throat. "I shall do myself the honor of calling upon you some other time when I have need of you. Good morning."

"Jocelyn," she said softly again when he already had the door of the bedchamber open. He looked back at her with haughtily raised eyebrows. "It was a wonderful night. You are lovely to sleep with."

He did not wait to discover if she mocked him or not. He stepped through the door and closed it none too quietly behind him.

Devil take it, he thought, noticing the clock in the hallway as he descended the stairs and noticing too with a grimace that Jacobs was waiting there to let him out, it was seven o' clock. He had been here for seven hours. He had been in her bed for seven hours, and he had had intercourse with her once. *Once!*

He bade the butler a curt good morning and strode off down the street, noticing with some satisfaction that the twinge of stiffness in his right leg was becoming less pronounced each day.

You are lovely to sleep with.

Jocelyn chuckled despite himself. She was right, goddammit. It had been a lovely night, and he felt more refreshed by his sleep than he had in a long while.

He would go home to bathe and change, he decided, and then go shopping—for a small pianoforte and for sketching and painting supplies. Perhaps the best thing to do about this whole extraordinary situation was to go along with it, let it happen, let it proceed in its own way and at its own pace to its inevitable conclusion. Sooner or later he would grow weary of Jane Ingleby. He had of every woman he had ever known or bedded. He would of her too—perhaps in a month, perhaps in two, perhaps in a year.

In the meantime, why not just enjoy the novel feeling of being—ah, yes, the fateful words that hovered in the background of his thoughts and threatened to verbalize themselves.

Why not?

Why not enjoy the feeling of being in love?

Why not revel in the ultimate foolishness for once in his life?

WORKING IN THE GARDEN later that same morning, enjoying the exercise, loving the brightness and heat of the sun on her back, Jane came to a decision.

She was in love with him, of course. Worse than that, she thought she was also growing to *love* him. There was no point in trying to deny her feelings and no use whatsoever in trying to fight them.

She loved him.

But it would not do, of course. She was not foolish enough to imagine that he would ever love her in return, though she knew that he was in the grip of a serious obsession with her. Besides, even if he ever did love her, there could be no happily-ever-after to expect. She was his mistress. And she was who she was.

But she could not live forever as a fugitive. She should never have given in to the cowardly impulse that had sent her scurrying into hiding in the first place. It had been so unlike her normal self. She was going to have to come out of hiding and do what she ought to have done as soon as she discovered that Lady Webb was not in London to help her.

She was going to find the Earl of Durbury if he was still in town. If he was not, she was going to find out where the Bow Street Runners had their headquarters and go there. She was going to write to Charles. She was going to tell her story to anyone who would listen. She was going to embrace her fate. Perhaps she would be arrested and tried and convicted of murder. Perhaps that would mean a hanging or at the very least transportation or lifelong imprisonment. But she would not give in meekly. She would fight like the very devil to the last moment—but not by running away and hiding.

She was going to come out into the open at last and *fight.*

But not just yet. That was the agreement she made with herself as she pulled weeds from about the rosebushes and turned the soil until it was a richer brown. A definite time limit must be set so that she would not continue to procrastinate week after week, month after month. She was going to give herself one month, one calendar month, starting today. One month to be Jocelyn's mistress, his love, though he would not be aware of the latter, of course. One month to spend with him as a person, as a friend in the den, if he ever returned there, as a lover in the bed upstairs.

One month.

And then she was going to give herself up. Without telling him. There might be scandal for him, of course, when it became known that he had harbored her at Dudley House for three weeks, or if anyone knew that she had been his mistress here. But she would not worry about that. His life had been one scandal after another. He appeared to thrive on them. She thought he would probably be rather amused by this particular one.

One month.

Jane leaned back on her heels to inspect her work, but Phillip was approaching from the direction of the house.

"Mr. Jacobs sent me, ma'am," he said, "to tell you that a new pianoforte just arrived and an easel and other parcels too. He wants to know where you want them put."

Jane got to her feet, her heart soaring, and followed him back to the house.

One glorious month, in which she would not even try to guard her feelings.

One month of love.

THERE FOLLOWED A WEEK during which Jocelyn almost totally ignored his family, the Olivers, the Forbeses, and all topics of gossip with which the *ton* continued to entertain itself. A week during which he rode in the park most mornings and spent an hour or two afterward breakfasting at White's and reading the papers and conversing with his friends, but during which he attended few social functions.

Kimble and Brougham were highly diverted, of course, and very inclined to ribaldry. Until, that was, the three of them were walking along a fortunately deserted street on the way from White's one morning and Kimble opened his mouth.

"All I can say, Tresh," he said, pretending to sound bored, "is that when the delectable Miss Ingleby has finally exhausted *you*, *you* may pass her on to me, if *you* please, and I will see if I can exhaust *her*. I daresay I know a trick or two she will not have learned from you. And if—"

His monologue was rudely interrupted when a fist collided with the left side of his jaw and with a look of blank astonishment he crashed to the pavement. Jocelyn looked with scarcely less astonishment at his own still-clenched fist.

"Oh, I say!" Conan Brougham protested.

Jocelyn spoke curtly to his friend, who was gingerly fingering his jaw. "Do you want satisfaction?"

"Oh, I say," Brougham said again. "I cannot be second to *both* of you."

"You should have told me, old chap," Kimble said ruefully, shaking his head to clear it before scrambling to his feet and brushing at his clothes, "and I would not have flapped my jaws. By Jove, you are in love with the wench. In which case the punch was understandable. But you might have been more sporting and warned me, Tresh. It is not the most comfortable of experiences to walk into one of your fists. No, of course I am not about to slap a glove in your face, so you need not look so damned grim. I meant no disrespect to the lady's honor."

"And I did not mean to endanger our friendship." Jocelyn extended his right hand, which his friend took rather warily. "It is all very well for you and Conan to tease, Kimble. I would do no less to you. But no one else is to be drawn into this. I will not have Jane publicly dishonored."

"I say!" Brougham sounded suddenly indignant. "You do not believe we have been spreading the word, Tresham? The very idea! I did not believe I would live to see the day when you would be in love, though." He laughed suddenly.

"Love be damned!" Jocelyn said gruffly.

But apart from that one incident, almost the whole of his attention for the week was taken up by the house where Jane lived and where he spent most of his time—in two separate but strangely complementary capacities. He spent his afternoons and several of his evenings in their den with her, almost never touching her. He spent his nights in the bedchamber with her, making love to her and sleeping with her.

It was a magical week.

A week to remember.

A week of such intense delight that it could not possibly last. It did not, of course.

But before it ended, there was that week....

17

ONCE OR TWICE THEY STROLLED IN THE GARDEN, and Jane showed him what she had already done with it and explained what she still intended to do. But most of the time they spent indoors. It was a misty, wet week anyway.

Jane had simply abandoned herself to sheer pleasure. She spent hours stitching by the fire, necessary because of the damp chill, the autumn woods spreading in glorious profusion across one corner of the linen cloth, then another. Sometimes he read to her—they had reached almost the halfway point of *Mansfield Park*. More often in the evenings he played the pianoforte. The music was almost all his own composition. Sometimes it was halting, uncertain at the start, as if he did not know where the music came from or where it was going. But she came to recognize the point at which it went beyond an activity of the mind and hands and became one simply of the heart and soul. Then the music flowed.

Sometimes she stood behind him or sat beside him and sang—mostly folk songs and ballads with which they were both acquainted. Even, surprisingly, a few hymns, which he sang with her in a good baritone voice.

"We were paraded to church every Sunday," he told her, "to cushion our superior backsides on the plush family pew—though never, at our peril, to squirm on it—while lesser mortals sat on hard wood and gawked in awe. And you, Jane? Were you orphans marched in a neat crocodile, two by two, to sit on backless benches and thank God for the many blessings He had showered on you?" His hands played a flourishing arpeggio.

"I always enjoyed church," she said quietly. "And there are always blessings for which to be thankful."

He laughed softly.

Most often during the afternoons he painted. He did not want after all, he decided, to paint just her face. He wanted to paint *her*, as she was. Jane had looked sharply at him when he said that, and he had raised his eyebrows.

"You think I am going to drape you in a lascivious pose on the floor, Jane, dressed only in your hair?" he asked. "I would put you to better use than to paint you if I did that, believe me. As I will show you tonight. Yes, definitely. Tonight we will have candles and nakedness and hair, and I will show you how to pose for me like the Siren you could be if you set your mind to it. I will paint you at your embroidery. That is when you are most yourself." He gazed narrow-eyed at her. "Quiet, industrious, elegant, engaged in creating a work of art."

And so he painted as she stitched, both of them silent. He always stripped off his coat and waistcoat before he began and donned a large, loose shirt over his good one. As the days passed it became smudged and streaked with paint.

He would not let her see the painting until it was finished.

"I let you see my embroidery," she reminded him.

"I asked and you said yes," he replied. "You asked and I said no."

To which logic there was no further argument.

She worked at her embroidery, but she watched him

too. Covertly, of course. If she looked too directly or stopped work too long, he frowned and looked distracted and grumbled at her. It was hard sometimes to realize that this man who shared her most intimate space with such mutual ease was the same man who had once told her he would make her wonder if starvation would not be better than working for him. The infamous, heartless Duke of Tresham.

He had the soul of an artist. Music had been trapped within him most of his life. She had not yet seen any product of his brush, but she recognized the total absorption in his work of the true artist. Much of the harshness and cynicism disappeared from his face. He looked younger, more conventionally handsome.

And entirely lovable.

But it was not until the fourth evening that he really began to talk, to let out in words the person who had lurked behind the haughty, confident, restless, wicked facade he had shown the world all his adult life.

HE WAS ENJOYING THE novelty of being in love, though he kept reminding himself that it was *just* novelty, that soon it would be over and he would be on safe, familiar ground again. But it saddened him, at the same time as it reassured him, that Jane would ever look to him just like any other beautiful woman he had once enjoyed and tired of, that the time would come when the thought of her, of *being* with her, both in bed and out, would not fill him with such a welling of gladness that it seemed he must have taken all the sunshine inside himself.

His sexual passion for her grew lustier as the week advanced. He could not be satisfied with the almost chaste encounters of their first two times together, but set out to teach her—and himself—different, more carnal, more prolonged delights. The previous week he might have exulted in the bed sport with his new mistress and proceeded with the rest of his life as usual. But it was not the previous week. It was *this* week. And this week there was so much more than just bed sport. Indeed, he suspected that bed was good between them just because there was so much else.

He dared do things he had craved as a boy—play the pianoforte, paint, dream, let his mind drift into realms beyond the merely practical. He was frustrated by his painting and exhilarated by it. He could not capture the essence of her, perhaps because he looked too hard for it and thought too much about it, he realized at last. And so he relearned what had once been instinctive with him—to observe not so much with his senses or even his mind but with the mindless, wordless aspect of himself that was itself part of the essence it sought. He learned to stop forcing his art to his will. He learned that to create, he somehow had to allow creation to proceed through him.

He would not have understood the concept if he had ever verbalized it. But he had learned that words were not always adequate to what he yearned to express. He had learned to move beyond words.

Gradually the woman who had become the grand obsession of his life took form on the canvas.

But it was words that finally took him into a new dimension of his relationship with his mistress on the fourth evening. He had been playing the pianoforte; she had been singing. Then she had sent for the tea tray and they had drunk their tea in companionable silence. They were both sitting idle and relaxed, one on each side of the hearth, she gazing into the fire, he gazing at her.

"There were woods in Acton Park," he said suddenly, apropos of nothing. "Wooded hills all down the eastern border of the park. Wild, uncultivated, inhabited by woodland creatures and birds. I used to escape there for long hours of solitude until I learned better. It was when I came to realize that I could never paint a tree or a flower or even a blade of grass."

She smiled rather lazily. For once, he noticed, she was leaning back in her chair, her head against the headrest.

"Why?" she asked.

"I used to run my hands over the trunks of trees," he explained, "and even stand against them, my arms about them. I used to hold wildflowers in the palm of my hand and run grass blades between my fingers. There was too much there, Jane. Too many dimensions. I am talking nonsense, am I not?"

She shook her head, and he knew she understood.

"I could not even begin to grasp all there was to grasp," he said. "I used to feel—how does one describe the feeling? Breathless? No, totally inadequate. But there was a feeling, as if I were in the presence of some quite unfathomable mystery. And the strange thing was, I never wanted to fathom it. How is that for lack of human curiosity?"

But she would not let him mock himself. "You were a contemplative," she said.

"A what?"

"Some people—most people, in fact," she said, "are content with a relationship with God in which they have Him pinned down with words and in which they address Him in words. It is inevitable that all of us do it to a certain extent, of course. Words are what humans work with. But a few people discover that God is far vaster than all the words in every language and religion of the world combined. They discover tantalizing near glimpses of God only in silence—in total nothingness. They communicate with God only by giving up all effort to do so."

"Damn it, Jane," he said, "I do not even believe in God."

"Most contemplatives do not," she said. "Or not at least in any God who can be named or described in words or pictured in the imagination."

He chuckled. "I used to think it blasphemous," he said, "to believe that I was more like to find God in the hills than at church. I used to delight in the blasphemy."

"Tell me about Acton," she said quietly.

And he did. He talked at length about the house and park, about his brother and sister, about the servants with whom he had had daily contact as a child, including his nurse, about his play, his mischief, his dreams, his fears. He resurrected a life he had long ago relegated to a dim recess of memory, where he had hoped it would fade away altogether.

There was silence at last.

"Jocelyn," she said after a few minutes, "let it all become part of you again. It *is* whether you wish it to be or not. And you love Acton far more than you realize."

"Skeletons, Jane," he told her. "Skeletons. I should not have allowed any of them out. You should not be such a restful companion."

"None of them seem very threatening," she commented.

"Ah," he said, "but you do not know what is crowding

behind them, Jane." He got to his feet and held out a hand for hers. "Time to put you to work upstairs." But he grinned at her when her eyes sparked. "And time for you to put me to work. Will you, Jane? Hard, physical labor? I'll show you how to ride me, and you can use me for your pleasure as long as you choose. Come and ride me to exhaustion, Jane. Make me beg for mercy. Make me your slave."

"What nonsense!" She got to her feet and set her hand in his. "I have no wish to enslave you."

"But you already have, Jane," he said meekly, his eyes laughing at her. "And never tell me my words have not aroused you. There is a certain telltale flush in your cheeks and breathlessness in your voice that I am coming to recognize."

"I have never pretended," she told him primly, "that duty is not also pleasure."

"Come and let me show you, then," he said, "how very pleasurable it will be to do the riding rather than always to be ridden, Jane. Let me show you how to master me."

"I have no wish—" But she laughed suddenly, a sound of delight he enjoyed coaxing from her. "You are not my master, Jocelyn. Why should I wish to be yours? But very well. Show me how to ride. Is it like a horse? I ride horses rather well. And of course *they* have to be taught who is in charge, wonderful creatures."

He laughed with her as he led her from the room.

HE FINISHED THE PORTRAIT on the last day of the first week, late in the afternoon. He had a dinner engagement during the evening, which fact was a disappointment to

Jane, but she expected that he would come back for the night. One week of her precious month was already over, though. There were only three left. She coveted every day, every hour.

She loved to watch him paint even more than she loved watching him play the pianoforte. With the latter, he very quickly entered a world of his own, where the music flowed effortlessly. At his easel he had to labor more. He frowned and muttered profanities as much as he was absorbed in his task.

But finally he finished. He cleaned his brush and spoke.

"Well," he said, "I suppose you have been sneaking peeks every time I leave the house."

"I have not!" she said indignantly. "The very idea, Jocelyn! Just because it is something *you* would undoubtedly do."

"Not if my word were given," he said. "Besides, I would never need to sneak peeks. I would boldly look. Come and see it, then. See if you like yourself."

"It is finished?" He had given no indication that he was nearing the end. She threaded her needle through the cloth and jumped to her feet.

"Come and discover the truth of my claim that I merely dabble," he said, shrugging as if he did not care what her verdict was, and busying himself with the task of cleaning his palette.

Jane was almost afraid to look then, afraid that indeed she would find an inferior product about which she would have to be tactful. Though he would tear her to pieces, she knew, if she were less than brutally honest.

Her first impression was that he had flattered her. She sat at her work, every line of her body elegantly arched.

Her face was in profile. She looked industrious and absorbed by what she was doing. But she never saw herself thus, of course. In reality it was a good likeness, she supposed. She flushed with pleasure.

Her second impression was that the likeness or otherwise of the portrait was really not the point. She was not looking at a canvas produced merely so that the sitter might exclaim at the flattering likeness. She was gazing at something—something more.

The colors were brighter than she had expected, though when she looked critically she could see that they were accurate. But there was something else. She frowned. She did not know what it was. She had never been a connoisseur of art.

"Well?" There were impatience and a world of hauteur in his voice. And a thread of anxiety too? "Did I not make you beautiful enough, Jane? Are you not flattered?"

"Where . . . ?" She frowned again. She did not know quite what it was she wished to ask. "Where does the *light* come from?"

That was it. The painting was an excellent portrait. It was colorful and tasteful. But it was more than just a painting. It had *life*. And there was light in it, though she was not quite sure what she meant by that. Of course it had light. It was a vivid daytime scene.

"Ah," he said softly, "have I done it then, Jane? Have I really captured it? The essence of you? The light is coming from *you*. It is the effect you have on your surroundings."

But how had he *done* it?

"You are disappointed," he said.

She turned to him and shook her head. "I suppose,"

she said, "you never had an art master. It would not have been allowed for a future Duke of Tresham. Jocelyn, you are a man in every sense that you think important. You must dare to be more fully a man as you have been in this room this week. You have an amazing talent as a musician, an awesome talent as a painter. You must continue to use them even when I am gone. For your own sake as much as that of the world."

It was typical of him, of course, to choose to comment on a very small point.

"You are going to leave me, then, Jane?" he asked. "Go to greener pastures, perhaps? To someone who can teach you new tricks?"

She recognized the source of the insult. He was embarrassed by her earnest praise.

"Why should I leave you," she asked briskly, "when the terms of the contract are so favorable to me provided you are the one who does the leaving?"

"As I will inevitably do, of course," he said, regarding her through narrowed eyes. "There is usually a week or two of total infatuation, Jane, followed by a few more weeks of dwindling interest before a final severance of the relationship. How long have I been totally besotted with you now?"

"I would like to have time to practice skills other than just embroidery," she said, returning to her chair and folding her silk threads to put away in her workbag. "The garden needs more work. There are all those books to be read. And there is much writing I wish to do. I daresay that once your interest dwindles, I shall find my days richer and filled to overflowing with any number of congenial activities."

He chuckled softly. "I thought," he said, "we were not supposed to quarrel in this room, Jane."

"I thought," she replied tartly, "the Duke of Tresham was not to be brought into the room. I thought we had agreed not to allow him over the threshold, nasty, arrogant man. The very idea of telling me *when* I might expect to find your interest in me waning and how long I might expect to enjoy your wearying favors after that. Come here looking as if you believe you are doing me a favor, Jocelyn, and you will be leaving faster than you arrived, believe me. I have to consent, remember, before you so much as touch me."

"You like the portrait, then?" he asked meekly.

She set down her workbag and looked at him, exasperated.

"Must you always try to hurt me when you feel most vulnerable?" she asked. "I love it. I love it because you painted it and because it will remind me of this week. But I suspect that if I knew more about painting I would love it too because it is great art. I believe it is, Jocelyn. But you would have to ask an expert. Is the painting mine? To keep? Forever?"

"If you want it, Jane," he said. "Do you?"

"Of *course* I want it. You had better go now or you will be late for your dinner."

"Dinner?" He frowned, then appeared to remember. "Oh, *dinner*. To hell with it. I shall stay here and dine with you, Jane."

One more evening of her month to hug to herself.

THEY DRANK TEA AFTER dinner and he read to her from *Mansfield Park* while she sat relaxed in her chair. But after that they sat in companionable silence until he started talking about his boyhood again, as he had done for the past two evenings. Having started, it seemed he could not stop.

"I believe you should go back, Jocelyn," she said when he paused. "I believe you need to go back."

"To Acton?" he said. "Never! Only for my own funeral."

"But you speak of it with love," she said. "How old were you when you left?"

"Sixteen," he told her. "I swore I would never go back. I never have, except for two funerals."

"You must have still been at school," she said.

"Yes."

She did not ask the question. That was so like Jane. She would not pry. But the question might as well have been shouted out. She sat quietly and receptively. Jane, to whom he had opened so much of himself in the past week.

"You do not want to know, Jane," he told her.

"I think perhaps," she said, "you need to tell."

That was all she said. He gazed into the fire and remembered the initiation. The moment at which he had become his father. And his grandfather. A true Dudley. A man.

"I was sixteen and in love," he said. "With a neighbor's fourteen-year-old daughter. We swore undying love and fidelity. I even managed to get her alone once and kissed her—on the lips. For all of three seconds. It was very serious, Jane."

"It is not always wise to mock our younger selves," she said, responding to his tone of irony as if she were an octogenarian. "Love is as serious and painful a business to the young as it is to older people. More so. There is so much more innocence."

"My father got wind of it and became apprehensive," he said. "Though doubtless if he had waited I would have been sighing over some other maiden two or three months later. It is not in the nature of a Dudley to be constant in love, Jane—or even in lust, for that matter."

"He separated you?" she asked.

"There is a cottage." He set his head back and closed his eyes. "I mentioned it to you before, Jane. With its inhabitant, an indigent female relative ten years my senior."

"Yes," she said.

"There was a pool not far from her cottage," he said. "Idyllic, Jane. At the foot of the hills, green with the reflections of trees, loud with birdsong, secluded. I used to go there often in the summer to bathe rather than frolic in the lake closer to the house. She was there one day before me, bathing, wearing only a thin shift."

Jane said nothing when he paused.

"She was suitably flustered," he said, "as she came out of the pool, looking as if she wore nothing at all. And then she laughed and joked and was charming. Can you picture it, Jane? The accomplished, well-endowed courtesan and the ignorant, virgin youth? That first time we did not even make it back to the cottage. We rutted on the grass beside the pool. I discovered what went where and what happened when it was in deep enough. I do believe all was accomplished inside thirty seconds. I thought myself one devil of a dashing fellow."

Jane's eyes were closed, he noticed when he opened his own.

"She was my first obsession." He chuckled. "The day

after that I went to the cottage, and the day after that again. I labored mightily on that last occasion, having quickly learned that I could make the pleasure last considerably longer than thirty seconds. I was proud and exhausted when I was finally finished demonstrating my prowess. And then she started to talk, Jane, in a very normal, very amused voice.

"'He is an apt pupil and shows enormous promise,' she said. 'Soon *he* will be teaching *me* tricks.' And then before I could get my head up to discover what the devil she was talking about, another voice, Jane. My father's. Coming from the doorway of the bedchamber behind me.

"'You have done very nicely, Phoebe,' he said. 'He was bucking lustily enough between your thighs.' He laughed when I jumped off the bed on the opposite side from my clothes as if I had been scalded. He was standing with one shoulder propped against the doorway as if he had been there for some time. He had, of course, been watching and assessing my performance, probably exchanging winks and leers with his mistress. 'No need for embarrassment,' he told me. 'Every man ought to be deflowered by an expert. My father arranged it for me; I have arranged it for you. There is no one more expert than Phoebe, though today is your last with her, my boy. She is off-limits as of this moment. I cannot have my son sowing his oats in my woman, can I, now?'"

"Oh," Jane said softly, bringing Jocelyn's mind back to the present with a jolt.

"I gathered my clothes up and ran out of the cottage," he said, "without even stopping to dress first. I needed to vomit. Partly because my father had watched something so terribly private. Partly because it was his *mistress* with whom I had been dallying, and he had planned it all. I had not known until then that he even had mistresses. I had assumed he and my mother were faithful to each other. There was never anyone more naïve than my boyhood self, Jane."

"Poor boy," she said quietly.

"I was not even allowed to vomit in peace." He laughed harshly. "My father had brought someone riding with him—his neighbor, father of the girl I fancied myself in love with. And out strode my father on my heels to share the joke in all its lurid details. He wanted to take us both to the village inn to toast my newly acquired manhood with a glass of ale. I told him he could go to hell, and I repeated the invitation at greater length when we were at home later. I left Acton the next day."

"And for this you have felt guilt ever since?" Jane asked. He discovered suddenly that she had got up from her place and crossed in front of the hearth to stand before his chair. Before he realized what she was about to do, she sat on his lap and burrowed there until her head was on his shoulder. His arms closed about her in sheer reflex action.

"It felt like incest," he said. "She was my father's *whore,* Jane."

"You were at the mercy of a ruthless man on one hand and a practiced courtesan on the other," she told him. "It was not your fault."

"I was in love with an innocent young girl," he said. "And yet I spared her not one thought as I rutted with a woman ten years my senior whom I thought to be a relative. I learned one valuable lesson from the experience, though, Jane. I was my father's son through and through. I *am* my father's son."

"Jocelyn," she said, "you were *sixteen*. No matter who you were, you would have had to be superhuman—or subhuman—to resist such a powerful temptation. You must not blame yourself. Not any longer. Those events did not prove that you have a depraved nature. Far from it."

"It took me a few years longer to prove that," he said.

"Jocelyn." He could feel her fingers playing with a button on his waistcoat. "Tell me something. Someday in the future when you have a son, will you ever do that to him? Initiate him with one of your own mistresses?"

He drew breath slowly and imagined it—the precious human who would be his son, product of his seed, and the woman with whom he would slake his appetites rather than remain true to his wife. Coming together, performing while he watched.

"I would sooner tear out my heart," he said. "My nonexistent heart."

"Then you are not your father," she said, "or your grandfather. You are yourself. You were a sensitive, artistic, romantic boy, who had been repressed and was finally cruelly seduced. That is all, Jocelyn. You have allowed your life to be stunted by those events. But there is much life left to you. Forgive yourself."

"I lost my father on that day," he said. "I lost my mother soon after, once I had arrived in London and learned the truth about her."

"Yes," she said sadly. "But forgive them too, Jocelyn. They were products of their own upbringing and experience. Who knows what demons they carried around inside them? Parents are not just parents. They are people too. Weak like all the rest of us."

His fingers were playing with her hair. "What made you so wise?"

She did not answer for a while. "It is always easier to look at someone else's life and see its pattern," she said, "especially when one cares."

"Do you care about me, then, Jane?" he asked, kissing the top of her head. "Even now you know those most sordid of all details about my past?"

"Yes, Jocelyn," she said. "I care."

They were the words that finally broke his reserve. He did not even realize he was weeping until he felt wet drops drip onto her hair and his chest heaved convulsively. He froze in horror. But she would not let him push her away. She wrapped her free arm about his neck and burrowed deeper. And so he sobbed and hiccuped ignominiously with her in his arms and then had to search for a handkerchief to blow his nose.

"Dammit, Jane," he said. "Dammit."

"Tell me," she said. "Do you have any kindly memories of your father? Anything at all?"

Hardly! But when he thought about it, he could remember his father teaching him to ride his first pony and playing cricket with him and Ferdinand.

"He used to play cricket with us," he said, "when we were young enough to saw at the air with our bats and hurl the ball all of six inches ahead when bowling. It must have been as exciting for him as watching grass grow."

"Remember those times," she said. "Find more memories like that. He was not a monster, Jocelyn. He was not a pleasant man either. I do not believe I would have liked him. But he was not a monster, for all that. He was simply a man. And even when he betrayed you, he thought somehow that he was doing something necessary for your education."

He kissed the top of her head again, and they lapsed into silence.

He could not quite believe that he had relived those memories at last. Aloud. In the hearing of a woman. His mistress, no less. But it felt strangely good to have spoken. Those ghastly, sordid events seemed less dreadful when put into words. *He* seemed less dreadful. Even his father did.

He felt peaceful.

"Skeletons are dreadful things to have in our past, Jane," he said at last. "I do not suppose you have any, do you?"

"No," she said after such a long silence that he thought she was not going to answer at all. "None."

"Come to bed?" he asked her with a sigh almost of total contentment. "Just to sleep, Jane? If I remember correctly, we were rather energetically busy most of last night. Shall we just sleep tonight?"

"Yes," she said.

He almost chuckled aloud. He was going to bed with his mistress.

To sleep.

His father would turn over in his grave.

18

JOCELYN WENT STRAIGHT HOME THE FOLLOWING morning, as he usually did, to bathe and shave and change before sallying forth to his clubs and engaging in his other morning activities. But Hawkins was waiting for him as he crossed the threshold, bursting with important information. Mr. Quincy wanted a word with his grace. At his earliest convenience.

"Send him to the library in half an hour," Jocelyn said as he made his way to the stairs. "And send Barnard up to me. Warn him that I feel no burning need of his personal company, Hawkins. Suggest to him that I will need hot water and my shaving gear."

Michael Quincy stepped into the library thirty minutes later. Jocelyn was already there.

"Well?" He looked at his secretary with raised eyebrows. "Some crisis at Acton, Michael?"

"There is a person, your grace," his secretary explained. "He is in the kitchen and has been there for two hours. He refuses to go away."

Jocelyn raised his eyebrows and clasped his hands at his back. "Indeed?" he said. "Do I not employ enough footmen to pick up this—this *person* and toss him out? Am I expected to do it myself? Is this why the matter has been brought to my attention?"

"He is asking about Miss Ingleby, your grace," Quincy explained.

Jocelyn went very still. "About Miss Ingleby?"

"He is a Bow Street Runner," his secretary told him.

Jocelyn merely stared at him.

"Hawkins referred him to me with his questions," Quincy explained. "I told him I knew nothing about any Miss Ingleby. He said he would wait and speak with you, then. When I told him he might have to wait a week before you found a moment to spare for him, he said he would wait a week. He is in the kitchen, your grace, and shows no sign of going away."

"With questions about Miss Ingleby." Jocelyn's eyes narrowed. "You had better show him up, Michael."

MICK BODEN WAS FEELING uncomfortable. Only very rarely did his work bring him to any of the grand mansions of Mayfair. Truth to tell he was rather in awe of the aristocracy. And the owner of Dudley House was the Duke of Tresham, reputedly the sort of man even his peers feared to tangle with.

But he knew he was close. The servants were all lying their heads off, every last one of them. None of them knew any Miss Jane Ingleby, including his grace's secretary, whom, to his shame, Mick Boden had taken for the duke himself at first, so grand a nob was he.

Mick knew when people were lying. And he knew why these people were lying. It was not that they were protecting her or hiding her but that they were servants who valued their employment. And clearly one rule of that employment was that one did not open one's mouth to strangers about any inhabitant of the house, even fellow servants. He could respect that.

And then the butler, a man who had the habit of

sniffing the air as if to catch the dirty odor of lesser mortals, appeared in the kitchen and fixed his disdainful eye upon Mick.

"Follow me," he said.

Mick followed him, out of the kitchen, up the steep stairs, and through the baize door that led into the back of the hall. The sudden splendor of the main part of the house fairly took his breath away, though he concentrated upon not showing that he was impressed. The secretary was waiting there.

"His grace will give you five minutes," he said. "I will show you into the library. I shall wait outside to show you off the premises when you have been dismissed."

"Thank you, sir," Mick Boden said.

He was a little nervous, but he strode purposefully enough into the library after the butler had opened the door. He came to a halt six steps inside the door and planted his feet wide on the carpet. He held his hat with both hands and bobbed his head civilly. He would not bow.

The duke—he supposed it must be the duke this time—was standing in front of an ornate marble fireplace, his hands clasped at his back. He was wearing riding clothes, but they were so well tailored and fit so perfectly that Mick immediately felt conscious of the cheapness of his own clothes, on whose nattiness he prided himself. He was being regarded steadily from eyes so dark Mick would swear they were black.

"You have a few questions for me," the duke informed Mick. "You are a Bow Street Runner?"

"Yes, sir. Mick Boden, sir." Mick resisted the urge to bob his head again. "I have been informed, sir, that you have a Miss Jane Ingleby in your service."

"Have you?" His grace raised his eyebrows and looked very forbidding indeed. "And who, may I ask, did the informing?"

"Madame de Laurent, sir," Mick Boden said. "A milliner. She employed Miss Ingleby until a month or so ago, when the young lady gave her notice and explained she was coming here to work for you."

"Indeed?" The duke's eyes narrowed. "And what is your interest in Miss Ingleby?"

Mick hesitated, but only for a moment. "She is wanted, sir," he said, "for dastardly crimes."

His grace's fingers found and curled about the handle of his quizzing glass, though he did not raise it to his eye.

"Dastardly crimes?" he repeated softly.

"Theft, sir," Mick explained. "And murder."

"Fascinating," the duke commented just as softly, and Mick, a good judge of character, knew without any doubt that this could be a very dangerous man indeed. "And a Banbury tale?"

"Oh, no, sir," Mick said briskly. "It is quite true. The name is an alias. In reality she is Lady Sara Illingsworth, who murdered Mr. Sidney Jardine, son and heir of the Earl of Durbury, and then ran off with the earl's money and jewels. You might have heard about the incident, sir. She is a desperate fugitive, sir, and it is my belief she is here in this house."

"Dear me," his grace said after a short silence. "I perceive that I am fortunate indeed not to have woken one morning during the past month to find my throat slit from ear to ear."

Mick felt intense satisfaction. At last! The Duke of

Tresham had as good as admitted that she was at Dudley House.

"She is here, sir?" he asked.

The duke raised his quizzing glass halfway to his eye. "*Was* here," he said. "Miss Ingleby was employed for three weeks as my nurse after I was shot in the leg. She left a couple of weeks ago. You must pursue your search elsewhere. I believe Mr. Quincy is waiting in the hall to show you out."

But Mick Boden was not ready to be dismissed just yet.

"Can you tell me where she went, sir?" he asked. "It is very important. The Earl of Durbury is beside himself with grief and will not know a moment's peace until his son's murderess has been brought to justice."

"And his jewels returned to his safe at Candleford," the duke added. "Miss Ingleby was a servant here. Am I to know where *servants* go after they leave my employ?" His eyebrows rose haughtily again.

Mick knew he had just slammed into a brick wall. He had come so close.

"That will be all?" his grace asked. "The interrogation is ended? I confess an eagerness for my breakfast."

Mick would have liked to ask more questions. Sometimes, even when people were not deliberately hiding information, they knew more than they realized. Perhaps the girl had said something about her future plans, dropped some hint, confided in some fellow servant. But it was unlikely, he admitted. She knew she was a fugitive. Doubtless she had heard, during her weeks in this house, that the Runners were after her.

"Well?" There was a force of arrogant incredulity behind the one word.

Mick bobbed his head again, bade the Duke of Tresham a good morning, and took his leave. The duke's secretary showed him out through the front door, and the Bow Street Runner found himself on Grosvenor Square, feeling that he was back where he had started.

Though perhaps not quite.

He had heard about the duel even before Madame de Laurent had mentioned it. The Duke of Tresham had been shot in the leg and incapacitated for three weeks. The rest of London's nobs had probably beaten a path to his door to keep him company. The girl had been his nurse. She must surely have been seen by some of those visitors. Some of them might be more forthcoming than the duke himself.

No, he had not come up against a brick wall after all, Mick Boden decided. Not yet at least.

He would find her.

ALL THE EVIDENCE HAD been staring him in the eyeballs, Jocelyn thought as he stood at the library window watching the Bow Street Runner make his slow way out of the square. Staring so closely, in fact, that it had thrown his mind out of focus and he had just not seen it.

She had clearly been brought up a lady. She had demonstrated all the attributes of a lady from the start except genteel dress. She spoke with a refined accent; she bore herself proudly and gracefully; she was literate; she could play the pianoforte with competence if not with flair; she could sing superbly—with a trained voice and a knowledge of composers like Handel; she could command and organize servants; she was not awed by a man with a title, like himself, even when he was overbearing by nature.

Had he for one moment believed her story that she had been brought up in an orphanage? For *one* moment, perhaps. But he had realized for some time that she had lied about her background. He had even idly wondered why. There was something about her past that she wanted to keep private, he had concluded. He had never been unduly curious about the secrets people chose to keep hidden.

Lady Sara Illingsworth.

Not Jane Ingleby, but Lady Sara Illingsworth.

His eyes narrowed as he gazed out onto the now empty square.

He had consistently misinterpreted the biggest clue of all—her reluctance to be seen. She had not wanted to venture outside Dudley House when she was here except into the garden; she did not want to venture outside the house where she was now. She had been very reluctant to sing for his guests. She had chosen to become his mistress rather than pursue what could undoubtedly be a brilliant career as a singer.

He had thought she was ashamed, first of what people would think her relationship to him might be and then of what that relationship really was. But she had shown no other sign of shame. She had negotiated their foolish contract with practical good sense. She had redecorated her house because she would not be made to feel like a whore living in a brothel. There had been no shrinking from her fate the afternoon of the consummation of their liaison, no tears or other sign of remorse afterward.

His mind should have worked its way around to understanding that she was afraid to be seen in public lest she be recognized and apprehended. He had simply not seen the obvious—that she was in hiding.

That she was wanted for theft and murder.

Jocelyn stepped back from the window, paced to the other side of the room, and set his hands flat on top of the oak desk.

He did not care a fig for the fact that he was harboring a fugitive. The notion that she was dangerous was patently absurd. But he cared the devil of a bit over the fact that he had discovered her identity too late.

Offering employment as his mistress to a penniless orphan or even to a destitute gentlewoman was a perfectly unexceptionable thing to do. Offering the same employment to the daughter of an earl was a different matter altogether. Perhaps it should not be. If they lived in a perfect society, in which all people were seen as equals, it would make no difference.

But they did not.

And so it did make a difference.

He had had the virginity of Lady Sara Illingsworth, daughter of the late Earl of Durbury of Candleford in Cornwall.

He was not at this particular moment feeling kindly disposed toward Lady Sara Illingsworth.

Damn her. He thumped one fist down hard on the desk and clenched his teeth. She should have told him. She should have enlisted his aid. Did she not realize that he was exactly the sort of man to whom she could openly admit the worst without fear that he would have a fit of the vapors and send for the Runners? Did she not understand that he must hold men like Jardine in the utmost contempt? The devil! He pounded his fist hard onto wood again. What had the bastard done to her to provoke her into killing him—if he *was* dead? What had she suffered since in guilt and fear and loneliness?

Damn her all to hell! She had not trusted him enough to confide in him.

Instead she had locked and bolted a shackle about his leg and thrown away the key. Even if it had been done unwittingly—in fact, *undoubtedly* she had not intended it since she trusted him so little—it had been done effectively indeed.

For that he would find it hard to forgive her.

Damn the woman!

And something else. Oh, yes, there was something else. He had bared his soul to her last evening as he had never done to any other human being. He had trusted her that much.

But she did not return his trust. Ever since he had first set eyes upon her, she must have been suffering unbearable torment. Yet she had kept it all from him. Even last night.

Skeletons are dreadful things to have in our past, Jane, he had said to her. *I do not suppose you have any, do you?*

No, she had replied. *None.*

Damn her!

Jocelyn's fist banged onto the desk once more, causing the inkpot to jump in its silver holder.

JOCELYN SPENT THE DAY at his clubs, at Jackson's boxing saloon, at a shooting range, at the races. He dined at White's and spent a couple of hours at an insipid soiree, at which his sister informed him that he had become quite the stranger and that she had talked Heyward into taking her to Brighton for a few weeks in the summer to mix with Prinny's set and sample the pleasures of the Pavilion. His brother, who also commented that he had become a stranger, was seething with indignation.

"The point is, Tresham," he said, "that the Forbeses are still hiding yet are still spreading the word that *you* are the one afraid to meet *them*. Not to mention what they must be saying about me hiding behind my big brother's coattails. What are you planning to do about them? That is what I want to know. I have never known you to drag your feet like this. If they do not show up within the week, I am going in search of them myself. And be-damned to that toplofty elder brother pronouncement that they are your concern. It was me they tried to kill."

Jocelyn sighed. Yes, he *had* procrastinated. All because of an infatuation for a woman.

"And me they hoped to humiliate," he said. "I will deal with them, Ferdinand. Soon." He refused to discuss the matter further.

But while he had been dallying with his *mistress* for the past week, talking and reading and dabbling with music and art, he had been allowing his reputation to tarnish. It would not do.

It was not until late evening that he finally contrived to get Brougham and Kimble alone. They were strolling together to White's from the soiree.

"You have not, either of you, mentioned the name of my mistress to anyone, have you?" he asked.

"The devil, Tresham." Brougham sounded irritated. "Do you need to ask when you requested us specifically not to?"

"If you do, Tresh," Kimble said with ominous calm, "perhaps I should plant you a facer. You have simply not been yourself lately. But maybe the question was rhetorical?"

"There is a person," Jocelyn explained, "a Runner with oiled hair and shudderingly awful taste in clothes but with shrewd eyes, who will very possibly be asking questions soon about Miss Jane Ingleby."

"A *Bow Street* Runner?" Brougham stopped walking.

"Asking about *Miss Ingleby*?" Even in the darkness of the street Kimble's frown was visible.

"Alias Lady Sara Illingsworth," Jocelyn explained.

His friends stared at him in silence.

"He will be questioning you among others," Jocelyn assured them.

"Miss Jane Ingleby?" Kimble's expression had become a blank mask. "Never even heard of her. Have you, Cone?"

"Who?" Brougham frowned.

"No, no," Jocelyn said gently, and began to walk again. His friends fell into step on either side of him. "It is known that she nursed me during my recuperation from my injury. I admitted as much this morning when the person was standing in my library doing his damnedest not to look servile. For three weeks. After which she left my employ. But who am I to have followed the progress beyond my doors of a mere servant?"

"*Was* there such a servant?" Brougham asked carelessly. "I confess I did not notice, Tresham. But I tend not to notice other people's servants."

"Was she the one who *sang* at your soiree, Tresh?" Kimble asked. "Pretty voice for those who like that sort of music. A pretty enough girl too for those who like simple country misses in muslin when all the ladies present are clad enticingly in satins and plumes and jewels. Whatever *did* happen to her?"

"Thank you," Jocelyn said briskly. "I knew I could trust you."

"I say, though, Tresham," Brougham asked, his voice returned to normal, "what *did* happen with Jardine? You are not about to ask us to believe, I hope, that Lady Sara murdered him in cold blood because he apprehended her stealing."

Kimble snorted derisively.

"I do not *know* what happened," Jocelyn said through his teeth. "She has not seen fit to confide in me. But let me say this. Jardine had better be dead as the proverbial doornail. If he is not, it will be my distinct pleasure to make him wish he were."

"If you need any help," Brougham offered, "look no further than yours truly, Tresham."

"What are you going to do about Lady Sara, Tresh?" Lord Kimble asked.

"Thrash her within an inch of her life," Jocelyn said viciously. "Get to the bottom of that ridiculous story. Get leg shackled to her and make her sorry for the rest of her life that she was ever born. In that order."

"Leg shackled." Conan Brougham winced. "Because she is your mistr—" He was overtaken suddenly by a fit of coughing, brought on perhaps by a sharp dig in the ribs from Viscount Kimble's elbow.

"Leg shackled," Jocelyn repeated. "But first I am going to get foxed. Inebriated. Drunk as a lord. Three sheets to the wind."

The trouble was, of course, that he never seemed able to get drunk when he wanted to, no matter how much he imbibed. He rather believed, by the time he left

White's alone at something past midnight, that he had consumed a vast quantity of liquor. But unless he was drunker than he realized, he was walking a straight line in the direction of his mistress's house, and he still felt only coldly furious instead of passionately angry. How could he thrash her—not that he ever could literally beat her or any other woman. How could he deliver one of his famous tongue-lashings, then, if he could feel no heat with his anger?

By the time he had reached the house and let himself in with his key, he could think only of humiliating her, of reminding her of her very subordinate position in his life. He was going to have to marry the woman, of course, even if she did not realize it yet. She would be his wife in name. But she would soon understand that always, for the rest of her days, she would be less to him than a mistress.

19

HE CAME AFTER MIDNIGHT, LONG AFTER JANE had given up expecting him, though she was still up, pacing from the den to the dining room to the sitting room, knowing that something was terribly wrong. She was in the den, gazing at his portrait of her, her arms wrapped defensively about her waist, when she heard his key in the outer door. She hurried to meet him, picking up a candlestick as she went. But she mustered the self-respect to step quietly into the hall. She was glad of that restraint a moment later.

He was wearing his black opera cloak. He removed his silk hat and gloves with careful deliberation before turning to look at her. When he did so, Jane found herself gazing at the Duke of Tresham—that stranger from her past. The dark, cold, cynical, and surely inebriated Duke of Tresham. She smiled.

"Upstairs!" he commanded with cold hauteur and a slight jerk of his head in the direction of the stairs.

"Why?" She frowned.

He raised his eyebrows and looked at her as if she were a worm beneath his foot.

"Why?" he asked softly. "*Why*, Jane? Have I mistaken the address, by any chance? But my key fit the lock. Is this not the house at which I keep my mistress? I have come to avail myself of my mistress's services. I need a bed in order to do that comfortably and her person on that bed. The bed is upstairs, I believe."

"You are foxed!" she said, matching him in coldness.

"Am I?" He looked surprised. "But not too foxed to find my way to my mistress's house. Not too foxed to climb the stairs to her bed. Not too foxed to get it up, Jane."

She flushed at his coarseness and stared at him while her heart felt too like a leaden weight to be capable of breaking. But it would break, she knew, once this night was over. Fool! Oh, fool, not only to have fallen in love with him, but to have dreamed that he had fallen for her too.

"Upstairs!" He pointed again. And then he nodded. "Ah, I have realized the reason for your hesitation. I forgot to say please. *Please* go upstairs, Jane. Please remove all your clothes and hairpins when you get there. Please lie on your back on the bed so that I may avail myself of your services. Please keep your end of our contract."

His voice was colder than ice. His eyes were as black as the night.

She had no good reason to refuse him. It had never been part of their bargain that he must love her before she would grant him her favors. But she felt suddenly disoriented, as if a week—the most precious week of her life—had just been erased without a trace. As if she had dreamed it. As if he had never become her companion, her friend, her lover. Her soul mate.

When all was said and done, she was merely his mistress.

She turned and preceded him up the stairs, the candlestick held high, her heart turned to stone. No, not that. A stone felt no pain. She blinked back tears. He would not see such a sign of weakness in her.

Never!

"I have come here, Jane," he said a few moments later, standing inside the door of her bedchamber, his expression quite inscrutable—except that there was something about him that spoke of inebriation and threatened danger, "to be entertained by my mistress. How are you going to entertain me?"

It felt again as if the past week had not been. If it had not, of course, she would have found nothing particularly offensive in his words. There *was* nothing offensive in them. She must not respond as if she thought there were. She must simply forget the past week. But she hesitated too long.

"You do not have a headache, by any chance, Jane?" There was heavy irony in his voice. "Or your courses?"

Her courses were due within the next few days, and she had been feeling a justifiable anxiety about them. But she would not worry before she must. She had known the consequences of such a liaison from the start. There was even a clause in the contract that dealt with children of their affair.

"Or are you simply repulsed by me tonight?" he asked, looking more dangerous than ever with his eyes narrowed on her. "Are you going to exercise your prerogative, Jane, and send me off to hell, my lust unsatisfied?"

"No, of course not." She looked at him calmly. "I will be pleased to entertain you, your grace. What else do I have to think of and dream of and plan for during all the long hours when you are not here, after all?"

"It is reassuring to discover, at least," he said as he strode toward her and the bed, "that you have not lost your saucy tongue, Jane. I would certainly not enjoy you meek and submissive on your back. Now, what sensual delights can you dream up for me?"

She had learned a number of skills during the past week and a half. She had learned not to be shy of her own sexuality or his. It was clear that he really was going to wait for her to entertain him. He took up a stand beside the bed, his feet apart, his hands clasped at his back, and gazed at her with raised eyebrows. It was more than a little disconcerting and very definitely upsetting in light of what she had hoped their next encounter would be like.

She undressed slowly, teasing him with tantalizing glimpses of naked flesh, a little at a time. She folded each garment and turned to set it down on a chair. When she was naked, she lifted her arms and drew the pins from her hair one at a time until it cascaded about her. She smiled. Perhaps after all she could tease him out of his embarrassment over last evening—if that was what this abrupt change in him was all about.

He was still wearing his cloak, but he had thrown it back over his shoulders. He made no effort to hide the telltale bulge of his arousal pushing at the tight fabric of his evening knee breeches. Yet he did not move. His expression remained impassive.

She undid the buttons at his neck and let his cloak fall to the floor behind him. But in doing so she brushed against him and discovered something she had not known before—that there was something erotic about being naked with someone who was fully clothed.

"Sit down," she invited him, indicating the bed.

He raised his eyebrows, but he sat on the side of it, bracing his feet apart, setting his hands behind him on the bed, supporting himself on his arms.

"You are learning wicked lessons that I have not taught you, Jane," he said, watching as she unbuttoned his breeches and freed him of their silken confines. "What do you have in store for me? Mouth play?"

She knew instinctively what he meant. And though with her mind she thought it disgusting, she knew with her body that it would not be so. But she did not believe she could do it, even so. Not yet. Not unless the time should ever arrive when they could come together as lovers rather than as man and mistress.

She took him in her hands, caressed him, stroked him while he watched what she did with narrowed eyes. Then she knelt astride him on the bed, placed him at her entrance, and bore down on him. She stayed upright, her spine slightly arched backward, her fingertips on the satin of his evening coat at his shoulders. She looked into his eyes.

"Good, Jane," he said. "Entertaining." But he still did not move. He was long and rigid inside her, but he did not move. She could smell liquor on his breath.

He had taught her to ride. But she had done it before while he lay flat and she had leaned over him. And he had ridden with her, stride for stride. They had both labored toward the ultimate pleasure.

Tonight he sat still and watched her with his dark, dangerous eyes.

She was slick and wet and pulsing with desire. She would have liked nothing better than to feel him respond in more than just simple arousal, to have allowed him to lead the way to completion. But he would not do it. There was a darkness in him that she could not seem to lighten. He was still punishing both himself and her, she thought, for what he must see as the humiliation of his disclosures the evening before.

She kept her weight on her spread knees and calves. And she rode him. Not as she had done before, inner muscles clenching and unclenching to the rhythm of ascent and descent. There was a certain defense in such motions, a certain control over the rising and cresting of passion—at least until the final moments. This time she moved without defenses, her inner muscles relaxed, no barrier against the rigid hardness onto which she impaled herself time and time again as she rode the rhythm of sex. She arched her spine more, tipped back her head, closed her eyes, and braced her hands on his silken knees behind her.

She tried to show him with her body that she cared, that she would withhold nothing from him when he needed her. And despite his strange, bleak mood, she sensed that he *did* need her.

She did not know for how many minutes she continued while he remained hard and motionless. But desire became a raw ache, and ache became indistinguishable from pain before finally—ah, blessedly—his hands came to her hips and clamped there so unexpectedly hard that her rhythm and all her control shattered even as he thrust urgently and repeatedly up into her, pumping past the barrier she had deliberately not erected. She could hear herself sobbing as if she listened to someone else a great distance away. She heard the growl of his climax and felt the hot gush of his seed.

Union. Ah, the blessed union. He would be consoled now. They would lie together, warm and sated, and talk. She would reassure him and he would be Jocelyn again instead of the dark, dangerous Duke of Tresham.

Tomorrow she would be able to confide her own dark secrets to him.

She was panting and damp and chilly with perspiration. She still straddled him on the bed, her legs wide and stiff. He was still embedded in her. She lifted her head and smiled dreamily at him.

"Vastly entertaining, Jane," he said briskly. "You are becoming skilled indeed at your profession. You are beginning to be worth every penny of your salary." He lifted her off him, turned her so that she sprawled on the bed, and got to his feet. He began to button himself up again.

He might as well have hurled a pitcher of ice water over her.

"And you, of course," she said, "have always been a master of the veiled insult. I perfectly well understand that this is what I am paid to do. You do not need to remind me just because you let down your guard last evening and embarrassed yourself by telling me things you deeply regret telling." She pulled the bedcovers up to cover herself. Suddenly she felt very naked indeed.

"You are insulted, Jane," he asked her, "to be told that you are remarkably skilled in bed? I do not often pay that compliment, you know." He was throwing his cloak about his shoulders.

"I am *insulted*," she told him, sitting up and holding the covers to her breasts, "that you would think it necessary to degrade me, your grace, with this talk of skills and salary. I am insulted that you are ashamed of having confided in me merely because I am a woman and your mistress to boot. I thought we had become friends—and friends *do* talk to each other. They do confide in each other and share their deepest secrets and their deepest wounds. I was mistaken. I should not have forgotten that you pay my salary for *this.*" She indicated the bed with one sweeping arm. "And now I am tired. I have been working hard earning my living. Kindly leave, your grace. Good night."

"Friends *confide* in each other, Jane?" He was glaring at her quite intently, his eyes very black. For a moment she felt frightened. She thought he was going to lean over and grab her. Instead he made her a sudden, ironically deferential bow and strode from the room.

Jane was left cold and trembling and lonelier and unhappier than she had ever been in her life before.

As he made his way home to Grosvenor Square, Jocelyn's mood was black indeed. He now thoroughly despised himself—a satisfyingly familiar feeling, at least. He felt as if he had raped her—though he had approached her in very much the way he had been accustomed to approaching his mistresses in the past. And he despised her. She ought not to have allowed him within touching distance of her tonight, but in fact she had serviced him like an experienced courtesan.

He hated her for lulling him all week into a belief that he had found a friend, a soul mate, as well as a damned good bed partner. For somehow inducing him to lower all his defenses, to share with her everything that was his most secret self. For somehow keeping him from noticing that she received but gave nothing except her body in return, that there was nothing reciprocal in their relationship.

She had taken his trust but had kept herself well hidden behind the position of mistress and the alias of Jane

Ingleby. Yet she had dared just now to lecture him on the nature of true friendship.

She had taken *everything* from him, even the love of which he had thought himself no longer capable.

He hated her for fooling him into hoping that after all life was worth living. For stripping away all the comfort of the hard cocoon inside which he had lived for ten years.

He hated her.

He could not even *think* of her as Sara.

She was Jane.

But Jane Ingleby did not exist.

He could feel the satisfying beginnings of a headache as he neared home. If he was fortunate, he would have the distraction of a colossal hangover by morning.

FROM HIS POSITION IN the shadows of a darkened doorway across the street, Mick Boden watched, first as the Duke of Tresham strode off down the street and then as the light in what must be the bedchamber of the house was extinguished. The house was clearly a love nest—the duke had let himself in with his own key, stayed long enough for a prolonged mount or two in that room where the candlelight had appeared just after his arrival, and had then stridden off homeward, looking well satisfied with himself.

It had been a long day. There was no point in hanging about any longer. It was scarcely likely that the mistress would emerge from the house to gaze after her lover, or even appear in the window since she had not done so in order to wave good night to him.

But she must come out sometime—probably tomorrow to go walking or shopping. All he needed was a glimpse of her. At least then he would know if the duke's fancy piece could possibly be Lady Sara Illingsworth, alias Miss Jane Ingleby. Mick Boden had a certain intuition about the female occupant of that house, and during his years as a Bow Street Runner he had learned to trust his intuition.

He would come back in the morning, Mick decided, and watch the house until she came out. He could set an assistant to such a mundane task, of course, since there were other courses of inquiry that he really should pursue, but his curiosity and even a certain respect for the woman had been aroused during his long, frustrating search for her. He wanted to be the first to see her and the one to apprehend her.

20

JOCELYN MISSED HIS USUAL MORNING RIDE IN THE park. He was too busy dealing with a fat head and a queasy stomach and a valet who opened back his curtains on bright sunshine and then appeared surprised to discover that his master was lying in his own bed, the sunlight full on his face.

But Jocelyn would not allow himself the luxury of nursing a hangover and terrorizing his staff for too long. There were things to do. Fortunately he had had a chance to talk with Kimble and Brougham the evening before. The same could not be said of the Earl of Durbury, who never appeared in public—just like his niece or his cousin or whatever Lady Sara Illingsworth was to him.

The man was still in town, though, and still at the Pulteney, Jocelyn discovered when he called there in the middle of the morning. And willing to receive the Duke of Tresham, though he might have been puzzled by the request. They had never had more than a nodding acquaintance, after all. He was standing in his private sitting room after Jocelyn had first sent up his card and then been escorted up by the earl's man.

"Tresham?" he said by way of greeting. "How do you do?"

"Very well, I thank you," Jocelyn replied, "when it is considered that I might at this moment be lying in my bed at home with my throat slit. Or in my grave, more like, since Lady Sara Illingsworth has been gone from my house for longer than two weeks."

"Ah, yes, have a seat. Let me pour you a drink." The Bow Street Runner had clearly reported to the earl recently, then. "Do you know where she is, Tresham? Have you heard something?"

"Nothing, thank you," Jocelyn said of the drink while his stomach churned unpleasantly. He availed himself of the offer of a chair. "You must understand that when she was in my employ she dressed the part of a servant and used an alias. She was a mere employee. It did not occur to me when she left to ask where she was going."

"No, of course not." The earl poured himself a drink and sat at the square table in the middle of the room. He looked disappointed. "Those damned Runners are not worth a quarter of what they charge, Tresham. Devilish incompetent, in fact. I have been kicking my heels here for well over a month while a dangerous criminal runs loose among an unsuspecting populace. And for three weeks of that time she was at Dudley House. If I had only known!"

"I was fortunate indeed," Jocelyn said, "to escape harm. Murdered your son, did she? My condolences, Durbury."

"Thank you."

The man looked distinctly uncomfortable. So much so, in fact, that Jocelyn, gazing keenly at him while giving an impression of almost bored indolence, drew his own conclusions.

"And robbed you to add insult to injury," he said. "Having spent three weeks at Dudley House, Lady Sara must be well aware that it is full of costly treasures. I have been apprehensive since learning her identity yesterday morning that she might attempt a burglary and murder me too if I am unfortunate enough to stumble upon her at the wrong moment."

The earl looked keenly back at him, but Jocelyn was long practiced in the art of giving nothing whatsoever away with his facial expression.

"Quite so," the earl agreed.

"I quite understand your, ah, *ire*," Jocelyn said, "in having had a mere female relative—and a dependent one too, I daresay—cause you such personal pain and expose your authority to such public ridicule. If I were in your shoes, I would be waiting as impatiently as you for her capture so that I could put my horsewhip to effective use about her hide before the law takes its turn. It is the only way with rebellious women, I have heard. I would mention two things to you, though—my reason for coming, in fact."

The Earl of Durbury looked unsure whether he had just been insulted or commiserated with.

"I have questioned some of my servants," Jocelyn explained—he had done no such thing, of course, "and they assure me that the nurse I knew as Miss Jane Ingleby had only one small bag of possessions with her at Dudley House. Which leaves a question in my mind. Where has she hidden the fortune in money and jewels that she took from you? Has the Bow Street Runner you employ thought of approaching the search from that angle? Find the treasure and there will surely be a clear trail to the woman."

He paused, eyebrows raised, for the earl to respond.

"It is an idea," his lordship conceded stiffly. Jocelyn

was confirmed in his suspicion that there *was* no treasure, or at least not any significant amount of it.

"He would certainly be better employed looking for the money and jewels than following me," Jocelyn added amiably.

The Earl of Durbury looked sharply at him.

"I suppose," Jocelyn continued, "he concluded from his interview with me yesterday morning that I am the sort of man who would derive a certain titillation out of bedding a woman who might rob me of my last farthing while I sleep and split open my skull with the sharp end of an ax for good measure. One can understand his conclusion. I do have a certain reputation for reckless, dangerous living. However, although I found it rather amusing yesterday to be followed wherever I went, I do believe I would find it tedious to have the experience repeated today."

The earl clearly did not know what his Runner had been up to most of yesterday. He stared blankly.

"Not that it has been happening yet today," Jocelyn admitted. "I daresay he is camped out again before the house of a certain, ah, *lady* whom I visited last night. The lady is my mistress, but you must understand, Durbury, that any mistress I employ is under my full protection and that anyone who harasses her will have me to answer to. You will perhaps consider it pertinent to explain this to your Runner—I am afraid his name escapes my memory at the moment." He rose to his feet.

"I most certainly will." The Earl of Durbury looked thunderous. "I am paying the Runners an exorbitant amount *to watch your mistress's house*, Tresham? This is outrageous."

"I must confess," Jocelyn said as he picked up his hat

and gloves from a table beside the door, "that it is somewhat distracting while one is engaged in, ah, *conversation* with a lady to know that the window is being watched from the outside. I will not expect such a distraction again tonight."

"No, indeed," the earl assured him. "I shall demand an explanation for this from Mick Boden, believe me."

"Ah, yes," Jocelyn said as he let himself out of the room, "that was the name. Wiry little man with well-oiled hair. Good day to you, Durbury."

He felt satisfied with the morning's visit as he sauntered down the stairs and out of the hotel, despite the headache that had settled in for a lengthy stay just behind his eyes. The morning was almost over. He just hoped that, untrue to form, she would not poke as much as her nose out through the door of her house before the watchdog was removed. But it was unlikely. She never went out except into the back garden. And now, of course, he understood why.

DURING A MORNING OF ferociously hard work tackling a corner of garden wilderness she had not worked on before, Jane convinced herself that the end had come. He had spoken of it himself—the infatuation, the gradual loss of interest, the final severance of all ties.

The infatuation was over, killed by his own indiscretion—or what he apparently saw as an indiscretion anyway. The loss of interest, Jane suspected, would not be gradual but sudden. Perhaps she might expect a few more night visits like last night's. But one day soon Mr. Quincy would arrive to make arrangements for the ending of the liaison. Not that there would be much to discuss. The contract took care of most details.

Then she would never see Jocelyn again.

She tore recklessly at a clump of nettles, which stung painfully even through her gloves.

It was just as well, she told herself. She was going to turn herself in to the Bow Street Runners anyway. Soon she would be able to do it without any encumbrance. Soon her fate would not much matter to her, though she would, of course, from sheer principle fight to clear herself of the ridiculous charges against her. Ridiculous except for the fact that Sidney was dead.

She reached for another clump of nettles.

She had convinced herself so well that she was surprised when Jocelyn arrived early in the afternoon. She heard the rapping of the door knocker as she was changing into a clean dress upstairs. She waited tensely to hear his footsteps on the stairs. But it was Mr. Jacobs's hesitant knock that sounded on her door.

"His grace requests the honor of your company in the sitting room, ma'am," the butler informed her.

Jane's heart sank as she set down her brush. They had not used the sitting room for over a week.

He was standing before the empty fireplace, one arm propped on the high mantel, when she stepped into the room.

"Good afternoon, Jocelyn," she said.

He was looking his usual dark, cynical, arrogant self, his eyes quite inscrutable. His mood had not improved since last night, then. And suddenly she realized why he had come. He would not send Mr. Quincy, of course. He would tell her himself.

This was the end. After just a week and a half.

He inclined his head but did not return her greeting.

"It was a mistake," she said quietly. "When you asked if you could see the room next door, I should have held firm and said no. You want a mistress, Jocelyn. You want an uncomplicated physical relationship with a woman. You are afraid of friendship, of emotional closeness. You are afraid of your artistic side. You are afraid to confront your memories and admit to yourself that you have allowed them to blight your life. You are afraid to let go of your image of yourself as a pure man. I should not have encouraged you to indulge your inner self. I should not have been your friend. I should have kept our relationship to what it was meant to be. I should have entertained you in bed and encouraged you to live all the rest of your life beyond the confines of this house."

"Indeed?" There was pure ice in his voice. "Do you have any other pearls of wisdom for me, Jane?"

"I will not hold you to our contract," she said. "It would be criminal of me to insist that you support me for four and a half years when our liaison has lasted a mere week and a half. You are free of me, your grace. As of this moment. By tomorrow I shall be gone. Even today if you wish."

It would be better today. To leave without having any time to think about it. To go to the Pulteney Hotel. Or to seek out the Bow Street Runners if the earl was not there.

"You are quite right," he said after staring at her in silence for an uncomfortably long time. "Our contract is void. It has a fatal flaw."

She lifted her chin a notch, realizing only as he spoke that she had been desperately hoping he would argue, try to persuade her to stay, be simply Jocelyn again.

"I believe," he said, "contracts are void if one of the parties uses an alias. I am no legal expert. Quincy would know. But I believe I am right, Sara."

Foolishly, she did not notice for a moment. There was only a strange chill at her heart. But it was only a moment. The name he had used seemed to hang in the air between them as if the sound of it had not died away with his voice.

She sat down abruptly on a chair close by.

"That is not my name," she whispered.

"I beg your pardon." He made her an ironic half bow. "I forget that you insist upon formality. I should have said *Lady* Sara. Is that better?"

She shook her head. "You misunderstand. It is not my *name*. I am Jane." But she spread her hands over her face suddenly and found they were shaking. She lowered them to her lap. "How did you find out?"

"I had a visitor," he said. "A Bow Street Runner. I understand that in his search for Lady Sara Illingsworth he called at the milliner's shop of a certain Madam Dee Lorrent. I suppose he meant Madame de Laurent. Coincidentally your former employer, Jane, as well as Lady Sara's. The Runner came to the intelligent conclusion that you were one and the same."

"I was going to tell you." She realized even as she spoke how lame her words sounded.

"Were you?" He raised his quizzing glass and regarded her through it with cold hauteur. "Were you indeed, Lady Sara? Pardon me for not believing you. You are as accomplished a liar as I have met. I am afraid of friendship and emotional closeness, am I? You ought not to have become my friend, ought you? To my shame

I became your dupe. For a short while. No longer." He dropped his quizzing glass and it swung on its ribbon.

The temptation was to beg him to believe her, try to explain that after the emotional intensity of his own disclosures two evenings ago she had decided to wait to tell her own story. But he would not believe her. She would not believe him if the situation were reversed, would she?

"Does he know where I am?" she asked. "The Bow Street Runner?"

"He followed me here last night," he told her, "and stood outside while you were pleasuring me upstairs. Oh, do not be alarmed. I have called off the hunt, at least in this particular place, though I do not imagine he is deceived. He is more intelligent than his current employer, I believe."

"Is the Earl of Durbury still at the Pulteney?" she asked. "Do you know?"

"He was there this morning when I called upon him," he said.

Her face felt cold and clammy. There was a ringing in her ears. The air she breathed felt icy. But she would not faint. She *would* not.

"Oh, I have not betrayed you, Lady Sara," he told her, his eyes narrowing.

"Thank you," she said. "I would rather turn myself in than be dragged in. If you will give me a minute to fetch my bag from upstairs, you may see me off the premises and assure yourself that I am gone. Unless you have told anyone that I am your mistress, no one need know. I daresay Mr. Quincy and the servants here are discreet. It would be a condition of their employment, would it not? The scandal need not touch you too nearly." She got to her feet.

"Sit down," he told her.

The words were so quietly spoken but with such cold command that she obeyed without thinking.

"Are you guilty of any of the charges against you?" he asked her.

"Murder? Theft?" She looked down at the hands clasped in her lap. Her fingers, she noticed dispassionately, were white with tension. "I hit him. I took money. Therefore, I am guilty."

"And jewels?"

"A bracelet," she said. "It is in my bag upstairs."

She would offer no explanations, no excuses. She owed him none now. Yesterday it would have been different. He would have been her friend, her lover. Now he was nothing at all.

"You hit him," he said. "With an ax? With a pistol?"

"With a book," she said.

"With a *book*?"

"The corner of it caught him on the temple," she explained. "He was bleeding and dizzy. If he had sat down all might have been well. But he came after me, and when I stepped aside he lost his balance and cracked his head on the hearth. He was not dead. I had him carried upstairs and tended him myself until the doctor arrived. He was still not dead when I left, though he was unconscious."

There, she had given in to the urge to explain after all. She was still watching her hands.

"He kept coming after you," Jocelyn said quietly. "Why was he coming after you in the first place? Because he had caught you stealing?"

"Oh, that nonsense," she said contemptuously. "He was going to ravish me."

"At *Candleford*?" His voice was sharp. "At his father's home? His father's ward?"

"They were gone," she told him, "the earl and countess. They had left for a few days."

"Leaving you alone with Jardine?"

"And with an elderly relative as chaperone." She laughed. "She likes her port, does Cousin Emily. And she likes Sidney too—*liked* Sidney, that is." There was an uncomfortable churning in her stomach. "He got her drunk and sent her off early to bed. There were only a few of his friends there that evening and his own servants."

"The friends did not defend you?" he asked. "And were not to be depended upon to tell the truth in an investigation into the death of Jardine?"

"They were all inebriated," she said. "They were urging him on."

"Was he not afraid," Jocelyn asked, "of the consequences of ravishing you after his father had returned?"

"I suppose," she said, "he counted upon my being too ashamed to say anything. He counted upon my meekly agreeing to marry him. And it would have been the earl's solution even if I had told. It is what they both wanted and had urged upon me ceaselessly until I almost *was* ready to go at them both with an ax."

"A reluctant bride," he said. "Yes, that would appeal to Jardine. Especially when she is as lovely as a golden goddess. I am not well acquainted with Durbury, though I did not find myself warming to him this morning. Why did you steal and run away and go into hiding under an alias and make yourself look as guilty as sin? It seems uncharacteristic of Jane Ingleby. But then she does not exist, does she?"

"I took fifteen pounds," she said. "In the year and a half since my father's death, the earl had given me no allowance. There was nothing on which to spend money at Candleford, he told me. I believe he owed me far more than fifteen pounds. The bracelet was my father's wedding gift to my mother. Mama gave it to me on her deathbed, but I asked Papa to keep it in the safe with all the other family jewelry. The earl had always refused to give it to me or to acknowledge it as mine. I knew the combination of the safe."

"Foolish of him," Jocelyn said, "not to have thought of that."

"I was not running away," she said. "I had had enough of them all. I came to London to stay with Lady Webb, my mama's dearest friend and my godmother. Lord Webb was to have been my guardian jointly with my father's cousin, the new earl, but he died and I suppose Papa did not think of having someone else appointed. Lady Webb was not at home and not expected back soon. That was when I panicked. I started to realize that Sidney might have been badly hurt, that he might even have died. I realized how the taking of the money and the bracelet would be construed. I realized that none of the witnesses was likely to tell the truth. I realized I might be in deep trouble."

"All the deeper," he said, "for your decision to become a fugitive."

"Yes."

"Was there no one at Candleford or in its neighborhood to stand your friend?" he asked.

"My father's cousin is the earl," she explained. "Sidney is—was—his heir. There was no one powerful enough to shield me, and my dearest friend was from home in Somersetshire on an extended visit with his sister."

"He?" The question was asked with soft emphasis.

"Charles," she said. "Sir Charles Fortescue."

"Your friend?" he said. "And beau?"

She looked up at him for the first time in several minutes. Shock was beginning to recede. He had no business interrogating her. She was under no obligation to answer him. She was merely his ex-mistress. And she had no intention of accepting any pay for the past week and a half or of taking with her any of the clothes he had bought her.

"And beau," she replied steadily. "We were to marry, but not for a long time. I am not permitted to marry without the earl's consent until I am five and twenty. We would have married on my twenty-fifth birthday."

"But will not now do so?" He had his glass to his eye again, but Jane would not be cowed by it. She continued to look steadily at him. "He will not fancy marrying a murderess, Lady Sara? How unsporting of him. And he will not marry a fallen woman? How unchivalrous."

"*I* will not marry *him,*" she said firmly.

"Quite right too," he said briskly. "The laws of our land prohibit bigamy, Lady Sara."

She *wished* he would not keep calling her that.

"Bigamy?" Had Charles met and married someone else? she thought foolishly without even stopping to wonder how she expected the Duke of Tresham to know that fact even if it were true.

"Sir Charles Fortescue," he said coldly, "would not be permitted by law to marry my wife. One hopes, I suppose, that his heart will not be broken, though I have not noticed him rushing about London, moving heaven and earth to find you and clasp you to his bosom. One hopes, perhaps, that *your* heart will not be broken, though frankly I cannot say that I much care."

Jane was on her feet.

"Your wife?" she said, her eyes wide with astonishment. "*Your wife?* How utterly preposterous. You think you owe me marriage just because you have suddenly discovered that I am Lady Sara Illingsworth of Candleford rather than Jane Ingleby from some orphanage?"

"I could not have phrased it better myself," he said.

"I do not know what you have planned for the rest of the afternoon, your grace," she told him, looking into his cold, cynical face and feeling the full chill of his total indifference to her as a person, "but I have something of importance to do. I have a visit to the Pulteney Hotel to make. If you will excuse me." She turned resolutely to the door.

"Sit down," he said as quietly as before.

She swung to face him. "I am not one of your servants, your grace," she said. "I am not—"

"*Sit down!*" His voice, if anything, was even quieter.

Jane stood staring at him for a few moments before striding across the room until she stood almost toe-to-toe with him.

"I repeat," she said, "I am not one of your servants. If you have something more to say to me, say it without this ridiculous posturing. My ears function quite well enough when I am on my feet."

"You try my patience to the limit, ma'am," he said, his eyes narrowing dangerously.

"And mine is already tried *beyond* the limit, your grace," she retorted, turning toward the door again.

"Lady Sara." His icy voice stopped her in her tracks. "We will have one thing straight between us. Soon—within the next few days—you will be the Duchess of Tresham. Your personal wishes on this matter are not to be consulted. I am quite indifferent to them. You will be my wife. And you will spend the rest of your life ruing the day you were born."

If she had not been so white with fury, she might well have laughed. As it was she took her time about seating herself in the nearest chair, arranging her skirts neatly about her before looking up into his eyes, her own carefully cool.

"How utterly ridiculous you make yourself when you decide to play the part of toplofty aristocrat," she told him, folding her hands in her lap and pressing her lips tightly together. She girded herself for the inevitable battle.

21

HE WAS SURPRISED BY THE FORCE OF HIS HATRED for her. He had never hated anyone—except perhaps his father. Not even his mother. It was unnecessary to hate when one did not feel strongly about anyone. He wished he could feel nothing but indifference for Lady Sara Illingsworth.

He could almost succeed when he thought of her by that name. But his eyes saw Jane Ingleby.

"You will not be forced to behold your ridiculous husband very often, you will be relieved to know," he told her. "You will live at Acton, and you know how fond I am of my main country seat. You will see me only once a year or so when it becomes necessary to breed you. If you are very efficient you will have two sons within the first two years of our marriage and I may consider them enough to secure the succession. If you are extraordinarily clever, of course, you may already be increasing." He lifted his quizzing glass and regarded her abdomen through it.

Her lips had already done their familiar disappearing act. He was glad she had pulled herself together. For a while she had looked pale and shaken and abject. He had found himself almost pitying her. She was glaring at him with her very blue eyes.

"You are forgetting one thing, your grace," she said. "Women are not quite slaves in our society, though they come dangerously close. I have to say 'I do' or 'I will' or whatever it is brides say to consent to a marriage. You may drag me to the altar—I will concede your superior physical strength—but you will be considerably embarrassed when I refuse my consent."

He knew he should be delighted by her obvious reluctance. But she had duped him, humiliated him, made a fool of him once. Her will would not prove stronger than his on this particular matter.

"Besides," she added, "I am not yet of age. And according to my father's will I cannot marry below the age of five and twenty without the consent of my guardian. If I do, I lose my inheritance."

"Inheritance?" He raised his eyebrows.

"Everything my father owned except Candleford itself was unentailed," she explained, "and his title, of course. His other estates, his fortune—everything, in fact—will be mine at the age of five and twenty, or my husband's if I marry with consent before then."

Which explained a great deal, of course. Durbury had the title and Candleford and control of everything else at the moment. He would have permanent control if he could persuade Lady Sara to marry into his family—or if he could make her life so uncomfortable that she would rashly elope with someone else before her twenty-fifth birthday.

"I suppose," he said, "if you break the rules Durbury himself inherits everything?"

"Yes."

"He may inherit everything, then," he said curtly. "I am enormously wealthy. I do not need my wife to bring me a fortune."

"I suppose," she said, "if I am convicted of murder I

will be disinherited. Perhaps I will even d-die. But I will fight to whatever end is in store for me. And I will marry no one, whatever the outcome. Not Charles. Not you. At least not until I am five and twenty. Then I will marry or not marry as I choose. I will be free. I will be dead or imprisoned or transported, or I will be free. Those are the alternatives. I will be no man's slave in the guise of wife. Certainly not yours."

He gazed at her in silence. She did not look away, of course. She was one of the few people, man or woman, who could hold his scrutiny. She held her chin high. Her eyes were steely, her lips still in their thin, stubborn line.

"I should have seen it sooner," he said, as much to himself as to her. "The essentially cold emptiness at the core of you. You are sexually passionate, but then sex is an essentially carnal thing. It does not touch the heart. You have the strange ability of opening yourself to other people's confidences. You convey an image of sympathy and empathy. You can take in and take in, can you not, like some cold-hearted creature warming itself with its victim's blood. One does not notice that in effect you give nothing back. Jane Ingleby, bastard of some unknown gentleman, reared in a superior orphanage. That was all you gave me—lies. And your Siren's body. I am weary of arguing with you. I have other calls to make, but I will return. You will stay here until I do."

"I have hurt you," she said, getting to her feet. "You will be pleased to know that you have had your revenge. If my heart was not cold before, it is now. I have given and given of my very self because your need has been so great. I was not given a chance to reach out for myself, for the comfort of your understanding and sympathy and friendship. There was not enough time—just one week and it ended so abruptly yesterday. Go. I am weary too. I want to be alone. You feel betrayed, your grace? Well, I do too."

He did not stop her this time when she turned to leave the room. He watched her go. He stood where he was for a long time.

His heart ached.

The heart he had not known he possessed.

He could not trust her. He would not trust her. Not again.

Had he betrayed her? *Had* it been sympathy and friendship and love she had given after all? *Had* she intended sharing herself with him as he had shared himself with her?

Jane.

Lady Sara Illingsworth.

Ah, Jane.

He strode from the room and from the house. It was only when he was some distance away that he remembered ordering her to remain until he returned. But she was not one to take orders meekly. He should have made her promise. Devil take it, he should have thought of that.

But surely she would not leave the house now. Surely she would wait.

He did not go back.

IF LADY WEBB WAS surprised when her butler handed her a card on a tray and informed her even before she could look at it that the Duke of Tresham was standing in her hall below requesting the honor of a few minutes of her time, she did not show it by the time Jocelyn was announced. She rose from a small escritoire, where she was apparently engaged in writing letters.

"Tresham?" she said graciously.

"Ma'am." He made her a deep bow. "I thank you for granting me some of your time."

Lady Webb was an elegant widow of about forty with whom he was acquainted, though not well. She moved in a more civilized set than any with which he usually consorted. He held her in considerable respect.

"Do have a seat," she offered, indicating a chair while she seated herself on a sofa close by, "and tell me what brings you here."

"I believe," he said, taking the offered chair, "you have an acquaintance with Lady Sara Illingsworth, ma'am."

She raised her eyebrows and regarded him more keenly. "She is my goddaughter," she said. "Do you have any news of her?"

"She was employed at Dudley House as my nurse for three weeks," he said, "after I had been shot in the leg in a, ah, duel. She came upon me in Hyde Park while it was happening. She was on her way to work at a milliner's at the time. She was using an alias, of course."

Lady Webb was sitting very still. "Is she still at Dudley House?" she asked.

"No, ma'am." Jocelyn sat back in his chair. He was experiencing extreme discomfort, a feeling relatively unknown to him. "I did not know her real identity until a Bow Street Runner came to speak with me yesterday. I knew her as Miss Jane Ingleby."

"Ah, Jane," Lady Webb said. "It is the name by which her parents called her. Her middle name."

Foolishly it felt good to hear that. She really *was* Jane, as she had told him earlier.

"She was a servant, you must understand," he said. "She had temporary employment with me."

Lady Webb shook her head and sighed aloud. "And you do not know where she went," she said. "Neither do I. Is that why you have come here? Because you are outraged to know that you were duped into giving sanctuary to a fugitive? If I knew where she was, Tresham, I would not tell you. Or the Earl of Durbury." She spoke the name with disdain.

"You do not believe, then," he asked, "that she is guilty of any of the charges against her?"

Her nostrils flared, the only sign of emotion. She sat straight but gracefully on her seat, her back not touching it. Her posture was rather reminiscent of Jane's—a lady's posture.

"Sara is no murderer," she said firmly, "and no thief either. I would stake my fortune and my reputation on it. The Earl of Durbury wanted her to marry his son, whom she held in the utmost contempt, sensible girl. I have my own theory on how Sidney Jardine met his end. If you are lending your support to Durbury by coming here in the hope that you will learn more from me than he did a few days ago, then you are wasting your time and mine. I would ask you to leave."

"Do you believe he is dead?" Jocelyn asked with narrowed eyes.

She stared at him. "Jardine?" she said. "Why would his father say he was dead if he were not?"

"*Has* he said it?" Jocelyn asked. "Or has he merely not contradicted the rumor that has been making the circuit of London drawing rooms and clubs?"

She was looking steadily at him. "Why are you here?" she asked.

All day he had wondered what exactly he would say. He had come to no satisfactory conclusion. "I know where she is," he said. "I found her other employment when she left Dudley House."

Lady Webb was on her feet instantly. "In town?" she asked. "Take me to her. I will bring her here and give her sanctuary while I have my solicitor look into the ridiculous charges against her. If your suspicions are correct and Sidney Jardine is still alive . . . Well. Where is she?"

Jocelyn had risen too. "She is in town, ma'am," he assured her. "I will bring her to you. I would have brought her now, but I had to be sure that she would find a safe haven here."

Her gaze became shrewd suddenly.

"Tresham," she asked, as he had feared she would, "what other employment did you find Sara?"

"You must understand, ma'am," he said stiffly, "that she gave me a false name. She told me she had been brought up in an orphanage. It was clear that she had had a genteel upbringing, but I thought her destitute and friendless."

She closed her eyes briefly, but she did not relax her very erect posture. "Bring her to me," she said. "You will have a maid or some respectable female companion with her when she arrives."

"Yes, ma'am," he agreed. "I do, of course, consider myself affianced to Lady Sara Illingsworth."

"Of course." There was a certain coldness in the eyes that regarded him so keenly. "It just seems a rather sad irony that she has escaped from one blackguard merely to land in the clutches of another. Bring her to me."

Jocelyn made her a bow, resisting the urge to don his usual expression of cynical hauteur. At least the woman had enough integrity not to be rubbing her hands with glee at the thought of netting the Duke of Tresham for her goddaughter.

"Enlist the help of your solicitor by all means, ma'am," he said. "In the meantime I will be doing my own part to clear the name of my betrothed and to release her from the bonds of an inappropriate guardianship. Good day."

He left her standing straight and proud and hostile in the middle of her drawing room. Someone to whom he could quite safely bring Jane. A friend at last.

JANE REMAINED IN HER bedchamber for a whole hour after Jocelyn had left, doing nothing but sit on the dressing table stool, her slippered feet side by side on the floor, her hands clasped in her lap, her eyes glazed as they gazed unseeing at the carpet.

Then she got up and removed all her clothes, everything that had been bought for her. She took from her wardrobe the plain muslin dress, the serviceable shift, and the stockings she had worn to London and dressed again. She brushed out her hair and braided it tightly so that it would fit beneath her gray bonnet. She pulled on the bonnet and matching cloak, slipped her feet into her old shoes, drew on her black gloves, and was ready to go. She picked up her bag of meager possessions—and the priceless bracelet—and let herself quietly out of her room.

Unfortunately Phillip was in the hallway below. He looked at her in surprise—she had never been out before, of course, and she was very plainly dressed.

"You are going out, ma'am?" he asked redundantly.

"Yes." She smiled. "Just for a walk and some fresh air, Phillip."

"Yes, ma'am." He hurried to open the door for her and looked uncertainly at her bag. "Where shall I tell his grace you have gone, ma'am, if he should return?"

"That I have gone for a walk." She retained her smile as she stepped out onto the doorsill. She immediately felt the panic of one who fears falling off the edge of the world. She stepped resolutely forward. "I am not a prisoner here, you know."

"No, of course, ma'am," Phillip was hasty to agree. "Enjoy your walk, ma'am."

She wanted to turn back to say a proper good-bye to him. He was a pleasant young man who had always been eager to please. But she merely walked on and listened to the sound of the door closing behind her.

Like a prison door.

Shutting her out.

It might have been just oversensitive nerves, of course. She realized that as soon as she sensed less than five minutes later that she was being followed. But she would not turn around to look. Neither would she quicken her pace—nor slacken it. She strode along the pavement at a steady pace, her back straight, her chin up.

"Lady Sara Illingsworth? Good afternoon, my lady."

The voice, reasonably pleasant, not raised, came from close behind her. She felt as if a reptile were crawling up her spine. Terror attacked her knees, nausea her stomach. She stopped and turned slowly.

"A member of the Bow Street Runners, I presume?" she said just as pleasantly. He certainly did not look the part. Neither tall nor large in girth, he appeared like nothing more than a poor man's imitation of a dandy.

"Yes, my lady. At your service, my lady," the Runner said, looking steadily at her, not making any obeisance.

Jocelyn had been wrong, then. He had not succeeded in lifting the watch on her house. He had described the Runner as shrewd, but he had not guessed that the man was too shrewd to allow himself to be ordered away from his prey when he knew she was close.

"I will make your task easy," she said, surprised by the steadiness of her own voice. Indeed, it was amazing how terror receded once one had faced it head-on. "I am on the way to the Pulteney Hotel to call upon the Earl of Durbury. You may escort me there and claim all the glory of having apprehended me, if you wish. But you will not come closer or touch me. If you do, I shall squawk very loudly—there are any number of carriages and pedestrians in sight. I shall make up every story I can think of to convince my audience that you are stalking and harassing me. Do we have an agreement?"

"It is like this, my lady." The Runner's voice sounded pleasantly regretful. "Mick Boden does not let criminals escape him once he has them in his sights. I don't foolishly let them off the leash just because they are ladies and know how to talk sweet. And I don't make bargains with them. You come quiet after I have tied your hands behind you under your cloak, and you will not embarrass yourself. I do know that ladies don't like to be embarrassed in public."

The man might be shrewd, but he certainly was not wise. He took a purposeful step toward Jane, one hand disappearing inside a deep pocket. She opened her mouth and screamed—and screamed. She startled even herself. She had never been a screamer, even as a child. The Runner looked both startled and aghast. His hand jerked out of his pocket, clutching a length of rope.

"Now, there is no need to take on so," he said sharply. "I'm not going to—"

But Jane never did discover what it was he was not going to do. Two gentlemen rode up at a smart trot and proceeded to dismount from their horses. A hackney coach stopped abruptly on the other side of the street, and its burly driver jumped down from the box while shouting directions to a young sweeper to hold the horses' heads. An elderly couple of respectable middle-class demeanor, who had passed Jane a few moments before, turned and hurried back. And a giant of an individual, who looked as if he might well be a pugilist, had materialized seemingly from nowhere and hugged Mick Boden from behind, pinioning his arms to his sides. It was this action that cut the Runner's sentence in half.

"He accosted me," Jane informed her gathering rescuers. "He was going to tie me up with *that*"—she pointed one genuinely shaking finger at the rope—"and abduct me."

Everyone spoke up at once. The pugilist offered to squeeze harder until the villain's stomach came spurting out his mouth. The coachman suggested taking him in the hackney to the nearest magistrate, where he would surely be sentenced to hang. One of the gentlemen riders gave it as his opinion that it would be a shame for such a slimy toad to swing before his facial features had been rearranged. The elderly gentleman did not know why such a villainous-looking thug should be allowed to roam the streets of a civilized city, terrorizing its womenfolk. His wife set a motherly arm about Jane's shoulders and clucked and tutted with mingled concern and outrage.

Mick Boden had recovered his composure even though he could not free himself. "I am a Bow Street Runner," he announced in a voice of authority. "I am engaged in apprehending a notorious thief and murderess and would advise you all not to interfere in the workings of justice."

Jane lifted her chin. "I am Lady Sara Illingsworth," she said indignantly, hoping that none of the gathered spectators had heard of her. "I am on my way to visit my cousin and guardian, the Earl of Durbury, at the Pulteney Hotel. He will be very vexed with me when I confess that I came out without my maid. The poor girl is nursing a chill. I should have brought a footman instead, of course, but I did not understand that desperate men will accost ladies even in broad daylight." She drew a handkerchief from the pocket of her cloak and held it to her mouth.

Mick Boden looked reproachfully at her. "Now, there was no need of all this," he said.

"Come, my dear," the elderly lady said, linking her arm through Jane's. "We will see you safely to the Pulteney Hotel, will we not, Vernon? It is not far out of our way."

"You go on, my lady," one of the riders told her. "We know where to find you if you are needed as a witness. But I've a mind to do the law's work for it without bothering any magistrate. You go on."

"Now see here," Mick Boden was saying as Jane took the offered arm of the elderly gentleman and proceeded along the street, protectively flanked by him and his wife. Under other circumstances she might have been amused. As it was, she felt a mingling of boldness—now at last she was *doing* something—and apprehension. He had been going to *tie* her hands.

She thanked her escort most profusely when they arrived before the doors of the Pulteney, and promised that never again would she be foolish enough to step out alone onto the streets of London. They had been so kind to her that she felt guilt at the way she had deceived them. Although she was, of course, no thief and no murderer. She stepped inside the hotel.

A few minutes later, she was knocking on the door of the Earl of Durbury's suite, having declined the offer to have his lordship informed of her arrival while she waited in a lounge downstairs. She recognized her cousin's valet, Parkins, who answered her knock, and he recognized her. His jaw dropped inelegantly. Jane stepped forward without a word for him, and he jumped smartly to one side.

She found herself in a spacious and elegant private sitting room. The earl was seated at a desk, his back to the door. Despite herself, her heart was thumping in her chest, in her throat, in her ears.

"Who was it, Parkins?" he asked without turning.

"Hello, Cousin Harold," Jane said.

JOCELYN INTENDED TO WASTE no time in taking Jane to Lady Webb's. It really would not do for her to remain where she was for a moment longer than necessary. He would have Mrs. Jacobs accompany her in his carriage.

But getting his carriage necessitated riding through Hyde Park. And in riding through the park he came quite coincidentally upon an interesting scene. There was a largish group of gentlemen on horseback some distance from the path along which he rode, several of them talking and gesticulating excitedly.

Some quarrel was brewing, he thought. Normally he would not have hesitated to ride closer and discover what was going on, but today he had more important matters to attend to and would have continued onward if he had not suddenly recognized one of the loudly gesturing gentlemen as his brother.

Ferdinand quarreling? Perhaps getting himself into deep waters from which his Dudley nature would not permit him to withdraw until he was in over his head? Well, the least he himself could do, Jocelyn decided with a resigned sigh, was go and lend some moral support.

His approach was noted, first by those who were not themselves involved in the loud altercation that was proceeding, but then even by its participants. The crowd turned as one man to watch him come and a curious hush descended on them.

The reason for it all was almost instantly apparent to Jocelyn. There they were at last, all five of them in a body together—the Forbes brothers. Terrified, no doubt, to show their individual faces anywhere in London, they were presenting a collective front to the world today.

"Tresham!" Ferdinand exclaimed. He looked about at the brothers in some triumph. "*Now* we will see who is a cowardly bastard!"

"Dear me." Jocelyn raised his eyebrows. "Has anyone here been using such shockingly vulgar language, Ferdinand? I am vastly relieved I was not present to hear it. And who, pray, was the recipient of such an uncharitable description?"

Although he was a prosy bore in a pulpit, the Reverend Josiah Forbes, to give him his due, was no sniveling, sneaky knave. He rode forward without any hesitation until he was almost knee to knee with Jocelyn, made a grand production of taking off his right glove, and then spoke.

"You were, Tresham," he said. "Cowardly bastard *and* debaucher of wedded virtue. You will meet me, sir, if you wish to dispute either of these accusations."

He leaned forward and slapped his glove across Jocelyn's cheek.

"Gladly," Jocelyn said with languid hauteur. "Your second may meet with Sir Conan Brougham at his earliest convenience."

The Reverend Forbes's place was taken by Captain Samuel Forbes, resplendent in his scarlet regimentals, and amid the buzz of heightened excitement among the spectators, Jocelyn was aware that the remaining Forbeses were forming a wavering queue behind. He yawned delicately behind one hand.

"And you will meet me over the matter of my sister's honor, Tresham," Captain Forbes said, and slapped *his* glove across the same ducal cheek.

"If fate permits me," Jocelyn told him gently. "But you will understand that if your brother has spattered my brains across a field of honor before I am able to keep our appointment, I will be forced to decline your invitation—or at least Brougham will on my posthumous behalf."

Captain Forbes wheeled his horse away, and it was apparently Sir Anthony Forbes's turn. But Jocelyn held up a staying hand and looked from one to the other of the three remaining brothers with careful disdain.

"You must forgive me," he said softly, "if I beg to decline the opportunity of meeting any of the three of you on a field of honor. There is no honor in attempting to punish a man without first challenging him face-to-face. And I make it a personal rule to duel only with gentlemen. There is nothing gentlemanly about attempting to wound a man by killing his brother."

"And nothing safe about it either," Ferdinand added hotly, "when that brother can stand up to answer the cowardly trick for himself."

There was a smattering of applause from the ever-growing circle of spectators.

"You three," Jocelyn said, raising his whip and pointing it at each of the brothers in turn, "will take your punishment at the end of my fists here and now, though I suggest we move to a more secluded area. I will take on all of you at once. You may defend yourselves since I *am* a gentleman and would not take unfair advantage even of rogues and scoundrels by having you tied down. But there will be no rules and we will have no seconds. This is *not* a field of honor."

"Oh, I say, Tresham," Ferdinand said with cheerful enthusiasm, "well done. But it will be two against three. This is my quarrel too and I will not be left out of the satisfaction of sharing in the punishing." He dismounted as he spoke and led his horse in the direction of the grove of trees toward which Jocelyn had pointed. Beyond it there was more grass but no paths, and so it was rarely used by those riders and pedestrians who frequented the park daily.

The three Forbes brothers, as Jocelyn had guessed, could not avoid the meeting without losing face. The other gentlemen crowded after them, delighted by the unexpected opportunity of watching a mill in Hyde Park of all places.

Jocelyn stripped off his coat and waistcoat while his brother did the same thing beside him. Then they both strode out into the grassy ring, formed by the crowd of acquaintances who had gathered to watch.

It really was a vastly uneven contest, Jocelyn realized with some disappointment and contempt before even two minutes had passed. Wesley Forbes liked to use his booted feet and clearly hoped to disarm his opponents with one well-placed kick to each. Unfortunately for him, Ferdinand, who had quick reflexes, caught his boot in midair with both hands just as if it were a ball and held him off balance while he used one of his considerably longer legs to poke the man sharply in the chin.

After that, and to enthusiastic cheering from the vast majority of the spectators, it was two against two.

Sir Anthony Forbes, who landed one lucky punch to Jocelyn's stomach, tried for some time to match his opponent strike for strike, but soon he began blubbering about its being unfair to fight him when it was Wes who had tampered with the curricle.

The crowd jeered.

"Perhaps it is poetic justice, then," Jocelyn told him as he jabbed at Sir Anthony's defenses and waited longer than was really necessary before delivering the *coup de grâce*, "that I should be punishing the wrong brother."

At last he let fly with a left hook and a right uppercut, which felled his opponent like a wicket going down before a cricket ball.

Ferdinand meanwhile was using Joseph Forbes's stomach as a punching ball. But hearing the general cheer as Sir Anthony went down, he ended his own bout with one pop to the man's face. Joseph's knees buckled under him and he rolled on the ground, clutching his bloody nose. He did not attempt to get up.

Jocelyn strode over to the other two brothers, who had watched in silence. He nodded courteously enough. "I shall await further word from Sir Conan Brougham," he said.

Ferdinand, without a visible mark on his body, was pulling his coat back on and laughing gaily. "One could have wished for all five," he said, "but one must not be greedy. Well done, Tresham. That was inspired. No duels for those three but simple punishment. And audience enough to tell the tale for weeks to come. We have reminded everyone of the consequences of annoying a Dudley. Come to White's?"

But Jocelyn had just grown aware of how much time had been used up in this encounter.

"Perhaps later," he said. "For now I have something of extreme importance to attend to." He looked assessingly at his brother, waving off the gentlemen who would have come to congratulate them and mounting his horse. "Ferdinand, there is something you can do for me."

"Anything." His brother looked both surprised and gratified. It was not often that Jocelyn asked something of him.

"You might spread the word," Jocelyn said, "subtly, of course, that it has turned out that Miss Jane Ingleby, my former nurse and the main musical attraction at my soiree, is in reality Lady Sara Illingsworth. That I have found her by happy chance and taken her to Lady Webb's. That all the rumors surrounding her name are about to be proved as exaggerated and groundless as most rumors are."

"Oh, I say." Ferdinand looked vastly interested. "How did you find out, Tresham? How did you find *her*? How—"

But Jocelyn held up a staying hand. "You will do it?" he asked. "Is there any grand *ton* entertainment tonight?" He was dreadfully out of touch.

"A ball," Ferdinand said. "Lady Wardle's. It is bound to be a horrid squeeze."

"Drop word there, then," Jocelyn said. "All you need do is mention the bare facts once. Twice perhaps for good measure. No more than that."

"What—" Ferdinand began, but Jocelyn had his hand up again.

"Later," he said. "I have to go take her to Lady Webb's. This is going to be a near-run thing, Ferdie. But we will pull it off."

It felt rather good, he thought as he rode onward, to have made the discovery that his brother could also be a friend, as he had been when they were boys.

So there were two more duels to face—after he had dealt with this whole damned mess with Jane. Would she out of sheer principle, he wondered, be as prickly about being escorted to Lady Webb's as she had been about everything else earlier on?

Dratted, exasperating woman!

22

THE EARL OF DURBURY WHIPPED AROUND, HIS eyes widening in astonishment.

"So," he said, getting to his feet, "you have been ferreted out at last, have you, Sara? By the Bow Street Runner? Where is he?"

"I am not perfectly sure," Jane said, strolling farther into the room in order to set her gloves and bonnet down on a small table. "The group of men who prevented him from abducting me had not decided what to do with him when I continued on my way here. I have come quite voluntarily to see you. To commiserate with you on your loss. And to demand what you mean by setting up a Bow Street Runner outside my house as if I were a common criminal."

"Aha," the earl said sharply. "He was right, then, was he? I might have guessed it. You are a strumpet, Tresham's doxy."

Jane ignored him. "Your hired Runner," she said, "who would have engaged in melodrama by dragging me here with my hands tied behind my back, called me a thief. What have I stolen, pray, that is yours and not mine? And he called me a murderess. In what sense am I criminally responsible for Sidney's death when he fell and banged his head while trying to grab hold of me so that he might ravish me and force me into marrying him? He was alive when I left Candleford. I had him carried upstairs to his bed. I tended him myself until the doctor *I sent for* arrived. I am sorry despite everything that he died. I would not wish for the death even of a despicable creature like Sidney. But I can hardly be held responsible. If you wish to try to have me convicted of his murder, I cannot stop you. But I warn you that you will merely make yourself look ridiculous in the public eye."

"You always did have a wicked, impudent tongue, Sara," her cousin said, clasping his hands at his back and glowering at her. "We will see whether the word of the Earl of Durbury carries more weight with a jury than that of a common whore."

"You bore me, Cousin Harold," Jane said, seating herself on the nearest chair and hoping that the shaking of her knees was not evident. "I should like some tea. Will you ring for service, or shall I?"

But he was given no chance to make a choice. There was a knock on the door, and the silent valet turned to answer it. The Bow Street Runner stepped into the room, breathing rather heavily and looking somewhat disheveled. His nose was as red as a beacon and surely swollen. In one hand he clutched a handkerchief on which Jane could see bloodstains. A thin red line trickled from one nostril. He glared accusingly at Jane.

"I apprehended her, my lord," he said. "But to my shame I confess she is more sly and dangerous than I had anticipated. I will tie her up here and now if it is your wish and drag her to a magistrate before she can play any more of her tricks."

Jane felt almost sorry for him. He had been made to look foolish. She guessed that such a thing did not happen often to upset his dignity.

"I shall be taking her back to Cornwall," the earl said.

"She will meet her fate there. We will be leaving tonight, as soon as I have dined."

"Then if I were you," the Runner advised, "I would not trust her to sit meekly beside you in your carriage, my lord, or to enter inns along the way without kicking up a fuss and having you set upon by a parcel of ignorant fools who would not see the truth if it peered into their eyes. I would not trust her not to bash you over the head as she did to your son as soon as you nod off to sleep."

"I really have hurt your feelings," Jane said pleasantly. "But you cannot say I did not warn you that I would scream."

He looked at her with dislike. "I would have her trussed up hand and foot if I were you, my lord," he said. "And gagged too. And hire a guard to travel with you. I know a woman who would be willing to take on the task. My lady here would not play any of her tricks on Bertha Meeker, believe me."

"How ridiculous!" Jane said.

But the earl was looking uneasy. "She always was headstrong," he said. "She was never biddable despite all the kindnesses we showed her after her father's passing. She was an only child, you know, and spoiled atrociously. I want her back at Candleford, where she can be properly dealt with. Yes, do it, Boden. Employ this woman. But she must be here within two hours or it will be dark even before I leave London."

Jane had been feeling an enormous sense of relief. It had all been a great deal easier than she had anticipated. Indeed, she had been finding it hard to imagine that she had been so unexpectedly craven for so long. She should never even have been tempted to go into hiding, to give in to the terrors of what might happen if none of the witnesses was willing to speak the truth of what had happened at Candleford that night.

Now once again terror assailed her. They were going to tie her up and send her back to Cornwall as a prisoner with a female guard. And then she was going to be tried for murder. The air felt suddenly cold in her nostrils.

"In the meantime," Mick Boden said, his gaze fastening nastily on Jane again, "we will confine my lady to that chair so that you may have your dinner in peace. Your man will help me."

Anger came to Jane's rescue. She shot to her feet. "Stay where you are," she commanded the Runner with such hauteur that for a moment he halted in his tracks. "What an utterly gothic suggestion! Is this your idea of revenge? I have just lost the final vestiges of respect I felt for you and your intelligence. I will accompany you to Candleford of my own free will, Cousin Harold. I will *not* be hauled there like a common felon."

But the Runner had that length of rope out of his pocket again, and the valet, after one uneasy glance at the earl, who nodded curtly, took a few steps toward her.

"Tie her down," the earl said before turning away to shuffle the papers on his desk.

"Very well." Jane gritted her teeth. "If it is a fight you want, a fight you will get."

But this time she could not scream. It would be too easy for the earl to convince would-be rescuers that she was a murderess resisting arrest. And of course she would lose the fight—she was pitted against two men with her cousin to add his strength to theirs if it became necessary. Within a few minutes she was going to find herself back on her chair, tied hand and foot and probably gagged too. Well, she would not go down without leaving a few bruises and scratches on each of her assailants. All fear had vanished, to be replaced by a strange sort of exhilaration.

They attacked her together, coming around both sides of the chair and grabbing for her. She hit out with both fists and then with both feet. She twisted and turned, jabbed with her elbows, and even bit a hand that came incautiously close to her mouth. And without even thinking she used language with which she had become familiar in the past few weeks.

"Take your *damned* hands off me and go to the *devil,*" she was saying when a quiet voice somehow penetrated the noise of the scuffle.

"Dear me," it said, "am I interrupting fun and games?"

By that time Parkins was hanging on to one of her arms while the Runner had the other twisted up painfully behind her back. Jane, panting for breath, her vision impaired by the hair that had fallen across her face, glared at her savior, who was lounging against the frame of the open door, his quizzing glass to his eye and grossly magnifying it.

"Go away," she said. "I have had *enough* of men to last me at least two lifetimes. I do not need you. I can do very well on my own."

"As I can see." The Duke of Tresham lowered his glass. "But such atrocious language, Jane. Wherever have you acquired it? Might I be permitted to ask, Durbury, why there is a male person—neither one a gentleman, I fear—hanging from each of Lady Sara Illingsworth's arms? It appears to be a strange, unsporting sort of game."

Jane caught sight of Mrs. Jacobs hovering outside the door, looking as if she were bristling with indignation. And Jane herself was feeling no less so. Why was it that two grown men, who had been quite ferocious enough to overpower her just a minute before, were now standing meek and motionless, looking as if for direction to one languid gentleman?

"Good day, Tresham," the earl said briskly. "Cousin Sara and I will be leaving for Candleford before dark. Your presence here is quite unnecessary."

"I came of my own free will," Jane said. "You are no longer responsible for me in any way at all, your grace."

He ignored her, of course. He addressed the Bow Street Runner. "Unhand the lady," he said gently. "You already have a nose that is painful to behold. Are you responsible, Jane? My compliments. I would regret to have to give you eyes to match, my fine fellow."

"Now see here—" Mick Boden began.

But the ducal glass was to the duke's eye again and his eyebrows had been raised. Much as it was a relief to have her arm suddenly released, Jane could feel only indignation against a man who could rule merely through the power of his eyebrows and his quizzing glass.

"Dismiss this man," the duke instructed the Earl of Durbury. "And your servant. Should this contretemps draw the attention of other hotel guests and employees, you might find yourself having to explain why a supposedly murdered man is alive and well and living at Candleford."

Jane's eyes flew to the earl's. He was looking thunderous and rather purple in the face. But for the moment he said nothing. He did not protest. He did not contradict what had just been said.

"Exactly so," the Duke of Tresham said softly.

"One would equally hate it to become public knowledge," the earl said, "that you have been harboring a common felon in the guise of mis—"

"I would not complete that sentence if I were you," Jocelyn advised. "You will dismiss the Runner, Durbury? Or shall I?"

Mick Boden drew audible breath. "I would have you know—" he began.

"Would you indeed?" his grace asked with faint indifference. "But, my good man, I have no wish to hear whatever it is you would have me know. You may wish to leave now before I decide after all to call you to account for the arm-twisting I witnessed a short while ago."

For a moment it seemed as if the Runner would accept the challenge, but then he replaced his length of rope in his pocket and stalked from the room with a great show of bruised dignity. The earl's valet followed him out willingly enough and closed the door quietly behind him.

Jane turned on the earl, her eyes blazing. "Sidney is *alive*?" she cried. "And *well*? Yet all this time you have been hunting me as a *murderess*? You have allowed me to believe since I arrived here in this room that he is *dead*? How *could* you be so cruel? And now I know why we were to return to Candleford instead of facing a magistrate here. You still believe you can persuade me to marry Sidney. You must have windmills in your head—or believe that I do."

"There is still the matter of a vicious assault, which kept my son hovering between life and death for many weeks," the earl retorted. "And there is still the matter of a certain sum of money and a certain costly bracelet."

"Ah," Jocelyn said, tossing his hat and cane onto a chair just inside the door, "it is gratifying to know that my guess was correct. Jardine *is* still an active member of this vale of tears, then? My congratulations, Durbury."

Jane turned her indignation on him. "It was a *guess?*" she said. "A *bluff*? And why are you still here? I told you I did not need you. I will never need you again. Go away."

"I have come to escort you to Lady Webb's," he told her.

Her eyes widened. "Aunt Harriet's? She is here? She is back in town?"

He inclined his head before turning away to address her cousin. "It will be an altogether more convenient place than Candleford at which to call upon my betrothed," he explained.

Jane drew breath to speak. How dare he! But Sidney was alive and well. Aunt Harriet was back in London. She was to go there. It was all over, this nightmare with which she had lived seemingly forever. She closed her mouth again.

"Yes, my love," Jocelyn said gently, observing her.

"Your betrothed?" The earl was pulling himself together. "Now see here, Tresham, Lady Sara is twenty years old. Until she is five and twenty she may not marry or betroth herself to any man who does not meet with my approval. You do not. Besides, this betrothal nonsense is humbug if ever I heard any. A man of your ilk does not marry his whore."

Jane watched wide-eyed as Jocelyn took a few leisurely strides forward. A moment later the earl's toes were scraping the floor for something against which to brace his weight while his cravat in Jocelyn's hand converted itself into a convenient noose. His face turned a deeper shade of purple.

"I sometimes believe," Jocelyn said softly, "that my hearing is defective. I suppose I should have it checked by a physician before punishing a man for what I merely suspect he said. But lest I find that I am unable to restrain myself despite good resolutions, I would suggest, Durbury, that in future you speak very clearly and very distinctly."

The earl's heels met the floor again and his cravat resumed its former function, though somewhat more crumpled and askew than before.

Jane would not have been human if she had been able to resist a purely feminine rush of satisfaction.

"Your permission must be granted before I may arrange my nuptials with Lady Sara Illingsworth?" Jocelyn asked. "I will have it then, in writing, before you leave for Cornwall, which I believe you will do no later than tomorrow morning?" He raised his glass to his eye.

"*That* I will not be bullied into doing," the earl said. "Sara is my responsibility. I owe it to her dead father to find her a husband more suited to providing her lasting happiness than you, Tresham. Remember too that she assaulted and almost killed my son. Remember that she robbed me of both money and jewels. She must answer for those actions in Cornwall, even if only to me. I am her guardian."

"Perhaps," Jocelyn said, "these charges should be made in London, Durbury. Lady Sara will doubtless prove a difficult prisoner on the long journey to Cornwall. I will help you haul her off to a magistrate now.

And then the *ton*, desperate for novelty at this stage of the Season, will be able to enjoy the entertainment of witnessing a gently nurtured lady being prosecuted for whacking and felling a man twice her size with a book. And for taking fifteen pounds from her guardian, who had deprived her for longer than a year of the allowance to which she was entitled. And for removing from a safe a bracelet that was her own while leaving behind what is doubtless a costly hoard of jewelry that will be hers at her marriage or on her twenty-fifth birthday. The *beau monde*, I assure you, sir, will be vastly amused."

The Earl of Durbury's nostrils flared. "Are you by chance attempting to blackmail me, Tresham?" he asked.

Jocelyn raised his eyebrows. "I do assure you, Durbury, that if I were attempting blackmail, I would choose to hold over your head the threat that my betrothed will charge you with neglect of your duty to protect her in your own home and your son with attempted ravishment. I am sure at least one of the witnesses could be persuaded to tell the truth. And I would add for good measure that if by some misfortune Sidney Jardine's path should ever cross mine during the remainder of both our lives, he will, within five minutes of such a meeting, be picking his teeth out of his throat. You may wish to convey that observation to him."

Jane felt another rush of unwilling satisfaction. It ought not to have been so easy for him. It was not fair. Why could no one stand up to the Duke of Tresham? All the bluster drained out of Cousin Harold when he understood that his plan to catch her, to lure her back to Cornwall, and to blackmail her into marrying Sidney was not going to work. And that even withholding his consent to her marriage would have consequences far worse than the loss of much of her father's property and most of his fortune.

While Jane sat in indignant silence, totally ignored as if her very existence were irrelevant, permission for the Duke of Tresham to marry Lady Sara Illingsworth was duly given in writing after Mrs. Jacobs and the valet had been summoned as witnesses.

After that, there was nothing left for Jane to do but smooth the creases from her cloak, put on her bonnet and gloves with slow deliberation while Mrs. Jacobs picked up her bag, and then march out of the room and down the stairs and out to the waiting carriage, with its ducal crest and cluster of servile sycophants waiting to bend and scrape and pay him homage. Jane climbed inside and seated herself, Mrs. Jacobs beside her. If it were really possible for a human being to burst with fury, Jane thought, she would surely do it. And serve him right too to have blood and brains and tissue raining down on the plush interior of his expensive town carriage.

He vaulted in and took the seat opposite.

Jane sat with straight back and lifted chin. She directed her gaze beyond the carriage windows. "I will avail myself of your escort to Lady Webb's," she said, "but we will be perfectly clear about one thing, your grace—and Mrs. Jacobs may be my witness. If you were the last man on earth and you were to pester me daily for a million years, I would not marry you. I *will* not do so."

"My dear Lady Sara." His voice was haughty and bored. "I do beg you to have some regard for my pride.

A million years? I assure you I would stop asking after the first thousand."

She pressed her lips together and resisted the urge to answer him with some sufficiently cutting remark. She would not give him the satisfaction of a quarrel.

He had come to her rescue—of course he had. It was the sort of thing the Duke of Tresham would do. She had left the house without his permission. She had been his mistress. He had determined that he would do the honorable thing and marry her. She was his possession.

But he did not believe she had been his friend.

He did not believe she would have made him hers by telling him the full truth about herself.

He did not trust her. He did not love her. *Of course he did not love her.*

Fortunately the journey to Lady Webb's was short. But it was only as the carriage drew to a halt that Jane really thought about her. She must know that Jane was on the way. Did she know everything else? Would she welcome her?

But she had her answer even as a footman was opening the carriage door and putting down the steps. The door of the house opened and Lady Webb came outside, not just onto the doorsill, but all the way down the steps.

"Aunt Harriet!"

Jane scarcely noticed Jocelyn descending from the carriage and handing her down. It seemed that within a single moment she was enfolded in the safe arms of her mother's dearest friend.

"Sara!" she exclaimed. "My dear girl. I thought you would never come. I have quite worn a path in the drawing room carpet, I declare. Oh, my dear, dear girl."

"Aunt Harriet."

Jane was sobbing and hiccuping suddenly and being led up the steps into a brightly lit hall. She had been taken up the staircase to the drawing room and seated in an elegant chair beside the cheerful fire there and handed a lace-edged handkerchief to dry her eyes before she realized that they were alone, she and Lady Webb.

He had gone.

Perhaps forever.

She could not have been more emphatic in her rejection of him.

And good riddance too.

There had perhaps not been any bleaker moment in her whole life.

IT WAS A BUSY morning. Jocelyn rode in the park, where he met Baron Pottier and Sir Conan Brougham. The latter had already spoken with the seconds of the two Forbes brothers and made arrangements for the duels to be fought on successive mornings one week hence in Hyde Park. He would single-handedly be bringing the park back into fashion as a venue for meetings of honor if he did not soon change the family of his dueling partners, Jocelyn thought wryly.

It was not a pleasant prospect. Two more men would be given their chance to snuff out his life. And he did not believe that the Reverend Josiah Forbes, at least, was one to be given the trembles by the famous black Tresham stare.

But Viscount Kimble joined them and then Ferdinand, and Jocelyn put the thought of the duels firmly behind him.

"Word spread last night like fire in a woodshed," Ferdinand said with a grin. "Miss Jane Ingleby turning out to be Lady Sara Illingsworth! It is the sensation of the hour, Tresham. Those people who were at your soiree and heard her sing were preening themselves at Lady Wardle's, I can tell you. Old Hardinge was trying to convince all who would listen that he had guessed it all along. She was far too genteel, he said, to be anyone but Lady Sara."

"Where did you find her, Tresham?" Baron Pottier asked. "And how did you discover the truth? When I think that every time we called on you at Dudley House, there she was. And we never so much as suspected."

"Is it true," Sir Conan asked, "that her name has been cleared, Tresham?"

"It was all a mistake." Jocelyn waved one careless hand and then tipped his hat to a couple of ladies who were riding in the opposite direction. "I spoke to Durbury last evening just before he set out for Cornwall. Jardine is not dead. Indeed, he has fully recovered from his little accident. Durbury came to town and hired a Runner to find Lady Sara simply to tell her there was nothing to worry about. The rumors spread, as rumors will, quite independently of him."

"But the theft, Tresham?" Baron Pottier asked.

"There was no theft," Jocelyn said. "How susceptible we all are to gossip. It makes one wonder if we need to find something better to do."

His friends laughed as if he had made the joke of the morning.

"But rumors have a nasty habit of lingering," Jocelyn continued, "unless there is something to take their place. I for one will be calling upon Lady Sara at Lady Webb's and even pursuing her acquaintance."

Baron Pottier roared with laughter. "Ho, Tresham," he said, "that will do it. That will create new gossip. It will be said that you are hankering after a leg shackle."

"Quite so," Jocelyn said agreeably. "One would certainly not wish the lady to be looked upon as someone who is somehow tainted, would one?"

"I will call upon her too, Tresham," Ferdinand said. "I want to take another look at Lady Sara now that I know she *is* Lady Sara. I say, this is famous!"

"It will be my pleasure to call upon her too, Tresh," the viscount said.

"I daresay my mother and my sister would be pleased to make her acquaintance," Sir Conan added. "I'll take them to call, Tresham. My mother has an acquaintance with Lady Webb."

His friends understood, Jocelyn was relieved to find. Kimble and Brougham had the advantage of knowing the full truth, of course, but even the other two seemed to realize there was a certain embarrassment in his having employed the lady as a nurse for three weeks. All were willing to do their part in drawing Jane into society, making her respectable, helping squash any vestiges of doubt about the charges that had been made against her.

The new sensation that would finally replace the old, of course, would be news that the Duke of Tresham was paying court to the woman who had once been his nurse.

All would be well. None of the few people who knew that Lady Sara Illingsworth had been his mistress would ever breathe a word of the fact. She would be safe, her reputation restored.

The conversation turned at length to a reliving of yesterday's fight.

He was at breakfast later, having decided to remain at home to read the papers before proceeding to White's, when Angeline arrived. She swept into the dining room unannounced.

"Tresham," she said, "whatever could you have been thinking of, you and Ferdie, to have taken on *three* of the Forbes brothers in the park yesterday? I was all aflutter when I heard. But how perfectly splendid that all three of them had to be carried to the nearest carriage, two of them quite insensible and the other with a broken nose. What a shame it was not all five. That would have been a glorious victory for the Dudleys, and I daresay you could have done it too. I suppose it is true that you have been drawn into dueling with the other two. Heyward says such information is not for a lady's ears, but he would not deny it so I daresay it is true. I shall not have a wink of sleep between now and then. You will be killed for sure, and what will I do then? And if you kill them, you will be forced to flee to Paris and Heyward *still* says he will not take me there, odious man, even though I would willingly forgo the pleasures of Brighton. And, Tresham, *what* is this I hear of the Ingleby woman's turning out to be Lady Sara Illingsworth?"

"Do have a seat, Angeline," Jocelyn said, waving one languid hand at the chair opposite, "and a coffee." He raised one finger in the direction of the butler at the sideboard. "And do remove that more than usually ghastly pea-green bonnet, I beg you. I fear it will interfere with my digestion."

"*Is* it true?" she asked. "Do tell me it is. It is just the sort of story we Dudleys revel in, is it not? You harboring an ax murderer as your nurse and presenting her to a select gathering of the *ton* as a nightingale. It is quite priceless." She went off into peals of merry laughter as Hawkins bent over her to fill her cup with coffee.

She had made no move to take off her bonnet. Jocelyn regarded it with distaste. "Lady Sara Illingsworth is now at Lady Webb's," he said. "I would be obliged if you would call upon her there, Angeline. The Lord knows why, but you are the only respectable Dudley—probably because a dry stick like Heyward married you and keeps you on some sort of rein, though heaven knows it is not a tight one."

She laughed merrily. "Heyward a dry stick?" she said. "Yes, he is, is he not? In public, at least."

Jocelyn's expression became more pained as her blush clashed horribly with the pink plumes of her bonnet.

"I shall certainly call at Lady Webb's," she said. "Heyward will escort me there this afternoon. I cannot resist having one more look at her, Tresham. Is she likely to be wielding an ax? How enormously exciting that would be. Heyward would be forced to risk his life in defending me."

"She hit Jardine over the head with a book," he said dryly, "when he was, ah, disrespectful. That is all, Angeline. The gentleman is alive and well, and it turns out that the stolen property was not stolen at all. A very dull story, in fact. But Lady Sara is not to be allowed to hover on the brink of society. She will need respectable people of good *ton* to draw her in."

"All of which Lady Webb will arrange for her," she

said. "Why should you be interested, Tresham?" But she stopped after an uncharacteristically brief monologue, stared at him for a moment, her cup halfway to her mouth, set it down in its saucer again, and resumed her hilarity. "Oh, Tresham, you are *interested*! How absolutely famous! Oh, I cannot wait to tell Heyward. But he has gone to the House, provoking man, and I daresay he will not return until it is time to take me visiting. Tresham, you are *smitten*."

Jocelyn used his quizzing glass despite the fact that it enlarged the garish bonnet. "I am delighted to have caused you such amusement," he said, "but *smitten* and the Tresham name are mutually exclusive terms, as you ought to be aware. I will, however, be marrying Lady Sara. You will be pleased to learn that you are the first to know, Angeline, apart from the lady herself, of course. She has said no, by the way."

She stared at him, and for one fascinated moment he thought she had been robbed of speech.

"Lady Sara has said no." She had found her voice. "To you? To the Duke of Tresham? How absolutely splendid of her. I confess I scarcely noticed her when she was your nurse. She looked so very drab in gray. Whoever would wear gray when there are so many other colors to choose among? I was quite struck with her when she sang at your soiree. And she knew how to waltz. That should have been a clue, but I confess I did not pick up on it. But now she has refused you. I am going to like her. She must be a woman of spirit. Just what you need. Oh, I am going to love her as a sister."

"She has said no, Angeline," he said dryly.

She looked at him in incomprehension. "You are a Dudley, Tresham," she said. "Dudleys do not take no for an answer. I did not. Heyward was quite averse to marrying me for all of one month after I was first presented to him, I do assure you. He thought me empty-headed and frivolous and too talkative. The fact that I had you and Ferdie for brothers did not endear me to him either. But he did marry me. Indeed, he was horridly dejected the first time he asked and I said no. I feared he would go home and shoot himself. How could he not have fallen for my charms when I was determined that he should?"

"How indeed?" he agreed.

He was subjected to almost half an hour more of her incessant chatter before she took her leave. But he felt that the morning had been well spent. Jane's respectability was assured. And by dropping a word in a fertile ear, he had lined up on his side powerful forces with which to storm the citadel of her mulish determination not to have him.

He did wonder briefly why he would want to storm her defenses. He could not admit, after all, to any personal need of her. It was just her very stubbornness, of course. Jane Ingleby had always had the last word with him.

Well, Lady Sara Illingsworth would not. It was as simple as that.

He found himself wondering what he would wear when he paid her an afternoon call. Just as if he were some moonstruck schoolboy.

23

"YOU ARE LOOKING PEAKED, SARA," LADY WEBB said. "It is quite to be expected, of course, after all you have gone through. We will soon put the roses back in your cheeks. I just wish we could go outside this afternoon for a walk or a drive. The weather is so lovely. However, this is one of the afternoons on which it is known that I am at home to visitors. Vexing as it may be, my dear, we must be ready to receive them."

Jane was wearing a fashionable, high-waisted dress of sprigged muslin. It had been in the trunk of her belongings that had been delivered during the morning by Phillip and the Duke of Tresham's coachman. Her hair had been dressed by the maid who had been assigned to her care. But ready as she appeared to be to face an afternoon of socializing, she broached the subject that was troubling her.

"Perhaps it would be best," she said, "if I remained out of sight of your guests, Aunt Harriet."

Lady Webb, who had been looking out through the window, came to sit down on a chair opposite Jane's. "That is precisely what you must not do," she said. "Although neither of us has put it into words, Sara, I am fully aware of how you have been living for the last little while. Appalling as it is that you felt driven to such a life, it is over. No one need know. You can be very sure that Tresham will silence anyone of his acquaintance who suspects the truth. And of course he means to marry you. He is a gentleman and knows he has compromised you. He is not only prepared to do the honorable thing but will doubtless try to insist upon it."

"He is very good at that," Jane said bitterly. "But he knows better than to believe it will work with me."

"The Duke of Tresham has possibly the most unsavory reputation of any gentleman in town," Lady Webb said with a sigh. "Though perhaps I exaggerate. He is not known for any particular vice but only for wildness and the tendency to be at the center of every brawl. He is exactly like his father before him and his grandfather before that."

"No!" Jane said more hotly than she had intended. "He is not."

Lady Webb raised her eyebrows. But before she could say anything more, there was a tap on the drawing room door and the butler opened it and announced the first visitors—Sir Conan Brougham with Lady Brougham, his mother, and Miss Chloe Brougham, his sister. They were followed not many minutes after by Lord and Lady Heyward, the latter of whom made it very clear that she had come for the specific purpose of talking with Jane and scolding her for hiding her true identity while she was at Dudley House.

"I was never more surprised in my life as when Tresham told me about it," she said. "And never more gratified than to know he had discovered you and brought you here, Lady Sara. The very idea that you were an ax murderer! I go off into peals of laughter whenever I think about it, as Heyward will testify. I daresay Mr. Jardine was unpardonably rude to you. I met him once and received the distinct impression that he was a slimy villain. It was most forbearing of you to slap him merely with a book, and very poor spirited of him to make a fuss about it and run sniveling to his papa. In your place I would have reached for an ax."

"Lady Webb has been offering you this chair for the last two minutes, my love," Lord Heyward said, leading his wife away.

A large number of guests arrived after that. A few were Lady Webb's friends. Many were people Jane had met at Dudley House on various occasions—Viscount Kimble, Lord Ferdinand Dudley, and Baron Pottier among them. It did not take Jane long to understand who had sent them all or why they had come. The campaign was on to make her respectable again. Far from gratifying her, the knowledge infuriated her. Did he really believe that she could not manage her own life without his helping hand? She only wished he would come in person so that she could give him a piece of her mind.

And then he did.

He arrived alone, looking immaculate in a blue coat and biscuit-colored pantaloons so well fitting that he must surely have been poured into them and Hessian boots that one might have used as twin mirrors. And he was looking insufferably handsome, of course, although when she had started to think of him as handsome Jane did not know. And suffocatingly male. And armed with all his detestable ducal hauteur.

She hated him with a powerful hatred, but of course good manners prevented her from either glaring at him or demanding that he leave. This was not her drawing room, after all. She was as much a guest here as he.

He bowed to Lady Webb and exchanged civilities

with her. He bowed distantly to Jane—just as if she were a speck of dust that had floated into his line of vision, she thought indignantly. He acknowledged with the lift of an eyebrow those of his relatives and friends who were clustered about her—Lady Heyward, Lord Ferdinand, Viscount Kimble among others. And then he proceeded to converse with Mrs. Minter and Mr. Brockledean for all of fifteen minutes.

She was *determined* not to speak to him, Jane had thought as soon as he was announced. How *dare* he give her no opportunity to ignore him? Of course, she also wanted a chance to tell him that he need not have bothered to send people here to visit her or to try to restore respectability to her life. How *dare* he not approach her to be upbraided and told to mind his own business?

"It is really a very splendid new curricle, Ferdie," Lady Heyward was saying. "It is far more dashing than the last one. But you are bound to accept a wager from someone to prove its superiority to any other. You must absolutely not accept. Only consider my nerves if there were another race like the last. Though I never tire of hearing about that final bend in the road, around which you accelerated despite all Tresham's and Heyward's warnings that you must drive with caution. I *do* wish I had been there to witness it. Is it not tiresome sometimes, Lady Sara, to be a woman?"

He had got up from his place, Jane saw with her peripheral vision. The Duke of Tresham, that was. He was about to take his leave. He had turned toward her group. He was going to approach and speak to her. She turned her head and smiled dazzlingly at his brother.

"I understand you are a famous whip, Lord Ferdinand," she said.

An eager, good-natured young man, whom she liked extremely well, he rose immediately to the bait.

"I say," he said, "would you care to drive in the park with me tomorrow afternoon, Lady Sara?"

"I would love to, thank you," she replied warmly, looking up into the dark eyes of the Duke of Tresham, who had stopped at the outer perimeter of her group.

But if she had expected to see annoyance in his face, she was to be disappointed. He had the gall to look faintly amused.

"I came to take my leave of you, ma'am," he told her, slightly inclining his head.

"Oh," she said, still smiling, "is it you, your grace? I had quite forgotten you were here." It was about the most ill-mannered thing she had said in public in her whole life. She was enormously pleased with herself.

"Ah," he said, holding her gaze and speaking only loudly enough to be heard by her and her group. "Not surprising, I suppose, when I am renowned for avoiding the tedium of paying afternoon calls. But for you I made an exception as I so rarely have the opportunity to take tea with a former employee."

He turned and strolled away, having enjoyed the satisfaction of having the last word, Jane had no doubt. She glared hotly at his receding back, good manners forgotten, while the members of her group either stared at one another in astonishment or pretended to a sudden deafness and a need to clear their throats. Lady Heyward tapped Jane's arm.

"Well done," she said. "That was a magnificent set-down and took Tresham so much by surprise that he descended to sheer spite. Oh, how *well* I like you."

The conversation resumed until a short time later the guests began to take their leave.

"Never has one of my at-home afternoons been such a success," Lady Webb said with a laugh when everyone had left. "For which I believe we have the Duke of Tresham to thank, Sara."

"Well," Jane said more tartly than she had intended, "I am grateful to him, I am sure. If he should ever come back and ask specifically for me, Aunt Harriet, I am not at home."

Lady Webb sat down and regarded her houseguest closely. "Did he treat you so badly, then, Sara?" she asked.

"No," Jane said firmly. "I was forced into nothing, Aunt Harriet. He offered and I accepted. I insisted upon a written contract, and he kept its terms. He did not treat me badly."

Except that he made me love him. And worse, he made me like him. And then he discovered the truth and turned as cold as ice and would not trust me even enough to believe that I would have made myself as vulnerable to him as he had made himself to me. Except that he stood all my emotions on their heads and left me empty and bewildered and as wretchedly unhappy as it is possible to be.

She did not speak her thoughts aloud, but she did not need to.

"Except to make you fall in love with him," Lady Webb said quietly.

Jane looked sharply at her, but she could not stop the despicable tears from springing to her eyes. "I hate him," she said with conviction.

"I can see that," Lady Webb agreed with a faint smile. "Why? Can you tell me?"

"He is an unfeeling, arrogant monster," Jane replied.

Lady Webb sighed. "Oh, dear," she said, "you really *are* in love with him. I do not know whether to be glad or sorry. But enough of that. All day I have been considering what is to be done to help you put the past quite behind you. I will present you at the next Queen's Drawing Room, Sara, and the following day I will give you a come-out ball here. I am as excited as a girl. It will almost certainly be the grandest squeeze of the Season. You are understandably famous, my dear. Let us start making plans."

It would be the come-out Jane had dreamed of just a few years ago. But all she could think of now was that Jocelyn had come this afternoon, looking cold and haughty, and that he had almost entirely ignored her until he had a chance to insult her. How many afternoons ago was it since he had finished her portrait and then poured out his heart to her and wept while holding her on his lap?

It felt like a lifetime ago.

It felt as if it must have happened to two other people.

She hated him.

She believed the heavy ache in her heart would never go away.

And then she felt sudden panic. *Her portrait.* Her precious painting. She had left home without it!

Home?

Home?

ALL THE FASHIONABLE WORLD rode or drove or promenaded in Hyde Park late in the afternoon during the spring Season. Everyone came to see and be seen, to gossip and be gossiped about, to display and observe all the latest fashions, to flirt and be flirted with.

Jane was wearing a blue dress and pelisse and a plain straw bonnet tied beneath her chin with a wide blue ribbon. She carried a straw-colored parasol, which Lady Webb had lent her. She was perched on the high seat of Lord Ferdinand Dudley's new curricle while he wielded the ribbons, conversed amiably with her, and introduced her to a number of people who approached for the specific purpose of meeting the notorious Lady Sara Illingsworth, whose story had drawing rooms and club lounges abuzz again.

She smiled and chattered. The sun was shining, after all, and she was in the company of a handsome young gentleman who was going out of his way to be charming to her. He bore a remarkable resemblance to his brother, which fact she would not hold against him.

It was the thought of his brother that kept her from truly enjoying herself. Despite all that had happened during the past forty-eight hours—the release from fear, the return to being herself, living in her own world—she almost wished she could will herself back one week. This time last week they had been together, he painting, she working at her embroidery. Growing comfortable together. Becoming friends. Falling in love.

All illusion.

This was reality.

And reality came riding up to Lord Ferdinand's curricle in company with Viscount Kimble. The Duke of Tresham, that was—it was even difficult now to think of him as Jocelyn—looking dark and morose and unapproachable, quite his usual self, in fact. He touched his whip to the brim of his hat, inclined his head to her, and bade her a good afternoon, while the viscount smiled and reached for her hand to carry to his lips and proceeded to make conversation for a few minutes. The duke's black, expressionless eyes rested on her the whole time.

Jane smiled and talked and twirled her parasol and agreed to come driving in the park again the very next day with Lord Kimble. Then they were gone and Jane, smiling gaily, fought the lump that had formed in her throat and the ache it sent up behind her nostrils and down into her bosom.

But there was no time to brood. There was Lord Ferdinand to listen to and other people with whom to converse. Only minutes after Jocelyn rode away, Lady Heyward drove up in an open barouche, introduced Jane to the Dowager Lady Heyward, and proceeded to talk.

"I am looking forward excessively to your come-out ball at Lady Webb's," she said. "Our invitation was delivered late this morning. I daresay Heyward will escort me, which is rare enough for him as he finds balls tedious. Can you imagine being bored by *dancing*, Lady Sara? And you may not roll your eyes in that odious way, Ferdie. I was not speaking to you. Besides, everyone knows that you prefer fighting to dancing. You will never know what palpitations I suffered on hearing that you and Tresham had fought three of the Forbes brothers the other day. Though as I told Tresham, the victory would have been sweeter had you fought all five. I do not know why the other two stood by to watch their brothers being slaughtered."

"Angie," Lord Ferdinand advised, "take a damper."

But Jane had turned sharply to look at him. "You and

his grace fought a few days ago?" she asked. "With *pistols*? And *you killed* three opponents?"

"Fists actually, ma'am." He looked decidedly embarrassed. "We rendered two of them unconscious, one apiece. The third was rolling on the ground nursing a broken nose. It would have been unsporting to hit him when he was down. You have no business speaking of such things in front of other ladies, Angie."

Lady Heyward rolled her eyes skyward. "I suppose it is ungenteel too, Ferdie," she said, "to be lying awake nights, my nerves positively shattered, because Tresham is to meet the other two Forbeses. I daresay it will be pistols. He will be killed for sure. Though I do think it rather grand of him to take on the *two* of them on two successive mornings. I have never heard the like before. One can only hope he lives to face the second meeting."

Jane felt as if every drop of blood in her body had drained downward to reside in her toes and set them tingling while the rest of her felt cold and clammy and faint.

"Angie," Lord Ferdinand said sharply, "that is gentlemen's business. If you have nothing better to talk about, I suggest you take that bird home that is perched on the brim of your bonnet and feed it birdseed before it expires. And water all those flowers while you are about it. How your neck can hold up all that clutter is beyond me. Good day, ma'am." He touched his hat to the dowager and gave his horses the signal to move on.

Jane was still not quite sure she would not pitch forward into insensibility. There was an annoying buzz in her ears. The pins and needles had found their way up to her hands.

"His grace is to fight another duel?" she asked. "*Two* more?"

"Nothing to bother your head over, Lady Sara," Lord Ferdinand said cheerfully. "I wish he would let me fight one of them, though, since it was me they tried to kill. But he won't, and when Tresham has his mind set on something, or against something as the case may be, there is no arguing with him."

"Oh, the foolish, foolish man!" Jane cried, anger saving her and sending the blood surging through her body again. "All for the sake of honor."

"Yes, precisely, ma'am," Lord Ferdinand agreed before very charmingly but very determinedly changing the subject.

Not one but two duels, Jane thought. On two successive mornings. He was almost certain to be killed. The odds against his surviving were double what they would normally be.

And it would serve him right too, she thought furiously.

But how would she be able to live on?

How could she live in a world that did not contain Jocelyn?

HE MISSED JANE MORE than he would have thought possible. Oh, he called at Lady Webb's that first afternoon, of course, and was goaded into being unpardonably rude to Jane before a sizable audience merely because she had been pert to him and had smiled so dazzlingly at Ferdinand while accepting his offer to drive her in the park that Jocelyn had been sorely tempted to plant his own brother a facer. And he had ridden in the park when he knew she would be there, first with Ferdinand and then with Kimble, and had greeted her and exchanged civilities with her. No more than that. He had sensed from her mulish look and set lips that had he tried to say more, he would merely have precipitated another sharp quarrel—which he would have been perfectly happy to do if only they could have been private together.

He was determined to have her, of course. Not least, perhaps, because she was determined not to have him. But he knew it would be useless to follow his usual practice and try to force his will on her. She must be allowed time in which to adjust her mind to the change in her fortune.

He must allow her time in which to miss *him*. Surely she would do so. Although when he had first learned her real identity he had concluded that her sympathy for him must have been a shallow thing, he was no longer so sure. He remembered the comfortable accord they had established in that room she called their den. And there had been no mistaking her sexual passion for him. He bitterly regretted those last two visits he had paid her—one by night, the other by day. He had not handled the situation well.

He would give her time, he had decided at first. And he would give himself time. He had two duels to face, both with pistols. He found he could not face them with the casual ennui with which he had approached the other four. He was startlingly aware this time that he could die.

Perhaps on those other occasions that fact had been of less significance to him. Perhaps now he had something to live for.

There was Jane.

But how could he pursue her now when he might die? And how could he pursue her when she was still so bitterly angry with him, and his own sense of betrayal was still like a raw wound?

And so in the days before the first of the duels, against the Reverend Josiah Forbes, Jocelyn deliberately avoided any close encounter with Jane. He went to the house once and found himself prowling around their private room. He looked at her unfinished embroidered cloth, still stretched over the frame, and pictured her sitting straight-backed and graceful before it as she worked. He picked up *Mansfield Park* from the table beside the chair where he had usually sat. He had never finished reading it. He played a melody on the pianoforte with his right hand without sitting down. And he gazed at the portrait he had painted of her.

Jane, with the light of life and love glowing from inside her and brightening the canvas. How could he ever have doubted her? How could he have treated her with cold fury instead of gathering her into his arms and inviting her to confide all her secrets, all her fears in him? She had not let him down. It was the other way around.

He summoned his lawyer to Dudley House and changed his will.

And was haunted by that mental image of what he ought to have done and had not done. He had not gathered her into his arms.

He might never have another chance to do so.

If he could do it just once more, he began to think with uncharacteristic sentimentality, he could die a contented man.

What utter, driveling balderdash, he thought in his saner moments.

But then he discovered from Angeline that she was to attend a sizable but private party at Lady Sangster's. Jane, that was. She was attending no public balls yet because she had neither been presented at court nor made her official come-out. But she had accepted her invitation to the soiree.

To which Jocelyn had also been invited.

The night before the first of his duels.

24

IT WAS QUITE UNEXCEPTIONABLE FOR JANE TO attend Lady Sangster's soiree, Lady Webb had assured her goddaughter. Indeed, it was desirable that she appear in public as much as possible before her official come-out. It must not seem that she had something to hide.

But it was the night before Jocelyn was to fight the first of his duels. Jane had not told Aunt Harriet. She had said nothing to anyone about it since quizzing Lord Ferdinand. She had scarcely slept or eaten. She could think of nothing else. She had considered going to Dudley House and begging him to stop the foolishness, but she knew it would be useless to do so. He was a man, with a man's sense of honor.

She went to the soiree, partly for Aunt Harriet's sake and partly for her own. Perhaps somehow it would distract her mind for the evening, even if not for the night ahead or the next morning until she had news. But even if he survived the morning, he had it all to do again the next day. She dressed with care in an elegant gown of dull gold satin and had her maid style her hair elaborately again. She even consented to having a little color rubbed artfully into her cheeks when her godmother commented that she looked beautiful but pale.

The Sangster soiree had been described as a private, select party. In fact, it seemed to Jane, it was a large gathering indeed. The double doors between the drawing room and a music room beyond had been thrown back, as had those leading to a smaller salon beyond. All three rooms were thronged with guests.

Lord and Lady Heyward and Lord Ferdinand were there, all three of them deep in animated conversation with other guests. How could they when they knew their brother was facing death in the morning, and on the morning following that? Viscount Kimble was there, smiling charmingly at a young lady with whom he was talking. How could he when one of his closest friends might die in the morning? He spotted Jane, made his excuses to the young lady, and came toward her to make his bow.

"I avoid insipid entertainments as I would the plague, Lady Sara," he said, smiling his attractive, dangerous smile at her. "But I was told that you were to be here."

"Is all the burden of lifting the evening above insipidity to be on my shoulders, then?" she asked, tapping him on the arm with her fan. Lady Webb had moved away to greet some friends.

"All of it." He offered his arm. "Let us find you a drink and an unoccupied corner where we may enjoy a tête-à-tête until someone discovers that I am monopolizing your company."

He was a charming and an amusing companion. Jane found herself over the next little while engaged in light flirtation and laughing a great deal—and all the while wondering how *he* could keep his mind on anything other than his friend's danger and how *she* could possibly force a laugh from her throat.

There was a loud buzz of conversation all around them. There was music coming from the middle room.

She was firmly back in her own world, Jane thought, looking about. It was true that her appearance had caused considerable interest, perfectly well bred, of course, but nonetheless unmistakable. But no one had looked askance at her or been shocked at her temerity in appearing at a superior gathering of the *ton*.

It felt like an empty victory.

"I am utterly crushed," Lord Kimble said. "My best joke, and it has been received without even a smile."

"Oh," Jane said, instantly contrite, "I am so very sorry. *What* did you say?"

His smile was gentler than usual. "Let us see if music will distract you more effectively," he said, offering his arm again. "All will turn out well, you know."

So he *did* care. And he did know that she knew. And that she cared.

Lord Ferdinand was in the middle room, among the people grouped about the pianoforte. He smiled at Jane, took her hand in his, and raised it to his lips.

"I must protest, Kimble," he said. "You have had the lady to yourself for too long. It is my turn." He tucked her hand through his arm and led her closer to the pianoforte.

He was so very like his brother, Jane thought. Except that he was somewhat more slender and long-legged. And where there was darkness in Jocelyn, there was light in Lord Ferdinand. He was an easygoing, happy, uncomplicated young man, she guessed. Or perhaps not. Perhaps it was just that she had had more of a chance to learn the secret depths of Jocelyn's character during the time she had been his mistress—and friend.

"There are more people here than I expected," she said.

"Yes." He smiled down at her. "I have almost as little experience with such select gatherings as you, Lady Sara. I usually avoid them."

"Why did you not on this occasion?" she asked.

"Because Angie said you were to be here." He grinned at her.

It was very much what Viscount Kimble had said earlier. Were these two gentlemen so smitten with her, then? Or did they both know exactly what she had been to Jocelyn?

"Will you sing?" Lord Ferdinand asked. "If I can persuade someone to accompany you, will you? For me, if for no one else? You have the loveliest voice I have ever heard."

She sang "The Lass with the Delicate Air" to the accompaniment provided by Miss Meighan. The crowd about the pianoforte listened with greater attention than they had given the other performers. And more people came crowding in from the other rooms.

Among them the Duke of Tresham.

He was standing in the drawing room doorway when Jane smiled about her in acknowledgment of the applause that followed her song. Looking elegant and immaculate and not at all as one would expect a man to look who was to face death within hours.

Jane's eyes locked with his for an endless moment while a curious sort of hush descended on the music room. Then she looked away and smiled again, and conversations resumed as if there had been no break in them.

"The devil!" Lord Ferdinand muttered from beside her as she made to move away from the pianoforte so that another young lady could take her place. "What in thunder is *she* doing here?"

Lady Oliver was standing beside Jocelyn, Jane saw when she looked again. She was smiling up at him and saying something. He was looking down at her and replying. She was setting one hand on his arm.

Lord Ferdinand had recovered himself. "There are refreshments in the room across the hall," he said. "Shall we go there? Will you allow me to fill a plate for you? Are you hungry?"

"Ravenous," she said, smiling dazzlingly up at him and taking his arm.

Five minutes later she was seated at a small table with a heaped plate in front of her and four fellow guests in addition to Lord Ferdinand with whom to converse. She never afterward knew what was said to her or what she said in reply. Or what she ate, if anything.

He had come. Just as if a duel were nothing at all. Just as if his life meant nothing to him. And he had allowed *that woman* to touch him and talk to him without loudly and publicly spurning her. Making himself look not only guilty but also lacking the good taste to keep his distance from his supposed mistress, a married lady. Did a man's honor stretch so far?

Finally Lord Ferdinand led her out of the refreshment room and back across the hall to the salon and the two adjoining rooms. Was it too early, Jane wondered, to find Aunt Harriet and suggest that they return home? But how was she to live through even one more hour here without fainting or giving in to a fit of hysteria?

Someone stepped into the doorway of the salon as they were about to enter it. Jocelyn. He grasped her right wrist and looked at his brother but said not a word to him. Lord Ferdinand said nothing either, but merely slid his arm away from Jane's and stepped into the room without her. And even she said nothing. It was a strange moment.

He led her back into the hallway and turned left, drawing her away from the lighted area of the party until they reached the darkened recess of a doorway. He turned her back against the door and stood in front of her, still holding her wrist. His face was all darkness and shadows. Except that she could see his eyes, which gazed back into her own with such an intensity of passion, sorrow, longing, and desperation that she could only gaze back, mute and heartsick.

Neither of them spoke. But the silence was pregnant with unspoken words.

I might die tomorrow or the morning after.

You might leave me. You might die.

This may be good-bye.

Forever. How will I face forever without you?

My love.

My love.

And then he gathered her into his arms and held her tightly, tightly, as if he would fold her right into himself. She clung to him as if she would merge with him, become eternally one with him. She could feel him and smell him and hear his heartbeat.

For perhaps the last time.

He found her mouth with his in the darkness, and they kissed with openmouthed passion, heedless of the proximity of so many of their peers in the nearby rooms. Jane felt his heat, his taste, his maleness, his essence. But all that mattered was that he was Jocelyn, that he was the air she breathed, the heart that beat within her, the soul that gave her life meaning. And that he was here, warm and alive and in her arms.

She would never let him go. Never.

But he lifted his head, gazed down at her for a long moment, then released her and was gone. She listened to the sound of his footsteps receding down the hall in the direction of the salon and was alone.

More alone than she had ever been in her life before. She stared blankly into the almost dark hall beyond the doorway.

Neither of them had spoken a word.

"There you are," a voice said gently perhaps a minute later. "Allow me to escort you to Lady Webb, ma'am. Shall I ask her to take you home?"

She could not even answer him for a few moments. But then she swallowed and stepped resolutely out of the doorway. "No, thank you, Lord Ferdinand," she said. "Is Lady Oliver still here? Do you know? Will you take me to her, please?"

He hesitated. "I don't believe you need worry about her," he said. "Tresham is not—"

"I know that," she said. "Oh, I know that very well. But I wish to talk to her. It is time *someone* did."

He hesitated, but he offered his arm and led her back to the soiree.

LADY OLIVER APPEARED TO be having some difficulty working her way into any group. She was standing alone in the middle of the drawing room, fanning herself and smiling rather contemptuously as if to say that it was beneath her dignity to join any of the groups there.

"I'll wager she did not even receive an invitation," Lord Ferdinand muttered. "Lady Sangster would not have invited both her and Tresham. But she would be too polite, I suppose, to turn the woman away. Are you sure you wish to talk to her?"

"Yes, I am," Jane assured him. "You need not stay, Lord Ferdinand. Thank you. You are a kind gentleman."

He bowed stiffly to Lady Oliver, who turned and raised her eyebrows in surprise when she saw Jane.

"Well," she said as Lord Ferdinand walked away, "the notorious Lady Sara Illingsworth herself. And what may I do for you?"

Jane had intended to try to draw her away to the refreshment room, but it seemed they were in a small island of privacy, enclosed by the noise of group conversations and the sound of music coming from the next room.

"You may tell the truth," she said, looking very directly into the other woman's eyes.

Lady Oliver opened her fan and plied it slowly before her face. "The truth?" she asked. "And to which truth do you refer, pray?"

"You risked your husband's life and the Duke of Tresham's because you would not tell the truth," Jane said. "Now you would risk the lives of two of your brothers and that of his grace again. All because you have not told the truth."

Lady Oliver visibly blanched and her hand stilled. There was no mistaking the fact that she had just been dealt a severe shock, that she had not known about the duels until this moment. But she was evidently made of stern stuff. She pulled herself together even as Jane watched, and began fanning her face again.

"I count myself fortunate that I have brothers to defend my honor, Lady Sara," she said coldly. "What do you want? That I should call them off and save your lover? You might be better served if he died in a duel. It would save you the ignominy of being shed like a soiled garment when he is done with you. That is what Tresham inevitably does with his doxies."

Jane regarded her coldly and steadily. "You will not divert me from what I have sought you out to say, Lady Oliver," she said. "The Duke of Tresham was never your lover. But he has always been a gentleman. He will die rather than contradict a lady and cause her public humiliation. The question is, ma'am, are you a lady? Will you allow gentlemen to suffer and perhaps die because a lie serves your vanity more than the truth?"

Lady Oliver laughed. "Is that what he has told you?" she asked. "That he was never my lover? And you believed him? Poor Lady Sara. You are an innocent after all. I could tell you things.... But no matter. You have nothing more to say? I will bid you good evening, then. I have friends awaiting me."

"You will have an unenviable life ahead of you," Jane told her, "if someone is killed on account of your lie. A life in which your conscience will plague you every single day and every night too. Even in sleep you will not be able to escape it. I pay you the compliment, you see, of believing that you do have a conscience, that you are vain rather than depraved. I will not bid you a good evening. I hope it is not good. I hope you will be tormented by the mental images of what may happen during one or both of those duels. And I hope that before it is too late you will do the only thing that is likely to win back the respect of your peers."

She watched as Lady Oliver snapped her fan shut and swept away into the music room. And then she turned her head to find Lady Angeline on her brother's arm, Lady Webb on Viscount Kimble's, all waiting to gather her up into their company.

"Come, Sara," Aunt Harriet said, "it is time to go home. I am thoroughly fatigued from so much pleasurable conversation."

"I will take upon myself the pleasure of escorting the two of you out to your carriage, ma'am," Lord Kimble announced.

Lady Angeline stepped forward and hugged Sara hard. Uncharacteristically, she said nothing.

Lord Ferdinand did. "I will wait upon you early tomorrow morning, Lady Sara," he said.

To tell her if Jocelyn were alive or dead.

JOCELYN THOUGHT THE NIGHT would never come to an end. But it did, of course, after endless hours of fitful sleep, vivid, bizarre dreams, and long spells of wakefulness. It was strange how different this duel felt from any of the four that had preceded it. Apart from an extra burst of nervous excitement on those other occasions, he could not remember having disturbed nights.

He rose earlier than necessary and wrote a long letter, to be delivered in the event that he did not return. After sealing it and pressing his signet ring into the soft wax, he raised it to his lips and closed his eyes briefly. He had held her once more in his arms. But he had been unable to utter a single word. He had been afraid of coming all to pieces if he had tried. He was not good at such words as had been needed. He had no previous experience.

Strange irony to have found love just when he had this morning to face. And tomorrow morning if he survived today.

Strange to have found love at all when he had not believed in its existence. When he had thought of marriage, even to her, as a trap.

He pulled on the bell rope to summon his valet.

JANE HAD NOT SLEPT. She had tried, but she had lain awake, staring at the shadowed canopy above her head, feeling dizzy and sick to her stomach. In the end it had been easier to get up, dress, and curl up on the windowseat of her bedchamber, alternately cooling a burning cheek against the windowpane and huddling for warmth inside a cashmere shawl.

She should have *said* something. Why had she remained silent when there was so much to say? But she knew the answer. There were no words with which to express the deepest emotions of the heart.

What if he should die?

Jane shivered inside the shawl and clamped her teeth hard together to prevent them from chattering.

He had come through four duels with no mortal injury. Surely he could survive two more. But the odds were against him. And Lord Ferdinand, who had been no match for Jane's determined quizzing during their drive in the park, had revealed not only the place and time of the meeting but also the fact that the Reverend Josiah Forbes, despite his calling, was a cold fish and a deadly shot.

Jane's thoughts were interrupted by a scratching on her door. She looked at it, startled. It was very early in the morning. The door opened quietly, and her maid looked cautiously around it in the direction of the bed.

"I am here," Jane said.

"Oh, my lady," the girl said, peering into the semi-darkness, "begging your pardon but there is a lady downstairs insisting on speaking with you. She got Mr. Ivy up out of his bed, she did, and he got me out of mine. She will not take no for an answer."

Jane was on her feet, her stomach churning, her head spinning.

"Who is she?" she asked. She *knew* who it must be, but she dared not hope. Besides, it was too late. Surely it was too late.

"Lady Oliver, my lady," her maid replied.

Jane did not pause to check her appearance. She dashed from the room and down the stairs with unladylike haste.

Lady Oliver was pacing the hallway. She looked upward when Jane came into sight and hurried toward the foot of the staircase. In the early dawn light, which was augmented by one branch of candles, Jane could see her agitation.

"Where are they?" she demanded. "Where are they to meet? Do you know? And when?"

"Hyde Park," Jane said. "At six."

"*Where* in Hyde Park?"

Jane could only guess that it would be the same place as before. But how could she explain exactly where that was? Hyde Park was a very large place. She shook her head.

"Why?" she demanded. "Are you going there?"

"Yes," Lady Oliver answered. "Oh, quick, quick. Tell me where."

"I cannot," Jane said. "But I can show you. Do you have a carriage?"

"Outside the door." Lady Oliver pointed. "Show me, then. Oh, quick. Run for a cloak and bonnet."

"There is not time," Jane said, hurrying past her visitor, grabbing her sleeve as she did so. "It must be well after five already. Come!"

Lady Oliver needed no urging. Within a minute they were seated in her carriage and on their way to Hyde Park.

"If he should die..." Lady Oliver dabbed at her nose with a handkerchief.

He could not die. He could not. There was too much living to be done. Oh, he could not die.

"He has always been the best of brothers," Lady Oliver continued, "and kinder to me than the others. He was the only one who would play with me as a girl and allow me to follow him around. He must not die. Oh, can that wretched coachman not go faster?"

They were in the park at last, but the carriage could not drive all the way to that private stretch of grass beyond the trees. The coachman, loudly berated by his mistress, set down the steps in haste, and Lady Oliver, looking reasonably respectable in cloak and bonnet and gloves, fairly tumbled out, followed by a bareheaded Jane in morning dress, shawl, and slippers.

"This way!" Jane cried, and broke into a run. She was not sure, of course. It might not be the right place. And even if it were, they might be too late. She listened tensely for the sound of shots above that of her own labored breathing and Lady Oliver's sobs.

It was the right place. As soon as they had stumbled

through the trees, they could see the gathered spectators, all of whom were silent.

There could be only one reason for their silence!

The Reverend Josiah Forbes and the Duke of Tresham, both clad only in shirt, pantaloons, and Hessian boots, were back to back, pacing away from each other, their pistols pointing at the sky. They were stopping. They were about to turn to take aim.

"Stop!" Jane cried. "STOP!" She obeyed her own command and came to a full halt, pressing both fists to her mouth as she did so.

Lady Oliver screamed and stumbled onward.

Both gentlemen stopped. Jocelyn, without turning or lowering his pistol, found Jane out with a single glance. His eyes locked with hers across the distance. The Reverend Forbes both turned and lowered his pistol, frowning ferociously.

"Gertrude!" he bellowed. "Go away from here. This is no place for a woman. I will deal with you later."

Lord Oliver, looking both flustered and embarrassed, stepped forward from among the spectators and would have taken his wife's arm and propelled her firmly away. But she jerked her arm free.

"No!" she declared. "I have something to say."

Jane, returning Jocelyn's stare unwaveringly, nevertheless listened. It took her only a moment to realize that Lady Oliver had chosen to play the part of brave martyr, sacrificing her own reputation for the life of her dear brother. But it did not matter. At least she was doing what she should have done long ago, before the meeting of her husband with the Duke of Tresham.

Strange, Jane thought dispassionately. If Lady Oliver had done the right thing at the start, she herself would never have met Jocelyn. How fragile were the moments of chance on which the whole course of one's life hinged.

"You must not shoot Tresham, Josiah," Lady Oliver implored. "Neither must Samuel. He has done no wrong. There was never anything between him and me. I wanted there to be, but he would have none of me. I wanted to be the subject of a duel—it seemed grand and romantic to me. But I was wrong, and I will admit it now. You must not shoot an innocent man. You would have it on your conscience for the rest of your life. So would I."

"Even now you would defend your lover, Gertrude?" the Reverend Forbes asked, using the voice he must use from the pulpit, Jane guessed.

"You know me better," she told him. "If it were true, I would not so abase myself before an audience. I have simply decided to do what is right. If you still do not believe me, you may speak to Lady Sara Illingsworth, who came with me this morning. She was a witness to the snub I received from Tresham when I called upon him after the last duel. He was never my lover. But he was too much the gentleman to call me a liar."

Jocelyn, who still had not moved, did not look away from Jane. But even across the distance she could see one eyebrow lift in mockery.

Her fists, she realized, were still pressed to her mouth.

The Reverend Josiah Forbes was striding across the grass toward his dueling partner. At last Jocelyn turned and lowered his pistol.

"It seems I was mistaken, Tresham." The Reverend Forbes was still using his pulpit voice. "I owe you an apology and I withdraw my challenge. If you feel that you have a grudge against me, of course, then we will continue this meeting. My family is responsible, after all, for a dishonorable plot to harm yours." Jane guessed that he had taken three of his brothers severely to task for the incident with Lord Ferdinand's curricle.

"I believe," Jocelyn said with a languid sigh, "that small matter has already been avenged, Forbes. And as for this, you were merely doing what I would do for my own sister." He transferred the pistol to his left hand and extended his right.

There was a collective sigh from the spectators as the two shook hands and Captain Samuel Forbes stepped forward to offer his own apologies and withdraw his own challenge. Jane slowly lowered her hands and realized that she had left the imprint of eight fingernails on her two palms.

Lady Oliver swooned elegantly into her husband's arms.

An honorable reconciliation had just taken place. Soon enough Jocelyn was alone again and looking toward the trees once more. He held up his left hand, palm out, to discourage his friends from approaching while at the same time beckoning Jane imperiously with the fingers of his right hand.

Everything fled from Jane's mind except a mind-numbing relief and an overpowering fury—fanned to breaking point by those beckoning fingers. As if she were a dog! As if he were incapable of coming to her. She hurried toward him until she stood almost nose to nose with him.

"You horrid man," she said, her voice low and trembling. "You *horrid*, arrogant, bull-headed man. I loathe you! You faced death here this morning, but you would have died without a word to me. Even last night—even then you spoke not a *word.* If I needed more evidence that you do not care *that* much for me"—she snapped her fingers in his face with a satisfyingly loud click—"I now have it in abundance. I never want to see you again. Do you understand me? Never. Stay away from me."

He looked back at her with lazy hauteur and no glimmering of remorse. "You came all this way at this hour of the morning and in this state of dishabille to command *me* to stay away from *you,* Lady Sara?" he asked with detestably cool logic. "You have flaunted propriety in order to tell me that I am *horrid*? Now, you will take my arm without further delay, and I will escort you to Oliver's carriage—I assume that is where the lady is being carried. I daresay that in the drama of the moment they will forget you if we do not hurry, and then you will be left with a score or two of gentlemen for your sole chaperons and escorts. It is not the sort of situation Lady Sara Illingsworth should find herself in when her reputation is still in a precarious state."

He offered his arm, but she turned away and began to stride in the direction of the carriage. He fell into step beside her.

"I suppose," he said, "all this was your idea? It made for wonderful drama. Saved in the nick of time."

"Not the nick of time part of it," she said coldly. "I merely suggested to Lady Oliver last evening that perhaps it was time to tell the truth."

"I owe my life to you, then." But his words were spoken haughtily and held no note of gratitude.

"You may return to your friends," she said as the carriage came into sight and it was clear that she would reach it in plenty of time to accompany the still-insensible Lady Oliver home again.

He stopped and bowed to her and turned away without another word. But she thought of something as he began to stride away.

"Jocelyn!" she called.

He stopped and looked at her over his shoulder, a strange light in his eyes.

"I left my embroidery behind," she said foolishly, unable even now to say what she wanted to say.

"I will bring it to you," he said. "No. Pardon me. You never wish to see me again. I will have it sent to you." He turned away.

"Jocelyn!"

Again the look over his shoulder.

"I left the *painting* behind."

It seemed to her that their eyes remained locked for long moments before he replied.

"I will have it sent," he said.

He turned and strode away from her.

Just as if last evening had never happened. And what *had* that been all about anyway? Just a stolen kiss between a man and his ex-mistress?

Jane turned and hurried toward the carriage.

25

HER EMBROIDERY, THE PAINTING, AND MANS-*field Park* were delivered the same day. Phillip brought them, though Jane did not see him. All she knew for certain was that he did not bring them himself. She was glad he did not. His behavior during the morning had been imperious and cold and offensive. She had simply imagined that there was tender yearning in his kiss last evening, she decided. His not coming in person with her belongings saved her from having to refuse to see him. She never wanted even to hear his name again.

Which argument was seen for the nonsense it was the following morning when Lady Webb was still in her dressing room and the butler brought the morning post into the breakfast parlor.

"There is a letter for you, my lady," he said to Jane.

She snatched it from his hand and looked with eager anxiety at the name and direction written on the outside. But her heart immediately plummeted. It was not in the bold, careless hand of the Duke of Tresham. In her disappointment she did not immediately realize that she did nevertheless recognize the handwriting.

"Thank you," she said, and broke the seal.

It was from Charles. A rather long letter. It had come from Cornwall.

The Earl of Durbury had returned to Candleford, Charles wrote, bringing with him the news that Sara had been found and was now staying with Lady Webb. She would be reassured to know that the announcement had been made from Candleford that Sidney Jardine, who had for a long time been reputed to be at death's door, was finally recovering his health.

"I have been more distressed than I can say," Charles wrote, "that I was away from home when all this happened so that you did not have me to turn to with your troubles. I would have followed you to London, but where would I have looked? It was said that Durbury had hired a Bow Street Runner but that even he could not find you. What chance would I have had, then?"

But he might have tried anyway, Jane thought. Surely if he really loved her, he would have come.

"Durbury is also spreading another piece of news," the letter continued, "though surely it cannot be true. My belief is that it is for my benefit, Sara, to hurt and alarm me. You know how much he has always despised our partiality for each other. He says that he has given his consent to the Duke of Tresham to pay his addresses to you. I daresay you will be laughing merrily when you read this, but really, Sara—Tresham! I have never met the man, but he has a reputation as surely the most notorious rake in all England. I sincerely hope he is not pestering you with unwanted attentions."

Jocelyn, she thought. Ah, Jocelyn.

"I am going to come up to London," Charles wrote, "as soon as I have dealt with a few important matters of business. I will come to protect you from the advances of any man who believes that this unfortunate incident has made you deserving of all manner of insult. I shall come to fetch you home, Sara. If Durbury will not consent to our marriage, then we will marry without his consent. I am not a wealthy man and so hate to see you deprived of your own fortune, but I am well able to support a wife and family in comfort and even some luxury."

Jane closed her eyes and bowed her head over the letter. She was dearly fond of Charles. She always had been. For several years she had tried to convince herself that she was fond enough of him to marry him. But she knew now why she had never been able to love him. There was no fire in his own love. There was only bland amiability. He obviously had no clear understanding of all she had suffered in the past weeks. Even now he was not rushing to her side. There were a few matters of business to be dealt with first.

Jane felt bleak almost to the point of despair as she folded the letter and set it beside her plate. She had not thought specifically of Charles since coming to Aunt Harriet's. She had known, of course, that a match between them was now impossible, but only now, this morning, had she been forced to face that reality before she was quite ready to deal with it.

She felt as if somehow a comfortable lifeline had been finally severed. As if she were now thoroughly and eternally alone.

And yet he was coming to London.

She would write immediately and tell him not to, she decided, getting to her feet even though she had eaten no breakfast. It would be a waste of time and expense for him to come all this way. And breaking the news to him that she could not marry him would be more easily done on paper than in a face-to-face encounter.

* * *

IT TOOK JOCELYN A few days to realize fully that there was no more imminent threat of death, that the Forbeses and apparently Lord Oliver too were satisfied that Lady Oliver had told the truth during her dramatic interruption of the duel.

When Jocelyn *did* realize it, in the library one morning while he was reading over the latest report from Acton Park, he discovered that he was somewhat short of breath. And when he rested his elbows on the desk and held up his hands, he found with some fascination that they were shaking.

He was very thankful that Michael Quincy was not present to witness the phenomenon.

It was strange really since none of his previous duels had succeeded in bringing him eyeball to eyeball with his own mortality. Perhaps it was because he had never before come face-to-face with life and the desire to live it to the full. For the first time reading the dry, factual report of his steward brought on a powerful feeling of aching nostalgia. He wanted to *go* there, to see the house again with adult eyes, to roam the park and the wooded hills, remembering the boy he had been, discovering the man he had become.

He wanted to go there with Jane.

He ached for her. He would leave her alone until after her presentation, he had decided. He would dance with her at her come-out ball and then pay her determined court until she capitulated, which she would surely do. No one could defy his will forever.

But there was still a whole week left before the ball. He could not wait that long. He was too afraid that she would be the one to defy him, if anyone could. And while he waited, the likes of Kimble and even his own brother were squiring her all over town, oozing charm from every pore, and drawing from her the sort of dazzling smiles she had been very sparing of in her dealings with him. And then he was furious at himself for admitting to jealousy of all things. If she wanted another man, let her have him. She could go to the devil for all he cared. He amused himself with mental images of fighting Kimble and Ferdinand simultaneously—with swords. One in each hand.

And a cutlass between his teeth, he thought in self-derision. And a black patch over one eye.

"Deuce take it!" he told his empty library, bringing the side of his fist down onto the desktop for good measure. "I'll wring her neck for her."

He presented himself at Lady Webb's that same afternoon but declined her butler's invitation to follow him to the drawing room, where other visitors were being entertained. He asked to speak to Lady Webb privately and was shown into a salon on the ground floor.

Lady Webb, he knew, did not approve of him. Not that she was ill bred enough to voice her dislike, of course. And it was perfectly understandable. He had not spent his adult years cultivating the good opinion of respectable ladies like her. Quite the contrary. She did not like him, but she clearly recognized the necessity of his making her goddaughter an offer.

"Though if she refuses you," she told him before sending Jane down, "I will support her fully. I will not allow you to come here bullying her."

He bowed stiffly.

Two more minutes passed before Jane appeared.

"Oh," she said, closing the door behind her back and keeping her hands on the knob, "it is you, is it?"

"It was the last time I glanced into a looking glass," he said, making her an elegant bow. "Whom did you expect?"

"I thought perhaps it was Charles," she said.

He frowned and glared. "*Charles?*" All his good intentions fled. "The milksop from Cornwall, do you mean? The bumpkin who imagines he is going to marry you? He is in town?"

Her lips did their familiar disappearing act. "Sir Charles Fortescue," she said, "is neither a milksop nor a bumpkin. He has always been my dearest friend. And he is coming as soon as he is able."

"As soon as he is able," he repeated. "Where has he been during the past month or so? I have not noticed him dashing about London searching for you, rescuing you from the clutches of your uncle or your cousin or whatever the devil Durbury is to you."

"Where would he have looked?" she asked. "If the Bow Street Runners could not find me, what chance would Charles have had, your grace?"

"I would have found you." He narrowed his gaze on her. "The world would not have been large enough to hide you, *Lady Sara,* if I had been searching."

"Don't call me that," she told him. "It is not my name. I am Jane."

His mood softened and for the moment he forgot the irritation of Sir Charles Fortescue, milksop and bumpkin.

"Yes," he agreed. "Yes, it is. And I am not 'your grace,' Jane. I am Jocelyn."

"Yes." She licked her lips.

"Why are you cowering there, grasping the doorknob?" he asked her. "Are you afraid I will make a grab for you and have my wicked way with you?"

She shook her head and advanced farther into the room. "I am not afraid of you."

"Then you should be." He allowed his eyes to roam over her. She was clad in pale-lemon muslin. Her hair glowed. "I have missed you." But after all, he could not allow himself such vulnerability. "In bed, of course."

"Of course," she said tartly. "Where else could you possibly mean? Why have you come, Jocelyn? Do you still feel honor bound to offer for me because I am Lady Sara Illingsworth rather than Jane Ingleby? You insult me. Is the name so much more significant than the person? You would not have dreamed of marrying Jane Ingleby."

"You have always presumed to know my thoughts, Jane," he said. "Do you know my dreams now too?"

"You would not have married Jane Ingleby," she insisted. "Why do you wish to marry me now? Because it is the gentlemanly thing to do, like facing death in a duel rather than call a lady a liar? I do not want a perfect gentleman, Jocelyn. I would prefer the rake."

It was one of the rare occasions when his own temper was not rising with hers. The fact gave him a definite advantage.

"Would you, Jane?" He made his voice a caress. "Why?"

"Because the rake has some spontaneity, some vulnerability, some humanity, some—oh, what is the word I am looking for?" One of her hands was making circles in the air.

"Passion?" he suggested.

"Yes, precisely." Her blue eyes gazed angrily back into

his. "I prefer you to be arguing and quarreling with me and insulting me and trying to order me about and reading to me and p-painting me and forgetting all about me and the rest of the world while you lose yourself in music. I prefer *that* man, odious as he can be. That man has *passion.* I will not have you acting the gentleman with me, Jocelyn. I *will* not."

He held his smile inside. And his hope. He wondered if she realized just how suggestive her final words had been. Probably not. She was still in a towering temper.

"Will you not?" He strolled toward her. "I had better kiss you, then, to prove how much I am not the gentleman."

"Come one step closer," she told him, "and I will slap you."

But she would not, of course, take one step back to put more distance between them. He took two steps closer until they were almost toe-to-toe.

"Please, Jane." He made his voice a caress again. "Let me kiss you?"

"Why should I?" Her eyes were bright with tears, but she would not look away. And he was not sure whether they were tears of anger or sentiment. "Why should I let you kiss me? The last time you made me believe you cared even though you said nothing. And then the morning after you *beckoned* with your fingers and looked cold and arrogant, just as if I were your dog being called to heel. Why should I let you kiss me when you do not care a fig for me?"

"A fig?" he said. "I do not even like figs, Jane. I like you."

"Go away," she told him. "You toy with me. I suppose I have much for which to thank you. Without you I would be in Cornwall now battling it out with Sidney and the Earl of Durbury. But I am not convinced you did not help merely for your pride's sake. You were not there for me when I really needed you to confide in. You—"

He reached out and set one finger across her lips. She stopped abruptly.

"Let me tell it," he said. "We grew close during that week, Jane. Closer than I have ever been to anyone else. We shared interests and conversation. We shared comfort and emotions. We became friends as well as lovers. More than friends. More than lovers. You convinced me without ever preaching at me that to be a whole person I had to forgive myself and my father too for what happened in the past. You convinced me that being a man does not consist of cutting off all one's finer feelings and more tender emotions. You taught me to feel again, to face the past again, to remember that there was joy as well as pain in my boyhood. And all this you did by just being there. By just being Jane."

She drew her head free of his finger, but he would not allow her to speak. Not yet. He cupped her chin in his hand.

"You told me," he said, "that you would have confided in me as I had in you if I had not discovered the truth about you just when I did. I should have believed you, Jane. And even when I first learned the truth, I should have reacted far differently than I did. I should have come to you. I should have taken you in my arms, as you had taken me the night before, told you what I had discovered, and invited you to tell me all, to trust me, to lean on me. I knew how difficult it was to relive some memories. I had got past that difficulty just the night before and should have been far more sensitive. I failed myself, Jane. And dammit, I failed you."

"Don't," she said. "You are despicable. I cannot fight you when you talk like this."

"Don't fight me," he told her. "Forgive me, Jane? Please?"

She searched his eyes as if to judge his sincerity. He had never seen her so defenseless. She was not even trying to hide her yearning to believe him.

"Jane," he said softly, "you have taught me that there really is love."

Two tears spilled over and ran down her cheeks. He blotted them with his thumbs, cupping her face with both hands, and then he leaned forward to kiss the dried spot on each cheek.

"I thought you were going to d-die!" she blurted suddenly. "I thought we would be too late. I thought I would hear a shot and find you dead. I had a feeling about it here." She patted her heart. "A premonition. I was desperate to reach you, to say all the things I had never said, to—to... oh, *why* can I never find a handkerchief when I most need one?" She was fumbling around at the pocketless seams of her dress, sniffing inelegantly.

He handed her a large white one.

"But you did reach me in time," he said, "and you did say all those things. Let me see if I can remember accurately. Horrid man? Arrogant? Bull-headed—that was a nasty one, Jane. You loathed me? I was never ever to come near you again? Have I missed anything?"

She blew her nose and then appeared not to know what to do with the handkerchief. He took it from her and put it away in his pocket.

"I would have died if you had died," she said, and he

had the satisfaction of seeing that she was growing cross again. "Horrid, loathsome man. If you ever again get yourself into a situation that invites a challenge from another man, I will kill you myself."

"Will you, my love?" he asked her.

She compressed her lips. "You are determined to have me, are you not?" she asked him. "Is this all a ruse?"

"If you knew what I am suffering, Jane," he said. "I am terrified that you are going to say no. And I know that if you do, there will be no shifting you. Have pity on me. I have never been in this position before. I have always been able to have my own way with ease."

But she would only look back at him with the same expression on her face.

"What is it?" he asked her, but she shook her head slightly. "Jane, I long to go home. To go back to Acton—with you. To start creating our own memories and our own traditions there. You thought you knew my dreams. But this is my dream. Will you not share it with me?"

She pressed her lips even harder together.

"Why have you stopped talking to me?" He clasped his hands at his back and leaned his head slightly closer to her. "Jane?"

"This is all about *you*, is it not?" she blurted. "About what you want? About your dreams? What about me? Do you even care about me?"

"Tell me," he said. "What about you, Jane? What do you want? Do you want me to go away? Seriously? Tell me if you do—but quietly and seriously, not in a passion, so that I will know that you mean what you say. Tell me to go and I will."

Even facing Forbes's pistol a few days before had not filled him with such terror.

"I am with *child,*" she cried. "I have no choices left."

He recoiled rather as if she had punched him on the chin with the full force of her fist. Good God! How long had she known? Would she have told him if he had not come today? Would she *ever* have told him? Ever have confided in him, trusted him, forgiven him?

She glared at him in the silence that followed her words. He clasped his hands so tightly behind his back that he felt pain.

"Ah, so," he said softly at last. "Well, this changes everything, Jane."

26

LADY WEBB OPENED JANE'S DRESSING ROOM DOOR and stepped inside. Dressed in midnight blue with matching plumed turban, she formed a marked contrast to Jane, who looked almost ethereal in a fashionable low-cut gown of white lace over white satin, silver thread gleaming on the scalloped hem, the sash beneath her bosom, and the short scalloped sleeves. She wore long white gloves and silver slippers and had a narrow white, silver-shot ribbon threaded through her golden hair.

"Oh, Sara, my dear," Lady Webb said, "you are indeed the daughter I never had. How fortunate I am. But how I wish your poor mother could be here to see you on surely the most important day of your life. You look positively beautiful."

Jane had been critically examining her appearance in the long pier glass in her dressing room. She turned to her godmother.

"You said exactly the same thing yesterday when I was forced to wear those horrid, heavy, old-fashioned clothes that the queen insists upon when one is being presented at one of her Drawing Rooms," she said. "I certainly feel better tonight."

"Your presentation at court was obligatory," Lady Webb said. "Your come-out ball is your personal, triumphant entry into society."

"Will it be a triumph, do you suppose?"

Jane picked up her fan from the dressing table. She was feeling a fluttering of anxiety about the evening ahead. All day there had been a great hustle and bustle in preparation for the ball. Since returning from a morning outing with her maid, she had watched in wonder as the ballroom was transformed before her eyes. It was decked out all in white and silver ribbons and bows and flowers, the only color provided by the lush green of leaves and ferns. The great chandeliers had been lowered and cleaned and filled with hundreds of new candles. The orchestra had arrived late in the afternoon and set up their instruments on the dais. The dining room had been set with all the best porcelain and crystal and silverware for a sumptuous supper banquet at midnight.

"Of *course* it will be a triumph," Lady Webb said, approaching Jane and hugging her, though not closely enough to rumple either of them. "How could it not? You are Lady Sara Illingsworth, daughter of the late Earl of Durbury and a great heiress. You are as lovely as the princesses of fairy tales. And you already have a considerable court of admirers."

Jane smiled ruefully.

"You could make any of a number of brilliant matches," her godmother told her. "Viscount Kimble, for example, has been markedly attentive and could be brought up to scratch, I believe. You need not feel obliged to allow Tresham to continue paying court to you—if he intends to do so, that is. He came and made you a decent offer—at least, I trust it was decent. But the choice is yours, Sara."

"Aunt Harriet," Jane said half reproachfully.

"But I will say no more on that subject," Lady Webb said briskly. "I have already said enough—perhaps too much. Come, we must go down to the ballroom. Our guests will be arriving soon. Cyril and Dorothy will be waiting for us."

Lord Lansdowne was Lady Webb's brother. She had invited him and his wife to help her host the ball. Lord Lansdowne was to lead Jane into the opening set of dances.

The ballroom had looked magnificent in the light of late afternoon. Now it looked nothing short of breathtaking. The candles had all been lit. They sparkled gold above all the white and silver, their light multiplied by the long mirrors along the walls.

It all looked, Jane thought, almost like a room prepared for a bridal ball. But it was her come-out they were celebrating tonight. And all must go well. Nothing must be allowed to spoil it. Aunt Harriet had given so much time and energy—as well as a great deal of money—to make sure that yesterday and today would be perfect for her goddaughter.

"Are you nervous, Sara?" Lady Lansdowne asked.

Jane turned to her with eyes that were tear-filled, despite herself. "Only insofar as I want everything to go well for Aunt Harriet's sake," she said.

"You look as fine as fivepence, I must say, my dear," Lord Lansdowne told her. "Now, if only I can disguise the fact that I have two left feet . . ." He laughed heartily.

Jane turned to Lady Webb, who was regarding her with a maternal eye. "Thank you so very much for all this, Aunt Harriet," she said. "My own mama could not have done better for me."

"Well, my dear. What can I say?" Lady Webb looked suspiciously dewy-eyed.

Fortunately, perhaps, there were some early guests arriving. The four of them hurried to form a receiving line outside the ballroom doors.

The next hour sped by in a blur for Jane as she was formally presented at long last—at the advanced age of twenty—to her peers in the *ton*. There were familiar faces among those of strangers. Some people she felt she already knew quite well. There was the very handsome and charming Viscount Kimble, who Aunt Harriet seemed to believe was a prospective suitor for her hand. There was the amiable Sir Conan Brougham, and a few more of Jocelyn's friends, who had visited him at Dudley House while Jane was there. There was Lord Ferdinand Dudley, who bowed over her hand, raised it to his lips, and grinned at her with his attractive boyish charm. And there were Lord and Lady Heyward. The former bowed courteously, said all that was correct, and would have moved on into the ballroom if his wife had not had other ideas.

"Oh, Sara," she said, hugging Jane tightly at risk of grave damage to both their appearances, "you *do* look lovely. I am *so* envious of your ability to wear white. I look like a ghost in it myself and simply must wear brighter colors. Though Tresham and Ferdie are forever criticizing my taste, odious creatures. Is Tresham coming tonight? He would not give me a direct answer when I met him in the park this afternoon. Have the two of you had words? How splendid of you actually to quarrel with him. No one has ever been able to stand up to him before. I do hope you will not forgive him too readily but will make him suffer. But tomorrow, you know—"

But Lord Heyward had grasped her firmly by the elbow. "Come, my love," he said. "The line will be stretched down the stairs and across the hall and out to the pavement if we stand here talking any longer."

"*Have* you quarreled with the duke, Sara?" Lady Webb asked as they turned away. "You had so little to say for yourself after he called on you last week. Do you know if he intends to come tonight?"

But there really was a line of people waiting to be presented. There was no chance for further private talk.

He did come. Of course he came. He was late, but not *too* late. Jane and Lady Webb were still standing outside the ballroom doors with Lord and Lady Lansdowne while all was abuzz inside and the members of the orchestra were tuning their instruments. He was dressed in a tailed black, form-fitting evening coat with gray silk knee breeches, silver-embroidered waistcoat, sparkling white linen, lace, and stockings, and black dancing shoes. He was looking formal and correct and haughty as he bowed in turn to everyone in the receiving line.

"Lady Sara," he murmured when he came to Jane. He grasped the handle of his jeweled quizzing glass but did not raise it quite to his eye as he looked her over slowly from head to toe. "Dear me. Looking almost like a bride."

Oh, odious, odious man! He knew very well that white was almost obligatory for any lady making her come-out.

"*Your grace,*" she murmured, emphasizing the words slightly in retaliation for his calling her Lady Sara. She dipped him a curtsy.

He did not linger but proceeded on into the ballroom. Jane turned her thoughts away from him. It was not easy to do but must be done. Tonight was for Aunt Harriet more than for herself.

Five minutes later Lord Lansdowne led her into the opening set of country dances. Jane relished the moment to the full. She was dancing at a grand London ball for the first time, and it was her own ball. It was a vigorous and intricate dance, one that had her flushed and laughing before it was over. Other couples had joined them on the dance floor, enough in fact to make it quite clear that tomorrow Aunt Harriet would be able to boast that the event had been a squeeze.

Jocelyn did not dance. Jane did not once look directly at him, but every moment she was aware of him, standing alone on the sidelines, dark and handsome, watching the dancing. At the end of the set, after Lord Lansdowne had returned her to Lady Webb's side and a few prospective partners had approached her, including Lord Ferdinand, she saw him turn and leave the ballroom.

JOCELYN PROWLED. THERE WAS no other word to describe his movements. Even he was aware of it as he moved from the ballroom to the card room to the refreshment room to the landing that connected all three rooms and back to the ballroom again. He could not settle anywhere, even though Pottier invited him to join a table of card players and Lady Webb offered to present him with a dancing partner. There was Ferdinand to deal with, of course. And Angeline.

"I do not know why you bothered to come, Tresh," the former said disapprovingly when they ran against each another on the landing while Ferdinand was on his way to the refreshment room and Jocelyn was about to enter the card room for the third time. "All you have done since you arrived is look damned morose and toplofty. If you have come to spoil the evening for her, I am here to tell you that I will not have it."

Jocelyn looked at his brother with pleased approval. Then he raised his quizzing glass to his eye. "You still have the same valet, Ferdinand?" he asked. "Despite the fact that he is still attempting to slice your throat? You are braver than I, my dear fellow."

Ferdinand frowned and fingered the small nick beneath his jaw on the right side while Jocelyn prowled off in the direction of the card room.

Angeline was a little more garrulous—but then, when was she not? It seemed that she applauded Jane for looking so radiantly happy when it was clear that Tresham must have quarreled with her. She hoped Jane would lead him a merry dance and never forgive him for whatever he had said to offend her. And he was no brother of hers if he did not immediately sweep Jane off her feet and make her an offer and positively refuse to take no for an answer.

"That is what I goaded Heyward into doing," she told him. She fanned her face while her brother looked at her with distaste.

"I wonder," he said, "if you are color blind, Angeline. It is the kindest explanation I can think of to account for your appalling choice of red and pink plumes to be worn side by side in your hair."

She ignored him. "You are going to marry Lady Sara in St. George's, Hanover Square, before the Season is over," she told him. "With all the *ton* in attendance. I absolutely insist upon it, Tresham. I shall plan it all myself."

"Heaven defend us," he murmured before bowing politely to her and continuing on his way into the ballroom.

It was almost time. A cotillion was coming to an end. A waltz was next. He stood close to the doors, his prowling forgotten, and watched Brougham lead a flushed and smiling Jane off the dance floor and return her to Lady

Webb's side. The inevitable court of hopefuls gathered around. It looked as if Kimble had won the race. He was smiling and saying something to Jane. Jocelyn strolled forward.

"This," he said firmly when he was close enough, "is my dance, I believe, ma'am."

"Too late, too late," Kimble said flippantly. "I spoke first, Tresham."

Jocelyn regarded his friend with haughtily raised eyebrows as the fingers of one hand grasped the handle of his quizzing glass.

"Congratulations, my dear fellow," he said. "But the lady's hand is mine nonetheless. Of course, if you care to argue the point—"

"Your grace," Jane began, sounding more embarrassed than angry. Jocelyn lifted his glass all the way to his eye and swung it in her direction. All the other bucks in attendance on her had frozen in place, he noticed, as if they were expecting fisticuffs to break out at any moment and were terrified that they might be involved.

"You have fought enough duels to last for the next decade or so, Tresh," Kimble said. "And I have no wish whatsoever to peer down the wrong end of your pistol, even if I know very well that you will shoot into the air when it comes to the point."

He bowed, had the temerity to wink at Jane, and strolled away.

"I cannot waltz, your grace," Jane reminded Jocelyn. "This is my come-out ball, and I have not yet had the nod of approval from any of the patronesses of Almack's to waltz at a public ball."

"Poppycock!" he said. "This is *your* ball, and you will waltz if you wish to. *Do* you?"

Lady Webb, who might have spoken up in protest, did not do so. The decision was Jane's. Did she have the courage? He looked directly into her eyes.

"Yes," she said, setting her hand on his sleeve. "Of course I do."

And so they took the floor together for the waltz, a move that drew considerable attention from most if not all of the gathered guests, Jocelyn noticed. He and Jane were an *ondit,* he realized, despite his efforts to see to it that they were not. And now he had goaded her into waltzing in defiance of the prevailing custom.

He did not care a tinker's damn what anyone thought. But she did, of course. This was her come-out ball, which Lady Webb had prepared for her with such selfless enthusiasm. He gazed intently at her as he took her in his arms. How could he possibly behave himself as a gentleman ought and act as if she meant nothing at all to him? How could he possibly disguise what he felt for this woman? Even just touching her, like this... But he held her the regulation distance from his body and concentrated on keeping the heat he was feeling out of his gaze.

"It was quite odious of you," she said, "to say what you did when you arrived."

"Lady Sara?" he said. "But you are. And I was on my best behavior. Besides, you retaliated without a blink, Jane."

"Not that," she said. "The other thing."

"About your looking like a bride?" he said. "You do. All white lace and satin and blushes."

"*Flushes,*" she said. "I have been dancing."

"With all your most loyal and persistent beaux," he agreed.

"Jealous?"

He raised his eyebrows and did not deign to answer. Instead, he drew her closer. Scandalously close, in fact. He could sense the gossips murmuring and muttering behind fans and lorgnettes and gloved hands. Jane made no protest at all.

They did not talk after that. It was a spirited waltz tune that the orchestra played, and the dance floor was larger than the drawing room at Dudley House, where they had last waltzed together. He moved her about the perimeter of the floor, twirling her to the rhythm, his eyes locked on hers the whole while, their bodies almost touching.

There was no need of words. They had spoken plenty during the weeks of their acquaintance. Enough that they could sometimes converse quite eloquently without a single sound issuing from their lips. Despite good intentions, he made love to her with his eyes, heedless of any audience they might still have. She pressed her lips together, but she did not once look away. He was not going to spoil the evening, her eyes told him. For Lady Webb's sake he was not. She might have been goaded into possible scandal by waltzing with him, but she would not be persuaded into looking back at him as he was looking at her. Or into quarreling with him. And yet her eyes said other things too. They were far more expressive than she realized.

"Well, Jane," he asked her when he knew the waltz was drawing to an end, "what is your assessment? Is this the happiest day of your life?"

"Of course." She smiled slowly at him. "How could it not be? Are *you* happy?" she asked him.

"Bedamned," he told her.

There was a stranger with Lady Webb, he saw as he took Jane's arm to lead her back to her godmother. A young man who was dressed with perfect decency and propriety but with not the slightest flair of elegance or fashion. Someone who lived almost exclusively in the country, it would appear. The milksop and country bumpkin, if his guess was not quite wide of the mark.

It was a suspicion that was confirmed almost immediately, as soon as Jane's attention was drawn away from someone who said something to her in passing. She looked ahead to Lady Webb, her hand stiffened on his arm, and she hurried forward.

"Charles!" she exclaimed, holding out both her hands to the bumpkin, who was glaring at him, Jocelyn, as if he would dearly like to take him apart limb from limb.

"Yes, Sara," the young idiot said, finally looking at the woman who was reputed to be the love of his heart and taking her hands in his own. "I have come. You are quite safe now."

"I HAVE COME," CHARLES said again. "And in the very nick of time, it would appear, Sara. I found that fellow offensive."

Jane had her arm linked through his and was leading him in the direction of the refreshment room. Yes, Jocelyn really had behaved rather annoyingly. He had become the Duke of Tresham even before she had introduced the two men, all haughty ennui, his quizzing glass to his eye. And when she *had* introduced them, he had spoken with faint hauteur.

"Indeed?" he had said, looking Charles over. "Lady Sara's champion, I gather? Her trusty knight, who rode at a gallop to her rescue when she was within the very jaws of the dragon?"

Charles had swelled up almost visibly with indignation, but he had found nothing better to say than that he had been away from home at the time and that when he had arrived back it was to learn that even a Bow Street Runner had been unable to find her.

"Yes, quite so," Jocelyn had agreed with an audible sigh before inclining his head to Jane and Lady Webb and strolling away.

To her shame Jane had wanted to laugh. She had felt nothing but dismay and chagrin at seeing Charles in Aunt Harriet's ballroom. Surely he must have received her letter before leaving Cornwall. But he had come anyway.

"Yes, you have come," she said. "But why, Charles, when I wrote and told you not to?"

"How could I stay away?" he asked her.

"And yet," she said quietly, accepting the glass of lemonade he had taken off a tray for her, "you did not come when I most needed you, Charles. Oh, yes, I know." She held up a staying hand when he would have spoken. "You did not see the point in coming when you did not know where to look. It was sensible to remain at home."

"Yes, exactly," he agreed. "I have come now when I can do some good. I am happy that Lady Webb has arranged this ball for you. It is only fitting that Lady Sara Illingsworth be presented to the *ton*. But it is unfortunate that an event such as this exposes you to every rake and fortune hunter who cares to ask a dance of you."

"The guest list was prepared by Aunt Harriet," Jane explained. "And every partner I have had tonight has been approved by her. You insult her by saying such a thing, Charles."

"Well," he said, "you were waltzing with the Duke of

Tresham, Sara, and he was taking inappropriate liberties with his eyes. Besides which, he had no business leading you into a waltz of all things. He will be causing you to be called fast. I know that he had a hand in finding you and bringing you here, so I suppose Lady Webb had no choice but to invite him. But he must not be encouraged. A man such as he has no honorable intentions toward any decent woman, believe me."

Jane sighed and sipped her drink. "Charles," she said, "I will not quarrel with you. We have always been friends, and I am grateful that you have cared enough to come all this way. But you really must not pass judgment on people you have not even met before, you know."

"His reputation is enough for me," he said. "Pardon me, Sara, but you have been gently nurtured and have lived a sheltered life far from places like London. I can understand that an experience like this tonight is exciting for you. But you must not abandon your roots. You belong in the country. You would not be happy here forever."

"No," she agreed, smiling softly into her glass. "You are right."

"Come home with me, then," he urged her. "Tomorrow or the next day or next week. Just come."

"Oh, Charles," she said, "I do wish you had read the letter I sent. I cannot go back to Cornwall. That phase of my life is over. I hope we can remain friends, but there—"

"He is not the one for you, Sara," he said urgently, interrupting her. "Believe me, he is not. He could bring you nothing but unhappiness."

"Which is exactly what I would bring you, Charles," she told him gently. "I feel a deep affection for you. But I do not love you."

"Love is something that grows between two married people," he said. "Affection is enough on which to start."

She set a hand on his arm. "This is neither the time nor the place, Charles," she said. "I have already missed one set of dances. If I do not return to the ballroom soon, I will miss another, and I would hate that."

"We will speak tomorrow, then," he said.

How she wished he had not come to London, she thought as he escorted her back to the ballroom. But she said no more.

Later in the evening, she was seated for supper at one of the long tables in the dining room, in company with friends and acquaintances, when Charles came to take the empty place opposite her. Jane smiled at him and introduced him to the people around them. He was quiet for a time while the rest of them chattered and laughed on a variety of topics.

Baron Pottier announced his intention of removing to Brighton for the summer, after the Season was over. It was where the Prince Regent went, and where half the *ton* followed him.

"Will you be going there, Lady Sara?" Lord Pottier asked.

"Oh, no, I think not," Jane said. "I would rather spend the summer in the country."

Viscount Kimble, seated at her side, caught her hand in his and raised it to his lips. "But Brighton would be empty of all attraction without you," he told her, his eyes twinkling. "I shall simply kidnap you and take you there myself."

"Oh, no, you will not," Lady Heyward said, laughing. "If there is any kidnapping to be done, it is I who will be doing it—with Heyward's help. Not that he would agree to do anything so dashing or dangerous, of course. With Ferdie's aid, then. We will kidnap Lady Sara and Tresham and bear them off to St. George's for a grand wedding. Will we not, Ferdie?"

Lord Ferdinand, seated across the table, next to Charles, grinned. "I would need the assistance of half a regiment of burly military types, Angie, if I were to try trussing up Tresham," he said.

Viscount Kimble sighed soulfully. "Alas," he said, "do not forget all about me or my heart will be broken, ma'am."

Jane laughed at him, and the conversation would doubtless have moved on to another subject. But Charles, perhaps not recognizing the light, teasing tone of the conversation, chose to speak up.

"As Lady Sara has said," he told the group, "she will be returning to the country for the summer. Perhaps sooner."

"Oh, yes," Lady Heyward agreed, laughing. "After the wedding. Now really, Ferdie—"

"Lady Sara will be returning to Cornwall. With me," Charles said with enough emphasis to attract the attention of everyone seated at their table. "We have long had an understanding."

"Charles!" Jane said sharply before explaining to the group at large. "We have been friends and neighbors all our lives."

"Tresham might have a thing or two to say about your *understanding*," Baron Pottier said. "Are you really going back to Cornwall, Lady Sara? Jardine notwithstanding?"

"I believe I will be able to protect my own betrothed

from any further impertinences from that direction," Charles said.

"Charles, *please* . . ."

"Oh, you are mistaken, sir," Lady Heyward said merrily. "Lady Sara is going to marry my brother even though they have quarreled and have danced together only once this evening—"

"Stow it, Angie," Lord Ferdinand said. "The lady is looking embarrassed. Let's change the subject. Let's talk about the weather."

But Charles was not to be deterred. He actually stood up, scraping back his chair with his knees. And somehow the action attracted general notice in the crowded dining room and the noise level dropped noticeably.

"Lady Sara Illingsworth will not be the object of any London buck's gallantries for much longer," he said, indignation vibrating in his voice. "I will be taking her home where she belongs. Not to Candleford, but *home*."

Jane would have closed her eyes in mortification, but she glanced first at a dark-clad figure standing in the dining room doorway. He must have been on his way out, but he was standing still now, his quizzing glass in one hand, his attention on Charles.

"Mr. Fortescue," Lady Lansdowne asked from the end of their table, "are we to understand that you are announcing your betrothal to Sara?"

Jane's eyes locked with Jocelyn's in the doorway.

"Charles—" she said aloud.

"Yes, ma'am," Charles said, raising his voice and speaking now to an audience of every single guest at the ball. "I have the honor of announcing my betrothal to Lady Sara Illingsworth. I trust everyone will wish us happy."

A swell of sound in the dining room replaced the silence. But then Jocelyn took one step forward and a hush descended once more.

"No, no, no," he said, every inch the Duke of Tresham again. "I would wager that Lady Sara has not consented, and it is not good *ton*, you know, Fortescue, to make such an announcement unless the prospective bride has done so."

"Of course she has consented," Charles said testily. "We have had an underst—"

"*Have* you, Jane?" The ducal quizzing glass swung her way. "How naughty of you, my love."

Jane heard a feminine gasp at the duke's use of the endearment. While Jocelyn was actually *enjoying* himself, Jane was wishing for a black hole to swallow her up.

"She is *not* your love," Charles retorted, "and I would thank you for not—"

"Ah, but she is," Jocelyn said, taking a few more steps forward and lowering his glass. "And I must protest most forcefully against your imagined betrothal to her, my dear fellow. You see, much as I commend you for the concern you have shown for her well-being, I really cannot permit you to marry my wife."

There was another swell of sound, but it died away quickly to a chorus of hushing noises. No one wanted to miss a word of this drama, which would be repeated endlessly and with blissful relish in dozens of drawing rooms and gentlemen's clubs for days, even weeks to come.

"*What?*" Charles had turned pale, Jane saw in a quick glance at him. He was looking at her across the table. "Is this true? Sara?"

She nodded almost imperceptibly.

He stared at her for a few moments while there was another small swell of sound and more hushing noises, and then he turned without another word and stalked from the room, brushing past the duke as he went.

"Come, Jane." Jocelyn held out a hand toward her and she went to him on legs that were not quite steady. He was smiling as she had never seen him smile before—openly, warmly, radiantly.

"Ladies and gentlemen," he said as his hand closed about hers, "allow me, please, to present my wife, the Duchess of Tresham. Ma'am?" He bowed to Lady Webb. "I do beg your pardon that my hand has been forced. Jane insisted that nothing be allowed to spoil yesterday and today for you since you have worked so tirelessly to plan her presentation and her come-out. Both, of course, would have had to change for a married lady. And so I agreed that we would delay our announcement until tomorrow."

He settled Jane's hand on his arm and covered it with his free hand before looking around at all the gathered guests, though his eyes rested on his brother and sister as he spoke again. "We were married by special license this morning. We had a quiet wedding, as we both wished, with only my secretary and her grace's maid in attendance as witnesses."

He smiled down at Jane—that warm, wonderful, defenseless smile again—and raised her hand to his lips. There was already noise and movement in response to his announcement.

"My love," he murmured while he still could, "I was already quite determined to have my bride in my own home and my own bed for what will remain of our wedding night when your ball is over. I am no saint, you see."

"I have never wanted a saint," she told him. "I have only ever wanted you, Jocelyn."

He leaned toward her, his eyes on fire, and whispered with passionate intensity in her ear. "My love and my life. My Jane. And at last and forever *my wife*."

There was only a moment—a timeless moment—in which to smile radiantly at him and to realize with a shock of reality that it was really true. She was married to Jocelyn, her love, her heart's desire, her soul's mate. She was happier than anyone had any right to be. He was *her husband*.

And there was no further need to hide the fact.

Then Aunt Harriet was hugging her and shedding tears over her and scolding her and laughing. And Lady Heyward was catching her in her arms and talking a mile a minute. Lord Ferdinand was grinning at her and kissing her cheek and calling her sister. Viscount Kimble was pretending to clutch his broken heart and was also kissing her cheek. Jocelyn's friends were all pumping his hand and slapping his shoulder. His sister was crying all over his waistcoat despite his protests and declaring that her nerves would not stand the shock and she had never been more happy in her life and she would organize a grand wedding ball for next week and just let Heyward try to stop her, provoking man.

Everything became a blur after that as everyone moved back to the ballroom, congratulating the newly married couple, bowing, curtsying, shaking hands, hugging and kissing as they went. The resumption of the dancing was considerably delayed.

Finally they were alone in the dining room with Lady Webb, Lord and Lady Lansdowne, Lord and Lady Heyward, and Lord Ferdinand. Jocelyn drew Jane's shining new wedding ring from a pocket of his waistcoat, lifted her left hand, and slid it onto her ring finger, where it had resided so briefly during the morning.

"With this ring, my love," he said, and dipped his head to kiss her lips in full view of their small audience. He looked up at Lady Webb. "Now, ma'am, do you suppose the orchestra can be coerced into playing another waltz?"

"Absolutely," Aunt Harriet said.

And so they waltzed again—alone for the first five minutes, while everyone watched.

"I repeat," Jocelyn said as the music began—a slow, dreamy waltz tune this time, "you look almost like a bride, Jane. In fact, you look exactly like a bride. Mine."

"And the ballroom looks as if it had been decked out for a wedding ball," she said, giving him back look for look. "Ours."

And then he did something truly outrageous. He dipped his head and kissed her hard. He lifted his head, smiled wickedly at her, and kissed her softly. And then again with all the yearning and all the hope and all the love Jane knew was in his heart—and her own.

"She will never reform the dangerous Duke of Tresham," some unidentified voice said with startling clarity as Jocelyn twirled Jane into the dance.

"But whyever would she want to?" a female voice called back.

No Man's Mistress

1

THE PICTURESQUE VILLAGE OF TRELLICK, NESTLED in a river valley in Somersetshire, was usually a quiet little backwater. But not on this particular day. By the middle of the afternoon it appeared that every villager and every country dweller for miles around must be out-of-doors, milling about the village green, enjoying the revelries.

The maypole at the center of the green, its colored ribbons fluttering in the breeze, proclaimed the occasion. It was May Day. Later, the young men would dance about the maypole with the partners of their choice, as they did with great energy and enthusiasm every year.

Meanwhile, there were races and other contests to draw attention to the green. Pitched about its perimeter were tented booths with their offerings of appetizing foods, eye-catching baubles, and challenging games of skill or strength or chance.

The weather had cooperated in magnificent fashion with warm sunshine and a cloudless blue sky. Women and girls had discarded shawls and pelisses they had worn in the morning. A few men and most boys remained in their shirtsleeves after engaging in one of the more strenuous contests. Tables and chairs had been carried from the church hall onto the lawn outside so that tea and cakes could be served in full view of all the merriment. Not to be outdone, on an adjacent side of the village green the Boar's Head had its own tables and benches set up outside for the convenience of those folk who preferred ale to tea.

A few strangers, on their way past the village to destinations unknown, stopped off for varying periods of time to observe the fun and even in some cases to participate in it before continuing their journeys.

One such stranger was riding slowly down toward the green from the main road when Viola Thornhill glanced up from serving tea to the Misses Merrywether. She would not have seen him over the heads of the crowd if he had not been on horseback. As it was, she paused for a second, more leisurely look.

He was clearly a gentleman, and a fashionable one at that. His dark blue riding coat looked as if it might have been molded to his frame. His linen beneath it was white and crisp. His black leather breeches clung to his long legs like a second skin. His riding boots looked supple and must surely have been made by the very best of boot makers. But it was not so much the clothes as the man inside them who attracted and held Viola's appreciative attention. He was young and slim and darkly handsome. He pushed back his tall hat even as she watched. He was smiling.

"You ought not to be serving *us*, Miss Thornhill," Miss Prudence Merrywether said, a customary note of anxious apology in her voice. "*We* ought to be serving *you*. You have been rushed off your feet all day."

Viola reassured her with a warm smile. "But I am having so much fun," she said. "Are we not fortunate indeed that the weather has been so kind?"

When she looked again, the stranger had disappeared from view, though he had not ridden on his way. His horse was being led away by one of the lads who worked in the inn stables.

"Miss Vi," a familiar voice said from behind her, and she turned to smile at the small, plump woman who had touched her on the shoulder. "The sack race is ready to begin, and you are needed to start it and award the prizes. I'll take the teapot from you."

"Will you, Hannah?" Viola handed it over and hurried onto the green, where a number of children were indeed wriggling into sacks and clutching them to their waists. Viola helped the stragglers and then directed them all as they hopped and shuffled into a roughly even line along the appointed starting point. Adults crowded about the four sides of the green to watch and cheer.

Viola had set out from home early in the morning looking ladylike and elegant in a muslin dress and shawl and straw bonnet, her hair in a neatly braided coronet about her head beneath it. She had even been wearing gloves. But she had long ago discarded all the accessories. Even her hair, slipping stubbornly out of its pins during the busy morning of rushing hither and yon, had been allowed finally to hang loose in a long braid down her back. She was feeling flushed and happy. She could not remember when she had enjoyed herself more.

"Get ready," she called, stepping to one side of the line of children. "Go!"

More than half the racers collapsed at their very first leap, their legs and feet all tangled up in sacking. They struggled to rise, to the accompaniment of good-natured laughter and shouted encouragement from relatives and neighbors. But inevitably there was one child who hopped across the green like a grasshopper and crossed the finish line before some of her less fortunate fellow contestants had recovered from their tumble.

Viola, laughing merrily, suddenly found herself locking eyes with the dark, handsome stranger, who was standing at the finish line, his own laughter emphasizing his extraordinary good looks. He looked her over frankly from head to toe before she turned away, but she discovered with pleased surprise that she felt amused, even exhilarated by his appreciation rather than repelled. She hurried forward to give out the prizes.

It was time then to hasten into the inn, where she was to judge the pie-baking contest with the Reverend Prewitt and Mr. Thomas Claypole.

"Eating pie is thirsty work," the vicar declared more than half an hour later, chuckling and patting his stomach after they had sampled every pie and declared a winner. "And if my observations have been correct, you have not had a break all day, Miss Thornhill. You go over to the church lawn now and find a table in the shade. Mrs. Prewitt or one of the other ladies will pour you tea. Mr. Claypole will be pleased to escort you, will you not, sir?"

Viola could have done without the escort of Mr. Claypole, who because he had proposed marriage to her at least a dozen times during the past year appeared to believe that he had some claim on her and the right to speak plainly to her on any number of issues. The best that could be said of Thomas Claypole was that he was worthy—a solid citizen, a prudent manager of his property, a dutiful son.

He was dull company at best. Irritating company at worst.

"Forgive me, Miss Thornhill," he began as soon as they were seated at one of the tables beneath the shade of a huge old oak tree and Hannah had poured their tea. "But you will not mind plain speaking from a friend, I daresay. Indeed, I flatter myself that I am more than a friend."

"What criticism of a perfect day do you have, then, sir?" she asked, setting her elbow on the table and her chin in her hand.

"Your willingness to organize the fête with the vicar's committee and to work hard to see that it runs smoothly is admirable indeed," he began, while Viola's eyes and attention drifted to the stranger, whom she could see drinking ale at a table outside the inn. "It can do nothing but earn my highest esteem. However, I have been somewhat alarmed to discover that today you look almost indistinguishable from any country wench."

"Oh, do I?" Viola laughed. "What a delightful thing to say. But you did not mean it as a compliment, did you?"

"You are hatless and your hair is down," he pointed out. "You have *daisies* in it."

She had forgotten. One of the children had presented her with a bunch gathered from the riverbank earlier in the day, and she had pushed the stems into her hair above her left ear. She touched the flowers lightly. Yes, they were still there.

"I believe it is *your* straw bonnet that is lying on the back pew of the church," Mr. Claypole continued.

"Ah," she said, "so *that* is where I left it, is it?"

"It should be protecting your complexion from the harmful rays of the sun," he said with gentle reproof.

"So it should," she agreed, finishing her tea and getting to her feet. "If you will excuse me, sir, I see that the fortune-teller is setting up her booth at last. I must go and see that she has everything she needs."

But Mr. Claypole would not have recognized a dismissal if it had doubled up into a fist and collided with his nose. He rose too, bowed, and offered his arm. Viola took it with an inward sigh of resignation.

Actually, the fortune-teller was already doing a brisk business, as Viola had been able to see from across the green. What she had also noticed, though, was that the stranger had strolled over to the throwing booth, which had been popular with the young men earlier in the afternoon. He was talking with Jake Tulliver, the blacksmith, when Viola and Mr. Claypole drew near.

"I was about to close down the booth, seeing as how we have run out of prizes," Jake said, raising his voice to address her. "But this gentleman wants a try."

"Well, then," she said gaily, "we will have to hope he does not win, will we not?"

The stranger turned his head to look at her. He was indeed tall, almost a full head taller than she. His eyes were almost black. They gave his handsome face a somewhat dangerous look. Viola felt her heartbeat quicken.

"Oh," he said with quiet assurance, "I *will* win, ma'am."

"Will you?" she asked. "Well, there is nothing so very surprising about that. Everyone else has won too, almost without exception. Hence the embarrassing lack of prizes still to give away. I daresay the targets were set too close. We must remember that next year, Mr. Tulliver."

"Set them back twice as far," the stranger said, "and I will still win."

She raised her eyebrows at the boast and looked at the metal candlesticks—the old set from the church vestry—which had been toppling all too readily before the ball the contestants had been hurling at them.

"Are you sure?" she asked. "Very well, then, sir, prove it. If you win—four out of the five must fall with just five throws, you understand—then we will return your money. It is the best we can do. All of today's proceeds go to the vicar's charities, you see, so we cannot afford to offer cash prizes."

"I will pay twice the entry fee," the stranger said with a grin that made him look both reckless and boyish. "And I will knock all five candlesticks down at twice their present distance. But I must insist upon a prize, ma'am."

"I believe we might safely offer the church spire without fear of denuding the church," she said. "It cannot be done."

"Oh, it can and will," he assured her, "if the prize is to be those daisies you wear above your ear."

Viola touched them and laughed. "A valuable prize indeed," she said. "Very well, sir."

Mr. Claypole cleared his throat. "You will permit me to point out that wagers are inappropriate to what is essentially a church fête, sir," he said.

The stranger laughed into Viola's eyes, almost as if he believed it was she who had spoken.

"Let us make sure that the church benefits well from this wager, then," he said. "Twenty pounds for the church whether I win or lose. The lady's daisies for me if I win. Move back the targets," he instructed Jake Tulliver, while he set a few banknotes down on the booth counter.

"Miss Thornhill." Mr. Claypole had taken her by the

elbow and was speaking earnestly into her ear. "This will not do. You are drawing attention to yourself."

She looked about to see that indeed people who had been awaiting their turn outside the fortune-teller's booth and had overheard the exchange were beginning to gather around. And their interest was attracting more. A number of people were hurrying across the green toward the throwing booth. The gentleman was removing his coat and rolling up his shirtsleeves. Jake was repositioning the candlesticks.

"This gentleman has donated twenty pounds to the vicar's fund," Viola called gaily to the gathering crowd. "If he knocks down all five candlesticks with five throws of the ball, he will win... my daisies."

She gestured toward them and laughed with the crowd. But the stranger, she saw, did not. He was rolling the ball in his hands, concentrating on it, and squinting ahead to the candlesticks, which now looked an impossible distance away. He could not possibly win. She doubted he could knock over even one.

But one toppled over even as she was thinking it, and the crowd applauded appreciatively.

Jake handed the stranger the ball again, and he concentrated on it as before. A hush fell on the gathered crowd, which had swelled even more in size.

A second candlestick teetered, looked as if it were about to right itself, and fell with a clatter.

At least, Viola thought, he had not totally humiliated himself. He looked more than handsome in his shirtsleeves. He looked... well, very male. She desperately wanted him to win his bet. But he had set himself a nearly impossible task.

Again he concentrated.

The third candlestick fell.

The fourth did not.

There was a collective moan from the crowd. Viola felt absurdly disappointed.

"It would seem, sir," she said, "that I get to keep my flowers."

"Not so hasty, ma'am." His grin was back and he held out his hand for the ball. "The wager was for five candlesticks down with five throws, was it not? Did it state that one had to go down with each throw?"

"No." She laughed when she understood his meaning. "But you have only one throw left, and two candlesticks are standing."

"Oh ye of little faith," he murmured with a wink, and Viola felt a pleased fluttering of awareness low in her abdomen.

Then he was concentrating again, and the crowd was being shushed by those who realized he had not yet admitted defeat, and Viola's heart was beating right up into her ears.

Her eyes widened with incredulity and the crowd erupted into a roar of wild cheering as the ball hit one upright candlestick, glanced sideways off it as it fell, and demolished the fifth with a satisfying crack.

The gentleman turned, bowed to his audience, and then grinned at Viola, who was clapping and laughing and realizing that this was by far the most exhilarating moment of the day.

"That bouquet is forfeit, I believe, ma'am," he said, pointing to her daisies. "I will claim them for myself."

She stood still while his fingers detached the small bunch of daisies from her hair. His laughing eyes did not waver from her own—they were a very dark brown, she could see now. His skin looked sun-bronzed. His body heat and a musky cologne reached out to envelop her. He carried the daisies to his lips, bowed with careless grace, and pushed the stems into a buttonhole of his shirt.

"A lady's favor at my breast," he murmured. "What more could I ask of the day?"

But she had no chance to respond to such blatant flirtation. The Reverend Prewitt's hearty voice intruded.

"Bravo, sir!" he exclaimed, stepping forward from the crowd, his right hand extended. "You are a regular good sport, if you will permit me to say so. Come over to the church lawn and my wife will pour you a cup of tea while I tell you about the charities that will benefit from your generosity."

The stranger smiled into Viola's eyes with a hint of reluctance and moved away with the vicar.

"I am vastly relieved," Mr. Claypole said, taking Viola by the elbow again as the crowd drifted away to sample other attractions, "that the Reverend Prewitt was able to cover up for the vulgarity of that display, Miss Thornhill, focused as the whole wager was on your person. It was not seemly. Now perhaps—"

She gave him no chance to complete his thought. "I do believe, sir," she said, "your mother has been beckoning you for the past ten minutes."

"Why did you not say so before?" He looked sharply in the direction of the church and hurried off without a backward glance. Viola looked at Hannah, who was standing close by, raised her eyebrows, and laughed aloud.

"Miss Vi," Hannah said, shaking her head, "he is as

handsome as sin. And twice as dangerous, if you were to ask me."

Clearly she was not talking about Mr. Claypole. "He is just a stranger passing through, Hannah," Viola said. "It was a very generous donation, was it not? Twenty pounds! We must be thankful that he broke his journey at Trellick. Now I am going to have my fortune told."

But fortune-tellers were all the same, she reflected when she came out of the booth some time later. Why could they not aim for at least some originality? This one was a gypsy with a reputation for being able to predict the future with remarkable accuracy.

"Beware of a tall, dark, handsome stranger," she had said after consulting her crystal ball. "He can destroy you—if you do not first snare his heart."

Tall, dark, and handsome indeed! Viola smiled at a child who had stopped to show her his new spinning top. What a lamentable cliché.

And then she spotted the stranger again, striding away from the church lawn in the direction of the inn stables. Ah, he was leaving, then. Continuing on his way while there was still some daylight left.

A *tall, dark, handsome stranger.* She laughed softly.

The sun was already low in the western sky. From the direction of the inn she could hear the fiddlers tuning their instruments. A couple of men were checking the ribbons about the maypole, making sure they were not tangled. She watched and listened with a certain wistfulness. The maypole dancing was always the joyful, exuberant climax of the May Day celebrations. But it was one activity in which she would have no part. It was not viewed as a genteel activity by the upper-class families of the village and neighborhood. A lady might watch, but she might not participate.

But no matter. She *would* watch and enjoy doing so, as she had last year—her first May Day at Trellick. In the meantime, she was expected at the vicarage for dinner.

BY THE TIME VIOLA stepped out of the vicarage again, darkness had fallen and bonfires were burning on three sides of the village green to provide light for the dancing. The fiddlers were playing, and young people were already twirling about the maypole in a merry, energetic dance. Viola declined an invitation to accompany the Reverend and Mrs. Prewitt as they strolled around the green. Instead, she moved onto the now-deserted church lawn to enjoy the spectacle alone.

It was amazingly warm for a spring evening. She had draped her shawl about her shoulders, but she did not really need it. Her bonnet was probably still on the back pew of the church. Hannah, her maid, once her nurse, had brushed out her hair before dinner and left it unbraided, tied back at the nape of her neck with a ribbon. It was more comfortable that way. Mr. Claypole would be scandalized indeed if he could see her, but fortunately he had taken his mother and his sister home at dusk.

The fiddling stopped and the dancers dispersed to the edges of the green to catch their breath and choose new partners. The moon was almost at the full, Viola saw, tipping back her head. The sky was brilliantly star-studded. She inhaled deeply of the clean country air, closed her eyes, and breathed a silent prayer of thanksgiving. Who could have predicted just two years ago that she would ever be living in a place like this? Belonging here, accepted here, generally liked here. Her life might have been very different now if . . .

"Now, what are you doing hiding here," a voice asked, "when you should be out there dancing?"

Her eyes snapped open. She had neither seen nor heard his approach. She had seen him go to the inn stables earlier and had assumed that he had long ago resumed his journey. She had assured herself that she was not disappointed. Why should she be, after all? He was merely an attractive stranger, who had passed briefly through her life and engaged her in a harmless flirtation over a bunch of wild daisies.

But here he was standing in front of her, awaiting her answer, his face in shadows. *Awaiting her answer.* She suddenly realized what it was he had said.

. . . you should be out there dancing.

It would be the perfect ending to a perfect day. Twirling about the maypole. Dancing with the handsome stranger. She did not even want to know who he was. She wanted the mystery preserved so that she could look back on this day with unalloyed pleasure.

"I have been waiting for the right partner, sir," she said. And then, more outrageously, as she lowered her voice, "I have been waiting for *you.*"

"Have you indeed?" He reached out a hand. "Well, here I am."

She dropped her shawl heedlessly to the grass and placed her hand in his. It closed firmly about her own before he led her away.

It was all pure enchantment after that. The green was lit by the flickering flames of the bonfires. The air was full of the pungent smell of wood smoke. Young men were already leading their partners forward and claiming the bright dangling ribbons. But the stranger secured two and put one in Viola's hand, his teeth flashing white in the darkness. And then the fiddles were scraping out a merry tune and the dance began—the light, tripping, intricate steps, the circular clockwise motion, the twirling and dipping and weaving while ribbons twined together and then miraculously untwined again, the pulsing, steady rhythm that thrummed with the blood through veins; the stars wheeling overhead; the fires crackling, throwing faces into mysterious shadow one moment, illuminating the gay animation in them the next; the spectators around the edges of the green clapping in time to the fiddles and the dancers.

And the focus of the enchantment—the handsome, long-legged stranger, still in his shirtsleeves, the wilting bunch of daisies adorning one buttonhole, dancing with light-footed grace and vibrant energy and merry laughter. And watching her own exuberance. As if the very universe revolved about the two of them just as surely as they circled the maypole.

Viola was breathless when the music ended and so happy that she thought she might well burst with it. And regretful too that now, finally, this magical day was at an end. Hannah would be eager to return home. The day had been as busy for her as it had been for Viola. She would not make her maid feel obliged to stay longer—though that generous impulse was quickly abandoned, at least temporarily.

"You look as if you would welcome a glass of lemonade," the stranger said, setting a hand at the small of her back and leaning down to smile into her face.

Tea was no longer being served on the church lawn. But two tables had been left outside, a large bowl of lemonade and a trayful of glasses on each. Not much of it was being drunk. Most of the older generation had gone home, and the younger people seemed to prefer the ale being served at the inn.

"I would indeed," she agreed.

They did not speak as they crossed the green and then the road to the church lawn and the table beneath the oak tree where she had found shade from the sun after judging the pie contest. He ladled out a glassful of lemonade for her and watched as she drank it, grateful for its tart coolness. Behind her, out of sight beyond the massive trunk of the old oak, the fiddlers were playing again, the sound of their brisk music mingling with the sounds of voices and laughter. Ahead she could see moonlight gleaming on the surface of the river, which flowed past the village behind the church.

It was a scene she concentrated deliberately upon remembering.

When she had finished drinking, he took the empty glass from her hand and set it on the table. It was on the tip of her tongue to ask him if he was not thirsty himself. But there was a certain spell, a certain tension between them that words might break. She had no wish to break it.

She had had no real girlhood—not after the age of nine, at least. No chance to steal away into the shadows for an innocent, clandestine tryst with a beau. There had been no chance for romance or even for light, harmless flirtation. At the age of five-and-twenty she suddenly felt like the girl she might have grown into, had her life not changed forever more than half a lifetime ago. She liked being that girl, however fleetingly.

He slid one arm about her waist and drew her against

him. With the other hand he grasped her hair below the ribbon and pulled on it with just enough pressure to tip back her head. Moonlight and tree branches were dappled across his face. He was smiling. Did he always smile, this stranger? Or was he merely indulging today, amid strangers he would never see again, in his own escape from more sober reality?

She closed her eyes when his face dipped down, and he kissed her.

It did not last long. It was not by any means a lascivious kiss. Although his lips parted over her own, he made no attempt to plunder her mouth. His one hand remained splayed firmly against the back of her waist, while the other cupped the ribbon at her neck. She did not for one second lose herself in passion, though she knew she could swoon into it if she chose. She would not so waste a single precious moment. What she did instead was carefully and deliberately savor and memorize each sensation. She felt his long, hard-muscled, leather-clad thighs against the softness of her own, his abdomen hard against hers, his chest firm against her breasts. She felt the moist intimacy of his lips, the warmth of his breath against her cheek. She breathed in the mingled scents of cologne and leather and man, and tasted on his mouth ale and something unidentifiable that must be the very essence of him. She heard music, voices, laughter, water flowing, a single owl hooting—all from a vast distance away. She twined her fingers in his thick, soft hair and felt with the other hand the well-developed muscles of his shoulder and upper arm.

Beware of a tall, dark, handsome stranger.

She drank her brief, clandestine draft of youthful romance from the brim to the very dregs. And then, when he raised his head and loosened his hold on her, she accepted the fact that the day was ended.

"Thank you for the dance." He chuckled. "And for the kiss."

"Good night," she said softly.

He looked down at her for a few moments longer. "Good night, my country lass," he said in answer, and strode past her, back in the direction of the green.

2

TRELLICK WAS A PRETTY VILLAGE. HE HAD SEEN that yesterday, gazing down on it as the main road dipped into the river valley. This morning, as he stood at the taproom window inside the Boar's Head sipping coffee, Lord Ferdinand Dudley noticed the whitewashed, thatched cottages with their neat, colorful flower gardens on two sides of the green. On the riverside stood the stone church, with its tall, slender spire and spacious lawn, in the middle of which stood a great old oak tree. The vicarage, its gray stone walls ivy-covered, was beside the church. He could not see the water from where he stood, just as he could not see the row of shops next to the inn, but he could see the forest of trees on the far side of the river, a pleasantly rural backdrop for the church and village.

He wondered where exactly Pinewood Manor was. He knew it must be reasonably close, since Bamber's solicitor had mentioned Trellick to him as the nearest village. But how close? And how large was it? What did it look like? A cottage like one of those opposite? A house like the vicarage? A larger building, as its name implied? A dilapidated heap? No one had seemed to know, least of all Bamber himself, who had not appeared to care much either.

Ferdinand fully expected the dilapidated heap.

He could have asked for directions yesterday, of

course—it was what he had ridden into the village to do, after all. But he had not done so. It had been well into the afternoon and he had persuaded himself that viewing Pinewood for the first time would be better left until the morning. The gaiety of the village fête into which he had ridden had been partly responsible for that decision, of course, as well as that country lass with the enticingly swinging braid whose laughing eyes he had met across the village green after the children's sack race. He had wanted to stay and enjoy himself—and see more of her.

Just two weeks ago he had not even heard of Pinewood. Now here he was on the verge of seeing it, and wondering what exactly there would be to see. A fool's errand, Lord Heyward, his brother-in-law, had predicted of his journey. But then, Heyward was never strong on optimism, especially where the escapades of Angeline's two brothers were concerned. He did not have a high opinion of the Dudleys, even though he had married one of them.

He ought not to have kissed that woman last night, Ferdinand thought uneasily. He was not in the habit of indulging in flirtations with innocent country wenches. And he suspected that she might be more than just a country wench. What if Pinewood Manor turned out to be very close, after all—and not in ruins? What if he should decide to stay there for a while? She might even turn out to be the vicar's daughter. It was entirely within the realm of possibility, since she had clearly been one of the prime movers of the festivities—and she had stepped out of the vicarage during the evening. He had not asked who she was. He did not even know her name.

Devil take it, but he hoped she was not the vicar's

daughter. And he hoped Pinewood was not so very close. That stolen kiss might yet prove an embarrassment.

Of course, she had been pretty enough to tempt a saint—and Dudleys had never been candidates for sainthood. Her dark red hair and perfect features in an oval face would give her a claim to extraordinary beauty even if one considered her only from the neck up. But when one added the rest of her to the picture... Ferdinand blew out his breath and turned from the window. *Voluptuous* was one word that leaped to mind. She was tall and slim but generously curved in all the right places. He had had evidence of that with his body as well as his eyes.

The memory itself was enough to make him uncomfortably warm.

He went in search of the landlord to ask about Pinewood. Then he summoned his valet, who had arrived with his coach and baggage in the middle of last evening, an hour after his groom had arrived with his curricle.

An hour later, freshly shaven and wearing clean riding clothes and boots so shiny that he could almost see his face in them, Ferdinand was riding across the river via a triple-arched stone bridge beyond the vicarage. Pinewood Manor, the landlord had assured him, was very close indeed. The river formed the boundary of its park on two sides, in fact. Ferdinand had not asked for further details. He wanted to see for himself what the place was like. He noticed suddenly that a number of the trees on the other side of the river were pines. *Pine*wood, of course. There was a footpath between the trees and the river, stretching away to his right until it was lost to view around a sharp bend in the river beyond the village.

It all looked very promising, but he must not get his hopes up prematurely.

It did not matter anyway, he told himself. Even if Heyward's gloomy predictions proved correct, he would be no worse off than he had been two weeks ago. All he would have missed was a week or so of the London Season and the arrival in town of his brother Tresham with his wife and children.

Ferdinand's spirits continued to rise when he found himself riding along a winding driveway shaded by overhanging trees—a driveway wide enough to accommodate even the grandest of carriages and displaying no sign of being overgrown from disuse.

He burst into song, as he sometimes did when alone, serenading the trees around him and the blue sky above. " 'Now is the month of Maying, when merry lads are playing. Fa-la-la-la-la, la-la-la-laaa. Fa-la-la-la-la-la-la. Each with his bonny lass.' "

But both the song and his forward motion came to an abrupt pause as he rode into the bright sunlight clear of the band of trees and found himself at the foot of a wide lawn. It was bisected by the driveway, which curved off to the left before it reached the house in the near distance.

House. Ferdinand whistled through his teeth. It was definitely more than that. It was closer to being a mansion, though that might be something of an exaggeration, he admitted, thinking of the imposing grandeur of Acton Park, his childhood home. Nevertheless, Pinewood was an impressive gray stone manor set in a sizable park. Even the stables and carriage house toward which the driveway turned were not negligible in size.

A flicker of movement to his left drew Ferdinand's eyes to two men, who were busy cutting the grass with scythes. It was only then that the neat, well-kept appearance of the lawn struck him. One of the men turned to gaze curiously at him, leaning both arms on the long handle of his scythe as he did so.

"That is Pinewood Manor?" Ferdinand pointed with his whip.

"Aye, 'tis, sir," the man agreed, respectfully touching his forelock.

Ferdinand rode onward, feeling somewhat euphoric. He resumed his singing as soon as he judged himself to be out of earshot of the grass cutters, though perhaps not with quite such cheerful abandon. " 'A-a-dancing on the grass,' " he sang, picking up the song where he had left it off. " 'Fa-la-la-la-laaa.' " He held the high note and noticed that the lawn did not stretch right up to the doors of the manor but ended before a low, neatly clipped box hedge with what looked like a formal garden beyond it. And unless he was much mistaken, there was a fountain in that garden. One that worked.

Why the devil had Bamber been so careless of such an apparently substantial property? Was the house a mere empty shell beyond the respectable outer facade? It was surely damp and horridly dilapidated from disuse, but if that was all that was wrong with it, he would count himself well blessed indeed. Why let the prospect of a little mildew dampen his spirits? He finished the verse of his song with a flourish.

" 'La-la-la-la-laaa.' "

There was a cobbled terrace before the front doors of

the manor, he noticed as he approached the stables. The formal garden, consisting of graveled walks, box hedges, and neat floral borders, was below it, at the foot of three broad steps. He was surprised, as he dismounted by the stables, to be met by a young lad coming out of one of the stalls.

The Earl of Bamber had never lived at this manor in remote Somersetshire or even visited it, if he was to be believed. He had denied any knowledge of it. Yet he seemed to have been spending money on its upkeep. Why else were there two gardeners at work on the lawn and a groom in the stables?

"Are there servants at the house?" he asked the lad curiously.

"Aye, sir," the boy told him as he prepared to lead the horse away. "Mr. Jarvey will see to you if you knock on the door. That was a right fine display of ball throwing, if you will pardon me for saying so, sir. I could only hit three of them candlesticks myself, and they was much closer when I tried."

Ferdinand grinned his acknowledgment of the compliment. "Mr. Jarvey?"

"The butler, sir."

There was a *butler*? Curious indeed. Ferdinand nodded affably, strode across the terrace to the double front doors of the manor, and rattled the knocker.

"Good morning, sir."

Ferdinand smiled cheerfully at the respectably black-clad servant who stood between the opened doors, a look of polite inquiry on his face.

"Jarvey?" Ferdinand asked.

"Yes, sir." The butler bowed respectfully and opened the doors wider before stepping to one side. His professional glance had obviously informed him that he was confronting a gentleman.

"Pleased to make your acquaintance," Ferdinand said, stepping inside and looking around with frank interest.

He found himself standing in a square, high-ceilinged hall with a tiled floor. The walls were tastefully hung with landscape paintings in gilded frames, and a marble bust of stern Roman aspect stood on a marble stand in an alcove opposite the door. There was an oak staircase with an ornately carved banister to the right, doors leading into other apartments to the left. The appearance of the hall certainly boded well for the rest of the house. Not only was it light, pleasingly designed, and tastefully decorated, but it was also clean. Everything gleamed.

The butler coughed with polite inquiry as Ferdinand strode to the center of the hall, his boots clicking on the tiles, and turned slowly about, his head tipped slightly back. "How may I help you, sir?"

"You may have the master bedchamber prepared for my use tonight," Ferdinand said, giving the man only half his attention, "and some luncheon conjured up an hour or so from now. Is that possible? Is there a cook here? Cold meat and bread will do if there is nothing else."

The butler regarded him with unconcealed astonishment. "The master bedchamber, sir?" he said stiffly. "I beg your pardon, but I have not been informed that you are expected."

Ferdinand chuckled good-naturedly and gave his full attention to the matter at hand. "I gather not," he said. "But then I was not informed that I was to expect *you*. I suppose the Earl of Bamber has not written or got anyone else to write for him?"

"The earl?" The butler sounded even more astonished. "He has never had anything to do with Pinewood Manor, sir. He—"

That was just like Bamber. To have known nothing about the place, not even that there were servants here. Not to have warned anyone that Lord Ferdinand Dudley was on his way here. But then, he had not appeared to know that there was anyone to warn. What a ramshackle fellow!

Ferdinand held up one hand. "You must be a devoted retainer indeed, then," he said, "if you have kept the manor and grounds in such fine order when he never comes to call you to account. Has he always paid the bills without question? I daresay you have grown to think of the house almost as your own, in which case you will soon wish me to the devil. All that is to change, you see. Allow me to introduce myself. I am Lord Ferdinand Dudley, younger brother of the Duke of Tresham, and the new owner of Pinewood."

Suddenly the truth of it took on a new reality to him. This was *his*. And it really did exist. In more than just name. There really was a manor and a park, and presumably farms as well. He was a member of the landed gentry.

The butler stared at him with stiff incomprehension. "The new owner, sir?" he said. "But—"

"Oh, I assure you the change of ownership is all legal," Ferdinand said briskly, his eye taken by the chandelier overhead. "*Is* there a cook? If not, I had better take my meals at the Boar's Head until there is. In the meantime, you may give the order about the master bedchamber while I take a look around. How many indoor servants are there?"

The butler did not answer his question. Another voice spoke instead. A female voice. A low, husky voice, which immediately sent shivers of recognition up Ferdinand's spine.

"Who is it, Mr. Jarvey?" she asked.

Ferdinand turned his head sharply. She was standing on the bottom stair, her left hand resting on the newel post. She looked altogether different today, dressed as she was in a dark green high-waisted walking dress, which hugged her magnificent figure in all the right places, her hair pulled back rather severely from her lovely face and braided into a coronet about her head. Today there was no mistaking the fact that she was no girl, but a woman. And no village wench, but a lady. For a moment she looked vaguely familiar, even apart from yesterday's acquaintance, but he was not at leisure to pursue that impression.

"Lord Ferdinand Dudley, ma'am." The butler, stiff and correct, made his name sound as if he were close blood kin to Satan.

Oh, Lord! Bamber had not given any hint about people being in residence. Had he *forgotten*? All the signs had been punching Ferdinand in the nose like a giant fist for the past half hour, but idiot that he was, he had recognized not a one of them. The house was *occupied*. And of all people, by the woman he had kissed last night. Possibly by her husband too. He had a pained mental image of pistols at dawn, grass for breakfast.

She had stepped down onto the tiled floor and was hurrying toward him, her right arm extended in greeting. She was smiling. And devil take it, but she was beautiful. He licked lips suddenly turned dry. There was no sign of a husband thundering down the stairs behind her.

"You!" she exclaimed. Then she seemed to hear the echo of what her butler had said to her and her smile faltered. "*Lord* Ferdinand Dudley?"

He took her outstretched hand in his and bowed over it, clicking his heels as he did so. "Ma'am," he murmured. *Bloody hell,* he added silently.

"I supposed that you had continued your journey this morning," she said. "I expected never to see you again. Do you have far to go? But how delightful that you have called on me first. Someone told you where I live? Do come up to the drawing room. Mr. Jarvey will have refreshments sent up. I was on my way out for a walk, but I am so glad you came before I left."

Where I live. His mind latched on to those three words. She *did* live here. She thought he had come to call on her on the strength of yesterday's acquaintance. Lord, what rotten bad luck. He dredged up a smile from somewhere deep inside himself, bowed again, and offered his arm.

"It would be my pleasure, ma'am," he said, instead of simply telling her what was what and having done with it.

This would teach him to avoid village fêtes and pretty country lasses, Ferdinand thought as she took his arm and led him toward the staircase. He tried to stuff aside the memory of her dancing with gay animation about the maypole on the village green, her face vibrant and beautiful in the firelight, her thick hair bouncing and swaying against her back below its confining ribbon. And of the kiss he had incautiously maneuvered, during which he had held her very shapely body flush against his own.

Devil take it!

3

HE HAD COME! HE WAS TALL AND LITHE AND elegant in crisply clean riding clothes different from yesterday's. He was smiling and handsome, and he was Lord Ferdinand Dudley. She remembered how the arm through which her own was now loosely linked had felt holding her close the night before. She remembered how his mouth had felt on her own.

He had come!

It was absurd, as well as undesirable, to imagine that he had come courting. He was merely a stranger passing through, who had danced with her and kissed her, discovered her identity, and come to pay a courtesy call. No, more than that, surely. He must have felt the sheer romance of the maypole dance and its aftermath, as she had. He had come to see her once more before riding on.

He had come!

Viola led Lord Ferdinand Dudley into the drawing room and indicated a chair beside the marble fireplace. She took one opposite him and smiled at him again.

"How did you discover my identity?" she asked. It warmed her to know that he had made the effort.

He cleared his throat and looked uncomfortable. How gratifying that she could discompose a *lord*. Her eyes sparkled with amusement.

"I asked the landlord of the Boar's Head for the direction to Pinewood Manor," he said.

Ah, so he had known yesterday who she was? She had not known his identity or sought to discover it. But she was glad he had come to introduce himself before riding on. She was glad their encounter yesterday had meant something to him, as it had to her.

"The fête was a great success," she said. She wanted him to talk about it, to mention their lovely dance.

"Quite so." He cleared his throat again and flushed. But before he could continue, the door opened and the parlormaid brought in a tray of coffee and set it down in front of Viola before bobbing a curtsy and leaving. Viola poured two cups and rose to set one down on the table beside Lord Ferdinand. He watched her in silence.

"Look here, ma'am," he blurted as she resumed her seat. "Has Bamber not written to you either?"

"The Earl of Bamber?" She stared at him in surprise.

"I beg your pardon, ma'am," he continued, "but Pinewood is no longer his, you see. It is mine. As of two weeks ago."

"Yours?" What *was* this? "But that is impossible, my lord. Pinewood Manor is mine. It has been for almost two years."

He reached into an inner pocket of his riding coat to draw out a folded sheet of paper, which he held out to her. "Here is the deed to the manor. It is now officially in my name. I am sorry."

She looked at it blankly without reaching for it, and foolishly all she could think of was that she had been mistaken. He had *not* come to call on her. At least, not because of yesterday. The contest for her daisies, the dance about the maypole, the kiss beneath the old oak had meant nothing whatsoever to him. Today he had come with the intention of ousting her from her home.

"It is a worthless piece of paper," she told him through lips that felt suddenly stiff. "The Earl of Bamber has made off with the price you paid for it, Lord Ferdinand, and is laughing at you from some safe distance. I suggest you find him and take up the matter with him." She felt the stirring of anger—and fright.

"There is nothing to take up," Lord Ferdinand told her. "The legality of the document is not in question, ma'am. It has been attested to by both Bamber's solicitor and my brother's—he is the Duke of Tresham. I was careful to verify the authenticity of my winnings."

"*Winnings?*" Oh, yes, of course. She knew his type—yes, indeed she did. He was the brother of the Duke of Tresham, with all of a younger son's weaknesses and vices—boredom, shiftlessness, extravagance, insensitivity, arrogance. He was probably impoverished too. But yesterday she had chosen to be beguiled by a handsome face and a virile male body, and to be flattered by his attentions. He was a gambler of the very worst kind, one who played deep without any concern for the human consequences of his addiction. He had won property that was not even his opponent's to lose.

"At cards," he explained. "There are any number of witnesses to the fact that Pinewood was fairly won. And I *did* have the document checked very thoroughly. I am indeed sorry for this inconvenience to you. I had no idea there was someone living here."

Inconvenience!

Viola leaped to her feet, her cheeks flooding with hot color, her eyes flashing. How dare he!

"You may take your *document* with you and toss it into the river as you leave," she said. "It is worthless. Pinewood Manor was willed to me almost two years ago. The Earl of Bamber may not have liked it, but there was nothing he could do to prevent it. Good day to you, my lord."

But Lord Ferdinand Dudley, although he too got to his feet, made no move to leave the room and her life, as any decent gentleman would have done. He stood before the fireplace looking large and unyielding and unsmiling. All his false geniality had been abandoned.

"On the contrary, ma'am," he said, "it is you who are going to have to leave. I will, of course, grant you sufficient time to gather your belongings and arrange for a destination, since Bamber has not seen fit to give you decent notice. You are a relative of his, are you? I suppose you should go to Bamber Court, then, unless somewhere else leaps to mind. He will hardly refuse you admittance, will he, though I daresay he is still in London. His mother lives there all the time, though, I believe. She will doubtless welcome you."

His words filled her with icy terror. Her nostrils flared. "Let me make one thing very clear to you, Lord Ferdinand," she said. "This is my home. You are a trespasser here and an unwelcome one, despite . . . well, despite yesterday. I understand clearly now that you are a gamer and an opportunist. I had evidence of those weaknesses yesterday but did not realize they were habitual. I do not doubt that you are also any number of other unsavory things. You will leave immediately. I will be going nowhere. I am already at home. Good day to you."

He gazed at her with those almost black eyes, which were quite unfathomable. "I will be taking up residence as soon as you have had time to pack up your belongings and remove yourself, ma'am," he said. "I would advise you not to delay too long. You would certainly not wish to be forced to spend any night beneath the roof of a single gentleman who is also a gamer and an opportunist, among other unsavory vices."

And she had danced about the maypole with this cold, unfeeling, obstinate man the night before and thought it surely the most glorious experience of her life? She had kissed him and thought she would warm herself with the memory for the rest of her life?

"I will simply not allow you to do this," she said. "How dare you expose me to public attention yesterday by wagering on my—my *daisies*! How dare you haul me onto the green to dance about the *maypole*! How dare you maul my person and k-*kiss* me as if I were a common milkmaid!"

His brows snapped together and she realized with some satisfaction that she had finally rattled him. "Yesterday?" he barked at her. "*Yesterday?* You accuse me of common assault when you *flirted* with me from the moment your eyes first alighted on me?"

"And how *dare* you have the audacity to come here today to invade my home and privacy, you . . . you Bond Street fop! You conscienceless rake! You callous, dissolute gamer!" She had lost control of both the situation and herself, she knew, but she did not care. "I know your sort, and I will *not* allow you to ignore my very existence. Get out of here!" She pointed toward the door. "Go back to London and your own kind, where you belong. We do not need you here."

He raised his eyebrows haughtily—and then lifted one hand and ran his fingers through his hair. He sighed out loud.

"Perhaps, ma'am," he suggested, "we should discuss

this matter like civilized beings instead of scrapping like a couple of ill-bred children. Your presence here has taken me by surprise. You know, it was unpardonable of Bamber not to have informed you that the property is no longer his. You of all people should have been the first to know. But—I beg your pardon—does he *know* you are living here? I mean . . . well, he did not *say* anything about you."

She regarded him scornfully. There was nothing to discuss, civilly or otherwise. "It is quite immaterial to me whether he knows or not," she said.

"Well," he said, "he should have informed both you and me, and so I shall tell him when I see him. It is a dashed awkward thing that I have descended on you like this without warning of any kind. Accept my apologies, ma'am. Is he a close relative of yours? Are you fond of him?"

"My affections would be sadly misplaced if I were," Viola said. "A man of *honor* surely does not pledge at a card game what does not belong to him."

He took one step closer to her. "Why do you claim that Pinewood is yours?" he asked. "You said it was willed to you?"

"When the Earl of Bamber died," she said. "This man's father."

"Were you there for the reading of the will?" he asked. "Or were you informed of the bequest by letter?"

"I had the earl's promise," she said.

"The old earl?" He was frowning. "He promised to leave you Pinewood? But you have no proof that he kept his promise? You were not there for the reading? You received no letter from his solicitor?" He shook his head slowly. "You have been hoaxed, I am afraid, ma'am."

Her clasped hands felt cold and clammy. Her heartbeat was thudding against her eardrums. "I was not there for the reading of the will," she said, "but I trust the word of the late Earl of Bamber, my lord. He promised me when I came here two years ago that he would change his will. He lived for more than a month after that. He would neither have changed his mind nor procrastinated. No one belonging to the present earl has been here or communicated in any way with me. Is that not proof enough that he knew very well the property is mine?"

"Why do you not have the deed in your possession, then?" he asked. "Why did both Bamber's solicitor and my brother's assure me that the property was indeed his before he wagered it and lost it to me?"

Viola's stomach somersaulted queasily. But she dared not give in to terror. "I have never thought about it," she said curtly. "The deed is merely a piece of paper. I trusted the word of the late Earl of Bamber. I still do. Pinewood is mine. I do not intend to discuss the matter further with you, Lord Ferdinand. I do not need to. You must leave."

He stared at her, the long fingers of one hand drumming a tattoo against the outside of his thigh. He was not going to go away quietly. Had she expected that he would? She had known from her first sight of him yesterday that he was a dangerous man. He was one who was accustomed to having his own way, she guessed. And he was the Duke of Tresham's brother? The duke was a notoriously ruthless man, whose will no one dared cross.

"There is an easy way to settle the matter," he said. "We can send for a copy of the old earl's will. But I would not hold out any hope of its saying what you wish it to say, if I were you, ma'am. If the old earl did indeed make you such a promise—"

"If? *If?*" Viola took an incautious step forward so that she was almost toe-to-toe with him.

He held up a staying hand. "Then I am afraid he did not keep it. There can be no doubt about it. I made very certain, before I left London to come down here, that Pinewood was Bamber's to lose. It is now mine."

"He had no right to wager away the house," she cried, "when it did not belong to him. It is *mine*. It was left to me."

"I can understand your agitation," he told her. "This was dashed irresponsible of Bamber—both Bambers: the father for making a promise he did not keep, the son for forgetting you were here. If I had only known of your existence, I could at least have given you ample notice before I came here in person. But I did not know, and so here I am, eager to acquaint myself with my new property. You really are going to have to leave, I'm afraid. There is no sensible alternative, is there? We cannot *both* live here. But I'll give you a week. Will that be long enough? I'll sleep at the inn in Trellick during that time. Do you have somewhere else to go? *Could* you go to Bamber Court?"

Viola clenched her hands even tighter. She could feel her fingernails digging into her palms. "I have no intention of going anywhere," she told him. "Until I see that will and it is proved to me that I am not named in it, this is where I belong. This is my house. My home."

He sighed, and she realized that he was too close for comfort. But she would not take a step back. She tilted her head and looked him straight in the eye—and had a flashing memory of standing even closer to him just the evening before. Could he possibly be the same man?

Beware of a tall, dark, handsome stranger. He can destroy you.

"If there is nowhere," he said with what she might have interpreted as kindness had the words not been so brutal, "I'll send you to London in my own carriage. I'll send you to my sister, Lady Heyward. No, on second thought, Angie is too scatterbrained to offer any practical assistance. I'll send you to my sister-in-law, the Duchess of Tresham, then. She will gladly offer you shelter while she helps you find some suitable and respectable employment. Or a relative willing to take you in."

Viola laughed scornfully. "Perhaps the Duchess of Tresham could do that for *you,* my lord," she suggested. "Find you respectable employment, that is. Gamblers frequently find their pockets to let, I understand. And gamblers are invariably gentlemen who have nothing more meaningful to do with their lives."

He raised his eyebrows and looked at her in some astonishment. "You *do* have a sharp tongue," he said. "Who are you? Have I seen you somewhere before? Before yesterday, that is?"

It was entirely possible. Though no one else in the neighborhood of Pinewood had. That had always been a large part of its charm. The only twinge of alarm she had felt at first downstairs—it seemed laughable now—had come with Mr. Jarvey's introduction of yesterday's handsome stranger as Lord Ferdinand Dudley—a member of the *ton,* possibly someone who lived much of his life in London and had perhaps done so for several years. She guessed that he must be in his late twenties.

"Viola Thornhill," she told him. "And I have never seen you before yesterday. I would have remembered."

He nodded, but his brows were still knitted in thought. He was obviously trying to remember where it was he had seen her before, if anywhere. She could have offered a few suggestions, though it was true she had never seen him before yesterday.

"Well," he said briskly, shaking his head, "I will take myself off back to Trellick, Miss Thornhill. It is Miss, not Mrs.?" She inclined her head. "For seven nights, though I must beg leave to intrude upon you here in the daytime. If you need my assistance in planning your journey, feel free to ask for it."

He strode past her across the room, all masculine arrogance and energy and power. Yesterday's dream transformed into today's nightmare. She looked after him with intense hatred.

"Lord Ferdinand," she said as his hand closed about the doorknob, "I do not believe you heard me a moment ago. Until I have seen that will, I am going nowhere. I will be remaining here in my own house and my own home. I will not give in to bluster and bullying. If you were a gentleman, you would not even ask it of me."

When he turned, she could see that she had angered him. His eyes looked very black. His brows had drawn together. His nostrils were flared, making his nose look sharper, almost hooked, and his lips were set in a grim line. He looked altogether more formidable than he had a moment before. Viola glared defiantly at him.

"If I were a *gentleman*?" he said, so softly that despite herself she felt a shiver of apprehension curl about her spine. "If you were a *lady*, ma'am, you would accept with grace what has happened through no fault of mine. I am not answerable for the failure of the late earl to keep his promise to you, or for his son's choosing to bet an estate instead of money on the outcome of a card game. The simple fact is that Pinewood Manor is *mine*. It was my plan a moment ago to inconvenience myself out of deference to your sensibilities and the awkwardness of your situation. It is no longer my plan. I will be taking up residence here immediately. It is *you* who will stay at the Boar's Head tonight. But as a *gentleman,* I will send a maid with you and have the bill sent to me."

"I will be sleeping here, in my own house, in my own bed," she told him, holding his gaze.

The air fairly crackled with the clashing of their wills.

His eyes narrowed. "Then you must share the house with me," he told her. "With someone you have accused of being less than a gentleman. Perhaps, as well as being a dissolute gamer, I am also possessed of unbridled sexual appetites. Perhaps last evening gave you only the glimmering of a hint of what I am capable of when my passions are aroused. Are you sure you wish to put your person and your reputation at such risk?"

She might have laughed if she had not been so incensed.

She took long, angry strides toward him until she was close enough to point a finger at him and jab it against his chest, like a blunt dagger, as she spoke. Her voice shook with fury.

"If you so much as attempt to lay one lascivious finger on me," she told him, "you may be surprised to discover that your sexual appetites will die an ignominious death and remain dead for all time. Be warned. I am no man's mistress. I am no man's abject victim, to be threatened and coerced into whimpering submission. I am my own mistress, *my lord,* and I am mistress of Pinewood. I will remain here tonight and every night for the rest of my life. If you truly believe you have a claim to the house, then I daresay you will stay here too. But I can guarantee that soon you will be glad enough to leave. You are a rake and a town fop and would be quite incapable of living more than a week in the country without expiring of boredom. I will endure you for that week. But I will not be bullied or threatened sexually without retaliating in ways you would not enjoy. And I will not be removed from my rightful home." She stabbed at his chest one more time—it was a remarkably solid chest. "And now, if you please, I wish to leave the room in order to resume my interrupted plan of walking out and taking the air."

He stared at her with the same angry expression—with perhaps also a suggestion of shock?—for several moments before standing aside, whisking open the drawing room door, and gesturing with a flourish toward the landing beyond it, while sketching her a mocking bow.

"Far be it from me to hold you against your will," he said. "But I in my turn can guarantee that within a week, or two at the most, you will be forced to abandon your rash determination to share a bachelor establishment with a rake. I will send for that damned will."

Viola ignored the blasphemy with cold civility and swept from the room. He had the deed of Pinewood, she thought as she climbed the stairs to her room. Something was terribly wrong. She had no written proof, only the word of a man long dead. But strangely, foolishly, the thought that crowded all else from her mind was that he—Lord Ferdinand Dudley, that is—had not known she lived here. He had made no attempt to discover who she was. He had not cared enough. Yesterday had meant nothing to him.

Well, it had not meant anything to her either!

4

VIOLA DID NOT, AFTER ALL, GO OUT WALKING. She sat for a long time on the window seat in her bedchamber. Hers was fortunately not the master bedchamber—at least they were not to fight over that and perhaps insist upon sharing the same bed. She had always preferred her present room, with its cheerful Chinese wallpaper and draperies and screens and its view over the back of the house rather than the front, over the kitchen garden and greenhouses, over the long avenue beyond them, culminating in the tree-dotted hill half a mile away.

Pinewood was hers. No one else had even been interested in it until it had become the subject of a card game. Lord Ferdinand Dudley would not be interested either once he recovered from the novelty of having won it. He was a city man, a dandy, a fop, a gamer, a rake—and probably many more nasty things. Once he went back to London, he would forget all about Pinewood again.

Once he went back to London . . .

Viola got to her feet, smoothed out her dress, straightened her shoulders, and left her room, bound for the kitchen.

"Yes, it is true," she said in answer to all the anxious, inquiring looks turned her way as soon as she walked in. They were all there—Mr. Jarvey; Mr. Paxton, the steward; Jeb Hardinge, the head groom; Samuel Dey, the footman; Hannah; Mrs. Walsh, the cook; Rose, the parlormaid; Tom Abbott, the head gardener. They must have been holding a meeting. "Though I do not believe it for a minute. Lord Ferdinand Dudley claims to be the new owner of Pinewood. But I have no intention of leaving. Indeed, I have every intention of persuading Lord Ferdinand to go away again."

"What do you have in mind, Miss Vi?" Hannah asked. "Oh, I *knew* that man was trouble the minute I set eyes on him. Too handsome for his own good, he is."

"How difficult can it be," Viola asked, "to convince a town tulip that the life of a country squire is not for him?"

"I can think of a few ways without even taxing my brains, Miss Thornhill," Jeb Hardinge said.

"So can I," Mrs. Walsh agreed grimly.

"Let's hear some of these ideas, then," Mr. Paxton suggested, "and see if we can come up with a plan."

Viola sat down at the kitchen table and invited everyone to join her.

A short while later, Viola was walking into the village. She was far too restless to sit still in any vehicle when she might be striding along, trying to keep up with the pace of her teeming thoughts.

How very different two days could be. Yesterday's dream had been very pleasant while it had lasted—more than pleasant. She had lain awake half the night reliving the dance about the maypole, when she had felt more vigorously alive than she had since she did not know when. And reliving his kiss and the feel of his lean man's body against her own.

More fool her, for allowing herself to indulge in dreams, she thought, lengthening her stride. Maybe that gypsy fortune-teller had not been so far off the mark, after all. She should have taken more heed. She should have been more wary.

She stopped first at the vicarage and found both the Reverend and Mrs. Prewitt at home.

"My dear Miss Thornhill," Mrs. Prewitt said when her housekeeper had ushered Viola into the parlor, "what a delightful surprise. I fully expected that you would remain at home, exhausted, today."

The vicar beamed at her. "Miss Thornhill," he said. "I have just now finished adding the proceeds from the fête. You will be delighted to know that we surpassed last year's total by almost exactly twenty pounds. Is that not significant? So you see, my dear, your daisies were sacrificed to a good cause."

He and his wife laughed over his joke as Viola took her seat.

"It was an extremely generous donation," Mrs. Prewitt said, "especially when one remembers that the gentleman was a stranger."

"He called on me this morning," Viola told them.

"Ah." The vicar rubbed his hands together. "Did he indeed?"

"He claims to be the rightful owner of Pinewood." Viola clasped her hands tightly in her lap. "Most provoking, is it not?"

Both her listeners stared blankly at her for a moment.

"But I was under the impression that Pinewood was yours," Mrs. Prewitt said.

"It *is*," Viola assured them both. "When the late Earl of Bamber sent me here almost two years ago, he changed his will so that it would be mine for the rest of my life. However, the present earl had the deed and chose to wager away the property in a *card* game at a *gaming hell* a short while ago, and lost it." She did not know where the card game had been played, but she chose to assume it had been at the shabbiest, most notorious hell.

"Oh, dear me," the vicar commented, looking down in some concern at his visitor. "But his lordship could not wager away property that does not belong to him, Miss Thornhill. I hope the gentleman was not too disappointed to learn how he had been deceived. He seemed pleasant enough."

"In a *card* game?" Mrs. Prewitt was more satisfyingly shocked than her husband. "We were deceived in him yesterday, then. I did think it very forward of him, I must confess, Miss Thornhill, to make you dance with him about the maypole when he had not been formally presented to you. What a dreadful turn you must have had when he called on you with his claim this morning."

"Oh, I have not allowed him to upset me greatly," Viola assured them. "Indeed I have a plan to persuade him that he would find life at Pinewood vastly uncomfortable. You may both help me if you will . . ."

A short while later she was outdoors again and continuing the round of visits she had planned. Fortunately everyone was at home, perhaps understandably so after such a busy day yesterday.

Her final call was at the cottage of the Misses Merrywether, who listened to her story with growing amazement and indignation. *She* had disliked Lord Ferdinand Dudley from the moment she first set eyes on him, Miss Faith Merrywether declared. His manners had been far too easy. And no true gentleman removed his coat in the presence of ladies, even when he was engaged in some sport on a hot day.

He was extremely handsome, Miss Prudence Merrywether conceded, blushing, and of course he had that charming smile, but one knew from experience that handsome, charming gentlemen were never up to any good. Lord Ferdinand Dudley was certainly not up to any if his intention was to drive their dear Miss Thornhill away destitute from Pinewood.

"Oh, he will not drive me away," Viola assured both ladies. "It will be the other way around. *I* shall get rid of *him*."

"The vicar and Mr. Claypole will see what can be done on your behalf, I am sure," Miss Merrywether said. "In the meantime, Miss Thornhill, you must come and live here. You will not be at all in the way."

"That is extremely kind of you, ma'am, but I have no intention of leaving Pinewood," Viola said. "Indeed, it is my plan to—"

But the description of her plan had to be deferred to a more convenient moment. Miss Prudence was so shocked at the mere idea of her returning to the house when there was a single gentleman in residence there that Miss Merrywether, made of sterner stuff herself, had to send in a hurry for their young maid to fetch burned feathers and hartshorn in order to prevent her sister from swooning dead away. Viola meanwhile chafed her wrists.

"There is no telling what such a libertine might attempt," Miss Merrywether warned Viola after the crisis had passed and a still-pale Miss Prudence was propped against cushions sipping weak, sweet tea, "if he were to get you alone with no servants in attendance. He might even attempt to *kiss* you. No, no, Prudence, you must not go off again; Miss Thornhill will not return to

Pinewood. She will remain here. We will have her things sent for. And we will lock all our doors from now on, even during the daytime. And bolt them too."

"I will be perfectly safe at Pinewood," Viola assured both sisters. "You must not forget that I am surrounded there by my own loyal servants. Hannah has been with me all my life. Besides, Lord Ferdinand will be leaving soon. He is about to discover that life in the country is simply not for him. You can both help me if you will . . ."

On the whole, Viola thought as she made her way homeward, she was pleased with her afternoon's visits. At least all the villagers with whom she was closely acquainted had heard her side of the story before he had had a chance to tell his own. And those she had not told would soon find out for themselves. News and gossip traveled on the wind, she sometimes thought.

As far as those families who lived in the country were concerned, well, she would be able to talk to several of them this evening when she dined at Crossings with the Claypoles.

Lord Ferdinand Dudley would dine alone at Pinewood. Viola smiled with sheer malice. But thinking of the man only served to remind her that she could no longer approach her home with the usual glad lifting of her spirits. She looked ahead up the lawn toward the house and wondered if he was standing at one of the windows, watching her. She wondered if she would encounter him as soon as she entered the house—in the hall, on the stairs, in the upper corridor.

It was intolerable to know that a stranger had invaded her most private domain. But there was no help for it, for the moment at least. And she could not afford to allow her footsteps to lag. She had an evening engagement to prepare for.

She was striding along the terrace from the stable side of the house several minutes later, determined not to tiptoe fearfully into her own home, when she was met by the sight of him striding onto it from the opposite direction. They both abruptly stopped walking.

He was still in his riding clothes. He was hatless. He looked disorientingly male in what she had made into her own essentially female preserve. And he was clearly making himself right at home. He must have been down by the river or out behind the house, inspecting the kitchen gardens and the greenhouses.

He bowed stiffly.

She curtsied stiffly—and then hurried on her way to the house without looking at him again. Whether he was coming in behind her or was still rooted to the spot or had gone to jump into the fountain, she neither knew nor cared.

"Mr. Jarvey," she said, seeing him pacing about the hall looking unaccustomedly lost. "Have Hannah come up to me, please."

She continued on her way upstairs, assuring herself with every step that she hurried only because there was little time left before she must leave for Crossings.

If only he were not so handsome, she thought. Or so young.

If only she had not flirted with him yesterday. Not that she had really *flirted,* of course. It had been her duty as a member of the fête committee to be pleasant to everyone, villager and stranger alike. She had merely been amiable.

Viola sighed as she hurried along the upper corridor

in the direction of her bedchamber. A spade might as well be called a spade. She had flirted with him.

She *wished* she had not.

She would not allow her mind even to touch upon that kiss. But she could feel the hardness of his thighs against her own and the warm softness of his lips parted over her own, and she could smell his cologne all the time she kept her mind off that particular incident.

"'EACH WITH HIS BONNY lass.'"

Ferdinand determinedly clamped his teeth together after singing just the one phrase and drew a leather-bound book randomly off a library shelf. He had sung the song with cheerful gusto as he approached the house for the first time many hours before. But it had stuck in his unconscious mind, as songs sometimes do, so that he had caught himself singing or humming snatches of it ever since, until he was heartily sick of it. It was a ridiculous song, anyway, with all its interminable fa-la-las.

And he was definitely not in the mood for music. He was rattled. And annoyed too—with himself because he had allowed *her* to dampen his spirits, with *her* because she had done the dampening. And with Bamber—no, make that plural. He was furious with the Bambers, father and son. What the devil sort of responsible heads of the family had either of them been? The one had sent her here with promises he had forgotten to honor—or had had no intention of honoring in the first place—and the other seemed unaware of her very existence.

He himself had allowed her to dig in her heels and put him in the embarrassing situation of sharing a house with an unmarried young lady. And a damned gorgeous one too, though that had nothing to say to the matter. He should have kicked her out. Or stayed at the Boar's Head himself until that infernal will could arrive and convince her that she had no claim to the property.

Ferdinand ran his fingers through his hair and glanced at the letters on the desk, sealed and ready to go in the morning. Perhaps he should simply go and get the will himself. Better yet, he should go and send it to her with a trusty messenger and a formal notice to quit. He would return after she had left.

But it would seem so damnably *weak* to turn tail and run and let someone else do his dirty business for him. It was just not the way he did things. It was not the Dudley way. If she could be stubborn, he could be ten times more so. If she was willing to risk her reputation by living here with him unchaperoned, on her own head be it. He was not going to worry *his* conscience over it.

He should go to bed before she returned from her dinner party, Ferdinand thought. He had no particular wish to encounter her again tonight—or ever again, if it came to that. But dash it all, it was not even midnight. He looked about him at the tastefully furnished library, with its cozy sitting area about the fireplace, its elegant desk, and its small but superior collection of books, which he had noticed were not even dusty. Did that mean she was a reader? He did not want to know. But he liked the library. He could feel right at home here.

Once she was gone.

He had not wanted to play for the wretched property in the first place, Ferdinand recalled, replacing the book on the shelf when it became obvious that his mind was too distracted to allow him to read tonight. He had never been much interested in card playing. He preferred physical sport. He liked the sort of extravagant dares with which the betting books at the various gentlemen's clubs always abounded—particularly the ones that involved him in the performance of some dangerous or daring physical feat.

He had played that night at Brookes's up to the limit he always privately allowed himself, and then he had risen to leave. There was a party he had half promised to look in on. But Leavering, who had accompanied him to the club, was just then being called away by the news that his wife was in childbed and likely to deliver at any moment, and Bamber, loud and obnoxious in his cups—as he invariably was, damn him—was accusing the prospective papa of making a lame excuse to leave with his winnings before he, the drunken earl, had had a chance to win them back. His luck was changing, he had declared. He could feel it in his bones.

Ferdinand had caught his friend by the arm just when the scene was threatening to turn ugly and was beginning to attract attention. He had offered to take Leavering's place and had tossed five hundred pounds onto the table.

A few minutes later he had been exclaiming in protest over the signed voucher Bamber had cast onto the table in place of money. It had represented the promise of property that no one in the card room had ever heard of—it was certainly not Bamber's principal seat or any of his better known secondary properties. Somewhere called Pinewood Manor in Somersetshire. Somewhere probably nowhere near as valuable as the five hundred pounds Ferdinand had thrown in, one of the players had warned.

Ferdinand would not have played any man for his

home—no true gentleman would. But Pinewood was apparently some subsidiary, inferior property. And so he had played—and won. And discovered the next day from both Bamber's solicitor and Tresham's that Pinewood really did exist and really was his. When in a pang of conscience, despite everything, he had called on Bamber the day after that to offer the return of the property in exchange for some monetary settlement of the gaming debt, the earl, nursing a colossal hangover from some orgy the previous night, had announced that talking made his head feel as if it were about to explode. Dudley would doubtless humor him by going away. And he was certainly welcome to Pinewood, which Bamber was unlikely to miss, having never set eyes on the place or seen a penny in rents to his knowledge.

And so Ferdinand had set out with a clear conscience to discover and inspect his new property. He had never owned, or expected to own, any land. He was the son of a duke, it was true, and enormously wealthy, to boot—his father had left him a generous portion, and both his mother and her sister had left him their not-insignificant fortunes on their deaths. But he was a younger son. Tresham had inherited Acton Park and all the other estates with the ducal titles.

Drat! Ferdinand thought suddenly, lifting his head and listening. The knocker had rattled against the front door and it was being opened. There was the sound of voices in the hall. More than one. More than two. Either all the servants had come upstairs to greet her return, or else she had brought people back with her. At almost midnight?

His first impulse was to stay where he was until they were all gone. But that butler fellow knew he was in here, and a Dudley could not have it said that he had skulked out of sight rather than establish from the outset that he was master of his own domain. He trod purposefully across the library and opened the door.

There were five persons standing in the hall—Jarvey, a small, plumpish woman who looked like a maid, Viola Thornhill, and two strangers, a man and a woman. The man was not entirely a stranger, though. He was the dry stick who had given it as his opinion yesterday that wagering was inappropriate to a church fête.

They all looked his way. Viola Thornhill herself did so by glancing over her shoulder at him, her eyebrows raised, her lips slightly parted. She was wearing a green silk opera cloak, the wide hood spread becomingly over her shoulders, her head with its high coronet of dark red braids bare of any covering or adornment.

Damn! Where the devil had he seen her before this trip to the hinterlands?

"Good evening." He stepped into the hall. "Will you present me, Miss Thornhill?"

The maid disappeared upstairs. The butler melted into the background. The three remaining people all gazed at him with undisguised hostility.

"This is Miss Claypole," Viola Thornhill said, indicating the tall, thin woman of indeterminate age. "And her brother, Mr. Claypole."

She did not introduce him to them. But then, it was probably unnecessary. He had doubtless formed the chief topic of conversation for the evening. Ferdinand bowed.

Neither visitor veered from the upright.

"This will not do, sir," Claypole said with pompous severity. "It is extremely improper for you, a single gentleman, to be occupying the home of a single, virtuous lady."

Ferdinand's right hand found the gilded handle of his quizzing glass and raised it to his eye. "I agree with you," he said curtly after a significant pause. "Or would if your facts were correct. But they are topsy-turvy, my good fellow. It is the single, virtuous female who is occupying *my* home."

"Now, see here—" Claypole took one aggressive stride toward him.

Ferdinand dropped his glass on its ribbon and held up his hand. "Take a damper," he advised. "You do not want to go that route, I do assure you. Certainly not in the presence of ladies."

"You have no need to rush to my defense, Mr. Claypole," Viola Thornhill said. "Thank you both for escorting me home in the carriage, but—"

"You will but me no buts, Viola," Miss Claypole said in strident tones. "This scandalous situation calls for an act of demonstrable propriety. Since Lord Ferdinand Dudley has chosen to remain at Pinewood instead of removing decently to the inn, then I will remain here as your chaperon. Indefinitely. For as long as I am needed. Humphrey will have a trunk of my things sent over in the morning."

Some of the tension had drained out of Claypole's body and flushed face. He had clearly realized how foolhardy it would be to come to blows. Ferdinand turned his attention to the sister.

"I thank you, ma'am," he said, "but your presence here will be quite unnecessary. I cannot answer for Miss Thornhill's reputation, but I can answer for her virtue. I have no intention of having my wicked way with her as soon as we are alone together—alone except for a number of servants, that is."

Miss Claypole appeared to add an extra couple of inches to her height as she inhaled audibly.

"Your vulgarity is boundless," she said. "Well, sir, I am here to guard Miss Thornhill's reputation as well as her virtue. I would not trust you one inch farther than I could see you. We have been informed today—my mother, my brother, and I—that you forced her to dance *about the maypole* with you last evening. Do not think to deny it. There were any number of witnesses."

"Bertha—" Viola Thornhill began.

Ferdinand had his glass to his eye again. "In that case," he said, "I will not perjure myself by denying it, ma'am. Now, I believe you and your brother are leaving?"

"I will not leave this house unless I am thrown bodily out," the lady said.

"You tempt me, ma'am," Ferdinand told her quietly. He turned his attention to Claypole. "Good night, sir. You *will* take Miss Claypole with you when you leave?"

"Miss Thornhill." Claypole possessed himself of one of her hands. "Do you see now the foolishness of insisting upon returning here? Was not my mama right? Bertha is your friend. I flatter myself that I am more than just a friend. Come back with us to Crossings until this matter can be settled."

"Thank you again, but I will not leave my own home, sir," she said. "And you must not upset yourself on my behalf, Bertha. I have Hannah and the other servants. I do not need a female companion."

"It is a good thing too," Ferdinand said briskly. "Because you won't be having one. Not in this house."

She looked at him with raised eyebrows and then turned away again to bid her companions good night.

"This is highly improper—" Claypole began.

"Good night." Ferdinand strode to the double doors, opened them with a flourish while Jarvey still hovered uncertainly in the background, and gestured toward the darkness outside.

They went unwillingly, but they did go. They had little choice without risking violence. The woman might have been game, Ferdinand judged, but the man certainly would not have been.

"I suppose," he said after he had closed the door behind them, turning on Viola Thornhill, who was removing her cloak and handing it to the butler, "he is your beau?"

"Do you?" she said. "Thank you, Mr. Jarvey, you will not be needed again tonight."

Ferdinand could have argued, since Jarvey was now *his* servant, but he would not appear petty.

"Claypole is a craven jackass," he said. "If the situation were reversed, I would have drawn the cork of any man who insisted on your being unchaperoned if you remained here. And then I would have dragged you out of here whether you wished to go or not."

"How comforting," she said, "to know that I am sharing a house with a caveman. I presume, my lord, that would have been by the hair, while you flourished a club in the other hand? Such a manly image."

He wished she had not removed her cloak. The darker green evening gown she wore beneath it was not in any way indecent. It fell in soft, shimmering folds from beneath her bosom to her ankles, and the bodice, though low, would have looked almost conservative in a

London ballroom. But the garment did nothing whatsoever to hide the alluring curves of the woman beneath it. And he knew just what those curves felt like pressed to his own body, dammit.

Lord! Perhaps he should have stayed at the Boar's Head after all, stubbornness notwithstanding.

"What you are doing," he said, "is insisting upon sharing a house with a man who knows what is what. And it is not at all the thing for you to be here with me. That idiot was right about that, at least."

She had crossed the hall to the staircase. She turned with her foot on the bottom stair.

"What, Lord Ferdinand?" she said. "Are you considering ravishing me after all, then? Must I race for my room? At least I must be thankful that I have a head start on you."

She had a saucy tongue. He had noticed it before.

"Believe me, ma'am," he said, "if I wanted to catch you, you would not even make it to the top of the staircase."

She smiled sweetly at him. "Did you enjoy your dinner?"

It was a strange question to ask at such a moment—until he understood the reason. They had both been out for the evening. She had had a dinner engagement, a fact he had learned with considerable relief, until the butler had informed him that since Miss Thornhill had not been expected to dine at home, all there was in the house to set on the dinner table for him was the leftover beef from two days ago, their having all dined in the village the evening before, his lordship would understand. But even though the beef still looked and smelled and even tasted unspoiled, the butler suggested that he should perhaps bear in mind that the weather *had* been unseasonably warm. And the pantry had never kept the food as cool as the cook would like, the butler had added as an aside. And no one could ever discover where the flies all managed to get in.

Ferdinand had announced his intention of dining at the Boar's Head. The food there had not been quite as appetizing as it had been yesterday, nor the service quite as prompt or friendly, but he had put those facts down to tiredness on the part of the staff after a day of celebrating.

Now, with a simple question, Viola Thornhill had made all clear to him. He must be a fool not to have realized sooner. He was already—both at Pinewood and in the village—carrying around the label of local enemy number one, was he?

"Extremely well, thank you," he said. "Did you?"

She smiled again and turned to climb the stairs without saying another word. In the light of the hall candles, the satin of her gown shimmered over the feminine sway of her hips.

Devil take it, but it was a hot night for May.

5

FERDINAND MIGHT HAVE BEEN CONVINCED THAT he had not slept all night had he not been woken so rudely while it was still dark. He shot out of bed rather as if a spring had broken through the mattress, catapulted him in an upward arc, and brought him down flat on his feet beside the bed.

"The devil!" he exclaimed, running the fingers of one hand through his disheveled hair. "What in thunder?" He had no idea what had disturbed him. For the moment he could not even recall where he was.

And then the raucous noise was repeated. He strode across to the open window, flung back the curtains, and thrust out his head. Dawn was the merest smudge of gray on the eastern horizon. He shivered in the predawn chill and for once wished he wore a nightshirt to bed. *There* it was, he saw as he glared downward, strutting along the terrace before the house as if it owned the universe.

A cockerel!

"Go to the devil!" Ferdinand instructed it, and the bird, startled out of its arrogant complacency, scuttled halfway along the terrace before recovering its dignity and crowing again.

Cock-a-doodle-doooo.

Ferdinand in his turn scuttled back to bed after closing both the window and the curtains. He had been unable to fall asleep after coming to bed at midnight. Partly, of course, that had been due to his knowledge that he was sharing his house with an unmarried young lady—who also happened to be voluptuous beauty personified—and had refused to allow her a companion to lend a measure of respectability to the situation. Mainly, though, it was because of the silence. He had lived all his adult years in London, ever since coming down from Oxford seven years before, at the age of twenty. He was unaccustomed to silence. He found it unnerving.

Why was a cockerel allowed to run loose so close to the house? he wondered suddenly. Was he to be woken thus every night (one could hardly call it morning, after all)? He thumped his pillow, which was about the most lumpy, uncomfortable specimen of pillowhood he had ever encountered, and tried to burrow his head into such a position in it that instant sleep would be induced.

Five minutes later he was still very wide awake.

He was remembering how she had looked in that shimmering satin evening gown. He was remembering how her shapely body had felt pressed against his own body, behind the oak tree in the village. And he thought about the fact that she was sleeping in a room not far from his own.

Ferdinand made the sudden discovery that it was the heaviness of the bedcovers that was preventing him from falling back to sleep. He pushed them aside, turned his hot pillow and thumped it again, tried to find a soft, cool nook for his head, failed miserably, and shivered in the chilly air, which was assaulting his naked body on three sides. The blankets were out of reach unless he sat up to grab them.

Devil take it, his sleep had been ruined. And she was

entirely to blame. Why had she not taken herself off as any decent woman would, or at least taken the week he had offered before he lost his temper, so that he might now be sleeping the peaceful sleep of the just at the Boar's Head in Trellick? Bedamned to her, he thought unchivalrously. She was going to have to learn who was master at Pinewood, and the sooner the better. Today she would learn—when today came. He grimaced as he looked about his bedchamber, into which not even the suggestion of daylight had yet penetrated.

He sat up on the side of the bed and thrust both hands through his hair again. Dammit, in his more normal life he often had not even gone to bed at this hour. Yet here he was, getting up. To do what, for God's sake? Eat his breakfast? It would serve those servants right—they had *deliberately* sent him off to the village for his dinner last evening—if he went downstairs, loudly demanding food. But they would probably just slap that cold green beef on a plate for him. Read, then? He was not in the mood. Write some letters? But he had scribbled off notes to Tresham and Angie last evening to be sent this morning with the letter to Bamber.

Ferdinand got to his feet, stretched, yawned until his jaws cracked, and shivered. He would go out for a ride and blow away some cobwebs before coming back and laying down the law. He *enjoyed* early morning rides, after all, he told himself grimly and not altogether truthfully. Anyway, he thought as he strode off in the direction of his dressing room, this hardly qualified as early morning. It was still the middle of the night, for God's sake.

He found his riding clothes in one of the wardrobes without ringing for his valet, dressed, and headed for the outdoors without stopping to shave. He had raced the sun, he saw grimly. Although it was no longer quite dark out, the world was lit only by a very gray twilight. It suited his mood to perfection.

He stalked off to the stables in the fervent hope that there would be a few sleepy grooms there to bark at.

THE COCKEREL HAD AWAKENED Viola even though her room was at the back of the house. But then, of course, she had been expecting it and had been sleeping lightly in anticipation of it. It seemed impossible to her that anyone in the house, especially someone whose room overlooked the terrace, could have slept through the alarum. She had chuckled with open malice when, ten or fifteen minutes later, she had heard a door open farther along the corridor and the sound of booted feet receding in the direction of the staircase.

And then she had dozed off again.

"His lordship was out the door, fit to be tied, not fifteen minutes after the first cock-crow," Hannah reported later as she helped Viola dress and braided and coiled her hair. "In a proper rage he was, apparently, when he took his horse out. And then he went galloping off, cursing and scowling, the Lord knows where. You stay out of his way, Miss Vi. You let us servants handle everything this morning."

"But I can hardly wait to witness his rage for myself, Hannah," Viola assured her. "I would not miss this morning for any consideration. Perhaps by noon he will be on his way back to London and we will be rid of him."

Hannah sighed as she straightened the combs and

brushes on the dressing table. "I wish it could be that easy, lovey," she said.

So did Viola. There was a yawning empty feeling somewhere in the region of her stomach that she was trying hard to ignore. This was not a game she played with Lord Ferdinand Dudley, after all. Her home, her income, her hard-won peace, her very identity were severely at risk.

VIOLA WAS SEATED AT the breakfast table later, still eating, when he strode into the dining room. Even though she had been expecting him and had steeled herself to having her privacy invaded, her heart felt as if it were hammering against her ribs. If this had to be happening at all, why could he not be an old man or an ugly man or in some way an unappealing man? Why should she be made to feel as if the very essence of maleness had just filled the room to suffocate her?

He had obviously come straight from his ride. His buff riding breeches hugged his long, well-muscled legs like a second skin. His boots must have been freshly polished last night and still shone. He was wearing a well-tailored brown riding coat with a white shirt beneath. She had spent enough years in London to recognize in him a regular top sawyer, an out-and-outer, as other gentlemen would call him. His dark hair was tousled from his hat and the outdoors. His face glowed with healthy color.

He was also smiling and looking annoyingly good-humored.

"Good morning, Miss Thornhill." He sketched her a bow. "And what a beautiful morning it is. I was awoken by a cockerel crowing beneath my window and so was out riding in time to watch the sun rise. I had forgotten how exhilarating life in the country can be."

He rubbed his hands together and looked about the room, hunger written all over his face. The sideboard was empty. So was the table, except for Viola's plate and cup and saucer. There were no servants present. He looked a little less cheerful.

"Good morning, my lord." Viola smiled placidly. "And to think that I tiptoed past your room a short while ago, believing that you must be sleeping on late in the country air. It *is* chilly in here, is it not? I'll have the fire lit and your breakfast brought up. I took the liberty of ordering what I thought you might like." She got to her feet and pulled on the bell rope beside the sideboard.

"Thank you." He took the chair at the head of the table, which she had left vacant for him, as she did not want the morning cluttered with unnecessary wrangling over precedence.

She still had eggs and sausage and toast on her plate—a far larger breakfast than her usual fare of toast and coffee. She picked up her knife and fork and continued eating, chewing each mouthful with slow relish, even though everything suddenly tasted like straw.

"The avenue behind the house must be delightful for walking as well as riding," he said. "The grass is well kept, and the trees on either side are as straight as two lines of soldiers on parade. It is a marvel of nature how they can hide an army of birds, is it not, so that one hears a thousand voices and yet is unable to see a single chorister until one of them decides to fly from one branch to another?"

"I have always enjoyed strolling there," she said.

"One can see for miles around from the top of the hill," he said. "I would have loved it as a boy. It reminds me a little of the hills at Acton Park, where I grew up. I would have been king of the castle and held it against all comers. Correction." He grinned, and Viola was unwillingly reminded of the dashing stranger at the fête. "I daresay my brother would have been king and I would have been his loyal henchman. But henchmen have the more exciting life, you know. They fight dragons and assorted other villains, while the king merely sits on his throne looking bored and supercilious and issuing orders and cursing foully."

"Gracious! Is that what your brother used to do?" She almost laughed.

"Elder brothers can be an abomination."

But Viola had no wish to hear about his childhood or his family. She did not want to see his boyish grin. She wanted him in a towering rage. She wanted *him* cursing foully. He was rather more frightening this way. Did he know it? Was this behavior deliberate? A cat toying with a mouse? He was drumming his fingertips on the table, though, and glancing at the door, sure signs that he did not feel as relaxed or as cheerful as he looked.

Viola popped a forkful of egg into her mouth.

"They are certainly taking their time in the kitchen," he said after a short silence. "I must have a word with Jarvey."

How dare he! Mr. Jarvey was *her* butler. The old Earl of Bamber had employed him specifically to serve her. But it was not part of her plan to quarrel with this man just yet.

"Does it seem a long wait to you?" She looked at him in cheerful surprise. "I am so sorry. The kitchen is at an inconvenient distance and the stairs are steep. Mr. Jarvey is not as young as he used to be and sometimes has trouble with his legs. The cook is a little slow too—and absentminded. But good servants are not easily come by in the country, you know, and one is wise to keep what one has even if it does not quite measure up to town standards."

The door opened as she spoke and the butler appeared, an uncovered plate in one hand, a vast tankard of ale in the other. Viola gazed at both with admiration. How had Mrs. Walsh been able to pile the plate so high without everything sliding off? And where had she found such an enormous and hideous tankard? As Mr. Jarvey set his load down on the table, she could see eggs, sausages, kidneys, and bacon as well as slices of toast balancing on one edge of the plate. But the pièce de résistance was a large, thick beefsteak, which must surely have been shown briefly on both sides to the fire and then slapped onto the plate. It was swimming in red juice.

She transferred her gaze to Lord Ferdinand's face, which looked somewhat astonished for a moment.

"I was sure you would enjoy a hearty country breakfast after a vigorous ride, my lord," she said—and remembered too late that she was supposed to have thought him still fast asleep in his bed as a result of the country air.

"Yes, indeed." He rubbed his hands together again, in apparent glee.

Was it possible that such a breakfast really did look appetizing to him? She waited with bated breath for him to taste it. But there was another detail to be taken care of without delay.

"Mr. Jarvey," she directed, "would you light the fire? His lordship is chilly."

The butler bent with agility to the task while Lord Ferdinand watched him. Viola hoped he was not noticing that there was no sign of creaky knees. And then she watched covertly as he speared a kidney with his fork and popped it in his mouth. She could have crowed with glee when he set his knife and fork down with a clatter.

"The food is cold," he said in astonishment.

"Oh, dear." She looked at him with apologetic concern. "I am so accustomed to it that I did not think to warn you. I daresay the cook prepared your food some time ago and forgot—again—to keep it warm in the oven until you came in. Is that what happened, Mr. Jarvey? Perhaps you would have it warmed up and brought back when it is ready. Will you wait for half an hour or so, my lord?"

The fire in the hearth crackled to life, and the butler straightened up and took one step forward.

"No, no." Lord Ferdinand held up one staying hand. "Never mind. I really do not need such a large breakfast. The toast will do me well enough. Fortunately, toast is appetizing even when cold. Normally I would prefer coffee to ale—perhaps you will remember that tomorrow, Jarvey?" He picked up a slice of toast and bit into it. It made a loud, crunching noise, suggesting to Viola that it was stone cold and crisp enough to smash into smithereens if he accidentally dropped it.

Viola, glancing toward the fireplace, raised her napkin to her nose and controlled her own reactions until Lord Ferdinand began to cough.

"Oh, dear," she said. The fireplace was belching smoke. "There must be a bird's nest in the chimney again. That is forever happening. And it always takes *days* to fetch a sweep to clean it out." She coughed into her napkin and felt her eyes begin to sting. "There is no chimney sweep in the village, you see, and the nearest town is eight miles away."

"One can only hope," Lord Ferdinand said, jumping to his feet and hurrying across the room to throw first one and then the other window wide, "that the nest is empty at this particular moment. Otherwise I daresay we can enjoy roast bird for dinner."

Something in his tone alerted Viola. He *knew* at last. He understood. But he was not going to lose his temper as she had hoped. He was going to play out the game, perhaps on the theory that good humor would annoy her far more than scowls and bellows. He was perfectly right too, of course. But it did not matter. At least he would understand now what he was facing—his lone person, and perhaps those of his handful of servants, pitted against a houseful of people bent on making his life as uncomfortable as they possibly could. She wondered how he had enjoyed his pillows last night.

"Sometimes," she said, shivering despite herself as a fresh breeze from the outdoors fluttered the edges of her napkin and wrapped itself about her person like an icy cloak, "I believe that the few advantages of living in the country are far outweighed by the disadvantages. You may leave, thank you, Mr. Jarvey. We must simply hope that the day will be warm enough that we can live without fires in only a moderate degree of discomfort."

The butler made for the door.

"Don't leave yet, Jarvey," Lord Ferdinand instructed him, staying close to the window. "Find me a good stout groom or gardener, will you? One with a head for heights? Perhaps one who is familiar with the rooftop and the chimneys? I daresay there *is* such a person. I would wager on it, in fact. I will go up there with him when I have finished my ale and see if we can rescue the poor homeless birds. Unless it is too late for them, of course, as undoubtedly it is for their nest."

Viola's eyes were watering and aching quite abominably. He was going to be a worthy foe, she realized with a sinking heart. Well, they would see who would win the final victory. He was grossly outnumbered. And she was no mean foe herself. She had far more to lose than he, after all—a thought that conspired to make her egg sit quite uncomfortably in her stomach.

"You will fall and kill yourself," she predicted before indulging in a prolonged coughing fit into her napkin. What on earth had Eli stuffed up the chimney? And why should she care if Lord Ferdinand came to grief?

"You must not fear for my safety, ma'am," he said as the butler slipped from the room. "One of my more notable escapades, though admittedly it was back in my salad days, was in response to a wager that I could not move from one end of a long London street to the other without once touching the ground. The dare was made more interesting by the fact that it was a wet, windy, moonless night, and there was a time limit of one hour. I did it in forty-three minutes."

"I suppose," she said more tartly than she intended, "you rode your horse."

"And took forty-three minutes?" He chuckled. "Alas, the men who issued the dare considered that possibility in advance. No form of conveyance was allowed except my feet. I did it over the rooftops."

"You have won my warmest admiration, my lord,"

she said, getting to her feet and doing nothing to hide her scorn.

"Where are you going?" he asked.

She raised her eyebrows and looked coolly at him through the gradually dispersing smoke haze. "My movements are none of your affair, my lord," she said—and then wished she had chosen different words. His eyes moved down her body, stripping her of clothes as they proceeded—or so it seemed. She clamped her teeth together and glared.

"Perhaps after I have dealt with the chimney," he said, "you will take a walk with me, Miss Thornhill."

"To show you the park?" she asked incredulously. "It is my private domain and is shown only to privileged visitors."

"Of which number I am not one," he said.

"Right."

"But I am not a visitor, am I?" he asked in that soft voice that insisted on curling itself about her spine despite all her determination not to be cowed by him.

"If you wish to find your way around the park, ask someone else to show you," she said, turning to the door.

"And find myself abandoned in a field with an ill-tempered bull?" he said. "Or in quicksand beside the river? I was not asking for a guided tour. I wish to talk with you, and the outdoors seems like the best venue. We need to forget the fun and games, Miss Thornhill, and come to some decision about your future—which will not be spent at Pinewood, by the way. There is no point in postponing the inevitable. Even if you insist upon staying here until a copy of the old earl's will arrives, you are going to have to deal with reality after that event. It would be best for you to be prepared. Walk with me."

She looked back at him over her shoulder. He had begun with a request but had ended with an order. He was so typical of his type. Lesser mortals existed merely to perform his will.

"I have household duties to perform," she said. "After that I will stroll down on the river walk. If you care to join me there, Lord Ferdinand, I will not turn you away. But you will be my guest. You will not issue commands to me—not now or ever. Is that understood?"

He folded his arms and reclined back against the windowsill, looking both relaxed and elegant as he did so. His lips were pursed and there was something that might have been amusement—or was it merely contempt?—lurking in his eyes.

"English has always been my first language," he said.

It was clear he did not intend to say anything else. She left the room, realizing as she did so that all the tricks she and the servants had dreamed up so far had only challenged him and caused him to dig in his heels, more determined than ever to stay. It had been perfectly predictable, of course. Games and tricks must be the breath of life to a bored London beau.

Well, they would see what he would do about everything else that was in store for him today.

WHAT WOULD SHE DREAM up next? Ferdinand wondered as he leaned back against the windowsill without making any attempt to put out the fire. It would burn itself down soon and he was well enough removed from the worst effects of the smoke. After last night's dinner offering, he should have been more alert to the significance of a cockerel apparently gone astray from the home farm and of a cold, undercooked breakfast. But it had taken the smoking chimney to open his eyes—or rather, to make them smart and water.

She actually thought she could drive him away.

His vigorous ride had blown away his irritation at being woken at such an ungodly hour. And toast—even cold, slightly burned toast—had always been sufficient to satisfy his hunger at breakfast. Smoking chimneys were simply a challenge. As for the threat of spoiled beef and flies' eggs last evening—well, he could take a joke as well as the next man. Indeed, he was tempted to join in the horseplay and dream up a few schemes of his own to convince Miss Viola Thornhill that it really was not a comfortable thing to be sharing a bachelor establishment with a man. He could easily tramp mud through the house, leave mess and mayhem behind him wherever he went, acquire a few unruly dogs, wander about the house only half dressed, forget to shave . . . well, he could be endlessly irritating if he chose.

But the trouble was, this was no game.

The devil of it was that he was feeling sorry for her this morning. And guilty, for God's sake, as if *he* were the villain of the piece. The very silliness of this morning's amateurish pranks—and yesterday's—was proof of how desperate she was.

She had shown no inclination to accept his offer to send her to Jane, Duchess of Tresham, his sister-in-law. She had not jumped for joy at the prospect of going to Bamber Court. She had not suggested any alternatives of her own. She seemed markedly unwilling to face up to reality. What else could he suggest? He was going to have to think of something. The only thing he was sure of was that he did not have the stomach to throw her out bodily or have her forcibly removed by a magistrate or constable. He had always been the weak member of the Dudley family in that respect, he thought uneasily. No backbone. But dammit, he felt *sorry* for her. She was a young innocent in the process of having all her comfort and security ripped away from her.

Ferdinand shook off his dilemma and pushed himself away from the windowsill. First things first. There being no hot coffee to tempt him to sit down at the table again—and he had to admit that the sight of that beefsteak made his stomach feel decidedly rebellious—it was time to go roof climbing.

AFTER GOING BELOWSTAIRS TO discuss the day's menu with Mrs. Walsh, Viola went to the library, where she intended to spend time bringing the household books up to date. But there was a letter on the desk, one that must have arrived with the morning post. She snatched it up and looked eagerly at the handwriting. Yes! It was from Claire. She was tempted to break the seal and read the contents without further delay, but of course the house was no longer her own. He might walk in upon her at any moment and ask one of his impertinent questions, as he had after breakfast. *Where are you going?* It was demeaning, to say the least.

Viola slid the unopened letter into the side pocket of her morning dress. There would be more privacy outdoors.

But the outdoors did not look particularly private when she stepped out through the unattended front doors. In fact, the box garden below the terrace was dotted with people—the butler, the head groom, the head gardener and both his assistants, the footman, Rose, Hannah, two male strangers who must be Lord Ferdinand's servants—all standing stock-still facing the house and gazing skyward. Rose had one hand over her eyes, a pointless affectation, since her fingers were spread.

No, Viola thought, correcting her first impression as she stood looking at them all for a moment, it was not skyward they were gazing, but *roofward*. Of course!

"It still don't make no sense why he didn't send for the sweep," she heard one of the undergardeners say to the other. "It don't make no sense to clean a chimney from the top."

"Eli'll fall right through and crack his skull in the hearth, you mark my words," the other predicted with ghoulish relish.

"Aye. *And* burn all his hair off."

Viola went down to join them at a run. He really had gone up there? He had not been bluffing? He and Eli, the groom's young apprentice? She did not want to look. She had no head for heights and could not imagine how anyone did.

"Hush your babbling!" the head gardener instructed his subordinates. "You'll distract their attention."

Viola turned and looked upward—and her legs turned to jelly. The attic window was opened wide onto the small balcony beyond it. But none of the tall chimneys could be reached from there. The rest of the roof was steeply sloped and covered with gray slates, which looked as smooth as an egg and twice as slippery. Lord Ferdinand Dudley and Eli were standing on the balcony, the former with his hands on his hips and his head tipped back to survey the roof above him. He had shed both his riding coat and his waistcoat.

"Jeb," Viola said in a loud whisper, "how did Eli plug the chimney? From below or from above?" She had assumed the former. She would never have consented to allowing him to clamber over the roof, putting his life at risk.

"The rags would have caught on fire if they were too low, Miss Thornhill," the groom explained to her. "He went up after he fetched the cockerel. Swore afterward that he didn't have the head to do it again, mind. But his lordship made him go."

Well, they had not stepped away from the relative safety of the flat balcony yet. The whispering and shushing were unnecessary.

"Eli!" Viola called, bracketing her mouth with her hands so that the sound of her voice would carry better. "Come down from there immediately before you break your neck. I do not care what Lord Ferdinand says to the contrary."

They both looked down. Viola could just imagine how precarious their safety looked from up there. It was bad enough from below.

"Come down!" she called again. "Both of you."

Even across the distance Viola could see Lord Ferdinand's grin as he set a hand on the boy's shoulder and said something that could not be heard from below. And then he swung first one long leg and then the other over the low rail that separated the balcony from the slate roof. He began the climb upward, using both his hands and his feet. Eli stayed where he was.

Rose stifled a shriek, and Mr. Jarvey admonished her sotto voce.

Viola would have sat down on the bench that circled the fountain if she could have moved the necessary six feet to reach it. As it was, she had to stand still, both hands pressed over her mouth. The fool! The imbecile! He would fall and break every bone in his body, and she would have his death on her conscience forevermore. That was probably what he wanted.

But he reached the peak of the roof without mishap. He pulled himself up beside the chimney that connected with the dining room fireplace among others and peered over the top of it—it reached up to his chest.

Foolish man. *Idiot* man!

"It won't do no good," Jeb Hardinge muttered. "He won't be able to reach down far enough."

Then Rose shrieked, the butler scolded, and Lord Ferdinand Dudley braced his hands on top of the chimney, pulled himself up until he could sit on the edge of it, and swung his legs to the inside.

"He won't be happy till he's killed himself," Hannah said.

"He's a jolly good sport, I must say," the footman observed, but Viola only half heard him. Lord Ferdinand Dudley was disappearing—had disappeared—inside the chimney.

He would fall through and kill himself. He would get stuck and die a slow and horrible death. If he survived, she would kill him with her bare hands.

It was probably two minutes, but felt more like two hours, before he reappeared—or at least a blackened version of him did. His face looked as black as his hair.

His shirt was gray. He held aloft a fistful of blackened rags with a black hand and grinned down at his audience, his teeth startlingly white even from such a distance.

"Not a bird's nest after all," he called out, "but some mysterious flying object, doubtless from the moon." He dropped the rags, which tumbled in slow disorder down over the roof and drifted off its edge to litter the terrace below.

How was he going to get down?

He did it in a matter of moments, loping carelessly, for all the world as if he were descending a grassy slope to a soft lawn below. When he reached the railing and the balcony where Eli still stood, he vaulted over the railing and turned to wave one hand. The boy was laughing and applauding.

"He has pluck. One must grant him that," Jeb Hardinge said.

"A jolly good sport," the footman agreed.

"He might have made Eli do it, like he threatened," the head gardener added, "but he did it himself. You won't find too many gents what would be as sporting as that."

"The thing of it is, you see," one of the strangers said, watching his master and Eli disappear through the attic window, "his lordship can't bear to stand by watching while someone else has all the fun. This was *nothing*. I could tell you—"

But Viola had heard enough. "Mr. Jarvey," she said coldly before setting off with purposeful strides for the terrace. "Perhaps it is time everyone got back to work?"

They were all admiring that act of utter foolhardiness. He was winning them over. Jolly good sport, indeed!

She marched into the house and up the stairs to the bedroom floor. She would have continued on up to the attic, but he was down already, standing with Eli on the clean, costly carpet of the corridor. If there was any soot left in the chimney, she would be surprised to hear it. It was surely all adorning his person.

"That was a reckless and disgusting display!" she cried, not reducing her pace until she was three feet in front of him. "You might have *killed* yourself!"

He grinned again. How could he possibly succeed in looking handsome and virile even at such a moment? The fact that he did merely fanned her ire.

"And *look* at the mess you are making on my carpet!"

"You may get back to the stables, lad," he told Eli. "And if you set so much as one toenail on that roof ever again, you will have a thrashing at my hands to look forward to when you come back down. Do you understand?"

"Yes, m'lord." And while Viola watched, outraged, the boy grinned cheekily at Lord Ferdinand and cast him a look of pure hero worship before turning and running down the stairs.

"You may eat your dinner tonight in both comfort and warmth, ma'am," Lord Ferdinand said, turning his attention back to Viola. "Now, if you will excuse me, I must go and face my valet's wrath. He will not be amused by the appearance of my boots."

"You did it deliberately," she said, her eyes narrowing, her hands closing into fists at her sides. "You made sure that everyone knew you were going up there before you went. You made sure you would be playing to an audience. You risked life and limb just so that everyone would gaze in admiration and call you a *jolly good sport*."

"No!" His eyes danced with merriment. "Is that what they were saying?"

"Life is nothing but a game to you," she cried. "You are probably *glad* you found me here and that I refused to leave. You are probably *glad* that everyone here is set on your discomfort."

"You must understand," he said, "that I have always been able to resist almost every temptation except a challenge. When you threw down the gauntlet, Miss Thornhill, I picked it up. What did you expect?"

"But this is not a game!" Her fingernails were digging painfully into her palms.

His almost-black eyes regarded her out of his blackened face. "No, it is not," he agreed. "But then, I was not the one who planned or executed the pranks, was I, ma'am? If there is a game afoot, you cannot expect me not to play it, you know. And I always play to win. You may wish to remember that. Give me half an hour or so. I am going to need a bath. Then we will take that walk you agreed to."

He turned and strode away. Viola watched him until his bedchamber door closed behind him. There was a decidedly grubby spot on the carpet where he had stood, she could see.

I always play to win.

He has pluck.

A jolly good sport.

She felt like throwing a major tantrum. Or weeping self-pityingly into her handkerchief. Or committing murder.

She did none of the three. Instead, she turned on her heel and made her way back downstairs. She was going outside to read her letter. She would go down onto the river walk. If he cared to, he could find her there. But she was not going to wait for him like an obedient scion.

6

SHE WAS READING WHEN HE FOUND HER. AT LEAST, she was folding up a letter, probably the one that had been on the library desk earlier. She was sitting on the grassy bank well north of the house, between the path and the river, her light muslin dress spread about her, her hair in its neat braided coronet. She was surrounded by daisies and buttercups and clover. She looked the perfect picture of beauty and innocence, at one with her surroundings.

Ferdinand felt wretched. He had heard that the late Earl of Bamber was a decent sort, though he had not known him personally. But obviously the man had been as much of a loose screw as his son.

She did not look up as he approached, though she surely must have heard him. She was slipping her letter into her pocket. Did she imagine he was going to snatch it away from her to read himself? His annoyance returned.

"Hiding from me, Miss Thornhill?"

She turned her head to look up at him. "With not a single tree to duck behind for cover?" she said. "If I chose to hide from you, my lord, you would not find me."

He stood on the grass beside her while she turned her gaze toward the river and beyond, her arms clasped about her updrawn knees. He would have preferred to walk with her, but she showed no inclination to get to her feet. He could hardly conduct a reasonable conversation with her, towering over her as he was. He sat down not far from her, one leg stretched out before him, an arm draped over the raised knee of the other.

"You have had a day and a night to think," he said. "You have had a chance to consult with your friends and neighbors. Although I have sent a request for a copy of the will to be sent down here, I believe you must realize now that Pinewood never was yours. Have you come to any decision about your future?"

"I am staying here," she said. "This is my home. This is where I belong."

"Your friends were right last night," he said. "Your reputation is severely at risk for as long as you stay here with me."

She laughed softly and plucked a daisy. He watched her split its stem with her thumbnail and then pluck another daisy to thread through it.

"If you are worried about propriety," she said, "perhaps you are the one who should go away. You have no right to Pinewood. You won its title in a *card game* at a gaming hell. Doubtless you were so drunk that you did not even know it until the next day."

"The gaming hell was Brookes's," he explained. "An eminently respectable gentlemen's club. And one would have to be a fool to gamble while foxed. I am no fool."

She gave him that low laugh again for answer—he recognized scorn in it—and her daisy chain acquired another link.

"The will may take a week to get here," he said. "If Bamber decides to send it or a copy of it, that is. He may choose to ignore my request. I really cannot have you staying here indefinitely, you know." Good Lord, her reputation would be in tatters, if it was not already. He would be expected to make reparation. And he knew what *that* meant. He was going to find himself leg-shackled to her if he was not very careful.

The very thought of a leg shackle was enough to make him break out in a cold sweat, warm May sunshine notwithstanding.

"Why are you so sure that the old earl meant to leave Pinewood to you?" he asked her. "Apart from the fact that he apparently promised to do so, that is."

"That he *did* do so," she corrected.

"That he did promise, then," he said. "Why would he promise such a thing? Were you a favorite niece or cousin?"

"He *loved* me," she said with quiet vehemence, plucking a number of daisies that were within her reach all at once and setting them down on the grass beside her before resuming her work.

"That does not always mean—"

"And I loved *him,*" she added. "Perhaps you have never loved or been loved, Lord Ferdinand. Love encompasses trust. I trusted him. I still do. I always will. He said that Pinewood was to be mine, and I do not doubt for one moment that it is."

"But the will?" He frowned and watched her hands. She had slim, delicate fingers. "If it gives proof that he did not keep his word, then you will have to accept the fact that he let you down."

"Never!" Her hands paused and she turned her head to glare at him. "All that will have been proved is that someone has tampered with it. Destroyed it, perhaps. I will never lose my trust in him because I will never stop loving him or knowing beyond any doubt that he loved me."

Ferdinand was silent, shaken by the passion with which she spoke of the love between herself and the old Earl of Bamber. What relationship had they had, for God's sake?

"That is a serious charge," he said. "That someone changed the will, I mean."

"Yes," she agreed. "It is." The daisy chain grew longer.

He did not really want to know more about her. He did not want her to become more of a person to him than she already was. He felt bad enough about her as it was. For a minute or two he fought his curiosity. A few stray curls of dark red hair lay enticingly against the back of her neck.

"Did you grow up in the country?" he asked despite himself.

"No." He thought for a few relieved moments that she would not elaborate, but she did. "I grew up in London. I spent all my life there until I came here almost two years ago."

"That must have been a shock to the system," he said.

"It was." She had denuded the grass within reach of daisies. She sat holding the two ends of the chain. "But I loved it from the first moment."

"Are your parents still living?" But if they were, why the devil were they not here with her? Or why was she not with them?

"My mother is."

"Were you very young when your father died?" he asked.

She spread the daisy chain across her lap, the ends trailing onto the grass on either side of her. Very deliberately she was arranging the daisies so that the blossoms all faced upward.

"My mother married my stepfather when I was nine," she said. "He died when I was eighteen—in a gaming hell brawl. He had been accused of cheating, and I daresay there was justice in the charge." Her voice was emotionless.

"Ah," he said. What else was there to say? He had won the home she had thought was hers in a card game. What a cruel irony of fate that must seem to her.

"I hated him," she said, meticulously continuing her task. "I could never understand why my mother doted on him."

"Do you have any memories of your real father?" he asked, being drawn inexorably into an interest in her life.

"Oh, yes." Her voice became more husky, as if she had forgotten his presence. Her hands fell still on the daisy chain. "I adored him. I used to watch for his coming home and run to meet him—sometimes right out onto the street even before he could come inside. My mother used to scold and remind me I must behave like a lady, but he used to snatch me up and twirl me about and tell me it was the loveliest welcome any man could wish for."

She laughed softly at the memory. Ferdinand sat very still. He felt almost as if he held his breath, eager to hear more, but suspecting that she would stop if she recalled to whom she was speaking.

"He used to take me on his knee while he and Mama talked," she said. "I would sit there patiently, because I knew that my turn would come. And even while he was taking no particular notice of me, I could feel the solid safety of his presence and smell the snuff he always used. And he would play absently with my fingers, his own hands large and capable. When he *did* turn his attention to me, he used to listen to all my little, insignificant pieces of news as if there were nothing more interesting in the world, and often he would have me read to him from my books. Sometimes *he* would read to me, but after a while he would always change the words of my favorite stories until I got indignant and corrected him. Then I would catch him winking at Mama. He used to call me his princess."

But he had died before she was even nine. The childhood idyll had ended. Ferdinand did not know why he should feel sad for her. It was a long time ago.

"It is important to be loved during one's childhood, is it not?" he said.

She turned her head to look at him then. "You must have been loved," she said. "You had two parents, did you not? And a brother to play with. And a sister?"

"We fought as fiercely as only Dudleys know how," he said with a grin. "But we were allies too whenever there was someone outside our threesome to terrorize. There was always someone—usually a tutor, sometimes a gamekeeper or a village notable—who had somehow incurred our wrath."

"You had a country home in which to grow up," she said, "and parents to love you and each other."

What a naïve assumption, he thought.

"Oh, they loved each other, all right," he said. "When one of them was at Acton Park, the other was in London. They alternated. They rarely spent more than a few hours in each other's company. Though I suppose I should be grateful that they did spend those few hours together at least three times in their married life. My brother, my sister, and I might not exist otherwise."

She was carefully joining together the ends of her chain.

"They had a perfectly civilized relationship," he said. "Really quite typical of married couples of the *ton*."

"How cynical you sound," she said. "Were you hurt by their near-estrangement?"

"Why should I have been?" He shrugged. "We were always quite happy when our father was away. He had been a hellion like us and so there was no deceiving him. And no escaping the birch cane he kept propped against the desk in his study. The one thing I was always grateful for was that my brother was his favorite and therefore was thrashed more often than I was."

"Your mother was kinder?" she asked.

"Our mother was bored by us," he said. "Or perhaps it was just the countryside that bored her. We did not see much of her—at least, my brother and sister did not. I was her favorite. She used to take me to London with her when I was old enough."

"You must have enjoyed that," she said.

He had hated it. It had brought about his early loss of innocence. It seemed to him that he had always known that his father kept mistresses. Somehow he had known—though he believed Tresham and Angie had not—that the poor relative living at Dove Cottage on the estate was no relative at all, but one of the mistresses. It was why they had not been allowed to visit her, of course, even though the cottage was below their beloved wooded hills and close to the pool where they bathed in summer despite the fact that they were strictly forbidden to do so.

What he had not known until he went to London

with his mother, whom he had adored, was that she too had lovers—legions of cicisbei who assembled in her dressing room both morning and evening to observe all but the most intimate stages of her toilette before squiring her about to all the routs and parties with which the London Season abounded, and a number of particular favorites with whom she shared a bed, though never at the house. She was never vulgar, his mother.

Infidelity in marriage, for both wives and husbands, was very much the norm in the *ton*, he had learned early. The vows brides and their grooms exchanged in the nuptial service were a sham. Marriages were for financial and dynastic alliances.

Ferdinand wanted none of it. The very idea of marriage sickened him. And unlike the naïve and gullible Miss Viola Thornhill, he did not believe in love and trust. Oh, he loved Tresham and Tresham's wife and children. He loved Angie and was even fond of Heyward. But not blindly, as Miss Thornhill loved and trusted. Perhaps after this disillusionment she would harden her heart and learn to trust no one but herself.

"Yes, I enjoyed it," he said in answer to her observation.

They seemed to have nothing more to say to each other after that. Ferdinand sat looking at her. He was annoyed with himself. He had sought her out so that they could talk about her future, make some sort of definite decision about her leaving. Instead they had talked about their childhoods. There was a light breeze blowing. It was lifting the short curls at her neck. He felt an absurd—and hastily quelled—desire to brush them aside with his hand and set his lips there.

"What are you planning to do with that daisy chain?" he asked her, getting to his feet.

She looked down at it as if she were noticing it for the first time. "Oh," she said.

He reached down a hand and helped her to her feet. He took the chain from her and looped it over her head.

"My wholesome country lass," he murmured, and bent his head to kiss her on the lips. He raised his head again sharply, but too late, of course. What sort of a blithering idiot had he turned into for that brief, thoughtless moment?

Color flamed in her cheeks, and her eyes sparked. He waited with an inward grimace for the crack across the cheek he fully expected—he would not defend himself, since he had undoubtedly been in the wrong. But she kept her hands to herself.

"Lord Ferdinand," she said, her voice cold and quavering, "you may have grounds for believing that Pinewood is yours. But I am not part of the package. My person is my own property. I believe I have said this before, but I say it again, lest you did not believe me the first time. I am no man's mistress. I am my own."

She turned and strode away, not along the river path but across it and up the steep bank beyond, to disappear over the top.

The devil! Ferdinand thought. What in thunder had possessed him? He had come out here to be firm, to assert himself, to get rid of the woman, and he had ended up kissing her and murmuring something so deucedly embarrassing that he did not care to remember the exact words.

My wholesome country lass.

Each word taken separately was enough to make him wince for a week.

Lord, but she had certainly been transformed before his eyes. A daisy-bedecked country lass one moment, a frosty, tight-lipped lady the next.

He wished suddenly that he could be as iron-willed and ruthless as Tresham would undoubtedly be in a situation like this. The woman would have been gone yesterday, forgotten today.

How the devil was he going to get rid of her?

He set off back along the river path, feeling all the frustration of having settled nothing but only compounded his problems. What he needed to do was sit down quietly somewhere and think for a few hours. Make plans. And then carry through on them. But as soon as he set foot inside the house, he knew that he was not going to get what he needed—not for a while anyway. The hall seemed crammed to capacity with people, all of whom turned at his entrance and gazed expectantly at him.

"Jarvey?" Ferdinand singled out the butler and raised his eyebrows in inquiry.

"Mr. Paxton is awaiting your return in the library, my lord," Jarvey told him. "And there are a number of persons who are requesting an audience with you."

"Paxton?"

"Pinewood's steward, my lord," Jarvey explained.

Ferdinand glanced about at all the silent persons who awaited an audience with him, and turned in the direction of the library.

"I had better see him, without further delay, then," he said.

* * *

Viola walked in the avenue until she felt she had calmed down sufficiently to risk meeting other people. She had talked with him, almost as if he were a friend. She had let him kiss her. Yes, she had allowed it. She had known somehow as soon as he took the daisy chain from her hands and looped it over her head that he was going to do it. She could have stopped him. But she had not. All the time he had been sitting beside her, half reclined on the grass, she had fought the effects of his attractiveness on her breathing, her heartbeat, her nerve endings.

She did not want to find him attractive. She wanted to hate him. She *did* hate him.

She turned her mind determinedly to her letter, slipping her hand into her pocket and closing her fingers about it. The answer was no—again.

"We are all very much obliged to you for your kind invitation," Claire had written. "You must know how we long to see you again after so long. Two years is *too* long a time. But Mama has asked me to express our deepest regrets on her behalf and to explain why we cannot go. She feels that she owes too much to our uncle, especially now that he has been generous enough to send Ben to school. She feels that she must stay here and help out as best she can. But she misses you dreadfully, Viola. We all do."

Viola felt bereft. She felt not so much her loneliness—she had learned to hold that at bay with her various activities and friendships at Pinewood—as her terrible aloneness. They would never come. Why did she keep on hoping they would?

It had been her dearest dream when she had come to Pinewood that soon her mother would recover from her anger and forget the dreadful quarrel they had had over Viola's accepting the earl's gift, that she would come to live with her daughter and bring Claire and the twins, Maria and Benjamin—Viola's half siblings—with her. But her mother was not ready to forgive her, at least not to the extent of coming here.

Mama and the children—though Claire was fifteen already and the twins twelve—did not have a home of their own. Viola's stepfather had died when she was eighteen and left nothing to his family except debts, which Uncle Wesley, Mama's brother, had paid off. He had taken them all to live at the coaching inn he owned, and they had remained there ever since.

"I am working now," Claire had continued. "Uncle Wesley has been showing me how to keep the account books, as you once did. He has said that he may let me serve in the coffee room too now that I am fifteen. I am happy to work for him, but what I really want to do is be a governess as you were, Viola, and help support the family with my earnings."

They had been proud of her, both Mama and her uncle, Viola recalled. Uncle Wesley had been disappointed when she had first announced that she would be leaving the inn, but he had understood her desire to help support her family. Two years ago her mother had not been able to understand why she was so eager to leave respectable, interesting, well-paid employment in order to accept charity. Charity, she had called the gift of Pinewood. . . .

"It feels good to help out," Claire had written. "Uncle Wesley really is most generous. Ben's school fees are considerable. In addition, he has bought new books for Maria, who is learning from Mama and is becoming more of a scholar than I ever was, and new clothes for her too. He bought me new shoes even though the old ones would have done for a while longer."

Only Uncle Wesley knew that the money for Ben's education and for many of the extra family expenses came from Pinewood rents. He had not wanted to be part of the deception. He did not want to take credit where it was not due. But Viola had pleaded with him in a letter she had written soon after coming to Somersetshire. Mama would never accept anything that came from Pinewood. But Viola needed to keep on helping her family. Claire and Ben and Maria must have a chance at a decent life.

"Bless you, dearest Viola," the letter had concluded. "Since we cannot go to Pinewood, can you not come to London for a visit? Please?"

But she had never been able to bring herself to go back there. The very thought made her shudder.

Upset over her encounter with Lord Ferdinand, and upset too over this letter, Viola gave in to a rare moment of self-pity and heard a gurgling in her throat. She swallowed determinedly. She did miss her family dreadfully. She had not seen them for two years, not since that dreadful quarrel she had had with her mother. Her one consolation had been that she was doing them some good while she lived here. But how would she continue to help out if Pinewood was no longer hers?

How would she be able even to support herself?

Panic tied her stomach in queasy knots as she turned her steps back toward the house. How she hated Lord Ferdinand. It was not just Pinewood he was trying to take away from her. It was everything. And how she hated herself for not merely turning a cold face away from him on the riverbank just a short while ago.

She might have gone into the house through the back door, since it was the closest entrance from the avenue. But she walked around to the front. She wanted to see if the plans for the rest of the day were being put into effect. Somehow she expected to find the hall deserted. But it was not. It was filled with people. Far more than she had expected or even hoped for. Was there a tenant farmer or a laborer who was *not* here?

Viola smiled broadly as all the men touched their forelocks or bowed awkwardly to her, and the few women bobbed curtsies. But they all grinned back at her in mass acknowledgment of the conspiracy afoot.

"Good morning," she said brightly.

Was it still morning? It certainly would not be by the time he had dealt with every petitioner and complainer who had demanded audience with the new owner of Pinewood. And before he could begin to admit them, he would have to listen to the speech of welcome and orientation that Mr. Paxton had doubtless stayed up half the night preparing. Mr. Paxton could be alarmingly ponderous when he set his mind to it. Lord Ferdinand would be fortunate indeed if he had time to snatch some luncheon before all the afternoon callers began to arrive to pay their respects to their new neighbor.

The Reverend Prewitt would talk about the church choir and next Sunday's sermon, Mrs. Prewitt about the ladies' sewing circle and the new kneelers they were busy making. The schoolmaster would drone on about the leaking schoolroom roof and the necessity of teaching something meaningful to the older pupils at the same time as he instructed the younger ones in the recitation of the alphabet. The Misses Merrywether would talk about the flower show coming up in the summer and the attempts of certain villagers to grow new or better strains of various blooms. Mrs. Claypole, Mr. Claypole, and Bertha—well, the Claypoles would simply be themselves. Mr. Willard had a bull who he claimed was in a state of deep depression over the demise—by butchering—of his favorite cow. Mr. Willard could—and would—wax marvelously eloquent on the subject of his cattle.

Mr. Codaire could put anyone to sleep on the subject of roads and toll gates and new methods of paving. Fortunately for Viola, he knew it and had offered it up as a suitable topic with which to regale the ears of Lord Ferdinand Dudley when the Codaires called upon him. Mrs. Codaire had just read a book of sermons she was sure his lordship would enjoy hearing paraphrased. And the Misses Codaire, aged sixteen and seventeen, had suggested accompanying their mama and papa and *giggling* at every available opportunity. Since the sight of a handsome young man was always opportunity enough for those girls even without an extra incentive, Viola was confident that they would grate upon every adult nerve in Pinewood's drawing room, most particularly upon those of Lord Ferdinand Dudley.

By this time tomorrow, Viola thought hopefully as she retired to her room, where she planned to spend a cozy afternoon reading, he might well be on his way back to London, having realized that country living would drive him mad within a week. He would still be the owner in the eyes of the law, she supposed, but chances were that he would never come back. If he tried to take the rents for himself, she would simply ignore him until he stopped asking. By this time tomorrow she might have her home to herself again.

And by this time tomorrow pigs might also have learned to fly, she thought with a sigh.

VIOLA DID NOT LEAVE her room until dinnertime. She had steeled herself to dine with him, consoling herself with the conviction that at least she would have his grumblings to listen to and enjoy. But the dining table was set for only one person, and the butler was standing behind Viola's usual chair at the head of the table, waiting to seat her.

"Where is Lord Ferdinand?" she asked him.

"He said he would dine at the Boar's Head, ma'am."

"I daresay," she said, smiling with relief and preparing unexpectedly to enjoy the meal, "he has had enough of making polite conversation for one day."

"I suppose so, ma'am," Mr. Jarvey agreed with a smirk, ladling soup into her bowl.

"Has he enjoyed his day, do you think?" She was feeling almost lighthearted.

"He *seemed* in a good enough humor whenever I stepped into the drawing room to announce another visitor," Mr. Jarvey told her. "He was smiling and talking and greeting the new arrivals as if he couldn't think of any better way to be spending his time. But I daresay that was just his cunning, so that I would not see that we had him bothered."

"Yes," Viola agreed. "I am sure you are right." But she would have far preferred to hear that he had been looking bored or irritable or weary or thunderous. "Have you spoken with Mr. Paxton?"

"His lordship demanded to see the estate books and then wanted to know who kept them so neat and precise, ma'am," Mr. Jarvey said. "Mr. Paxton told me he asked a number of questions that were more intelligent than what Mr. Paxton had expected. His lordship took the books upstairs with him when he left. He said he wanted to study them more closely. And then instead of having all those people sent into the library one by one, he took a chair out into the middle of the hall, his lordship did, and sat down and talked to everyone at once. I was there, ma'am, and you will be pleased to hear that he doesn't seem to know the first thing about farming. He is a downright ignoramus, in fact."

"Indeed?" Viola said, vexed that Lord Ferdinand had thought of a way of saving himself from being overwhelmed by numbers, but also pleased that his presence in the hall had allowed the butler to be witness to all his inadequacies and embarrassment.

"Yes, indeed, ma'am," the butler said. "But he does know how to listen, he does, and he knew just exactly what questions to ask. He can tell a joke too. He had everyone laughing more than once. Even I almost smiled at the one about the town rake and the country parson. It seems that—"

"Thank you, Mr. Jarvey," Viola said firmly. "I am not really in the mood for jokes."

"No, ma'am." Mr. Jarvey retreated into his more normal poker-faced manner as he cleared away her empty soup bowl.

Viola felt guilty then for being so surly. But really! Was he winning everyone over? Could not everyone see that he was a practiced charmer, who would do anything to cut the support from under her feet so that she would have no choice but to leave?

The thought destroyed the little appetite she had.

Perhaps he would stay late at the inn tonight and get obnoxiously drunk. Perhaps he would make a spectacle of himself and show himself in his true colors. Perhaps she would even hear a commotion from the direction of the Boar's Head when she came out of the church after choir practice this evening. How very satisfying that would be. All the other choir members would hear it too.

But that faint, uncharitable hope was dashed an hour later when Viola left the horse and gig at the vicarage stables and walked into the church. She was almost late. Every other member of the choir was already present.

So was Lord Ferdinand Dudley.

7

IT HAD NOT TAKEN FERDINAND LONG TO UNderstand what was going on. His day had been planned for him with meticulous care, beginning with the cockerel crowing at the very crack of dawn. It was probably intended to end with the world's worst dinner at Pinewood. If his breakfast was any indication of the cook's ingenuity in serving up culinary stomach-churners, he would be better off eating at the Boar's Head, even if he was not exactly welcome there either.

The strange thing was, he thought as he ate his steak and kidney pie in a private parlor at the inn, that he had almost enjoyed the day. Almost, but not quite. There was Viola Thornhill, the thorn in his conscience, to spoil his fun. But the morning horseplay had been entertaining once he had adjusted his mind and body to being up even before the proverbial lark. And he had found his talk with Paxton and his cursory perusal of the estate books interesting. He looked forward to learning more. It was already evident to him that in two years the estate had developed from a run-down, slovenly kept, unprosperous business to just the opposite. Paxton was obviously an able steward.

He had enjoyed talking with the estate laborers and tenants, distinguishing real problems from petty complaints, observing the various personalities, picking out those who were leaders, those who were followers. He had enjoyed joking with them and watching their initial hostility begin to thaw. Paxton, of course, had not been so easily swayed. He was loyal to Miss Thornhill.

Afternoon visits had always been something to avoid. But today's had been vastly amusing, especially since each caller had come with the express purpose of boring his head off.

The thing was, though, that he had long been fascinated with new developments in road construction. And talk of cattle could easily be turned into talk about horses, one of Ferdinand's favorite topics. Ladies who formed sewing circles were naturally interested to learn that the infant Lord Ferdinand had once talked his nurse into teaching him to knit and that within a week he had produced a scarf that had grown progressively narrower as he gradually dropped stitches but that had stretched the whole length of the nursery when laid flat on the floor after he had finished it. As for the pupil at the village school who had asked the schoolmaster for Latin lessons—well, Ferdinand had graduated from Oxford with a degree in Latin and Greek. Perhaps he could offer his services as a teacher.

All the people he had met today, of course, had been determined not to like him. Many probably still did not and perhaps never would. Their hostility was a tribute to Viola Thornhill, who appeared to have won everyone's respect and even affection in the two years she had been at Pinewood. But Ferdinand did not despair. He had never had difficulty relating to all kinds of people, and he had always been gregarious.

He rather thought he was going to enjoy life in the country.

The vicar had said there was to be a practice for the

church choir tonight. His wife had even invited Ferdinand to join them, though she had said it in such a way that he knew she did not expect him to accept. But why not? he thought, pushing away half the suet pudding he had been brought for dessert. He did not want to return to Pinewood yet. That would mean either making conversation with Miss Thornhill in the drawing room or slinking off to hide in a room where she was not—and he had never been a slinker. Neither did he want to spend another whole evening drinking in the taproom.

The choir practice it would be, then.

The practice was not in the church itself, he discovered as soon as he opened the door and stepped inside. But he could hear the sound of a pianoforte being thumped upon and followed it down a steep flight of stone steps to the church hall below, a gloomy apartment with a few windows high on three of the four walls. There were fifteen or twenty people gathered in groups, talking. None of them was taking any notice of the pianist, a thin woman of indeterminate age and faded, frizzed fair hair, who was peering at the music propped before her through small wire-framed spectacles. She was one of the spinster sisters who had called during the afternoon with the vicar and his wife, Ferdinand recalled—Merryfield? Merryheart? *Merrywether*—that was it. While her sister had talked at great, droning length about the growing of prize blooms, this one had apologized whenever she had been able to work a word into the conversation, assuring Lord Ferdinand Dudley that he could not possibly be interested in such rural concerns but must be simply longing to return to town.

"It is in four parts," she was saying to no one in particular but with every appearance of extreme anxiety as

Ferdinand's eyes alighted on her. "Oh, dear, can we manage four parts?"

Perhaps someone would have answered her had not everyone at the same moment noticed the new arrival and fallen silent.

"I have accepted my invitation, you see, sir," Ferdinand said, singling out the vicar and striding toward him, his right hand outstretched.

The Reverend Prewitt appeared slightly flustered, but gratified. "That is very obliging of you, I am sure, my lord," he said. "Do you sing?"

But Ferdinand had no chance to answer. There was a slight stir among the choir members, whose eyes had all moved from Ferdinand himself to some point beyond his left shoulder. He turned to see Viola Thornhill coming down the stairs, a look of pure astonishment on her face. She was part of the choir too?

He bowed as he looked up at her—and something snatched at the edges of his memory again. Damn, but he had seen her somewhere. She was looking rather regal, her chin raised, her face a mask of controlled dignity—a far cry from the laughing lass of the maypole.

"Lord Ferdinand," she said, stepping down onto the stone floor of the hall, "I did not expect to find *you* here."

"I trust you had a pleasant day, ma'am," he said. "The vicar's wife was kind enough to invite me to choir practice."

She looked at the clergyman with what might have been silent reproach, and Ferdinand turned away to address the pianist.

"You were saying as I came in, Miss Merrywether," he

said, "that the piece of music before you is in four parts. It that a problem?"

"Oh, not a *problem*, exactly, my lord," she assured him, her voice breathless with apology for bothering him with such a slight concern. "But Mr. Worthington is our only tenor, you see. Not that I am saying he does not have a fine voice, for he does. Very fine indeed. It is just that—well, he does not like to sing alone, and I do not blame him, I am sure. I would certainly not wish to do it. Not that I have a tenor voice, of course, being a woman, but—"

"He is easily distracted by the basses and sings along with them," a round woman Ferdinand had not encountered before said more bluntly.

There was general laughter.

"We have never claimed to be professional singers," the vicar added. "But what we lack in musicality we make up for in enthusiasm."

"And volume," someone else added, to the accompaniment of more laughter.

"All we can ask of ourselves," the vicar said genially, "is that we make a joyful noise unto the Lord."

"You would not enjoy listening to us," Viola Thornhill told Ferdinand.

Smiling into her eyes, he offered his services. "I sing tenor," he said quite truthfully. He had sung with a university choir and enjoyed the experience enormously. "No one has ever accused me of having extraordinary talent, but I have never noticed particularly pained expressions on the faces of those within earshot of my singing voice either. Shall Worthington and I put our heads and our voices together and see if we can hold our own against the basses?" Worthington, a balding, freckled redhead, was one of the tenant farmers who had camped out in his hall during the morning, he recalled.

"We would not put you to so much trouble, my lord," Miss Thornhill said firmly. "You surely wish to—"

He did not wait to hear what it was he would wish.

"But it is no trouble at all," he assured everyone. "I love nothing better than an evening of music, especially when I may be a participant rather than a mere listener. However, I must ask if I am being presumptuous—are there auditions?"

That question drew a burst of hilarity from most of the choir members. Even Miss Merrywether tittered.

"No one with a desire to sing with us has ever been turned away, my lord," the vicar assured him. "We should get started, then."

It was certainly not a particularly musical group. Someone who was nominally a contralto was tone deaf but sang heartily nevertheless, one of the sopranos sang with a shrill vibrato, the bass section proceeded under the apparent assumption that it was their primary function to drown out the rest of the choir, and Mr. Worthington did indeed display a tendency to join forces with them when he was not inventing a tune all of his own. Miss Merrywether was heavy-handed on the pianoforte, and the conductor slowed or speeded up the rhythm with bewildering and unpredictable frequency.

But despite it all, music was created.

Ferdinand amused himself by imagining the reactions of his friends if they could see him now. They would bundle him up and cart him off to Bedlam as a raving lunatic. Tresham would fix him with one of his famous black stares. No—perhaps not. Tresham had been playing the pianoforte again during the past few years—since his marriage, in fact—instead of smothering his talent as he had done most of his life. Their father had brought them up to the belief that the most deadly of all sins for a Dudley male was anything that hinted at effeminacy. Music, art, an overindulgence in intellectual pursuits—all had been ruthlessly stamped out, with the aid of that infamous birch cane when necessary.

Ferdinand had enjoyed both the singing and the company. And obviously he had cooled the hostility of at least a few of the neighbors with whom he was going to have to consort during future years. It was the habit of several of the male members of the choir, it seemed, to take a glass of ale at the Boar's Head on choir evenings. Worthington suggested that he join them.

"Singing dries the throat," he added by way of explanation and excuse.

"It does indeed, and I would be delighted," Ferdinand replied. "But Miss Thornhill, did you walk here? May I escort you home in my curricle first?"

"I brought the gig, thank you, my lord," she said, and he could tell from the stiffness of her voice that she was furious. She must feel let down by her friends, who were not repulsing him as they ought.

And so he went off to drink with six other male choristers and the realization that country life was very different from town life. More egalitarian. More genial. More to his taste—a strange thought, considering the fact that he had spent the years since Oxford kicking up every lark that fell his way and generally leading a fast, wild existence in London.

If only there were not Viola Thornhill. In some strange way he felt indignant on her behalf that the people who were her friends had allowed him within the space of one day to begin to inveigle himself into their lives. For, after all, they could not both live here, he and Miss Thornhill. One of them was going to have to leave, and that one, of course, was she. But her friends should be furious with him. They should be making life sheer hell for him.

"He could not really have enjoyed choir practice," Viola said. "Could he, Hannah?"

"I don't know, Miss Vi," Hannah said, drawing the brush in one firm stroke from the crown of Viola's head to the ends of her hair below her waist. "I just don't know."

"Well, I do," Viola said firmly. "Gentlemen like him just do not enjoy the company of people like that, Hannah. And they certainly do not enjoy singing church music with a choir like ours. He must have been excruciatingly bored. In fact, I really believe that it turned out for the best that he decided to go. After today he is sure to realize that this corner of Somersetshire has nothing whatsoever to offer a sophisticated and dissipated London rake. Do you think?"

"What I think, Miss Vi," Hannah said, "is that that man has as much charm as he has good looks and that he knows how to use both to his advantage. And I think he is a dangerous man because he will not ever admit defeat. If you had not been here when he came, he would likely have gone off again to wherever he came from within a week. But you are here, you see, and you have challenged him. That is what I think."

It was so exactly what Viola herself thought that there was nothing to add. She merely sighed as Hannah brushed back the hair from her face and began to plait it for the night.

"The thing is, Miss Vi," Hannah said when she had almost finished the task, "I thought in the village the other day that he had an eye for you. In fact, I am sure he did, him playing for your daisies and taking you onto the green to dance about the maypole and all that. And then he turned up here next morning just like fate had brought him, not knowing it was your home. And now when you have tried your best to drive him away, he has risen to the task and shown that he is your equal. I think he is *enjoying* the challenge—just because it is you, Miss Vi. Perhaps you should change your tactics, not try to drive him away, but—"

"Hannah!" Viola cut her off midsentence. "What on earth are you suggesting? That I lure that man into falling in love with me? How would that get rid of him, even if it could be done and even if I wished to do it?"

"I wasn't thinking of your getting rid of him, exactly," Hannah said, twisting a length of ribbon about the end of Viola's braid.

"You were not—"

"The thing is, Miss Vi," Hannah said, turning to put away the dress and other garments Viola had just removed, "I cannot accept that your life is over. You are still young. You are still lovely and sweet and kind and... Your life cannot possibly be over, that is all."

"Well, it *is*, Hannah." Viola's voice was shaking. "But at least it has been a peaceful half existence I have been living here. He is determined to drive me away. Then there will be nothing left. Nothing at all. No life, no home, no dream. No income." She swallowed convulsively. Panic had her stomach tied in knots.

"Not if he fell in love with you, he wouldn't," Hannah said. "And he is already partway there, Miss Vi. You could see to it that he fell all the way."

"Gentlemen do not house their mistresses on their country estates," Viola said tartly.

"Not mistress, Miss Vi."

Viola turned on the stool and stared incredulously at her maid. "You think he would *marry* me? He is Lord Ferdinand Dudley, Hannah. He is a gentleman, a duke's son. I am a *bastard*. And that is the kindest thing that can be said about me."

"Don't upset yourself," Hannah said with a sigh. "Stranger things have happened. He would be the lucky one to win your hand."

"Oh, Hannah." Viola laughed rather shakily. "Ever the dreamer. But if I ever were to seek a husband, you know, it would be someone far different from Lord Ferdinand. He is everything I most abhor in a gentleman. He is a *gamer*. A reckless one who plays for high stakes. I will survive somehow without even attempting to make such a dreadful sacrifice. And I have not admitted defeat yet. If he wishes to be rid of me, he will have to have me dragged away. Perhaps then everyone will think a little less of his *charm*," she added bitterly.

"That they will." Hannah was using the soothing voice she had once used on the child Viola when something had happened to make her believe her world had come to an end. Yet that had been the golden time, when really the world had been a very solid, secure place and love had been real and seemingly eternal. "You get into bed now, Miss Vi. There is nothing a good night's sleep will not solve."

Viola laughed and hugged her maid. "At least I have

you, the very best friend anyone ever had," she said. "Very well, then, I will go to bed and to sleep like a good girl, and tomorrow all my problems will have vanished. Perhaps he will be so drunk when he leaves the Boar's Head that he will ride for London and forget all about Pinewood. Perhaps he will fall off his horse and break his neck."

"Lovey!" Hannah said reproachfully.

"But he did not ride to the village," Viola said. "He took his curricle. All the better. He has farther to fall."

She lay in bed a little while later, wide awake, staring up at the shadowed canopy over her head, wondering how life could have changed so completely within two days.

IT WAS AFTER MIDNIGHT when Ferdinand returned home. The house was in darkness. *Indignant* darkness, he thought with a grin. She probably expected him to come staggering home, roaring out obscene ditties off-key and slurring his words. But the knowledge that it was not really a game they played soon wiped the grin from his face. He wished it were something that harmless. She was an interesting opponent.

Jarvey was still up. He came prowling into the hall as Ferdinand let himself in through the unlocked door, a branch of candles held aloft in one hand, its shadows across his face making him look somewhat sinister.

"Ah, Jarvey." Ferdinand handed the man his hat and cloak and whip. "Waited up for me, did you? And Bentley did too, I daresay?"

"Yes, my lord," the butler informed him. "I'll send him up to your room immediately."

"You may send him to bed," Ferdinand said, making for the library. "And go to your own too. I'll not need either of you again tonight."

But he did not really know why he had come to the library, he thought after he had shut the door behind him. It was just that soon after midnight seemed a ridiculously early hour at which to retire. He shrugged out of his coat and tossed it over the back of a chair. His waistcoat joined it there. He loosened and then removed his neckcloth. Now he was comfortable enough to settle into a chair with a book—except that he did not feel in the mood for reading. It was too late. He wandered over to the glass-fronted cabinet in one corner of the library and poured himself a brandy, but he did not particularly feel like drinking it, he realized after the first sip. He had had three glasses of ale at the Boar's Head. He had never been much of a solitary drinker. Or much of a heavy drinker at all, in fact. He was not an advocate of thick morning heads, having experienced a few of them during his youth.

There must be a solution to her problems, he thought, throwing himself into one of the chairs grouped about the fireplace. He just wished she would help him find one instead of clinging to the notion that the will would exonerate her—or that the will had been tampered with.

Why was he worrying about her problems? They were not his. They had nothing to do with him. He was giving himself a headache, a grossly unfair consequence of drinking only three glasses of ale over two and a half hours.

She had friends here. She was well liked here. If he was not much mistaken—he would know for sure when he had studied the estate books more closely and spoken with Paxton again—she had been involved in running and improving the estate. She was involved in community activities. What she should be doing was staying here.

She could stay if she married that ass and prize bore, Claypole.

She could stay if . . .

Ferdinand stared at the dark painting hanging over the mantel. No! Definitely not that—*definitely*! Where the devil had that idea popped out from? But the devil that had nudged the strange idea into his mind spoke on.

She is young and beautiful and desirable.

So were dozens of other girls who had set their caps for him anytime during the past six or seven years. He had never for a moment considered matrimony with any of them.

She is fresh and innocent.

Any woman who married him would have a duke for a brother-in-law. She would be marrying into the *ton*. She would be marrying a very wealthy man. Freshness and innocence would disappear in a trice once the pleasures of society were tasted and once there were other men, more personable than Claypole, to admire her. She would be no different from any other woman in a similar marriage.

She believes in love. She trusts love, even when to all appearances it has betrayed her.

Both love and trust would disappear with innocence.

You want her.

Ferdinand closed his eyes and spread his hands on the armrests of the chair. He breathed deeply and evenly. She was an innocent. She was living unchaperoned in his house. That was scandal enough without his lusting after her.

She has a body to die for.

And he would die too before giving up his freedom merely in order to possess it.

Her problems would be solved and your conscience would be appeased if you married her.

Damn Bamber, Ferdinand thought vehemently. And damn Bamber's father. And damn Leavering for having impregnated his wife just when he had, so that *he* had not been the one to play for Pinewood instead of Ferdinand. Damn Brookes's.

He was *not* going to play the gallant by offering her marriage. The very idea had him reaching up to tug at his overtight neckcloth—only to discover that he had removed it before he sat down. He was in a bad way, indeed.

He was going to go to bed, Ferdinand decided, getting determinedly to his feet. Not that he was going to be able to sleep, even though he had ordered Bentley to find him different pillows or, failing that, to set a block of marble at the head of his bed, since marble could not be less comfortable than what he had slept on last night. But there was nothing else to do *except* go to bed.

He snuffed the candles, having decided that there was quite enough moonlight beaming through the windows to light his way upstairs. With one finger he hooked his coat and waistcoat over his shoulder and left the room.

He fervently hoped he would rise in the morning in a more sensible frame of mind.

8

THE UPPER CORRIDOR WAS DARKER THAN THE hall and staircase. There was only one window at the far end. But, preoccupied with his thoughts as he was, it did not occur to Ferdinand to regret not bringing a candle with him until he went plowing into a table, the corner of which caught him painfully in the middle of the thigh.

"Ouch!" he exclaimed loudly before letting loose with a few other, more profane epithets and dropping his coat and waistcoat in order to rub his leg with both hands. But even in the near-darkness he could see that further disaster was looming in the form of a large urn, which was wobbling on the table in imminent danger of toppling to its doom. He roared and lunged for it—and then whooped with self-congratulatory relief when he righted it. He pressed a hand to his injured leg again, but his absorption with the pain was short-lived. Somehow a large painting in a heavy, ornate frame had been dislodged from the wall and crashed to the floor, its descent made more spectacular by the fact that it brought the urn down with it, smashing it to smithereens, and overturned the table into the bargain.

Ferdinand swore foully and eloquently at the mess around him, though he could scarcely see the full extent of it in the darkness. He stepped back from the debris and rubbed his leg. And then suddenly there *was* light, illuminating the scene and momentarily dazzling him.

"You are *drunk*!" the person holding the candle informed him coldly.

Ferdinand put up a hand to shade his eyes. How *exactly* like a woman to jump to that conclusion.

"Devilish foxed," he agreed curtly. "Three sheets to the wind. And what's it to you?" He returned his attention to the disaster he could now see clearly, rubbing his thigh at the same time. The painting looked as if it weighed a ton, but he waded in among the debris and somehow hefted it back up to its position on the wall. He picked up the table and set it to rights. There was no apparent damage to it. But he could do nothing except grimace at the scattered remains of the urn, which lay in a few thousand separate pieces.

Her candle had been dazzling him the whole while. And she had been coming closer. When he looked at her, feeling still annoyed but also decidedly sheepish, he could see her clearly for the first time.

Good God! She had not stopped either to dress or to throw on a dressing gown. Not that there was anything particularly indecent about her appearance. Her white cotton nightgown covered her from neck to wrists to ankles. She wore no nightcap, but her hair was scraped back from her face and lay in a thick braid down her back.

She did not look indecent at all, even if her feet *were* bare. She looked like chastity incarnate, in fact. But still and all, it *was* just a nightgown, and one could not prevent oneself from imagining what was—or, more to the purpose, what was not—beneath it. Nothing whatsoever, at a guess. Ferdinand's temperature soared and he rubbed harder at his bruised thigh.

"What is it to me?" she asked, repeating his question, her voice tight with self-righteous indignation. "It is the middle of the *night*. I am trying to *sleep*."

"It is a downright stupid place to keep a table—in the middle of the corridor," he said, careful not to look fully at her and then noticing his coat and waistcoat on the floor. He was clad only in shirt and breeches and stockings himself. Oh, Lord, Lord, Lord, he could have done without this. They were alone together after midnight in the darkened corridor outside both their bedchambers—and he had thoughts crowding his mind that had no business being there at all.

Lustful thoughts.

She herself was safely armed with indignation—at least for the moment. She had probably never even heard of lust. "The table was standing against the wall, my lord," she pointed out with cold civility. "The painting was hanging *on* the wall. If there was any stupidity involved in what has happened here, it was yours in lurching along the corridor without a candle while you were drunk."

"Deuce take it," he said, "I suppose that urn was worth a king's ransom."

"At least that much," she agreed. "It was also unspeakably hideous."

He grinned directly at her when she said that and then wished he had kept his eyes averted. She had the sort of face—a perfect oval with high cheekbones, a straight nose, large eyes, and soft, kissable lips—that actually looked more beautiful without the distraction of curls and ringlets to dress it up. Her usual coronet of plaits gave her a regal air. Tonight's loose braid gave her a youthful look, an aura of innocence and purity. His temperature edged up another notch as he determinedly returned his attention to the sad remains of the urn.

"Where will I find a broom?" he asked. Perhaps sweeping up the pieces would restore his equilibrium.

But she did exactly the wrong thing. She looked directly up at him and laughed, her eyes dancing with merriment.

"I am almost tempted to tell you," she said. "It would be priceless to see you wielding a broom. But you had better forget that impulse. It is after midnight."

Which fact he was trying diligently—and futilely—to ignore.

"What should I do, then?" he asked, frowning.

"I think you ought to go to bed, Lord Ferdinand," she said.

If only the top could have blown off his head, some heat might have escaped harmlessly into the air above and saved him. But it did not, of course. And instead of taking her advice and scurrying off in the direction of his room and sanctuary, his eyes on the doorknob every step of the way, he made the mistake of looking down at her again and locking eyes with her and seeing that finally her mind had attached itself to the atmosphere that had been sizzling around them ever since she had ventured outside her room.

He did not notice himself taking the candlestick out of her hand, but it was definitely his own hand that was setting it down on the table. And then he was turning and cupping her chin with the same hand, which was sending impressions of warm softness sizzling up his arm.

"Ought I?" he asked her. "But who is going to put me there?"

Even at that late moment he might have answered his own question and scampered off with all haste to put himself to bed. Or she might have helped restore sanity to them both by making some caustic remark about his supposed inebriation before effecting a dignified retreat. Or she might have delivered this morning's speech about the sanctity of her person again. Or she could simply have turned and bolted on her bare feet, leaving the candle to him as a trophy.

Neither of them took any of the easy—and sensible—ways out.

Instead she did something totally unexpected. Her teeth sank into her soft lower lip, and in the flickering light of the candle it seemed to Ferdinand that the brightness of her eyes might have been attributable to unshed tears. The words she spoke confirmed that impression.

"I wish," she said softly, "you had gone away after that day and that evening. I wish I had never known your name."

"Do you?" He forgot danger. He forgot propriety. He even forgot that they were locked in an insoluble conflict. All he saw was his lovely, vibrant lass, who had once worn daisies in her hair but who now had tears in her eyes—because of him. "Why?"

She hesitated and then shrugged. "It would have been a pleasant memory," she said.

Had he been thinking rationally, he would have left her answer uncommented upon. But he really was not thinking at all.

"*This* memory?" He lowered his head, touched his lips

to hers, and was irrevocably lost in sensation. Sweet, wholesome innocence and beauty. The enticing smells of soap and cleanliness and woman. And the memories of firelight and fiddle music and bright, twining ribbons. And of the laughing, lovely face of the woman he had taken behind the oak tree to kiss.

This woman.

He kissed her for only a few moments before drawing back his head and gazing down into her eyes. The candlelight flickered across her face as the firelight had done on the village green. Her eyes gazed dreamily back into his. The tears were gone. She raised one hand and set her fingertips lightly against his cheek, sending shivers of raw desire coursing downward through his body to center in his groin. And yet the hunger he felt was not purely carnal in nature. She was not just any lovely woman with whom he had found himself alone under provocative circumstances.

She was Viola Thornhill, the laughing, lovely, vibrant woman who danced with joy, as if she had drawn all the music and all the rhythm of the universe into her body, the relative of Bamber's who had been promised Pinewood and then betrayed, the child who had run to meet her father and poured out all her childhood secrets to him.

"Yes," she whispered at last in answer to the question he had almost forgotten asking. "I wanted that memory."

"When the real man is right here to provide others?" He forgot for the moment that she would remember her every association with him after May Day with a bitterness that would last a lifetime.

He set his hands on either side of her waist and drew

her closer. She did not push him away. On the contrary, she cupped his elbows in her palms and arched herself in toward him, pressing thighs, abdomen, and breasts against his body. She was all soft, alluring curves. His arms slid tightly about her waist, and hers twined about his neck. Any doubt of the nakedness that lay beneath the virginal white of her nightgown was put to flight. So was any doubt that she was a willing participant in what was happening.

This time when he kissed her, he opened his mouth over hers and licked her parted lips and the soft, moist flesh behind them. He was consumed by sweet, raw hunger. Sweet because he knew with a deep, innate integrity that he would not take the embrace far enough to destroy her innocence—he would not take her virginity. Raw because he wanted and wanted and wanted. He wanted her beneath him on a bed, yes. He was already hard with arousal. He wanted to press himself deep inside her and bring her pleasure and himself ease. But more than that simple animal urge, he wanted... Ah, he simply *yearned.*

"Sweet," he murmured, moving his mouth from hers, feathering kisses over her closed eyes, her temples, her cheeks, drawing the lobe of one ear between his teeth and rubbing his tongue over the tip, burying his face in the warm, soft hollow between her neck and shoulder. He wrapped both arms even more tightly about her, lifting her until she stood on her toes.

"Yes," she murmured, her voice low velvet, her cheek rubbing against his hair, the fingers of one hand entwined in it. "Ah, sweet."

They clung for endless moments.

He was releasing his hold on her at the same moment

as she set her hands against his shoulders and pushed him away, not violently, but firmly.

"Go to bed, Lord Ferdinand," she said before he could speak. "Alone." Yet she was not angry. There was something in her voice that spoke of a yearning to match his own. He knew that part of her—a weaker part—wanted him to argue.

"I was not headed down that road," he said softly. "Seduction was not on my mind. Your maidenhood is perfectly safe with me. But it would be best for us not to meet like this again. I am only a man, when all is said and done."

She picked up her candlestick. "I will have those pieces swept up in the morning," she said. "Leave them for now." She did not look at him again but made her way back to her room, her braid swinging back and forth across her back like a pendulum. She looked infinitely enticing.

He had lost all faith in innocence and purity and fidelity, and even love, long before he left his boyhood behind. He had never been in love or ever enjoyed anything more than a light, bantering sort of friendship with any woman. Women were for sex and children. He did not want children.

But perhaps, after all, Ferdinand thought as the door of her bedchamber closed behind her and the corridor was plunged into darkness again, there were such qualities as goodness and innocence and uncomplicated wholesomeness.

Perhaps there was even love.

And fidelity.

And perhaps he was simply tired, he thought as he located his abandoned clothes in the faint moonlight and picked them up before making his way toward his bedchamber. It had been a long day, after all, and an extraordinarily busy one.

There was a way for both of them to remain at Pinewood, he thought as he stepped inside the room and closed the door behind him. But he would not pursue that thought tonight. Or tomorrow either, if he was wise.

He was a perfectly contented bachelor.

Ah, sweet, she had just murmured to him, her voice throaty with passion, her cheek resting softly against his head.

Yes. Sweet, indeed.

He strode purposefully into his dressing room.

VIOLA GREETED THE ABSENCE of Lord Ferdinand Dudley from Pinewood the following morning with both relief and dismay. Through a long, almost sleepless night, she had not known how she was going to face him over the breakfast table. On the other hand, his absence was due to the fact that he had ridden out with Mr. Paxton to visit the home farm. It seemed that he was interested in the running of the estate, at least at present. Viola felt his absence on such a mission as a huge intrusion. From the first she had been personally involved in making Pinewood an efficient, prosperous concern. She had done rather well at it, with Mr. Paxton's help and advice. She had loved it.

There were no great schemes to put into effect today. Only the one this afternoon, which already seemed lame and doomed to failure. Just to accentuate her mood of depression, the lovely warm, sunny spell seemed to have deserted Somersetshire. There was a light drizzle misting the windows and heavy gray skies to darken the breakfast room.

The trouble was, she did not know for which of two evils she must blame herself more. She had capitulated to the enemy, allowing him to hold her and kiss her. And partly—oh, more than partly—that had happened because he had looked irresistibly attractive in his shirtsleeves, with his evening knee breeches skintight about his long, muscled legs, and because she had felt unbearably lonely and loveless. How could she excuse herself for giving in to desire for such a man? And yet she would prefer to accuse herself of unbridled lust than the other.

For even though she had been half lost in passion while she was in his arms, she really had been *only* half lost. The other half of herself had watched dispassionately as she arched against him, bringing her breasts against his hard chest, her thighs against his, her abdomen against the hard bulk of his erection. She had known the effect she was having on him, the power she had over him. She could have enticed him into bed with almost no effort at all. But though the passionate woman had longed for just that, to lie spread beneath him, brought to pleasure by his clean, youthful virility, the calculating woman had weighed the possibility of enticing him in an entirely different direction—toward love and even marriage.

Viola was deeply ashamed of that half of herself.

"Yes," she said when the butler stepped closer to her, "you may clear away, Mr. Jarvey. I am not hungry this morning."

She went to the library and seated herself behind the

desk. She would write home. At least she need not fear interruption for the rest of the morning.

How could she even be tempted to try to make him fall in love with her? She disliked and despised him. Besides, it was impossible. Not to engage his feelings, perhaps, but to marry him. Though it was not that practical consideration that made her feel slightly nauseated, but the moral implications of trying to trick a man into marriage. She picked up the quill pen from the desk, tested the nib, and dipped it in the inkwell.

Beware of a tall, dark, handsome stranger. He can destroy you—if you do not first snare his heart.

Why had those words of the gypsy fortune-teller chosen to pop into her mind at this particular moment?

She would not do it, she thought with firm resolve. She would not do a single thing deliberately to attract his admiration—or lust. But what if she did not have to do a thing? What if his obvious attraction to her person developed quite freely into something deeper? What if . . .

No, not even then, she thought, writing, "Dearest Mama, Claire, and Maria," with a flourish across the top of a blank sheet of paper. She forced her attention onto her letter.

He had *not* been drunk, she thought after writing five words. She had tasted ale on his tongue, it was true, but he had not been drunk. And he had told her that he had not been bent on seducing her, that she was quite safe with him. Worse, she had *believed* him. Still did.

No, she would not be distracted, she thought, writing doggedly on. And she would *not* allow herself to like him.

But later that afternoon she knew there was no danger of that at all. He was, in fact, quite the most contemptible man she had ever known.

It had been her idea, more than a year before, to begin a sewing circle for the women of the village and neighborhood. There were several places and events to bring the men together, but very few for the women. They had met weekly in the church hall ever since. But Viola had hit upon the happy idea two days ago of inviting the group to meet in Pinewood's drawing room instead. There could surely be nothing, she had thought then, more calculated to send a town tulip hastening back to London than to discover a few dozen women gathered over their needlework and conversation in the drawing room he considered his property.

"This is really a remarkably good idea of yours, Miss Thornhill," Mrs. Codaire said as she spread her embroidery threads about her. "Even apart from your main motive, this is a far more convenient meeting place than the church hall. No offense to you, Mrs. Prewitt."

"None taken, Eleanor," the vicar's wife assured her graciously.

"I must say, though," Mrs. Codaire added, "that his lordship seemed a perfectly amiable gentleman when I called here with Mr. Codaire and the girls yesterday."

"He insisted upon escorting me home after choir practice last evening," Miss Prudence Merrywether said breathlessly. "I would have preferred to walk alone, for I could not think of a single intelligent thing to say to a duke's brother and would have been quite tongue-tied if he had not asked me to explain what soil is best for planting roses in. But it was very obliging of him to consider my safety, even though it is quite absurd to think of *not* being safe in Trellick. And who would think of assaulting me, anyway, when I am neither young nor beautiful nor rich?"

"It was just his cunning, Prudence," her sister said firmly, to Viola's satisfaction. "He wants us all to *like* him. I have no intention of falling for his charms."

"Quite right too, Miss Merrywether," Mrs. Claypole said. "No proper gentleman would insist upon living at Pinewood before Miss Thornhill has had a chance to move out. It is quite scandalous, and I blame him entirely. He is not a man of breeding."

"He flatly refused to allow me to stay here as dear Viola's chaperon two evenings ago," Bertha added. "He was remarkably rude."

"He smiles too much," Mrs. Warner said. "I noticed that at the village during the fête."

"Though it *is* a lovely smile," Miss Prudence said, and blushed.

Miss Merrywether, better organized than most of them, was already hard at work. "If Lord Ferdinand Dudley does not like having us here today, Miss Thornhill," she said, "and comes in here and orders us to leave, we will inform him that we are here to chaperon our friend and intend to remain for the better part of the afternoon."

"You always were braver than I, Faith," Miss Prudence said with a sigh. "But you are right. You are always right. Never fear, Miss Thornhill. If Lord Ferdinand chooses to scold you in our hearing—well, we will scold right back. Oh, dear, if only we dare."

They all settled to their work after that, and half an hour passed while the room hummed with the usual feminine conversational topics—the weather, everyone's health, household tips, the newest fashions as displayed in fashion plates received from London itself, the next assembly.

Then the drawing room door opened and Lord Ferdinand stepped inside. He was looking quite immaculate, Viola saw when she glanced up from the bridal kneeler she had undertaken, dressed in a green superfine coat of expert cut with buff-colored pantaloons and tasseled, highly polished Hessian boots and his usual white linen. His hair had been freshly brushed and looked thick and shiny. He must have been warned, she realized. But instead of hiding away until all the ladies had left, he had gone upstairs to change and had come back down to make his entrance with all the appearance of easy good humor.

"Ah." He included everyone in his graceful bow. "Good afternoon, ladies. Welcome to Pinewood for those of you I did not meet here yesterday."

Viola set her work aside and rose to her feet. "The ladies' sewing circle is meeting here this week," she explained. "When one is privileged enough to own a manor of this size, you see, one must be prepared to use it for the common good and give up some of one's privacy."

He turned his eyes—his *laughing* eyes—on her. "Quite so," he agreed.

"I believe," she said pointedly, "the library is free."

"It is," he said. "I have just been in there finding a book of which I have heard many good opinions."

He was holding a book in one hand, Viola noticed for the first time.

"It is called *Pride and Prejudice,*" he said. "Has anyone heard of it?"

"I have," Mrs. Codaire admitted. "But I have not read it."

Viola had—more than once. She thought it easily the best book she had ever read. Lord Ferdinand strolled farther into the room and smiled about him with easy charm.

"Shall I read some of it aloud," he asked, "while you ladies sew? We men are not nearly as diligent or as skilled with our hands, you see, but perhaps we are good for something after all."

Viola glared indignantly at him. How dare he bring his charm into this female preserve instead of slinking about outside working himself into a temper as any decent man would?

"That would be very kind of you, I am sure, Lord Ferdinand," Miss Prudence Merrywether said. "Our papa used to read to us, particularly on dark evenings when time might otherwise have hung heavily on our hands. Do you remember, Faith, dear?"

He did not need further encouragement. He seated himself on the only remaining seat, an ottoman almost at Viola's feet, smiled about him once more as the ladies settled back to their work, opened the book, and began to read:

"'It is a truth universally acknowledged that a single man in possession of a good fortune must be in want of a wife.'"

Three or four of the women laughed, and he read on—surely knowing that more than three or four of them were thinking of how that opening statement of the novel applied to him. Not that he had a good fortune in all probability. But he had Pinewood. And she, Viola, had made it prosperous. She gazed bitterly down at him for a few minutes before resuming her work.

He read well. Not only did he do so clearly and with good pacing and expression, but he also looked up at frequent intervals to reveal his reactions to the narrative with his facial expressions. He was enjoying both the book and his audience, his manner said—and his audience was enjoying *him*. A glance about the room assured Viola of that.

How she hated him!

He stayed after he had read for half an hour to discuss the book with the ladies and to take tea with them and examine and admire their work. By the time the sewing group dispersed for another week, he had all but the strong-minded few veritably eating out of his hand. He even accompanied Viola out onto the terrace to see them all on their way. The rain had stopped, but the clouds still loomed gray and cheerless overhead.

Viola could have cried, and perhaps would have done so except that she was not going to give him the satisfaction of knowing that he had bested her—again.

"What a charming group of ladies," he said, turning to her when they were alone on the terrace. "I must see to it that they are invited to meet here each week."

"So must I." Viola turned sharply away and hurried back into the house, leaving him standing on the terrace.

9

FERDINAND WOULD HAVE ENJOYED THE FOLLOWING week if it had not been for Viola Thornhill. He had not anticipated the intense sense of belonging he felt at Pinewood. He had considered several careers after university—the army, the church, the diplomatic service—but nothing had appealed to him. But the result of doing nothing had been inevitable boredom and involvement in all sorts of madcap escapades and a general sense of purposelessness. He had not even realized it until he came to Pinewood and discovered that the life of a country landowner fit him like a glove.

But there was Viola Thornhill. He assiduously avoided any further encounter like the one the night he broke the urn. He even more firmly avoided all thoughts of matrimony. That would be a solution bought at too dear a price. And so they continued to inhabit Pinewood together.

He began to return his neighbors' calls. He continued to make friends of them and tried not to admit to himself that he was disappointed to discover how easy it was in most cases. They ought to have been more loyal to Miss Thornhill. He heartily disliked the tedious, pompous Claypoles and believed he would have disliked them under any circumstances. But their stiff, cold civility won his respect. Claypole fancied himself to be Miss Thornhill's suitor, Miss Claypole was her friend, and

Mrs. Claypole doted on her children. To them Lord Ferdinand Dudley was simply the enemy.

He set about familiarizing himself with the workings of his estate. He had little knowledge and no experience, having never expected to be a landowner. But he was determined to learn rather than leave everything to a steward. Besides, he might soon be without a steward. Paxton was Miss Thornhill's loyal employee. He made that clear when Ferdinand called on him at his office over the stable block one morning, the estate book tucked under one arm.

"The books are very well kept," Ferdinand said after exchanging greetings with the steward.

"She keeps them herself," William Paxton said curtly.

Ferdinand was surprised, though he might have guessed that the small, neat handwriting was a woman's. It was not a pleasant surprise, though, to know that she had had a direct part in the running of the estate. Worse was to come.

"You have done remarkably well," he said. "I have noticed how everything has changed for the better during the last two years."

"*She* has done well," the steward replied, passion vibrating in his voice. "*She* has performed the miracle. She tells me what to do and I do it. She often asks my advice, and she usually takes it when I offer it, but she does not need it. She could have done it all without me. She has as good a head on her shoulders as any man I have ever known. If she goes from here, I go too, I am here to tell you right now. I'll not stay to see the place go to wrack and ruin again."

"But why should it?" Ferdinand asked.

"We all saw you betting recklessly on almost certain

failure in the village," Paxton said, not even trying to disguise the bitterness in his voice. "And we all know how you acquired Pinewood through another wild wager."

"But I did not fail," Ferdinand pointed out, "at either venture. I do not deal in failure. I find it too depressing."

But Paxton was launched on mutiny. "You promised all sorts of things the other morning when we went to the home farm," he said. "The estate cannot afford them yet. *She* understands that. She does things gradually."

"The laborers need new cottages, not just repairs upon repairs," Ferdinand said. "The estate will not pay for them. I will."

Paxton looked at him suspiciously. Doubtless with the label of gambling wastrel put upon his person went that of impoverished aristocrat, Ferdinand thought.

"However," he added, "I will need the advice and assistance of a good steward. Was it Bamber who hired you?"

"The old earl," Paxton said, nodding. "He sent me here, but he made it clear to me that I would be *her* employee, that Pinewood was hers, not his."

Viola Thornhill was not the only one who had been given that impression, then? The late earl really had intended that the property be hers.

Paxton, like the Claypoles, was someone he came to respect during that week.

He involved himself with other neighborhood concerns. The church choir was one. The school was another. The roof of the schoolhouse leaked during wet weather, he learned during a visit to the schoolmaster. There was still not enough money in the village fund to have it replaced, even though Miss Thornhill had made a generous donation. Ferdinand put in what remained to be raised, and immediate arrangements were made for the job to be done. So that classes would not have to be interrupted, he offered Pinewood as a temporary schoolhouse for the appointed day. He told Viola Thornhill about it at dinner.

"But how can it be done?" she asked. "There is not enough money. I was hoping that within the next three or four months—" But she clamped her lips together and did not complete her sentence.

"You could afford it?" he suggested. "I have contributed what remains."

She stared mutely at him.

"I *can* afford it," he told her.

"And so of course you *will*." There was annoyance in her voice. "You will do anything to make a good impression here, will you not?"

"I suppose," he suggested, "I could not be doing it because I believe in education?"

She laughed derisively. "And school is to be held here while the work is being done?"

"Will that inconvenience you?" he asked.

"I am surprised you ask," she told him. "Pinewood is yours—according to you."

"And to law," he added.

He hoped Bamber would not simply ignore his plea to send a copy of the will. He even sent another letter, urging him not to delay. The present situation was ridiculous and impossible—and definitely dangerous. He was compromising the woman by living in this house with her. But it was not just that. He only had to set eyes on her to feel his temperature take an upward swing. Indeed, he did not even have to set eyes on her.

The nights in particular were a trial to him.

Once the will had arrived and she could see for herself

that Bamber had left her nothing, she would have no choice but to leave.

It could not be soon enough for Ferdinand.

IT WAS A WEEK of near-despair for Viola. One by one she had to let go of her comfortably negative illusions about Lord Ferdinand Dudley. He was a wastrel who would care nothing about the well-being of the estate or neighborhood, she had thought. His actions proved her wrong on both counts. He was an extravagant, impoverished younger son, she had thought, a man who gambled recklessly and probably had huge debts. But he was going to build new cottages for the farm laborers, Mr. Paxton reported—out of his own money. He was going to pay half the cost of a new schoolhouse roof.

He was not to be driven away either by foolish pranks or by boredom. She suspected that he genuinely liked most of her neighbors. And it was obvious that he was winning their friendship. Under other circumstances, she thought grudgingly, she might even like him herself. He seemed good-natured. He had a sense of humor.

He was idle and empty-headed, of course. She clung to that illusion after all the others. But even that she was forced to abandon before the week was out.

The schoolmaster had marched the children in an orderly crocodile from the village to Pinewood on the appointed morning, and classes had been set up in the drawing room. As she often did, Viola helped out by supervising some of the younger children as they practiced their penmanship. But when a history lesson began, involving all the children, she went downstairs to the library to see if there were any letters.

The library was occupied. Lord Ferdinand sat on one side of the desk, one of the older boys on the other.

"Excuse me," she said, startled.

"Not at all." Lord Ferdinand got to his feet and grinned at her—with the sunny smile that was beginning to play havoc with both her digestion and her sleep. "Jamie is late for the history lesson. Off you go, then, lad."

The boy hurried past Viola, bobbing his head respectfully as he passed.

"Why was he here?" she asked.

"To learn a little Latin," Lord Ferdinand explained. "Not necessary for the son of a tenant farmer destined to take his father's place one day, one might think. But there is no accounting for the desires of the intellect."

"*Latin?*" She knew all about Jamie's brightness and scholastic ambitions, for which his father had neither sympathy nor money. "But who can teach him?"

Lord Ferdinand shrugged. "Yours truly, I am afraid," he said. "An embarrassing admission, is it not? It was my specialty at Oxford, you see. Latin and Greek. My father would have been ashamed of me if he had still been alive."

Gentlemen went to Oxford or Cambridge almost as a matter of course, unless they went into the army instead. But they went mainly to socialize and carouse with their peers—or so she had heard.

"I suppose," she said more tartly than she intended, "you did well."

"A double first." He grinned sheepishly.

A *double first*. In Latin and Greek.

"My brain," he said, "is so full of dry matter that if you

knock on my skull you can watch the dust wafting from my ears and nostrils."

"And *why*," she asked him, "have you been wasting your time climbing over wet roofs at night and gambling?"

"Sowing my wild oats?" His eyes smiled into hers.

She did not want him to be intelligent, studious, wealthy, generous, good-humored, conscientious. She wanted him to be a wild, indigent, unprincipled hellion. She wanted to be able to despise him. It was bad enough that he was handsome and charming.

"I am sorry," he said meekly.

She turned without a word and left the library. She went back to the drawing room to hear about Oliver Cromwell and the Roundheads and the Interregnum. Music was to follow history. She usually helped out with that too.

But the drawing room door opened just as the history lesson was nearing its end, and the schoolmaster clapped his hands for everyone's attention. Viola turned her head to see Lord Ferdinand standing in the doorway.

"We will dispense with the usual music class," the schoolmaster said. He frowned ferociously when someone was unwise enough to begin applauding. "For today *only*, Felix Winwood. Lord Ferdinand Dudley has suggested that since we have the lawns of Pinewood at our disposal and it is a sunny day, we should have a games lesson instead."

"We are off outside for a cricket game," Lord Ferdinand Dudley added. "Is anyone interested?"

It was a foolish question, if ever Viola had heard one. "These children do not even know how to play cricket," she protested.

He turned his eyes on her. "But this is to be a games *lesson,*" he said. "They will be taught."

"We do not have the necessary equipment," she said.

"Paxton has bats, balls, and wickets among his things," Lord Ferdinand said. "Long gathering dust, it would seem. He is fetching them."

"But what are *we* going to do while the boys play cricket?" one of the girls asked plaintively.

"What?" Lord Ferdinand grinned at her. "Girls cannot hold a bat or throw a ball or catch one or run? No one ever told my sister that, which was probably just as well. He would without a doubt have ended up with a black eye and a beacon for a nose."

One minute later the children were filing two by two down the staircase, bound for the outdoors, Lord Ferdinand leading the way, the schoolmaster bringing up the rear. Viola trailed downstairs after them. Even the children were coming over to his side.

"His lordship has been down to the kitchen this morning, ma'am," Mr. Jarvey said from the back of the hall. "He has wheedled Mrs. Walsh into making up a batch of sweet biscuits. They are to be served to the children with chocolate to drink before they go home."

"Wheedled?"

"He smiled and said please," the butler said sourly.

Yes, he would. He would not be content until he had all the servants worshiping and adoring him too.

"He is a dangerous gentleman, Miss Thornhill," the butler added. "I have said it from the start."

"Thank you, Mr. Jarvey." Viola wandered to the front doors, which stood open. They were down on the lawn beyond the box garden. There was a great deal of noise and commotion, but order was being created out of chaos, she could see, without Mr. Roberts having to step in with his loud schoolmaster's bellow. Lord Ferdinand Dudley was gathering everyone about him. He was explaining something and gesticulating with both arms. And everyone was listening.

She might have guessed that he would be good with children, Viola thought bitterly. After all, he was good with everyone else. She stepped outside, drawn as if by a magnet.

By the time she had descended the steps to the box garden and taken a meandering route through its gravel paths to the low hedge dividing the garden from the lawn, the children had been divided into groups. Mr. Roberts was throwing the ball out to a widely scattered group, who were practicing catching it and throwing it back as quickly and accurately as possible. Mr. Paxton—the traitor!—was leading a group in batting practice. Lord Ferdinand Dudley was showing another group how to bowl.

Viola watched him lope up to the near wickets, throw the ball in one fluid overarm motion, and shatter the far wickets every time. He had stripped down to his shirt and breeches and boots again, she could not fail to notice—he was wearing the same tight black leather breeches he had worn when she first saw him in Trellick. He was patiently and good-naturedly instructing his group, none of whom displayed the smallest suggestion of talent. Then he spotted her.

"Ah, Miss Thornhill." He strode toward her, his right hand extended. "Allow me to help you over the hedge. Have you come to join us? We need another adult. How would you like to take the schoolmaster's place while he instructs the batters and Paxton sets out the pitch ready for a game?"

Viola had very little experience with physical sports. But she had been caught by the gaiety of the scene. She set her hand in his and stepped over the hedge, smiling gaily before she could think of reacting any other way. A few minutes later she was throwing the ball underhand, silently lamenting her inability to throw it nearly as far as Mr. Roberts had done, but nonetheless enjoying the fresh air and exercise.

"You will have more success if you throw overarm," a voice said from directly behind her.

"But I have never been able to throw that way," she told Lord Ferdinand Dudley. To prove her point, she bent her arm at the elbow and hurled the ball with all her might. It hurtled ahead at a downward angle and landed with a thud on the grass perhaps twelve feet away.

He chuckled. "The motion of your arm is all wrong," he said. "You will do better if you do not clutch your upper arm to your side and tighten all your muscles as if for a feat of great strength. Throwing has little to do with strength and everything to do with timing and motion."

"Huh!" she said derisively. The children, she half noticed, were all running toward Mr. Paxton, who was about to explain some of the basic rules of the game to them.

"Like this," Lord Ferdinand said, demonstrating first without a ball in his hand and then with. The ball arced out of his hand and landed some distance away. He went and got it and held it out to her. "Try it."

She tried and achieved perhaps thirteen feet. "Huh!" she said again.

"Better," he said. "But you let go of the ball too late. You are also locking your elbow. Let me help you."

And then he was right behind her, holding her right arm loosely just below the elbow and making the throwing motion with her.

"Relax your muscles," he said. "There is nothing jerky about this."

The heat of his exertions radiated from his body. His vitality somehow wrapped about her.

"Next time open your hand as if throwing," he said. He chuckled softly again a moment later. "If you had had the ball that time, it would have bounced right at your feet. Throw when your arm is just coming to the highest point. Ah, yes, now you are getting it. Try it on your own—with the ball."

A few moments later she laughed with delight as the ball arced upward out of her hand and sailed an impressive distance before curving in for a landing. She turned to share her triumph with him. His eyes were smiling into hers from a mere few inches away. Then he went striding after the ball and she crashed into reality.

She did not join in the noisy, vigorous game that followed. But she did stay out on the lawn, cheering batters and fielders with indiscriminate enthusiasm. After the first few minutes Lord Ferdinand took over the bowling when it became obvious that none of the children could pitch the ball anywhere near the batter. He threw with gentle ease, not to shatter the wickets, but to give each batter a chance to hit the ball. He laughed a good deal and called out encouragement to everyone, while the schoolmaster and Mr. Paxton were more inclined to criticize.

Viola unwillingly watched Lord Ferdinand. She could tell that he had a real zest for life. And he was genuinely kind. It was a bitter admission.

A procession of servants was coming from the house, she could see at last, surely long before the hour could be up. But the game was over, and everyone sat down on the grass, enjoying the rare luxury of steaming chocolate and sweet biscuits. Lord Ferdinand seated himself cross-legged right in the middle of a dense mob of children and chatted with them while they ate.

Then the schoolday was over and the long crocodile of children, walking in orderly pairs, was marched off down the driveway by Mr. Roberts while the servants carried the empty cups and plates inside and Mr. Paxton disappeared back in the direction of his office. Lord Ferdinand was pulling on his coat when Viola turned back to the house.

"Miss Thornhill," he called, "would you care to join me in a stroll? Along the avenue to the hill, perhaps? It is too lovely a day to be spent indoors."

They had been avoiding each other since the night when they had kissed and her attraction to him had warred with the temptation to lure him into falling in love with her. Neither had referred to the incident since. The broken pieces of the urn had been swept up before she left her room the morning after. Another vase had appeared on the table in its place.

It would be as well if they continued to avoid each other. But they could not go on indefinitely like this, inhabiting the same home, each claiming ownership. She just feared that when one of them left, as one of them inevitably must, it was going to be her. She would never be able to prove that the will had been changed or lost.

His eyes were smiling at her. It was another of his gifts—the ability to smile with a straight face.

"That would be pleasant," she said. "I'll go and put on a bonnet."

10

DRAWING HER INTO THE CRICKET LESSON HAD been a mistake. So had teaching her how to throw a ball overarm, especially cozying up behind her to demonstrate the correct motion of the arm with her. Suddenly it had felt like a mid-July day during a heat wave. But even more dangerous than her sexual appeal had been her laughter and her exuberant glee when she had finally hurled the ball correctly. When she had turned her sparkling smile on him, he had only just stopped himself from picking her up, twirling her about, and laughing with her.

And now he had invited her to walk with him.

She was wearing a straw bonnet when she came back outside. It fit snugly and attractively over her coronet of braids. The pale turquoise ribbons, which matched the color of her dress, were tied in a large bow beneath her left ear. She looked purely pretty, Ferdinand thought.

They conversed about trivialities until they were on the avenue behind the house. It was already Ferdinand's favorite part of the park. Wide and grassy, it was bordered on both sides by straight lines of lime trees. The turf was soft and springy underfoot. Insects were chirping in the grass, birds singing in the trees.

She walked with her arms behind her back. He could scarcely see her face beyond the poke of her bonnet. The devil of it was, he thought unexpectedly, he was going to miss her after she left.

"You have been helping teach at the village school for some time," he said. "Where were you educated?"

"My mother taught me," she said.

"I understand from Paxton," he said, "that you have been keeping the account books."

"Yes."

"And have taken an active role in the running of the estate."

"Yes."

She was not going to be forthcoming on that topic, he could see. Or perhaps on any topic. But she turned her head to look up at him just as he was thinking it.

"Why do you want Pinewood, Lord Ferdinand?" she asked. "Just because you won it and believe it to be yours? It is not a large estate and it is far from London and the sort of life you appear to have been enjoying there. It is far from any intellectual center too. What is there for you here?"

He breathed in the smells of nature as he considered his answer.

"A sense of fulfillment," he said. "I have never resented my elder brother. I always knew that Acton Park and all the other properties would be Tresham's and that I would be the landless younger son. I considered various careers, even an academic one. My father, had he lived, would have insisted on a commission with some prestigious cavalry regiment. It is what Dudley second sons have always been expected to do. I have never known what it is I want to do with the rest of my life—until now. I know now, you see. I want to be a country squire."

"Are you wealthy?" she asked. "I think you must be."

It did not occur to him to consider the question impertinent.

"Yes," he said.

"*Very* wealthy?"

"Yes."

"Could you not buy land elsewhere, then?" Her head was angled away from him so that he could not see her face.

"Instead of remaining at Pinewood, do you mean?" he asked. Strangely enough, buying land and settling on it was something he had never considered. "But why should I? And what would I do with this property? Sell it to you? *Give* it to you?"

"It is mine already," she said.

He sighed. "I hope within the next day or two that question will finally be settled beyond doubt," he said. "Until then, perhaps the least said, the better. Why are you so attached to Pinewood? You grew up in London, you told me. Do you not miss it and your friends there? And your mother? Would you not be happier back there?"

For a long time it seemed she was not going to answer at all. When she spoke, her voice was low, her head still averted.

"It is because *he* gave it to me," she said. "And because the difference between living here and living in London is the difference between heaven and hell."

He was startled—and not a little disturbed.

"Is your mother still in London?" he asked.

"Yes."

She was not going to elaborate on that monosyllabic answer, he realized. But going to live with her mother seemed to be another solution.

They were almost at the end of the avenue. The hill rose steeply in front of them.

"Shall we climb?" he asked.

"Of course." She did not even break stride, but lifted the hem of her dress with both hands and trudged upward, her head down, watching where she set her feet. She paused for breath when they were still not quite at the top, and he offered a hand. She took it, and he drew her up the rest of the slope until they stood on the bare grassy top.

He made the mistake of not immediately releasing her hand. After a few moments it would have been more awkward to let go than to hold on to it. Her fingers were curled firmly about his.

"When I stood on top of the highest hill in Acton Park as a boy," he said, "I always imagined it as the roof of the world. I was master of all I surveyed."

"Imagination is the wonder and magic of childhood," she said. "It is so easy to believe in forever when one is a child. In happily-ever-afters."

"I always believed happily-ever-after could be earned through honorable deeds of heroism and derring-do." He laughed softly. "If I killed a dragon or two, all the treasures of the universe would be mine. Is not childhood a gifted time? Even though disillusion and cynicism must follow?"

"Is it?" she asked, gazing about at the wide view over fields and river and the house below, centered perfectly between the trees of the avenue. "If there were no illusions, there would be no disillusionment. But then one would have no fond memories either, with which to fortify oneself against the pain of reality."

Her hand was soft and warm in his. A light breeze

fluttered the poke of her bonnet and the ribbons that dangled from the bow beneath her ear. He wanted desperately to kiss her and wondered if he was in love with her. Or was it the tenderness of pity that he felt? Or merely lust? But he did not feel particularly lustful at the moment.

She turned her head to look at him. "I have wanted to hate and despise you," she said. "I wanted you to be all the nasty and dissolute things I thought you must be."

"But I am not?"

She answered with another question. "Is gaming your *only* weakness? Even if it is, though, it is still a serious one. It was the vice that ruined my mother's health and happiness and destroyed my life. My stepfather was a compulsive gambler."

"I never wager more than I can afford to lose," he said gently. "Gaming is not a compulsion with me. It was only because a friend of mine was called away by his wife's confinement that I played against Bamber that night."

She laughed, though there was no amusement in the sound. "And so the last of my illusions must be abandoned?" It was not really a question.

He gazed into her eyes and then raised her hand and held it to his lips. "What am I going to do with you?"

She did not answer, but then he had not really expected her to. He bent his head closer to hers, his heart thumping painfully, not so much with the knowledge that he was about to kiss her as with the realization of what he was about to say and seemed powerless *not* to say. There was really only one solution to this situation he had found at Pinewood, and at the moment it was looking like a rather desirable one. It was time perhaps to trust again, even to love again, to take a leap of faith.

"Miss Thornhill—" he began.

But she snatched her hand from his and turned her back on him.

"Gracious," she said, "luncheon must have been ready ages ago. I forgot all about the time when you invited me for a walk. I suppose it was because of the chocolate and biscuits. I am glad you thought of refreshments. Some of the children have a long walk home from the village."

She did not want to be kissed. She did not want to listen to any sort of declaration. That was perfectly clear. Perhaps she would feel differently once she knew she had no other option except to leave Pinewood. But he felt a certain sense of relief, Ferdinand admitted to himself. A huge sense, in fact. He had no wish to marry. He had always been very firm in his intention never to do so. And pity was not a strong enough reason for changing his mind. It must be pity that had impelled him. It could not be love. *Love* was a word his father had always used with contempt—it was for females. His mother had used the word all too frequently. For her, Ferdinand had learned in his formative, impressionable years, love was self-absorption and manipulation and possessiveness.

He must avoid being alone with Viola Thornhill in the future. He had just had a narrow escape. Yet a part of himself gazed at her with a certain yearning. He would miss her when she left Pinewood. She was the only woman he had come close to loving.

"Shall we return to the house, then?" he suggested.

"Do you need a hand?" The slope down to the avenue seemed even steeper when viewed from the top.

"Of course not," she said, gathering her skirts above her ankles with both hands and beginning a gingerly descent.

Ferdinand loped down ahead of her and turned close to the bottom to watch her progress. She was running with small steps, and even as he watched she came faster, shrieking and laughing. He stepped in front of her and caught her as she came hurtling down. He lifted her off her feet, both arms about her waist, and swung her around in a complete circle before setting her down on her feet. Both of them were laughing.

Ah, he was a weakling indeed, he thought a moment later as he kissed her, first lightly, then fiercely. He was a man who could not force his emotions and behavior to his will. But she did not resist him as she had done at the top of the hill. She clutched his shoulders and kissed him back.

They released each other after a while, their eyes averted, their laughter gone, and began the walk back to the house side by side, not talking. Ferdinand's mind was in turmoil again. Should he or should he not? Did she wish him to or did she not? Would he regret it or would he not?

Did he love her?

It was on that question that his mind stuck. He knew so little about love—about *real* love, if there was such a thing. How could he recognize it? He liked her, he respected her, admired her, wanted her, pitied her—ah, yes, he *pitied* her. Pity was not love. He knew that much, at least. But was pity the dominant emotion he felt for her? Or was there more?

What was love?

He was still pondering the question when they circled the house to enter by the front doors. Jarvey was in the hall, looking important.

"You have a visitor, my lord," he announced. "From London. I have put him in the salon."

Ah, at last! Was it Bamber's solicitor or Bamber himself? Finally the question of ownership was to be settled. But even as Ferdinand turned toward the salon, the door opened and the visitor stepped out into the hall.

"Tresham!" Ferdinand exclaimed, striding toward his brother, his boots ringing on the tiles, his right hand extended. "What the devil are *you* doing here?"

His brother shook his hand, raised his eyebrows, and grasped the handle of his quizzing glass with the other hand. "Dear me, Ferdinand," he said, "am I not welcome?"

But Ferdinand was not to be cowed by the ducal hauteur, which could have almost every other mortal on the face of the earth quailing in terror. He squeezed his brother's hand and slapped him on the shoulder.

"Did you come alone?" he asked. "Where is Jane?"

"In London with the children," the Duke of Tresham replied. "Our younger son is a mere two months old, you may remember. Being away from them is a severe trial to me, Ferdinand, but your need sounded greater than mine. What *is* this coil you have got yourself into, pray?"

"No coil at all," Ferdinand assured him heartily, "except that it did not occur to me when Bamber lost the property that there might be someone already in residence here."

He stepped aside and turned to make the introductions. He noticed that Tresham was already looking at Viola Thornhill across the hall and even raising his glass to his eye, the better to peruse her.

"Miss Thornhill," Ferdinand said, "allow me to present my brother, the Duke of Tresham."

Her face was an expressionless mask as she dipped into the slightest of curtsies. "Your grace," she murmured.

"This is Miss Viola Thornhill," Ferdinand said.

"Ah." Tresham spoke with faint hauteur. He inclined his head but did not bow. "Your servant, ma'am."

There! Ferdinand thought indignantly. Now if only he could have behaved like that on the very first morning, she would have been gone within the hour. But at the same time he felt annoyed. This was *his* house and *his* problem. He did not need Tresham coming here to bedeck the poor woman with icicles at a single glance.

She was half smiling, Ferdinand saw before he could step into the breach and create a more civil atmosphere. It was a strangely chilling expression and made her look quite different from usual.

"Excuse me," she said. She disappeared upstairs with straight spine and uplifted chin, very much on her dignity.

Tresham was gazing after her with narrowed eyes.

"Dear me, Ferdinand," he muttered, "what *have* I walked in upon?"

VIOLA WENT STRAIGHT TO her room and rang for Hannah. She stood at the window while she waited and gazed along the avenue where she had walked just a few minutes ago.

She felt cold through to the very heart.

As soon as she had known who Lord Ferdinand Dudley was, she had thought he resembled his brother. She had met the Duke of Tresham once. They had been at the same dinner party—it must be four or five years ago. Both brothers were tall and dark and slender and long-legged. But there the resemblance ended, she realized now after seeing them side by side. While Lord Ferdinand was handsome, with an open, good-humored countenance, the duke was none of those things. His face was harsh and cold and arrogant. It was easy to understand why everyone feared him.

Just there, she thought, her eyes on the distant hill, Ferdinand had held and kissed her hand and begun to ask her to marry him. She had not allowed him to speak more than her name, but she was convinced that that was what he had been about to do, presumptuous as it might be to believe it. For a moment she had been very, very tempted. It had taken all her willpower to snatch away her hand and turn the moment.

He can destroy you—if you do not first snare his heart.

She had not been able to bring herself to do it.

And there, just there, she thought, moving her eyes lower, she had run shrieking and laughing into his arms and had kissed him with all the passion she had ruthlessly denied just a few minutes before. It had been one of those magical moments, like the throwing contest at the fête and the maypole dance and the kiss behind the oak. One more brief memory to tuck away for future comfort. Except that comfort would be all mingled up with pain.

It would have been easy to snare his heart. And easier still to lose her own.

The door opened behind her.

"Hannah," she said, "the Duke of Tresham has just arrived from London."

"Yes, Miss Vi." Hannah did not sound at all surprised.

"He recognized me."

"Did he, lovey?"

Viola drew a slow, deep breath. "You might as well pack my things," she said. "I think you might as well, Hannah."

"Where will we be going?" her maid asked.

Again the slow breath. But it did not keep the tremor from her voice when she spoke. "I don't know, Hannah. I'll have to think."

"COME INTO THE LIBRARY," Ferdinand said, leading the way. He felt a little embarrassed being caught returning from a walk with Viola Thornhill as if it were the most proper thing in the world to be sharing a house with a single young lady and living on amicable terms with her. He poured his brother a drink.

Tresham took the glass and sipped from it. "You get yourself into the most unbelievable scrapes," he said.

Ferdinand felt irritated again. He was three years younger than his brother, and Tresham had always been autocratic, especially since inheriting the title and all the responsibilities that went with it at the age of seventeen, but Ferdinand was no longer a boy to be criticized and scolded—especially in his own home.

"What was I supposed to do?" he asked. "Throw her out on her ear? She is convinced that Pinewood is hers, Tresham. Bamber—Bamber's father, that is—promised it to her."

"Are you sleeping with her?" his brother asked.

"Am I... Good Lord!" Ferdinand's hands closed into fists at his sides. "Of *course* I am not sleeping with her. I am a gentleman."

"My point exactly." Tresham had his quizzing glass in hand again. If he raised it to his eye, Ferdinand thought, he would be sorry.

"It was rash of her to insist upon staying here with me, of course," Ferdinand said. "But it is also a measure of the trust she has placed in me as a gentleman. She is an innocent, Tresham. I would not sully that." He thought guiltily of the kisses he had shared with her.

His brother set down his glass on a library shelf and sighed. "You really don't know her, then," he said. "You have not recognized her. I suspected as much."

And Tresham *did* know her? Ferdinand stared as him transfixed, a premonition of disaster holding him motionless.

"She has looked familiar from the start," he said. "But I just cannot place her."

"Perhaps," the duke said, "if she had introduced herself by her real name, Ferdinand, your memory would not have played such tricks on you. She is better known in certain London circles as Lilian Talbot."

Ferdinand stood where he was for a moment longer before turning sharply and crossing the room to the window. He stood there with his back to the room, all the cloudy layers ripping away from his memory.

He had been at the theater in London one evening several years ago, sitting in the pit with some friends. The play had already begun, but even so, there had been a sudden noticeable stir from the boxes and a buzz from the predominantly male preserve of the pit. Ferdinand's nearest companion had dug him in the ribs with an elbow and pointed with his thumb toward the party arriving late in one of the boxes. Lord Gnass, an aging but still notorious roué, was removing the russet satin cloak of his female companion to reveal a shimmering gold gown beneath—and a daring amount of the voluptuous flesh of the woman inside the gown.

"Who is she?" Ferdinand had asked, raising his quizzing glass to his eye, as a large number of other gentlemen were doing.

"Lilian Talbot," his friend had explained.

It was the only explanation necessary. Lilian Talbot was enjoying enormous fame even though she was rarely seen in public. She was said to be lovelier and more desirable than Venus or Aphrodite or Helen of Troy all rolled into one. And almost as unattainable as the moon.

Ferdinand had been able to see that reports of her had not been exaggerated. Even apart from her glorious, shapely body, she had a classically beautiful face and hair of a rich dark red set in elaborate but elegant curls high on her head and trailing down onto her long, swanlike neck. She sat down, set one bare arm along the velvet edge of the box, and directed her gaze toward the action on the stage as if she were unaware that the attention of almost the entire audience was on her.

Lilian Talbot was London's most celebrated, most sought-after, most expensive courtesan. But part of her allure was the fact that no one, not even the wealthiest, highest ranked, most influential lord of the *ton,* had ever been able to persuade her to become his mistress. One night was all she would grant of her favors to any man.

Some said that no one could afford more than that anyway.

Lilian Talbot. Alias Viola Thornhill.

I am no man's mistress.

"I saw her only once at the theater," Ferdinand said, staring at the fountain in the box garden without seeing it. "I never met her. Did you?"

"Once," Tresham said.

Once? "Did you—"

"No," his brother replied coolly, without waiting for the question to be completed. "I preferred to mount mistresses for long-term comfort rather than one-time-only courtesans for sensation and prestige. What the devil is she doing here?"

"She is a relative of Bamber's," Ferdinand said, bracing both hands on the windowsill. "His father must have been fond of her. He sent her down here and promised to leave her Pinewood in his will."

The duke laughed derisively. "She must have serviced him well if he was prepared to offer her such an extravagant gift after one night," he said. "Doubtless he paid her outrageous fee as well. But he came to his senses in time. It is why I am here, Ferdinand. You might wait until doomsday for Bamber to exert himself. I called on his solicitor and persuaded him to let me see the will. There is no mention in it of either Viola Thornhill or Lilian Talbot. And the present Bamber has never heard of the former, though perhaps he has of the latter. He was clearly unaware that she was living here. Pinewood Manor is without a doubt yours. I am pleased for you. It appears to be a pretty enough property."

Not a relative, but a satisfied customer.

He loved me. Ferdinand could hear her voice down on

the riverbank as if she were still speaking. *And I loved him.*

Pinewood had been the impulsive gift of a grateful, dazzled man, who had just been well serviced in bed.

I will never lose my trust in him because I will never stop loving him or knowing beyond any doubt that he loved me.

Even the most experienced courtesan could be naïve on occasion, it seemed. Bamber had changed his mind. Her trust had been misplaced.

"You can order her off the premises without further ado," the duke said. "I daresay she is even now packing her trunks—she knows the game is up. She could see that I recognized her. I will be eternally thankful that I did not bring Angeline with me. She wanted to come since Jane had to remain with the baby, but it has long been my practice to endure our sister's incessant chatter only in small doses. Besides, I believe Heyward said no even before I did, and for some reason I still have not fathomed—it is certainly not fear—Angeline obeys him."

But Ferdinand was not listening.

It is because he gave it to me, she had said only an hour or so ago when he had asked why she loved Pinewood. London's most celebrated courtesan had fallen in love with one of her clients—and had made the cardinal mistake of believing that he loved her in return.

"Where will she go?" he asked, more of himself than his brother. If she was no relative of Bamber's, her options were cut down considerably.

"To the devil, for all I care," Tresham said.

Ferdinand's hands closed more tightly about the sill.

"Good Lord, Ferdinand," his brother said, "you have

not conceived a *tendre* for the woman, have you? If this does not beat all—my brother infatuated with a whore!"

Ferdinand gripped the sill as if for dear life. "Whatever she is," he said without turning, "she is under my protection while she is beneath this roof, Tresham. You will not use that word either of her or to her while you remain here, or you will answer to me."

"Good God!" the Duke of Tresham said after a short, pregnant silence.

11

VIOLA DRESSED CAREFULLY FOR DINNER IN A pale blue silk evening gown, fashionably high-waisted and low at the bosom, but neither overdaring nor dowdily demure. It was one Mrs. Claypole herself had commended. Viola had Hannah dress her hair in a smooth, elegant chignon. She wore no jewelry, but only an evening shawl about her shoulders.

She had no idea whether Lord Ferdinand and the Duke of Tresham intended to dine at home. She had no idea if she would be denounced and banished from the dining room if they were there. But she was no coward. She would not hide away in her room. Neither would she go quietly if they tried to rid themselves of her company for dinner. After all, she was still living here under the assumption that she belonged here, that it was they who were the usurpers. No proof to the contrary had yet been shown her.

They were both in the dining room, both wearing black evening clothes with white linen, looking very much like the sons of Satan. They rose and bowed at her entrance.

They dined together, the three of them, in a strange charade of civility. Both gentlemen were meticulously polite, making sure that she had everything she needed, careful not to choose any topic of conversation that might exclude her. Under other circumstances, Viola thought, she might have enjoyed herself. But these were not other circumstances. She was scandalously alone with two gentlemen. One of them knew who she was—or who she had been. It was impossible to tell if the other did too. But he would soon.

Viola did not afterward know quite what had been served for dinner or how many courses there had been. All she took away with her was the impression that Mrs. Walsh had excelled herself in deference to the presence of a duke at Pinewood. She found the meal interminable and rose to her feet as soon as she decently could.

"I will leave you to your port, gentlemen," she said. "If you will excuse me, I will bid you good night and go straight to my room. I have a slight headache. I trust you are happy with your room and have everything you need, your grace?"

"Everything, thank you, ma'am," he assured her.

"Miss Thornhill." Lord Ferdinand Dudley drew a folded piece of paper from a pocket of his evening coat. "Would you oblige me by reading this in your own time?"

The will? But it was just a single sheet. The Earl of Bamber's will would surely be a fat document.

"Yes." She took it from him.

It was not the will, she discovered when she had reached her room. It was not really a letter either. It was some sort of declaration, written in a bold, black hand. It stated that although the will of the late Earl of Bamber was not for copying or perusal by anyone unconnected with its contents, it had been produced and read in its entirety by the Duke of Tresham, his claim to an interest in its contents having been acknowledged. The paper asserted that beyond any doubt the will made no specific mention of Pinewood Manor in Somersetshire and none of Miss Viola Thornhill. It was signed by the duke in the same bold, black hand, and by George Westinghouse, solicitor of the late Earl of Bamber.

Viola folded the paper and held it in her lap for a long time while she stared into space. He simply would not have changed his mind. And he would not have delayed. He had known that his health was poor. He had not expected to live more than a month or two longer. He would not have forgotten.

She would not lose faith in him—not again.

The will must have been changed without his knowledge. But there was no way on earth she was going to be able to prove that, of course. And so she had lost Pinewood. How sad he would be if he could know! She felt as sad for him at that moment as for herself—she could feel only numbness for herself. He had thought she was safe and secure for life. He had been cheerful, even happy, as he had bidden her good-bye forever—they had both known it was forever.

A tear plopped off Viola's cheek and darkened the fabric of her skirt.

THE DUKE OF TRESHAM stayed only until early afternoon of the following day. He was interested in seeing the house and park and home farm, all of which Ferdinand showed him during the morning, but he was eager to return to London and his family. The baby was colicky, he explained, and Jane needed his support during the nights of disturbed sleep. Ferdinand listened to the explanation in some fascination but without comment. Was it not a nurse's job to stay up with a fussy baby? Did Tresham really allow his sleep to be disturbed by a child?

Was it really possible that a marriage that had begun four years ago as an apparent love match had continued as such? With Tresham, of all people? Could he possibly be steadfast in his devotion? And faithful to Jane? Could she be faithful to him? Even now, after she had dutifully borne Tresham two sons—an heir and a spare, to use the vulgar parlance? Jane was a beautiful woman, and a spirited one too.

Was there really such a thing as true, lasting marital love? Even within his own family?

But it was too late to take any real interest in learning the answer. One day too late. Yesterday she had been Viola Thornhill, wholesome, lovely, innocent. Today she was Lilian Talbot, beautiful, experienced—and deceitful to the core of her cold heart.

"I wish you had let me have a word with her this morning, Ferdinand," the duke said as they stood together outside his traveling carriage. "You lack the necessary resolve for performing unpleasant tasks. And you are emotionally involved. I could have had her out of here by now."

"Pinewood is mine, Tresham," Ferdinand said firmly. "And everything concerned with it, even its problems."

"Take my advice and don't allow her to spend another night here." His brother laughed shortly. "But Dudleys have never taken well to advice, have they? Will we be seeing you in London before the Season is over?"

"I don't know," Ferdinand said. "Probably. Maybe not."

"A decisive answer indeed," Tresham said dryly, and took his seat in the carriage.

Ferdinand raised a hand in farewell and watched until the carriage disappeared among the trees. Then he turned and walked back into the house with firm strides. It was time to get rid of the intruder. It was time to harden his heart and behave like a man. Like a Dudley.

The butler was hovering in the hall.

"Jarvey," Ferdinand said grimly, "have Miss Thornhill in the library within the next two minutes." But he paused when his hand was on the doorknob and the butler was already on the second stair. "Jarvey, ask Miss Thornhill if she will wait upon me in the library at her earliest convenience."

"Yes, my lord."

He stood at the library window, looking out, until he heard the door open and close behind him. He had not even been sure she was at home. He turned to look at her. She was dressed very simply in a light muslin day dress. Her hair was in its usual neat coronet of braids. He looked her over from head to toe. Perhaps after all Tresham had been mistaken, and his own memory had played tricks on him.

"Good afternoon, Miss Talbot," he said.

She did not answer immediately. But his foolish hope died an instant death. A faint smile played about her lips. It was just the expression she had worn at the theater—and in the hall yesterday when he had presented her to Tresham.

"You address me by a name that is not my own," she said.

"You knew very *well* where I had seen you before," he

said, his eyes raking her again, with anger this time. How dare she look just so at him! He had been kind to her. But then, she would despise kindness. Good Lord, he thought as if realizing it for the first time, he had been sharing a house with *Lilian Talbot*.

"On the contrary." She raised her eyebrows. "Where *did* you see me, Lord Ferdinand? It was not in any bed you have ever occupied. I believe I might have remembered that. Of course, despite your claim to be wealthy, you probably could not have afforded me, could you?"

Her eyes were sweeping over him as she spoke, giving him the peculiar notion that he was being stripped naked and found wanting—rather as if he had regressed ten years or so to the time when he had shot up to a gangly, spindly height, all legs and sharp elbows and teeth too large for his face.

"At the theater," he said. "With Lord Gnass."

"Ah, yes, Lord Gnass," she said. "He *could* afford me and liked demonstrating the fact."

He could hardly believe how she had been transformed before his eyes.

"I suppose," he said curtly, "Viola Thornhill is an alias. No wonder Bamber has never heard of you. I suppose no one at Pinewood or in the neighborhood knows your real identity."

"Viola Thornhill is my real name," she said. "Lilian Talbot died a natural death two years ago. Are you disappointed? Were you hoping to sample her favors before you toss me out? I was always too expensive for you, Lord Ferdinand. I still am, no matter how large your fortune is."

She was regarding him with that sensuous, scornful

half smile. He was repulsed by it and by her words. But he felt his temperature rise despite himself.

"I would waste not a penny of my fortune on purchasing the favors of a whore, Miss Talbot," he told her. He probably would have felt instant shame at his choice of words if she had shown any sign of mortification or even anger. But the look on her face merely deepened to amusement.

"I could not be tempted," he added.

She came closer then, stopping just beyond touching distance—and after he had taken an involuntary step back until his heels clicked against the base of the wall behind him. Her eyes had become heavy-lidded. Bedroom eyes, he thought. With a voice to match, he observed a moment later when she spoke again.

"That sounds very much like a challenge," she said. "I am very, very skilled, my lord. And you are very, very male."

She seemed somehow to have sucked half the air out of the room, leaving precious little to supply the need of his lungs.

"Would you care to make a wager?" she asked him.

"A wager?" He felt deuced uncomfortable, though he would not take another step back even if he could. He was already trapped against the window, looking like a bloody idiot. How had he maneuvered himself into this awkward position anyway? He was the one who had summoned her. He had been going to give her a piece of his mind before ordering her to leave before sundown.

"That I can seduce you," she said. "Or not. However you want it phrased. Bed you. Pleasure you. Cater to all your deepest and darkest sexual fantasies."

Fury held him speechless. *This* was the woman he had

pitied? Grown to like? Even fancied himself half in love with? Considered marrying? Was he indeed so gauche? Such a dupe? So easily manipulated? For he could see clearly now that he had been clay in her hands from the first. She had soon realized that she could not drive him away and so had planned a different solution to her problems. She had accomplished her goal with humiliating ease—humiliating for him. If Tresham had not arrived when he had and recognized her, there was no knowing what the rest of the day might have accomplished for her. He might be betrothed to her now. He might at this moment be at the vicarage, arranging to have the first banns read on Sunday.

Now, without a blink, she had changed tactics yet again, but this time she was comfortably within the realm of her expertise. She had made a handsome living on her back. Famed for her beauty and her seductive charms and her prowess in the sexual arts—and for the clever ploy of granting each client only one night of her favors—she had been in greater demand than any other courtesan within living memory.

She chuckled low in her throat. "I *can* seduce you, you know." She moved another step closer, set one forefinger lightly against his chest, and traced a light path upward with it, over his neckcloth toward his bare throat.

He clamped a hand about her wrist and returned her arm to her side. Anger and desire and revulsion all warred within him. "I think not, ma'am," he said. "I prefer to make a free choice of my bed partners."

"Ah, but you do enjoy a wager," she said. "Especially when the stakes are high."

"If you are suggesting that I wager Pinewood," he said, "you are wasting your breath. You would lose."

"But according to you, I already have lost," she said, turning away and crossing the room to run her fingers over the bare surface of the desk. "You really appear to have won, do you not?"

"I dashed well have," he said, glaring at her. "And you have diverted me from my purpose in summoning you down here."

"Ah," she said, turning her head to smile at him, "but you changed your summons to a request, Lord Ferdinand. Mr. Jarvey told me so. You like to think of yourself as a gentleman, do you not? And you consider yourself weaker than your brother, who does not care what anyone thinks of him."

She was uncannily perceptive. But then, an understanding of men must have been necessary in her career.

"I want you out of here before nightfall," he said. "I do not care whether that gives you enough time to pack your things or not. You will leave. Today."

She was still looking at him over her shoulder. "What, Lord Ferdinand?" she said, amusement in her voice when he had steeled himself for either tears or anger. "You are afraid to accept a wager? Afraid that you will lose? How you would be derided in all the gentlemen's clubs if word were to get out that you were afraid of being bested by a woman. By a whore!"

"Don't call yourself that," he said before he could stop himself.

Her smile deepened and she turned to face him fully, her fingertips still lightly stroking the desktop.

"Give me one week," she said. "If I cannot seduce you within that time, I'll never again challenge the authenticity of that will. I will go away and never trouble either your person or your conscience again—I *do* trouble your conscience, do I not? If you lose, of course"—she caught him completely off guard by smiling dazzlingly at him—"then *you* will be the one to leave. You will also relinquish your claim to Pinewood in my favor—and in writing. With witnesses."

"Nonsense!" he said. But the thought struck him at the same moment that it would be an easily enough won bet and that in one week he—and his conscience—would be permanently rid of her.

"But before you left, Lord Ferdinand," she told him softly, her voice sultry again, "you would enjoy a night of such exquisite pleasure that you would spend the rest of your life pining for more."

Despite the revulsion her boast caused him, he also felt an unwilling surge of pure lust. Had she been dressed like a harlot—as she had been at the theater—he would more easily have resisted her. One *expected* an expensive harlot to speak in such a way. But she was clad in a dress of virginal white. Her hair was dressed for elegance and practicality. She was Viola Thornhill, for God's sake. Talking about going to bed with him.

"I never disappoint," she said, lifting her hand away from the desk, moistening her forefinger slowly with her tongue and running it along her lower lip. More of the air seemed to have gone from the room, leaving Ferdinand gasping for breath and fighting to disguise the fact.

"By God!" he blurted, his temper snapping. "I want you out of here. Now. *Sooner.*"

"Would it not be better to have me leave quietly after one week than screaming and biting and kicking and shedding copious tears today?" she asked him.

"And stopping in the village to scream and weep some more?"

"Do they *know*?" He frowned at her and for the first time took a few steps farther into the room. "Do these people know who you are?"

"Who I *am*? Yes, of course," she said. "I am Viola Thornhill of Pinewood Manor. They know that I am a connection of the Earl of Bamber's."

"They believe a lie, in fact," he said indignantly. "They do not know you are a whore."

"Present tense?" She laughed softly. "But no, they do not *know*. And what a weapon I have just handed you. You may reveal my dreadful secret, Lord Ferdinand, and doubtless they will gather behind you in a righteous mob to run me out of Somersetshire."

He glared at her, white with fury. "I am a *gentleman*," he reminded her. "I do not go about spreading such unsavory tidings. Your secret is safe with me."

"Thank you," she said with mocking carelessness. "Is that a promise, my lord?"

"Devil take it!" he retorted. "I have said it is so. A gentleman does not need to promise."

"And yet," she reminded him, "it would be an easy way to rid yourself of me for all time, would it not?"

"That is already done," he said. "I daresay you read the declaration signed by both Tresham and Westinghouse that I handed you last evening. Bamber changed his mind, if ever he intended to make you a permanent gift of Pinewood. I daresay he thought it too extravagant a gift for the services you had rendered him."

She stood very still, her finger still resting against her lower lip, staring at him blankly, her faint, contemptuous smile fading. And then she returned her hand to the desk and smiled again.

"You will never know," she said, "unless you avail yourself of those services, Lord Ferdinand. You can only take my word for it that you will not consider Pinewood too extravagant a wager at all. I am very, very good at what I do. But you are convinced, of course, that you can resist me. And perhaps you can. Or perhaps not. It would be an interesting wager. You will forever consider yourself a coward if you refuse to accept it. Come." She walked toward him, her right hand extended. "Shake my hand on it."

"You would lose," he warned her weakly instead of simply repeating his order that she leave before nightfall.

"Perhaps. Perhaps not." She held her hand steady. "Are you *really* afraid of losing to a woman? Having won Pinewood at cards, are you now afraid of losing it at love?"

"*Love?*" he asked with undisguised revulsion.

"A euphemism," she admitted. "Lust, if you prefer."

"I am not afraid of losing anything at all to you, ma'am," he told her.

"Well, then." She laughed and looked for a disconcerting moment like the Viola Thornhill with whom he was more familiar. "You have nothing to fear. This will be the easiest won wager you have ever agreed to, Lord Ferdinand."

"Dammit!" He slapped his hand onto hers and squeezed it so hard that she visibly winced. "You have your wager. One that you will lose, I do assure you. You have one more week here. If I were you, I would use the time wisely and begin to pack and make plans. You will not be staying one day longer than a week. That is a promise."

"On the contrary, my lord," she said, drawing her hand free of his. "It is you who will be leaving—the morning after you bed me and turn over the deed of Pinewood and sign the necessary papers."

She turned then and left the room. Ferdinand stood where he was, looking at the door through which she had disappeared. What in thunder had he just agreed to? Another week spent under the same roof as Viola Thornhill? No—Lilian Talbot.

He had just made a wager with *Lilian Talbot*. A wager that she could seduce him within a week, Pinewood as the prize if she succeeded.

His temper had got the better of him, as it often did. And his inability to resist a wager.

He would win, of course, as he always did.

But he did not want to share a house with Lilian Talbot. Especially when she looked almost identical to Viola Thornhill—to whom he had come within a whisker of offering marriage just yesterday. What a fortunate escape he had had, he thought suddenly.

But he did not feel fortunate. He felt somehow bereft.

VIOLA MADE HER WAY upstairs, thankful that the butler was not in the hall as she passed through it. Her hands were shaking, she noticed when she held them before her, her fingers spread. She really had thought Lilian Talbot was dead, consigned forever to the dust. But how very easily she had been resurrected. How quickly she had bundled all that was herself deep inside so that he would not see her raw pain in confronting her past.

He had called her a whore—after objecting to her calling herself that.

She had begun—oh, yes, there was no point in denying it—to fall a little in love with him.

He had called her a whore.

Hannah was still in her dressing room, packing the large trunk Viola had brought with her from London two years before.

"What happened?" she asked sharply. "What did he want?"

"Only what we expected," Viola told her. "He gave me until nightfall to leave."

"We will be ready long before then," Hannah said grimly. "He *knows*, I suppose. That duke told him?"

"Yes." Viola sat down on the dressing table stool, her back to the mirror. "But we are not leaving after all, Hannah. Not now or ever."

"Is there any point, Miss Vi?" her maid asked. "You read me that paper last night. There is no court in the land that will believe you."

"We are not leaving," Viola said. "I am going to win Pinewood from him. I have a week to do it."

"How?" Hannah straightened up from the half-packed trunk, her expression suddenly suspicious. "*How*, lovey? You are not going back to work?"

"I have talked him into a wager," Viola said. "One I intend to win. Never mind about the details, Hannah. Put my clothes back in the wardrobe. They will get creased in the trunk. And have the trunk put away in the attic again. We are staying."

"Miss Vi—"

"No, Hannah." Viola looked at her with set jaw and hard eyes. "No! This is where I belong. This is where he wanted me to be. I *will* not give in just because there has been some fraud. Lord Ferdinand Dudley has made a wager with me, and he will abide by its terms. That at least I can be sure of. He is a gentleman, you see—almost to a fault. It is a wager I will not lose."

Hannah came and stood in front of her, her head tipped to one side. "I don't think I want to know exactly what you are up to," she said, "but I do know you need to lie down for an hour or so. You are as white as any ghost. Turn around and I will brush out your hair for you."

That had always been Hannah's solution to any problem. Viola could not remember a time when her former nurse had not soothed her by brushing her hair. She turned on the stool and felt Hannah's capable hands unpinning and then unraveling her braids.

Just yesterday, Viola thought, closing her eyes, she had run down the hill into his arms, and he had twirled her about and kissed her with a fierce passion to match her own. Today he had called her a whore and ordered her to get out of Pinewood.

Tomorrow or the next day or the next she was going to entice him into bed and pleasure him there with the cold sensual arts she had learned and practiced to perfection.

She was going to do those things with Lord Ferdinand Dudley. *To* him.

One more time.

And then she was going to have to live with herself for the rest of her life. At Pinewood. It would be hers—indisputably and forever.

But would there be any dreams left to dream?

12

DURING THE NEXT TWO DAYS FERDINAND BEgan to think that perhaps the week would pass faster and more painlessly than he had expected after agreeing to that mad wager. Perhaps she had come to regret it herself. Certainly if she intended to win it, she was going a strange way about it. He scarcely saw her.

He had a dinner engagement the first evening. It was only when he returned that he learned she had been out too, and still was. He went to bed, taking a book up with him. He heard her walk past his room an hour or so later. Her footsteps did not slow outside his door.

He saw her briefly at breakfast the following morning. She was finishing her meal as he entered the dining room after an early ride. She was looking her usual neat, wholesome self. She would be gone most of the day, she informed him. It was her regular day for visiting the sick and elderly. It struck him that it was not the way one would expect Lilian Talbot to spend her time, but he was happy enough that she would not be going to the school to help out. He had already promised that he would go there himself to give another lesson to Jamie, the would-be Latin scholar.

He intended to call on the boy's father afterward to see what could be arranged for the boy's future education. Jamie needed to be at a good boarding school. Ferdinand was quite willing to finance the whole venture himself, but he had a parent's pride to deal with. He would have to talk of scholarships, Ferdinand thought, rather than financial assistance.

"Will you be attending the assembly tomorrow evening?" Viola Thornhill asked before she left.

There was to be a dance at the assembly rooms above the inn. He had heard about it wherever he went. He certainly planned to attend. It was important to him to be an active participant in village life.

"Yes, indeed," he said. "You may ride in my carriage with me."

"Thank you." She smiled. "But I will be dining at Crossings and will go to the assembly with the Claypoles."

The Claypoles, he thought, would have a heart seizure apiece if they knew the truth about her.

He did not see her again for the rest of the day. He dined at home, but she did not. He went to choir practice at the church, but she did not. He learned when he returned home that she had been delayed at the cottage of one of the laborers, helping to care for five young children while their mother delivered a sixth.

She was going to be missed when she left Pinewood, Ferdinand knew. His neighbors treated him politely. A few had even warmed to him. But he sensed that most of them still resented the fact that he had come to turn their Miss Thornhill away.

This time he did not hear her come home. He fell asleep with his book open and his candle still alight. She had returned at four o'clock in the morning, he learned at breakfast—from which meal she was absent.

When he came back to the house after a session with Paxton, she had already left for the school.

He did see her during the afternoon, when the ladies'

sewing circle gathered in the drawing room again. She was sitting demurely sewing when he went in there, shamelessly to charm the ladies and to read them another few chapters of *Pride and Prejudice.* Viola Thornhill stitched on through it all, just as if he were not there, her neck arched delicately over her embroidery frame. The sunlight pouring through the windows picked gold and auburn highlights out of the predominantly dark red braids of her hair. She was wearing one of her simple, pretty muslins.

If Tresham had not said it, he thought, he would be doubting the evidence of his own eyes now. How could she be the same woman as that voluptuous courtesan in Gnass's box, with her haughty, contemptuous half smile? Or the same woman who had forced a wager on him two days ago?

He dined alone before proceeding to the assembly. She had gone off with the Claypole ladies. Five more days after this one was over, he thought. Then he would be free. She would be gone, and he would never see her again.

Five more days.

But the thought did not cheer him nearly as much as it ought.

DURING HER WORKING YEARS, men—titled, wealthy, powerful, influential men—had pursued Lilian Talbot relentlessly. Viola Thornhill had no idea how to entice a man who was determined not to have her. It was not that Lord Ferdinand did not want her. She knew he did. He had kissed her on four separate occasions. On the night he had broken the urn, he had come very close to going beyond mere kisses. No, it was not lack of desire that would make him difficult to seduce. It was his love of a wager, his determination to win it at all costs.

She could use none of her more obvious seductive arts on him. They just would not work. He would resist them. The best way to proceed, she had decided that very first day, was to convince him that she was not proceeding at all. It would be best to confuse him with the illusion that she was Viola Thornhill, that Lilian Talbot was indeed dead and gone. It would be best to tease him with only the occasional glimpse of her when he must expect to be bombarded with her company and full-blown sexual allure.

She would win the wager. She was determined to do so. Her resolve strengthened after she received a letter from Maria, telling her how much Ben was enjoying school, how much he wanted to work hard and become a lawyer when he grew up, how very kind it was of Uncle Wesley to pay his school fees.

There would be no more money to send. Pinewood's income was now Lord Ferdinand Dudley's. The little money Viola had brought with her to Pinewood had gone into the estate and to her family. What the estate had earned in two years had gone back into further improvements—and to her family. Uncle Wesley would continue to care for them, of course. They would not be destitute. But Ben would have to leave school, and there would be very little money for all the extras that added comfort to life.

There would be no more money to send unless she won her wager. She was determined to win it.

She dined at Crossings the evening of the assembly. Mr. Claypole took her aside before they left for the village and proposed marriage to her yet again. For a moment she was tempted, as she never had been before. But only for a moment. Marrying Thomas Claypole would not really solve her problems. She would live in comfort and security as his wife, but she could not expect him to pay for Ben's schooling or to help support her family. Besides, he did not know the truth about her, and she would not so deceive him as to marry him.

She refused his offer.

Soon she was in the carriage with the Claypoles, on the way to the assembly. Lord Ferdinand Dudley would be there, she thought. She would see him for a few hours at a stretch.

She wished—oh, she wished, wished, *wished* she had not been forced to make that wager with him. But there was no other way.

THE VILLAGE ASSEMBLIES WERE always jolly affairs. All the sets here were country dances, performed in circles or lines, some slow and stately, others fast and vigorous, all with precise, intricate patterns, which everyone knew from long practice.

Ferdinand danced every set. So did Viola Thornhill. He talked and laughed with his neighbors between sets. So did she. He ate supper in company with a group of people who had invited him to take a seat at their table. So did she.

They scarcely looked at each other. He was aware of almost no one else. They did not exchange a word. Yet he heard her low, musical voice and her laughter even when the whole room separated them. They did not share a table, yet he knew that she ate only one-half of a buttered scone and drank only one cup of tea. He did not ask her to dance, yet he noticed the light, graceful way in which she performed the steps and pictured her with a maypole ribbon in one hand.

This time next week she would be gone. The next time there was an assembly he would be able to concentrate the whole of his attention on the pretty girls with whom he danced. He hated this constant awareness, this constant alertness for the move she must surely make soon if she hoped to have any chance at all to win her wager before time ran out. He wished fervently that she had assaulted him with all her tricks on that very first day. He had been angry enough then to resist her with ease.

He was talking with the Reverend Prewitt and Miss Faith Merrywether when Viola touched his arm. He looked down and was somewhat surprised to see that her fingers had not burned a hole through the sleeve of his evening coat. He looked into her face, flushed from the exertions of dancing.

"My lord," she said, "Mr. Claypole has had to take his mother home early. The heat has made her feel faint."

"Mrs. Claypole does not have a strong constitution," Miss Merrywether commented disapprovingly. "She is fortunate indeed to have such a doting son."

But Viola Thornhill had not removed her eyes from Ferdinand's. "They were to escort me home," she said. "But Mr. Claypole thought it wise not to take such a wide detour on his way to Crossings."

"I would be delighted to call out my carriage for your convenience, Miss Thornhill," the vicar assured her. "But I daresay his lordship will squeeze you into his."

She looked mortified and smiled apologetically. "Will you?"

Ferdinand bowed. "It would be my pleasure, ma'am," he said.

"Not just yet, though," she said. "I would not drag you away early from the dancing. There is still one more set. I was to dance it with Mr. Claypole."

"I would lead you out myself," the Reverend Prewitt said with a hearty laugh, "if I had any breath and any legs left, but I confess I have neither. His lordship will see to it that you are not a wallflower, Miss Thornhill. Will you not, my lord?"

The color in her cheeks deepened. "Perhaps his lordship has another partner in mind," she said.

But there was that glow of color in her face, and her eyes were still sparkling from an evening of dancing. Her hair, dressed in curls tonight rather than the usual coronet of braids, was still tidy, but a few wavy tendrils of hair teased her neck and temples. There was a slight sheen of perspiration on her cheeks and on her bosom above the neckline of her evening gown.

I have been waiting for a suitable partner, sir. He could hear again the low, saucy words she had spoken to him when he had sought her out to dance about the maypole with him. *I have been waiting for you.*

"I was prepared to be a wallflower myself," he said, offering her his arm, "believing that your hand had already been engaged."

She set her hand on his sleeve and he led her onto the floor to join the long lines that were forming for the Roger de Coverly.

The dance consumed all their energy and concentration. There was no chance to talk, even had they wished to. But she glowed and laughed with delight when it was their turn to twirl between the lines and lead the procession around the outside to form an arch with their arms for everyone else to dance beneath. He could not take his eyes off her.

He was still more than halfway in love with her, he realized. How could he not be? What he should do on the way home was tell her to forget that outrageous wager. He should just marry her so that they could both remain at Pinewood. Forever after. Happily ever after.

But she had been Lilian Talbot. And the courtesan in her still survived—he had seen it for himself just two days ago.

He could not simply forget and pretend that she was Viola Thornhill as he had known her for the first week. She had deceived him.

A great heavy sadness seemed to lodge itself suddenly in the soles of his dancing shoes.

Fortunately, the music drew to an end within the next few minutes. Less fortunately, it was the final set. He was handing her into his carriage only minutes later. What did all the neighbors think of the situation at Pinewood? he wondered. He would not have to worry about it for much longer, though, would he?

Five more days.

VIOLA WAS BEGINNING TO hate herself. Or perhaps it would be more accurate to say that she was beginning to hate herself *again.* There had been two years of healing, but really, she had discovered in the past few days, the gaping wound of her self-loathing had only filmed over, not knitted into wholeness at all.

It was so easy to play a part, to send herself into deep hiding and become someone else. The trouble was that this time the part she played and her real self were so similar to each other that sometimes she got them confused. She was wearing down his defenses by playing the part of Viola Thornhill. But *she was Viola Thornhill.*

Mr. Claypole really had decided to take his mother home early, but he had wanted to escort Viola home on their way. She had refused by lying. She had told him it was all arranged for her to return to Pinewood in Lord Ferdinand Dudley's carriage.

She had wanted to dance with Lord Ferdinand. She had wanted to remind him of the evening at the fête. But acting had got all jumbled up with reality. She had enjoyed herself immensely and been hopelessly miserable at the same time.

She sat silently beside him until the carriage wheels had rumbled over the bridge.

"Do you ever feel lonely?" she asked him softly.

"Lonely?" The question seemed to surprise him. "No, I don't think so. Alone, sometimes, but that is not the same thing as loneliness. Aloneness can actually be pleasant."

"How?" she asked.

"One can read," he said.

It had surprised her to realize that he did enjoy reading. It seemed out of character somehow. But then, so did the fact that he had graduated from Oxford with a double first in Latin and Greek.

"What if there are no books?" she asked.

"Then one thinks," he said. "Actually, I have not done a great deal of that for many years. I have not been much alone either. I used to be when I lived at Acton. So was

Tresham. It used to be like an unspoken conspiracy sometimes—he would go off to his favorite hill and I would go to mine. It was furtive. Dudley males admitted only to being hellions, not to being thinkers, brooding on the mysteries of life and the universe."

"Is that what you did?" she asked.

"Actually, yes." He chuckled softly. "I used to read a great deal, though not openly when my father was at home. He did not approve of bookish sons. But the more I read, the more I realized how little I knew. I used to gaze out at the universe feeling all the frustration of my smallness—especially the smallness of my brain. And then I would gaze at a blade of grass and tell myself that if only I could understand *that,* then perhaps I could penetrate the larger mysteries too."

"Why have you not done that for many years?" she asked.

"I don't know." But he had obviously thought more deeply about her question before he spoke again. "I have been too busy being busy, perhaps. Or perhaps I realized when I was at university that I could never know everything and so gave up the attempt to know anything. Perhaps I have been in the wrong place. London is not conducive to thought—or wisdom."

The interior of the carriage became a little lighter as it moved clear of the trees. The conversation had not taken the course she had expected. More and more she was realizing that Lord Ferdinand Dudley was not at all the man she had taken him for when he first arrived at Pinewood. She wished she did not like him. Liking him was making things very difficult for her.

"What about you?" he asked. "Are you ever lonely?"

"No, of course not," she said. Why were people so reluctant to admit to loneliness? she wondered. It was almost as if it were something shameful.

"That was a hasty answer," he said. "Too hasty."

"Loneliness can be a balm to the soul," she said, "especially when one considers some of the alternatives. There are far worse afflictions than loneliness."

"Are there?" In the faint light she could see that his face was turned toward her.

"The worst thing about loneliness," she said, "is that it brings one face-to-face with oneself. That can also be the best thing about it, depending upon one's character. If one is strong, self-knowledge can be the best knowledge one can ever acquire."

"Are you strong?" His voice was soft.

She had thought she was. She really had thought so.

"Yes," she said.

"What have you learned about yourself?"

"That I am a survivor," she said.

The carriage rocked to a halt on its comfortable springs, and the door opened almost immediately. Lord Ferdinand's groom set down the steps.

Mr. Jarvey had waited up and took her cloak and Lord Ferdinand's cloak and hat when they stepped into the hall. He disappeared with the garments.

"Come into the library for a nightcap?" Lord Ferdinand asked her.

She could probably accomplish her goal tonight if she set her mind to it. They would share a drink and more conversation, and then he would escort her upstairs. She would pause outside his room and thank him for bringing her home. She would sway toward him so that he would be kissing her before he even had a chance to realize his danger. It would all be over within an hour after that. Tomorrow he would be gone. Pinewood would be hers.

She felt the soreness of unshed tears in her throat and chest and shook her head.

"I am tired," she said. "Thank you for bringing me home. Good night."

She did *not* sway toward him. Neither did she offer her hand. But there it was in his, and he was raising it to his lips, and his eyes were regarding her over the top of it, a faint smile softening their darkness.

"Thank you for the dance," he said. "But it is the maypole dance for which I will always remember you."

She fled, not even pausing to take a candle from the hall table. Had she done that deliberately? Caused him to kiss her hand and look at her like that and speak so softly about always remembering her? It was what she had set out to do. It was *exactly* what she had hoped to accomplish. But she had not really done it, had she? She had simply been herself.

Or had she been the Viola Thornhill who intended to throw him off guard sufficiently that he would not realize that when he bedded her he would be losing his wager to Lilian Talbot?

She no longer knew who was herself and who was the courtesan. She no longer knew whether she wanted to win that wager or not. She dreaded—*dreaded*—being in bed with him, feeling him coming inside her while she coaxed him to a pleasure so prolonged and so intense that he would never after feel cheated. How could Viola Thornhill hide deeply enough in the persona of Lilian Talbot to allow it to happen?

Viola Thornhill—the real Viola—wanted to join herself with him in love. It was something she had never experienced and could not really imagine experiencing. For the physical joining of man and woman was an ugly, demeaning act. But dreams were not quite dead after all, she was finding. And her dreams wove themselves about his person in a way that had nothing to do with any wager.

What she should do, Viola thought as she fled along the upper corridor in the darkness, was go back down to the library and announce to him that their wager was off, that she would leave Pinewood tomorrow. But she kept going until she was inside her room, the closed door firmly and safely between her and temptation.

13

FOR THE NEXT TWO DAYS VIOLA WENT ABOUT her daily round of activities with her usual energy and cheerful smile, but her mind and emotions were in turmoil. Perhaps, she thought sometimes, she should go away to somewhere other than London and seek employment. But Hannah and her family would have to fend for themselves, then. Why should she have to bear all the responsibility? But the thought of relinquishing her family to their own resources consumed her with guilt.

She could win Pinewood with her wager, and life would be back to normal again. But she could not bear the thought of seducing Lord Ferdinand—it nauseated her and filled her with self-loathing. He was a decent man.

But remaining at Pinewood was not just about money. It was her *home,* her legacy. She simply could not face leaving it.

On the third morning after the assembly, with two more days to go before she must either win her wager or leave Pinewood, matters were severely complicated by the arrival of another letter from Claire. It was lying on the desk in the library when Viola returned from a morning walk along the avenue. She snatched it up eagerly and took it with her to the box garden. She sat on the bench that surrounded the fountain, after checking to see that the seat was dry. It had rained all the day before, though the sun was shining again today.

Everyone was well, Claire reported. She was working every day for their uncle. She liked serving in the coffee room best, where she met and talked with travelers and a few local people who came there regularly. One gentleman in particular had begun to come quite often. He was extremely pleasant and always thanked her for her kind service and gave her a generous tip. She had not recognized him at first, not having seen him for many years, but Mama and Uncle Wesley had.

Viola clutched the single sheet of paper with both hands and suddenly felt her heart beat faster. She sensed what was coming even before her eyes confirmed her premonition.

"He is Mr. Kirby," Claire had written, "the gentleman who used to frequent the inn when you worked here and then was obliging enough to recommend you for a governess's position with his friends. Mama and Uncle Wesley are delighted to see him again."

Viola clenched her eyes tightly closed. Daniel Kirby. Oh, dear God, what was he doing back at her uncle's inn? She opened her eyes and read on.

"He has asked about you," the letter continued. "He had heard you had left your position, though he did not know you are now living in the country. He gave me a message for you yesterday. Let me see, now. I want to get it just right. He had me repeat it after him. He said that he hopes that you will come back to town for a visit soon. He has discovered another paper that he is certain would be of interest to you. He said you would know what he meant. He also said that if you were not interested in seeing it, then he would show it to me instead. Was that not a provoking thing to say, for now of course I long to know what is in that paper. But he would not tell me no matter how much I pleaded. He would only laugh and tease me. But you see, dear Viola, we are not the only ones who long to see you again. . . ."

Viola stopped reading.

Another paper. Oh, yes, indeed, she knew what he meant. He had "discovered" another bill to be paid, even though he had sworn in writing that he had produced them all, that they had all been settled. They were her stepfather's numerous unpaid bills, most of them gaming vouchers, which Mr. Kirby had purchased after his death.

He had become a regular customer at the White Horse Inn after Viola's family moved there. He had been very amiable, very kind, very generous. And then one day he had told Viola he could help her to find more interesting employment than she had. He had friends, new to town, who needed a governess for their four children. They preferred to choose someone from a personal recommendation than go to an agency or put an advertisement in the papers. He would arrange for an interview if she wished.

If she wished. She had been ecstatic. So had her mother. And Uncle Wesley had raised no objection. Although he would be losing help at the inn, it pleased him that his niece would be in employment more suited to her birth and education.

She had gone to the interview, escorted by Mr. Kirby. And she had found herself in a dingy house in a shabby part of London, confronting a woman whose orange hair and painted face had made her look frighteningly grotesque. Sally Duke would train her for her new profession, Mr. Kirby had explained—and he had made no bones about what that profession was to be. Viola had flatly refused to proceed, of course. She could remember now the terror she had felt, the fear that she was a prisoner and would not be allowed to go free. But Mr. Kirby had assured her in his usual kindly manner that she was free to leave whenever she wished, but that her mother and her young sisters and brother faced long incarceration in debtors' prison if they were unable to pay off all their debts. He named the total to her, and she had felt all the blood draining downward until her head was cold and her ears were ringing and the room began to spin about her.

She had been nineteen years old. She had a mother who was in a state of nervous and physical collapse after the death of her husband. Claire had been nine years old, the twins six. Uncle Wesley had already paid off a few debts, which seemed trifling in comparison with these—there was no way he could pay them. And Mr. Kirby, of course, knew it. Viola had been able to see no way out but compliance with his demands.

The arrangement had been that eighty percent of all she earned was to go toward the reduction of the debt. She was to live on the remaining twenty percent. It behooved her, then, to work hard, to establish a reputation for herself, so that her twenty percent would enable her to keep body and soul together.

Later, when she was already working, she had been informed that only twenty of Mr. Kirby's eighty percent could be applied to debt reduction. The remaining sixty paid Mr. Kirby's fee for housing her, procuring clients for her, and looking after her best interests. To all intents and purposes, Viola had been a slave. But she had used the little power she had to insist upon working no more than one night a month and to refuse to be any man's exclusive mistress. She had quickly become more sought after than any other courtesan in London.

By some strange miracle, she had kept the secret from all of her family. Only to Hannah had she rashly poured out her heart as soon as she knew the truth of what her future held. Hannah had insisted upon going with her even though Mama had warned that a governess would not be allowed to have her own personal maid. Her family still believed she had been a governess for four years before coming to Pinewood. Her mother had been furious with her for leaving such respectable employment in order to accept the gift.

The debts had not been significantly reduced in four years. The interest had eaten up the bulk of her payments. She had known Mr. Kirby would hold her in thrall for the rest of her working years, but she had not been able to think of a solution. It had seemed that she was caught in a lifelong trap. But then she had met the Earl of Bamber. And he had discovered the truth—she had poured her heart out to him one night, seated beside him on the plush sofa in her living room, his arm securely about her shoulders, her head nestled on his shoulder. She had told him everything she had kept bottled inside for four long years, and he had kissed her cheek and told her she was a good girl and he loved her.

A good girl. Love.

The words had been like a spring of pure water in the middle of a desert. Balm to an aching soul.

He loved her. She was loved. She was a good girl. She was three-and-twenty years old and a veteran at her profession. But she was a good girl and she was loved. He loved her.

He had called on Daniel Kirby and persuaded him to produce all the bills still owing. He had paid them all off and obtained a signed, witnessed note that there were no more. And then he had asked Viola if she would like to go to Pinewood Manor to live. It was a long way away, in the middle of nowhere, to use his own words, and as far as he knew it was probably shabby. Certainly it did not fill his coffers with income. But he would send her there if she wished, and he would send a good steward down to get everything sorted out for her, and a good butler to set the house to rights and hire other servants. The manor would be hers. He would leave it to her in his will.

She had buried her face in the hollow between his shoulder and neck and wrapped her arm about his portly middle. She had felt safe and loved and strangely clean for the first time in four years.

"Oh, yes," she had said. "Oh, yes, please. But I don't want to leave you." She had known he was gravely ill.

He had patted one large hand against the side of her face and kissed her temple. "I will be going home to the country to die," he had said gently. "My wife is there."

Grief and love and gratitude and happiness had soaked his cravat and neckcloth with a flood of tears.

The sound of booted feet on stone brought Viola back to the present with a jolt. She was sitting on the bench in the box garden at Pinewood, Claire's letter clutched in both her hands. Lord Ferdinand was striding toward the house from the direction of the stables. He always looked his most enticing in riding clothes, she thought. He paused for a moment, seeing her, and touched the brim of his hat with his whip. She half raised one hand in greeting. He did not come down the steps to join her but continued on his way into the house. She breathed a deep sigh of relief.

Claire was in terrible danger. The meaning of the message was very clear. Daniel Kirby wanted Viola to return. Although she was twenty-five years old, rather aged for a courtesan, she had retired at the height of her fame. She would still be remembered. There would surely be a rush of prospective clients, at least for a while, if word spread that she had returned to town—and Mr. Kirby would see to it that that happened. She could earn far more money for him, at least for a year or two, than Claire could do as a raw novice, who might never take as well as her sister even after training.

Viola swallowed once, and then again. For a minute or two she had to concentrate very hard not to vomit. The very thought of Claire . . .

If she did not return, he would use Claire. That was the threat he held over her head. He had kept back at least one of the bills. She was going to have to pay it off by going back to work.

Unless she owned Pinewood.

It was prospering. It was true that she had planned to put most of the profits back into improvements. It would be many years—if ever—before she could consider herself a wealthy woman. But the profits did not *have* to be reinvested. They were hers, to be spent as she wished. She could make payments on the debt. They would be endless payments, of course, but there was little she could do about that. She could . . .

But Pinewood was not hers. It was Lord Ferdinand's.

Unless . . .

Viola closed her eyes and crumpled the letter in her hand.

Yes, *unless.*

FERDINAND WOULD HAVE DINED at the Boar's Head except that he had been told that Viola Thornhill was to spend the evening with the Misses Merrywether. He was counting down the days. There were two to go. He was stubborn to a fault. He knew that. He had made a decision, but even so he was going to torture himself for two more days with brief glimpses of her—like this morning in the box garden—and short encounters with her. He wanted her with every beat of his pulse, but he was determined to win his wager, to be able to throw that, at least, in her teeth.

She was being very foolish, of course. There had been no glimpse of Lilian Talbot since the day of their wager. Only of Viola Thornhill. How could she hope to seduce him like this?

He dressed for dinner even though he would be dining alone—it was the habit of a lifetime. He was humming as he entered the dining room, but he stopped abruptly. She was standing by the sideboard, talking with Jarvey, and there were two places set at the table. She was wearing a gold silk gown without any jewelry or other adornment. The garment itself was of such simple design that Ferdinand knew at a glance that it was very costly indeed. It shimmered over her curves in a way that would have made further adornment quite redundant. Her hair was a smooth, shining, dark red cap over her head. Her braids were coiled at the back, low on her neck. She was beauty and elegance personified.

Ferdinand checked his stride. For a moment he misplaced the rhythm of his breathing. She smiled, and he was not at all sure whether she was Viola Thornhill or Lilian Talbot. He suspected that she was wearing one of the latter's gowns. But it was a sweet smile.

"I thought you were dining with the Misses Merrywether," he said.

"No."

There was nothing for it, then, but to seat her at the table, take his own place, and make the best of the situation. They conversed politely on a number of topics. She told him how she had started the ladies' sewing group as a social outlet for the women of the neighborhood and observed with a smile that even when they were being sociable, women liked to be useful too. He told her about Tattersall's and the horse auctions that were held there every week.

They talked about the weather.

She told him how the river walk had been so overgrown when she first came to Pinewood that she had thought the area was mere wilderness. When she had discovered that there was a well-defined path there, she had set the gardeners to work and had even sent some of the farm laborers to help them. He told her about Oxford and the delight he had taken in the libraries there and the conversation of men who were unashamedly intellectual.

"It is a wonder," she said, "you did not stay there and become a lecturer or a professor or don."

"No." He laughed. "By the time I had finished my studies, I was vowing never to open another book in my life. I wanted to *live*."

They talked about the weather.

She told him that her one real extravagance since coming to Somersetshire had been buying books. She sent to London and Bath for them. Several of the books in the library had been added during the past two years, including the copy of *Pride and Prejudice* from which he was reading to the ladies. He talked about the book, and they embarked on a brief but spirited discussion of its merits.

They talked about the weather.

When she rose at the end of the meal and announced that she would leave him to his port, he breathed a silent sigh of relief. It was over for another day. She was incredibly beautiful. She was also charming and intelligent and an interesting companion. It was easy to relax into the pleasure of her company and forget that after two more days he would never see her again.

He found it a rather depressing thought.

He left the dining room a mere ten minutes later, not having drunk any port, and made his way to the library. But Jarvey intercepted him.

"I have carried a tea tray up to the drawing room, my lord," he said, "at Miss Thornhill's request."

Did she expect him to join her there? But it would be churlish of him not to.

"She asked me to inform you," the butler added.

She was pouring a cup of tea for herself when he entered the room. She looked up, smiled, and poured another for him.

"You did not stay long," she said.

She took her own cup and saucer and sat down to one side of the fireplace. She had had the fire lit, he saw, even though it was not a cold night. But it was almost dark outside and the candles were lit. The fire added coziness to the room. He took the chair at the other side of the hearth.

She did not speak. She was drinking and gazing rather dreamily into the flames. She looked relaxed and elegant at the same time.

"Why did you become a courtesan?" he asked, and could have bitten out his tongue as soon as the words were spoken.

She transferred her gaze to his face and her expression changed so slowly and so subtly that for a while he was unaware of it. He was aware only of acute discomfort.

"Why else does one work?" she asked him. "For money, of course."

He had been pondering the question a great deal during the past few days. He had never thought much about whores and their motivation. But when he *did* think about them, he concluded that they must enter their profession for one of two reasons—love or money. Which had it been for her? She had answered the question. But she had been London's leading courtesan for a long time, and she had charged a fortune for a fee. Surely after the first year or so she had not needed to continue to work for money. She must have made enough on which to retire quite comfortably.

"Why did you need the money?" he asked.

Her smile, he realized suddenly, was not Viola Thornhill's. "Asked like a true son of the aristocracy," she said. "I had to eat, my lord. Food is necessary to survival. Had you not realized that?"

"But you must have made a fortune," he said.

"Yes," she agreed. "Yes, I did."

"Did you *enjoy* it? Your profession, I mean?" He understood now that he was talking to Lilian Talbot—the amusement in her eyes was faintly mocking. Her voice had become lower pitched, more velvet in tone.

She laughed softly and began to run one finger lightly along the neckline of her gown, beginning at one shoulder. "Everyone, male and female, hungers for sex," she said. "Is it not a dream profession to work and earn one's living doing what one most enjoys? It is far preferable to making up beds and emptying chamber pots for a pittance."

He was slightly shocked. He had never heard a lady use the word *sex* or speak openly about sexual hunger.

"But with so many different men?" He frowned.

"But that is part of the allure," she told him. "It is said, you know, that no two men are identical, that each has unique gifts. I can vouch for the truth of that."

Her finger had paused at the slight shadow indicating the valley between her breasts. She hooked the fingertip down inside the fabric of her dress. He felt an uncomfortable tightening in his groin.

"And it was the challenge of my profession," she said, "to satisfy the individual needs of each client. To give so much pleasure that each man would plead for more. And never forget me."

Who had started this? he wondered, leaning farther back in his chair as if to put more distance between himself and her. And why the devil had the fire been lit on such a warm night?

She seemed to be having the identical thought. "It is very warm in here, is it not?" she asked, and she reached down a little farther into her décolletage to pull the silk of her bodice away from her flesh before returning it and sliding the finger up inside the bodice to her shoulder again.

He was mesmerized by the sight of that long finger. When he looked up into her eyes, they laughed knowingly at him.

"I should have had my maid dress my hair up off my neck," she said, raising both arms and sliding her fingers beneath the coiled braids there. She closed her eyes briefly and tipped back her head. And then he realized that her fingers were working at the braids, her movements quite unhurried. She drew out pins and set them down neatly on the table beside her. The braids uncoiled and then fell, two of them, down her back. She drew one over her shoulder and unraveled it. Thick, wavy hair spread over her bosom and down to her waist as she drew the second braid over her other shoulder and unraveled that too. She shook her head when the task was completed, and her hair fell about her in luxurious, disordered waves.

Ferdinand's mouth was dry. He had not taken his eyes from her. Neither of them had spoken a word for several minutes.

"That is better," she said, looking across at him with heavy-lidded eyes. The sharp, mocking look had gone. "Are you overwarm too? Why do you not remove your neckcloth? I will not mind. There are just the two of us. I have told Mr. Jarvey that we do not wish to be disturbed."

He was not so dazzled that he did not know exactly what was happening. She had decided that tonight was the night, and she had gone into action. She intended to bed him within the next hour and banish him tomorrow. For all the heavy sensuality of her eyes, he could not miss noticing their essential emptiness. She was working. This was business to her. And she was an experienced worker.

But very, very good. Every bit as good as she had promised. She had not even touched him yet. She was sitting several feet away from him. She was fully clothed; so was he. But he was wearing silk evening breeches. It would have been foolish to try to disguise his arousal. How would he do it? Grab a pillow and set it on his lap? He made no such attempt. Her eyes had not dipped, but he felt no doubt at all that she knew very well what effect her voice and actions would have on any red-blooded male.

He might have fought her. He might have jumped to his feet, fully aroused though he was, and walked from the room. He had always had good control over his sexual urges. But it was perhaps part of her skill, he thought as he reached up and unknotted and removed his neckcloth, that she could seduce even a man who knew he was being seduced and had sworn it could not happen.

The point was that perhaps it would be better this way. He had decided that he was going to give her Pinewood, that he was going to walk away from it, figuratively as well as literally, and buy himself property elsewhere. He would give her what was rightfully hers—the old earl should never have promised and broken his promise. A gentleman just did not act that way. The trouble was, she might spurn the gift from him. There was no predicting her reaction when he told her.

Perhaps he should simply let her win her wager.

And he wanted her. Desire had become indistinguishable from pain. His erection pressed against the tight, confining fabric of his breeches.

"Open your shirt at the neck," she said, leaning back in her chair and laying her head against its rest so that it looked in the candlelight as if she were already laid back against pillows, her hair spread in a dark red cloud of waves about her. "You will feel cooler."

He doubted it, but he did as she suggested and ran one hand inside his shirt. His chest was damp. She was watching him and moistening her lips, the tip of her tongue moving slowly across her upper lip.

"Has anyone told you how beautiful you are?" she asked him.

No one had. He was deeply embarrassed. What man would enjoy being called beautiful? At the same time, it felt as if Jarvey must have crept in invisibly and built the fire halfway up the chimney.

"You *are*, you know," she said. "Incredibly beautiful. Even with your clothes on."

He shot out of his chair then and closed the distance between them in a few strides. He held out a hand for hers, and she placed her own in it and allowed him to draw her to her feet and straight into his arms.

"Witch!" he said, before fastening his open mouth to hers.

But she drew back her head and set her two forefingers against his lips.

"You are impatient," she said. "I wanted to make love to you with words for an hour or longer, but I cannot do that when you are touching me. Do you not like making love with words?"

"I think we had better go to bed," he said. "I want

action, not words. I am conceding defeat, you see. You win. I will pay dearly for you. Pinewood in exchange for one night in bed with you. You have promised that I will never regret it. Live up to your promise, then."

He tried to kiss her again, but she cupped his face with both hands, holding it away from her, and gazed into his eyes. An extraordinary thing happened then. Lilian Talbot gradually dissolved into Viola Thornhill. He tried to draw her closer again. He was desperate for her. But she broke from his grasp and turned to run with stumbling steps toward the door.

"Viola—" he called.

But she was through it and gone before he could say any more.

14

VIOLA DID NOT STOP RUNNING UNTIL SHE WAS inside her bedchamber, the closed door against her back.

She could have won the wager within the hour. Indeed, he had already conceded defeat.

She had just not been able to do it.

She did not understand why. He was merely one more man; it was merely one more night of work.

She had not been able to do it.

She pushed herself away from the door and moved toward her dressing room, peeling off her gold silk gown as she went. She reached for her nightgown, but her hand stilled before she touched it. She could not bear to lie down here, to try to sleep, knowing that in time he would come up to his own room, not far from hers. She dressed quickly in one of her day dresses. She drew a warm cloak about her shoulders and as an afterthought pulled down the blanket that was always kept folded on top of the wardrobe.

The hard part was leaving her room again. She set her ear to the edge of the door and listened. There was no sound. She opened the door a crack and peeped out. Nothing and no one. She darted along the corridor, her heart thumping, ready to run back to her room if she should see him on the stairs. But they were deserted and she ran down, pausing when she reached the drawing room floor and gazing warily at the closed door. It remained shut. She darted down to the hall, which was mercifully deserted, slid back the bolts on the front doors as quickly and quietly as she could, and slipped outside. She pulled the door closed slowly, trying not to make a sound.

A minute later, she was half running along the terrace and down the sloping lawn until the trees that shaded the river walk hid her from view. Then she slowed. She had to. The moonlight did not penetrate here and she had to find her way to the path by touch and memory. Even the path itself was dark—almost frighteningly so. But she made her way along it, telling herself that ghosts and goblins were preferable to the inside of Pinewood Manor tonight. Soon enough she had walked past the trees and there was light by which to see where she was going. It was even sparkling on the surface of the river.

She sat down in the exact spot where she had made a daisy chain a week or ten years ago. It was not a chilly night, but she wrapped both her cloak and the blanket about her—she was shivering. She hit the black depths of despair as she sat. There was no glimmering of hope left. She drew her knees up, wrapped her arms about them, and rested her forehead on them.

The fight had gone out of her and she did not know how she would ever find the energy to get up from where she was. But it would not take a great deal of energy, she thought fleetingly, to move the few feet from where she was to the riverbank. The water was deep and fast-flowing. All she would have to do . . .

But even escape into oblivion was not an option. If she died, Claire would have to take her place. . . .

A twig snapped and her head shot up from her knees.

"Don't be alarmed," a voice said. "It's just me."

She would have preferred the ghosts and goblins. *Far* preferred.

"Go away," she said wearily, returning her forehead to her knees.

He did not answer her. Neither did he go away. She sensed rather than heard him sitting on the bank beside her.

"How did you know I was here?" she asked.

"I saw you," he said, "from the drawing room window."

And he had pursued her, his lust unsatisfied. But he was all out of luck. Lilian Talbot was dead. Oh, she would have to be resurrected soon enough, but not tonight. Not here. And never with him.

She sat in silence. So did he. He would go away eventually, she thought, and she would be left to concentrate on her despair. It frightened her. Even at her darkest moments, she had never been much given to self-pity.

And then every muscle in her body tensed. His hand had come to rest on her head, his touch so light that for a moment she was not sure that her senses were not playing tricks on her. But then she felt his fingertips, feather-light, massaging her scalp through her hair.

"Shhh," he said, though she had not spoken a word.

She dared not move. She did not *want* to move. His touch felt so very good, so very soothing. She had always been the pleasure giver. None of her clients had ever considered her pleasure. Why should they? Besides, personal gratification had always been the farthest thing from her mind while she had been at work. She let go of despair and accepted the brief gift of the present moment. She was relaxed in every muscle when his hand lifted and brushed her hair over to the side farthest from him. Then his lips were against the back of her neck, warm, soft, light. She should have felt threatened—he had also moved closer to her side—but instead she felt immeasurably comforted.

"I am Viola Thornhill," she said without lifting her head. She had not intended to speak. But it was as well that he know, just in case he had come with any idea of resuming what she had abandoned in the drawing room.

"Yes." His voice was a whisper of sound against her ear. "Yes, I know that, Viola."

The sudden yearning she felt was as piercing, as painful as the despair that had preceded it. She lifted her head and turned her face to him. He was only inches away. She could not see his expression in the darkness.

"I know," he said again, and then his mouth was on hers.

She hugged her knees and allowed the kiss. She did not participate except to relax her lips and teeth. She stood back mentally and emotionally, rather as she had done the night of the fête, except for different reasons, to observe. And to take the kiss to herself as a gift. She felt gifted.

He was not fierce and impatient, as he had been earlier in the drawing room. He kissed her slowly and with infinite gentleness, his mouth open, warm, and moist, his tongue tracing the line of her lips and then penetrating slowly, exploring, touching, teasing, sending darting spirals of sensation down into her throat and even into her breasts. One of his hands cupped the side of her face and then smoothed the hair back from her temple.

She had little previous experience with gentleness. She was helpless against it.

"Viola," he whispered when he finally drew back his head.

"Yes."

A question had been asked and answered. But she was no longer outside herself, observing. She had spoken the one word from a deep inner need—for someone gentle and tender, for someone who asked the question with her name, for someone who did not demand that she perform for him.

He touched her then, drawing her upward until they were both on their knees, facing each other. He unbuttoned her cloak and let it fall. She lifted both arms as he drew her dress off over her head. He did not immediately remove her shift too. He set his hands on either side of her waist—they were trembling, she noticed—and lowered his head to kiss her beneath one ear, at the base of her throat, on the rise of one breast. When his mouth closed over the nipple and suckled her, she tipped back her head, closed her eyes, and buried her fingers in his hair.

And then she lifted her arms again while he removed her shift.

She was almost a total stranger to physical desire. She felt it now in the almost painful tightening of her breasts and in the raw, pulsing ache in her womb and down between her thighs. She was pressed to him from her waist to her knees, and through the thin silk of his knee breeches she could feel again the hard bulk of his erection.

She would do nothing except surrender. She knew exactly what to do to bring him crashing to pleasure, but she would do nothing. She was Viola Thornhill tonight, not that other woman. But she did not know what to do with her own desire.

Please. Please, please.

"Please."

He had been suckling her other breast, but he lifted his head at the sound of her voice and gazed into her eyes.

"Yes," he whispered. "Let me spread your cloak on the grass. And roll my coat for a pillow."

He was taking it off as he spoke. He arranged their bed while she knelt and watched, and then stood to undress while she lay down and waited for him. He was even more beautiful without his clothes, she saw as first his waistcoat and shirt and then his stockings and breeches came off. But she said nothing and made no move to touch him. She rested her hands palm-down on either side of her naked body. He removed his underdrawers and knelt down beside her. He was large. She could see that even in the near-darkness. A pulse throbbed between her legs. She did not want to wait any longer. She willed him not to want any more foreplay.

"Viola." He leaned over her and spoke against her lips. "I want to be inside you. Now."

"Yes." She spread her legs on the cloak as he came over her. He settled between them and on top of her. He was heavy. His weight was almost robbing her of breath. The ground was hard against her back. She had never before done this anywhere except on a bed, but she was glad the whole experience was to be different. She was glad the ground was hard. She was glad there were stars above. She was glad she could hear the sound of rushing water.

He slid his hands beneath her, and she raised her knees and braced her feet on the ground. He came into her with one deep, hard thrust. He held very still in her for a few moments before sliding his hands away and lifting some of his weight onto his forearms. He looked down into her eyes and touched his mouth to hers.

She was aching and throbbing from her thighs up to her throat. She wanted to wrap her legs about his, tighten her inner muscles about his hardness, and spread her hands against his back so that she could arch upward and touch his chest with her hardened nipples. But she lay still and relaxed.

"Tell me it feels good," he whispered.

"It feels good."

"I want to go now," he said, his voice tense and breathless. "I *must* go. But I want it to be good for you."

"It will be good." She lifted her hands from the cloak and spread them lightly over his buttocks. "It *is* good."

He came hard and fast then. It was over within moments. But it did not matter. Her pain reached a point beyond which it could not be borne. She cried out and the stars above her shattered into a million shards of light. At the same moment she heard him call out his own release.

The sense of peace and well-being that followed negated any discomfort the hard ground at her back and his full relaxed weight might have brought. She listened to the water flowing past the bank and watched the stars re-form themselves above her head and hugged the moment to herself with all her will.

He inhaled deeply and released the breath on a sigh before rolling to one side of her. She thought it was over, but he reached for the blanket, pulled it over them, and drew her against him, one arm pillowing her head. She breathed in the scents of cologne and sweat and man and relaxed. His body was warm and damp against hers. She thought she might sleep if she just concentrated upon the moment and did not allow her thoughts to drift to tomorrow or any more distant future. *The present moment is, after all, the only moment we ever have,* she thought.

She was at the point of dozing when one reality of what had just happened struck her with absolute certainty.

He had been a virgin.

FERDINAND DID NOT SLEEP. He had been a dismal failure, he thought. If he had timed himself—he had not done so, thank God—he would surely have discovered the humiliating truth that the whole thing had been over within one minute. Less than a minute from mount to release. He felt mortified indeed. He just had not fully imagined what it would be like to feel her soft, wet heat sheathing him. He had thought he knew, but his expectations had fallen lamentably short of reality.

He had wanted to be gentle with her. He had wanted her to feel that he was doing something for her, not just for his own pleasure. He had wanted her to feel less like a whore and more like a woman.

Instead he had gone off half-cocked, like a damned schoolboy.

She had burrowed her head into the hollow between his neck and shoulder and appeared to be sleeping, which was at least a promising sign. He kissed the top of her head and twined his free hand into the luxurious thickness of her hair.

There was a certain feeling of relief despite his embarrassment. He was twenty-seven years old. He had known when he was still a boy that he could never marry, since there was no such thing as marital fidelity among his own class. The idea of marital infidelity had always sickened him. But it was only when he was older—when he was at university, in fact—that he had learned to his alarm that while he had perfectly healthy sexual urges, he could not satisfy them with a whore. He had tried a few times. He had gone to brothels with his friends and ended up paying the girl of his choice on each occasion for nothing more than her time. The thought of the physical act without any emotional component had chilled him. The thought of doing it with a whore, who knew no sentiment at all, gave him the shudders.

He had begun to think there must be something wrong with him. At least now he knew he could do it. In under one minute—he grimaced. He had probably broken some record, for God's sake.

He wished he could have made it better for her. She had needed comforting, and he had offered comfort. It had been more than just sex. Yes, he was sure it had.

"Mmmm," she said on a long sigh as she moved and stretched against him.

He felt the stirrings of renewed desire and smiled when she tipped back her head to look up at him, the moonlight on her face.

"Viola."

"Yes."

He half expected her to berate him with his inadequacy as a lover, but she looked almost happy. He could feel himself growing hard again. She must feel it too—her body was against his—but she did not draw away. He wanted to be inside her again, to feel that feeling again, to see if he could make it last longer than one minute.

And then she did move—to kneel up beside him. He felt foolish. Once had obviously been more than enough for her.

"Lie on your back," she said.

At first he felt alarmed. The moonlight showed her in all her glorious beauty—firm, voluptuous breasts, small waist, very feminine hips, shapely legs, her hair a dark, loose cloud about her face and down her back. But the moonlight lit her face too, and there was nothing there of the contemptuous half smile he feared to see. She was not playing the part of courtesan.

He turned onto his back and she came astride him and leaned over him, setting her hands flat on the grass beside his head. Her hair fell about him like a fragrant curtain. He felt the tips of her breasts touch his chest as she kissed him openmouthed, and he hardened into full arousal.

He kissed her back, his hands spread over the outsides of her thighs. He did not know what else to do. He did not know where to touch her or how. Had she been a novice, like him, he could have experimented until he learned what best pleased her. But he was afraid of being gauche.

She knelt upright even as he was thinking it, spread her legs wide, caressed him lightly with both hands, and brought herself down onto him until she was sitting on him, fully impaled. He inhaled slowly, fighting for control.

Then she moved, her fingertips light against his stomach, her head tipped back while she rode to a rhythm that pulsed with the beating of his blood. He bent his legs at the knee to brace his feet on the ground, and he rode with her.

There could be no greater sensual delight. While he pulsed with desire, with the urge to drive up into her until his seed sprang, he also felt powerful, detached from his need, in control of it. He wanted the act to last a long, long time. All night. He wanted this to go on forever. He wanted *her* forever. He watched her. Her eyes were closed, her lips parted. He was giving her pleasure, he thought, and the realization made him happy. He was redeeming himself.

He listened to the rhythmic suck and pull of their mating, to her labored breathing and his own, and wondered how she could hold her legs wide for so long without cramping. He massaged his hands over her thighs, and she lifted her head to smile down at him. Somehow it was the most intimate moment of all.

And then she did something that had him gripping her thighs. She clenched inner muscles about him as he reached the peak of his thrust and then relaxed them as he withdrew . . . and clenched again as he entered. He had never in his life known such exquisite agony. The rhythm became faster and more frenzied until she broke it suddenly, holding still when he expected her to move, relaxing her muscles when he expected her to clench them.

He spilled in one hot thrust and fell off the edge of the world.

Somewhere out in the vast reaches of the universe came the echo of her wordless cry. And two spoken words.

"My love."

In his voice.

When he awoke, they were both tangled in her cloak and the blanket. His feet were chilly, though the rest of him was warm—he had her for an extra blanket. She was still on top of him. He was still inside her. A strand of her hair was tickling his nose.

"Are you awake?" he asked.

"No." Her voice was sleepy.

"Well." He chuckled. "You have won our wager in fine fashion, have you not?"

He knew he had made a mistake as soon as the words were out. She did not stiffen. She did not move at all or say anything. But he knew he had said the wrong thing. He tried again, his voice more gentle.

"Pinewood is yours," he said. "I could not deprive you of it, you see. I will give you the deed in the morning. I'll have the legalities attended to in London and then it will be official. Your home is yours, Viola. For the rest of your life. Your nightmare is over." He kissed the top of her head.

She still said nothing.

"I'll be relinquishing every claim to Pinewood," he said. "Winning it at cards does not quite match the promise you were made, does it?"

"But the winning of wagers is more important to you than almost anything else," she said, speaking at last. "This is one you have lost. I have won. I knew I had a better chance to seduce you as Viola Thornhill than as Lilian Talbot. But I could have done it as either one tonight, could I not? You did not stand a chance. It was a foolish wager to agree to."

He felt a lurching of doubt. But dammit, he had hurt her. He had said the wrong thing. They had been making love, for God's sake. The wager had been the farthest thing from his mind. And from hers too, he was quite sure.

"I was not thinking of the wager when I came out here after you, Viola," he said.

"Then the more fool you." She disengaged herself from him as she spoke and pushed up onto her knees to lift herself off him. She gathered up her clothes, stood up, and began to dress. "I had a week. I did not need that long. I could have bedded you anytime during the past five days. You have lost, Lord Ferdinand. I wonder." She looked down at him, pushing her hair to one side so that her face would not be in shadow. "Do you feel cheated? Or do you feel that what you have had from me tonight more than compensates you for the loss of Pinewood?"

The devil! Dammit! It was Lilian Talbot who was looking down at him as she straightened her dress at the shoulder. That ghastly half smile was playing about her lips. And her voice had become a velvet caress.

"I believe," he said curtly, "we were making love."

She laughed softly. "Poor Lord Ferdinand," she said. "It was the illusion of love. What it was in reality was very good lust. Very good for you, that is. Men always like to believe that their prowess in bed can crumble the defenses of even the most hardened whore. It is necessary for their pride's sake to give the impression that one has received as much pleasure as one has given. Did I do well?"

"Viola—" he said sharply.

"I am a *very* hardened whore," she said. "You were foolish to tangle with me."

It had been an act? The whole of it? And in his foolish inexperience he had thought they were making love? Was it possible? Or was she merely covering up for the hurt of being told that she had won their wager? He had intended to follow up by telling her that it had been his intention all day simply to give her Pinewood.

He watched her go without even attempting to call after her or follow her. He had already stuffed one of his shoes into his mouth. He would doubtless ram the other one in too if he tried to rectify the situation. He had so little experience in dealing with the sensibilities of women. He had expected her to be amused at the reminder of their stupid wager. He had expected her to laugh.

Dammit, was he *mad*?

He was going to have some major humble pie to eat in the morning, he thought ruefully. He had better sit up for what remained of the night composing some speech that would mollify her and keep his footwear out of his mouth. Not that her good opinion should matter a great deal to him. It would not take long, after all, to hand over the deed and the note he would sign and have his valet witness even before he went down to breakfast. He would leave right after breakfast. He might even eat at the Boar's Head. It would not really matter what she thought of him.

Except that it mattered one devil of a lot.

And the prospect of leaving tomorrow and never seeing her again caused his stomach to clench into knots of panic.

Dammit!

He had never expected to fall in love. He had never wanted to. By what joke of fate, then, had he fallen in love with a notorious ex-courtesan?

And fallen hard too.

Goddammit all to hell!

15

VIOLA HAD LEFT HER CLOAK AND THE BLANKET behind. But she did not feel the chill of the night air as she hurried along the river path, scrambled up through the trees and over the lawn, and half ran along the terrace.

You have won our wager in fine fashion, have you not?

And she *had* won it. Except that the wager had been that she would *seduce* him. That had not been seduction.

But to him it had. To him what had happened had been nothing but sex. What had she expected?

My love, he had said against her ear.

So what? That was just the sort of nonsense many men babbled in sexual climax. Oh, Sally Duke had been quite right. One must never, *never* equate sex with love. No matter what passionate declarations a man might utter while in bed, sex was simply physical gratification to him, the woman only the instrument of his pleasure.

Viola made her way to the servants' quarters as soon as she had entered the house.

He was going to give her the deed to Pinewood in the morning. Her winnings, her pay for the services she had rendered twice down by the river. She would no longer owe her home to the dead Earl of Bamber, but to Lord Ferdinand Dudley, satisfied client.

No!

She tapped on Hannah's door and eased it open, hoping not to startle her maid into screaming.

"Don't be alarmed," she whispered. "It's just me." Exactly the words he had used a few hours ago, she remembered, wincing.

"Miss Vi?" Hannah shot up in bed. "What is it? What has he done to you?"

"Hannah," she said, still whispering, "we are leaving. You will need to get dressed and pack your things. If you finish before I do, you may come and help me, if you please. But come quietly."

"Leaving?" Hannah said. "When? What time is it?"

"I have no idea," Viola admitted. "One o'clock? Two? The stagecoach passes above the village very early, and it does not stop unless there are passengers waiting by the side of the road. We must be there."

"What happened?" Hannah peered at her in the darkness. "Did he hurt you? Did he—"

"He did not hurt me," Viola said. "There is no time for talk, Hannah. We must catch the stage. I cannot stay here another day. We will take only what we can carry. I do not want anyone to know we are leaving."

She left before Hannah had a chance to ask any more questions, and hurried in the direction of her own room. There was no sign of him as she went. Perhaps he had remained down by the river. Perhaps he was sleeping again. Perhaps she had serviced him that well, she thought bitterly.

She would not cry. There was nothing on this earth worth shedding a tear over, least of all her own foolish heart.

* * *

IT WAS SURPRISING HOW quickly one could become attached to a place, Ferdinand thought. He was standing at the window of his bedchamber, looking out over the box garden and the lawns and trees beyond. Over the tops of the trees he could just see the spire of the church at Trellick.

He did not want to leave.

But his bags were packed, and he was dressed in his riding clothes. Bentley had just shaved him. While he was having breakfast—though he was not at all hungry—his carriage would be loaded up and would set off for London with Bentley. His groom would accompany it on Ferdinand's horse. He himself would drive his curricle.

He should perhaps have left earlier. She probably would not want to see him again, and it would be just as well if he did not see her. But he owed it to her to place the deed of the manor in her hand and also the letter he had written, assuring the world in case of his sudden death within the next few days that he had given her Pinewood Manor. He needed to explain that even if last night had not happened he would still be giving it to her and would still be leaving, never to bother her again.

He did not want to leave.

It pained him to think that he would see her only once more. It was just that she had been his first sex partner, he tried to tell himself, and that he could not imagine bringing himself to do it with anyone else after her. But he was not sure he was being truthful.

He moved resolutely from the window and went down for breakfast. It was early, but she was usually an early riser. He was disappointed not to find her in the dining room. He had steeled himself for meeting her there. He had planned exactly how he would look at her and exactly what he would say.

He forced himself to eat two slices of toast and drink a cup of coffee. He dawdled over a second cup, but she still did not come down. Perhaps she was avoiding him, he thought. Undoubtedly she was, in fact. Perhaps he should simply leave. Even so, he paced the hall, his boots ringing on the tiled floor, for half an hour or so after leaving the dining room. His carriage and servants and baggage had left long before.

She had had a late night. It had been after two o'clock when he came back to the house not long after her. She was sleeping late. Or more likely, she was deliberately keeping to her room until he left. He had told her last night, had he not, that he would be going away today? He had offended her with his foolish notion of a joke, and she was not going to forgive him.

Well, he would wait no longer, he thought eventually. The morning was already well advanced. He was wasting precious traveling time. He strode into the library. He would leave the deed and the letter on the desk. He knew she looked there every morning for incoming mail. He would tell Jarvey to make sure she checked there.

There was a letter already lying on the otherwise bare surface of the desk. Had this morning's post already come, then? It was addressed to him, he saw as he picked it up—and recognized the small, neat hand that kept the estate books. What the devil? She could not face him this morning and so had written to him instead? He unfolded the letter.

"We each conceded victory to the other in the drawing room last evening," she had written. "It was a stalemate. Our wager was void. What happened afterward had nothing to do with any wager. Pinewood is yours. I am leaving." There was no signature.

Ferdinand strode to the door.

"Jarvey!" he bellowed. For once the butler was not hovering in the hall. He came soon enough, though. Probably everyone in the house had heard the summons. "Go fetch Miss Thornhill *now.*"

The butler retreated in the direction of the stairs, but Ferdinand knew it was hopeless. She would not have put that letter there before going to bed. She would have put it there, as he had been going to put his, as she was leaving the house.

"Stop!" he called, and the butler turned on the bottom stair. "Never mind. Find her maid. And fetch Hardinge from the stables. No, forget it, I'll go there and talk to him myself." He did not wait to see Jarvey's reaction to such confused and conflicting orders. He hurried from the house to the stables.

There was no carriage missing but his own. No horse either. And the groom looked as blank as Jarvey had when Viola Thornhill's name was mentioned. So did young Eli. Damn the woman. Goddamn her! Unless he had missed something in her letter—but how could he have, when it was as terse a letter as any he had ever seen—she had given no clue to her destination. She had simply gone. Probably to London.

"Is there a stagecoach that stops in Trellick?" he asked.

"It used to come right down to the Boar's Head, m'lord," Hardinge explained, "but there were too few passengers getting on and off there, so now it passes on by and just stops to drop off the odd passenger on the main road."

"Or pick up the odd passenger who happens to be standing there?"

"Yes, m'lord."

Goddammit!

She had escaped. She had slipped through his fingers. She had punished him in the worst possible way for what he had said last night—*as a joke,* for God's sake. He had made light of what had happened between them by telling her she had won their wager. She had punished him by disappearing without a trace, leaving him in possession of an estate he no longer wanted. Neither did she, it seemed.

Did anyone in this godforsaken place know where she might have gone? How the deuce was he going to find her so that he could stuff the deed down her throat? Before he throttled her, that is.

Devil take it, he had been *joking*. They had been making love—at least that was what he had been doing. He could not speak for her—he was pathetically low on experience. But surely she would not have taken such stupid offense if she had not been making love too. If she just had a spark of humor in her body she would have been crowing all over him long before he made his stab at a joke. She would have been teasing him to death about one of the few wagers he had lost in his entire life—and to a woman. She could have made much of that.

One did not joke with a woman, he guessed, wincing inwardly as he strode back to the house, when one had just finished making love to her. It was probably wiser to whisper sweet nothings. He would remember that next time.

Next time—ha!

THE STAGECOACH GUARD RIDING up behind the coach blew his yard of tin as a signal of something—that they were approaching an inn for a change of horses or that someone was about to pass them in one direction or the other or that there were sheep or cows or some other obstruction on the road ahead or that they were approaching a tollgate. The horn had been blasting at frequent intervals throughout the long, uncomfortable day. Sleep was impossible. Whenever Viola had come close to nodding off, she had been rudely jolted awake again.

"What is it this time?" Hannah mumbled from beside her. "I'll give that man a piece of my mind, I will, when we stop next."

A fellow passenger agreed. Another hoped that the sound meant an inn and refreshments ahead—he was starved. They had been allowed only ten minutes at the last stop. The cup of tea and meat pasty he had ordered had not come in time. A spirited litany of complaints followed.

Viola looked out through the window beside her. There was no sign of any town or village ahead. But there was another vehicle passing them—from behind. The road was not wide at this point, and the coachman did not draw his vehicle to one side or even slacken its speed to let the other pass. This happened all too often, she thought, holding her breath and involuntarily shrinking back from the window as if to allow the curricle more room to pass. The road abounded with discourteous stagecoach drivers and reckless, impatient gentlemen with their sporting vehicles.

This particular curricle passed at high speed. It remained clear of the stagecoach by a mere few inches. The gentleman plying the ribbons drove with consummate skill and with criminal disregard for his own safety and that of the stagecoach passengers. Viola glanced up to the high seat of the curricle. Its driver glanced down into the interior of the coach at the same moment and their eyes met for the merest fraction of a second.

Then both he and his curricle were past.

Viola sat sharply back in her seat and closed her eyes.

"The fool!" someone said. "He might have killed us all."

What on earth was he doing on the road to London? Had he not read her letter? Had he seen her? *Of course he had seen her.*

Viola kept her eyes firmly closed as her thoughts and emotions swirled. All day she had been remembering the night before and trying desperately not to remember. But the only other thing to think about was the future and all it would hold for her. . . .

The guard blew the horn again and a passenger cursed. Hannah scolded him and reminded him that there were ladies present. The coach was slackening speed. It was an inn this time. And the first thing Viola saw as the stagecoach drew into the crowded yard was the curricle that had passed them on the road ten minutes earlier. An ostler was changing the horses.

"Hannah!" Viola grabbed her maid's wrist as the steps were set down and the passengers scrambled to get out and make the most of the short time they would be allowed. "Stay here, please. You are not desperate for anything, are you? We will wait until the next stop."

Hannah looked surprised, but before she could question Viola's strange request, someone had come to stand in the doorway and was extending a hand toward Viola.

"Allow me," Lord Ferdinand Dudley said.

Hannah drew in a sharp breath.

"No," Viola said. "Thank you. We do not need to get out."

But he was not the smiling, good-natured gentleman she was most familiar with. He was the grim, hard-jawed, arrogant, demanding aristocrat he had been that first morning at Pinewood. His eyes looked very black.

"Hannah," he said, "get down, please. Go inside the coffee room and order yourself a meal. You need not hurry. There will be plenty of time to eat it. The stagecoach will be continuing on its way without the two of you."

"It most certainly will not." Viola bristled with indignation. "Stay where you are, Hannah."

"If you wish to scrap with me in the inn yard with a score of people looking on, I am game," he said grimly. "But you will not be continuing your journey on this stagecoach. I suggest we go inside to the private parlor I have reserved and scrap there. Hannah, please?"

Hannah took his hand without further argument and scrambled down from the coach. She disappeared in the direction of the inn without even looking back at Viola.

"Come." He had reached his hand back inside.

"Our bags—" she said.

"Have already been taken down," he assured her.

She was angry then. "You have no right," she said,

brushing aside his hand and descending to the cobbled yard without his assistance. Her bag and Hannah's were indeed standing side by side on the ground. "This is bullying. This—" She encountered the grinning face of an interested groom and clamped her mouth shut. He was not the only one who had stopped work in the obvious hope of witnessing a fight.

"Runaway wives need firm handling," Lord Ferdinand remarked cheerfully, obviously for their further amusement. He took her elbow in a firm grasp and propelled her toward the inn while she listened indignantly to the purely male laughter behind them.

"How dare you!" she said.

"It's dashed fortunate I caught up to you before you reached London," he said. "What the devil did you mean by running off like that?"

He led her down a long, low-beamed corridor to a small room at the back of the inn. There was a fire crackling in the hearth. A table in the middle of the room had been set with a white cloth and laid for two.

"I would be obliged if you would watch your language," she said. "And my movements are none of your business. Or my destination in London. Excuse me. I have to fetch Hannah and have our bags put back on the coach before it leaves without us."

He ignored her. He closed the parlor door and stood against it, his long, booted legs crossed at the ankles, his arms folded across his chest. He was looking less grim now.

"Was it that stupid joke I made?" he asked her. "About your winning our wager? It was a *joke*."

"It was *not* a joke," she said, taking up her stand on the far side of the table. "You said you were going to give me the deed to Pinewood today. Don't tell me you were going to do it out of the goodness of your heart. Or out of a pang of conscience."

"But I was," he said.

"Was I *that* good?" She glared scornfully at him.

"I decided it yesterday," he said, "long before I knew whether you were good or not."

Her eyes flashed. "Liar!"

He stared at her for such a long time that her fury evaporated and a cold chill crept up her spine in its place.

"If you were a man," he said at last, "I would call you out for that."

"If I were a man," she retorted, "I would accept."

He reached into a pocket of his coat and drew out some folded papers. He held them out to her. "Yours," he said. "Come and take them. We'll eat, and then I'll reserve a room here for you and your maid tonight and hire a private chaise to take you both home tomorrow."

"No." She stayed where she was. "I don't want it."

"Pinewood?"

"I don't want it."

He stared at her for a few moments before striding toward the table and slapping the papers down on it.

"Goddammit!" he said. "If that doesn't beat all. What the devil *do* you want?"

"Watch your language!" she said again. What she *did* want was to rush around the table, cast herself into his arms, and sob out all her misery. But since that was not an option, she regarded him coldly. "I want you to go away and leave me alone. I want you to take those papers with you. And if it is not too late, I want to get on the stagecoach."

"Viola," he said, his voice so gentle suddenly that he almost broke her reserve, "take Pinewood. It is yours. It was never mine. Not really. I daresay the old earl meant it to be yours but just forgot to change his will."

"He did *not* forget," she said stubbornly. "He would not have done so. He did it. It was the wrong will that the Duke of Tresham read."

"Well, then." He shrugged and she knew she had not convinced him. "All the more reason for you to take the papers and go back home. I'll continue on my way to London and make the transfer right and tight. Let me tell the landlord we are ready for dinner."

"No!" He had already taken a couple of steps toward the door. He turned to look at her in some exasperation. "No," she said again. "It would be a gift from you. Or the prize for a wager won. I will not accept it either way. Things would never be the same. It was a gift from *him*."

"Very well, then." He was definitely annoyed now. "We will just say that I am setting matters right."

"No."

He ran the fingers of one hand through his hair, leaving it disheveled and unconsciously making himself look more gorgeous than ever.

"What do you want, then?" he asked her.

"I have told you."

"What are you going to do in London?"

She smiled at him even though every muscle in her face felt stiff. "That is not any of your business," she told him.

His eyes narrowed and he looked menacing again. "If you are planning to go back to whoring," he said, "it dashed well is my business. You were happy enough at Pinewood until I came along. I am not going to have you on my conscience every time I see you about town with the Lord Gnasses of this world. You had better marry me."

Her insides somersaulted, and for a moment she stared at him in utter astonishment. He looked hardly less surprised himself. She forced herself to smile again.

"I think I had better *not* marry you," she said. "The Duke of Tresham would devour you for breakfast."

"I don't care a tuppenny toss what Tresham says," he said. "Or anyone else. I'll marry whomever I want to marry."

"Unless she says no." She felt engulfed in a huge wave of sadness as she continued to smile. "And she does say no. You think you know the worst about me, Lord Ferdinand, but you do not know all. I am a bastard, you see. When my mother married my stepfather, it was her first marriage. Thornhill was her maiden name. You do not want to be marrying a bastard *and* a whore."

"Don't do that." He frowned. "Don't smile like that and call yourself names like that."

"But they are true names," she said. "Come, admit that you are relieved by my refusal. You spoke entirely without forethought. You would be horrified if I said yes."

"I would not," he said, but he spoke without conviction.

Viola smiled again.

"You are not going back to whoring," he told her.

"How vulgar!" she said. "I was never a whore. I was a courtesan. There is a world of difference."

"Don't *do* that," he said again. "Do you have any money?"

She stiffened. "That is none—"

"And *don't* tell me it is none of my damned business," he said. "You don't, do you?"

"I have enough," she told him.

"Enough for what?" he asked. "Your fare and your maid's to London? A few meals along the way?"

That was about it.

"If you won't go home to Pinewood and if you won't marry me," he said, "there is only one thing left for you."

Yes, she knew that. But she felt as if the weight of the universe had settled on her shoulders again. Had she really been hoping that he would be more persuasive over one of the other options?

"You are going to have to be my mistress," he said.

16

THEY WERE DRIVING INTO LONDON IN FERDInand's carriage, everyone else in their entourage having been banished to horse or curricle. They were sitting side by side, as far apart as space allowed, gazing out of opposite windows. They had not spoken to each other for more than an hour. It was early evening.

Ferdinand did not feel as he imagined a man ought to feel with a new mistress. Not that she had yet agreed to accept the position. But she had adamantly refused to go back to Pinewood. She had insisted upon paying for her own room at the inn and had tried to purchase tickets for herself and her maid on today's London stage. That was after breakfast. He had threatened to revive the story about her being a runaway wife if she tried it. He would take her over his knee in some very public place and wallop her a good one, and there would not be a man or woman at the inn who would not applaud him.

She had retaliated with an icy stare and an assurance that if he laid so much as a fingernail on her she would inform everyone within earshot exactly *why* she had run away from her husband. He would not care to discover how very inventive she could be, she warned him, but he was welcome to find out, if he so desired. However, she *would* accept a ride in his carriage to London, since he had caused her to miss yesterday's stagecoach, for which she had paid.

"I suppose," she said now, breaking the long silence between them, "you have not thought this thing through, have you? I suppose you do not know where you would take me. We cannot go to a hotel. It would not be respectable. You cannot take me to your rooms. Your neighbors would be scandalized. I have no rooms of my own—I gave them up two years ago."

"There you are wrong," he told her. "Of course I know where I am taking you. You are going to be my mistress, and I intend to house you in style. But I have just the house in mind for tonight and the next few days."

"I suppose," she said, "it is where you always house your mistresses."

"Well, it is not," he said. "I am not in the habit of mounting mistresses. I prefer to... Well, never mind." She had turned to look at him, her expression faintly amused. She was such an expert at that look, and it never failed to irritate him and make him feel like a gauche schoolboy. "The house is Tresham's."

"Your brother's?" She raised her eyebrows. "It is where he houses *his* mistresses? Are you sure there is no one in residence?"

"It is where he *did* house them," he said, "before his marriage. I don't know why he has never sold the house, but to my knowledge he still has it."

"How long has the duke been married?" she asked.

"Four years," he said.

"Are you quite sure, then, that the house is not occupied?" she asked.

It had damned well better not be. If it was, he would rearrange Tresham's nose for him so that it projected inward instead of outward. Not that one could really challenge one's brother for being unfaithful to one's sister-in-law. But Ferdinand had not realized until that moment how much he was depending upon his brother to restore some of his faith in love and marriage. Tresham's had almost certainly been a love match. But could it stand the test of time? Tresham had always changed mistresses dizzyingly often.

"You really are not sure, are you?" Viola Thornhill asked him. "You had better let me down at a clean, cheap hotel, Lord Ferdinand. You can go back to Pinewood or back to your usual life here in London and forget all about me. You are not responsible for me."

"I am," he said. "I played cards with Bamber and turned your life upside down." Not to mention his own.

"If it had not been you," she said, "it would have been someone else. You are not responsible for me. Set me down and I will get on with my life. I will not be destitute. I have work awaiting me."

"As a whore?" He frowned fiercely at her. "You could do better than that. There are all sorts of other things you could do."

"But whoring is so lucrative," she said, her voice pure velvet amusement. He *hated* it when she did that.

"You are going to be my mistress," he said stubbornly. "It was settled yesterday. It has been settled again today. I don't want to hear any more arguments."

"It was settled and is being settled unilaterally," she said. "Do I have no say in the matter? Because I am a woman, perhaps? A nonentity? A thing? A toy? You do not want a mistress, Lord Ferdinand. And I have never been one. I have always belonged to myself."

"There is no point in telling me yet again that you are no man's mistress," he said. "You are now. And you are going to be for some time to come. You are *my* mistress. Look at me."

She looked at his chin and smiled as she settled her shoulders across the corner of the carriage.

"Into my eyes. Look into my eyes."

"Whyever should I?" She laughed softly.

"Because you are not the sort to enjoy being called a coward," he said. "Dash it all, look into my eyes."

She did.

"Now tell me," he said. "Would you prefer to go whoring with a different man each night than to be my mistress?"

"It would be the same thing," she said.

"It would *not*." He did not know why he was arguing with her. She kept insisting she was not his responsibility. Why not take her at her word? "Being a man's mistress is respectable employment. And it would not be uncongenial to you to be *my* mistress, would it? You did not mind two nights ago. I believe you even enjoyed it."

"I am very skilled at feigning enjoyment, Lord Ferdinand," she said.

He turned his head away. Yes, of course she was. He had doubtless been mortifyingly fumbling and awkward and ignorant. What did he know about pleasing any woman, not to mention a skilled, experienced courtesan? And why was he trying to pressure such a woman into accepting regular employment from him? How would he hold her interest—or incite it in the first place? Not that a man was required to do that with his mistress, of course. She was the one being paid. It was her job to hold *his* interest. Except that he did not believe he would be able to do those intimate things with a woman who did them with him only because she was being paid.

She touched his arm then. "But I did not have to feign it two nights ago," she said.

Well, there. He felt absurdly pleased, though she might well have said so just out of kindness.

"You will stay at that house of Tresham's until I can find a place of my own for you," he said.

"Very well," she said quietly. "Take me there. But I will stay only as long as we both wish to continue the liaison. We must both be free to end it at a moment's notice."

It chilled him to think of ending the affair even before it had begun, but he had no objection. Of course she must be free to leave when she tired of him. He must be free to leave when he tired of her. It would happen at some time, he supposed. He could not imagine ever tiring of Viola Thornhill, but he was naïve and inexperienced.

"We have a deal, then," he said, and he reached out and took her hand in a firm clasp. She did not return the pressure of his fingers, but neither did she pull away. "You will be my mistress and under my protection. All we have left to discuss is your salary."

He could not bear the thought of paying her to bed with him. But dammit, he had offered her Pinewood and she had refused. He had offered her marriage and she had refused. What other choice had she left him?

"Not now," she said, turning her head away to look out through her window. "We can talk about that tomorrow."

There should be some definitive moment, he thought, to mark the beginning of their liaison. He should draw her into his arms and kiss her soundly. But the carriage was well into London already. Indeed, they would be stopping outside Dudley House within a minute or two. He would wait until he had her inside Tresham's house—the other house, that is. He would kiss her soundly then. No, he would take her to bed and consummate their new relationship—employer and employee, man and mistress.

Lord, but there was something strangely depressing about the thought. He was not at all sure . . .

The carriage turned onto Grosvenor Square and rolled to a halt outside Dudley House.

"Stay here," he said, releasing her hand as his coachman opened the door and set down the steps.

"FERDINAND!" THE DUCHESS OF Tresham came hurrying toward him as soon as he strode into the drawing room in the wake of the butler's announcement. "What a delightful surprise!" She set both her hands in his and kissed him on the cheek.

"Jane." He squeezed her hands and looked her over. "As lovely as ever. Have you fully recovered your health after your confinement?"

She laughed. She was a golden beauty, whose figure looked just as good to Ferdinand now as it had four years ago, when he first met her.

"Jocelyn warned me before he married me that Dudley babies give their mothers a hard time even before they are born," she said. "He said it to shock me at the time, but he was perfectly right. I have, however, survived the ordeal twice."

His brother was in the room too, Ferdinand saw then.

He was holding a tiny baby against one shoulder and patting its back.

"I never thought I would live to see the day, Tresh," Ferdinand said with a grin, strolling closer to admire his newest nephew, whose eyes were open but fixed, as if he were very close to sleep.

"Yes, well, Dudley babies are not finished with giving their parents a rough time once they are out of the womb, Ferdinand, as we should well remember," his brother said. "Don't waggle your fingers at him like that, if you please. I do believe he is about to nod off after deafening me with his cries for all of an hour past. Have the joys of country living palled already? I thought you had found your vocation at last. I came home from Somersetshire and told Jane so."

"What Jocelyn means," Jane said, "is that we are delighted to see you, Ferdinand. You must join us for dinner, which will be ready as soon as Christopher is returned to the nursery. Nicholas is already asleep. You must come and see him tomorrow."

"I am not here to stay," Ferdinand said. "I wondered if I might have a word with you, Tresh."

"Alone?" his brother asked. "With something that is not for the duchess's ears? Dear me. Did you rid yourself of that woman, by the way? I hope she did not persuade you into paying her a large bribe."

"Miss Thornhill is no longer at Pinewood," Ferdinand said stiffly.

"Then I am proud of you," his brother said. "Particularly if you did *not* bribe her. I'll take Christopher up to his bed, Jane. Ferdinand may accompany me and divulge his secret."

"I'll say good night, Jane," Ferdinand said, bowing to

her, "and call on you tomorrow at a more proper hour, if I may."

"You may call here at any hour you please, Ferdinand," she said, smiling affectionately at him. "I want to hear all about Pinewood Manor."

"Well, speak," Tresham said when they were on the stairs. "What scrape are you in now? And do not waste your breath assuring me that there is no scrape. Your face has always borne a distinct resemblance to an open book."

"I would like a loan of your house," Ferdinand said abruptly. "Your other house, that is. If you still own it, but I believe you do. And if there is no current occupant."

"There are two," his brother said. "Mr. and Mrs. Jacobs, butler and housekeeper. No mistress, Ferdinand, if that is what you meant, and I daresay it was. I have a wife. Now, let me guess and let me hope I am well wide of the mark. You *do* have a mistress. Lilian Talbot, by any chance?"

"Miss Thornhill," Ferdinand said. They turned in the direction of the nursery, but Tresham made no move to go inside. "She needs somewhere to live. She won't take Pinewood and I won't be responsible for her returning to whoring."

"She won't take Pinewood." Tresham did not make the remark into a question. "I suppose you developed a chronic case of bleeding heart, Ferdinand, and offered it to her free of charge. And she had too much pride to accept. Good for her."

"She won it," Ferdinand said. "We made a wager. But she would not accept her winnings. Then she ran away. What was I to do? A gentleman cannot lose a wager and then retain what he wagered. It would just not be honorable."

The baby, whose eyes were now closed, made stirring noises, but Tresham patted him on the back and he settled again.

"I am not going to ask what the wager was," the duke said. "And please do not volunteer the information, Ferdinand. I have a strong suspicion that I do not want to know. She ran away, you ran after her, and now she is your mistress—but you have nowhere to take her. It all makes perfect sense," he added dryly.

"I need the house for a night or two," Ferdinand said. "Until I can get something of my own."

"If you want my advice, Ferdinand," his brother said, "which of course you do not because you are a Dudley, you will pay her handsomely and turn her off. She will not starve. She will be mobbed by prospective protectors as soon as it is known that she is in town. Go back to Pinewood so that you will not have to listen to all the men who will boast of having had her. I believe you belong at Pinewood. I was surprised to realize it, but realize it I did."

"All I want," Ferdinand said through his clenched teeth, "is permission to use your house for a day or two. Will those servants let me in?"

"They will if I write a note," his brother said, "which I will do as soon as I have turned Christopher over to his nurse's care. Have *you* had her yet, Ferdinand? No, don't answer. I suppose you are still besotted with her?"

"I was never—"

But Tresham had opened the nursery door and proceeded inside. Ferdinand followed him. The children slept in the same room, Nicholas in a bed, the baby in a crib. Ferdinand went to look at the sleeping boy while his brother set the baby down and the children's nurse hurried in from an adjoining room and curtsied.

Just a few years ago, Ferdinand thought, gazing down at the tousled head of his sleeping nephew, one could not have imagined Tresham domesticated. It would certainly have been impossible to picture him with a baby in his arms or bent over a crib as he was now, tucking a blanket warmly about the tiny form.

All appearances suggested that his elder brother was a contented family man. Ferdinand felt an unexpected pang of envy as he bade the nurse a good evening and led the way out of the nursery.

But why the devil had Tresham never sold that house? Did Jane even know about it?

"Come to the library for a moment," Tresham said, "and I'll write that note for you. Where have you left her?"

"Outside in the carriage," Ferdinand said.

His brother did not comment.

VIOLA DID NOT MOVE from the carriage even though after Lord Ferdinand disappeared inside the Duke of Tresham's house she was very tempted to get out. His curricle had come to a stop behind the carriage and Hannah sat there with his groom. It would be easy enough to call her maid, find their bags among all the other luggage, and walk away into the gathering dusk.

But perhaps not. Perhaps after all she would discover that she was a type of prisoner. Perhaps one of his servants would make a fuss, try to stop her, knock on the house door to raise the alarm. Not that any of them could or would detain her for long against her will, of course. But she would embarrass Lord Ferdinand in front of his servants and the duke's—perhaps in front of his brother too.

She would not do that to him.

She might at this moment be back at Pinewood, Viola thought. Alone. The undisputed owner. She was a fool to be here instead. But Pinewood would no longer have the power to bring her any sort of peace or security. She had thought, after she first read Claire's letter, that Pinewood rents would pay off the debt to Daniel Kirby even if the estate was impoverished in the process. But she had realized since that he would not accept that arrangement. He wanted her back working for him, earning him a fortune. If she failed to come, he would punish her by using Claire.

Lord Ferdinand would agree to pay her a large salary as his mistress. She had no doubt about that. But Viola knew Daniel Kirby would not accept a share of that either. He wanted to control her career.

All the way to London she had pondered the situation and all the possible choices she had. But however her mind approached the problem, it always ended up with the same conclusion—the only possible one. She had to go back to her life as a courtesan.

Besides, she could not bear the thought of being Lord Ferdinand's mistress. She did not want to do with him what they had done by the river as a condition of employment. She did not want to earn her living by lying with him. Ah, dear God, not with Ferdinand.

The carriage door opened and interrupted her train of thought. Ferdinand took his seat beside her again. She turned her head, but darkness was already falling and the interior of the carriage was dim. Even so, she shivered at the sight of him and wished after all that she had had the courage to make her escape with Hannah while he was inside the house. She could not bear this.

"We will be there in a few minutes," he said as the carriage lurched into motion. "You must be weary after such a long journey."

"Yes."

He took her hand in his, curling his strong fingers about her own. But he made no attempt to draw closer to her, to kiss her, or even to converse with her. His hand did not relax. She wondered if he regretted what he believed they had agreed to. She wondered if the Duke of Tresham had tried to talk him out of it. But it did not matter. Nothing mattered. Tomorrow he would be able to go back to Pinewood. He belonged there—it was a bitter admission. He would soon forget her.

Tomorrow she would set the future in motion.

That left tonight. She closed her eyes and rested her head against the squabs of the carriage. Oh, yes, she would allow herself tonight.

The house in which the Duke of Tresham had housed his mistresses was in a quiet, respectable neighborhood. The manservant who answered Lord Ferdinand's knock also seemed like the kind of servant one might find in any respectable home. So did his wife, who came into the hall to discover who the late callers were, and curtsied first to Lord Ferdinand and then to Viola after he had introduced her and explained that she would be living there for a short while. They looked at her as she had become accustomed to being regarded, as if she were a lady worthy of respect. They would have been trained to behave that way, of course. The Duke of Tresham would not tolerate servants who treated his mistresses like doxies.

"I will show Miss Thornhill around," Lord Ferdinand informed the butler. "Have her bags taken up and her maid shown to her rooms, will you?"

"Have you been here before, then?" Viola asked him as he ushered her into a room to their left.

"No," he admitted. "But it is not a large house. I do not expect I will get lost."

The sitting room in which they found themselves was tastefully furnished and decorated in delicate shades of gray and lavender. It was a very feminine room, even if it lacked some warmth. It was a good place, she decided, looking about with a practiced eye, for a mistress to entertain her employer before they adjourned to the bedchamber.

The room next door was less pretty, but far cozier. There were some comfortable armchairs arranged about the fireplace as well as a small but elegant desk and chair. There was a pianoforte and a bookcase filled with books. There was an empty embroidery frame before one of the chairs and an artist's easel propped against one wall.

The Duke of Tresham's mistresses, Viola thought, or one of them, at least, had been people in their own right. How strange, that she of all people should feel some surprise at that fact. This room had an air of having been lived in, perhaps even happily. Maybe, after all, being a mistress was preferable to the sort of life she had led for four years. Perhaps there was a chance of some relationship. But whoever the poor woman was who had been happy here with the duke, she was gone now. He had married the duchess.

"I like this room," she said. "Someone made a home here."

Lord Ferdinand was looking about too, his eyes pausing on each object, a slight frown between his brows. But he did not comment aloud. He ushered her into the dining room and then upstairs.

The bedchamber took her quite by surprise. Although it was opulently decorated in satins and velvets and had a thick carpet underfoot, it did not look like a typical love nest. Men invariably liked scarlet as an accompaniment to their sensual delights. Lilian Talbot's bedchamber had been predominantly scarlet. This one was decorated in varying shades of moss green, cream, and gold.

One would feel less like a mistress in this room and more like a lover, she thought. She was glad it was here she would spend her last hours with Lord Ferdinand. She would not be his mistress, because she was not going to be paid, but she was glad their surroundings would help her see him as a lover rather than as a client.

The door that must lead into the dressing room, slightly ajar when they entered the bedchamber, was pulled firmly closed from the other side.

Viola turned to look at Lord Ferdinand. He was hovering in the doorway, his hands at his back, his long legs slightly apart. He looked handsome and powerful and slightly dangerous—and very obviously uncomfortable. This, of course, she realized, was all new to him.

"Will it do until I can find something else?" he asked.

"Yes, it will do."

His eyes shifted away from hers. "You must be very tired," he said.

"Yes, rather."

"I will leave you, then," he said. "I will return tomorrow to see that you have settled comfortably. I daresay the rest of your belongings will arrive within the next few days. I sent a message back to Pinewood yesterday."

He was going to leave her out of deference to her weariness after two days of travel. She had not expected this. How easy it would be. She could see the last of him forever now, within the next few minutes, before she had time to think. But she could not bear to be alone tonight. It was too soon. She had not had a chance to steel her mind to it. Tomorrow she would be ready, but tonight . . .

She crossed the room and set her fingertips against his chest. He did not move as she smiled into his face and arched her body inward until she touched him from her hips to her knees.

"I *am* tired," she said, "and ready for bed. Are you?"

He flushed. "Don't do that," he said, frowning. "Don't *do* it, do you hear me? If I wanted a damned whore, I would go to a brothel. I don't want Lilian Talbot. I want *you*. I want Viola Thornhill."

She had donned her other persona without conscious thought, she realized, desperate to shield herself from pain. It was strange, she thought, and just a little frightening, to realize that Lilian Talbot repelled him, that it was Viola Thornhill who drew him to intimacy. It was Viola he wanted as his mistress. She drew away from him and let her arms fall to her sides. Without her customary mask, all her emotions felt naked.

"Let us at least be honest with each other," he said. "Must there be artifice and tricks and games just because we are embarking on a sexual relationship? You *know*, do you not? I suppose it was embarrassingly obvious that you were my first woman. Let me be Viola Thornhill's first man, then. Let us look for some comfort from this relationship as well as pleasure. Perhaps even some companionship? Will it be possible, do you suppose?"

But she could only shake her head, while unshed tears balled themselves into a lump in her throat and welled into her eyes.

"I do not know," she whispered.

"I am not interested in Lilian Talbot," he said. "She would make me feel gauche and inadequate, you see. And rather dirty. I want you or no one at all. Take it or leave it."

It was time for the truth. Time to tell him that she had tricked him earlier in the carriage, getting him to agree that she was free to end the liaison at a moment's notice. Time to tell him that she intended to use that freedom tomorrow morning.

She stepped against him again and pressed her face into his neckcloth.

"Ah, Ferdinand," she said.

17

He was in deep waters. His instinct was to wade out so that he could stand upon the shore and view the situation from a safe distance. If he went back to his own rooms, he would be able to digest what was happening to him. It was not even late. He could change his clothes and go to White's, find some of his friends, discover what entertainments the evening offered, and pick one or two to attend. Life would be familiar and comfortable again.

Was this how all men felt about their mistresses at first? As if their very souls yearned for union, for comfort, for peace? For love? Did all men suffer from the illusion that the woman was the other half of their soul?

He must be naïve indeed to be feeling as he was feeling. But he knew with blinding clarity that what had happened between him and Viola two evenings ago on the riverbank at Pinewood had merely confirmed what he had known about himself most of his life. He would rather go celibate through life than engage in sex for its own sake.

He wrapped his arms about her and kissed her mouth when she raised her face to his.

"Do you want me to stay?" he asked her. But he set one finger over her lips before she had a chance to answer. "You must be honest. I'll never bed you unless you want it too."

Her lips curved beneath his silencing finger. "What if I never want it?"

"Then I'll have to find some other solution for you," he said. "But you are not going back to your old life. I'll not allow it."

Her smile was purely Viola's, not that other woman's, he was glad to see. It seemed to be tinged with sadness. "Do you have any say in the matter?" she asked him.

"I dashed well do," he told her. "You are my woman."

Not mistress—*woman*. There was a difference. He had spoken without forethought, but he knew that he had spoken a true thing. He was responsible for her. He had no legal obligation to her and no legal right to demand obedience from her. Nevertheless, she was his woman.

"Stay with me," she said. "I do not want to be alone tonight. And I do want you."

She could trust him, he almost told her. Through most of his life he had trusted no one but himself, knowing that even those people nearest and dearest to him could let him down at any moment and make the firm earth beneath his feet feel more like quicksand. He had trusted in himself and had never done anything he considered truly shameful or dishonorable. She could trust him too. He would be the Rock of Gibraltar for her. But how could he say the words without sounding like a foolish, boastful boy?

He would have to *show* her that he was to be trusted, that was all. Only time would accomplish that.

In the meantime, she had told him that she wanted him. And by God, he wanted her too. She had been pulsing like a fever in his blood all day long. And yesterday too when he had come chasing after her.

He drew her into his arms and kissed her hungrily. She wrapped her arms about him and kissed him back in the same way. But he remembered suddenly that until less than half an hour before she had been sitting in his carriage since their last posting stop.

"Go into your dressing room and make yourself comfortable," he said. "Come back in ten minutes' time."

She smiled slowly at him. "Thank you," she said.

He was glad almost fifteen minutes later that he had done it. He was sitting on the side of the bed, the covers turned back, when she returned. He had stripped down to his riding breeches. She was wearing a nightgown, perhaps the same one she had worn the night he broke the urn. It was white and virginal and covered her from neck to wrists to bare feet. Her hair had been unbraided and brushed until it shone like copper. It was loose and billowed down her back almost to her bottom. She could not have looked more desirable if she had come to him naked. Or if the single candle had been gleaming off the scarlet trappings he had half expected to find in this bedchamber.

She came toward him, and he spread his knees and reached out his hands so that she could come right to the edge of the bed and stand against him. He set his hands on either side of her small waist and rested his face in the valley between her breasts. The nightgown had a freshly washed smell. So did she. The most enticing feminine perfume, he discovered in that moment, was soap and woman. Her fingers smoothed lightly through his hair.

"Do you want me to undress?" she asked him. "I was not sure."

"No." He got to his feet and pulled the bedcovers back

farther. "Lie down. Let me see you there before I blow out the candle."

"You want to blow it out?" she asked him as she lay down and smoothed her nightgown over her knees.

"Yes."

It was not that he did not want to see her. It was certainly not that he would be embarrassed by his own nakedness. After all, they had been naked together just two nights before in moonlight. He was not quite sure why he wanted darkness. Or why he wanted her to keep her nightgown on. Perhaps there would be more of fantasy in it—the illusion that they were not man and mistress having sex for his pleasure, but a couple, finding warmth and comfort in each other's bodies in the bed where they slept together.

He blew out the candle, removed his breeches and drawers, and lay down beside her. He slid one arm beneath her head, and she turned against him and found his mouth with her own.

"Make love to me, Ferdinand," she said. "As you did two nights ago. Please. No one else had ever made love to me. Just you. You were the first."

His hands moved over her warm curves, on top of the nightgown. "I don't know how to please you," he said. "But I'll learn if you will be patient with me. I want to please you more than anything else in life."

"You pleased me," she told him. "More than anyone or anything ever has done before. And you please me now. You feel good. You smell good."

He laughed softly. He had washed, but he did not have any of his colognes with him. She did not mind his inexperience, he realized. Perhaps it was something that appealed more than expertise would have to Viola Thornhill.

It was Viola Thornhill with whom he was making love. In some strange way she had come virgin to him. He felt gifted—and vaguely disturbed. But he pushed back the latter feeling. It was only as his mistress that he could keep her safe.

She did not mind his inexperience and so he relaxed and did not mind it himself any longer. He explored her with his hands, learning every curve of his woman, while desire heated his blood and tightened his groin and stiffened his erection. He began to discover the places—some of them unexpected—that drew soft purrs of pleasure or slow gasps of desire from her. He began to know her.

And then he slipped his hand beneath her nightgown and moved it upward, along her slim, smooth legs to the heart of her. She was hot and moist. She parted her thighs and her hands fell still on his body as his fingers explored her, learned the folds and the secrets of her, slid inside her. He hardened to almost unbearable arousal as her inner muscles clenched about his fingers.

And then by some instinct the pad of his thumb found a small part of her at the mouth of her opening and rubbed lightly over it. He knew immediately that he had discovered perhaps her most intense pleasure spot. She trembled, her hands gripping his sides, and cried out as she shuddered into what could only be a feminine orgasm.

He laughed softly after she had finished. "Can I possibly be that good?" he asked her.

She laughed with him, her voice breathless and a little

shaky. "I think you must be," she said. "What did you *do*?"

"That is my secret," he said. "I find that I have hidden talents. I am one devil of a fine lover, in fact."

They laughed together as he raised himself on one elbow and leaned over her. They had not drawn the curtains across the window. He could see her faintly, her face surrounded by a cloud of dark hair on the pillow.

"And enormously modest," she said.

"Well. Enormous, anyway." He rubbed his nose across hers.

She tutted. "I rest my case."

The laughter was unexpected. And unexpectedly good.

"Give me a moment," he said, "and I'll show you that I speak only the truth."

He did not peel her nightgown all the way off. The fantasy felt more erotic than nudity. He moved over her and settled himself between her thighs.

"Show me, then," she said, "and I'll pass judgment. I *think* you are merely boasting."

He thrust hard and deep—and fought the urge to bring himself to a fast completion. But he had known what to expect this time. It was a little easier. He wanted to take his time. He wanted to give her time to enjoy it with him.

"No," she said, her voice sounding startlingly normal, "it was no boast."

Minx. Jade. Witch. Woman.

He raised himself onto his forearms and grinned down at her. "Five minutes?" he said. "Or ten? Which do you think me capable of?"

"I do not wager when I have no hope of winning," she

said. "But which do I *think* you capable of? Let me see. Both added together, I believe. Fifteen." She laughed.

He moved in her then, settling much of his weight on her, working her with slow, rhythmic strokes, enjoying the feel of her, the smell of her, the sounds of their coupling, the knowledge that she was enjoying the same things about him and what they did together.

Together. It was the key. United. As one. Bodies joined in the deeply intimate, infinitely pleasurable dance of sex. And not just bodies. Not just any man with any woman.

"Viola," he whispered against her ear.

"Yes."

They kissed openmouthed without breaking the rhythm of their loving. But she knew—of course she knew—what he had said to her with the single word of her name. She said it back to him timeless moments later.

"Ferdinand."

"Yes."

They kissed again. And then he buried his face in the silky fragrance of her hair and quickened and deepened his pace until he felt her tighten every muscle and strain closer to him and closer and closer until . . .

The thing was, he thought some time later, a moment before he realized he was lying on top of her like a dead weight and lifted himself off—the thing was that there was only a before and an after and a knowledge of a placeless, nameless, eventless somewhere and sometime in between that left one peaceful and exhausted and utterly convinced that it was heaven one had spied and forgotten all in the same eternal momentless moment.

It had happened to them together. He had not consciously heard her, but he knew she had cried out. So had he. He had little experience, but instinct told him that what they had shared was rare and precious. They had glimpsed heaven together.

His friends would cart him off to Bedlam and leave him there if ever he started spouting such embarrassing nonsense in their hearing, he thought. His acquaintances' conversations about women were altogether more earthy and bawdy.

He lowered Viola's nightgown and cradled her against him. He kissed the top of her head.

"Thank you," he said.

THE NIGHT HAD BEEN sweet agony. They had been hungry after making love and had dressed and gone downstairs for a cold supper Ferdinand had asked for earlier. It was late after they had finished and talked for a while. Viola had expected him to leave. But he had asked her, reaching across the small round table to set one hand over hers, if she wanted him to stay, and she had said yes.

They had slept together. They had also made love twice more, once when they went back to bed, once before they got up in the morning. But it was the actual sleeping together that Viola had found most agonizing. She had slept in fits and starts, and every time she awoke she was aware of him, sometimes turned away from her, more often with his arms about her, the bedcovers all tangled about them. Simply being together like that had seemed more intimate to her than the sex. And more seductive.

Her head was aching now as they sat at breakfast. He

was wearing yesterday's clothes and was not turned out as immaculately as usual. His hair was still looking rather tousled, even though it had been combed. He was unshaven. He was looking altogether adorable.

"I have a number of things to do today," he was saying, "not least of which is to go home and change my clothes." He grinned and rubbed a hand over his jaw. "And get rid of this beard. Perhaps I'll be able to call in here this afternoon, though. We need to discuss your salary, and then we will be able to forget about it and not mention it again. I do find that part of our arrangement a little distasteful, don't you?"

"But quite essential." She smiled at him and memorized him with her eyes—the restless, rather boyishly eager manner that was so typical of him, the ready grin, which she had at first thought was rakish, the confident air, tinged with an unconscious arrogance that came from his birth and upbringing, the hint of reckless danger that always saved him from being a soft touch.

"I daresay Jane—the duchess, that is—will invite me for dinner tonight," he said. "I have promised to call sometime today to see the children—they were sleeping last evening. Or if it is not Jane it will be Angie—Lady Heyward, my sister. She will ferret me out fast enough once she knows I am back in town."

Viola held on to her smile. He had family, of whose members he was fonder than he realized. His voice told her that he was looking forward to seeing them again. The gulf between her and him was enormous, insurmountable. As his mistress she would be on the very periphery of his life, performing a base, if essential, service. And even that would be just for a few weeks or months, until he tired of her. His family was his forever.

Such thoughts confirmed her in her resolve.

"I won't stay late, though." He reached across the table, as he had the evening before, and took her hand in a warm clasp. "I won't let them persuade me to go off with them to whatever balls or soirees or concerts are scheduled for tonight. I'll come back here after dinner." He squeezed her hand. "I can hardly wait."

"Me neither." She smiled at him.

"Really, Viola?" His dark eyes were gazing into hers. "It really and truly is not just a job to you? You really—"

"Ferdinand." She raised their clasped hands and brought his against her cheek. His uncertainty and vulnerability, in such contrast to the image he presented to the world, broke her heart. "You cannot believe that. Not after last night. Please don't believe that. Not ever."

"No." He chuckled. "I won't. I just don't like this setup, though, Viola, and I don't mind telling you so. You ought to be back in the country—Miss Thornhill of Pinewood Manor. Or my wife—Lady Ferdinand Dudley. You really ought. I don't care that you have no father or that you did what you did because you had to eat. And I don't care what people might say. I'm the sort of fellow everyone expects to get into scrapes anyway."

"Marrying me would hardly be a scrape, Ferdinand," she said past the great lump in her throat.

"Let's do it," he said eagerly. "Let's just *do* it. I'll purchase a special license and—"

"No!" She turned her head to kiss the back of his hand before releasing it and standing up.

"It is what Tresham and Jane did," he said quickly, getting to his feet too. "They just went off one morning and got married while Angie and I were devising schemes for getting him to offer for her. He announced their marriage in the middle of a ball that night. I don't think they have ever regretted it. I think they are happy."

To be Ferdinand's wife. To be able to go back to Pinewood with him . . .

"It would not work for us, dear," she said gently, and then was jolted by the realization that she had spoken the endearment out loud. "You must be on your way. You have things to do."

"Yes." He took both her hands in his and raised them one at a time to his lips. "I wish I had met you six or seven years ago, Viola. Before . . . well, *before*. What were you doing then?"

"Probably serving coffee at my uncle's inn," she said. "And you were in the dusty depths of a library somewhere at Oxford studying Latin declensions. Go now."

"Later, then." He was still holding her hands. He leaned forward and touched his lips to hers. "I could become addicted to you. Be warned." He grinned at her as he turned and strode from the room.

It was appropriate, she thought, that her final sight of him was almost identical to her first—or nearly the first. He had been smiling just like that when her eyes had met his across the village green at the conclusion of the sack race.

A handsome, dashing stranger then.

The love of her heart now.

She stood where she was beside the dining room table until she heard the front door open and then shut behind him. She closed her eyes tightly and clutched the back of her chair.

Then she took a deep breath and went in search of Hannah.

18

IT WAS MIDMORNING BY THE TIME FERDINAND set off for the offices of Selby and Braithwaite. Fortunately, Selby was free to see him no more than five minutes after he arrived.

"Ah, my lord." The solicitor met him at the door of his office and shook his hand warmly. "Come up to London for the rest of the Season, have you? I hope you found Pinewood to your taste. I heard from his grace about the spot of bother you had when you arrived there, but that has all been cleared up, I trust. Have a chair and tell me what I may do for you."

Matthew Selby, middle-aged, genial, woolly-haired, looked like everyone's image of an upright, respectable father figure. He was also one of London's toughest solicitors.

"What you may do, Selby," Ferdinand said, "is transfer ownership of Pinewood Manor to Miss Viola Thornhill. I want it done legally and in writing so there can never be any argument about it."

"She is the lady you found living there," the solicitor said, frowning. "His grace mentioned her by name. She has no legal claim on the estate, my lord. Even though his grace insisted upon calling at Westinghouse and Sons in person, I did conduct my own investigation too, since you are a valued client of mine."

"If she had a legal claim I would not need to come,

would I?" Ferdinand said. "Draw up any papers that are necessary and I will sign them. I want it done today."

Selby removed the spectacles that were usually perched halfway down his nose and regarded Ferdinand with paternal concern, as if he were a boy who could not possibly make a rational decision on his own.

"Might I respectfully suggest, my lord," he said, "that you discuss the matter with the Duke of Tresham before doing anything hasty?"

Ferdinand fixed him with a stare. "Does Tresham have any claim on Pinewood?" he asked. "Is he my guardian?"

"I beg your pardon, my lord," Selby said. "I merely thought he might help you reach a wise decision."

"You are agreed," Ferdinand continued, "that Pinewood is mine? You have just said so. You investigated the matter and discovered that there can be no possible doubt."

"None whatsoever, my lord. But—"

"Then Pinewood is mine to give away," Ferdinand told him. "I am giving it away. To Miss Viola Thornhill. I want you to do the paperwork for me, Selby, so that I will know everything is done properly. I don't want anyone else to ride up to Pinewood in two years' time, claiming to have won the damned property in a card game and kicking her out. Now, can you do it for me, or shall I go elsewhere?"

Selby looked across the desk at him with gentle reproach as he put his spectacles back on his nose.

"I can do it, my lord," he said.

"Good." Ferdinand sat back and crossed his booted legs at the ankles. "Do it, then. I'll wait."

He thought about Pinewood and Trellick while he waited—about choir practice proceeding without him this week, about Jamie going without his Latin lessons, about the ladies straining their eyes sewing in the poorly lit church hall instead of in the drawing room at Pinewood, about the building of the laborers' cottages being delayed. About a certain spot on the riverbank where the river rushed past and daisies and buttercups grew in the grass, about a hillside down which a woman had run out of control, laughing and shrieking. About a village lass with daisies in her hair.

Well, he decided later as he strode away from the offices, there was no point in thinking about it all any longer. It had nothing to do with him. This time she would have to accept the gift. She would have no choice. He would take her the deed this afternoon. Of course—his footsteps lagged and some of the spring went out of his step—it would mean that she would no longer need to be his mistress. But that had been very much a last-resort offer on his part anyway.

He did not really want Viola Thornhill as his mistress. He wanted her . . . well, he simply wanted her. But he would damned well have to learn to do without her, wouldn't he? That was all there was to it. Of course . . .

"Wool-gathering, Ferdinand?"

He looked up to see his brother on horseback, riding along the street in the opposite direction from the one he was taking.

"Tresham," he said.

"And looking decidedly glum," the duke said. "She would not agree to terms, I suppose? Women of her sort are not worth brooding over, take my word for it. Do you want to come to Jackson's boxing saloon and try your luck sparring with me? Throwing a few punches can be a marvelous cure for bruised pride."

"Where is Jane?" Ferdinand asked.

His brother raised his eyebrows. "Angeline took her shopping," he said. "This will mean one new bonnet at the very least, I daresay. For our sister, that is. One wonders why Heyward is still complaisant enough to pay the bills. She must have a bonnet for every day of the year, with a few to spare."

Ferdinand grimaced. "It is to be hoped that Jane will steer her away from her usual garish choice," he said. "Our sister was born with the severe handicap of no taste whatsoever."

"She was wearing a puce monstrosity today," his brother said, "with a canary yellow plume at least a yard tall nodding above it. I made the mistake of looking at it through my quizzing glass. I was thankful it was my duchess who was to be seen in public with her and not me."

"I'll say," Ferdinand agreed fervently. He continued without giving himself time to think. Tresham was not the most comfortable person in the world to be telling such things to, even though it was none of his business. "I called on Selby just now. I have made Pinewood over to Miss Thornhill."

His brother looked down at him with an inscrutable stare. "You are a fool, Ferdinand," he said at last. "But one must look on the bright side. She will return there and be out of your life. It is not wise, you see, to fall in love with one's mistress. Especially one of such notoriety."

Something clicked in Ferdinand's brain. That room last night—the one with the pianoforte and the easel—and the embroidery frame. There was something about it that had teased at his mind. Tresham played the pianoforte. He also painted. But they had both been hidden, repressed talents until Jane had gone to work on him. Their father had brought his sons up to believe that art and music were effeminate pursuits. He had made his heir ashamed of indulging his talents. Even now Tresham rarely played for anyone but Jane. And he painted only when she was with him, sitting quietly in a room with him, working on her embroidery. She was wonderfully skilled with her needle. *That room.*

"But *you* did it," he said, looking up with narrow-eyed intensity into his brother's eyes. "You fell in love with *your* mistress, Tresham. You married her."

He found himself at the receiving end of one of Tresham's famous black stares.

"Who told you that?" Tresham's voice was always at its quietest and most pleasant when he was at his most dangerous.

"A certain room in a certain house," Ferdinand told him.

But it was not just the one room. There was the bedchamber too, with its unexpectedly elegant green and cream colorings. He would bet a pony Jane was responsible for that room. She had exquisite taste in design and color. She had been Tresham's *mistress.* He understood now at least why his brother had not sold the house.

"I had better rent the house from you, Tresham," he said while his brother continued to gaze at him, tight-lipped. "It won't be for long, I daresay. She will probably go back to Pinewood once she knows that it is hers whether she likes it or not. You will be able to relax then. Your little brother will be safe from the clutches of a notoriously wicked woman. Unlike you. Everyone thought *your* mistress was an ax murderer."

"By God, Ferdinand." Tresham leaned one arm across the pommel of his saddle and tapped his whip against one boot. "Are you deliberately courting death? Some advice, my dear fellow. Point a pistol between my eyes and pull the trigger if you must, but cast no aspersions on the good name of my duchess. It is not allowed."

"And I, *damn* you, will have none cast on that of Miss Thornhill," Ferdinand said.

His brother straightened up. "What is this all about, Ferdinand?" he asked. "Will it upset you so very much to see her go?"

Life was going to be empty without her, that was all. There was not going to seem much point to it. But he would soldier on, he supposed. One did not die of such a ridiculous malady as a broken heart. And when had he started to feel quite this way about her, anyway? After sleeping with her? It was probably just lust that was bothering him. Nothing more serious than that.

"The thing is," he said, "that I can't help thinking that if I had not made over the property to her this morning or if I failed to hand her the deed, she would stay and be my mistress. I can't help being tempted. But it would be wrong. It would, Tresh. I don't care what she has done in the past. I daresay she had her reasons. But *now,* you see, she is Miss Thornhill of Pinewood Manor. She is a lady. And I can't bear it because I have already defiled her and because I want to keep on doing so when she belongs back there. And I damned well can't *bear* the thought of her going. And make one sneering remark about this babbling drivel that is spouting out of my mouth and I'll drag you down from your horse and punch out all your teeth. I swear I will."

His brother stared broodingly at him for a few moments before dismounting to stand beside him. "Come to Jackson's," he said, "and pound the stuffing out of me, if it will make you feel better—and if you can. Preferably not my teeth, though, if it's all the same to you. Strange—I did not think you were into the petticoat line, Ferdinand. But perhaps that is the whole point. Perhaps I should have guessed that when you eventually fell, you would fall hard."

It was much later in the afternoon before Ferdinand went back to the house. He had gone home with Tresham after they had sparred to a stalemate at Jackson's. Angie had been there and had talked his ear off and forced both him and Tresham to view her new bonnet. He had played a vigorous wrestling game with his nephew, whom Tresham had brought down from the nursery for tea. Angie and Jane had vied for his company at dinner. Angie had won, though he had assured her that he would not go on to the Grosnick ball with her afterward—Heyward was to accompany her, she had explained, but Ferdie knew how much he danced, provoking man, which was absolutely not at all, while Ferdie was a divine dancer and would make her the envy of every other lady present.

Finally he arrived at the house. He was not really sure how he was going to proceed. Hand her the deed immediately and tell her Pinewood was hers whether she wanted it or not? Or keep the news until tonight? Perhaps they could go to bed this afternoon. Would it be dishonorable? Dash it, but honor could sometimes be a dreary killjoy of a weight on the conscience.

"Tell Miss Thornhill that I am here," he instructed Jacobs after he had been admitted to the house. "Where is she?"

"She is not in, my lord," the butler said, taking his hat and cane.

Damnation! He had not considered the possibility that she might be out. But it was a pleasant afternoon. She must have felt the need for some air and exercise.

"I'll wait," he said. "Did she say when she would be back?"

"No, my lord."

"Did she take her maid?" Ferdinand frowned. She was in London now. He would not have her walking about outside without a chaperon.

"Yes, my lord."

He went into the room with the pianoforte and looked about him. How on earth had he not realized the truth yesterday as soon as he set foot in here? he wondered. It had Jane and Tresham-with-Jane written all over it. It was a strangely cozy room, even though the embroidery frame and the easel and music stand were all empty. He would enjoy spending time here with Viola. She would feel like his companion as well as his mistress in here. They would talk and read and be comfortable together. She would feel almost like a wife.

But he did not want a wife, he reminded himself—or mistress either. He wanted Viola to be back at Pinewood, lady of the manor again. Even if it meant never seeing her again, because that was what she wanted.

He wandered restlessly from the room and upstairs to the bedchamber. He sat on the side of the bed and ran one hand over the pillow where her head had lain last night. He hoped—he swallowed the lump that had formed in his throat—he hoped she would go back home. Perhaps after some time had passed he could go down there, stay at the Boar's Head, call on her, court her....

He wandered into her dressing room. It looked empty. She had brought only the one bag with her from Pinewood, it was true, but there surely should have been a comb or brush or something on the dressing table. All that was there, propped against the mirror, was a folded piece of paper. He crossed the room with hesitant steps, knowing very well what it was. It had his name written on the outside in the now-familiar neat handwriting.

It was as terse as the last one.

"We agreed that we were both free to end our liaison at a moment's notice," she had written. "I am ending it now. Go back to Pinewood. It is where you will find the fulfillment for which you have been searching all your adult life, I believe. Be happy there. Viola."

So she had escaped after all. She had intended it from the start, he realized. Now that he thought about it, he could recall that she had never said explicitly that she would be his mistress, only that she would come here with him and must be free to go whenever she chose. She had disappeared into the vastness of London. Last night had meant nothing to her. *He* meant nothing to her. She preferred the life of a courtesan. It made no sense whatsoever to him. But did it need to?

Would he never learn?

He crumpled the paper and dropped it to the floor.

"Goddamn you," he said aloud.

And then he surprised and embarrassed himself—almost as if there were an audience—by sobbing once and then again and finding it impossible to stem the flow of his grief.

"Goddamn you to hell," he said between sobs. "What do you *want* from me?"

The silence answered him loud and clear.

Nothing at all.

VIOLA WAS GOING HOME. Home to her uncle's inn to see her mother and sisters. And to meet Daniel Kirby and come to some arrangement with him about her future. But even though she would not put herself through the agony of hoping, she intended to fight as far as she was able. Bag in hand, Hannah beside her, she made her way first in the opposite direction to the inn. She had a call to make.

She sat and waited stubbornly for three hours in a dingy outer office of Westinghouse and Sons, Solicitors, before being admitted for one whole minute into the presence of the most junior partner and assured that the late Earl of Bamber's will made no mention whatsoever of Miss Viola Thornhill.

"Well, Hannah," she said as they were leaving, "I did not expect anything different, you know. But I had to hear it with my own ears."

"Where are we going now, Miss Vi?"

Hannah had been disapproving of last night's destination. But this morning she had disapproved of their leaving. She had wanted Viola to throw herself upon Lord Ferdinand's mercy, to tell him everything, to beg him to lend her the money with which to pay Daniel Kirby. Ferdinand was more than halfway in love with her, according to Hannah. He could be brought to offer for her if Miss Vi just played her cards right.

Never! She would not beg money from him, she would

not burden him with her problems, and she would not entice him into a marriage he would bitterly regret for the rest of his life.

"We are going to call on the Earl of Bamber," she said in answer to Hannah's question.

It was halfway through the afternoon by the time they arrived there. It was very probable he would not be home. It was even more probable that she would be denied admittance even if he were. It was a shocking thing for a lady to call upon a single gentleman, even though she was accompanied by her maid. The look with which the earl's butler regarded her when he opened the door to her knock confirmed her fears. She probably would not have succeeded in setting so much as a foot over the doorstep if chance had not brought the earl home while she was standing there arguing.

"Who do we have here, then?" he asked, coming up the steps behind her, his eyes raking over her.

He was short, portly, fair-haired, and florid of complexion. He bore no discernible resemblance to his father.

"I am Viola Thornhill," she said, turning to face him.

"Well, damn me." His brows snapped together. "The woman herself, standing on my doorstep. I am mortally sick of hearing your name. I'll not have you bothering me, I say. Take yourself off. Shoo!"

"My mother was once your governess," she said.

For a moment she thought he was going to tell her again to shoo, but then an arrested look came over his face.

"*Hillie?*" he said. "I only ever had one governess—before I went to school. She was Hillie."

"Rosamond Thornhill," Viola said. "My mother."

She watched the glimmer of understanding come into his rather bloodshot eyes.

"You had better come inside," he said ungraciously, and he led the way into the house and across the hall to a small salon. Hannah followed them and stood quietly inside the door after the earl had shut it.

"Who the devil are you?" he asked.

"My mother was your father's mistress for ten years," she said. "He was my father too."

He stared at her, his expression grim.

"What do you want from me?" he asked her. "If you have come here begging for money—"

"I met him shortly before he died," she said. "He was determined to provide for me. He sent me to Pinewood Manor. It was one of his smaller, unentailed holdings, he said. He had never even been there himself. But he thought it was in a suitably secluded corner of England and could offer me a decent living if it was well managed. He was going to change his will so that it would always be mine."

"Well, he did not do so," he said. "The very idea—"

"He loved me," she said. "He always loved me. I never doubted his affection while I was a child, before my mother married. I doubted it afterward because suddenly he did not come anymore or even write. But that was my mother's fault, I learned later. She had broken off her relationship with him and refused to let him even see me. She destroyed all the letters and gifts he sent me. It was quite by chance that I saw him in the park.... But no matter. The details can be of no interest to you. Did you persuade Mr. Westinghouse to erase the new clause from his will?"

The explosive blasphemy that was his first reaction

convinced her that he was not the villain of this piece. "Get out of here," he told her, "before I throw you out."

"Could he have made a new will with someone else?" she asked, ignoring his wrath. "You see, it is not only Pinewood that is at stake. There was another paper, which he said he would file officially with his solicitor so that the matter could never be disputed. He paid off some debts to release me from an obligation and keep my mother out of debtors' prison. He had the man who held the debts sign a paper stating that all the bills had been paid in full, that there were no more, and that he waived the right to claim for any other unpaid bill that preceded the date of the agreement."

"What the devil!" the Earl of Bamber said.

"That man has now discovered other debts," Viola said, "and is demanding payment."

"And you expect me—"

"No!" she said. "My father rescued me . . . from the life of prostitution I had been forced into so that I could pay back the debt. He provided for my future so that I could live in peace and security for the rest of my life. I ask nothing of you, my lord. I ask only that my father not be denied his dying wish. That paper is of vital importance to me. Your father loved me. I was as much his daughter as you were his son, you see, even though I was born on the wrong side of the blanket."

He stared at her for a while and then ran the fingers of one hand through his hair before turning abruptly away to stare into the unlit coals of the fire.

"Damn me," he said. "Why did I go to Brookes's that night? I have had nothing but trouble over that worthless property ever since. Well, he didn't change his will, and that's all about it. And there is no paper. Westinghouse would have said so. He would at least have recognized your name, wouldn't he?"

"And there is no possibility there was someone else?"

He drummed his fingers on the mantel above his head. "I wonder if m'mother knew about Hillie," he muttered. "And about you. I bet she did. M'mother always knows everything."

Viola waited.

"I'm sorry," he said eventually, turning abruptly to face her. "I can't help you, you know. And I can't send you back to Pinewood even if I wanted to—which I don't particularly. Why should I? You are just m'father's by-blow. Pinewood is Dudley's. Go beg from him. I'm expected somewhere for dinner. You will have to leave now."

There was nothing further to say. Viola left with Hannah. There was no way to save herself from her inevitable future, it seemed.

They began the long walk home.

19

"I HAVE NEVER KNOWN YOU SO OUT OF SORTS, Ferdie," Lady Heyward complained. "I expected you to be bubbling over with stories about Pinewood and your two weeks in the country. But whenever one asks you a question, you say nothing whatsoever of any significance."

"Perhaps, Angie," he said irritably, "it is because trying to get a word in sideways in your company is an exercise in futility. Besides, the dinner is good and to be savored. Convey my compliments to your cook, will you?"

"Unfair!" she cried. "Is he not being unfair, Jane? Tell me, have I or have I not plied Ferdie with enough questions to get him talking about Pinewood? And have I or have I not paused each time to allow him all the time in the world to answer?"

"There really is not—" Ferdinand began.

"Of *course* there must be a great deal to say," she said. "Who are your neighbors there? What—"

"Angie," Ferdinand said firmly, "Pinewood no longer belongs to me. It is hardly worth talking about the place."

"Jocelyn told me you have legally made over the ownership to Miss Thornhill, Ferdinand," the Duchess of Tresham said. "I *do* admire you for doing something so very honorable."

"You have done *what,* Ferdie?" His sister's eyes were wide with astonishment.

"He has given Pinewood back to Miss Thornhill," Jane explained, "because he believed it was more hers than his. I am very proud of you, Ferdinand. Jocelyn told me that it is a lovely place."

"Was that wise, Ferdinand?" Lord Heyward asked. "It might have been a prosperous estate for you."

"Now everything makes perfect sense!" Angeline cried. "Ferdie is in *love*!"

"Oh, good Lord!" he was startled into saying.

"You are in love with this Miss Thornhill," she said. "How absolutely splendid. And so of course you have made the magnificent gesture of returning Pinewood to her. But you *must* go back there. She is sure to fall into your arms and dissolve into tears of gratitude. I simply must be there to see it. Do take me with you. Heyward, *may* I go? You spend all your days at the House of Lords anyway, and you know it will be a relief not to have to escort me to evening entertainments for a week or two. There will be time before the Season ends to organize a grand wedding at St. George's. We will have a great squeeze of a ball here. Jane, you must help me. I was deprived of the opportunity of doing it for you and Tresh when he whisked you off to marry you one morning with absolutely no one in attendance but his secretary and your maid. What a waste that was. For Ferdie I am determined to do much better."

"Angie!" Ferdinand said firmly. "Take a damper." He caught his brother's eye across the table. Tresham merely raised his eyebrows, pursed his lips, and addressed himself to the food on his plate.

"I do believe you are embarrassing your brother, my love," Lord Heyward said.

"Men!" Angeline exclaimed. "Always embarrassed at any mention of love and marriage. Are they not ridiculous creatures, Jane?"

"I have frequently said so," the duchess agreed, looking with some amusement at Tresham, who did not rise to the bait. "But Ferdinand, who *is* Miss Thornhill? Jocelyn did tell me she is beautiful."

"It was, of course," Tresham said, "the first question Jane asked when I returned home."

"Oh, not the *first*, you odious man," she protested.

"She is the most irritating female I have ever known," Ferdinand said. "She talked me into making a wager with her, Pinewood as the prize—and she won. She would not take it. Then I gave it to her as a gift. She ran away. I followed her and caught her before she reached London. Today I had Selby make the change of ownership legal, but when I went to tell her so, she had disappeared again. It seems she really does not want it."

"How extraordinary!" Jane said.

"You must go back tomorrow, then, and get Selby to reverse the procedure," Heyward said. "You ought to have come to me or Tresham before you did it anyway, Ferdinand. You have a strong tendency to act impulsively. It is the Dudley blood in you."

"People are always impulsive when they are in love," Angeline said. "Ferdie, you must find her. You must comb London for her. Hire a Bow Street Runner. How very romantic."

"I have no wish to find her," he said.

"Do you have no idea where she is?" Jane asked.

"None," he said curtly. "And I have no wish to know.

Pinewood is hers. If she does not want it, that is her concern. It may rot, for all I care."

And then a thought popped into his head as if from nowhere—a thought spoken in her voice…

Probably serving coffee at my uncle's inn.

He had asked her what she would have been doing six or seven years ago if he had met her before she became a courtesan. At the time his mind had scarcely registered her answer.

"I believe her uncle owns an inn," he said.

Angie was all eagerness to know what kind of inn, where in London it might be situated, what the uncle's name was. She—and Jane, to a lesser degree—seemed determined to find in the whole situation a romance that must be given a happy ending. He could stand it no longer after a few minutes.

"There is no question of finding her," he said. "I offered her Pinewood and she would not take it. I offered her marriage and she would not accept me. I offered her… protection and she ran away. She would prefer to return to her old way of life."

"What is that?" Angeline asked.

Ferdinand was aware of his brother's black stare across the table.

"She was a courtesan," he said. "A very successful one until she went to Pinewood two years ago. And she is illegitimate into the bargain. So you might as well take a damper, Angie, and go matchmake for someone else. Now let's change the subject, shall we?"

"Oh, the poor lady," Jane said softly. "I wonder what is driving her back to her old life."

"Me," Ferdinand said.

"No." She shook her head, frowning. "No, Ferdinand. Not that."

"A lady with a scarlet past and a murky secret," Angeline said, clasping her hands to her bosom. "How irresistibly intriguing. You can be sure she loves you as desperately as you love her, Ferdie. Why else would she have run away from you twice?"

Women! he thought as Heyward launched into a long, dry monologue about a speech he had delivered in the House that very day. The older he grew, Ferdinand thought, the less he understood women. Angie and Jane should be in the middle of a fit of the vapors apiece.

An innkeeper. He dared not even guess how many inns there might be in London. Her uncle—maternal or paternal? How slender was the chance that he bore the same last name as she? He had been an innkeeper six or seven years ago. Was he still?

She had no wish to be found—until she surfaced again as Lilian Talbot, he supposed. And he had no wish to find her. She had deceived and rejected him one time too many.

How many inns *were* there?

He was not really going to waste his time searching, was he?

I wonder what is driving her back to her old life.

Jane's words echoed and reechoed in his mind.

A COACH WAS LEAVING the White Horse Inn with a great deal of din and bustle. Viola and Hannah stood aside to let it turn out onto the street before stepping into the cobbled yard. The innkeeper was standing outside the door, bellowing something to a distant ostler. But he turned and saw the two women, and his scowl was replaced by a broad smile.

"Viola!" he exclaimed, spreading his arms wide.

"Uncle Wesley!"

Soon she was enveloped in his strong arms and crushed against his broad chest.

"So you *did* come," he said, holding her at arm's length. "But why did you not let us know when? Someone would have met you. Hello, Hannah. Rosamond and the girls are going to be delighted." He called through the open door of the inn, "Claire! Come and see what we have here."

Viola's sister came rushing through the door a moment later. She was looking remarkably pretty, Viola noticed at once. She had blossomed into a slender, shapely beauty with shining blond tresses. Then they were in each other's arms, hugging and laughing.

"I *knew* you would come!" her sister exclaimed. "And Hannah is with you. Oh, do come upstairs. Mama will be ecstatic. So will Maria." She took Viola by the hand and turned back toward the inn door. But then she stopped and looked anxiously at her uncle. "*May* I go up with her, Uncle Wesley? Everything is quiet now that the coach has left."

"Up with you both," he said jovially. "Away you go."

Viola was led up to the private living quarters on the upper floor and into her mother's sitting room. Her mother was seated by the window sewing, while Maria sat at the table, a book open before her. But a moment later, all was movement and squeals and laughter and hugs and kisses.

"We *knew* you would come," Maria cried when some

sanity had been restored to the scene. "Oh, I do hope you will be living here now."

Maria had changed from a child to a young girl with some promise of beauty to come.

"You must be weary," their mother said, linking an arm through Viola's and leading her to a love seat, where they seated themselves side by side. "Have you just traveled up from Somersetshire? I wish we had known it was today we were to expect you. We would have come to meet you. Maria, dear, run downstairs and bring up a tea tray and some cakes, there's a good girl."

Maria went obediently, even though she looked reluctant to miss even a moment of her eldest sister's homecoming.

"It is so lovely to be back here and to see you all," Viola said. For the moment she allowed home and family to wrap themselves about her like a cocoon, where she could be safe from all the menaces of the outside world. And from all the memories. She wondered if Ferdinand had returned to the house yet and discovered her gone.

"All will be well." Her mother took her hand and patted it.

"But it seems that you were all expecting me," Viola said, puzzled.

Her mother squeezed her hand. "We have heard," she said, "about Pinewood's turning out not to belong to you after all. I am so sorry, Viola. You know I was opposed to your accepting it from—f-from Bamber when you were doing so well at your governess's post, but I am sorry he deceived you so."

Despite the bitter quarrel they had had before she left for Pinewood, Viola had had enough experience of life not to pass too severe a judgment on her mother. She had been got with child—with her, Viola—while she was governess to the Earl of Bamber's son. The earl had whisked her off to London and kept her there as his mistress for ten years before she fell headlong in love with Clarence Wilding and married him. The change in Viola's life was total and severe. There was no more contact with her father, whom she had adored. There was the impatience and contempt of her stepfather instead. Sometimes, when he was drunk and her mother was not present, he called her "the bastard." She had had to ask Hannah the meaning of the word.

It was not until almost thirteen years later, when she recognized her father driving in the park one afternoon while she was walking and had impulsively hailed him, that she had discovered the full truth. Her father had not abandoned her. He had tried to see her. He had written to her and sent her presents. He had sent money for her support. He had wanted to send her to a good boarding school before arranging a respectable marriage for her. Everything had been returned to him.

And so he had discovered the truth about his daughter and the life she was living and the reason for it. He had arranged a meeting with Daniel Kirby and paid off all the remaining debts of the man who had taken his mistress and his daughter from him. And then he had given Viola the precious gift of a new life. He had given her Pinewood.

Her mother had been incensed. At first Viola had been much inclined to blame her. What right had she to keep Viola from her own father? But she had learned enough about life by that time to know that the human heart was a complex organ and frequently led one in the wrong direction without any really cruel intent. Also she recognized that her mother was reacting without full knowledge of all the facts. Her mother believed that Viola had respectable employment as a governess.

She had forgiven her mother long ago.

"He did not deceive me, Mama," she said. "But how did you know about Pinewood?"

"Mr. Kirby told us," her mother said.

Just the sound of his name made Viola's stomach lurch.

"Do you remember him?" her mother asked. "But of course you must. He comes to the inn to take coffee quite frequently, does he not, Claire? He is still very amiable. I have gone down once or twice to converse with him. He commiserated with us over your loss. Naturally, we were mystified. That was when he told us about the Duke of Tresham's brother winning the property from the earl and going down to Somersetshire to claim it. What is the brother's name? I cannot recall."

"Lord Ferdinand Dudley," Viola said.

Daniel Kirby had heard, then. But *of course* he would have heard. He made it his business to know everything. This explained why he suddenly discovered a new debt. He knew she would be returning to London. He knew he could exercise power over her again.

"What is Lord Ferdinand like, Viola?" Claire asked.

Handsome. Full of laughter. Gregarious, charming, impossibly attractive. Daring and dashing. Kind. Honorable. Innocent—strangely innocent.

"I did not know him long enough to form any lasting impression," she said.

Maria came back then, carrying a tray, which she set down on a table close to the love seat.

"Well," their mother said as she poured the tea, "you are home now, Viola. That part of your life is in the past and best forgotten. Perhaps Mr. Kirby will help you again. He knows a great many influential people. And of course your former employers may be willing to give you a good recommendation even though you left them rather abruptly."

Viola shook her head when Maria offered the plate of cakes. She felt quite nauseated. For that, of course, was just what was going to happen. Daniel Kirby would come here soon and the two of them would talk and come to some arrangement for the resumption of her career. They would set about spinning a suitable yarn for her family so they would never know the truth.

Perhaps, Viola thought as she sipped her tea and listened to Maria's prattle about the latest news from Ben, she should tell them herself—now, before her life became a web of lies and deceit again.

But she simply could not do it. All their lives would be ruined. Uncle Wesley had been enormously kind to them over the years. He had never remarried after his young wife died giving birth to their stillborn child only one year into their marriage. His sister and her family had become his own. He had supported them cheerfully and without complaint. Viola could not see him destroyed. And there were Claire and Maria and Ben, who must be allowed a future of pleasant prospects. Her mother's health was not strong. She would not be able to support the burden.

No, she could not do it.

20

IT WAS FERDINAND'S SECOND DAY OF RIDING from inn to inn on a search that he fully expected to be futile. He would waste a week or so in this way until finally he would either see her—in the park or at the theater—or hear of her from his acquaintances. Lilian Talbot was back, the story would go, as beautiful, as alluring, as expensive as ever. Lord So-and-so had been the fortunate one to secure her services first, Lord Such-and-such second...

If he was wise, Ferdinand kept telling himself, he would return to Selby and get him to tear up the papers transferring ownership of Pinewood, and he would go back there himself—and stay there for the rest of his life.

He never had been renowned for his wisdom.

He had arrived at the White Horse Inn at just the wrong time, he thought as he rode into the cobbled yard. A stagecoach was preparing for departure. There were people, horses, and baggage everywhere, and a great deal of noise and commotion. But one stablehand recognized him as a gentleman and hurried toward him to ask if he could take his horse.

"Perhaps," Ferdinand said, leaning down from his saddle. "But I am not sure I have the right place. I am looking for an innkeeper by the name of Thornhill."

"He is over there, sir," the lad said, pointing to the

densest throng of people close to the coach. "He is busy, but I'll call him if you like."

"No." Ferdinand dismounted and handed the boy a coin. "I'll go inside and wait."

The innkeeper was large in both height and girth. He was exchanging pleasantries with the stagecoach driver. His name was Thornhill. Could the search possibly end this easily? Ferdinand wondered.

He ducked through the doorway and found himself in a dark, beamed porch. A slender, pretty young girl with a tray of used dishes in her hands curtsied to him and would have proceeded on her way if he had not spoken.

"I am looking for Miss Viola Thornhill," he said.

She looked far more directly at him then. "Viola?" she said. "She is in the coffee room, sir. Shall I call her?"

"No," he said. He was feeling almost dizzy. She was *here*? "Which room is that?"

She pointed and stood to watch him as he proceeded toward it.

There must still be some time left before the stagecoach was due to depart, he thought as he stood in the doorway. It was still half full. But he saw Viola immediately, seated at the far side of the room, facing toward him. Opposite her sat a man, to whom she was talking.

Ferdinand stood watching them, torn between feelings of relief, anger, and uncertainty. He never had decided how he would proceed if he found her. He could stride toward that table now, if he chose, place the papers beside her saucer, make his bow, and leave without saying a word. He could then get on with his life, his conscience appeased.

But two things happened before he could make up his mind to do it.

The man turned his head sideways to look out through the window. Ferdinand could not see him full-face, but he could see enough to realize that he knew him. Not personally, but he supposed there were not many men of his class who would not recognize Daniel Kirby. He was a gentleman, though not a member of the *ton*. He hung about places like Tattersall's and Jackson's and various racetracks—places frequented primarily by men. A small, round-faced, jovial fellow, he was nevertheless well known for the weasel he was. He was a moneylender, a blackmailer, and other unsavory things. Wherever there was money to be made by shady means, Daniel Kirby was there.

And Viola Thornhill was in conversation with him.

The other thing that happened was that she looked beyond the shoulder of her companion and her gaze locked with Ferdinand's for a moment. But although she stopped talking for that moment, her expression did not change. There was no look of surprise, anger, embarrassment—or anything else. Then she returned her attention to Kirby and continued with what she was saying as if nothing had happened.

She did not want Kirby to know he was there, Ferdinand concluded. Only seconds must have passed, he realized, when he turned to find the young maid still standing where she was, holding her tray.

"Does she live here?" he asked.

"Yes, sir," the girl said.

"And her mother too?"

"Yes, sir."

"What is her name?"

"My mother's?" She frowned.

"*Your* mother's?" He looked more intently at her. "Is Miss Thornhill your sister?"

"My half-sister, sir," she said. "I am Claire Wilding."

He had not even known that she had a sister. The girl was small and slender and blond. He made an impulsive decision.

"Will you ask Mrs. Wilding if she will receive me?" he asked. He drew out one of his visiting cards from his coat pocket.

She looked at it as he set it on the tray.

"Yes, my lord." She curtsied and blushed. "I'll ask her."

She spoke with a refined accent, he noticed, just as Viola did. Clearly she could also read.

LIFE COULD GET NO bleaker, Viola thought as Daniel Kirby took his leave. When her uncle had come upstairs earlier to announce his arrival, he had been smiling. Her mother had smiled too and insisted on coming down to the coffee room with Viola to pay her respects to him.

The conversation had turned to business once the two of them had been alone together, of course. The terms were the same as they had been before. Viola had not given in without protest, but she had known it was hopeless. When she had mentioned the receipt Mr. Kirby had signed and given to her father, he had regarded her kindly but blankly.

"Now, what receipt would that be?" he had asked her. "I recollect no such thing."

"No, of course. You would not," she had replied coldly.

He was to find her rooms. He was to put about the

word that she was back in town. He was to engage clients for her. He granted her a week's holiday to spend with her family while he made all the arrangements.

"After all," he had said, "your family might find it strange if I were to find you a governess's post too soon. And we would not wish to upset your family, would we?"

But if the interview with Daniel Kirby was not trouble enough for one morning, there was the other ghastly thing that had happened while she was sitting talking to him. She had looked up, conscious that someone was standing in the doorway, and for a moment had completely lost the trend of what she was saying.

In the split second before she had pulled herself together, all she had thought of was that he had *found* her, that he had come for her, that she could rush into his arms, and he would hold her there safe forever. Then she *had* pulled herself together and looked away. When she had glanced up again a few seconds later, he had gone.

She had felt enormous relief.

She had also hit the depths of despair.

She got up from the empty table. She had promised to help out in the office with some of the paperwork Claire so abhorred. But first, she thought, she must go to her room to spend some time alone.

How had he found her?

Why had he come?

Why had he gone away again without a word?

Would he come back?

Hannah was in her room, hanging up her newly laundered and ironed traveling dress.

"Your mother asked that you go to her as soon as *that man* left," she said.

Viola sighed. "Did she say what she wanted, Hannah?"

"No," her maid said, though Viola had the feeling that she knew very well.

She sighed again. Her mother probably wanted to share her delight at Mr. Kirby's promise to help her daughter find employment, Viola thought as she opened the sitting room door and stepped inside.

Lord Ferdinand Dudley was sitting by the fireplace.

"See who has come to call upon me this morning, Viola," her mother said, getting to her feet and hurrying closer. "He needs no introduction to you, of course."

He rose and bowed as her mother turned to smile warmly at him.

"Miss Thornhill," he said.

"Lord Ferdinand has just traveled up from Somersetshire," her mother explained, "and has come to pay his respects to me. Is that not a kind courtesy, Viola? He has been telling Maria and me how highly thought of you are at Pinewood."

Viola looked at him with silent reproach. "It was kind of you to call, my lord," she said. *How did you find me? Why did you find me?*

"Do sit down again," her mother told their guest as she drew Viola to sit beside her on the love seat. "I have been explaining, Viola, why you could not join us immediately." She looked back at their visitor. "My father was a gentleman, you see, but he lost his fortune in some unwise investments, and so my brother had to forge his own way in the world, as did I. I was a governess too. Viola's father was a gentleman. So was my late husband."

Her mother was on the defensive, Viola thought.

"No one who saw Miss Thornhill manage a country

fête could possibly doubt that she is a lady, ma'am," Lord Ferdinand said, his eyes smiling into Viola's.

He proceeded to tell her mother and Maria about the May Day celebrations at Trellick. He soon had both of them laughing and exclaiming in delight. The ability to charm almost any audience was one of his personal gifts, of course. It had annoyed her at Pinewood. It annoyed her now.

"We are glad to have Viola home with us again," her mother said at last. "Of course, she will probably be teaching again soon. Mr. Kirby has promised to help her find a respectable position, as he did once before."

Viola watched Lord Ferdinand, but he gave no sign of knowing the name.

"I came to town just in time, then, ma'am," he said. "I might have missed Miss Thornhill if I had postponed my visit to a later date."

"Yes, indeed," her mother agreed.

"I wonder if I might beg the favor of a private word with your daughter, ma'am?" he asked.

Viola shook her head imperceptibly, but no one was looking at her. Her mother got to her feet without any hesitation.

"Of course, my lord," she said, sounding inordinately pleased. "Come along, Maria. We will see what help we can offer downstairs."

Mama thought he had come *courting*, Viola thought as her mother, her back to their visitor, gave her a significant look. Then she left, taking Maria with her.

The clock ticked with unnatural loudness on the mantel.

Viola spread her hands in her lap and looked down at them.

"How did you find me?" she asked.

"You said your uncle was an innkeeper," he said.

Had she told him that?

"I started searching yesterday morning," he said. "I began with the coaching inns and the slim hope that your uncle was still in business and bore the name of Thornhill."

She looked up at him. "Why?"

He had got to his feet when her mother rose. He stood now in front of the fireplace, his hands at his back. He looked large and powerful. She felt at a distinct disadvantage. She saw him draw a deep breath and release it slowly.

"Mainly for this reason, I suppose," he said, reaching into his coat pocket and bringing out a sheaf of papers.

"How many times do I have to say no before you will believe me?" she asked.

"Pinewood is yours," he said. "I have had the title legally transferred to you. It is yours whether you want it or not, Viola."

He held out the papers, but she made no move to take them. It was too late. Daniel Kirby had heard about his winning Pinewood and had concluded that if her father had not changed his will, he had probably not kept that receipt either. He had guessed that he had her in his power again. Pinewood would not be able to help her now. He would make sure that the rents were not quite enough to cover payment on the debts.

Lord Ferdinand moved toward the table and set the papers down beside Maria's books.

"It is yours," he said again.

"Very well," she said, her eyes on her hands again.

"Your task has been successfully accomplished. Good day to you, my lord."

"Viola," he said softly, and she heard him sigh with exasperation.

The next moment, she saw his riding boots almost toe-to-toe with her slippers, and then he came down on his haunches and captured both her hands in his own. She had little choice but to look into his eyes, on a level with her own.

"Do you hate me so much?" he asked her.

The question almost broke her heart. Perhaps she had not realized until this precise moment just how much she loved him. Not just how much she was *in* love with him, but how much she *loved* him.

"Do you find it so hard to believe," she asked in return, "that I could wish to be my own person rather than your mistress?"

"I offered you Pinewood," he said. "You told me it meant so much to you only because the late Earl of Bamber gave it to you. Did you love him so much more than me, then? He must have been old enough to be your father."

His words might have been funny under other circumstances.

"Fool!" she said, but she spoke gently. "Ferdinand, he *was* my father. Do you think I would have accepted a gift like that from a lover?"

His hands tightened about her own and he stared at her in astonishment. "Bamber was your *father*?"

She nodded. "I had not seen him since my mother married Clarence Wilding. He had been in poor health for years. He did not come to London often. He came then to consult a physician, but it was hopeless. He knew he was dying. I will forever be thankful that I saw him and recognized him in Hyde Park and called out to him before I could stop myself. He explained why I had not heard from him during all those years. And he tried to atone, to do for me what he would have done if we had not been estranged by my mother's marriage. It was too late for him to arrange a decent marriage for me—I had been working for four years. But he gave me Pinewood and the chance of a new life. It was a precious gift, Ferdinand, because it came from my father. It was a gift of pure love."

He bent his head and closed his eyes. "This explains why you will not believe that he neglected to change his will," he said.

"Yes."

Ferdinand lifted her hands one at a time to his lips. "Forgive me," he said. "I behaved like a prize ass when I came to Pinewood. I should have gone away immediately. You would still be happy there now."

"No." She gazed earnestly at him. "You behaved quite reasonably under the circumstances. You might have thrown me out that very first day."

"Go home," he urged her. "Go back there. Not because I want you to but because your father did. And because that is where you belong."

"Perhaps I will," she said.

"No, dash it." He got to his feet and drew her to hers. "I can tell by the look on your face that you are humoring me. You have no intention of going there, have you? Because it comes from *me*. It brings me back to my original question. Do you hate me so much?"

"I don't hate you." She closed her eyes.

It was a mistake. He stepped closer, wrapped his arms

about her, and set his mouth, open, over hers. She was powerless to end the embrace, even though he did not hold her imprisoned. She twined her arms about his neck and allowed all the defenses she had erected about herself in the past few days to crumble away. She kissed him back with all the yearning, all the passion, all the love in her heart.

For those few moments, impossibilities seemed possible. But passion did not have the power to drown out reality for very long.

"Ferdinand," she said, drawing back her head, though she kept her arms about him, "I cannot be your mistress."

"No, you dashed well cannot," he agreed. "The position is no longer open. It was all wrong anyway. I was not made to have mistresses. I cannot bed a woman and carry on with the rest of my life as if she did not exist. I want you to marry me."

"Because I am the daughter of the Earl of Bamber?" she asked, her hands slipping to his shoulders.

He clucked his tongue. "*Illegitimate* daughter. You forgot that juicy detail," he said scornfully. "No, of course not for that reason. I asked you once before, long before I knew who your father was. I want to marry you, that is all. I miss you."

He had not said he loved her, but he did not need to. It was there in the way he looked at her, in the way he held her, in the words he spoke. Viola knew a few moments of intense temptation. For she knew that with one word—*yes*—she could turn her whole life around. He loved her. He wanted to marry her. She could tell him everything—he already knew the worst about her. She had no doubt that he could and would pay off all of

Clarence Wilding's debts and so free her family from the threat of ruin. She herself would be freed forever from the power of Daniel Kirby and a life of prostitution.

But she *loved* him. He could not marry her without sacrificing everything that was dear to him—his family, his position in society, his friends. He might think now that he did not care—he always had that reckless, dangerous eagerness to take up any challenge—the more outrageous, the better. But this was a challenge he could not win. He would be unhappy for most of the rest of his life. And therefore, so would she.

"Ferdinand," she said, and she retreated behind the contemptuous half smile that was second nature to her whenever she needed to protect herself from hurt, "I refused to marry you because I have no wish to marry you or any man. Why should I, when I can have any man I please whenever I please and still retain my freedom? I never did agree to become your mistress. I slept with you the night we arrived in London because you seemed to want it so badly. And it was pleasant, I must admit. But you really do not know yet—forgive me—how to please a woman in bed. I would become restless within a week or two if I stayed with you. I have been feeling restless at Pinewood for some time. You did me a favor by coming there and forcing me into doing what I have been wanting to do—resuming my career, that is. I find the life exciting."

"Don't *do* that." He was gripping her arms hard enough to leave bruises. He was also glaring into her eyes, his own suddenly very black. "Goddamn you, Viola. Don't you *trust* me? If you loved me, you would. I thought perhaps you did love me."

"Oh, Ferdinand." She smiled and spoke softly. "How foolish of you."

He swung away from her and picked up his hat and his cane from a chair inside the door.

"You could have trusted me, you know." He looked back at her when his hand was on the doorknob. "If he has some sort of power over you, you could have told me so. Dudley men know how to protect their women. But I can't force you, can I? And I can't make you love me if you don't. Good day to you."

The door was closing behind him as she reached out one arm toward him. She clapped her hand over her mouth so that she would not call after him. The ache in her throat was almost too painful to bear.

He *did* know who Daniel Kirby was.

You could have trusted me…you could have told me so. Dudley men know how to protect their women.

She did not know where he lived. She would not know where to find him if she changed her mind.

Thank God she did not know. Temptation was beyond her reach.

21

FERDINAND HAD STILL NOT QUITE ADJUSTED HIS mind to thinking of his brother as a family man. But when Tresham's butler led him all the way up to the nursery of Dudley House and announced him, he walked in to find Tresham actually down on the floor building a precarious-looking castle out of wooden blocks with his three-year-old while the baby lay on a blanket beside them—out of range of falling masonry—kicking his legs and waving his arms. Their nurse was nowhere in sight. Neither was Jane.

The arrival of an uncle was more appealing, at least for a few minutes, it seemed, than the castle. Nicholas came hurtling across the room, and Ferdinand scooped him up and tossed him at the ceiling.

"Hello, old sport," he said as he caught the shrieking child. "By gad, I almost missed you. You weigh a ton."

"Again!"

Ferdinand tossed him again, made a great to-do about staggering and roaring with alarm as he caught the boy, and then set him down before bending to tickle the baby's stomach.

"Where is Jane?" he asked.

"Calling on Lady Webb—her godmother," Tresham explained, in case Ferdinand had forgotten. "Angie went with her and so I did not. About the only common sense our sister has ever shown is her attachment to Jane. This notion that during the Season it is bad *ton* for husbands and wives to be seen anywhere together, or at least to remain together for longer than two minutes after their arrival at any entertainment, is damnably irritating, Ferdinand. I am taking my duchess back home to Acton at the earliest opportunity."

This was what his brother had become? Ferdinand thought, looking at him in some fascination. A man who spent much of his time with his children and grumbled when his wife was not with him? After four years, Tresham was still not fretting against his leg shackle?

"I need some information," Ferdinand said with deliberate casualness. "I thought you might know."

"Well, the devil!" his brother exclaimed as the castle suddenly came crashing down. "Was that my fault, Nick? Or was it yours? Did you poke it with your finger again? You did, you rascal." He caught his giggling son before he could escape and wrestled with him on the floor.

Ferdinand watched with some wistfulness.

"Now." Tresham got to his feet and brushed at his clothes, even though he looked as immaculate as ever. "What is it, Ferdinand?"

"You know Kirby, I suppose," Ferdinand said. "Do you know where I might find him? Where he lives, I mean?"

His brother paused midbrush and looked up in obvious surprise. "Kirby?" he said. "Good God, Ferdinand, if it is a woman you want, there are far more direct—"

"Did he manage Lilian Talbot's career?" Ferdinand asked.

The duke looked sharply at him. "Pick up the blocks and put them away, Nick," he said, "before Nurse comes back." He glanced at the baby, who appeared contented enough, before crossing the room to stand facing the window. Ferdinand joined him there.

"They were talking together this morning," Ferdinand said. "Kirby and Viola Thornhill, that is. And then her mother told me that he is helping her daughter find a governess's position, as he did once before. She seemed to believe it too."

"I assume, then," Tresham said, his hand closing about the handle of his quizzing glass, though he did not raise it to his eye, "that your question about his being her former manager was rhetorical?"

"I need to find him," Ferdinand said. "I need to ask him none too gently what hold he has over her."

"Has it occurred to you," his brother asked, "that *she* might have contacted *him* because she wishes to return to work?"

"Yes," Ferdinand said curtly. He gazed down at his brother's crested town carriage, which had drawn to a stop outside the front doors. His sister and his sister-in-law were descending from it. "But that is not the way it is. She knows Pinewood is hers, but she will not go back there. She was *happy* there, Tresham. You should have seen her the first time I did, organizing a sack race on the village green, flushed and laughing, her hair in a plait down her back, a bunch of daisies here." He gestured to a point above his left ear. "She was *happy,* dammit. And now she insists she does not love me." It was a non sequitur that he did not even notice.

"My dear Ferdinand—" His brother sounded genuinely concerned.

"She is lying," Ferdinand said. "Devil take it, Tresham, she is *lying.*"

But their conversation was cut short by the opening

of the nursery door and the appearance of Jane and Angeline. For a few minutes there was a great deal of noise and confusion as the children were picked up and hugged and Nicholas prattled loudly to his mother and his aunt about building a castle as tall as the sky and Uncle Ferdie throwing him up so high that he almost dropped him—and the baby set up a loud wailing. Fortunately, the children's nurse arrived on the scene to rescue the adults, and they were able to retreat to the drawing room for tea.

"Well, Ferdie," Angeline asked as soon as they were settled there, "have you found her yet?"

"Miss Thornhill?" he said warily. He was not sure how willing Heyward would be to have Angie fed information about one of London's most notorious courtesans. "Yes. At the White Horse Inn. Her uncle owns it. Her mother and half-sisters live there too."

"How splendid," she said. "Are they dreadfully vulgar?"

"Not at all," he said stiffly. "Thornhill is actually a gentleman by birth. So was Wilding—Miss Thornhill's stepfather."

"*Clarence* Wilding?" Tresham said. "I remember him. Got himself killed in some brawl, if I remember correctly."

"But a gentleman nonetheless," Ferdinand said, realizing even as he spoke that he was on the defensive, just as Mrs. Wilding had been earlier. "Miss Thornhill is the natural daughter of the late Earl of Bamber."

Tresham raised his eyebrows. Angeline looked ecstatic.

"Oh, Ferdinand," Jane said, "that would explain why

she was at Pinewood Manor. Now I am more glad than ever that you have given it back to her."

"An *earl's* daughter!" Angeline exclaimed. "How utterly splendid. It will be quite unexceptionable for you to marry her, Ferdie. The very highest sticklers may frown upon natural sons and daughters, but perfectly respectable people marry them all the time. And Miss Thornhill was recognized by her father before he died. He gave her property—I am sure he meant to do it even if he forgot to say so in his will, and now that you have given it back to her, no one will be any the wiser anyway. She will be known simply as Miss Thornhill of Pinewood—until she becomes Lady Ferdinand Dudley, of course. Jane, we must waste no more ti—"

"Angie!" Ferdinand said sharply. "Her illegitimacy is not the worst charge the *ton* would level against her. Not that I would care the snap of two fingers, and I would defend her honor against anyone who chose to argue the point. But *you* would care. At least you would by the time Heyward had finished with you."

"Pooh!" she said. "Heyward does not rule me. Besides, he would not be so stuffy."

"Ferdinand." Jane leaned forward in her chair. "You *are* fond of her, are you not? Are you going to marry her? *We* will never disown you if you do. Will we, Jocelyn?"

"Will we not?" he asked, looking at her with one of his black stares.

Her eyes sparked. It had always fascinated Ferdinand to see that not only was Jane uncowed by that look, which could cause even the strongest man to quake in his boots, but that it provoked her into giving as good as she got. Perhaps, he had concluded long ago, that was why Tresham had married her.

"You claim to be a *Dudley* and yet ask such a question?" she cried. "I will not disown Ferdinand, even if *you* do. And I will not disown Miss Thornhill either if he should choose to marry her. She cannot help her birth. And who knows why she chose the career she did? Women become courtesans and mistresses and . . . and *whores* for a number of reasons. But it is *never* from personal choice. No woman would freely choose such degradation. If Miss Thornhill has won Ferdinand's respect and admiration and love, then she is worthy of recognition by his family. She will have *my* recognition, if no one else's."

"Indeed, my love!" Tresham said softly before turning his eyes on his brother. "So there you have it, Ferdinand. We are Dudleys. And if society tells us that something is impossible, then of course we have been provoked into proving that we do not care *that* much for society's good opinion." He snapped his thumb and middle finger with a satisfyingly loud crack.

"Bravo, Tresh!" Angeline said. "The White Horse Inn, did you say, Ferdie? Jane, we must call on Mrs. Wilding and Miss Thornhill there. I cannot wait to see her, can you? She must be extremely beautiful, to have caught Ferdie's eye. Heyward says he has never been in the petticoat line, which of course he ought not to have said in my hearing, but I persuaded him years ago that I am no delicate bloom and will not faint away at the merest provocation. What we will do, Jane, is invite them here for some grand reception to introduce them to society. Ferdie can announce his betroth—"

"Angie!" Ferdinand was on his feet. "Take a damper, will you? She won't marry me."

For a rare moment she was speechless. She stared at him, her mouth still open. But she recovered quickly.

"Why not?" she asked.

"Because she does not *want* to," he said. "Because she would prefer to retain her freedom and live her own life. Because she does not care for me. Because she does not *love* me." He ran the fingers of one hand through his hair. "Deuce take it, I cannot believe I am discussing my personal life with my family."

"Is she going back to Pinewood, then?" Jane asked.

"No," he said. "She dashed well won't do that either. She is going back to her old way of life, if you must know. There! End of discussion. For all time. I will take my leave now. Thank you for tea, Jane." He had not touched a drop of it.

"Angeline." Jane spoke to their sister-in-law, but she was looking at Ferdinand. "I like your idea. We will call at the White Horse Inn tomorrow morning. I think we ought not to delay any longer than that. Don't forbid me to go, Jocelyn. I would simply defy you."

"My love," he said, his voice deceptively meek, "I cannot have it said that I am one of those sad men who cannot control their own wives. I issue commands only when I have a reasonable expectation that they will be obeyed."

Ferdinand heard no more. He had left the room and closed the door behind him. But he had not had an answer to the question he had come to ask, he thought as he ran down the stairs.

He would just have to find Kirby himself. It should not be impossibly difficult. He just hoped Kirby would be reluctant to talk. He hoped the man would need considerable persuasion, in fact.

* * *

VIOLA WAS IN THE small office of the White Horse Inn the next morning bringing the account books up to date, making sure that the columns of figures balanced. She had dressed in one of her plainest morning gowns, one she had left behind at the inn years ago. It was not particularly out of fashion, simply because it had never been in fashion. She had had Hannah dress her hair in a tight coronet of braids.

She wanted to feel, at least for the rest of this week, as if she were nothing more than her uncle's secretary and bookkeeper. She did not want to look either ahead or back. She kept her mind ruthlessly focused on the figures before her.

Yet the mind is a strange thing. It can concentrate on a mechanical task while at the same time wandering in the most undisciplined way.

To her meeting with Daniel Kirby.

To the upsetting confrontation with Ferdinand.

To all that had happened afterward.

Her mother had come back to the sitting room soon after he had left. So had Maria and Claire and Uncle Wesley. They had all been beaming expectantly.

"Well?" her mother had asked.

"He brought me the deed of Pinewood," she had told them, indicating the papers on the table. "He has had ownership transferred to me. It was always more mine than his, he said."

"That is all?" her mother had asked, clearly disappointed.

"Oh, Viola," Maria had said, "he is so *handsome*."

"He offered me marriage," Viola had told them. "I refused."

She had not been able to explain any of her real reasons, of course, and so had been forced to allow her mother to draw the conclusion that it was her illegitimacy that had led her to refuse. Mama had wept. But she had not been able to understand why that fact should mean so much to Viola when clearly it did not to Lord Ferdinand Dudley.

"Mama," Viola had said at last, "I do not love him."

"Love? *Love?*" Her mother's voice had risen. "You refuse a lord, the son of a *duke,* when you might marry him and be secure for life? When you might do something for your sisters? How *can* you be so selfish?"

"How can you not love him," Maria had wailed, "when he is so *gorgeous*?"

"Hush, Maria!" Claire had said sternly. "Mama, do dry your eyes and let me bring you some tea."

"Oh," their mother had said after blowing her nose, "I am the selfish one. Forgive me, Viola. You always sent us money from your governess's salary. You were kind to us."

"And since then too, Rosamond," Uncle Wesley had said. He had continued despite Viola's shake of the head. "I am not the one who has been paying Benjamin's school fees, you know. Viola has. And other things too that you have thought came from me. It is time you knew. You do not have to marry any wealthy aristocrat you do not even like, niece. And you do not have to go out as a governess again either if you do not want to. The inn will support my sister and her children just as it would have supported Alice and our children if she had lived."

They had all ended up in tears, except Uncle Wesley, who had slipped off back downstairs. No one had mentioned Ferdinand again—except Hannah, who had still been in Viola's room when she returned there.

"Well?" she had asked. "Did he come to take you back to that house? Or has he come to his senses and offered you something better?"

"Something better, Hannah," Viola had told her. "He has given me Pinewood. Perhaps one day, when Mr. Kirby can make no more money out of me and decides that the debt is paid off, we will go back there, you and I. Everyone needs some hope. Lord Ferdinand Dudley has given it to me."

"And he didn't offer to make an honest woman of you?" Hannah had asked. "I thought better of him, I must confess."

"An honest woman." Viola had sighed and then laughed. "He *did* offer, Hannah, and I refused. No, don't look at me in that mulish manner. You of all people must know why I refused, why I could never marry him or any other man. I could not do that to him."

"Why not, lovey?" Hannah had asked.

It was really a rhetorical question, but Viola had answered it anyway.

"Because I *love* him, that is why," she had cried. "Because I l-l-love him, Hannah." She had sobbed in her old nurse's arms, which were wonderfully comforting but which had somehow lost their magical ability to make all better.

She had definitely added up that column correctly, she thought now, her head bent over the account book. She had added it three times and arrived at the same total each time. The trouble was that there was no more paperwork to do and she did not want it to be at an end. She wanted to lose herself in work.

But the door opened suddenly and Maria's flushed, excited face appeared around it.

"Viola," she said, "you are to come up immediately to Mama. She has sent me to fetch you."

"Why?" Viola was immediately suspicious.

"I am not going to say." Maria smirked importantly. "It is a secret."

Viola sighed in exasperation. "He has not come back, has he?" she asked. "Tell me if he has, Maria. I do not want to see him and you may go back and tell Mama so."

"I am not saying," her sister said.

As Viola made her way upstairs, it suddenly occurred to her that perhaps it was Daniel Kirby who had called. But Maria would not be so excited about that, surely.

"You will never guess," she said from just behind Viola.

There were two ladies in the sitting room with her mother, who was looking almost as flushed as Maria. Two very grand ladies, both dressed in the first state of fashion, the one quietly and expensively elegant, the other brighter and more flamboyant.

"Viola." Her mother stood, as they both did too. "Come and make your curtsy to these ladies, who have been kind enough to call upon me and ask to make your acquaintance too."

Maria slipped past her into the room, but Viola stood just inside the door.

"This is my eldest daughter, Viola Thornhill," her mother said. "Her grace, the Duchess of Tresham, and Lady Heyward, Viola." She indicated first the elegant, golden-haired lady and then the other.

Viola was never sure afterward if she curtsied or not. She did know that somehow her hands found the doorknob behind her back and gripped it as if for dear life.

Both ladies were smiling at her. The duchess spoke first.

"Miss Thornhill," she said, "I do hope you will forgive us for calling on you and your mama without any warning. We have heard so much about you from Ferdinand, you see, and longed to make your acquaintance."

"I am his sister," Lady Heyward said. "You are every bit as lovely as I expected. And younger."

Did they know? *Did they know?* Did Ferdinand know they were here? *Did the Duke of Tresham?*

"Thank you," Viola said. "How very obliging of you to call upon Mama."

"Her grace has invited us to take tea with her at Dudley House tomorrow afternoon, Viola," her mother said. "Do come and sit down."

Did they know?

"Actually, Mrs. Wilding," the duchess said, "we would like to take Miss Thornhill for a drive with us today. It is far too lovely a day to be spent indoors. Can you spare her for an hour?"

"I am working on my uncle's books," Viola said.

"But of *course* you can be spared," her mother said. "Run and change into one of your pretty dresses. I cannot imagine where you found that old thing you are wearing. Whatever will her grace and Lady Heyward think of you?"

"Please come," the duchess said with a warm smile for Viola.

"Yes, please do," Lady Heyward added.

There seemed to be no other choice but to go and

change. Ten minutes later Viola was seated in a very luxurious open barouche beside Lady Heyward while the duchess sat on the seat opposite, her back to the horses.

Please not to the park.

But the barouche turned in the direction of Hyde Park.

"We have disturbed and upset you," the duchess said. "Please do not blame Ferdinand, Miss Thornhill. He did not send us. He told us you had refused his marriage offer."

"You must have seen from your visit to my uncle's inn how unsuitable such a match would have been," Viola said, clasping her gloved hands in her lap so that she would not fidget.

"Your mother is a real lady," the duchess said, "and your younger sister delightful. We did not meet the older girl. You have a half-brother at school too, I believe?"

"Yes," Viola said.

"We were so very curious, you see," Lady Heyward said, "to meet the lady who has stolen Ferdie's heart. You *have* stolen it, Miss Thornhill. Did you know that? Or did he neglect to tell you, as gentlemen so often do? They can be such foolish creatures, can they not, Jane? They will make a perfectly decent marriage proposal in which they list all the considerable advantages of making a match with them and neglect to mention the only one that really matters. I refused Heyward when he first offered for me, even though he went down on one knee very prettily and looked very foolish, the poor darling. Everyone says he is just a dry old stick—at least Tresham and Ferdie say it, because of course he is so very different from them. He is not really stuffy, at least not when one is private with him, but when he first offered for me he made not the slightest hint of a mention of love. He did not even try to steal a kiss. Can you imagine anything so provoking? How could I have accepted him, even if I *was* head over heels for him? Now, what was it I set out to say?"

"You wondered how I could have refused Lord Ferdinand," Viola said. The barouche was turning into the park, and her heart was beating faster. Of course, this was not the fashionable hour, which would draw the whole of the *ton* into the park in a few hours' time, but even so, she might be recognized at any moment. "There are very compelling reasons, believe me, none of which have anything to do with the regard in which I hold him. Not the least of those reasons is that I am not a daughter of my mother's marriage. Perhaps you wondered why my name is different from hers. It is her maiden name, you see."

"You are a natural daughter of the late Earl of Bamber," Lady Heyward said, taking Viola's hand in her own. "Which is nothing to be ashamed of. Natural sons cannot inherit their fathers' titles and entailed property, of course, but apart from that it is as respectable to be a natural child as to be one born within wedlock. *That* need not keep you from wedding Ferdie. Do you love him?"

"There is a reason," Viola said, turning her head away so that her face would be hidden by the brim of her straw bonnet, "why that question has no relevance at all. I cannot marry him. And I will not explain to you. You must take me back to my uncle's inn, please. You would not wish to be seen with me. The duke and Lord Heyward would not wish it."

"Oh, Miss Thornhill, do not distress yourself," the duchess said. "I am going to tell you something that very few people know. Even Angeline will be hearing it for the first time now. Before I married Jocelyn, I was his mistress."

Lady Heyward's hand slipped away from Viola's.

"He kept me in the house where Ferdinand took you on your return to London," the duchess said. "Jocelyn has kept the house. We always spend an afternoon or two there when we are in town. It holds many fond memories. It was there we learned to be happy together. But that does not alter the fact that I was a mistress. A fallen woman, if you will."

"Jane!" Lady Heyward exclaimed. "How utterly, splendidly romantic. Whyever have you never told me?"

So they *did* know, Viola thought. How rash of them to bring her out with them like this, in an open carriage.

"It was always a matter of pride with me," she said, her head averted again, "to keep on asserting that I would be no man's mistress. You knew one man, your grace. During the four years I worked, I knew so many men that I lost count. I never even tried to keep count, in fact, or wanted to. It was work. It was entirely different from your situation. I was famous. I was much in demand. I might still be recognized at any moment. Take me back home."

"Miss Thornhill." The duchess leaned forward and took Viola's hand in both her own. "We three are women. We understand things that men will never understand, even the men we love. We understand that what brings men pleasure by the very nature of the act can bring us none unless it is more an emotional than a physical experience, unless there is some sort of love commitment from and to our partner. We understand that *no* courtesan embarks on her career with a free or joyful heart. We know that no woman could enjoy such a life. And we know too—as men most certainly do not—that the woman, the *person,* is something quite distinct from what she does for a living. You are uncomfortable with us. You probably resent us. But I know—I sense—that I will like you very much indeed if you will allow me to. Do you love Ferdinand?"

Viola turned her head sharply to glare at the duchess and pulled her hand away. "Of course I love him," she said. "*Of course* I do. Why else would I have refused him? It would be a magnificent coup, would it not, for an illegitimate whore to marry the brother of a duke? Well, this illegitimate whore will not do it. I can do only one thing in my life to demonstrate how very much I love him. *One thing*—I can refuse him. I can make him believe that the prospect of returning to my old life is more enticing than the possibility of marrying him. If you love him, you will take me home now and go back and tell him how coldly and disdainfully I received you. I have feelings. I have *feelings,* and I cannot stand much more of this. Take me home."

The duchess turned her head and called new instructions to the coachman. Then she turned back to Viola.

"I am so sorry," she said. "We are such meddlesome creatures, Angeline and I. But we both love Ferdinand, you see, and hate to see him miserable. Now it breaks my heart to see that you are every bit as unhappy as he. We chose the park deliberately as our destination. We *wanted* to be seen with you. We want to make you respectable."

Viola laughed bitterly. "You do not understand."

Lady Heyward touched her arm. "Oh, yes," she said, "we do. But Jane chose the wrong word. We are not going to make you respectable, Miss Thornhill, but *respected.* We Dudleys have never been respectable, you see. I would never be a simpering miss. Tresham was forever fighting duels before Jane intervened one time and caused him to get shot in the leg—and it was always over women. Ferdie can never resist the most outrageous and dangerous challenges. But we never wanted to be respectable—how dull that would be! We are respected, though. No one would dare *not* respect us. We could make you respected too if you would give us the chance. How exciting it would be. I would give a grand ball—"

"Thank you," Viola said quietly but firmly. "You are both very kind. But no."

Conversation lapsed until the barouche turned into the inn yard again. The duchess's coachman jumped down from his perch to assist Viola to alight.

"Miss Thornhill." The duchess smiled at her. "Please come for tea with your mother tomorrow. I believe she would be disappointed if you refused."

"I am delighted," Lady Heyward said, "to have met Miss Thornhill of Pinewood Manor at last."

"Thank you." Viola hurried into the inn before the barouche turned to leave again.

She had a new plan. It had come to her full-blown after they had left the park. It filled her mind with dizzying hope and bleak despair both at the same time. She needed to think through a few details.

22

FERDINAND ROSE FROM HIS BED THE FOLLOWING morning much later than he had intended. Of course, he had been out most of the night, dragging John Leavering and a few of his other friends from party to party—not the sort he normally attended—and even to a couple of the more notorious gaming hells. But there had been no sign at any of them of Kirby.

He intended to spend the day at Tattersall's and a few other places where the man was likely to be. He would have to be patient, he decided, though patience was not a virtue he had much cultivated. If Kirby was seeking clients for Viola, then he must do so in the places Ferdinand intended to haunt.

He was just finishing breakfast when his valet announced that a visitor had called. He handed his master a calling card.

"Bamber?" Ferdinand frowned. Bamber up and about before noon? What the devil? "Show him in, Bentley."

The earl strode into the dining room a few moments later, looking as ill-natured as ever and more dissolute than usual. His hair was disheveled and his eyes bloodshot. He was unshaven. He must surely have been up all night, but he was not wearing evening clothes. He was dressed for travel.

"Ah, Bamber." Ferdinand got to his feet and extended his right hand.

The earl ignored it. He strode up to the table, reaching into a capacious pocket of his carriage coat as he did so. He pulled out a couple of folded papers and slapped them down.

"There!" he said. "It was an ill wind that blew me to Brookes's that night, Dudley. I wish I'd never set foot there, and that's the truth, but I did, and it can't be helped. Damn you for all the trouble you have caused me." He was reaching into an inner pocket as he spoke. He brought out a sheaf of banknotes and set them down beside the other papers. "Here is an end of the matter, and I hope not to hear another word about it for the rest of my days—from *anyone*."

Ferdinand sat back down. "What is this?" he asked, gesturing to the papers and the money.

Bamber picked up one of the papers and unfolded it before shoving it under Ferdinand's nose.

"This," he said, "is a copy of the codicil m'father made to his will a few weeks before he died and left with m'mother's solicitor in York. As you can see for yourself, he left Pinewood to that chit, his by-blow. The property was never mine, and so it was never yours, Dudley." He tapped his forefinger on the money. "And *this* is five hundred pounds. It is the amount you set on the table against the promise of Pinewood. It is in payment of my debt to you. Are you satisfied? It is not one fraction the worth of Pinewood, of course. If you want more—"

"It is enough," Ferdinand said. He took the paper and read it. His eyes lingered on four of the words written there—"my daughter, Viola Thornhill." The late earl had made this public acknowledgment of his relationship to her, then. Ferdinand looked curiously at the other man.

"Have you just come from Yorkshire, Bamber? It looks as if you have been traveling all night."

"I damned well have," the earl assured him. "I may be a ramshackle fellow, Dudley. I may be known as something of a loose screw, but I'll not have it said that I have been a party to any fraud or cover-up. As soon as the chit said she had met m'father here just before he died—"

"Miss Thornhill?"

"She had the effrontery to come calling on me," Bamber said. "You could have knocked me over with a bald feather. I didn't know she existed. Anyway, I knew as soon as she said it that if he *had* been going to do anything to his will he couldn't have done it that week he was here. I remember because I asked him to go to Westinghouse to have my allowance raised. I was living on *pin* money, for the love of God, and old Westinghouse always made a great to-do about giving me an advance on the next quarter. Anyway, m'father told me he had been to see Westinghouse the day before but he had not been there. His mother had died in Kent or something inconvenient like that and he had gone off to bury her. M'father left London the same day. He sometimes went to my mother's solicitor on small matters. It struck me that he might have gone to him about this—and that other matter the chit mentioned too. In fact, she seemed more concerned about that than about the will." He tapped the other folded paper.

"Why did these not come to light before now?" Ferdinand asked.

"Corking is not the brightest light," Bamber said carelessly. "He forgot all about them."

"*Forgot?*" Ferdinand looked at him incredulously.

The earl leaned both hands on the table and looked narrow-eyed at Ferdinand.

"He *forgot,*" he repeated with slow emphasis. "My questions jolted his memory. Leave it at that, Dudley. He *forgot.*"

Ferdinand understood immediately. The York solicitor was primarily the Countess of Bamber's. The late earl had used him out of desperation because Westinghouse had been gone from London and Bamber had known he did not have much time left in which to make all secure for his newly restored daughter. The countess had found out about the codicil, and she had persuaded her solicitor to say nothing about it. Whose decision it had been not to destroy the papers, Ferdinand could not even guess. He could merely feel grateful that one or both of them had not been prepared to go that whole criminal length.

"I don't know where to find the chit," Bamber said. "And quite honestly, I don't intend to put myself out trying. I don't feel any obligation whatsoever to her even if she is m'half-sister. But I won't do her out of what is rightfully hers either. I daresay you know where she is. Will you take her these?"

"Yes," Ferdinand said. He had no idea what the content of the other paper was or why she had said it was more important to her than the will. She was going to be ecstatic to learn that her unwavering faith in Bamber had not been misplaced. So she did not owe Pinewood in any way at all to him, he thought wryly.

"Good," Bamber said. "That is it, then. I'm going home to sleep. I hope never to hear the names Pinewood or Thornhill ever again. Or Dudley either, for that matter. Corking has sent a copy of the codicil to Westinghouse, by the way."

He turned to leave.

"Wait!" Ferdinand said, an idea popping into his head. "Sit down and have some coffee, Bamber. I haven't finished with you yet."

"Devil take it!" the earl said irritably, pulling a chair out from the table and plumping himself down onto it none too elegantly. "I would set a light to Brookes's with m'own hands today, and stand around to watch it burn to the ground too, if it were not somewhat akin to shutting the stable door after the horse had bolted. What now?"

Ferdinand looked assessingly at him.

VIOLA FELT HORRIBLY EXPOSED as she approached the front doors of Dudley House on Grosvenor Square. She was terrified that they would open and the duchess would step out—or that the duchess would be looking out through one of the many windows that overlooked the square. After she had lifted the knocker and let it fall against the door, she was afraid the duchess might be in the hall.

A very superior-looking butler opened the door. His eyes alit on her and then went beyond her to note that there was no carriage and no companion, not even a maid. He looked back at her.

"I wish to see his grace," she said. She felt as breathless as if she had run a mile uphill. Her knees were unsteady.

The butler raised his eyebrows and looked at her as if she were a little lower on the social scale than a worm. Viola had realized, of course, that the very strong chance the duke was away from home so close to the middle of the day was not the least of her worries.

"Kindly inform him that Lilian Talbot wishes to speak with him," she said, holding his gaze with a confidence she did not feel. She reminded herself that she was still wearing the clothes she had worn for the drive in the park. They were the clothes of a lady, the clothes Viola Thornhill of Pinewood Manor had worn for afternoon visits.

"I believe," she said, "he will agree to see me."

"Step inside," the butler said, after such a lengthy pause that she feared any moment to have the door slammed in her face. "Wait here."

She had hoped he would show her into a room to wait. At any moment one of the doors that lined the hall might open to reveal the duchess. Or she might come down the grand staircase that the butler was now ascending. Viola stood just inside the front doors with one silent liveried footman for company. She stood there for what felt like an hour at the very least but was perhaps five minutes. Then the butler came back downstairs.

"This way," he said as frigidly as he had spoken before. He opened a door to her right, and she stepped into what was obviously a reception room—a square, elegant apartment with chairs arranged about the walls. "His grace will be with you soon." The door closed.

Another five minutes passed before he came. Viola thought a dozen times at least of bolting, but she had come this far. She would see it through to the end. If the Duke of Tresham was the man she thought he was, he would agree to her suggestion. Then the door opened again, and she turned from the window.

She felt a strange shock as soon as he stepped into the

room. He was as austere, as forbidding, as . . . frightening as he had been at Pinewood. Yet he was holding a tiny baby. The child was against his shoulder, making fussing noises and sucking loudly on one fist. The duke was patting its back with one long-fingered hand.

"Miss . . . Talbot?" he said, raising his eyebrows.

She curtsied and lifted her chin. She would not be cowed. "Yes, your grace."

"And how may I be of service to you?" he asked her.

"I have a proposition to make to you," she said.

"Indeed?" His voice was soft, but all her insides jerked with alarm.

"It is not what you think," she said hastily.

"Am I to feel flattered or . . . shattered?" he asked her. He cupped his hand over the back of the baby's head when the child fussed in an obvious attempt to find a more comfortable position. There was gentleness in that hand, she thought. But there was none whatsoever in his face.

"I do not know," she said, "if you are aware that Lord Ferdinand Dudley has restored Pinewood Manor to me. Or that he has offered me marriage."

His eyebrows rose again. "But do I need to be aware?" he asked her. "My brother is seven-and-twenty, Miss . . . Talbot."

She hesitated before continuing. "And I do not know," she said, "if you are aware that the duchess and Lady Heyward called upon my mother this morning and then took me driving in the park. Or that the duchess has invited my mother and me to tea here tomorrow. I do not wish to cause any trouble for them," she added.

Two of his long fingers were rubbing lightly over the baby's neck. "You need not fear," he said. "I do not make a habit of taking a whip to my wife. And my sister is Lord Heyward's responsibility."

"I am aware," she said, "that my presence in London can be nothing but an embarrassment to you."

"Are you?" he said.

"I might have been seen in your barouche this morning," she said. "I might have been seen coming here. I might be seen tomorrow when I come with my mother. And recognized."

He appeared to consider for a moment. "Unless you wear a mask," he agreed, "I suppose that is a distinct possibility."

"I am prepared to go back to Pinewood," she said. "I am prepared to live there for the rest of my life and repel any attempt Lord Ferdinand may make to write to me or to see me there. This I will swear to—in writing, if you will."

His stare was as black as his brother's, she thought during the silent moments that followed. No, blacker. For Ferdinand's stare always gave evidence of some emotion behind it. This man seemed as cold as death.

"This is extremely magnanimous of you," he said at last. "I assume there is a condition attached? How much, Miss Talbot? I suppose you are aware that I am one of the wealthiest men in England?"

She named the sum baldly, without any explanation or apology.

He strolled farther into the room and turned half away from her. The baby—its eyes were blue—stared sleepily at her. The neck-rubbing was putting it to sleep.

"Apparently," the duke said, "you do not realize *how* wealthy, Miss Talbot. You might have asked for considerably more. But it is too late now, is it not?"

"It is a loan I ask for," she said. "I will pay you back. With interest."

He swung around to look at her again, and for the first time his eyes looked less than opaque. She had sparked his interest, it seemed.

"In that case," he said, "I am ensuring the respectability of my name and my family at remarkably small cost. You surprise me."

"But you must do something else for me," she said.

"Ah." He tipped his head to one side to note that his child was sleeping. Then he looked back at Viola. "Yes, I am sure there is. Proceed."

"The money is to be used in payment of a debt," she said. "I want you to pay it for me—in person. I want you to get a receipt stating that the debt has been paid in full and that there are no others. I want you to send me a copy at the White Horse Inn, signed by both you and him."

"Who?" His eyebrows were raised again.

"Daniel Kirby," she said. "Do you know him? I can give you his direction."

"Please do." He spoke softly. "Why, if I am permitted to ask, can you not pay him yourself if I give you the money?"

She hesitated. "It will not be enough," she explained. "He will discover other unpaid bills or he will claim that I was mistaken about the interest rate. If *you* go to him, the amount will be right. You are a powerful man."

He stared at her for a long time while his child slumbered peacefully against his shoulder.

"Yes," he said at last. "I believe I am."

"You will do it?" she asked him.

"I will do it."

She closed her eyes. She had not really expected him to agree. She had not been sure if she would be more relieved or disappointed if he would not. She was still not sure. She had not yet permitted herself to look ahead to the rest of her life, when she must keep her side of their bargain.

"I will wait for that receipt to be delivered to my uncle's inn, then," she said after giving him Daniel Kirby's address. "Do you wish to say now, your grace, in what installments you will expect the loan to be repaid? And what interest will be acceptable to you? Shall I sign something now?"

"I think that will be unnecessary, Miss Talbot," he said. "I am sure I can trust you to repay your debt in a timely manner. I know where you may be reached at any time during the rest of your life, after all, do I not? And I am, as you observed a short while ago, a powerful man."

She shivered.

"Yes. Thank you," she said. "I will leave for Pinewood on the next stagecoach after the receipt has been delivered into my hands."

"I am sure you will," he said.

She hurried across the room and opened the door. The butler was in the hall. He opened the front doors, and a few moments later she was out on the steps, gulping in fresh air. It had been so very easy.

She had just been saved from what had appeared to be an unavoidable future.

Mama and Uncle Wesley had been saved.

So had Claire.

She hurried out of the square, her head down, the warmth of bright sunlight soaking into her. Why did life still appear bleaker than bleak? Why was she cold through to her very soul?

THE DUCHESS OF TRESHAM looked around the open door of the reception room before stepping inside.

"She has gone?" she asked unnecessarily. "Why did she come alone and ask to speak with *you*, Jocelyn? Why did she use a false name?" The duchess had been looking out through the nursery window earlier while nursing the baby and had observed the arrival of Viola Thornhill. She had remarked on it to her husband, who had been reading their elder son a story.

"Lilian Talbot was her working name," he said.

"Oh." She frowned.

"She has persuaded me," he said, "to pay her off so that she will go back to Pinewood and never be seen or heard from again."

"And you *agreed*?"

"Ah, but it is only a loan, you see," he said. "We will not be permanently impoverished, Jane. She is to pay me back."

"She thinks this is what is best for Ferdinand?" she asked. "How foolishly noble."

"She did apologize for letting me know that you and Angeline took her driving in the park this morning," he said. "But I promised not to whip you, you will be relieved to know."

"Jocelyn!" She tipped her head to one side. "You have been terrifying the poor lady. You are not serious about this, are you? You are not going to be odious and break Ferdinand's heart?"

"It is just the effect I have on people, you see," he said.

"You are the only one who has ever defied me, Jane. I married you so that you would be forced to obey me, but we both know how successful I have been at that."

She smiled with amusement despite herself. "I see that Christopher is asleep," she said. "How do you *do* it, Jocelyn? I resent it. I am his mother, but he does nothing except squirm and wail when I try to rock him to sleep."

"He is wise enough to understand that he can expect no meal from me, you see," he said. "There is nothing else to alleviate his boredom than to nod off. Dudleys are never so foolish as to waste negative energy. They merely fall asleep and store it up for future mayhem. Christopher is going to be more of a handful than Ferdinand and I were combined—with Angeline thrown in. I believe Nick may prove to be more biddable."

She laughed but then sobered.

"Are you really going to send her back to Pinewood?" she asked. "Ferdinand may well challenge you if he discovers what you have done."

"That would make a change," he said. "I have not been challenged for over four years. I have forgotten the peculiar excitement attached to gazing down the wrong end of a pistol. I had better go and find him and give him the opportunity."

"Jocelyn, do be serious," she said.

"I was never more so," he assured her. "I must find Ferdinand. I have to confess that being head of the family has never been more interesting. Take this rascal, will you, Jane? If I am not much mistaken, he has dampened my sleeve. Not to mention the soggy patch on my shoulder."

He kissed her swiftly as she took their sleeping son from him.

* * *

FERDINAND WASTED A GOOD part of the afternoon looking for Daniel Kirby—without success—before deciding that as usual he was allowing impetuosity to lead him by the nose instead of harnessing his wrath and using it in a measured and effective way.

There was sure to be a *much* more effective way. He would need some assistance, though. He did not have to think too deeply before deciding that his brother was his best possible choice. And so he made his way to Grosvenor Square.

Both the duchess and his grace were away from home, Tresham's poker-faced butler informed him. The duchess was attending a garden party with Lady Webb. His grace was simply out.

"Damnation!" Ferdinand said aloud, flicking his riding whip impatiently against his boot. "I'll have to go searching for him, then."

Fortunately he did not have to look far. Tresham's curricle turned into the square just as he was swinging himself up into the saddle.

"Ah," Tresham called, "just the man I have been looking for. And you were on my doorstep all the time."

"You have been looking for me?" Ferdinand dismounted, and his brother vaulted down from the high seat of his curricle and tossed the ribbons to his groom.

"Combing the streets of London," Tresham said, setting a hand on his brother's shoulder and walking back up the steps to the house with him. He took Ferdinand into his library, closed the door, and poured them both a drink. "I have a confession to make, Ferdinand. My duchess believes it highly probable that you will slap a glove in my face as soon as I tell you." He handed Ferdinand one of the glasses.

Ferdinand was bursting with his own news, but his brother's words arrested him. "What?" he asked.

"I have agreed to pay Miss Thornhill a largish sum to withdraw to Pinewood and never communicate with you again," Tresham said.

"By God!" Ferdinand's fury finally found an available target. "You might have heeded Jane's warning. I'll kill you for this, Tresham."

His brother sat down on a leather chair beside the hearth and crossed one booted leg over the other. He looked damnably unconcerned. "Actually," he said, "it was Miss Thornhill's suggestion. And it is to be a loan rather than a gift. She will repay every penny plus interest. It is the additional request she made of me as part of our bargain that will be of particular interest to you."

"Well, it will not be," Ferdinand said, setting his glass down. "I do not want to hear it. I don't care what sum you have bribed her with, and I do not care what promises she has made you. I will pay your damned money back, and then I am going to release her from her promise. Maybe she will never have me. But she is going to be free to say yes if she means yes and no if she means no. Damn you, Tresham. I'll never speak to you again after today. I am too disgusted even to kill you, damn you." He turned toward the door.

"She wants me to deliver the money personally into Kirby's hands," Tresham said, ignoring the outburst. "And to extort from him a written statement to the effect that all debts have been fully and permanently paid off. Jane was right, you see. That scoundrel had her working off debts for a number of years. And having heard that she was returning to London, he no doubt discovered other debts—the ones I have agreed to pay off for her by advancing her a loan. I have told you all this with the greatest reluctance, Ferdinand, merely because it seemed selfish to hoard to myself all the pleasure of dealing with Kirby. I thought perhaps you might consider your claim to take the first, er, *shot* at him superior to my own."

Ferdinand looked over his shoulder at his brother for a few moments before reaching into a pocket and drawing out the second of the two papers Bamber had put on his breakfast table earlier. He had hesitated about reading it at first, since it belonged to Viola, but it had been unsealed and he had been unable to resist the temptation. He crossed the room and handed it to his brother, who read it carefully from beginning to end.

"Where did you get this?" he asked.

"From Bamber," Ferdinand said. "It was put into the safekeeping of the countess's solicitor in York together with a codicil to the late Bamber's will leaving Pinewood to his daughter. The solicitor, doubtless encouraged by the countess, conveniently *forgot* about both documents until Bamber went up there and reminded him. He arrived back in town this morning and came straight to me."

"Bamber Senior paid off all the debts two years ago," Tresham said, looking back at the paper. "*All*. And this is an interesting detail, Ferdinand. They were debts incurred by Clarence Wilding. Having had a slight acquaintance with the man, I can believe they were large enough. They became as deep as the ocean, no doubt, by the time Kirby acquired them and added interest of several hundred percent. Does *Mrs.* Wilding know of these debts? Do you know?"

"I don't think so," Ferdinand said. "She seems genuinely to believe that Kirby found Viola a governess's job once upon a time and is finding her another now."

"She took the whole burden on her own young shoulders, then," Tresham said. "There are younger half-brothers and -sisters, I seem to recall?"

"Three of them. They must have been mere children at the time," Ferdinand said. "Viola was a young lady by birth and education. Her illegitimacy would have been no great barrier to a decent future. Her father was an earl, after all. She could have expected to make a respectable match. Kirby took that chance from her and plunged her into hell instead."

"You must understand," Tresham said, "what a great sacrifice I am making, Ferdinand, in granting you precedence in this matter. I would offer to be your second, but I do not believe this man has earned the right to an honorable challenge, do you? Let me assist you, though. And a suggestion? I will not call it advice or you must reject it out of sheer principle. A bullet between the eyes is too easy. Besides, it will involve you in all sorts of annoying complications and you may find yourself obliged to spend the next year or two kicking your heels on the Continent. Pick up your drink again and have a seat and together we will contrive some suitable punishment."

"Even death would not be *suitable* for what he has done," Ferdinand said savagely. "But it is the best substitute I can think of."

"Ah," his brother said softly. "But we must think of what is best for your Viola too, Ferdinand. You cannot afford to make a mistake there or she will lock herself behind Pinewood doors and never come out again."

Ferdinand picked up his glass and sat down.

23

VIOLA SAT READING THE NEXT MORNING WHILE her mother gave Maria an arithmetic lesson. At least she held an open book in her lap and even remembered to turn a page now and then. But her hands were like ice and her heart was thudding and her mind was in turmoil.

All she needed was that piece of paper in her hands. There was a stagecoach leaving for the west country from another inn during the afternoon. She could be on it. Hannah already had their bags packed. Her mother would be disappointed, of course. She had her heart set on going to Dudley House for tea. She firmly believed that Lord Ferdinand would renew his addresses and that this time Viola would have the good sense to accept. But Mama's disappointment would have to be borne.

Surely his grace would call on Daniel Kirby this morning. Or perhaps he had gone yesterday but had waited until today to send her the receipt. Surely he would not let her down when the alternative for him might be acquiring Lilian Talbot as a sister-in-law.

She turned a page with a cold, clammy hand.

And then the sitting room door opened to admit Claire, waving a letter. Viola leaped to her feet, and her book clattered to the floor.

"Is it for me?" she cried.

"It is. A messenger brought it." Claire was smiling.

"Perhaps it is from Mr. Kirby, Viola. Perhaps he has found you a position."

Viola snatched the letter from her sister's hand. Her name on the outside was written in bold black letters, like the duke's writing as she had seen it at Pinewood.

"I'll read it in my room," she said, and hurried away before anyone could protest.

Her hands were shaking as she sat down heavily on her bed and broke the seal. She and Hannah would be in time to catch the afternoon stage.

She would never see him again.

Two papers fluttered into her lap. She ignored them while her eyes scanned the brief note that had enclosed them.

"With my compliments," it said. "Both papers were filed with a solicitor in York shortly before the late Earl of Bamber's passing. F. Dudley."

It was Ferdinand's handwriting, then.

She picked up the top paper from her lap and unfolded it.

Oh, God! Oh, God, oh, God! Her hand shook so violently that she had to grip the paper with the other hand too. It was the receipt her father had made Daniel Kirby sign, declaring that the late Clarence Wilding's debts had been paid in full and for all time. There were the two signatures as plain as could be. And the signatures of two witnesses too.

She was free. They were all free.

But there was the paper lying folded in her lap. She set aside the one she had just read on the bed beside her and unfolded the second. She stared down at it until her vision blurred and one tear plopped onto a corner of it. She had not doubted him. Not even for a moment. But it was sweet—ah, it was sweet indeed—to hold the documentary evidence in her hands.

Father. Oh, Papa, Papa.

She was weeping openly when her bedroom door opened and her mother first peeped around it and then came hurrying inside.

"Viola?" she said. "Oh, what is it, my dear? Is the letter from the duchess? Has she changed her mind about this afternoon? It really does not matter. Oh, goodness me, what *is* it?"

She had come close to the bed and would have gathered her daughter in her arms, but Viola held out the codicil to her father's will.

"He *did* love me," she wailed. "He *did*."

Her mother read it before folding it and returning it to Viola's lap. "Yes, of course he did," she said softly. "He adored you. Long after our relationship turned sour he came just to see you. I truly believe he loved you more than anyone else in the world. When I married your stepfather, I wanted nothing more to do with him. I was in love and I was very proud. I ignored your needs. He was my lover, but he was your father. There is a world of difference—I know that now. I suppose my anger with you for accepting Pinewood Manor from him arose from my guilt. I am so sorry. Can you ever forgive me? I am glad you were right and he really did leave Pinewood to you. I *am* glad, Viola."

Viola pulled a handkerchief out of the pocket of her dress and held it to her eyes, but for the moment at least she could not seem to stop crying.

"What is *this?*" her mother asked suddenly in a strange voice.

The other paper. Viola slapped a hand onto the bed

beside her, but it was too late. The paper was in her mother's hands, and she was reading it with wide, dismayed eyes.

"Bamber paid off Clarence's debts?" she said. "What debts? To Mr. *Kirby*?" She lifted her gaze to Viola's face.

Viola could think of nothing to say.

"Explain this to me." Her mother sat down beside her.

"I did not want to worry you," Viola said. "You were so ill after my stepfather died. And it would not have been fair to Uncle Wesley to have burdened him. I—I tried to pay the bills myself, but there were so many of them. M-my father was kind enough to pay them all off for me."

Leave it at that, Mama.

"*You* were paying Clarence's debts, Viola?" her mother said. "*Gaming* debts? Out of a governess's pay? *And* you were helping to support us?"

"I needed very little for myself," Viola said. *Please leave it at that.*

But her mother had turned noticeably paler. "What *did* you do during those years?" she asked. "You were not a governess, were you? He was not our friend, was he?"

"Mama—" Viola laid a hand on her mother's arm, but her mother shook it off and gazed at her in horror.

"What did you do?" she cried. "Viola, *what did he force you to do?*"

Viola shook her head and bit her upper lip as her mother clapped a shaking hand over her mouth.

"Oh, my child," she said, "what have you done for us? What did you do *for four years?*"

"Uncle would have been ruined," Viola said. "Please try to understand. The children would have ended up in debtors' prison with you. Mama, *please* try to understand. Don't hate me."

"*Hate you?*" Her mother grabbed her, held her tightly, and rocked her. "Viola. My sweet child. What have I done to you?"

Some time passed before Viola drew away and blew her nose firmly. "I think I am glad you know," she said. "It is horrid to have dark secrets from one's own family. But it is all over now, Mama. He has no more power over me—or Claire."

"Claire?" her mother cried.

"He would have used her if I had not come back to London," Viola explained. "But she is safe now, Mama. The receipt has been found. And Pinewood belongs to me. I am going to go back there. After I have settled again, perhaps you and the children will come and live with me. All is well that ends well, you see."

"Where did these papers come from?" her mother asked.

"Lord Ferdinand Dudley sent them," Viola said. "He must have gone looking for them."

"Oh, my love." Her mother touched her arm. "He knows? Yet he still cares for you? Surely you must feel some affection for him."

Viola got to her feet and turned her back on her mother. "You must understand now, Mama," she said, "why such a match is a total impossibility. Besides, he will not renew his addresses. He sent these papers with a messenger." And signed himself F. Dudley.

Her mother sighed. "It is his loss, then," she said. "Did Bam— Did your father know everything, Viola?"

"Yes."

"And so he freed you from your burden and gave you

Pinewood so that you could start a new life," her mother said. "He was always a generous man. I cannot deny that. My complaints must have seemed cruel indeed to you. Come to the sitting room and we will have a cup of tea together."

But Viola shook her head. "I have a letter to write, Mama," she said. "And Hannah and I will be leaving for Pinewood this afternoon."

She had to write to the Duke of Tresham first. If the letter arrived in time, she would save him some effort and herself some money. But the letter would assure him that she would keep her part of their bargain regardless.

She was going home.

DANIEL KIRBY SETTLED HIMSELF in the high seat of the curricle that had long been the envy of the male half of the ton and smiled genially at the man beside him. "I always did suspect you had an eye for the best, your grace," he said.

"The best in sporting vehicles?" the Duke of Tresham asked.

"That too." Kirby chuckled.

"Ah." His grace flicked the ribbons and his horses stepped smartly out onto the street, leaving Kirby's lodgings behind in a matter of moments. "You were referring to female charms. Yes, I have always had an eye for the very best."

"Which is precisely what you will get with Miss Talbot," the other man said. "She is more alluring than ever after a two-year absence. But perhaps your grace's brother has informed you of that, since he must have met her at Pinewood."

"Indeed," the duke said.

"She will be ready to start entertaining within the week," Kirby said. He clung to the rail beside him as the curricle turned into Hyde Park. "Of course, you must know that she is expensive, but one must always be prepared to pay for the best."

"I have always said so," his grace agreed.

Kirby chuckled. "And there will be an extra charge to her first client," he said. "It will be worth it, your grace. You will acquire considerable prestige in the eyes of your acquaintances as the first to bed the delectable Lilian Talbot in two years."

"One always likes to bolster one's prestige in a worthy cause," Tresham said. "Miss Talbot is, ah, eager to return to work?"

"Work!" Kirby laughed heartily. "She calls it pleasure, your grace. She would start tonight if I would let her. But I wanted to give her to someone . . . ah, shall we say, *special,* the first time?"

"I do like to consider myself special," the duke said. "Dear me, whatever is going on up ahead of us, I wonder?"

Up ahead of them, on the grass to one side of the path along which they drove, there was a considerable gathering of people. It was strange, really, as all were on foot and this particular part of the park, shaded by trees and hidden from much of the rest of it, was not one of the most frequented. As they drove closer it became clear that all the people were men. One of them, a little apart from the others and lounging at his ease against a tree trunk, his arms crossed over his chest, was in a shocking state of semi-undress. He wore a white shirt with tight leather riding breeches and boots, but if he had worn a waistcoat and coat and hat into the park, there certainly was no sign of them now.

"A fight?" Kirby suggested, his voice brightening with interest.

"If so, there seems to be only one participant," Tresham said. "And dear me, it appears to be my brother." He slowed the pace of his horses until they came to a halt altogether beside the relaxed figure of Lord Ferdinand Dudley.

"Ah," he said with a grin, "just the man I want to see."

"Me?" Kirby asked, pointing to his own chest when it became obvious that Lord Ferdinand's gaze was not directed at his brother. He eyed the gathered throng, all of whom had fallen silent. "You wished to see me, my lord?"

"You *are* Lilian Talbot's manager, are you not?" Ferdinand asked him.

Daniel Kirby smiled jovially, if a little self-consciously. "If *that* is what you wish to see me about," he said, "you are going to have to stand in line behind his grace, your brother, my lord."

"Let me understand you," Ferdinand said. "You manage Lilian Talbot, whose real name is Viola Thornhill."

"I like to grant her some privacy, my lord, by keeping mum about that second name," Kirby said.

"Natural daughter of the late Earl of Bamber," Ferdinand added.

There was a murmuring from the spectators, to whom that detail appeared to come as news. For the first time, Kirby looked uneasy.

"Bamber." Ferdinand had raised his voice. "Is this true? Lilian Talbot is really Miss Viola Thornhill, your father's natural daughter?"

"He acknowledged her as such," the Earl of Bamber agreed from close by.

"I did not—" Kirby began.

"Miss Thornhill lived quietly and respectably with her mother and half-brother and -sisters at her uncle's inn until you bought up the debts of Clarence Wilding, her late stepfather?" Ferdinand asked.

"I don't know what this is about," Kirby said, "but—"

He was about to clamber down from his seat, but the duke set four gloved fingertips lightly on his arm, and he changed his mind.

"You offered her the chance of saving her family from debtors' prison?" Ferdinand asked.

"Here, here," Kirby said indignantly, "I had to recover that money somehow. It was a large sum."

"And so you created Lilian Talbot," Ferdinand said, "and put her to work and took her earnings. For *four years*. They must have been astronomical debts."

"They *were*," the other man said indignantly. "And I did not take more than a small fraction of her earnings. She lived in the lap of luxury. And she enjoyed what she did. There are men here who can vouch for the fact."

"Shame!" several of the gentlemen present murmured. But Ferdinand held up a staying hand.

"Miss Thornhill must have been disappointed, then," he said, "when Bamber, her father, discovered the truth, paid off all the debts, received a written receipt to that effect from you, Kirby, and gave her Pinewood Manor in Somersetshire, where she could live out her life in a manner suited to her birth."

"There was no such receipt," Kirby said. "And if she says so—"

But Ferdinand had held up his hand again.

"It would be wise not to perjure yourself," he said. "The paper has been found. Both Bamber and I have seen it—and Tresham too. But when I won Pinewood from Bamber, you assumed that the late earl had played her false, did you not, and that the receipt had been discarded or lost. A foolish assumption. Bamber has discovered that his father did indeed change his will. Miss Thornhill is mistress of Pinewood."

There was a smattering of applause from behind him.

"You discovered more debts when you believed her to be destitute," Ferdinand said. "You have been attempting to force her return to prostitution, Kirby."

The murmur behind him was louder and uglier now.

"I have not—"

"Tresham?" Ferdinand asked coolly.

"I was to have her within the week," the duke said. "At something over and above her usual high fee, since apparently it would add to my prestige and make me appear, ah, *special* to be her first client after two years."

Ferdinand's jaw tightened.

"I was about to decline when I spotted this interesting gathering," Tresham continued. "The duchess, it is to be understood, would carve out my liver without bothering to kill me first."

There was a burst of laughter from the spectators. But Ferdinand did not join in. He was gazing at a clearly nervous Daniel Kirby, his eyes very black, his jaw hard, his mouth a thin line.

"You have terrorized and ruined a gently born lady, Kirby," he said, "whose only fault has been love of her family and a willingness to sacrifice her honor and her very self for their freedom and happiness. You are looking at her champion, sir."

"Look," Daniel Kirby said, his eyes darting about as if to search out a friendly face or an escape route, "I don't want any trouble."

"Quite frankly," Ferdinand said, "I do not care what you want, Kirby. It is trouble you have found this morning—six years too late for Miss Thornhill. Get down from there. You are going to be punished."

"Your grace." Kirby turned frightened eyes on Tresham. "I must call upon you to protect me. I came with you in good faith to arrange an assignation."

"And an assignation has been arranged," the duke said, vaulting down from his seat and tossing the ribbons to his groom, who had been up behind the curricle. "This is it. Get down from there or I will come around and help you down. You will be given five minutes to strip to the waist and prepare to defend yourself. No, don't look so alarmed. We are not all about to pounce upon you like a pack of wolves. The idea has considerable appeal, it is true, but most of us *gentlemen* are constrained by a damnable sense of honor, you see. All the pleasure of the encounter falls to Lord Ferdinand Dudley, who has appointed himself Miss Thornhill's champion."

There was loud jeering from the spectators while Daniel Kirby sat where he was. There was laughter and then cheers as the Duke of Tresham stalked around his curricle and Kirby scrambled hastily down. Ferdinand pulled his shirt off over his head and tossed it to the grass. Kirby cast one horrified glance at his hard torso and rippling muscles and looked away again. Even though no one touched him, he was being herded onto the grass by the sheer menace of a few dozen gentlemen moving purposefully to form a ring about an ominously empty area of lawn.

"Strip down," Ferdinand said tersely, "or I'll do it for you, Kirby, and I'll not stop at your waist. It will be a fair fight. If you can fell me, you are free to go. No one here will stop you. I am not going to kill you, but I *am* going to thrash you within an inch of your life—with my bare hands. If you imagine that going down will save you, you are mistaken. It will not. You will be unconscious by the time I have finished with you. So I will say the rest of what I have to say now. After you have recovered from your beating well enough to travel—it may take a week or two—you are to travel until there is an ocean between you and me. That ocean will remain between us for the rest of your life. If I ever hear of your returning, I will hunt you down and punish you all over again—to within *half* an inch of your life. I will not ask if you understand me. You are a weasel, but you are obviously intelligent too—intelligent enough to choose a young, vulnerable, loving girl as your victim. This is going to be for her—to restore her honor in the sight of these witnesses. *Get* that shirt off."

A moment later, Daniel Kirby, small, pudgy, and pasty-skinned, stood shivering within the hostile, jeering ring of spectators. He was visibly shaking as Ferdinand strode toward him. He fell to his knees and clasped his hands together.

"I am not a fighter. I am a peaceable man," he said. "Just let me go. I'll be gone from London before the day is out. You'll never see me again. I'll never trouble you again. Just don't hit me. Arrgghh!"

Ferdinand had reached out and grasped Kirby's nose between the middle and forefinger of one hand. He twisted and raised his arm until Kirby was standing on his toes before him, his hands flailing helplessly, his mouth wide open to gasp in air. There was a roar of mirth from the spectators.

"For God's sake, man," Ferdinand said in the utmost disgust, "stay on your feet and throw at least one punch. Show some self-respect."

He released his hold and for a moment stood before the other man, within arm's length, his own arms at his side, unprotected. But Kirby merely covered his injured nose with both hands.

"I am a peaceable man," he wailed.

And so it was punishment pure and simple. And coldly and scientifically meted out. It would have been easy to render him unconscious with a few powerful blows. And it would have been easy to pity a man whose physical stature and condition gave him no chance whatsoever of winning the fight. But Ferdinand did not allow himself either the luxury of fury or the weakness of pity.

This was not for himself or for the spectators. This was not sport.

This was for Viola.

He had said he was her champion. He would avenge her, then, in the only way he could, inadequate as it was—with his physical strength.

She was his lady, and this was for her.

The spectators had grown strangely quiet and Ferdinand's knuckles on both hands were red and raw by the time he judged Daniel Kirby to be within the proverbial inch of his life. Only then did he draw back his right fist and drive it up beneath the man's chin with enough force to send him into oblivion.

He stood looking down at the plump, unconscious body, his hands still balled into fists at his sides, his mind bleak with sorrow and near-despair as the men around him, his friends and acquaintances, his peers, clapped slowly.

"If anyone," he said without looking up—there was instant silence so that everyone could hear what he had to say—"has any doubt in his mind that Miss Viola Thornhill is a lady deserving of the deepest honor and respect and admiration, let him speak now."

No one spoke until Tresham broke the silence.

"My duchess will be sending out invitations within a day or two to a reception at Dudley House," he said. "It is our hope that the guest of honor will be Miss Thornhill of Pinewood Manor in Somersetshire, natural daughter of the late Earl of Bamber. She is a lady we wish to have the pleasure of presenting to society."

"And it is my hope," the Earl of Bamber said unexpectedly, "that she will arrive at Dudley House under my escort, Tresham. M'half-sister, you know."

Ferdinand turned and walked away to where he had left his clothes in the keeping of his friend John Leavering. He dressed in silence. Although there was now an excited buzz from those who had watched the punishment, no one approached him. His black mood, so uncharacteristic of him, was too obvious to them all. But his brother clasped his shoulder as he pulled on his waistcoat.

"I am prouder of you today than I have ever been before, Ferdinand," he said softly. "And I have always been proud of you."

"I wish I could have killed the bastard," Ferdinand

said, pushing his arms into the sleeves of his coat. "Perhaps I would feel better if I had killed him."

"You have done much better than that," his brother told him. "You have restored life to someone deserving of it, Ferdinand. There is not a man here who would not gladly kneel to kiss the hem of Viola Thornhill's garments. You have shown her as a lady who sacrificed all for love."

"I have done damn all," Ferdinand said, gazing at his raw knuckles. "She suffered for four years, Tresham. And again in the last few weeks."

"You will have to spend a lifetime soothing the pain of those four years, then," Tresham said. "Shall I come with you to the White Horse?"

Ferdinand shook his head.

His brother squeezed his shoulder hard and comfortingly once more before turning away.

24

THE GUARD HAD ALREADY BLOWN ONE LONG blast on his horn—the final warning for any laggards among the passengers to scramble on board the stagecoach before it pulled out of the inn yard and began its journey west. But only one outside passenger had yet to board. The guard slammed the door on the inside passengers and moved to take his place at the rear of the coach.

Mrs. Wilding stepped back, a handkerchief pressed to her lips. Maria clung to her free arm. Claire, smiling bravely, raised one hand in farewell. Viola, seated beside the window, smiled back. Farewells were so hard. She had tried to persuade them not to come with her and Hannah from the White Horse Inn, but they had insisted.

She would see them all again, of course, perhaps soon. Her mother had declared adamantly that her home was with her brother, that it was with him she would stay. But she had agreed to come to Pinewood for a visit later in the year. Maria and Claire could stay longer if they wished, she had said. Maybe Ben would wish to spend a part of his summer holiday there.

But the moment of parting was still hard.

She was leaving London behind forever. She would never see him again. He had sent her those precious papers this morning, but he had not seen fit to bring them in person. And in the accompanying note he had signed himself merely F. Dudley.

She had heard nothing from the Duke of Tresham. It did not matter. If he had already paid Daniel Kirby, then she would repay the loan.

She was going *home,* she reminded herself as the guard blew another deafening blast on his yard of tin as a warning to anyone on the street outside to make way. She had been happy there and would be happy again. Soon the memories would begin to recede, and she would start to heal once more. All she needed was time and patience.

Ah, but the memories were fresh and raw now.

Why had he not come? She had not wanted him to, but why had he not? Why had he sent the papers with a servant?

Ferdinand.

The coach lurched into motion and the *clop-clop* of the horses' hooves drowned out all other sounds. Mama was crying. So was Maria. But they were all smiling too and waving. Viola smiled determinedly and raised her hand. Once the coach had turned onto the street and she could not see them anymore, she would feel better.

But just when she expected it to begin its turn, it jerked to a sudden halt and there was a great deal of shouting and general commotion from the direction of the street.

"Lord love us," Hannah said from beside Viola, "what now?"

The man opposite them, who was facing the horses, pressed the side of his head against the glass and peered forward.

"There be horses and a carriage of some sort drawn

across the entrance," he announced to his fellow passengers. "He'll be in trouble, that driver will. Be he deaf?"

It might be to his benefit if he was, Viola thought, noting that her family were no longer looking at her but at the cause of the delay. Even the walls and windows of the coach could not keep out the blistering profanities with which the coachman, the guard, and several of the outside passengers were berating the hapless man who had driven his carriage across the entryway of the inn yard despite the horn's warning and had apparently stopped there, blocking the stagecoach's path.

And then the sounds of merry laughter and another voice dominated all others.

"Come, now," the voice called gaily, "you can do better than that, my fine fellow. You have not yet turned the air blue. I have business with one of your passengers."

Viola scarcely had time to feel shock before the carriage door was wrenched open.

"In the nick of time," Lord Ferdinand Dudley said, peering inside and then reaching up a gloved hand to her. "Come, Viola."

A moment ago her heart had felt as if it were breaking in two because she would never see him again. Now she was furiously angry. How dare he!

"What are you doing here?" she asked. "How did you know—"

"I went to the White Horse Inn first." He grinned. "I have just put terror into half of London by springing my horses through its streets. Come down."

She clasped her hands firmly in her lap and glared at him. "I am going home," she said. "You are holding up the coach and making a spectacle of us both. Please shut the door, my lord."

If the coachman had not turned the air blue before, he must surely be doing it now. Other men were shouting indignantly too. Only the inside passengers remained quiet, their attention focused on the interesting scene before them.

"Don't go," he said. "Not yet. We need to talk."

Viola shook her head while one of the female passengers informed the others in an awed whisper that the gentleman was a *lord.*

"There is nothing more to say," Viola said. "*Please* go away. Everyone is terribly angry."

"Let them be," he said. "Come down and talk to me."

"You go with him, love," the same passenger advised aloud. "He's a right handsome gent, he is. I'd go with him myself if he would take me instead."

There was a burst of appreciative laughter from those within hearing distance.

"Go away!" Viola said, angry and embarrassed.

"Please, Viola." He was no longer smiling. He was compelling her shamelessly with his dark eyes, which gazed very deeply into her own. "Please, my love. Don't go."

The other passengers awaited her reply with bated breath.

Hannah touched her arm. "We had better get out, Miss Vi," she said, "before we are thrown out."

The coachman and a few other men were still swearing ferociously. The guard had jumped down from his place and was advancing menacingly on Lord Ferdinand.

"If you insist upon staying where you are," Ferdinand said, grinning suddenly again, "I'll follow the coach, Viola, and accost you at every tollgate and every stop between here and Somersetshire. I can make a very public nuisance of myself when I choose. Take my hand now, and get down."

He had made it impossible for her to remain in the coach. How would she look her fellow passengers in the eye during the long hours ahead? How would she be able to face the coachman and guard at the various stops along the way? She stretched out her hand slowly until it was resting in Ferdinand's. He grasped it tightly, and the next moment she was descending to the inn yard while all the inside passengers, a few of the outside ones, and a sizable ring of spectators cheered and applauded.

"Toss down the lady's bags and her maid's, if you will, my man," Ferdinand said, grinning at the guard and pressing a gold coin into his hand. With one glance at it, the guard forgot his wrath and did as he had been bidden. Ferdinand, meanwhile, was assisting Hannah to alight and then stretching up an arm to appease the coachman with another coin. His curricle and horses, Viola noticed, were still blocking the gateway, his groom holding the horses' heads.

She stood mutely watching while the curricle was pulled ahead and the stagecoach finally rumbled out of the yard—without her—and turned onto the street. The grooms and other spectators were dispersing.

"Ma'am." Lord Ferdinand was addressing her mother. "May I have your leave to take Miss Thornhill for a drive?"

She did not *want* to drive with him. At this particular moment she hated him. The worst should be over now. She should be on her way home.

"Of course, my lord," her mother said warmly. "Hannah will return to the White Horse with us."

They were all smiling, Viola saw when she looked

from one to the other of them—just as if they were witnessing the beginning of a happily-ever-after. Even Hannah was beaming. Did they not *understand*?

He was offering her his arm. She took it without a word and went with him out to the street, where he handed her up to the high seat of his curricle before striding around to the other side and climbing up beside her. He took the ribbons from his groom's hand.

"I am very vexed with you," she said curtly when the curricle was in motion.

"Are you?" He turned his head to look briefly at her. "Why?"

"You had no business stopping me from doing what I had decided to do," she said, "and what I *wanted* to do. This morning, when there were important papers to deliver to me, you sent them with a servant and a note signed *F. Dudley*. Now suddenly this afternoon you need to speak with me urgently enough to drag me from a stagecoach."

"Ah, this morning," he said. "I had a very important commitment this morning that made it impossible to call on you in person. But it struck me that you had a right to see those papers at the earliest possible moment. I had time only to dash off a quick note. Did I really sign myself that way? Were you offended?"

"Not at all," she said. "Why should I be?"

He merely flashed her a grin.

"There is nothing more to be said," she told him. "I have already sent a letter thanking you for the papers. Where did they come from, by the way?"

"Bamber," he said. "He went to Yorkshire to call upon the countess's solicitor. It seems that his father used his services occasionally. He did so just before his death because Westinghouse was away from London when you left for Pinewood. The York solicitor neglected to bring the papers to light afterward, though, probably at the countess's urging. Bamber did not know where to find you with them, and so he came to me."

"I would have expected him to keep his mouth shut too," she said tartly. "He cannot feel kindly toward me, after all."

"He is a ramshackle fellow," Ferdinand said, "but not dishonest."

"Everything has been said, then." She turned her head away from him. "It could have been explained just as well in a letter. You did not need to see me again. I wanted to be on that stagecoach. I wanted to go home. I did not want to see you again."

"We have to talk," he said—and then was silent.

"Where are we going?" she asked after a few minutes.

"Somewhere where we can talk," he said.

Her question had been rhetorical. It was clear that they were headed in the direction of the Duke of Tresham's house—the one where his grace housed his mistresses. The curricle drew to a stop there a couple of minutes later and Ferdinand jumped down before coming around to her side.

"I won't," she said firmly as her feet touched the pavement.

"Sleep with me?" he said, grinning down at her. "No, you dashed well won't, Viola. Not today anyway. We need to talk."

Alone together. Here, of all places, where they had spent one night of delirious happiness.

She hated him with an intense anger.

* * *

HE TOOK HER TO the room he liked best—the back room with the pianoforte and books, where Jane and Tresham must have spent a great deal of time. She took off her outdoor garments and went to sit primly in the armchair beside the hearth. Her face was pale and expressionless. She had not once looked at him since they entered the house.

"Why didn't you trust me?" he asked her. He stood some distance from her, his hands clasped at his back. She had lost weight and bloom since that day of the village fête. But somehow she looked as beautiful as ever. Or perhaps it seemed so because he was no longer able to see her objectively. "Why did you go to Tresham instead?"

She looked up at him sharply then. "How do you know that?"

"He told me so," he said. "Did you think he would not, Viola?"

She stared at him. "Now that I think of it," she said, "I can see that it is something he *would* do. He would want to tell you how I was willing to bargain with him and take money from him in exchange for refusing to marry you. Yes, I can see that he would get satisfaction from telling you how calculating and mercenary I am. Does he know about the receipt the Earl of Bamber brought you? How disappointed he must have been—and how terrified that after all I might accept a marriage offer from you."

She was still angry, he could see. He had learned early that Viola Thornhill was not easily dominated. She would not readily forgive him for forcing her to get down from that stagecoach.

"Why did you not trust me?" he asked her again. "Why did you not ask me for the money, Viola? You must know that I would have helped you."

"I did not want you to," she said. "I did not want you to know why I worked for Daniel Kirby. I wanted you to believe that I was Lilian Talbot because I liked being her and doing what she did. I wanted you to abandon the foolish notion that we could marry. I still wish it. I *was* Lilian Talbot, even though I hated every moment of her life. And I remain what she was. I wish the Duke of Tresham had not told you. Better yet, I wish I had not gone to him or had waited another day. That receipt has set me free, you see. But not free to live here or to associate with people like you."

"I can never ever be worthy of you, you know," he said. She looked at him in astonishment, but he continued. "When I learned as a boy of the life my mother and father lived, as well as most of their friends, I was so disillusioned with love that I shrank from it forever after and withdrew into cynicism. Apart from my studies I have done nothing worthwhile in all the years since. Certainly I have not given love. You, on the other hand, have stuck steadfastly by love even though it has hurt you immeasurably. And you keep on sticking by it. You are intent upon not hurting me, are you not?"

She turned her head away. "Don't make a saint of me," she said. "I did what I had to do. But I am a whore nonetheless."

"I think," he said, "that I have done *one* worthwhile thing in my adult life."

"Yes. You gave Pinewood back to me before you knew

it was mine anyway," she said. "I will always remember you kindly for that."

"Kirby won't be troubling you again," he said.

"No." He saw her shudder.

"I would have killed him for you, Viola," he said quietly. "I would *like* to have killed him."

"Oh, no." She was on her feet then and closing the distance between them. She set one hand on his sleeve and looked earnestly into his face. "Don't get into any trouble on my behalf, Ferdinand. He has no more power over me."

He covered her hand on his arm with his own. "Oh, I did not say that he has gone unpunished," he said.

She looked at his hand as he spoke, and then she looked down at the other, her eyes widening. "Oh, Ferdinand, what have you done?"

"I have punished him," he said. "No punishment could be adequate for what he has done to you, not even death. But I believe it will be several days before he can get up off his bed. Once he *is* up, he will be taking himself beyond these shores for the rest of his life."

She raised his hand and set her cheek gently against his raw knuckles. "How dreadful of me to feel glad," she said. "But I do. Thank you. But I hope no one else hears of this, especially the Duke of Tresham. You should not be seen to have any involvement with me. But no matter. I will leave for home tomorrow, and no one will ever hear from me again. I did not want to see you today, Ferdinand, but I am glad after all that you caught up to me in time. I will have this as a last memory of you."

"Actually, Tresham does know," he said. "He is the one who brought Kirby to me in the park."

She looked at him in horror. "He *knows*? In the *park*?"

"With fifty or so other chosen witnesses," he told her. "By now there is probably no one in the *ton* who does not know."

She stepped back from him, her face suddenly pale. Then she tried to rush past him to the door, but he caught her arm and held her.

"By now," he said, "everyone knows of your courage and selfless devotion to your family when you were little more than a girl. Everyone knows that the villain who preyed upon you has been publicly humiliated and punished. Everyone knows that the powerful and influential Dudleys, led by the Duke of Tresham himself, have taken your part and devoted themselves to restoring your good name and celebrating your heroism. And everyone knows that Lord Ferdinand Dudley has appointed himself your champion."

"How could you?" she cried. "How *could* you? To have exposed me to such public..." She could not seem to think of the right word. Her eyes flashed at him.

"Do you not see that it is the only way?" he asked her gently. "Tresham is going to invite the *ton* to a reception at Dudley House. He wants you to be the guest of honor. Everyone will come, Viola. They will all be agog to catch a glimpse of you. But it is our version of you they will come to see. It is the real Viola Thornhill they will meet. You will become all the rage."

"I don't want to be all the rage," she snapped at him. "Ferdinand, I was a courtesan for four years. I am illegitimate. I—"

"Bamber hopes to escort you to the reception and present you to the *ton* as his half-sister," he said.

"What?" She stared at him. "*What?*"

"He was in the park too," he told her.

"So were a dozen or more of my former clients, I daresay." She glared indignantly at him.

"Yes." He drew a slow breath and tested the idea in his mind. It really did not matter to him. "But not one of them will reveal the fact by so much as a flicker of an eyelash, Viola. You will be the acknowledged half-sister of the Earl of Bamber. You will be the protégée of the Duke and Duchess of Tresham. You will be my lady—or so I hope."

He could see the moment at which anger drained out of her and a certain wistfulness took its place, parting her lips and making her eyes more luminous.

"Ferdinand," she said softly, "it cannot be, my dear. You must not do this." Tears welled into her eyes.

He possessed himself of both her hands. What he was about to do might look ridiculous, but he felt an overwhelming need to pay homage to her courage and loyalty and unfailing love—to her superiority over him. He went down on one knee and set his forehead against the backs of her hands.

"My love," he said. "Do me the honor of marrying me. If you truly do not love me, I will understand. I will send you home to Pinewood in my own carriage the day after the reception. But I love you. I'll always love you. It is my dream that you will marry me and that we will go home to Pinewood together and raise a family there."

She drew her hands free of his, and he waited for rejection. But then he felt them come to rest lightly on his head, like a benediction.

"Ferdinand," she said. "Oh, my dear love."

He was on his feet then and scooping her up into his arms with a whoop that had her laughing. He twirled her about and carried her to the chair by the fireplace, where he sat with her cradled in his arms, her head nestled in the warm hollow between his neck and shoulder.

"Of course," he said, "everyone will be expecting our betrothal announcement at Tresham's reception. Angie will want to insist upon a grand wedding in St. George's and a lavish breakfast for five hundred or so afterward. All of it preceded the night before by a great ball."

"Oh, no," she said, real horror in her voice.

"Ghastly thought, is it not?" he agreed. "She will be even more eager this time because Tresham foiled all her grandiose plans by marrying Jane quietly by special license."

"Can *we* marry quietly?" she begged him. "At Trellick, perhaps?"

He chuckled. "You don't know my sister," he said, "though I daresay you soon will."

"Ferdinand." She tipped back her head and gazed up at him. "Are you sure? Are you quite, quite—"

There was only one way to deal with such foolishness. He covered her mouth with his own and silenced her. After a few moments her arm crept up about his neck and she sighed her surrender.

Ferdinand found himself thinking all sorts of mindless drivel—about being surely the happiest man in the world, for example.

25

VIOLA WAS SEATED IN THE EARL OF BAMBER'S opulent town carriage, her mother beside her, the earl opposite. They were on their way to Dudley House.

It had been a turbulent week. The Duchess of Tresham had called at the White Horse Inn the day after Ferdinand stopped Viola from leaving on the stagecoach. She had issued a formal invitation to Viola and her mother to attend the reception she and her husband were giving. She had stayed for twenty minutes and had shown an interest in Claire, who was not working downstairs at the time. Her grace had mentioned that her godmother, Lady Webb, was considering employing a companion to live with her—she spent half the year in London and the other half in Bath. The duchess had wondered if Claire would be interested in the position.

The day after, Claire had gone with their mother, by invitation, to call upon Lady Webb, and the two had appeared delighted with each other. Claire was to begin her new position in two weeks' time and had looked during the past few days as if she were walking on air.

"This is very kind of you, my lord," Viola's mother said to the earl.

He was looking stout and florid and very fine indeed in his evening clothes. He must be eight or nine years her senior, Viola guessed. She had not asked her mother how it had come about that she had progressed from being the boy's governess to becoming his father's mistress. That was her mother's private, secret life.

"Not at all, ma'am," he said, stiffly inclining his head.

He too had called on them during the week. His manner to his former governess had been distant, but not discourteous. With Viola herself he had been scrupulously polite. He had requested the honor of escorting both ladies to the Duke of Tresham's reception. Viola wondered now why he was doing it. Her mother had been his father's mistress, and she was the offspring of that illicit union. But he answered her question even as she thought it.

"M'father wanted Miss Thornhill to be recognized as a lady," he said. "I will have no part in thwarting his wishes."

"She *is* a lady," Viola's mother said. "My father . . ."

But Viola was not listening. She was nervous. Yes, of course she was. It would be pointless to deny it. Even without her scarlet past—and even if she had been Clarence Wilding's legitimate daughter—she could never have hoped to be on her way to a *ton* party. Although both he and her mother were of the gentry class, they were not high enough on the social scale to mingle with the *beau monde*.

But she refused to give in to her nerves. She had decided to trust Ferdinand and his family to know what they were doing. In a sense, it was a relief to have everything out in the open. To have no more secrets. No more hidden fears. And no more doubts.

She was wearing a white satin gown with a delicately scalloped hem and short train but with no other adornment. She had been to several tedious fittings during the week with one of Bond Street's most prestigious dressmakers. The gown, as well as the silver slippers and gloves and fan she had chosen to wear with it, had been exorbitantly costly, but the loan she had asked of Uncle Wesley until she could send the money from Pinewood had turned into a gift. Her mother had told him everything and he had been angry with Viola—but in a tearful, hugging sort of way. It had hurt him that she had borne the burden of her stepfather's debts instead of going to him.

She had scarcely seen Ferdinand all week. He had called once formally to ask her mother's and her uncle's permission to marry her, even though she was twenty-five years old and he need not have asked at all. She had seen him only once—briefly—since then. Her hands closed firmly about her fan, and she smiled.

Tomorrow she was going home.

The carriage turned into Grosvenor Square and rolled to a halt before the doors of Dudley House.

SHE LOOKED LIKE MISS Thornhill of Pinewood Manor. That was Ferdinand's thought as he watched her through much of the evening. She was the picture of understated elegance in her deceptively simple white gown. She wore her hair in the familiar braids, but they were looped and coiled in an intricate design. She bore herself with regal grace. If she was nervous—and she undoubtedly was—she did not show it.

He kept his distance. Everyone at Dudley House—and the drawing room and the adjoining salons beyond it were thronged with the crème de la crème of society—

would know what he had done on her behalf in Hyde Park the week before. He would not have it said, then, that she had to cling to him tonight, that without him she could not have done what she clearly was doing quite magnificently.

She was mingling with the *ton*. She was conversing with ladies whom one might expect under other circumstances to avert their faces from her and gather their skirts about them lest they rub against her. She was talking and laughing with gentlemen who had known her in her other, now-dead persona.

And she was doing it alone.

It was true that Bamber, distinguishing himself by his good manners as he had perhaps never done before, hovered at her elbow for the first hour until he had personally introduced her to every guest as his half-sister. And Jane, Angie, Tresham, and even Heyward made sure that one of them was always in any group that gathered about her.

But she behaved like Miss Thornhill of Pinewood. However she was feeling inside, she appeared to be perfectly at her ease.

Ferdinand watched her, at first with some anxiety, then with pride.

He had not been at all sure that day he had stopped her from leaving London that she would agree to the daring scheme he and Tresham had conceived. Perhaps in her own way, he thought, Viola was as drawn to a difficult challenge as irresistibly as he ever was. Nothing had been more chancy than her appearance here tonight.

But she had done it, and it had worked. Oh, he knew she had no wish to mingle with the *ton* after tonight. He knew she longed to go home to Pinewood and to resume her life there. But she had done this first, and now it would be known that society had accepted her and she could return anytime she wished.

"Well, Ferdie." His sister had come up beside him without his noticing. "I can see now why she was always so celebrated for her beauty. If I were a few years younger and still on the marriage mart, I would doubtless hate her." She laughed merrily. "Heyward said you were mad, you and Tresh, and that you could never pull this off. But you have, as I told him you would—and of course Heyward is pleased about it. He says he always knew that when you finally did fall in love, it would be with someone wildly ineligible, but that he was going to have to throw his support behind you because you are my brother."

"That is magnanimous of him." He grinned.

"Well, it *is*," she agreed. "There is no higher stickler than Heyward, you know. I believe it is why I decided the first time I set eyes on him that I would marry him. He was so *different* from us."

It had always been a source of amusement to Ferdinand and his brother that their shatterbrained, chatterbox Angie and a dry old stick like Heyward were locked up tight in a love match.

"Ferdie." She set one gloved hand on his arm. "I simply *must* tell you, even though Heyward said I must not because it would be vulgar to talk about such a thing at a public event. Just you, though. I have already whispered it to Jane and Tresh. Ferdie, I am in an *interesting condition.* I saw a physician today and it is quite, quite certain. After *six years.*"

Her eyes were swimming with tears, he saw when

he looked down at her and set his hand warmly over hers.

"Angie," he said.

"I hope," she said. "Oh, I *do* hope I can present Heyward with an heir, though he says that he does not mind if it is a girl as long as both she and I come safely through the ordeal."

"Of course he will not mind," Ferdinand said, raising her hand to his lips. "He loves you, after all."

"Yes." She searched out her husband with her eyes and beamed at him while he looked back with an expression of pained resignation—he knew very well, of course, that she was spreading the embarrassing news of his impending fatherhood. "Yes, he does."

She chattered on.

There was a formal supper later in the evening, during which Ferdinand sat with Mrs. Wilding and Lady Webb, who had taken Viola's mother under her wing during most of the evening. Viola was at the opposite side of the room with Bamber and Angie and Heyward. But they were very aware of each other. Their eyes met halfway through the meal, and they smiled at each other—though it was more a smile of the eyes than of the face.

I am so proud of you, his look said.

I am so happy, hers replied.

I love you.

I love you.

And then Tresham was touching his shoulder and bending his head to speak quietly.

"You want the announcement made, then?" he asked. "And you still want me to make it?"

"It is your house and reception," Ferdinand said. "And you are the head of the family."

His brother squeezed his shoulder, straightened up, and cleared his throat. The Duke of Tresham never needed to do more than that to command the attention of a large number of people. The room was silent within moments.

"I have an announcement to make," his grace said. "I daresay most, if not all of you, have half guessed it."

There was a murmuring as all eyes moved between Ferdinand and Viola. His own were on her. She was flushed, her gaze lowered.

"But only half," Tresham continued. "Lord Ferdinand Dudley asked me several days ago if I would announce his betrothal to Miss Viola Thornhill this evening."

There was a swell of sound and a smattering of applause. Viola was biting her lower lip. Tresham held up one hand for quiet.

"I prepared a suitable speech," he said, "of congratulation to my brother, of sincere welcome to our family of my future sister-in-law. But we Dudleys can never behave ourselves as we ought, you know."

There was laughter.

"My sister and my duchess were already planning a grand wedding at St. George's and a breakfast and ball," Tresham continued. "It was to be the event of the Season."

"What do you mean by *were* and *was,* Tresh?" Angeline cried, her voice filled with sudden suspicion. "Ferdie has not—"

"Yes, I am afraid he has," Tresham said. "This morning I was informed an hour after the event that Ferdinand and Miss Thornhill were married by special license, his valet and her maid the only witnesses. Ladies and gentlemen, I proudly present to you my brother and sister-in-law, Lord and Lady Ferdinand Dudley."

VIOLA HAD FOUND THE courage to look up while the duke spoke. She gazed across the room at Ferdinand, handsome and elegant in his crisp black and white evening clothes, and so very, very dear.

Her husband.

How she had longed for him all day. But she had had the reception to prepare for, and he had had business to attend to so that he could be ready to leave with her for Pinewood tomorrow morning. And they had wanted no one to know except her mother and the duke, whom they had told after their brief, achingly beautiful wedding early in the morning.

How she had longed all evening to go to him, to have him come to her. But she had insisted, and he had agreed, that this evening was something she must do for herself, in her own person. She would not hide behind anyone's coattails. The evening had been incredibly hard, but she had felt his powerful, comforting presence at every moment of it, and she had done it—for herself and for him. He had taken a great gamble, marrying her this morning before he knew for sure that the *ton* would not spurn her and turn its back on him.

She gazed at him now across the room and rose to her feet as he came striding toward her, his dark eyes alight, one arm lifting as he drew close. She set her hand in his, and he raised it to his lips.

It was only then that she became fully aware of the noise about them—voices and applause and laughter.

But then the noise died away again. The Duke of Tresham—her *brother-in-law*—had not finished speaking.

"There has not been a great deal of time," he said, "but my duchess is a resourceful lady—I did share the secret with her, of course. And we have able servants. We ask you all to join us in the ballroom after supper. But before we adjourn . . ." He lifted his eyebrows in the direction of his butler, who was standing in the doorway, and the man stood aside for two footmen, who were carrying between them a white and silver three-tiered wedding cake.

"The devil!" Ferdinand murmured, gripping Viola's hand and drawing it through his arm. "I might have known it would be fatal to say anything before tonight." His eyes were dancing with merriment when he looked down at her. "I hope you won't mind too much, my love."

For the next half hour she felt too overwhelmed to know if she minded or not. Her mother came to hug them both, as did Jane and Angeline—who each insisted that she must now call them by their first names—and even the duke. Lord Heyward and the Earl of Bamber hugged her and shook hands with Ferdinand. But then Jane insisted it was time to cut the cake and carry it around on a silver platter so that all the guests could have a chance to congratulate them and wish them well.

It was the very fuss they had hoped to avoid by marrying quietly.

It was wonderful.

Gradually the guests drifted away from the dining room until only Jane and Angeline and Viola's mother were left apart from the newlyweds. Angeline was complaining bitterly about two brothers who had foiled her dearest wish to organize a grand wedding. But interspersed with the complaints were tears and hugs and an assurance that she had never been happier in her life.

"Besides," she added, "if I have a daughter I will be able to give her the grandest wedding anyone has ever seen. Then you will know what you and Tresh missed, Ferdie."

"We should go and join everyone else," he suggested, smiling so warmly into Viola's eyes that her heart turned over.

"Why the ballroom?" she asked.

"A question I have been trying not to ask myself," he said with a grimace. "First, though, a matter of importance that I should have seen to as soon as Tresham made his announcement, love." He drew her wedding ring out of a pocket of his evening coat and slid it onto her finger—where it had lain for such a brief spell during the morning. He kissed it. "For all time, Viola."

The ballroom was large, imposing, and quite breathtaking, Viola saw. The guests stood about the edges of the dance floor. An orchestra occupied a dais at the other end of the room. Three large chandeliers overhead glistened with all their candles alight. The walls and windows and doorways were adorned with masses of white flowers, greenery, and silver ribbons.

There was renewed applause as Viola and Ferdinand appeared in the doorway. The Duke of Tresham stood on the dais, waiting for quiet.

"An impromptu ball, ladies and gentlemen," he said, "in celebration of a marriage. Ferdinand, lead your bride into the opening waltz, if you please."

Ferdinand turned his head and looked down at Viola as the orchestra began to play. He looked embarrassed and pleased—and also slightly amused.

"Now, what are you doing hiding here," he murmured to her, "when you should be out there dancing?"

She was struck by the familiarity of the words and then remembered where and when he had spoken them before. She smiled back at him.

"I have been waiting for the right partner, sir," she replied. And, more softly, "I have been waiting for *you*."

She set her hand on his and he led her onto the dance floor and set one arm about her waist. He moved her into the lilting rhythm of the waltz while their wedding guests watched. His eyes smiled into hers.

And then she remembered something else from that fateful May Day about the village green in Trellick.

Beware of a tall, dark, handsome stranger. He can destroy you—if you do not first snare his heart.

If you loved *More than a Mistress* and *No* [illegible] *Mistress*, get ready to learn how it all started in [illegible]

The Secret Mistress

Coming soon from Delacorte Press in hardcover

Turn the page for a sneak peek inside.

Man's

1

LADY ANGELINE DUDLEY was standing at the window of the taproom in the Rose and Crown Inn east of Reading. Quite scandalously, she was alone there, but what was she to do? The window of her own room looked out only upon a rural landscape. It was picturesque enough, but it was not the view she wanted. Only the taproom window offered that, looking out as it did upon the inn yard into which any new arrival was bound to ride.

Angeline was waiting, with barely curbed impatience, for the arrival of her brother and guardian, Jocelyn Dudley, Duke of Tresham. He was to have been here before her, but she had arrived an hour and a half ago and there had been no sign of him. It was very provoking. A string of governesses over the years, culminating in Miss Pratt, had instilled in her the idea that a lady never showed an excess of emotion, but how was one not to do so when one was on one's way to London for the Season—one's *first*—and one was eager to be there so that one's adult life could begin in earnest *at last,* yet one's brother had apparently forgotten all about one's very existence and was about to leave one languishing forever at a public inn a day's journey away from the rest of her life?

Of course, she had arrived here ridiculously early. Tresham had arranged for her to travel this far under the care of the Reverend Isaiah Coombes and his wife and two children before they went off in a different direction to celebrate some special anniversary with Mrs. Coombes's relatives, and Angeline was transferred to the care of her brother, who was to come from London. The Coombeses arose each morning at the crack of dawn or even earlier, despite yawning protests from the junior Coombeses, with the result that their day's journey was completed almost before those of more normal persons even began.

The Reverend and Mrs. Coombes had been quite prepared to settle in and wait like long-suffering martyrs at the inn until their precious charge could be handed over to the care of His Grace, but Angeline had persuaded them to be on their way. What could possibly happen to her at the Rose and Crown Inn, after all? It was a perfectly respectable establishment—Tresham had chosen it himself, had he not? And it was not as if she was quite alone. There was Betty, her maid; two burly grooms from the stables at Acton Park, Tresham's estate in Hampshire; and two stout footmen from the house. And Tresham himself was sure to arrive any minute.

The Reverend Coombes had been swayed, against his better judgment, by the soundness of her reasoning—and by the anxiety of his wife lest their journey not be completed before nightfall, and by the whining complaints of Miss Chastity Coombes and Master Esau Coombes, aged eleven and nine respectively, that they would *never* get to play with their cousins if they had to wait here forever.

Angeline's patience had been severely tried by those two while she had been forced to share a carriage with them.

She had retired to her room to change out of her travel clothes and to have Betty brush and restyle her hair. She had then instructed her drooping maid to rest awhile, which the girl had done to immediate effect on the truckle bed at the foot of Angeline's own. Meanwhile Angeline had noticed that her window would give no advance notice whatsoever of the arrival of her brother, so she had left the room to find a more satisfactory window—only to discover the four hefty male servants from Acton arrayed in all their menacing largeness outside her door as though to protect her from foreign invasion. She had banished them to the servants' quarters for rest and refreshments, explaining by way of persuasion that she had not noticed any highwaymen or footpads or brigands or other assorted villains hovering about the inn. Had they?

And then, alone at last, she had discovered the window

she was searching for—in the public taproom. It was not quite proper for her to be there unescorted, but the room was deserted, so where was the harm? Who was to know of her slight indiscretion? If any persons came before Tresham rode into the inn yard, she would simply withdraw to her room until they left. When Tresham arrived, she would *dash* up to her room so that when he entered the inn, she could be descending the stairs, all modest respectability, Betty behind her, as though she were just coming down to ask about him.

Oh, it was very hard not to bounce around with impatience and excitement. She was nineteen years old, and this was almost the first time she had been more than ten miles from Acton Park. She had lived a *very* sheltered existence, thanks to a stern, overprotective father and an absentee overprotective brother after him, and thanks to a mother who had never taken her to London or Bath or Brighton or any of the other places she herself had frequented.

Angeline had entertained hopes of making her come-out at the age of seventeen, but before she could muster all her arguments and begin persuading and wheedling the persons who held her fate in their hands, her mother had died unexpectedly in London and there had been a whole year of mourning to be lived through at Acton. And then *last* year, when all had been set for her come-out at the indisputably correct age of eighteen, she had broken her leg, and Tresham, provoking man, had flatly refused to allow her to clump into the queen's presence on crutches in order to make her curtsy and her debut into the adult world of the *ton* and the marriage mart.

By now she was ancient, a veritable fossil, but nevertheless a hopeful, excited, impatient one.

Horses!

Angeline leaned her forearms along the windowsill and rested her bosom on them as she cocked her ear closer to the window.

And carriage wheels!

Oh, she could not possibly be mistaken.

She was not. A team of horses, followed by a carriage,

turned in at the gate and clopped and rumbled over the cobbles to the far side of the yard.

It was immediately apparent to Angeline, however, that this was not Tresham. The carriage was far too battered and ancient. And the gentleman who jumped down from inside it even before the coachman could set down the steps bore no resemblance to her brother. Before she could see him clearly enough to decide if he was worth looking at anyway, though, her attention was distracted by the deafening sound of a horn blast, and almost simultaneously *another* team and another coach hove into sight and drew to a halt close to the taproom door.

Again, it was not Tresham's carriage. That had been apparent from the first moment. It was a stagecoach.

Angeline did not feel as great a disappointment as might have been expected, though. This bustle of human activity was all new and exciting to her. She watched as the coachman opened the door and set down the steps and passengers spilled out onto the cobbles from inside and clambered down a rickety ladder from the roof. Too late she realized that, of course, all these people were about to swarm inside for refreshments and that she ought not to be here when they did. The inn door was opening even as she thought it, and the buzz of at least a dozen voices all talking at once preceded their owners inside, but only by a second or two.

If she withdrew now, Angeline thought, she would be far more conspicuous than if she stayed where she was. Besides, she was enjoying the scene. And besides again, if she went upstairs and waited for the coach to be on its way, she might miss the arrival of her brother, and it seemed somehow important to her to see him the moment he appeared. She had not seen him in the two years since their mother's funeral at Acton Park.

She stayed and assuaged her conscience by continuing to look out the window, her back to the room, while people called with varying degrees of politeness and patience for ale and pasties and one or two instructed someone to look sharp about it, and the someone addressed replied tartly that she had only one pair of hands and was it *her* fault the coach was running an hour late and the passengers had been given only a ten-minute stop instead of half an hour?

Indeed, ten minutes after the coach's arrival, the passengers were called to board again if they did not want to get left behind, and they hurried or straggled out, some complaining vociferously that they had to abandon at least half their ale.

The taproom was soon as empty and silent as it had been before. No one had had time to notice Angeline, a fact for which she was profoundly grateful. Miss Pratt even now, a full year after moving on to other employment, would have had a fit of the vapors if she could have seen the full taproom with her former pupil standing alone at the window. Tresham would have had a fit of something far more volcanic.

No matter. No one would ever know.

Would he *never* come?

Angeline heaved a deep sigh as the coachman blew his yard of tin again to warn any persons or dogs or chickens out on the street that they were in imminent danger of being mown down if they did not immediately scurry for safety. The coach rattled out through the gates, turning as it went, and disappeared from sight.

The gentleman's carriage was still at the far side of the yard, but now it had fresh horses attached. He was still here, then. He must be taking refreshments in a private parlor.

Angeline adjusted her bosom on her arms, wiggled herself into a more comfortable position, and proceeded to dream about all the splendors of the Season awaiting her in London.

Oh, she could not *wait*.

It did seem, however, that she had no choice but to do just that.

Had Tresham even left *London* yet?

The gentleman whose carriage awaited him at the far side of the inn yard was not taking refreshments in a private parlor. He was doing so in the public taproom, his elbow resting on the high counter. The reason Angeline did not realize he was there was that he did not slurp his ale and did not talk aloud to himself.

Edward Ailsbury, Earl of Heyward, was feeling more than slightly uncomfortable. And he was feeling annoyed that he had been made to feel so. Was it *his* fault that a young woman who was clearly a lady was in the taproom with him, quite alone? Where were her parents or her husband or whoever it was that was supposed to be chaperoning her? There was no one in sight except the two of them.

At first he had assumed she was a stagecoach passenger. But when she had made no move to scurry outside when the call to board again came, he noticed that of course she was not dressed for the outdoors. She must be a guest at the inn, then. But she really ought not to have been allowed to wander where she had no business being, embarrassing perfectly innocent and respectable travelers who were trying to enjoy a glass of ale in peace and respectability before continuing the journey to London.

To make matters worse—*considerably* worse—she was leaning forward and slightly down in order to rest her bosom on her forearms along the windowsill, with the result that her back was arched inward like an inverted bow, and her derriere was thrust outward at a provocative angle. Indeed, Edward found himself drinking his ale less to slake the thirst of the journey than to cool an elevated body temperature.

It was a very shapely derriere.

And to make matters even worse, if that were possible, the dress she wore was of fine muslin and clung to her person in places where it would be kinder to innocent males for it *not* to cling. It did not help that the dress was of a bright, luminous pink the likes of which shade Edward had never before encountered in a fabric or anywhere else for that matter. The woman could have been seen with the naked eye from a distance of five miles. He was considerably closer to her than that.

He was further annoyed over the undeniable fact that he was ogling her—or one part of her anatomy, anyway. And, while he was ogling her with his eyes, his head was fairly humming with lascivious thoughts. He resented both facts—and her. He prided himself upon always treating ladies with the utmost respect. And not just ladies. He treated *women* with respect. Eunice Goddard had once pointed out to him during one of their many lengthy conversations—not that he could not have worked it out for himself—that women of all walks of life were *persons,* despite what the church and the law might have to say to the contrary, and not mere objects to cater to man's baser instincts.

He respected Eunice's opinions. She had a fine mind, which she had cultivated with extensive reading and thoughtful observations of life. He hoped to marry her, though he realized that his family might find his choice disappointing now that he was Earl of Heyward instead of plain Mr. Edward Ailsbury.

His carriage—his ancient embarrassment of a carriage, which his mother had begged him to bring to London because she could never seem to get comfortable in any newer one she had ever ridden in—was ready to leave, Edward could see through the window over the pink lady's head. He had intended to eat something as well as drink before resuming his journey, but she had ruined that plan. It was not right for him to be here with her—though it was not *his* fault that he was placing her in such a potentially compromising position. And it was not *his* fault that the ale was not cooling his blood one iota.

Though Eunice might argue with that, about its not being his fault, that was. The woman had done nothing to provoke his reaction, after all, beyond being here with her bright-pink-clad derriere elevated in his direction. And he could have gone to the dining room to eat, though he would then have felt obliged to order a full-blown meal.

He set his not-quite-empty glass down on the counter as silently as he could and straightened up. He would leave and take his grudge against her with him. He had not even seen her face. She might be as ugly as sin.

An unworthy, spiteful thought.

He shook his head in exasperation.

But then, before he could take a step toward the outer door and freedom from temptation and other ills, the door opened from the outside and a man stepped inside.

Edward recognized him, though *he* clearly did not recognize Edward. That was hardly surprising, since Edward was quite unremarkable in his own person, and his title had been lending him consequence only for the past year, since the death of his far more imposing and charismatic older brother, Maurice. And the year of mourning had been spent at Wimsbury Abbey in Shropshire, where Edward had stayed to familiarize himself with his new duties and gird his loins for the inevitable removal to London this spring to take his seat in the House of Lords—and to take a bride, a step his female relatives deemed essential despite the fact that he was only twenty-four years old. Maurice and Lorraine had produced only one daughter before Maurice's demise, and the succession must be secured. Edward was the spare of his particular generation. He had two sisters but no other brothers.

The new arrival was Lord Windrow, a member of Maurice's old circle of friends and acquaintances, and as wild and rakish as the best of them. Tall and handsome, neither of which attributes Edward shared to any noticeable degree, Windrow moved with an indolent swagger and regarded the world from cynical eyes over which his eyelids habitually drooped as if he were about to nod off to sleep at any moment. He was dressed in the height of fashion.

Edward would have liked nothing better than to nod genially at the man and be on his way. But he hesitated. The pink lady was still present and was still posed as before. And if *he* had ogled her, what would Windrow do?

It was absolutely none of his business what Windrow might do, Edward told himself. And the pink lady was certainly none of his concern. Let her look to the consequences of her own indiscretions. Let her family look to them. Besides, this was the public taproom of a respectable inn. No real harm would come to her.

He urged himself to be on his way.

But he found himself instead resting his elbow on the counter and picking up his glass again.

Confound his misplaced sense of social responsibility. The fact that Eunice might applaud him for staying was no consolation.

The landlord appeared behind the counter and served Windrow a tankard of ale before disappearing again.

Windrow turned to survey the room, and his eyes alit almost immediately upon the pink lady. But how could they not unless he was totally blind? He leaned back against the counter, resting his forearms back along it while clutching his tankard in one hand. His lips pursed in a silent whistle.

Edward was all the more annoyed at the blatantly sensual look on the man's face because his own must have looked very much like it just a few minutes ago.

"Sweetheart," Windrow said softly, obviously having dismissed Edward as a man of no account whatsoever—or perhaps he had not even noticed him, "may I persuade you to share my ale? Better yet, may I persuade you to share it and a meat pasty? There is only one comfortable-looking chair over by the fireplace, I see, but you may sit on my lap and share that too."

Edward frowned at him. Could he not see that the woman was a *lady*? The evidence was glaring enough in the fine muslin of her dress, despite the bright shade, and in the intricacy of her coiffure of dark hair. He glanced at her, expecting to see her stiffen with horror and fright. She continued to stare out the window. She either assumed that the invitation was directed at someone else, or—was it possible?—she simply did not hear the words at all.

He should *leave,* Edward decided. *Right now.*

He spoke instead.

"I doubt you know the lady," he said. "Calling her *sweetheart,* then, would be inappropriately impertinent."

Maurice had often called him, affectionately enough most of the time, a staid old sobersides. Edward half expected to see dust emerge from his mouth along with the words. But they were spoken now, and he would not recall them if he could. *Someone* had to speak up for defenseless female innocence. If she *was* innocent, that was.

Windrow's head swiveled slowly, and just as slowly his lazy eyes swept Edward from head to toe. His perusal aroused no discernible alarm in him.

"You were speaking to me, fellow?" he asked.

Edward in his turn looked slowly about the room.

"I must have been," he said. "I see no one else present except the two of us and the lady, and I am not in the habit of speaking to myself."

Slight amusement showed in the other man's face.

"*Lady,*" he said. "I take it she is not with you. She is alone, then. I wish she *were* a lady. It might be mildly less of a yawn to frequent London ballrooms and drawing rooms. You would be wise, fellow, to address yourself to what remains of your ale and mind your own business."

And he turned back to regard the woman's derriere again. She had changed position. Her elbows were now on the sill, and her face was cupped in her hands. The effect of the change was to thrust her bosom into more prominence in one direction and her derriere in the other.

If she could only step back and see herself from this position, Edward thought, she would run screaming from the room and never return, even with a dozen chaperons.

"Perhaps this *lady* would care to sit in my lap while I call to the landlord to bring *her* a pasty and ale so that *she* may share with *me*," Windrow said with insolent emphasis. "*Would* you, sweetheart?"

Edward sighed inwardly and moved one degree closer to an unwilling confrontation. It was too late to back off now.

"I really must insist," he said, "that the lady be treated with the respect that any female ought to be accorded as a matter of right by anyone claiming the name of gentleman."

He sounded pompous. *Of course* he sounded pompous. He always did, did he not?

Windrow's head turned, and his amusement was quite unmistakable now.

"Are you looking for a fight, fellow?" he asked.

The lady seemed finally to have realized that she was the subject of the conversation behind her. She straightened up and turned, all wide, dark eyes in a narrow, handsome face, and all tall, shapely height.

Good God, Edward thought, the rest of her person more than lived up to the promise of her derriere. She was a rare beauty. But this was no time to allow himself to be distracted. He had been asked a question.

"I have never felt any burning desire to enforce gentility or simple civility with my fists," he said, his tone mild and amiable. "It seems something of a contradiction in terms."

"I believe," Windrow said, "I have the pleasure of addressing a sniveling coward. And a stuffy windbag. All wrapped in one neat package."

Each charge, even the last, was an insult. But Edward would be damned before he would allow himself to be goaded into adopting swashbuckling tactics just to prove to someone he despised that he was a *man.*

"A man who defends the honor of a lady, and who expects a gentleman to behave like one and confronts him when he does not, is a *coward,* then?" he asked mildly.

The woman's eyes, he was aware, had moved from one to the other of them but were now riveted upon his face. Her hands were clasped to her bosom as though she had been struck by some tender passion. She looked remarkably unalarmed.

"I believe," Windrow said, "the suggestion has been made that I am not a *gentleman.* If I had a glove about my person, I would slap it across your insolent face, fellow, and invite you to follow me out to the inn yard. But a man ought not to be allowed to get away with being a coward *and* a stuffy windbag, gloves or no gloves, ought he? Fellow, you are hereby challenged to fisticuffs outside." He jerked his thumb in the direction of the inn yard and smiled—very unpleasantly indeed.

Once more Edward sighed inwardly.

"And the winner proves himself a gentleman worthy of

the name, does he?" he said. "Pardon me if I disagree and decline your generous offer. I will settle for an apology to the lady instead before you take yourself off."

He glanced at her again. She was still gazing fixedly at him.

He had, as he was fully aware, backed himself into a tight corner from which there was no way out that was not going to prove painful. He was going to end up having to fight Windrow and either give *him* a bloody nose and two black eyes to take to London with him, or suffer his opponent to dish out the like to himself. Or both.

It was all very tedious. Nothing but flash and fists. That was what being a gentleman was to many of the men who claimed the name. Maurice, unfortunately, had been one of them.

"Apologize to the *lady*?" Windrow laughed softly and with undisguised menace.

That was when the lady decided to enter the fray—without uttering a word.

She seemed to grow three inches. She looked suddenly regal and haughty—and she shifted her gaze to Windrow. She looked him up and down unhurriedly and appeared to find what she saw utterly contemptible.

It was a masterly performance—or perhaps a mistressly one.

Her wordless comment was not without its effect, even though Windrow was half grinning at her. Perhaps it was a *rueful* grin?

"I misjudged you, alas, did I?" he asked her. "Because you were alone in here and leaning nonchalantly on the windowsill and dressed like a bird of paradise, I suppose. I cannot persuade you to share a pasty and a glass of ale with me? Or to sit on my lap? A pity. And it would seem I cannot persuade this sniveling coward to defend your honor or his own with his fists. What a sad day to have encountered, when I had such high hopes of it when I awoke this morning. There is nothing for it, I see, but to resume my tedious journey and hope for a brighter tomorrow."

And he pushed himself away from the counter, setting down his empty tankard as he did so, and would have sauntered out of the inn without a word more or a backward glance. He found an obstacle in his path, however. Before he could reach the door, Edward was there ahead of him and standing in front of it, blocking the way.

"You have forgotten something," he said. "You owe the lady an apology."

Windrow's eyebrows rose and amusement suffused his face again. He turned back to the room and made the lady a deep and mocking bow.

"Oh, fair one," he said, "it pains me that I may have distressed you with my admiration. Accept my humble apologies, I beg you."

She neither accepted nor rejected them. She gazed coldly at him without relaxing her regal demeanor.

Windrow winked at her.

"I shall look forward to making your official acquaintance at some future date," he said. "It is my fervent hope that that will not be far in the future."

He turned to Edward, who stood out of the way of the door.

"And likewise for you, fellow," he said. "It will be a distinct pleasure."

Edward inclined his head curtly to him, and Windrow left the inn and closed the door behind him.

That left Edward and the lady in the taproom together again. But this time she knew he was there and so the impropriety could not be ignored or even silently fumed over. He was freshly annoyed with her—and with himself for having become embroiled in such an undignified episode.

She was gazing at him, the regal demeanor vanished, her hands clasped at her bosom again.

Edward inclined his head curtly to her and made his way outside. He half expected to find Windrow lying in wait for him in the yard and was almost disappointed to see no sign of the man.

Less than five minutes later he was inside his carriage again and on his way toward London. Ten minutes after that, the carriage passed a far smarter one—of course, it would have been difficult to find one shabbier—traveling with reckless speed in the opposite direction. He caught a glimpse of the coat of arms emblazoned on the door. The Duke of Tresham's. He breathed a sigh of relief that at least he had been spared having to encounter that particular gentleman at the Rose and Crown in addition to Windrow. It would have been the final straw.

Tresham was not his favorite person in the world. And, to be fair, he did not doubt that he was not Tresham's either. The duke had been another of Maurice's friends. It was in a curricle race against him that Maurice had overturned his own and killed himself. And then Tresham had had the effrontery to turn up at Maurice's funeral. Edward had made his opinion known to him there.

He wished anew that he could have stayed at Wimsbury Abbey. But duty called in London. And there was consolation, for Eunice was there too. She was staying with Lady Sanford, her aunt, and he would see her again.

It struck him suddenly that Tresham was driving in the opposite direction from London. Perhaps he was on his way to Acton Park. Perhaps he was going to remain there throughout the spring. It was something to be hoped for.

Who the devil *was* that lady back at the inn? *Someone* needed to take her in hand and teach her a thing or two about what was what.

But devil take it, she was a rare beauty.

He frowned as he shifted position in a vain attempt to get comfortable.

Beauty was no excuse for impropriety. Indeed, beauty called for more than usual discretion.

He still felt entirely out of charity with her, whoever she was. Unlike Windrow, he did *not* look forward to making her official acquaintance. He hoped rather that he would never see her again. He hoped she was traveling away from London rather than toward it.

Preferably to the highlands of Scotland.